# SEAL FIRSTS

### First Books in Four Series

SHARON HAMILTON

# SHARON HAMILTON'S BOOK LIST

## SEAL BROTHERHOOD BOOKS

### SEAL BROTHERHOOD SERIES
Accidental SEAL Book 1
Fallen SEAL Legacy Book 2
SEAL Under Covers Book 3
SEAL The Deal Book 4
Cruisin' For A SEAL Book 5
SEAL My Destiny Book 6
SEAL of My Heart Book 7
Fredo's Dream Book 8
SEAL My Love Book 9
SEAL Encounter Prequel to Book 1
SEAL Endeavor Prequel to Book 2
Ultimate SEAL Collection Vol. 1 Books 1-4 /2 Prequels
Ultimate SEAL Collection Vol. 2 Books 5-7

### SEAL BROTHERHOOD LEGACY SERIES
Watery Grave Book 1

### BAD BOYS OF SEAL TEAM 3 SERIES
SEAL's Promise Book 1
SEAL My Home Book 2
SEAL's Code Book 3
Big Bad Boys Bundle Books 1-3

### BAND OF BACHELORS SERIES
Lucas Book 1
Alex Book 2
Jake Book 3
Jake 2 Book 4
Big Band of Bachelors Bundle

### BONE FROG BROTHERHOOD SERIES
New Year's SEAL Dream Book 1
SEALed At The Altar Book 2
SEALed Forever Book 3
SEAL's Rescue Book 4

SEALed Protection Book 5

## SUNSET SEALS SERIES
SEALed at Sunset
Second Chance SEAL
Treasure Island SEAL
Escape to Sunset
The House at Sunset Beach

## SILVER SEALS SERIES
SEAL Love's Legacy

## SLEEPER SEALS SERIES
Bachelor SEAL

## BONE FROG BACHELOR SERIES
Bone Frog Bachelor
Unleashed

## STAND ALONE BOOKS & SERIES
SEAL's Goal: The Beautiful Game
Nashville SEAL: Jameson
True Blue SEALS Zak
Paradise: In Search of Love
Love Me Tender, Love You Hard

## NOVELLAS
SEAL You In My Dreams Magnolias and Moonshine

# PARANORMALS

## GOLDEN VAMPIRES OF TUSCANY SERIES
Honeymoon Bite Book 1
Mortal Bite Book 2
Christmas Bite Book 3
Midnight Bite Book 4

## THE GUARDIANS
Heavenly Lover Book 1
Underworld Lover Book 2
Underworld Queen Book 3

Redemption Book 4

**FALL FROM GRACE SERIES**
Gideon: Heavenly Fall

**NOVELLAS**
SEAL Of Time Trident Legacy

All of Sharon's books are available on Audible, narrated by the talented J.D. Hart.

# ABOUT THIS SEAL FIRSTS BOOK BUNDLE

This book contains all four full-length books in four of Sharon's most popular SEALs Series:

Accidental SEAL, from the SEAL Brotherhood Series (Book 1)
SEAL's Promise, from the Bad Boys of SEAL Team 3 Series (Book 1)
Band of Bachelors: Lucas, from the Band of Bachelors Series (Book 1)
New Years SEAL Dream, from the Bone Frog Brotherhood Series (Book 1)

More information about these four series can be obtained on Sharon's website:
Authorsharonhamilton.com

# ACCIDENTAL SEAL

## SEAL Brotherhood
## Book 1

## SHARON HAMILTON

# CHAPTER 1

CHRISTY NELSON WORKED to keep her breakfast down as Wayne Somerville came lurking around her cubicle. He'd pestered her every day since she'd been introduced as the newest agent at the Patterson Realty sales meeting three days ago. His soft, flabby torso was repulsive, and those distinctive hair plugs, installed at an angle on Wayne's shiny salmon-colored forehead, were distracting. Her gaze followed rows of black dots receding into his dyed-black hair. A life-sized version of Mr. King's Chuckie.

Wayne winked at her again, and her blood turned to ice.

His horse teeth and foul breath could raise the dead. He'd made it clear he wanted to mentor her, but she suspected he had more in mind than real estate contracts and short sales. He was persistent, though. She'd give him that.

He draped his bulky frame against the back of her chair. She wanted to duck for cover. The eerie need to protect her neck put her radar on high alert as she visualized violence and fangs.

"I've coached quite a few of the new agents over the years." Wayne's look lasted too long—hungry and inappropriate. Christy didn't trust one single hair plug.

"Well," she said, resisting the urge to escape, "I do need a good open house.

*Now, why did I say that?*

"I've got the perfect one! Great little short sale." Wayne launched into his routine, oblivious to the fact she'd become dizzy from the smell of the garlic fries he'd apparently had for lunch. "The house is a little rough around the edges, but in a super neighborhood. The sellers are about to lose it." He threw her a mock frown. She could see him singing a hymn, asking for money on TV.

*Perhaps a second career.*

"No sign on the lawn yet and it's not even in the computer," he continued. "You can snatch all those buyers for yourself." He leaned in and whispered as if it were a national secret. "And I could help you with the paperwork. You know, show you how it's done."

*Male alert. If he touches me, he'll get a knee to his groin.* She swung her chair to angle for quick action.

He stepped back just in time. She exhaled, grateful for the distance.

"Doing short sales is a real art," he added with a frown, stiffening. His shiny suit fit like one of those unfortunate animals in a teddy bear factory, stuffed into its fur. The silver glint of the fabric reminded her of fish scales.

*Run, Christy, run. You could be the one who got away...*

She had never in her life paid a favor with sex and wasn't about to start. She would hold his new listing open, but only if she could do it without owing him.

Besides, she had to do something to drum up business. Her move to San Diego marked the beginning of her new professional career as a Realtor. Being the top salesperson at Madame M's lingerie boutique on Maiden Lane in San Francisco barely paid the bills. She'd loved Madame and had thrived as a sales clerk, but recognized the time for a real career. She trained in real estate, and then moved to San Diego after her mother passed. Christy inherited the condo.

Though she'd been comfortable selling to the rich and powerful of the City by the Bay, Wayne, even if he was half the success he claimed he was, made her nervous.

*This is a very bad idea. Just say no.*

"Fine." It sounded like it came from the cubicle next to her.

But then she spotted Wayne's dimples and canines.

*Oh. My. God. I've just said yes.*


CHRISTY'S RED HONDA looked like a wet cherry lollipop, polished to perfection. Cute and shiny on the outside, but hot and sweltering on the inside. Sitting in the cramped front seat, she stopped and squinted to make out house numbers, comparing them to the address Wayne minutely scribbled on the back of his business card. Then she found it.

The house appeared nicer than he'd described. The advertised price, he said, was the lowest in the neighborhood, going back ten years. Hopefully she'd pick up a young couple out looking for their first home, complete with good credit and a wad of cash from Mommy and Daddy. Wouldn't it be great to make a sale on her very first day on the job?

She parked in the driveway, popped the trunk, and brought out three sandwich signs with the Patterson Realty logo, on loan from Wayne. He was out with his family today. She hoped the Somervilles didn't stop by since she'd feel uncomfortable looking into the eyes of Wayne's wife, a woman he'd probably cheated on and would again if he got the chance. One of Christy's other rules: no married men. She wasn't about to change that, either.

A perfumed late spring breeze blew softly against her face and neck, sending a thrill up her spine. The air ripened with possibility. This was her favorite time of year.

The walkway looked freshly swept. After placing one sign in the front yard, she stacked the other two beside the front door and inserted Wayne's key. While the lock accepted the new shiny silver metal, the tumblers stayed in place, frozen.

*Way to go Wayne. Waste my time and give me the wrong key!*

Irritation bubbled, ruining her cheerful, spring-induced mood. She yanked on the front handle and pushed against it out of frustration. It opened.

"Anybody home?" her voice wavered like that of a small child. She waited. No answer.

Christy stepped inside, onto a striped cotton rug lying cockeyed behind the front door. The smell of fried food hit her. She walked across the wooden floor of the living room, her stilettos clacking. She cracked open a window. Air scented by fresh blossoms poured in, diluting the smells of ordinary life. She grabbed the newspaper tossed on top of an ottoman and folded the crinkling pages under her arm, aiming for the kitchen to find a trashcan. She passed the dining room table, which was strewn with a map of the area, a couple of felt-tipped pens, and a letter-sized yellow lined tablet. She collected these items as well and made her way to the kitchen.

Christy threw the tablet and newspaper onto the tiled countertop and placed her hands on her hips to assess the scene before her. She squinted at several days' worth of dishes piled high in the sink. Next to it, a large stainless steel bowl sat encrusted with dark green and purple leaves at the bottom, evidence of a salad—several days old.

Maybe Wayne had neglected to tell the sellers about the open house. She decided it was entirely possible. "How can you expect to sell a house this way?" she muttered, then sighed and removed her jacket, slinging it over the back of a clean-looking kitchen chair. She decided to take a tour of the place, checking for other things to clean or straighten before she'd be ready to hold it open.

But this house was such a mess, an uneasy darkness chilled her. She tiptoed down the carpeted hallway, feeling like an intruder, past empty rooms to a closed door at the end.

*Probably the master bedroom.*

Something about the whole scene was strange. These people left in a hurry without cleaning up dinner from several days before. She'd been told short sale houses rarely showed pride of ownership, but this felt absolutely creepy, like she'd stepped on someone's grave. The hair on the back of her neck bristled as she gripped the doorknob. She lightly tapped with her other hand and then opened the door.

A naked body lay on the bed.

*Holy crap.*

Hesitant to look at first, she pushed through her fear. She saw movement. Tanned skin, a muscular male chest that rose and fell. Earphones were wired to a phone balanced on his open palm. The man was very much alive, and healthy. Her eyes drifted further down to a dusting of dark brown hair that led to an impossible-to-miss erection. His penis stood at attention, like a deep rose-colored light standard under a matching fireman's hat of deeper pink.

Blood pumped to her ears, making them ring, as her heart raced. A wave of anger coursed over her at the realization she had been the victim of a very sick joke perpetrated by Wayne and one of his disgusting friends.

Christy silently closed the door and tiptoed back down the carpeted hallway, her three-inch heels wobbling on the thick, padded surface. Her knees knocked against each other as she picked up speed, her anger building. She grabbed her jacket, keys, and purse, and crossed the living room, headed toward the front door. She was almost free.

Christy wouldn't give the prankster the satisfaction of knowing she had even seen him. She wanted to stomp her foot and kick something through the window. This was Wayne's doing.

*That sonofabitch and his lopsided plugs will pay for this.*

She pulled the door handle and was rewarded by the smells of a warm spring day bleeding through the inch-wide crack she'd created. An enormous hand and forearm came from behind her and slammed the door shut. She saw a familiar blue-green tattoo of some animal tracks on his muscled forearm just before his other hand gripped her mouth. Callused fingers pinched the sides of her cheeks. The grip hurt.

She panicked at first; then her self-defense training kicked into gear. She struggled to duck and turn, digging her nails into the man's arm. He locked her tightly in a choke hold, which immobilized her upper torso. She attempted a muffled cry, but the chokehold pulled against her windpipe and allowed her only a weak, high-pitched whine. He was good at the mouth grip, not giving her any room to bite the way she'd been taught. His mountainous shoulders were so large she couldn't find his face to scratch at his eyes.

That left her lower body somewhat free. Christy balanced herself like a stork on one high heel, leaned against the wall of his chest, and dug the other heel backward into his knee. She felt him jerk in a sharp inhale. He didn't cry out. She knew she'd hurt him, but cursed her inability to land the steel tip of her new three-inch stilettos into the soft tissue area of his thigh, going for his femoral artery. Christy moved to deliver a second blow and was pulled backward, tight against his chest. They tumbled to the floor. He took the brunt of the fall, and then pitched her body like a tiny twig in the wind, climbing on top of her.

Though they faced each other, her hair was everywhere, covering her eyes, but by the anatomical placement of his body pressed against hers, she knew he was the naked stranger from the bedroom. It took only one large paw to hold both her wrists and pin them high above her head.

With the weight of his packed and well-developed body immobilizing her, she feared a more sinister intent. She mentally prepared herself for the worst: a brutal rape or murder, or perhaps both.

*Think, dammit. There's always a solution.*

But the universe remained mute.

Out of options, she vowed deep in her heart she would cause him damage, maybe spill some of his blood so that when the police detectives looked over her lifeless body at the crime scene, there would be forensic evidence.

*So this is the way I will be remembered: at a crime scene, outlined in yellow chalk.*

Maybe she wouldn't survive, but she would help get him caught and save another innocent woman from this sexual sicko. She couldn't see his eyes, which was a minor blessing. She didn't want him to know her fear.

He adjusted himself and shifted off her lower body. Her skirt rode halfway up her thighs. Christy used the opportunity to maneuver her stocking-covered knee between his legs and punch his groin. To her horror, her knee felt the warmth of his naked skin. His yell, accompanied by a string of obscenities, interrupted her repulsion. She was pleased not all the blood from his cock had drained, meaning the hit had caused him pain. He lifted his hand off her mouth and balled it into a fist under her head, gripping her hair at the scalp.

"You bastard..." She growled from deep inside her chest, surprised at her own bravado, then decided to scream. Immediately, the hand clamped over her mouth again. This time she bit down through the soft tissue between his thumb and forefinger and tasted the warm metallic liquid from his broken skin. But he still didn't flinch and pressed down even harder. His other hand released her wrists and pulled her hair back with a tug at the nape of her neck, forcing her chin up toward the ceiling. She tried pushing him away with her arms, but his were longer.

She arched her chest in defiance, but this gave him a full view of her breasts. The buttons on her sheer ivory blouse popped open. She muttered a curse. The fleeting thought that he would now ruin her two-hundred-dollar bra and be spurred on to ravish her further flashed through her mind.

He immobilized her arms above her head with one forearm and pinned her thighs with his own that were easily twice the size of hers. She had no way to move and no ability to scream for help. But his blood dripped on the wooden flooring, and it coated the inside of her mouth. Maybe that would be enough to land him a spot in San Quentin. Tired and resigned, she sighed, knowing she could not win the physical tussle, and allowed her body to go limp.

He responded by whispering a question in her ear. "Who *are* you?"

For a second, her ears buzzed. Then she mumbled through his fingers, seeking the soft fleshy part of his palm with her canines again, but failing. She was unable to give him an intelligible answer, but if she could, it would be, "*Who the fuck are you?*"

"I'm going to take my hand away, and you will tell me who you are and whom you work for." His voice came across calm and steady. Practiced. Measured. She'd have to say, commanding.

This surprised her, but she still didn't trust him. She gave a short nod, but intended to get away at the first opportunity. He removed his hand and brought it between their bodies. She sucked in her breath and straightened her spine, even though it hurt. She prepared for him to grip her breasts and rip her clothing to shreds. She clenched her abdomen and waited for the pain.

But instead, she caught a filtered view through her tresses of one heavily veined hand reaching to his tensed pectoral muscle, removing her Patterson Realty nametag that speared him there. He sniffed the pin as he thumbed over the embedded letters of her name, and then tossed it. The pin skidded across the floor until it hit a baseboard.

"This gonna make me pass out?" He made it sound like a legitimate question. He touched the pinprick wound on his chest and then yanked back the strands of her hair he still held wrapped in his fist. She couldn't see much of his face.

"What?"

"You an agent?"

"Yes, I'm...I'm a r-r-r..."

"Business or political?"

Christy furrowed her brow, squinting. "Business!"

He reached under her skirt, pulling down her pantyhose so quickly that he got her lace panties too. Cold fear snaked in her belly and shivered up her spine. She shrieked, but it did no good. He removed her remaining heel and then ripped her under things off in one fluid movement. Christy attempted to scream again but was silenced by his hand squeezing her neck, his thumb pressing against her voice box.

"Stop it. I don't want to hurt you."

*That's what they say just before they kill you.*

She couldn't move. She couldn't breathe and tried to cough, hoping death would come soon, *before* he raped her. But then he relaxed his grip, allowing spring air to flood her lungs. For a grateful few seconds, everything was right with the world.

With his other hand, he took the now shredded pantyhose and wrapped them around her wrists that he held up over her head. The knot he tied cut off circulation to her hands, but at least she could move her torso a little. Her neck tensed up from the fall, and her tailbone hurt.

"Please, I'm j-just…here…for…the open house."

"What open house?"

"W-Wayne…said…I…should…"

"Who the hell is Wayne? He your handler?"

Now this pissed her off. "God damn it. I'm an independent contractor!" She'd heard it so many times while she was studying for her license that the phrase was the first thing that popped into her mind. "Wayne is another agent. I'm a Realtor."

"Sure you are."

Christy drilled him with a look he wouldn't be able to mistake, if he could see it. Hair still covered her face.

He chuckled. "This part of your sales training? They teach you how to bite men, break into houses, knock out their knees, and puncture them with poisonous needles?" His subtle mocking fueled something bubbling in her stomach.

She shifted slightly, noticing the still rather large package between her legs that might have been welcome in another time and place. She shook her head to the side, clearing the hair from her face with the aid of her bound hands; she then stared into deep blue eyes, a crooked nose, and soft full lips pressed together in a straight line. A tiny scar resided on his high cheekbone just under his left eye.

He swallowed as he looked down on her and watched her follow the trek of his Adam's apple. When she looked back into his eyes, his body seemed to soften. A few errant strands of hair were caught in her lipgloss. He removed them with two hardened fingers. His eyes explored her face, tracing all her features, as if memorizing every one.

Her heart beat against her chest wall, echoing his, for several long seconds. He didn't look like a criminal. Or a practical joker type. As she studied him closer, she realized something didn't add up.

He righted himself, released his hold on her, and then sat crouched, covering his exposed groin with the throw rug. He seized her purse and turned it inside out in seconds by pulling apart the lining and dumping the contents on the floor.

"Hey! That's a Coach bag, you…"

He gave her another glare, reminding her she was physically outmatched. She closed her mouth mid-sentence, choking down renewed anger. He sifted through the contents, opened a lipstick tube and sniffed the pink shaft, then carefully retracted it and replaced the top.

"Sorry." He directed his apology to the floor and didn't glance up.

*That's it? Can't even look at me, you horrible son of a bitch?* She decided it was still unsafe, so kept her thoughts to herself.

*He's crazy. A psycho. A sociopath. No wonder he has financial issues and has to sell his house.*

Christy sat up, her spine ramrod straight, and held out her hands, encumbered by the torn pantyhose that hung like moss from a tree. It was not a beg but a demand to be released of her bonds. To her surprise, he gently leaned over and untied her. She buttoned her blouse, noting before she could finish that his last-minute stolen peek gave him a good view of her lacy beige bra.

She returned a poisonous look she hoped would stop any ideas from forming on his part, and then she noticed a tiny trickle of blood coming from the pinprick in his chest. A much larger ribbon of blood dripped to a small puddle on the floor where her heel had done damage to his knee. Below that was a tattoo of thorns ringing his bulging calf. As if she asked, he raised his palm, showing her a nice bloody semicircle of teeth marks.

"You're lethal," his voice was soft, but measured. He arose, all six-foot-something of him, then fisted the throw rug to his groin. He turned, exposing his muscled buttocks, and looked over his shoulder at her. He shook his head and smirked as he watched her stuff the lining back into her purse and replace the spilled contents.

"I don't think it's funny at all," she huffed. "Get someone else to hold your damn open house."

He didn't say anything but continued staring down at her as he offered a hand, which she refused. She clamored to stand up, barefoot.

"And if you think this is a good way to meet a girl," she said as she wedged her bare feet into her heels, "well, I hope the bank takes your house and I hope your wife finds out what kind of sick games you play."

She headed to the door. She was relieved he was going to actually let her go. Without looking back, she swung the door wide open.

"This isn't my house, and I'm not married," she heard him call just before she slammed the door behind her, finally free at last.

# CHAPTER 2

NAVY SEAL KYLE Lansdowne threw down the rag rug and stalked naked to the place where the woman's nametag landed next to the wall. He traced the letters again and examined the nametag's construction, looking for—*what?*

"Christy Nelson," he said as he focused on the indentations the letters made in the smooth white plastic tag. He had the funny feeling he'd met this woman before. Or maybe she reminded him of someone he'd known in his past.

He dropped his shoulders and arched backward to give his spine a good crack. Holding the light plastic badge in his fingertips, he was careful not to let it puncture him again. He leaned forward, aimed for the dining table, and tossed the nametag so it landed in one bounce at the center.

He checked the front window, confirming that the car he'd heard leaving was hers and that he was now alone. He locked the dead bolt on the front door and made his way back to the bedroom.

*I'm losing it, man.* He cursed himself for his carelessness. The naked meditation he engaged in usually heightened his senses, but this time he'd fallen asleep. Next thing he knew he was smelling her perfume. Still could smell it. Had she not been a woman, he could have hurt her, or worse. On the other hand, if she'd been hired to neutralize him, she could have taken him out in an instant.

His Team buddy, Armando Guzman, was missing. Gone. Never showed up at ProDev. He'd made it out of Afghanistan with the rest of SEAL Team 3, but instead of doing the five days decompression in Hawaii with the rest of the guys, he'd booked a flight to Puerto Rico for some family emergency.

*Where the fuck are you?*

Mysteriously, Armando met them at the airport in San Diego when they arrived from Hawaii, talking about seeing everyone at ProDev the next day. And then he didn't show. Timmons, their chief, was freaked, worried to hell. It just wasn't like Armando to do this. No way would he disappear voluntarily without alerting Kyle and the chief.

Day before yesterday, when Timmons told him Armando never checked in, Kyle thought perhaps he'd just found himself a lady to share a little time with, disappear for a day or two. Something they were trained to do: get lost. Wouldn't have been the first time Armando had gone to dark. And Kyle couldn't blame him. He'd done it a time or two himself, but never without checking in with his buddy first.

*Something is very wrong.*

Armando was known all over Coronado as the Latin Lover of SEAL Team 3. So good looking he could capture a girl's attention simply by walking down the street. His linguistic training allowed him to sound Aussie, French, Brit, Eastern European, Spanish, Pashtoon or Afghani. He could charm the pants off anyone on the phone as well as in person. He'd even been "captured" by a Marine unit who mistook him for a foreign interpreter trying to infiltrate the U.S. forces. Some of Team 3 still called him *"Tarjumah,"* the translator.

More than a couple of Senior Officers' wives, took long, dangerous looks at him when he wore his dress whites. He was the Antonio Banderas type of good looking, with a fashion sense and love of stylish clothes that made him look more like a cover model than a SEAL. The Team guys nicknamed him "Armani."

But when Timmons told Kyle his buddy never checked in before he left base, Kyle knew some serious shit had hit the fan. Nobody ever did that unless there was an attitude issue. Attitudes didn't last long on the Teams. Armando had a history from his youth, growing up with a Puerto Rican gang, but the Navy had pretty much drummed that out of him. Legendary for his nerves of steel, Armando could disarm a bomb while blowing bubbles with his bubblegum. Could save the whole team from extinction while thinking about what he would have for dinner that night.

So, Mr. Cool and Lethal wanted to be followed, and found. It was as obvious as if Armando had sent him a registered letter.

"What the hell are you up to, Armani?" Kyle whispered.

He'd spent days buried in sand with the man. They'd put their lives on the line for each other as well as for the rest of the team. Having spent three tours in Afghanistan and Iraq together, he and Armando had survived the battle of Fallujah when their unit reported record kills without losing many of their own. He could practically read Armando's mind. They'd been scared shitless together. They'd cried over a fallen Team guy and still had the presence of mind to jump in and save someone else the next minute. That kind of brotherhood couldn't be taught. It had to be *lived.*

Without Armando as his swim buddy, Kyle knew he never would have completed the grueling BUD/S training, the qualification all Navy SEALs had to pass in order to begin their real training. He owed his gold Trident, the insignia of a SEAL, to this man. Armando's problem, whatever it was, would now become Kyle's problem.

Armando swam like a fish with the explosive strength of a bull. He used to joke with the members of his unit how he could bring a cruise ship to port in his native Puerto Rico by holding the tie line with his teeth.

Kyle and a couple of other teammates had been granted ten days leave, and Kyle intended to spend every day of it searching for Armando. He knew deep in his soul that the guy would do the same for him. Kyle and his chief had a silent understanding. If he needed more time he would have to ask for it, and the request would be denied. If Kyle couldn't find Armando, no one could. But the Navy could hardly afford to have one missing SEAL; two missing men could get a commander stripped or booted.

His thoughts wandered to the girl.

The scent of her perfume lingered on his skin. He couldn't get the little hellcat out of his mind. No denying his body liked what Christy felt like under him; his erection had never fully settled down, even with the pain above his knee. His traitorous body part now started rising again, as if it had been summoned.

Damn. It had been too long since he'd held a woman that close. Was his training such that consorting with females ended up posing a danger to their health? He hated how he'd treated her. He shook his head, thinking of how the woman seemed to be one of those feisty, angry types who wouldn't allow herself to become a victim. This woman, a stealth survivor of the love wars, did a damn good job at self-defense.

Except she shouldn't have experienced this today. She was an innocent. She didn't deserve to be tied and treated like a suspect. The honor in Kyle's chest, the vow he made to protect the innocent even if it meant his own life, was wounded. He'd have to make it right somehow. He'd caused her the fright of her life, and he needed to make amends. Later.

But maybe she *was* somehow involved. Otherwise, why would she break into Armando's house? And why had she mentioned something about a bank and a wife?

Would Armando be losing his house? Kyle didn't think this was possible. Armando was frugal as all hell, even managing to send money home to parts of his family still in Puerto Rico. Kyle also doubted he would sell it.

*Who is this Wayne guy? Does he know Armando?*

Kyle stepped into the shower and washed the glorious smell of her off his skin, pouring over the other questions in his mind.

Enough of that.

That kind of lapse in concentration could get a good squid killed. He needed to stay sharp, not distracted by the fantasy of a woman he barely knew. A woman who he didn't believe was involved in his friend's disappearance. He'd been trained to challenge other warriors, and if his time came, trained to take several bad guys with him. Not like this, mistreating an innocent.

He shut the water off and thought of his deep admiration for Armando. It made no sense that the man would just walk away from his country, his proud heritage, his family, and his SEAL community. Kyle doubted any one man would be able to take Armando down without a big fight, something so high profile it would alert one of their friendlies.

Even on leave, his team would email or text or run into several of their buddies every day. They hung out in the same bars owned by former members, got their tattoos at the same parlors, even picked the same beaches in San Diego to hang out on—away from the base, of course—but never far away from another Team member. The community was their family, and the blood in their veins pumped to protect it. They never even considered the cost.

So something very wrong happened, he thought as he dried off. A quick sniff to the towel told him a tiny amount of her perfume remained a scented shadow. Yeah, he'd wait a day or two before washing that towel. He hung it on the back of the door.

Staring at his image in the bathroom mirror, he didn't see the face of a killer. It was his warrior persona, his part of an exclusive brotherhood. Hesitation had been drummed out of him. Was he succumbing to fuzzy judgment of the female kind? Thank God he'd been able to accurately assess the danger she didn't pose to him before he'd caused her unintentional harm. Other than scaring the wits out of her, of course.

He decided to shave tomorrow. He straightened the bed, then threw on some mid-calf khakis and a green T-shirt. Today was a flip-flop-out-of-uniform kind of day, as it usually was whenever he was home. He had one pair of non-military dress shoes and they hurt his feet. His BUD/S trainers told him he'd develop webbed feet eventually, and although it was a big joke, it had a ring of truth to it.

He completed his dress by adding a sweatshirt hoodie, then took the dark wire-rimmed sunglasses from the pouch in his duty bag and smoothed them across his eyes.

As he left, he noted the two red sandwich signs leaning against Armando's front porch. Then he spotted the one in the front lawn, and added it to the other two, leaving all three of them there. He knew it would be a mistake to try to track her down.

*Leave the poor woman alone.* He hoped she would come by when he was gone.

Kyle hit the button on his key fob and his black Hummer squawked. It reminded him of a greeting a good horse would make. As if saying the machine was ready to do his master's bidding. He hardly washed the beast, and knew the salt air wasn't a friend, but he just couldn't bring himself to drive something clean and sanitized and smelling like hospitals, the one place he tried to avoid.

He'd parked across and down the street from Armando's house. He'd intended to bring the Hummer inside the garage after dark, erasing evidence he was there in case bad guys watched the house. He'd checked the garage when he'd first arrived. It smelled like it had been a couple of days since a gas-fired engine had turned over there. Armando's Land Rover was missing.

Not a good sign.

Kyle hopped into the Hummer and headed toward Coronado.

He came to the strip, one block off the beach, and passed familiar haunts, cruising past a couple of Team guys watching girls and drinking beer at an open-air cafe. He honked and was rewarded with two three-finger salutes, which he returned. His anxiety lessened somewhat by that quick check-in with fellow Team guys.

Up and down the strip he looked for Armando's Rover, but without any luck. He headed to Gunny's gym.

He liked the iron smell of rusty, well-used equipment that assaulted his nostrils the instant he pushed his way through the glass door and tinkled the bell. But he hated bells.

The DOR, or Drop On Request, bell they used during their BUD/S training didn't survive the class. He'd had his share of looking at that damned thing, tied to the back of a pickup truck that headed down the beach as some poor Team hopeful tried to catch it to end his torment and pain. There was no shame in quitting. Not everyone was cut out to do this job. Even at the beginning of Hell Week, the new class of recruits were one in ten thousand regular Navy guys who would gladly trade places with them for a shot at becoming a SEAL. But, the instructors didn't make it easy to drop out. DOR guys had to chase the damned thing a mile down the beach, catcalls being shouted at them from the back of the pickup, like these hopefuls were sissies.

Not a surprise to anyone that he and Armando had given that bell a really good deep-sea burial. Out of the 190 who started their class, they were part of the twelve who'd successfully graduated. That bell was homage to the 178 brave souls who'd given it a shot. God bless them for trying.

He and Armando worked out at Gunny's almost every day when they were home. The smell of sweat and the ancient equipment suited him just fine. No Nautilus stuff here, no digital anything except a scale that couldn't be rigged. The house rule reigned: when you finished with the dead weight, you had to throw it on the black rubber matted ground so it would bounce, not just place it carefully at your feet. That part he liked best about the place. And of course, he could always spot a Team or former Team guy there.

Gunny had been Marine Recon, a Gunnery Sergeant. He'd gone in just as troops were pulling out of Viet Nam, but saw a little combat at the tail end. He called himself a serial husband, and had a pack of ex-wives and kids littering the whole globe. Some of them didn't even speak English.

Everyone knew, including his ex-wives and their lawyers, that Gunny didn't have anything but his pension and this crusty, run-down gym that barely broke even. Gunny had told Kyle if any of his kids wanted to see him, they'd have to come to San Diego. There were no birthday or Christmas cards exchanged, and as far as Kyle knew, Gunny had never met any of his progeny, except one.

Gunny was known for rescuing Team guys at bars in the middle of the night if they were too drunk to drive. He'd get them home safe, keeping them from the local or military police looking to make a trophy bust. Gunny made sure no one got booted for a DUI or Acts Unbecoming, and called the MPs and even regular police who were also ex-military "Rent-A-Cops." He held them with about as much respect as he had for security guards. Kyle guessed there would be some interesting reading if he ever got his hands on Gunny's personnel jacket.

Gunny was violating his own sign, a cigarette full of ash protruding out the right side of his mouth. But the gym was empty today.

"Thought you'd have quit by now. You got that scare last year, Gunny."

"Nah, I'm gonna burn it out." Gunny's grizzled gray chin stored a line of sweat in the deep crease under his lower lip.

"But you dodged the bullet, right?" Kyle knew the gym had closed for a week when Gunny went in for lung surgery. Later, Gunny had gotten a tattoo over the scar that read, *I Already Gave*, just in case anyone would have some crazy idea to harvest his lungs and heart upon his demise.

"What do you think, kid?" Gunny gave Kyle a wary look and continued. "Not one of us gets out of this tour alive."

So Kyle knew the rumor was true. They'd opened Gunny up and then put him back together again. No cure. That's why he'd never lost his hair. No further treatment. Team guys had been making bets on what Gunny would look like—maybe pink and hairless like a newborn, since his normal pelt made him resemble a grizzly. Kyle and Armando just figured Gunny's system was too ornery for the chemo to affect him.

"I'm not happy to hear this, Gunny."

"Hear what? I never told you nothing." Gunny grinned, showing his stained teeth, then removed the cigarette and put it out in the palm of his hand. He shook the ashes into a wastebasket by the entry glass display case filled with Gunny's Gym T-shirts bearing the picture of Popeye holding up a barbell with an anchor tattoo prominent on his forearm.

"You don't look like you're here to work out," Gunny stated the obvious fact.

"No. I'm looking for Armando. You seen him last day or two?" Kyle watched the old man's eyes flash with alarm, and then the older man shook his head.

"Not a good sign," Gunny said as he looked at the floor. "What are you thinking?"

"He's never done this before. Timmins is freaked. Armando left the base without checking in with him." Kyle leaned toward the older man. "And I didn't tell you that, either."

"Got it."

The tinkling bell over the door broke the awkward silence. Two older ex-Team guys entered, carrying their well-worn workout bags. In their late forties, they still bore developed chest and arm muscles, maybe even more than the younger guys. Both of them sported graying ponytails and were covered in tattoos.

"Hey, guys," Gunny said, addressing them.

"Shit, Gunny, you've been smoking again," one of them said as he propped open the door. "All your brains go south on you?"

"There's a reason I have twelve kids and five ex-wives."

Kyle laughed inside at this comment. He knew Gunny well enough to know he married every one of those women before he had sex with them. This was a little known fact he and Armando had been privy to—hardened and tough Gunny was also a gentleman. He'd even married one in a jungle temple in Southeast Asia, the rites performed by a yellow-robed priest who'd painted both the bride and groom with symbols. Gunny told Kyle he couldn't wait and had consummated his marriage on the way back to the family celebration in the covered litter pulled by water buffalo, piloted by his new wife's brother. They had a hard time calming her mother down when she saw the disarray of their intricate face paintings, meant to ensure good luck, fertility, and great fortune.

The two men nodded at Kyle and went about selecting the equipment for their workout. Gunny motioned to the outside, so Kyle followed him through the entryway.

"So, what have you found out?"

"Timmons is tracking down Armando's cell signal. Said it would take a day, maybe two. But this is Sunday and Timmons has to wait until tomorrow to call it in."

"The waiting must be a sonofabitch."

"I don't do 'wait' very well." Kyle thought about the waiting they used to do, buried in sand, perched on rooftops. Waiting for the enemy to show up. Waiting to be told to get the hell out of there. But this was worse.

"Looks like he's trying to leave a trail of breadcrumbs. Not checking in with Timmins might be his first clue. I just don't know where to go from there. I'm missing something important."

"He didn't tell you anything?"

"I'm thinking about the last few times we were together. He got a lot of text messages, but I'm not sure from who," Kyle continued in a whisper, "Now that I think back on it, he didn't look too pleased when he got them."

"Can't get the cell location any sooner?"

Kyle's thoughts exactly. "Timmons says to wait until we have a location. Don't want to alarm the locals or ask them for help."

"Understood. Meantime, you're hoping he'll show up somewhere and it was all a false alarm."

"Exactly."

"Possible he got offed?"

"Nah. No fucking way. Not alone, anyway."

"He have a girl?"

"Between girls."

"Someone who pulled him back into the dark ages?"

Kyle recognized this as Gunny's way of dosing out a bit of his personal philosophy about not getting permanently involved with women. Gunny felt women were the biggest threat to a man's freedom and always told the men to steer clear, advice he seldom took himself. Kyle tended to agree with him.

"No. The only people outside the community who could pull him away like this would be someone from his family in Puerto Rico."

"Then you start with them." Gunny leveled a dead-serious stare. "Kyle, they don't know how many months I got. I never made it to your ranks, but I feel like a father to all you Team guys. If you want me, I'll help."

# CHAPTER 3

C HRISTY STRADDLED THE line between fury and fear all the way back to her condo. She checked her rear view mirror every thirty seconds to make sure that cretin hadn't followed her home. Trying to remember evasion strategies she'd read in some of her favorite thriller novels, she'd doubled back, turned right, then drove for ten minutes in the opposite direction, finally headed for her place. She planned never to go back to that damned house or even the street again for the rest of her life. She'd just take that page and rip it from her Thomas Brothers Map Book. She would familiarize herself with all the other streets and buildings of San Diego County except for the ones on page 68.

Then she remembered she'd left all three of Wayne's red Patterson Realty signs back at the house.

"Damn!" Well, it served Wayne right. Christy wasn't entirely sure of Wayne's involvement in this afternoon's caper. *Let him go back and get those signs.* She chuckled at the thought of Wayne finding the naked crazy guy at the front door. Now that would be a sight she would go back to see.

She drove into her condo garage, double-checking dark corners of the structure for evidence of someone lurking there. She'd never worried about this before.

All kinds of possibilities and scenarios ran through her mind as she rode the elevator to her floor. Perhaps Wayne wasn't who she thought he was. Could there be a jealous husband or jilted lover from one of the affairs Christy imagined he'd had?

Wayne must have been the real target, she thought. After all, the worst thing she had done was help some guy max out his credit card at Madame M's lingerie shop. She was the shop's best saleswoman. Last she checked, this wasn't a crime.

Once inside, she put the whole afternoon's incident out of her mind by stripping her clothes and donning her workout gear, and then she headed for the upscale gym on the top floor of her condo complex.

Every area of the complex had a terrific view of San Diego Harbor. A few minutes into her spin class, her body was covered in glistening sweat as she worked out to her iPod playing her favorite *Secret Garden* piece. The beauty of the poignant viola speared her heart. Tears streamed down her cheeks.

*Damn, I'm lonely.*

All her relationships with men ended badly. And the guy she'd just met had some sort of sick death wish for her. She barely knew him, well, except for how nicely he fit between her legs. Though she tried, she couldn't get that image out of her head. Why were all these weird men coming into her life now, just when she wanted to embark on a professional career?

"You okay, Christy?" Marla, her personal trainer, touched her arm.

Christy realized the class had stopped for a water break. She looked up and saw the concern in Marla's eyes. Christy buried her face in the white towel around her neck. "No. I'm not alright," she said, her voice muffled through the towel so Marla couldn't hear the waver there. Memories flooded in—how she'd tried to scream and how that big hand had covered her mouth, how she'd felt with him pressed down onto her body, and how she'd reacted to those damn blue eyes that seemed to drink in her face. She could easily mistake it for attraction. What was going on?

"Aw, honey." Marla wrapped her arms around Christy's waist. "Take a break. Come on, let's go into my office for a bit."

Christy nodded and let Marla lead her into a private office off the spin room. Marla motioned to a chair in front of her desk, and Christy collapsed there, continuing to wipe her face and neck with the towel. Marla punched the phone and spoke softly.

"Marla here. Hey, can Trey finish my spin class for me? Something's come up." Marla locked eyes on Christy.

"I'm fine. Don't do this, Marla," Christy whispered.

"Okay? Good. Tell him I owe him one." Marla hung up the phone. "Not a problem. Happens all the time." She pulled her desk chair over and held Christy's hands in both of hers. "Come on, spill it. Don't make me dig."

"Today was supposed to be my first open house."

"Yup, you were excited about it."

"Yes, I was…until I got there…" Tears welled up in her eyes and her lower lip quivered.

"Christy, what happened?"

"There was this crazy guy there who was asleep in the master bedroom, stark naked."

"Did he touch you?"

"Yes…" Christy's chest was heaving and she found it difficult to breathe.

"The creep. Did he hurt you?"

*Did he hurt me?* "He scared me, that's all."

"You call the cops?"

"No. I mean, he thought I was breaking into his house. I couldn't call the cops. Maybe Wayne set it up…I'm just not sure what happened."

"Who's Wayne?"

"The agent whose listing it is."

"Tell me honestly, Christy. Were you hurt?"

"He ripped off my pantyhose and messed with my purse, but no, I'm not hurt."

"Jeez, Christy. What do you mean messed with your purse? Screw the purse. He scared you to death!"

The two women looked at each other. Christy's composure was coming back, but Marla seemed to be losing hers.

"I know. He could have killed me, but he didn't."

"Exactly. And you're giving him a pass for acting like a Neanderthal? Why would he rip off your pantyhose?"

"He used them to tie my hands together."

"Oh, this just keeps getting better and better. That's assault, Christy. That man should go to jail."

"Yes, I understand, and under normal circumstances, I would agree. But somehow I got that this guy was simply reacting to what he thought was a threat. Maybe he's not right in the head. I don't want to have anything more to do with him. I just want to stay away. He let me go and he didn't really hurt me, just scared me is all. I don't know, but I somehow don't feel it's entirely his fault." She looked up at Marla. "Does that sound crazy?"

"Absolutely. You're not thinking straight at all, Christy."

"He secured my wrists to keep me quiet...so he could talk to me."

"That sick bastard."

"No. I mean I was pretty hysterical and I did bite him and even spiked his knee with my high heel. I fought as hard as I could, Marla. He attempted to get information out of me, like he thought I was some sort of undercover agent or something, like I was there to do him harm. His mind had it all screwed up."

Marla nodded.

"Are there lots of paranoid whackos like this in San Diego?"

"Not generally. But then, I don't seem to attract them like you do."

"Thanks a lot."

Marla rubbed her hands with her thumbs. "How did you get hired to hold this open house?"

"Wayne." Christy winced as she forced herself to say the name again. "He told me they were expecting me. I don't want to think he purposely set me up, but you know, I can't figure it out otherwise."

"What can I do to help?" Marla's sincere voice soothed.

Christy stood up and gave her a hug. "Thanks, Marla. You already have." At the door, she turned. "I'm going to report this to my manager tomorrow as soon as I get into the office. If I felt I was in danger now, I would call the police."

Marla shook her head. "I'd say call them just in case, Christy. Don't be a wimp. That's how come these creeps stay out there. Nobody turns them in."

"I'll do it tomorrow, I promise. Tonight, I'm going to take a hot bath and go to bed early. Thanks again, Marla."

Marla handed her a business card with her home and cell number on it. "Call me tonight if you need company. Honest. If you have trouble sleeping, that's a gut check that you need to call the cops, okay?"


THE WARM BUBBLES in Christy's bath sluiced all the tension from her muscles and bones. But every time her eyelids closed and she began drifting off to sleep, she saw those blue eyes staring down at her, his full lips, slightly upturned at the edges, and his swallow that had forced her attention to wander down his tanned neck and rest just under his stubbled chin. She could smell the muskiness of this man's heaving chest as he arched over her while she peeked at the trail of light brown hair that led downward to the place where their bodies touched. When he'd whispered in her ear, asking who she was, he had pressed his cheek next to hers. She'd had to endure his scent all the way home in the car. There was a part of her that wanted to reach up and—do what? Kiss him?

*Get a grip!*

After the bath, she went to bed with a big glass of warm milk, taking her favorite romance novel with her. The bath had done its job and she fell asleep, waking up at midnight to turn off her reading light.

She lay back again, deciding to put up with the fear while she studied him in her memory—every inch of him, and fell asleep for the second time.

MR. SIMMS CAME in early, so Christy made sure to arrive first, just a little before eight o'clock. She knew no one else except the office staff would likely come in until well past ten.

"Good morning, Christy," he said as he passed by her cubicle. "Nice to see you here bright and early. That's a good sign." He appeared in a chipper mood and Christy didn't pick up any indication he was somehow involved in the fiasco the day before.

*Good. I'll just tell him, then.*

"Mr. Simms, I have something to speak with you about. It's urgent."

"Oh? Something happen?"

"Yes." Christy was surprised at her forcefulness.

"Okay, come on in." He indicated she should follow him to his office. Once inside, he closed the glass sliding door behind her.

Christy took up a chair in front of the red cherrywood desk. Plaques from various agencies, awards from the Board of Realtors, as well as several service groups, including Rotary, decorated the walls. An impressive collection, Christy had to admit, not quite sure why she hadn't noticed them before.

"Shoot." He waited without expression on his face, hands folded over the calendar desk blotter. On the back credenza sat a picture of a woman, two children, and a black Labrador retriever. A family like she'd always wanted.

"I went to do the open house on Sedgeway yesterday for Wayne. You know, his new listing?"

"Oh, that's a great one. Bank sale, right?"

"Um, yes. Short sale."

"So what happened?"

"Well, I got attacked."

Mr. Simms fell back in his chair and almost toppled over. He righted himself and let out a big sigh. "Did he...did he...hurt you?"

"Yes and no."

"Meaning?"

"He didn't rape me, but he, he..." Christy's eyes stung in reflex, trying to create tears that would no longer come. Her lower lip trembled. Her throat was parched.

Mr. Simms was quick to make it around his desk. He knelt in front of Christy and placed his hands on her upper arms with care, as if he didn't want to appear inappropriate. "I'm so sorry, Christy. Have you been to the police?" he asked, his demeanor genuine and tender. She appreciated that.

"No."

"Why?" He rubbed her arms gently and then took her hands in his. His moist, warm hands were a comfort to her. "We *have* to report this. You know that," he said softly. "Could you identify him?"

*Oh yes, I could. I can't get the look and smell of him out of my mind.*

"Mr. Simms, I'm thinking there was some sort of a mistake. Maybe even a prank. I don't want to blame Wayne, but this guy was like, waiting for me. He was...he was...naked."

Simms removed his hands from her arms and stood up, shaking his head.

"Bastard. Did he say he knew Wayne?"

Christy could tell Simms was considering Wayne's involvement, which further underscored some of her own hesitation to be anywhere near the man.

"No, he didn't. In fact, the guy acted like he'd never heard of Wayne."

The appearance of a very angry Wayne, puffed up and red, tore apart their conversation. He pulled open the sliding glass door without being given the nod of approval from Simms, and wedged himself into the room, making it feel suddenly very stuffy.

"What the hell happened, Christy? My clients called me, and they're so mad they want to cancel the listing." His tiny bloodshot eyes darted back and forth between Christy and their manager.

"Wait a minute, Wayne." Simms put a palm on Wayne's sausage-shaped chest, holding him back from coming any closer to her. "Christy here was just explaining what went on yesterday, and I have to say, I find it highly disturbing."

"Disturbing? Disturbing? I'll tell you what's disturbing!" Wayne said, looking like he wanted to crash through Simms and grab Christy himself.

*Great! Another man wants to attack me.*

"I work damned hard to get a good listing, then try to take my wife and kids to the zoo—just try to take one Sunday off to be with them the way I never do—and I drive by the house on our way home and, voila, no open house signs. No sign of Christy anywhere. Then I get home and I get this irate message on my answering machine telling me I'm fired."

"Wayne, you sack of shit." Christy's own surprise wasn't half of what got reflected on Wayne's and Mr. Simms' faces. One of the office staff came running to check the ruckus so Christy toned down her voice. "I was going to hold it open, but there was this naked crazy guy who came after me and...and..."

"What?" Wayne looked genuinely shocked.

Simms interrupted. "Apparently, Christy was attacked, Wayne. That's what she was trying to tell you."

"No way."

Christy hated the man now. Genuinely hated him. His sense of morals, his scheming, his lack of sensitivity to her and what she was going through, and the way he'd pushed his oversized body into Mr. Simms's office. Anger boiled in her stomach. Christy had reached her limit.

"I'm not putting up with this. I quit. No way can I work in the same office with this...this...idiot." She pointed to Wayne, wanting to say something nastier but thinking better of it.

Christy tore around her manager and sneered at Wayne as she pushed him with one hand, which sent him careening against a bookshelf with a loud crash. Christy saw the ruckus had attracted every staffer in the area. Simms bolted past Wayne, who tried to right himself, still thrashing in a nest of books and files.

"Christy," Wayne called after her. "Christy, wait a minute. This is all wrong."

She turned and glared at him. "That's the first truthful thing I've heard all morning."

She dug in her heels and whirled around to exit, then ran straight into the chest of one very solid wall of man, holding a bouquet of flowers in one hand and three red open house signs in the other.

# CHAPTER 4

**"Y**OU!" CHRISTY SAID, suddenly aware of the understatement. His blue eyes melted her bones. She needed air and pushed against him to step back a safe distance, if that was possible.

She wondered if he felt the electric ripple that traveled with lightning speed all over her skin's surface.

*Probably not.*

His face had that soft smirk, and he held his head at an angle. He looked more uncomfortable holding the flowers than the three metal open house signs.

"I came to apologize for the misunderstanding," his deep voice, cracking just a little, was dripped in honey and ensnared her as if he'd tied her up with pantyhose again. She shivered at the very thought that this might be something she could look forward to.

"Good. Saves me the trouble of calling the police." As soon as she'd said it, she wondered why. Calling the police was not what she was really thinking.

"That won't be necessary. Just hear me out first, and if you still want to call them, I won't be able to object. It's your right. But I'm sorry about…"

"This him?" Simms immediately stepped next to Christy, and, after sizing up the physique and bearing of the stranger, pegged him. "Navy, right?"

"Yes, sir."

Wayne appeared at the end of the hallway, but his ego had turned to pudding. He hovered in the shadow, half protected by a wall.

Simms continued. "I'm Carl Simms, the manager here. Ms. Nelson was just telling me how you terrorized her yesterday. Scared this nice young lady to death. I've advised her to call the police, and if she doesn't, *I* will." Simms delivered this with determination, but Christy noted he stayed a healthy two steps away from the large Navy man.

The visitor had been looking at Simms, but in the silence that followed, his blue gaze turned back on Christy, as if to beg for time alone with her. And damn, she was going to give it to him too. There was something there she needed to find out about. She had too many questions about the day before to be consistently angry. And how could she, when he looked at her like that?

"Why don't we go to the conference room and discuss this?" Christy offered softly.

"That sounds fair to me," the stranger replied. He didn't take his eyes off Christy when he added, "Simms, you can join us if you like."

"Christy?" Simms asked.

"I think I'll be okay. Thanks."

"Can someone take these please?" the man said, holding up the heavy metal signs like they were a carton of Chinese food.

"Those are mine." Wayne darted from the shadows and grabbed them away without looking at the stranger. The signs clattered and he almost dropped them.

"I'm guessing you must be Wayne."

Wayne shot him a murderous look, then adjusted his bravado and walked away, carrying the signs awkwardly in both hands. He was swearing under his breath, his sport coat stretching across his shoulders and his knees bumping the metal signs as he lumbered off.

Christy drew back the sliding door to the conference room as the stranger passed by too close. A fresh soap scent made her eyes flutter and her nose itch. He found a spot at the head of the table facing out to the reception area and remained standing until Christy slid the door closed. When she took the chair at his left, he sat in tandem with her.

He pushed the flowers in her direction across the laminate tabletop. She noticed again the tattoo of footprints from some unknown three-toed creature that traversed up his forearm.

"These are yours. Once again, I am very sorry." His voice, raspy and soft, drew her complete attention. His large hand squeezed the plastic outer wrap with a delicious crunch. The package displayed a colorful spring gathering of daffodils, stock, and baby green chrysanthemums. A few sprigs of lavender had been added for garnish. The glorious smell of the bouquet filled the room. The flowers had obviously been hand selected and the bouquet freshly made. She noticed things like that. Some of her past boyfriends hadn't even bothered to take the price tags off the supermarket bunches. This bouquet probably set him back a good twenty dollars.

*A whole lot cheaper than bail.* Some of her anger returned, but she gave him a curt thank you.

He pulled his hand back and leaned against the table. He took a deep breath, and then exhaled as he began his story. "My name is Kyle Lansdowne. I am in the Navy. I'm looking for my Navy buddy and best friend, who is missing."

"Okay."

"The house…where we…met…belongs to my friend, Armando. I'd begun to look for him and thought I would start there."

"Naked?"

"Well." Kyle suppressed a grin and nodded his head. "I understand this may not make sense, but I actually meditate like that all the time. I didn't expect company." He flashed those blue eyes up at her again.

"Obviously."

"Look, I'm sorry, but I'm really not a weirdo."

Christy knew she had to break eye contact or she would never get through this. She rubbed her temples and closed her eyes.

Mr. Simms popped his head into the conference room. "Everything all right?"

Christy realized how weary she must have looked from her night of tossing in her sleep. The stress of the last twenty-four hours had gotten to her. She could barely hold it together.

"It's okay," she said to Simms.

Simms nodded, staring back at Kyle, but leaving them alone again as he closed the door. Kyle rubbed his palm where her teeth marks remained clearly evident. When he noticed her looking at them, he stopped and buried his hands under the table.

"So why the questions about all this covert stuff? The tying me up with my pantyhose? What was that all about?"

"Again, please let me apologize. I thought maybe you were involved with Armando's disappearance."

"Me?"

Kyle rolled his shoulders. "I just assumed you might be one of the bad guys."

"You think I look like a bad guy?"

"Of course not. I see that now."

Christy glared at him. She decided he was telling the truth so she backed down. "Well, I still don't see what the big deal is. Maybe your friend went out on a bender—it happens, you know."

"Not to us."

"I'm *sorry*?"

"We're SEALs."

"Oh."

"And we never disappear without someone else from the SEAL community knowing about it. We're trained to disappear, but that's not how this happened. Something's wrong."

"Sounds a little over the top. Don't you guys have a life?"

"That's exactly what we've got."

Christy watched Kyle survey the top of the conference table, his eyes sweeping up to the flowers laying flat against the Formica surface.

"Staying alive is the goal," he said.

Christy didn't know what else to say.

"Well, I've taken enough…" He started to rise.

"No. Wait a minute. That was unkind of me."

Kyle shrugged, and then sat back down. He looked at his lap.

"What can I do to help?" she asked.

Kyle folded his hands neatly in front of him and a crooked smile angled up to the left, causing a dimple. "Nothing you can do. I'm here because you never should have been involved in the first place and I wanted to personally apologize for my behavior."

Some of the pieces started to connect. She rolled her neck back and forth and felt some of the tension leave.

"Did I injure you? I tried not to." His eyes were steady as he raised his brows, forming crease lines on his forehead. "You hurt anywhere?"

*Good question.* "No. I'm fine." She didn't understand why he chuckled at this and nodded his head twice.

"You're a very strong young lady."

"I've been told that a time or two."

"I can imagine." He scanned her face like he had yesterday when they were on the floor. She could tell he wanted to look at her farther down, but held himself in check. She liked that about him.

He looked to the side as if thinking about something before he spoke again. "I would like to make it up to you, if you'll let me." He turned on the blue-eyed charm again and smiled. "Give me a chance for you to see my decent side, not my animal side."

She was thinking about his animal side. Did he know?

"Well, I don't normally bite people when I first meet them, either." She found it in herself to smile and enjoyed that he returned her smile, focusing on her lips.

An awkward silence followed, but she determined not to break it. His move and how he played it would indicate if she would trust him.

"Maybe I could buy you lunch sometime. Tomorrow?"

She'd been hoping for dinner but knew lunch was the right answer. "That would be fine." She wanted to say "nice" but was pleased she made the last-minute word substitution. No denying her attraction to this man, but it would be dangerous to let him see it.

"Okay, then. Can I pick you up here tomorrow at, say, noon?"

"If I still have my job."

"What do you mean?" he asked.

"I technically quit," she whispered, peering down at her hands. "I thought Wayne did this."

"And so now you know. It was my fault. Entirely."

"Yes, I see that now. Okay, I'll see you here tomorrow."

They stood as she gathered up the flowers, burying her nose in them, inhaling the delicious scent. He caught her little lapse in judgment and smiled.

"I thought you'd like them. They look like you."


CHRISTY DIDN'T REMEMBER when or how she said good-bye. She'd been numbed by his words...*they look like you*. For the rest of the day she operated out of the comfortable cocoon that warm numbness created, that shielded her from ordinary life.

She didn't completely trust or believe Kyle, but looked forward to tomorrow with eagerness she hadn't known in years.


KYLE'S FIRST STRING of second thoughts rushed in before he got into his Hummer. He stopped halfway there, almost turning back to call the whole thing off.

*You've got no business doing this. You are one messed up sailor if you think someone like her is fair game.*

He wondered why in the world he'd asked her out for lunch. Well, being honest, he knew why. She reminded him of someone from his past.

He couldn't stop thinking about her and the way her eyes held him courageously, staring at the possibility of her own death. She didn't beg— a true fighter.

*Just like me.*

That kind of a person deserved an apology, and more. Her defiance in the face of mortal danger reached in and grabbed him. She commanded respect. Sure, he was marking time, waiting for Timmons to get the information on Armando's cell phone, but something else was going on, and he couldn't quite identify it. Or, maybe he didn't want to.

He continued telling himself that buying her lunch was the right thing to do, his way of an apology. After all, he'd terrorized her, a civilian, an innocent—something he never thought he was capable of. He was half-surprised she'd said yes.

Hanging around a woman like Christy was dangerous. Would it set things in motion Kyle knew were better off buried? It was difficult enough dealing with Armando's disappearance. Did he need this complication as well?

Despite what he tried to suppress, he realized she enchanted him. There was something about her fiery attitude and that leveling gaze that made his heart drop to his knees. He couldn't wait for tomorrow.

# CHAPTER 5

K YLE CHECKED IN with his chief, but was disappointed to hear from Timmons that finding Armando's cell phone location would take at least another day. He bought a sandwich and went out to look at the boats berthed at the wharf. He liked studying the expensive toys of the privileged—no trace of anything military. Being at the water's edge always calmed him, helped him think. It was either watch boats or practice meditation again, but since the last practice hadn't turned out so well, he was reluctant to try again.

He shook his head. *What were the odds his meditation would have drawn such an audience?*

He watched a man and a boy, who was probably the man's young son, coming down the wooden pier. The boy looked about six, skipping along, holding hands and trying to keep up with the man, who rolled a small ice chest down the planks with a bumpity-bump. At one point the boy tripped, getting the front rubber bumper of his tennis shoes caught between a gap in the wood. Before he could skid and get a splintered scrape to his knees, the man hauled him up to safety. The boy squealed with a giggle and then kept up his incessant chatter as they made their way down the dock.

This wasn't anything that happened in Kyle's life. There were no picnics down by the harbor, no father-son outings, no camping trips. Happy afternoons fishing with his father had never happened as he was growing up. He got other things that made him strong and hard: a leather belt on his rear or the back of his dad's hand. It wasn't until he'd joined his SEAL team that he learned about the meaning of family.

He'd called for a meeting with two other members of Charlie Team, along with Gunny. They agreed to gather early at the Rusty Scupper, which meant the place would be nearly deserted. There were only two reasons the community came into this favorite Team hangout. If a group of Team guys sat out front at one of the tables, tilted on indestructible chairs, they were passing time, watching the meat parade meandering down the sidewalk.

Even high schoolers, totally off limits, of course, but hotties nonetheless, were only too willing to tease them. The skirts got shorter, and the shorts showed everything. Skimpy clothes were worn so tight a guy could tell if they wore panties, thongs, or nothing. Tops were becoming practically nonexistent. Girls wore kids sizes, too, so a firm three- to four-inch swath of tanned skin without a single stretch mark bounced deliciously around pierced belly buttons. Just a hint of a tattoo poking up from underneath sometimes, or perhaps a little black lace. It was distracting for sure, if a guy looked for that sort of thing.

The other reason to go to the Scupper was to plan something without prying eyes. The Scupper's dark corner at the back of the bar was perfect for such a meeting. That's where Kyle sat, waiting for his guys to show up, watching the bubbles traveling up the side of his glass of beer.

His apprehension about Armando grew the more he considered all the clues or, rather, lack of them. He also worried about being too late. He faced the reality that in waiting too long for their only clue, the location of the cell signal, he might have put Armando in further danger. Perhaps grave danger.

*Nah. Not Armando. Guy is a fuckin' warrior machine.*

Kyle had never had an unsuccessful mission. This wasn't going to be his first. Not today. Not this week. He hoped to God never.

*Help me out here, buddy. Give me another sign. Don't try to do this alone, Armando.* Kyle knew the missing SEAL would find a way to steer him in the right direction. And he knew Armando still lived. He could feel it in his bones.

Cooper walked into the bar first, followed by his ever-present sidekick, Fredo. Coop, a farm boy from Nebraska, had graduated as the tallest SEAL at over 6'4". He still looked like he walked around in his overalls, had a loping gait, and needed to duck under every doorway in his path. Raised nowhere near the ocean, Cooper still swam second fastest on the Team. Second to Armando. Coop had spent the summer before Indoc learning. Had hired a former Olympic coach who told him he might have a shot at a medal if he washed out of BUD/S.

Fredo, short and built like a soccer player, which was how he'd spent his youth in LA, took two steps for every one of Cooper's strides, but beat the giant and almost everyone else at timed runs, either long or short. Best wrestler on the Team also went to Fredo. And he liked to cheat, touching a guy someplace he didn't want to be touched, causing a serious lack of focus and getting the resulting quick take down.

The unlikely pair of friends hunkered down across the table from Kyle. They were served a couple of beers by the new girl with the nice hands. Cooper ordered mineral water with lots of ice and lime. He told Kyle he'd leave his for Gunny. At last Gunny showed up, red-faced, as if he'd been on a bender. He arrived a full fifteen minutes late, and Kyle suspected he'd jogged to make up time, but didn't have the lung capacity for much of a run.

"Sorry, gents. Got caught up at the gym with a late arrival," Gunny said as he pointed to a beer.

"Got your name on it, Sarge," Cooper said.

Gunny downed half of it quickly. Too quickly, Kyle thought. Gunny must be in some pain and had decided to douse it. He noted Gunny might not be much help on this mercy mission.

"Armando's gone missing."

"Fuck me. When?" Fredo asked.

"Friday night, maybe Saturday." Kyle watched as his words sunk in.

"You're just now fuckin' telling us?" Fredo's brow contorted. Prune face, Kyle had said on more than one occasion. But a good question, and one that deserved an answer.

"I wasn't sure. Thought maybe he was having a little honeymoon, without the ring and the preacher."

Everyone laughed.

"That would be Armani." Coop chuckled.

"Timmons asked me to look into it."

"You try calling him?" Fredo asked. Everyone immediately turned and growled at the Mexican-American SEAL, who shrugged his shoulders and added, "I'm just sayin'."

"Timmons is waiting for the cell tracking." Kyle looked at Coop, who had gone alert.

Coop answered. "I definitely can help you there."

Kyle knew Cooper had done a rotation at the CIA and had some friends there.

"I got his number right here."

Kyle handed Armando's number over to Coop on a white piece of paper. "No strings. Invisible."

"Of course." Cooper frowned. "Probably get it later tonight. I'm gonna make the call now."

"Thanks." Kyle watched as the giant SEAL unfolded from the table, stood, and went outside to make the call. Cooper's huge frame completely blocked sunlight from coming through the doorway of the Scupper.

Two young ladies sauntered past Coop, and they must have looked back at the handsome farm boy because Cooper waved, wiggling his fingers and grinning, with the cell phone clutched to his ear.

"What's the plan, boss?" Fredo wanted to know.

"First we get the location, and then we get Armando out. Just like the snatch and grabs we did overseas."

"Sounds cool," said Fredo.

"Got nothin' else to do," said Gunny.

Coop came back. "Take a few hours at the most. My friend in DC will have the coordinates on Armani's cell—if it's still on." He gulped down his water, crushing ice with his molars. "So I suppose now we hurry up and wait?" He dumped a lopsided grin on Kyle.

"Exactly. We've got our team. We go when we get the location. Not a breath to anyone but Timmons. No other Team guys, you got it?"

They nodded in agreement.

"And you get some rest. Not sure what's in store, but we gotta be alert and strong and ready to go. Get your gear in order in case we need it. I'll check back with you boys tomorrow sometime after noon. But be ready to take off as soon as I call."

He watched them leave behind their unfinished drinks. He hoped his call to action wouldn't cost them their careers—or their lives.

# CHAPTER 6

C HRISTY KNEW SIMMS wasn't expecting her early, so she slept in. She shaved, oiled her skin after her steamy shower, blow-dried her blond hair, and then curled it in ringlets, extra fluffy.

She pulled out her special Lady Parisienne bra with the skin-like padding and silky butterfly stitching. Madame M gave her the delicate garment as a gift when Christy made that thousand-dollar sale to the San Francisco mayor who bought lingerie for his new girlfriend. He had been one of the shop's regular customers. The mayor liked his girls extra full on top, so Madame M always had a fully stocked DD section with nothing but the most expensive lingerie.

She leaned forward and lifted the soft pillows of her breasts into the creamy cups, leaving just enough cleavage to distract the average male. But Kyle wasn't an average male. She doubted he'd ever seen a woman in a three-hundred-dollar bra. That part about men she could read like a school primer. Her trouble happened with the after-the-first-date-thing. She decided not to fall too quickly for him, even though she already had, and he hadn't done anything but tie her up on the floor with her hands above her head, lay across her body with his package between her legs, covering her chest with his muscled torso, and spread her legs with the strong muscles of his thighs. And then he gave her flowers and asked for a lunch date.

*Pretty unbeatable combination.*

Her sex quivered in anticipation as she slipped the satin and lace matching panties over her hips and centered the small frilly triangle in front. She applied her makeup with patience and skill, thinking about kissing him, wondering what the feel of his tongue would be like opening her lips and plunging in to play with hers. She imagined what those strong hands could do around her waist, then sliding down the front of her abdomen into her panties.

She sprayed perfume in the air and walked through it, coating her flesh with scent. She was a lethal combination of female determination and need. She would make him pay for yesterday's transgression. She'd make him beg, and then she'd decide what to do next. Logic told her she should hold out and not let him touch her. But her heart and her body craved the caress of the man with three-toed footprints running up his muscled arm.

After she finished dressing, she drove her Honda into the office parking lot. Sounds of sea birds and a foghorn in the distance reminded her the ocean was not far. It never got hot in San Diego. The moist late morning air caressed her cheeks. She turned and found him leaning against a shiny black Hummer, legs crossed at the ankles, arms crossed as well. He'd been watching her get out of the car. She hoped she'd been graceful.

A slight smile lit up his face. She tweeted her car closed, slung her purse over her right shoulder, and walked straight for him without taking her eyes from his. He made no apology for watching every moving body part she had, including her mouth, when she stopped in front of him and licked her lips.

*So far so good.*

Something registered on his face. A loneliness and hunger resided inside his vacant eyes, something dead and now coming back to life. He appeared so confident, so well trained and measured. Probably he'd learned to cut off his soft side from his survival side.

She had a sudden urge to soften him.

*Where did that come from?*

"I wasn't sure you'd come," he said. One eye twitched. His long dark lashes, thick and shiny, outlined the blue gaze he leveled at her. It almost made her faint. Her ears buzzed and her stomach lurched.

"I promised you lunch," she answered. "I keep my promises. Always."

"So do I."

His masculine cologne wafted toward her. Erotic goose bumps slipped down the front of her blouse like cool fingers touching her white flesh. She felt naked and blushed, looking down.

His chest heaved and then stilled. Had he caught himself reacting to her blush?

*A man of control.*

She read all the little signs of a man's arousal. Even without dwelling on the considerable tent in his pants, she knew she turned him on by her fragrance and appearance.

And she loved it.

He assembled all six-foot something of himself and walked around to the passenger side of the Hummer, then opened the door. She bent her left knee, gripping the chrome handle on the doorframe for the high step. He stopped her with a hand to her shoulder.

"Here, let's use this." He retrieved a white plastic stepstool no larger than a shoebox, bent down, and placed it on the pavement at her feet. He uncoiled his muscled frame less than four inches in front of her and just as slowly let his eyes wander over her body, from her knees all the way up to her chest.

"Better?" he asked with a hint of a smile.

Her knees wobbled, knocking against each other. "Much," she said as she leaned in, almost brushing against his chest, close enough to feel the heat from his body. She was careful not to make contact, though her insides argued with her willpower.

She step-mounted into the front seat of the vehicle. The black leather groaned. His scent filled the air. Smiling, he handed her the seatbelt, tossed the step into the rear, and slammed the door. Something told her life was about to change—for the good.

*Strap in and get ready.*

They didn't talk as he drove down toward the wharf. She focused on the Celtic ring tattoo that peeked below the right sleeve of his T-shirt. Staring at the tattoo helped with the not-wanting-to-look-at-his-chest-neck-and-Adam's-apple stuff. And it definitely helped her not focus on his lips.

*Does he know I'm sneaking little looks?*

Maybe he was used to it. Maybe he liked it. Maybe he didn't notice. In any case, he never looked back at her.

They walked into a tiny sandwich shop by the water. Holding out her chair, he stood guard as she seated herself, then he leaned against her back and put a palm on her shoulder as she settled in. On his way to take up position across the table from her, Kyle waved at a couple sitting on the opposite side of the room. The other guy sported a series of ringed tattoos on his forearm, too.

Clean place but not fancy, she observed. The menu specialized in seafood sandwiches and soft shell tacos.

"The turkey chili is what they're known for, even though this is a seafood place," Kyle said over the top of the paper menu. "But you'd probably like the crab salad sandwich." His blue eyes flashed on her and a ripple of energy traveled all the way down her spine. He showed perfect white teeth beneath slanted, full lips, which ended with a curl at one side she found so distracting. He had to be fully aware he was turning on the charm. *The Blue Charm.*

"I've heard about this spot," Christy said. "A few of the Realtors in my office come here for dinner and drinks after work."

"Only if they're single. This place is a real meat market at night," he replied.

"Well, that never seemed to stop some." She fanned herself with the menu as she looked out over the bay.

Kyle chuckled. "I've never seen Wayne here, not that I would notice. But then, this is a pretty young crowd."

"Hmm. Exactly. No, this wouldn't be his kind of place."

"So, you're single then, Christy?" He glanced at his water glass.

"Very much so. And enjoying every minute of it." She'd rehearsed this line in the shower a dozen times just in case it came up. But as she watched him raise his eyes, it sounded ridiculous, but still earned her a smile from his tanned face.

"I catch your drift. I'm the same." He'd turned serious. Honest. Totally kissable.

Their waiter came over and gripped Kyle's outstretched palm like they'd probably done hundreds of times. "You're back, and you don't even smell like a camel."

"Goat. No camels. Goats."

The two men laughed.

"Christy, this is Griz. Griz, Christy. I'm going to taste-test all your food now that I know he's on."

"Bro, I got your back. You've done enough defending the ladies for a while. Time for some R and R." Griz nodded in Christy's direction.

The crab sandwich tasted better than any she'd eaten, but she could only take a few bites. Her anticipation of this meeting completely eliminated her appetite.

The couple from across the way dropped by their table and Kyle introduced them. Without Kyle telling her, she knew the man was another Team guy.

"You seen Armando anywhere?" Kyle asked, adding a quick shrug. The eye contact seemed urgent between the two men, despite what Christy saw as Kyle's attempt to be casual.

"Nope. You try LuLu's?" The Team guy gave Christy a wink, but she could tell all was not well.

"Stopped by yesterday, but they hadn't seen him either."

"Well, look, if I catch sight of his sorry ass, I'll tell him his lover needs to get a call from him, 'kay?" the Team guy said, walking backward, holding the girl's hand. "Nice to meet you." He waved at Christy.

"Later." Kyle waved back.

"So your friend is still missing?" Christy asked.

"Yep. Probably holed up somewhere. When we don't want to be found, nobody can find us."

"But you're worried," she insisted.

"He never checked in with me before he left. We always do that. We talk to each other every day."

"*Every* day?"

Kyle lowered his head. She could see remnants of a grin he didn't want to show her. "Yep. Every day. We're practically married."

Christy's cheeks heated. This was totally unexpected.

Kyle looked up. "Hey! Don't worry," he said. "I only go for the ladies. Please don't get me wrong."

"Sorry. Seems like all the best looking guys are gay…"

"Then I'll take that as a compliment."

His perfect grin made her glad she was sitting down.

She watched him take the final bite of his chili, tipping the bowl to get the last drop into his spoon. She couldn't keep her eyes off him or anything that he did. He must have noticed how she watched him. He took a long time to dab his mouth with the white paper napkin, his eyes averted. He licked his lips and swallowed. She followed his Adam's apple down his tanned throat, and then she fell into his gaze as he searched her face. That smile again—it roped her in.

*Get a grip, Christy.*

"How long has it been?" she asked. Her face blazed heat involuntarily at the unintended innuendo. But he acted as if he didn't notice. *Or maybe he liked it.*

"Three days. Maybe four."

"So what are your thoughts?"

Kyle leaned in, setting aside his dishes, and rested his forearms on the table. "I know he's in some kind of trouble. I'm sure it's nothing he caused. There's a lot of gang activity here in Coronado, and some of the bangers try to hang around our community, looking for Team guys who might have an axe to grind. Misfits."

"Community? I don't understand."

"Our SEAL community."

"Misfits?" she asked.

"Stress does things to a guy. Makes him question all sorts of things." He looked out at the bay and squinted. "But that's not Armando."

"So you think he's like been kidnapped or something? Held for ransom?"

"Don't know. And we're not supposed to be talking about this."

His blue eyes pinned her again. She'd never felt so good being helpless.

She wiped her hands on the warm, wet washcloth, soaked in lemon juice, and then handed it to Kyle. They touched for a moment and he slid his forefinger along hers in an obvious caress she didn't back out of. They looked into each other's eyes, and something understood passed between them. Then his face formed a question.

"Want a coffee? Like a cappuccino or something?" he asked.

"Sure."

"C'mon. I have a great place in mind, unless you…"

"I don't really know the area well," she interrupted, and then thought maybe she sounded too eager.

He left money on the table. It seemed natural that he put his arm on her shoulder again, which she liked, but then he quickly dropped it. Kyle walked behind as they exited to the salty afternoon air.

"Duckies is just down the street," he said, pointing. "Let's walk. Parking around here is nonexistent."

Rubber duckies of all shapes and all states of dress littered the coffee shop. The barista wore a Hawaiian flowered shirt covered in sun-glassed yellow ducks. Jimmy Buffett blared from the speakers. After getting their drinks, Kyle waved to a group of four guys in the corner, who flipped him the bird when they thought Christy wasn't looking. Kyle directed her to be seated in the opposite corner in front of an opened bay window. They both sat just as a gentle bay breeze tickled the back of her neck.

"So, Christy, you from here?"

"No, I've just moved down from San Francisco."

"Just moved down, as in maybe the last three or four days?" he asked.

"Yes."

"I saw you at the airport." He leaned back in his chair and gave her an admiring grin.

Christy remembered seeing that muscled arm with the tats, and how hard his chest felt as she almost fell into him that day at the baggage claim.

*Holy Guacamole. It's him. That guy.*

Christy regained her composure. Her cheeks flushed recalling the two times she had been so close to him.

*Think, Christy. Get hold of yourself. It's just lunch.*

"My mother died last year and I inherited her condo, so I decided to try San Diego for a spell. She loved it here, even though she was sick."

"Sorry to hear that," Kyle said with a frown. "Sounds like you were close."

"I have a brother I don't see much. Never knew my dad."

"Well, that sorta makes two of us." He looked out at the water, tightening his jaw.

"How about your mom? Where does she live?"

"She's gone, too. I have no one," he said it to her with a blank look, but Christy could tell he had steeled something inside him. He seemed practiced at hiding, at being private.

"That probably makes it easier to do what you do. I have a lot of respect for your profession."

He nodded into his coffee cup as she said this. He probably got this line a lot and had grown immune to the words, so she decided to add some levity. "Even though we both know you are a dangerous killer who ravishes females and ties them up with their pantyhose."

He laughed. The sunshine of his face warmed her all the way to her toes.

"Not today, though. Don't think you're wearing any." He leveled the blue charm on her mercilessly.

*He'd noticed?*

His simple comment made her wet. She'd told herself she would let him beg. She would stay aloof, make him grovel to get back in her good graces, but his effect on her was the opposite. Everything he did made her crave more. She even wished she'd worn pantyhose.

The pause became the most awkward since their meeting, more awkward than the position of his body over hers as he'd incapacitated her on the floor of Armando's house two days ago.

"You live here in San Diego, too, right?" she had to ask.

"I'm between places. Was planning to stay at Armando's while I looked for a condo."

His blue eyes scanned her lips and then searched the side of her face. "Maybe you could help me."

*God, yes I could.*

"I don't handle leases, but if you're looking to buy…"

"I have a bonus coming and I thought now would be a good time."

"The absolute best. There are bank sales and foreclosures all over the county. Even some in my complex."

"Which one is that?"

"The Infinity, down by the harbor."

"Nice place. Too expensive."

"Not as much as you think. I could show you."

Her stomach clenched. She had crossed a line. He'd get scared off now. But she'd wait to see his response before she retreated.

He leaned back in his chair and nodded with a mock frown. "Okay, we could do that. What about this afternoon?"

His blue eyes pierced her again—with what he *didn't* say.


THEY RETRIEVED CHRISTY'S Honda at the real estate office and Kyle followed her over to the Infinity complex.

"Some of these places went for close to a million dollars when they first came up for resale," Christy said as she let them inside the furnished model with her passkey. "My mother was one of the first to buy. She got in under a special housing density program." They both stepped into a beautifully staged great room and kitchen. Through tall picture windows, the bay gleamed as if covered with shattered glass. He opened the sliding glass door and stepped onto the balcony.

"Nice place. Doubt I could afford it." He turned, resting his back against the black iron railing, his bulging package prominent. He cocked his head, removed his sunglasses and asked, "How much?"

"This one's five sixty. But we could make them an offer. It's owned by the bank. If you have some sort of down payment, this could be financed

VA."

"Not sure I have enough." He walked past her and waited by the slider opening.

"Want to see the rest of the place? It has a nice big bedroom."

She slipped through the door, close to his body, and heard his inhale. He didn't move out of the way.

"I don't care about the big bedroom. I like a big bed," he whispered, his voice husky.

She melted and didn't dare look back at him, but instead kept walking down a short hallway, past a guest bath, and into a bright bedroom. A full-sized bed, covered with a flowered green bedspread, sat against the far wall. She stopped at the foot and immediately felt his heat behind her.

"Too small," he whispered. When she turned to look, his eyes focused on her lips. Her knees were shaking. She melted when she heard him murmur, "But it will have to do." He leaned in and kissed her.

She raised her arms up over his shoulders and loved the feel of his firm chest pressed against her breasts, the way one arm wrapped around her waist and pulled her to his groin. His other hand fisted in her hair at the back of her head. His wet kiss opened more than her lips. It opened her soul. He plunged his tongue into her mouth, lacing over her teeth, searching. She granted him full access to everything in the moan she couldn't help but give him.

He pulled her tighter against the rock wall of his upper torso. She spread her legs and rubbed herself against his thigh with a need she'd not felt in years. Her fingers entwined the short, curly hair at the nape of his neck, then slid around to trace down under his jaw. She pulled away to look at him, needing to see his eyes.

Without saying anything, she held his face in her hands and stared into the azure sparkles of his soul. One vein pulsed at his forehead as he allowed her to examine the questions written there, the traces of need and pain, of hurt and loss. He let her see it all. And she knew she could heal him.

She stepped on tiptoes and leaned against him again, as his hand slipped under the skirt of her sundress and smoothed over the lace panties she so carefully had put on for him.

He kneeled and buried his head under her skirt, licking the smooth satin fabric and then poking his tongue around the elastic to find the slit of her sex.

"Oh, God, Christy," he whispered, as he sought her nude opening.

And then the roughness of his tongue laved her, deepening their connection. She released herself to his hungry mouth.

Her thighs trembled, her hands clutching the hair at the top of his head as she leaned into him, pressed into him, and begged him. She begged him to take all of her, anything he wanted, as much as he wanted.

*Anything.*

He came out from under the cotton fabric, a wet grin on his face, eyes blazing, and slowly rose, standing in front of her. He slipped her dress off like lifting a piece of tissue paper from a lingerie box, then stared at her bra and panties. It registered what she had done for him. That she anticipated him seeing those lovely lacy things.

And she could tell it thrilled him.

Christy removed his T-shirt, and then let her palms slide over his hairless ribcage and nipples as she squeezed the heavy muscles underneath. His broad shoulders were more massive than she had remembered. Her fingers snaked around his thick neck as she pulled him down to her lips and made him cover hers.

She moved her hands to the button fly on his jeans, squeezing his erection, which earned her another moan. His hands kneaded her ass, pulling her to him and pinning her arms between their bodies, palms to his chest.

"Should we go to my place?" she asked.

He smirked and looked her over as she stood before him, clad only in her lacy underwear, and shook his head slowly. "Too late. Maybe later." He stepped closer, holding her head with one warm palm that turned her ear to his lips. "Maybe tonight. Maybe all night?"

"I might need you all night."

"I can deliver whatever you need. I promise."

She needed his pants off right now. She slipped them down his nonexistent hips and then over huge thighs, taking off his briefs with them. His warm cock bounced to life. She palmed the entire length of his shaft and squeezed the moist tip. She sat at the edge of the bed and put her lips over the helmet of his crown and tasted him.

His breath came harder as she worked on him, his fingers sifting through her hair, pushing her head into his groin. Then he lifted her under the arms and lay her back on the bed. He made short work of her panties, leaving her bra in place. His fingers massaged her opening as he climbed on top of her. His gaze searched her eyes, and then sought her mouth. First one, and then a second finger tucked into her folds and she thought she would explode. Christy stroked his length and helped guide him, pushed the head of his shaft against the wetness of her sex. And rubbed.

*God, I need this.*

A shrill voice came from the living room. "Okay, now we have this one here. It's a little on the small side."

Christy and Kyle looked at each other in panic as they realized a Realtor was in the next room showing the home. Kyle quickly leapt off the bed and slammed the door, which drew a resounding "Oh" from a female on the other side.

They dressed and straightened the bed. Christy's cheeks were on fire as she looked at Kyle. She swallowed, and then opened the door to face their audience. A portly woman too large for her height stood armed with an expression of surprise and disgust.

"Sorry. We had to use the bathroom," Christy said, realizing too late the water to the unit had probably been turned off.

The Realtor looked at them as if they were road kill, but the young couple behind them grinned from ear to ear.

"Hey, no problem, guys," the man said. "It happens." He squeezed his wife's shoulder.

Christy handed the Realtor the passkey and realized as she did so that her panties hung around her wrist. The older woman inspected her hand and shot back a hateful look with black, beady eyes. "This is way out of line, missy. I'm going to have to report this."

Everyone else but Christy jumped in with a comment. Then Kyle grabbed Christy's hand and they escaped together down the hallway to the elevator.

"I can't believe I just did that," she said, looking at the floor.

Inside the elevator, Kyle took the panties from her fist and buried his nose in them, then gave her a smirk. She grabbed them back, stuffing them inside her bra. He was enjoying her turmoil way too much.

"Regrets?" Kyle asked as he stepped close to her, tracing the form of her right breast with his forefinger and then squeezing her nipple.

She had to admit that even if she lost her job, which most assuredly could happen, it was worth it. She squeezed his package as she pressed herself to his chest again. "Not one. You?"

"Only one, but I'm going to fix that right away." His deep, penetrating kiss turned her bones to rubber as the doors to her floor whooshed open.

# CHAPTER 7

**K**YLE PRESSED HIMSELF against Christy's backside as she worked the lock on her door. He flipped her scented blonde hair off her shoulder and kissed her soft neck. She arched her rear into his groin, rubbing against his shaft. He was so hot for her, he wondered if they would make it to the bedroom.

The door gave way and Christy turned to face him, her eyes fixated on his lips. She then threw one arm about his neck and kissed him. He kicked the door closed and she dropped her purse. Staring at each other, they began to disrobe. He watched her lithe body unsheathe itself from her dress. The bra was his to remove. He pulled her hands from her back and stuck them down his unzipped jeans. Her fingers found him and then pushed his pants over his hips. At last they embraced fully naked, flesh on flesh.

He picked her up and she encircled his waist with her legs, pressing against him, rubbing her sex against his cock, kissing first the line under his jaw and then full, on his lips as he inhaled her.

After he placed her down on the bed, he whispered in her ear, "I need protection. Let me go…"

"Shh. I have some." She arched and rolled over to her tummy, exposing her plump ass as she reached for the bedside table and pulled open a drawer. He could see the little fruit of her sex, hairless and wet. He rose up and covered her body, pushing his shaft into the crease between her legs, begging for entrance. She flipped to her knees, raising herself up off the bed just high enough so he could slip a hand there and plunge two fingers inside her wet opening.

She gasped and spread her knees out wider, arched up and slapped her palms against the wall. He spotted a red foil packet in her right hand.

He removed his fingers, slid his thighs under hers, and pressed his chest against her back. He grabbed the packet and quickly covered himself, while she moaned and leaned back against him, turning her head, giving him a mouthful of blond tresses until her lips found his.

Ready and poised at her opening, he stopped, and then tenderly removed the hair that separated their cheeks and pressed his forehead to the side of her face by her temple.

"Christy, Christy," he murmured. He wanted to be covered in her scent, wanted every part of his body rubbing against hers. He wanted her to rub off all the roughness, all the little scars and nubs of his soul.

*Make me clean. Bring me back to life.*

He plunged in from behind, watching the long curls fall down the silky softness of her back. He brushed them aside and kissed one vertebra at a time while his cock slowly had its way with her, drawing back and plunging in, back and forth in a rhythm he would not be able to sustain for very long.

She had gone liquid, as if made without bones or cartilage. Her body pressed against him, needing him, drawing him deeper inside her. She gasped for air as he slid to the hilt and then slowly drew out. With gentle rhythms he rode her, loving the feel of her flesh covering his cock, loving how each wave of pleasure brought him to the edge and then back again as he withdrew and plunged again and again.

He clutched her breasts as he pumped her. He held her by the waist and moved her up and down on his shaft as he arched his groin into her. At last, the muscles in her sex tensed and then released as she shuddered. He moved even slower, in and out, as every delicious ripple of her orgasm washed over both of them.

At last he could hold on no longer, and with one last plunge to answer her soft, satisfied whimper, he burst forth and came, rooting and planting himself deep inside her. She squeezed every drop from him as he continued to pump and then lurched one more time. They collapsed on the bed, his body covering hers.

He wanted to be careful with this delicate creature lying beneath him, the one who smelled of lavender and vanilla, of the sweet sweat of her arousal. His hands were too callused to rub across her soft breasts and down her arms, but he needed to feel the smoothness of her skin, as if the more he stroked her, the more he would be healed.

He nuzzled and found the back of her neck and kissed her there, feeling the vibrations of her sigh, her chest moving down into the bed as his body could do nothing but follow her. He continued to nuzzle, kiss and give her little bites, tasting the salt of her skin along her neck, under her ear. His tongue found the upturned curl of her closed lips and he could tell she was smiling. He begged for her to open to him again.

She rolled to the side and faced him as he pulled out and then repositioned himself, covering her chest and lower abdomen from on top. His hands held her face as his thumbs traced over her cheekbones, her lips. He slid his fingers behind her head and cupped her, raising her up to meet his lips again in a long, languid kiss. She studied him deeply and he saw her face was wet with tears.

"Hey. Are you okay?" He wondered if he had hurt her in some way. The glittering moistness in her eyes drew him in and he wanted to forget who he was and where he was. Almost, but not quite.

He could tell she wanted to say something as he watched her think, but she chose to stay silent. Some day he might want to let a woman tell him things of her heart, but not today. It was way too soon. This was just beautiful sex.

Yet, something had shifted. Certain words would have to remain unspoken for now. But he knew he'd found someone very rare and very lonely, like he was. It would be difficult to let her go, like she belonged to him already. Or maybe he needed something she had. Something he would protect.

They rested, then made love again as the raging orange sunset streamed through her bedroom window. All he wanted to do was watch her face as she came, as he shot her full of his seed. He couldn't be deep enough inside her, touch enough of her skin, or hear enough of her little moans and whimpers as he poured out everything he had. He slid in and out of her and watched her bloom for him, open to him, need him. And he could do this. He could be there for her, could send them both into ecstasy. Every soft brushing of her lips on his flesh brought on a new wave of strength and the desire to own every inch of her body—the desire to give her all of his body in return.

They played in the shower until the hot water ran out, then they dressed and went to the harbor and ate at the Salty Dog cafe that overlooked boats of every size. The moonlight shimmered on the still waters of the inlet.

Kyle turned back to her face, which was lit by the table candle that flickered, sending dancing shadows like a fan dance that first covered up and then revealed her sweet smile. He wanted her all over again, but that was foolish. He braced for the cold blast of reality to follow. This was wrong. He needed to find Armando first. The Navy came second. There was no room for a third option.

*So what's going on with you? Wake up, Kyle. You know better. You've warned other men on your team about this. It's nice being with her, but let's not get lost here.*

"You come to this place a lot?" she asked, as if testing the waters.

"Actually, I've never been. Don't normally hang out in this part of town. But I can tell you about every dive on Coronado."

"I'll bet."

Two large bowls of seafood chowder delivered to their table broke the silence in the nick of time. The chowder tasted hot and delicious and was accompanied by warm steaming French bread and melted butter, which was the way he liked it. They ate in silence. He'd been starved.

"They fly in the French bread from San Francisco," she said between bites.

"No wonder you like it here."

"It's close. My mom and I used to come here when I'd visit her."

"That must have been nice."

When they finished, he avoided her gaze but could tell she was trying to engage eye contact, so he pulled out his phone and checked to make sure the ring was on. No messages, either.

"It's late and I'm going to have to be going. If you're done, I'll walk you back."

She flinched but seemed to catch herself. Her eyes held lots of questions. Things she had a right to know. A regular tangle of things he wouldn't be able to answer.

*Get out before you get dragged in, Kyle.*

"I was hoping you'd stay the night," she delivered her words with steely coolness.

She was watching him. He knew it was important how he responded. He sensed she was trying her hardest not to look disappointed. Forced casual.

*Here it comes. Damn. This is harder to do than I thought.* "Sorry. I don't do the overnight thing…"

"But you said…"

"I'm sorry. I seem to do a lot of apologizing to you." He looked away quickly. Her body shook as he noticed her composure crumble. He saw the glistening tears out of the corner of his eye.

*Give her a chance to recover in private. Being direct is being merciful. Don't lie to her. It's cruel to linger.* "C'mon, let's get you home, safe and sound."

He felt awkward and ashamed he'd crossed the line with her, that he'd made her think there was more to it than just the sex. The *incredible* sex.

*God, I wish there was.*

At the lobby of her building, he kissed her. "Thank you. This was nice, Christy."

"I'd like to do it again sometime."

She was masking again, trying not to plead. But damn, if he didn't love the way she wanted him, and how hard he felt she was fighting to cover it up.

*Me, too. Fuck. I could do this every night.* He shifted his weight and stepped on his own foot to wake himself up—a trick he'd learned in the BUD/S training.

"Let's not get ahead of ourselves here." It hurt to say it, but it had to be said. After all, he was a dog. And she deserved way better.

As she opened the heavy glass door, she turned and asked him a question. "Kyle, *will* I see you again?"

He didn't want to answer it. He didn't want to lie. But what was the truth, after all? He sighed. "I think so." Then he shrugged. "Just not sure when." He looked down at his feet, then up to her face. "Best not to expect too much out of this."

She got the message. He saw it in her eyes, in the flicker that showed she had felt the spear of rejection. He could see she wasn't used to getting it. And she wasn't used to giving so freely of herself.

He'd been honest with her, at least. He'd done what had to be done, no question about it. But he still felt like a complete heel. He hoped her anger would help her forget him.

He knew it would be impossible to ever forget her.

# CHAPTER 8

THE NEXT MORNING, Kyle didn't have time for shame. He threw it in the back of his mind like he used to throw his wetsuit and surfboard in the back of the battered old truck with the rusty headlights. His old but reliable vehicle had been crumbling, with parts sloughing off it for years. This flawed hunk of metal had served him well while he became a man. She was always by his side, proving to be much more reliable than any of the girls he'd dated.

His heart hadn't gotten seriously snagged on any of the lovelies from his past. But the truck was different. He nearly cried the day he'd sold her to a friend, the sale signaling the end of his carefree but tumultuous life—the same day he'd reported to the Indoc center. Not once did he ever wash her. She was perfect the way she was.

He took a shower, then checked Armando's refrigerator for something unhealthy. No luck. A little nonfat yogurt and greens. No milk for cereal, if he even had cereal. No bread for toast. He found some cheese and cut a slice. It tasted terrible, like rubber tires. He read the label.

*99% nonfat? What the hell is up with that?*

Armando was a food Nazi, all right. Kyle grabbed a bruised apple from a bowl on the kitchen counter and walked around, surveying the house, sure he missed something. Armando had nothing frilly to indicate a woman's presence. All hard steel stuff. No pictures of frogmen jumping out of airplanes or US flags either.

*When I was a child I thought like a child. But when I became a man, I put away childish things.* It was one of the quotes he and Armando loved, and that had sustained them all during his training and during some of the darkest days overseas in the Middle East. On those days he'd look out over the sand and hear the kids playing, the goats bleating, and wonder if this dusty hellhole was going to be his killing field, where he would end his days on earth.

He and Armando had the shared experience of getting up close and personal with Death. And just like at BUD/S, neither of them would quit.

*Wherever you are, Armani, I'm coming. I'm bringing you home.* Armando had to know Kyle would do this, or die trying.

He thought about the lovely woman he'd shared his passion with last night. How her face was filled with tears from the intensity of their lovemaking. He caught a very brief glimpse of what life would be like with a woman like her. But all too quickly the picture turned, and once more he'd humiliated Christy, exposed her to the dark side of his chosen life. All she'd done was peek her head around the doorway of his vacancy—try to smooth him a bit with that soft skin and those little squeals she made when she came.

He hoped she had a mess of friends to take care of any wounds he couldn't help but create. He didn't want her brooding over something she couldn't control. Hell, he couldn't control it either, and it was damned unhealthy. He hoped she was the kind of woman who could take it like a man. Take the hard truth. He'd let his guard down this time. He'd had no business getting her involved, even if it was only one incredible night of sex. And he'd almost spent the night, even promised her he'd pump her all night long. Not like he didn't want to. He needed the sex. But he didn't need the entanglement.

He checked his cell again. Still no word from Timmons. He'd have to go see his chief this morning.

*Damn. Armani, where are you?* The silence didn't reveal an answer. He was alone again, with the visions of a magical few hours of lovemaking and something that couldn't be.

The afternoon and evening with Christy had tipped the earth on its axis for him. Damn, it was a close one. If ever there was a woman for him, she'd look and act and smell and sigh and need just like Christy did. He wished he'd met her about six years ago, before he'd become a polar bear. Before the dinosaur skin. Before he became a trained killer. Before Armando had disappeared. She'd have been a welcome distraction in those days.

*She can do way better. She deserves it.* Some day. Some day the timing would be right for that kind of woman. In the meantime, it would be best if he left her completely alone. He swallowed, his throat parched. He knew he would never call her back. He knew, too, being without her would get easier every day and week that passed, until he would only have that warm glow and smile at the memory of a really nice time with her. When he couldn't remember what she looked like and how she tasted. When the pain got buried.

He pulled himself back to the task at hand: finding Armando. He flipped open his cell.

Gunny answered after a coughing spell.

"Shit, Gunny. You gonna croak on me today?"

"Not on your fuckin' life. You'll go before me."

"Now, how's that?"

"I should ask you, Kyle. What the hell are you doin'? I got reports from no less than three groups of your webfoot buddies that you found yourself a honey pot and went MIA yesterday. You're not going to find Armando between her legs. Nothing there but pain an' misery," Gunny spewed out.

*Well said.*

"I had apologies to make. I shook her up a little when she came into Armando's house *by accident* and found me."

"Accident, my ass. You know better than to hook up with a sexy cat burglar."

Kyle laughed, enjoying the banter they shared. No one else except Armando could talk this kind of disrespect and trash to him.

"Well, I was asleep on the bed. Naked."

A series of croaks and wheezes sounded between some Navy swear words, assaulting his ears, words Kyle hadn't heard since one of the early Team reunions. What came next on the other end of the line was not intelligible, followed by deep hacking and a release of some phlegm-wad probably large enough to knock a man down. Gunny's condition was worsening by the minute, and it worried him.

"Heard from Timmons yet?" Gunny rasped.

"Nope."

Gunny let out a series of thick, rheumy coughs that sounded like his lungs had turned inside out.

"You need to smoke more, Gunny. The burning-it-out-of-you isn't working."

"Tell me about it." Gunny wheezed and then continued. "I got Cooper and Fredo waiting until we could find you. Coop's guy got us some intel. We could meet up. That is, unless little miss fancy pants is in heat."

*Perceptive. Almost like that.* Kyle could see Christy's face as he filled her to the hilt, as he held her jaw and lips with one hand, as he squeezed them into soft pillows he could suck down. He could see her fingernails dragged against his butt cheeks, pulling him into her while he tasted the salty sweat between her perfect breasts. He felt like turning his Hummer around and driving to her house, then taking her again, but that was ridiculous. If he were another man, they'd just ride off together and get lost.

But he wasn't that kind of man.

"No comment. But Gunny, it's all about Armando now."

They arranged a meeting at a local beer pub for later that evening.

Kyle checked Armando's stash of guns in the concealed weapons box he'd built under the floorboards of his bedroom, hidden by the carpeting. Everything looked untouched, as Armando would have left it. The guns were oiled, with hardly a speck of dust anywhere. Clips and rounds were separated from the weapons. Kyle would have to deal with them if Armando didn't turn up soon. Besides, unless entirely necessary, it would be best not to enrage the locals by carrying weapons in his vehicle, other than his own in his vehicle. It wasn't protocol to carry a big stash unless a Team guy was on his way to ship out, but everyone did it anyway.

He found Christy's nametag still on the dining table where he'd tossed it three long days ago. Kyle picked it up again and traced over the indented letters that represented the woman he couldn't get out of his mind.

He released a sigh and put the plastic tag back. He surveyed the dirty kitchen sink and ruled it unacceptable. Adding hot water and soap, he rinsed off the crusty dishes and loaded them into the dishwasher, then turned it on.

Cleaning always helped him center his thoughts. Armando had a vacuum in the storage closet, and Kyle lost himself in the dull buzz of the machine while he removed a week's worth of dust and dirt. He wiped down the countertops, then looked at the damp rag and wet formica surface, wondering if he'd just removed evidence.

*Not likely.*

If Armando had been taken against his will, there'd be holes in the wall, missing windows, and a few large carving knives stuck into cabinet doors. And there'd be blood. Lots of it. No question.

No. Armando had left in a hurry, but he'd left on his own.

Kyle went back to the table and looked at the yellow tablet he remembered seeing the day he'd been waiting at Armando's. There were scribbles on the top and a folded street map tucked under several sheets. He hadn't noticed the deep grooves where something important had been pressed into a sheet that had been removed. He recognized it as Armando's writing. He became annoyed he'd missed this obvious clue two days ago when he first came to the house.

Rubbing the No. 2 pencil over the surface, he found a phone number with the area code of an adjacent county. He picked up Armando's landline, holding it with a towel, and hit redial. The same number came up.

"Hola? Armando?" said a panicked voice on the other line.

"No," Kyle said. "*¿Está Armando allí?*"

"No, Armando is not here." He did not recognize the voice.

"Kyle? Kyle is that you? Armando is not with you?"

"Ah, Mama Guzman. Didn't recognize the number."

"*Sí.* I'm at my daughter's. Where is Armando? Please, you will tell me now he is with you and he scares his mama for no good reason?"

"No. Sorry. I'm looking for him too. I'm sure he'll turn up." Kyle wondered if she believed the lie.

*Probably not.*

"Kyle. I am worried. He is coming to my house, but he never come. I am sick with worry."

"When was this?"

"Five, six days ago. Mia, you know Mia, Armando's sister?"

"Yes." Kyle assumed the stories of Mia's poor choice in men and lifestyles were true.

"Mia is in some trouble again," her voice started out calm, but her strength collapsed at the end, like a row of dominoes. Through ragged catches of breath, the creaking sound of the phone in Kyle's ear told him she was pacing anxiously, beside herself.

"So what happened? Did you call him?"

"Yes. I told him Mia is gone. And now Armando. I am here at Mia's apartment. I have no choice but to go to the police next. But they will laugh at me. And I don't want to tell them about Armando and the Navy."

"No. You did the right thing. We can handle this."

"You think so? He was mad, very, very mad when I told him."

"Mama, what? What did you tell him?"

"Mia is pregnant. She got pregnant with that bastard Caesar. She went off to tell him the good news." She mumbled something in Spanish Kyle didn't understand. "And I think Armando is thinking Caesar didn't take it very well. He has girls all over, but no, Mia loved him, she says. She says he will be different with her, with the baby when it comes."

*Not fucking likely.*

Kyle knew exactly what Armando had done. Gone dark. But why hadn't he told his mother? This question niggled and worried him. So that was what all the texting was about. Kyle didn't like it either.

"Mama, you need to get back to your own house. What if he's tried to call you there?"

"Yes. Yes, I will do that now. Nothing here for me. I just came to see if they were...here..." her voice trailed off again. Kyle knew Mama Guzman had thought she'd find them in a bloody pile.

"Anything look out of order?" He had to ask it, the picture in his head was too strong.

"No. Looks just like she went to work."

"Best get out of there. I'm not sure it's safe. You need to get home."

"Yes. Yes I will."

"Bring her key, okay? I might need it."

"*Si.*"

"You have a cell phone?"

Kyle heard a streak of swear words he thankfully couldn't understand.

"I'll give you my home number. I don't want to get the ear cancer."

"Mia have one?"

"Yes, of course."

Kyle wrote both numbers down. "I'm going to get some friends, and we're going to go find them. You stay by the phone, okay, Mama?" He gave her his personal cell number, not his overseas phone. "You won't get me, but leave a message there."

He could hear her chicken scratches, mumbling the numbers in translation to herself.

"When I call you, it won't look like a regular number. So, pick up anything that looks strange. Don't want you screening out my call. Leave me a message. I'll get back to you when I can."

"Yes. No caller ID, like Armando."

"Right."

He hung up, and then programmed her home number and Mia's with a quiet code ring and ran to Armando's bedroom to change into some gear and dark clothes. On his way out the door, he checked the phone calls and messages, leaving them just in case the police got dragged in. He noticed the last call out was five days ago, Mia's number. He wrote down the two previous numbers as well and the date and times they were made. He saw the calls from Mrs. Guzman and two blocked calls incoming earlier in the day.

He thought about Armando's stash of guns under the corner in the bedroom and decided against taking them in case his buddy made it back and needed the firepower. He grabbed his black duffel bag that contained everything he'd brought and slung it over his shoulder, then headed to the door.

Kyle looked around to say goodbye to Armando's home.

He might not ever return here. That same thought was always on his mind each time he deployed.

He flipped the lock and almost shut the door, but then remembered Christy's nametag. In three long strides, he reached the table. He grabbed the little badge and placed it in his left breast pocket and closed the Velcro flap.

After leaving the house, he hung out under the darkened overhang to see if anyone watched the house. The quiet street held only a couple of parked cars that dotted the curb, but none of them were close. He made it across the street to his beast and drove away. He had to check in with Timmons back on base.

KYLE SWORE UNDER his breath when he saw Petty Officer III$^{rd}$ Carlisle Channing, decked out with his usual asshole attitude, manning the front gate like he guarded the Alamo.

"Well, here he is, the second coming. How many times you jerk off in the bathroom today, sailor? Or do you just whip it out and show all the girls—"

"Shut the fuck up, Car-LILE."

"Need to see your ID, you prick."

Kyle dug out his military issue card. Before Channing could put his well-manicured paws on it, Kyle let it slip through his fingers to the ground.

"Oops. I'm sorry about that," Kyle said sarcastically as he opened the door of his Hummer, catching Petty Officer III$^{rd}$ Channing in the groin.

That made the guard hop around. "I'm going to write you up for that," he said as he held himself with both hands.

Kyle knew the Naval police would add the infraction to the other forty they had. Really important ones, like not showing respect to the regular Navy guys. Kyle couldn't hold anything against someone who tried one day of BUD/S. Took balls to even consider going through the hell of becoming a SEAL. So, the ones who thought they'd drawn some kind of cushy police job, trying to hold the real warriors back as if they were a danger to the general public, well, he carried no respect for those assholes.

He'd gotten a dozen slips for riding a bicycle without a helmet after he'd taken his Hummer into the shop for an alteration and it was getting fixed. One slip for scuffed shoes. One for stopping just over the line at the gate. These guys just itched to bust him. Carlisle had a whole six-pack of associate flunkies he terrorized on a regular basis. Like monkeys at the zoo. Kyle felt sorry for the whole lot of them.

"Make sure you write that I hit you in the crotch. My reputation is at stake."

"One of these days, sailor, you're gonna need a friend and I'll be sitting back, watching you squirm, on my way over to screw your woman," Carlisle said as he handed Kyle back his ID.

"Geez, Carlisle, I'd have to wear Kevlar if I had a friend like you." Kyle slipped his card inside the pocket that held Christy's nametag. "And as for the girls, well, I thought you knew I like guys. But in your case, I'd share. All you had to do was ask."

He puckered his lips and blew a kiss at Carlyle, revved the motor, and tore off through the parking lot before he got a dent in his door.

*I'll have to tone it down a bit soon. This one is a war without winners.* Kyle knew well enough what a man would do if pushed too far, and Carlisle looked just like one of those guys with no control. But he was a comrade, a member of the same Navy Kyle served. And that was worth something, after all.

*Another set of amends I need to make.* But not today. Today was still all about Armando and getting his ass safely back on base. Kyle marched down the buffed vinyl floor tiles leading to Timmons's office.

Timmons frowned down at a half-inch report, his thick glasses perched atop his shiny forehead, which told Kyle he wasn't reading a thing. Timmons mumbled and tapped his pencil.

"Sir?" Kyle said as he rapped on the open door.

"Lansdowne. You got anything good for me today?"

"Sir? I was hoping you had the last cell coordinates."

"We got some of the best equipment known to man, and we still have to wait on the fuckin' phone company."

"Coop's friend said the signal's dead."

"Dammit, Kyle. I told you not to involve the locals or the Feds."

"It was off the record."

"Sure it was. Nothing is off the record, son. So what good news *do* you have?"

"Wish I did, Mister. I got another number for you to check, though. This one belongs to Mia, Armando's sister. No news at all. Just a big fucking mystery, getting worse."

Timmons nodded his partially bald head, the shiny nut-brown skin of his scalp all too visible and getting more so by the day. Kyle noticed he looked a little pudgy too.

"Why are we tracking the sister?" Timmons asked, staring at the piece of paper like it was a dead cockroach.

"His sister's gone missing. Talked to his mom. She's major freaked."

"So this is some kind of stinking foul play. What—"

"No sir, it wasn't Armando's doing. I'd stake my career on it. He's gone after his sister. Nothing's disturbed at his place and the same for hers, according to his mom. It's like they just walked into the sunset together."

"Except that never happens."

"I understand, sir."

"I don't want to get the local cops involved. Or the regulars either, if we can help it."

"Completely agree, sir."

"How could two people disappear without any clues?"

"Disappearing is what we're trained to do. When we don't want to be found, we aren't found."

Timmons nodded again, then gazed back at his report and pulled down his glasses. Then he yanked them off, leaned back in his chair, and nibbled on a well-chewed plastic temple. "One problem with that fuckin' theory, son."

"What's that, sir?"

"When Armando didn't check in, that's like painting a great big fucking red SOS sign on a destroyer." He leaned forward, his forearms on the desk, and stared at Kyle. "He wanted to be found from the day he left."

# CHAPTER 9

C HRISTY TORE INTO cleaning her condo with complete abandon. She'd washed three loads of laundry, including the sheets full of the scent of him. She added five lavender-scented dryer sheets just in case a trace of the man remained.

On her hands and knees, she scoured the bathroom floor. She removed almost everything from her refrigerator and cleaned her glass shelves with hot, soapy water. Searching through her closet, she filled a garbage bag full of clothes she would give away to the women's shelter. Purging her bathroom vanity drawers, she gathered up little bottles of shampoo and soap from her hotel stays and threw them into the giveaway bag.

*Damn him. How dare he come waltzing in here, disrupting my life? Everything had been just f—*

But no. Everything hadn't been *fine*. Her eyes, already sore from crying, painfully filled with tears again. She felt cheap, furious with herself for allowing a romp in the hay without commitment.

*What were you thinking?*

After checking her phone at the office for messages, she forwarded calls to her cell. She went online and answered several emails that had piled up over the last two days.

Kyle Lansdowne lacked for nothing, of course—the asshole had screwed her good and plenty and then had left. No way she'd let him treat her this way. Her insides still smoldered, but she'd landed on her feet.

*God damn you. Who gave you the right? How could I have felt as if something wonderful were happening?*

The option of giving up and going back to San Francisco to nurse her wounds was out of the question. He'd left a rather stern message this afternoon. She needed another cup of coffee to dredge up the guts to return his call. No doubt that Realtor they'd run into at the model had told a compelling story and had probably even embellished it.

Well, she had to just suck it up and deal. They'd all be surprised. She'd throw herself into her work even more than before. Be the best goddamned salesperson in the whole office, if given a second chance. After all, she'd had lots of training selling upscale bras and panties that cost as much as most people's car payments.

She would make it her mission to go looking for someone else to wipe the memory of Kyle out of her mind, someone else to kiss her all over and make her shudder with pleasure. Couldn't be *that* hard to do.

Working for Madame M in San Francisco had exposed her to a clientele of wealthy older men who would often ask her to dinner or the theater. One had even asked her on a cruise. But the answer had always been the same. She'd done her share of flirting, part of her customer service, and Madame M had showed her how the clients liked it. Happy clients bought more things. But Christy never took their interest seriously. She knew they were seeking a replacement to a loss in their lives as the result of either widowhood or divorce. Madame M had called them the "real DDs."

Christy didn't mind being the familiar face associated with happier times when they bought lingerie for their wives or long-term companions. But she didn't want to be a *step* anything, wanting to have her own family someday with someone who hadn't made that choice before. Christy wanted to be someone's *only*.

She sank into her leather couch and leaned back. A cobweb she had missed dangled in the corner, almost winking at her. Christy jumped up and threw a rag at it, then collapsed back into the couch and had a good cry. Although she'd tried, despite all the scrubbing, cleaning and purging, only one man's face popped up on her radar screen—the one with the three-toed tattoo tracks running up his arm.

*Get a grip, Christy. Life moves on. Apparently he has too.*

But she could have sworn he'd felt something.

She jumped up, stormed into the kitchen, and threw her rag into the suds in the kitchen sink, which sent a splash of gray water all over her countertop and onto the floor.

Maybe another Team guy could fill the bill, someone Kyle even knew. That would get him. And it would serve him fucking right. Let him imagine her screwing the other guy senseless every time Kyle had to look at the guy. Every time they had to go on a training mission.

*See how it feels to be discarded.*

First things first. She dialed her manager's office.

"Christy. Thanks for calling back. I was a little worried. I hadn't seen or heard from you in a couple of days. You okay?"

"Yes. Been working, but out of the house," she lied.

"Good. That's good. Say, I got this very disturbing call yesterday afternoon from Connie at the Infinity sales office," Simms said.

"Yeah, I thought maybe she would call." Christy sucked it up and just decided to tell the truth. If she lost her job over it, well, she hated hanging around Wayne and the way he stared through her clothes, anyway.

"Mr. Simms." She surprised herself how confident she sounded. So she turned it up a notch and continued, "I owe you an apology."

"Oh? How's that?"

Christy heard doubt in his voice, and continued. "I was so relieved when that SEAL turned out to be…he had a legitimate reason for being at the house. I was the one in the wrong place at the wrong time."

"I thought it was Wayne's fault. But he insists he gave you the right address."

"Whatever. It isn't important anymore."

"Never happened before here. Very strange. I'm glad you weren't really hurt."

"No. Just scared out of my gourd. But it was my fault, I guess. Anyway, the tension was getting to me a little, and I wanted to give him a chance to apologize. So, we agreed to have lunch. Well, one thing led to another, and…" She had to tell the little white lie to keep her job. "All we did was kiss. I know what you're going to say. It was a complete lapse in judgment on my part."

Simms chuckled into the phone. "Yeah, those guys can get pretty wound up. Nice lookin' fella. I can't say as I blame you. But…Christy…she said it went way beyond kissing. She said…"

"Just how would she know?" Christy interrupted. "I can't deny the fact that we were engaged in a very passionate kiss, but, honestly, Mr. Simms, do you really believe we would… It was the *model*, and, you know… I live right upstairs. If…"

He sighed. "Yeah. Look, Christy. I get it. Older agent versus a new, young, pretty agent. She thinks you get your business by screwing your clients. Unfortunately, I've heard that one before too."

"Well, it wasn't very professional of me. Not right that her clients had to be witness to my little indiscretion."

"Oh, hell, they probably didn't mind it, although she said different."

"They were laughing. I'm sure she blew it out of proportion. I don't even want to know what she told you."

Christy knew Simms was blushing even though she couldn't see his face.

*Yeah, the old biddy told him about the panties.*

"Well, I'm satisfied. As long as you clarify one more thing with me," Simms words came across short and clipped. Christy braced herself.

"Sure. What?"

"Did you enjoy the rest of the afternoon?" He chuckled again.

"As a matter of fact, I did." She hung up.


TOTAL TRUTH, CHRISTY couldn't stop thinking about Kyle. The hair at the back of her neck and all the way down her spine tickled deliciously where he had kissed her, where she needed him to kiss her now. She stood at a crossroads between spending energy trying to bury her feelings for him and…what?

*Oh. My. God. Am I actually thinking about running after him?*

Something she'd never done. She wasn't going to beg. Besides, he'd made it clear. For her sake, he would say no.

He'd walked right back into her life with those damned red signs and the flowers, and had made a nest in her heart. And then something had made him stop. Something Christy knew she didn't cause.

*What?*

Maybe if she could find him, they could talk it over. Take it slow. She could tell him she didn't expect a lifetime, just a casual friendship. A *little* relationship, not a big one. A friendship with benefits.

*How do I do this? Where do I find him?* He knew how to reach her, but she had no clue how to find him. She couldn't just hang around a bunch of bars, hoping for him to show up.

Could she have offended him in some way? Had he misunderstood her? She just couldn't let it go. She didn't do "wait" very well. Wait until he decided to waltz back into her life?

*Never!* But if she didn't talk to him perhaps he would ship out or worse, find someone else.

*No.*

She'd have to go back to that street Armando lived on. Back to the page of the Thomas Bros. guide she had already mentally ripped out of her book.

Though she was nervous, she had to go back to Armando's house to search for some evidence of where Kyle was staying.

Christy's red Honda puttered down the tree-lined street of Armando's neighborhood. The sun hung low and on its way to retiring. She drove by the house quickly at first, making sure there wasn't a car in the driveway. A vacant brown beat-up Buick was parked down the street two doors away. Other than that, the neighborhood seemed empty. A jet streaked across the sky and sent a rumble through the air.

*Fly boy.*

Christy pulled into the driveway in case she needed to make a quick exit. The front door to the house was locked. As she walked around the side, trying the wood sash windows, she heard something inside clatter to the floor. She listened through a window that had closed drapes, but heard no other noise.

She continued along the side of the house to a wooden gate leading to the rear yard. She pulled a wire latch, and a shallow garden oasis with a lap pool came into view. Everything was neatly maintained, although the grass looked a little long. A few dozen leaves floated in the turquoise water, out of place.

A pair of concrete steps on the back porch led her to the rear sliding glass door, and, to her surprise, the door was unlocked. She slid it open without making a sound.

As soon as she stepped into the large open kitchen, she knew she'd made a mistake, but her curiosity had been piqued. The house had been ransacked. Things had been tossed everywhere; a chair left upended, cabinet doors flung open, and several dishes lying smashed across the kitchen floor.

She turned and went down the hallway leading to the now-infamous rear bedroom. Inside the room she found all the sheets had been ripped from the mattress and tossed about. The mattress top was sliced open. Clothes from Armando's closet were strewn haphazardly all over the place.

All of a sudden, she heard the front door open and slam shut, and then heard footsteps running outside. Through the living room window she saw two men jump into the brown sedan that had been parked down the street. They pulled a U-turn and left the area.

Christy quickly checked the rest of the house without touching anything. She was alone. A message light blinked on the phone machine. Using the edge of her jacket, she pushed the button to play it back.

"Amigo," a thickly accented voice said. "Thirty minutes. Foothills. Smell fire. They got at least ten. Loaded. Left..." The line went dead. Christy knew she'd just heard the voice of Armando, and he sounded stressed. He'd spoken in some sort of code. She didn't have time to put together the pieces, but she knew she had to get the message to Kyle right away. Something told her it could mean a matter of life or death. She jotted down the words, replaying the message until she got it right.

Would Kyle believe her? Well, yes, if he heard the message. But knowing he wanted to disappear, would she even be able to find him?

She remembered what he'd told her about the community, and how the buzz traveled like the Underground Railroad. Everyone knew about everyone else somehow. So, if she gave one of the Team guys a message, Kyle would come. She was counting on it.

Christy drove to the Golden Bear Café and searched for square-shouldered, stern-looking men with tattoos and didn't spot one. But she saw the cook Kyle knew. Griz. Maybe he'd have a suggestion.

Griz's unshaved chin was heavily scarred on the right side. His steel blue eyes wandered carefully up and down her torso with a glint of appreciation for another man's lady. At least that's how she interpreted it, anyway.

"Well, hello there. You flying solo today, or is he meeting up with you later?" Griz asked her while wiping his hands on his stained apron.

"I was hoping you'd remember me," Christy said as she looked down at her sandaled feet with the pink toenail polish, and then back up to his face before her tears burst loose.

*Damn those pink toes.*

"You're not exactly easy to forget." He smiled, but didn't look at her cleavage, though she could tell he wanted to. She liked that part about this community, the respect they showed her. The direct look without flinching, not hiding the effect she had on him.

"You wanna beer?" he finally said.

"No, thanks."

"Well then, Missy, what can I do you for?" He chewed on a toothpick as he nodded to a couple just entering the diner.

"I'm looking for Kyle. It's important."

"Well, I haven't seen him since yesterday. With you. Doubt he'll be here tonight either. Not his scene."

"If you could put the word out. I need to talk to him about a friend of his."

"Um hum. This a message he's going to want to hear?" The man pinned her with his eyes, being careful, protective of Kyle.

"Yes. He's looking for someone. You know, Armando. I may have some information."

"'Kay. So you have some information about Armando. Where should he contact you *if* I hear from him?"

Christy fished out her business card. "My cell phone's at the bottom."

Griz flipped the card back and forth against his other thumb, obviously thinking. He looked as if he wanted to say something, but stopped himself. Christy felt the awkwardness of the two of them standing in a nearly empty room.

"Well. I've got to go. I'm going to drive around and see if I can spot his Hummer."

He nodded. "You two have a little tiff?"

"That's an off-limits question."

"Could be, but then Kyle's a special operator and we look out for each other."

"I know about that. Any idea where he's staying?"

"You're asking me? I'm surprised he let you escape."

Griz grinned full out, but lopsided and apologetic. She saw the heart of gold inside the rough-hewn man of steel.

Christy scratched the back of her head, hoping to break the tension and change the mood. "I'm sorry I bothered you. I'll be off now. But if you think of anything, please give me a call."

Christy's shoulders stiffened as she drove back and forth along the strip lined by little shops across the street from a white expanse of beach. Several times she thought she felt eyes watching her, but upon checking in the rear view mirror, she found no sign of the black Hummer. She ran into three young men in shorts and flip-flops with matching wrap-around sunglasses that screamed military issue at the frozen yogurt stand. She also gave them one of her cards since they hinted they might know Kyle but said they weren't sure.

*They're lying.*

She checked her phone to see if she'd missed a call, but her voicemail was empty. The afternoon wafted away from her, so she decided to return home. She hoped to see a black Hummer inside the automatic gate at the underground garage, but no such luck. She stepped into the elevator after parking and made it up to the fourteenth floor.

A maid vacuuming the hallway nodded a greeting as Christy let herself in the condo.

Dropping her purse and kicking off her shoes on her way to the bathroom, she automatically massaged the back of her neck, which was still so tight. She recalled how Kyle had protected her head when he leveled her to the ground that first day. This must be some resulting swollen tissue, she thought.

She slipped off her clothes and prepared a bubble bath. She placed her cell phone to the tub's edge and picked up a current romance novel she had yet to finish. She'd just submerged in the warm bubbles and lain back against a towel when her cell rang. A strange combination of numbers, not from an area code around San Diego, appeared in a sequence on the screen.

"Hello?"

"Hi, Christy."

A shot of electricity traveled down her spine. She'd done a pretty good job of thinking she could maintain her composure until she heard Kyle's voice. Her will turned to butter.

"I know you don't want to have anything to do with me, but—"

"That's not true, and you know it."

*Damn the man.*

"I went over to Armando's house today," she said.

"Now why would you go and do that? Not very smart."

"No. But then you know how smart I am, don't you?"

"I think you're one of the smartest girls I've ever met, but it was dumb to go over to that house. You must promise me you won't do it again. Ever. It's dangerous."

"I think I know that now. Don't worry."

Kyle paused. In a soft voice, he asked, "What are you saying?"

"There were two men there."

Christy moved around in the water.

"Where are you?"

"In the bathtub."

"Oh." He paused. "So, what did the men look like?"

"Dark-haired. Young. They ran out the front when I went in the back."

"You went into the house?"

"Yes. The place is a mess. I think they were looking for something. But I scared them off."

Kyle chuckled at that. "I could see how you would make a man go weak at the knees. Even two men. Two very bad men."

"Not funny. Don't make fun of me."

"I'm not. So after you scared them off, what did you do?"

"I listened to Armando's phone message on the answering machine."

"What the hell? Christy, you have no business getting involved. You stay out of this, understand?"

"So do you want to hear the message?"

Kyle hesitated, breathing hard into the receiver. God she wished he was breathing against the side of her face, kissing her there, looking at her and touching…

"Yes."

"He said 'Foothills and thirty minutes.' Then he said 'Got ten loaded.' He started to say he *left* something and then the line went dead."

Christy could hear her heart pounding, wondering if he heard it too.

"Thanks," he whispered.

More silence. She would make him talk next, if he wanted to. That's what she needed to hear. Did he want to or not?

"I understand you went out of your way to find me. I appreciate that."

"Because it's the right thing to do, Kyle." She hoped it didn't sound too strong, so she added as soft and sexy as she could muster, "Because it was important to you."

There, she'd said it. Time to figure out if she would have to do a rescue mission on her own heart. A girl's night out? A romantic movie that made her cry all night long?

"Well, I thank you."

She could tell he had difficulty saying it.

"So, if you're free tonight, I am." God, she hoped he'd say he was.

"No. We have things we have to do. I'll give you a call sometime."

Her heart fell to the bottom of the tub. That was the answer she had expected. At least her attempt had been worth the try.

"Okay then, sailor. You know where I live." She found the courage to hang up on him first. She lay back in the tub and placed a wet washcloth over her eyes, which absorbed the welled-up tears and those continuing to fall.

No, she didn't do "wait" very well. She needed to move on.

# CHAPTER 10

KYLE STEPPED INTO Jimmy's, the place where the Wall of the Fallen took Kyle's breath away every time he saw it—all the faces of young, handsome men, cut short in their prime. He usually looked at every one of their pictures as if he were looking right into their eyes, and said a thank you.

Every time.

The inscription in the middle, translated from a rough-hewn carving by some anonymous artisan at the graveyard on Iwo Jima read:

*When you go home,*
*Tell them for us, and say,*
*For your tomorrow,*
*We gave our today.*

As tough as he knew his community was, he didn't know a single Team guy who didn't choke up reading that.

Being a SEAL wasn't all about rah rah or politics. Wasn't about highs and lows of armed warfare, man on man. Wasn't about knowing your limits or having a band of brothers. It was about life and death.

When he and Armando got their very first tattoo together, his band of barbed wire thorns around his calf, the old artist looked Kyle right in the eyes and said, "So you want to make friends with death, son?"

He could answer the old man today. But not that day.

Kyle sat and waited for his team to arrive.

"I'VE TALKED TO Armando's mom," Kyle began, after the group had gathered, "and I think he linked up with this guy, Caesar, who Mia has been hanging around. Apparently, she's pregnant. Armando went to go find her."

"That could be good news. Maybe this asshole won't hurt her," Fredo tossed that statement into the mix.

"Can't count on that, Fredo." Kyle worked to keep panic out of his voice.

Gunny swore and shook his head. "The man must be an animal. I'd say put him down."

"Whoa! Gunny. We're not talking about doing anything like that," Kyle shot back, alarmed.

"Be doing the female population a favor, you ask me. But then you didn't, did you?"

Cooper narrowed his eyes at Kyle and then winced. "You think they're still in the area?"

Kyle nodded. "The message said something about the foothills and thirty minutes away. Said there were ten. Well-armed." He sighed. "Can you get your friend to track this cell phone?" Kyle handed Cooper a yellow Post-It note with Mia's cell phone number.

"Sure. No problem. How old is this?"

"I think only a couple of hours. This morning there was nothing on the answering machine. But..." He didn't want to tell them how he got the message. "Well, the message came in sometime after noon. I'm guessing he used Mia's cell phone, since they took or destroyed his."

"You listen to it?" Fredo asked as Cooper got up, presumably to call his friend in the DOJ.

"Nah. Someone else did. And there's another thing. Armando's house has been trashed."

"Hey, boss, you got someone else working on this job? Someone we need to know about?" Fredo asked.

Kyle looked down at his folded hands. He wanted a beer, but he knew he'd need his wits about him in case they got a location. "The lady I was with yesterday afternoon came looking for me." He didn't want to make eye contact.

"Uh huh. Like I said, you gotta start thinking with your other head, boss."

"I never had that problem," Gunny inserted, laughing at Kyle's obvious discomfort.

"So Gramps, you knew about this too?" Fredo asked.

"Shit, yes. My gym's like a fuckin beauty parlor. I learn everything about the crap you guys get into just from keeping my ears open. Always some newbie or wanna-be who is only too quick to tell me about all your dumb-ass moves." Gunny coughed. "Although this time, he gave me a full description of the lady in question, like she was naked."

Kyle almost grabbed Gunny by the shirt collar. He drank water and crunched on ice cubes instead.

"So Kyle, I gotta ask. Are you okay?" Fredo looked at him hard.

Not the question he wanted to hear. Were they feeling him starting to slip? Was he starting to slip? Was it wrong to want to feel the soft flesh of a woman next to his and not be able to get her out of his mind?

No, it wasn't wrong. It was right. But it interfered with his mental clarity, and was so unfair to her.

"No worries, gentlemen. I'm right as rain. Got all the cum lovingly worked outta me real good last night. Now I'm ready for a fight." Kyle hoped they believed him.

"Sounds like she didn't get enough, though," Fredo barked.

"Oh, yeah she did." Kyle grinned. "She just wants more."

Finally Fredo laughed and nodded his head. "Tell her I'm available."

Kyle punched Fredo's bicep, this time a little harder than usual.

Coop returned with the news he'd left a message for his DOJ friend in two places. "He'll call me back, I hope tonight."

"Okay, so now that we know Armando's alive, we're gonna only have one chance to break him out. I want this kept tight, just between us. And when we're ready to roll, we go."

The team nodded in agreement.

"Gentlemen, we got only three days to do this. Then I'll go it alone," Kyle said.

"The hell you will. I'm with you all the way," Gunny said.

There was a pause as Gunny looked back into three cowed faces. Nothing more needed to be said. "Fuck it, fellas, I can drive a car, shoot a gun, I don't wear glasses. And the ladies don't distract me like some people sitting at this table."

Everyone laughed, except Kyle. He was thinking of the way Christy's breasts filled his palm, how she tasted under her ear, and how he'd tried to sleep with the largest boner he'd ever had just from the feel of her hair on his chest as he snuggled next to her in bed. The mere memory of her scent had kept him awake all night.

Gunny snapped his gnarled fingers in front of Kyle's face. "You've got it bad, kid. That kind of a lapse in concentration can get you killed, you know."

A harsh thing to say, but it was the truth. Kyle looked at the pock-marked and ruddy red complexion of one of the ugliest men he'd ever met and knew Gunny would give his life to protect him. Gunny had a heart the size of the Pacific Ocean and wanted to go out like a hero.

But Kyle hoped he wouldn't have to.

KYLE DECIDED TO get a motel room and watch movies all night. He knew he wouldn't be able to sleep. He couldn't get drunk or go clubbing because he had to be able to hear his phone. There were some nights he couldn't wait to press his body into a throng of strangers and dance to oblivion, but tonight wasn't one of them. He knew what he wanted to do.

*If you're available, I'm available.*

It wasn't the right thing, but it was the *only* thing he could think about. How she whimpered under him, how he loved to watch her and feel her shuddering with climax. He loved watching how he made her feel.

A really good guy would stay away.

*But I'm just a man. A dog.*

So he turned around and headed off the island toward Old Town.

CHRISTY HEARD A knock at her door. She'd fallen asleep and the bathtub water had turned ice cold. She got out of the tub and quickly dried off, her heart pounding in her throat. With hair still dripping wet around the sides of her face, she slipped on her flowered silk robe, headed down the hall, then viewed Kyle's face in profile through the peephole of her front door.

She quickly ran to her bedroom and made her bed, throwing her clothes behind the closet door. She put on some hand cream and then wished she'd gotten her legs and feet as well. She applied cherry lip-gloss and a spritzer of *L'Interdit*.

*He came back.*

She slowly walked back to the front door, took a big gulp, and pulled the door open, raising her gaze from his beltline up the hard chest encased in a baby blue T-shirt, up the thick clean-shaven neck to a square jaw, to the full lips and two light blue eyes. He stared back at her like he had the first time they'd made love. His need came across stronger than his control, and seeing that, she felt hope.

In an instant, he'd moved through the doorway and had kicked the front door closed behind him. His hands were suddenly inside her robe, exploring her flesh and igniting her passion. She tugged at his pants, and then kneeled to unbutton his fly. He stripped off his T-shirt and removed his shoes. She kissed the head of his cock, and then took his full length into her mouth, peeling his jeans down his tight cheeks to his ankles. She sucked him hard as he pulled her robe away and threw it into the corner. He leaned over her kneeling form, running his hands down her spine, over her shoulders and under her chin as she worked her tongue over him.

He moaned something she couldn't make out.

He withdrew and kneeled in front of her. She didn't care that she showed him how much she'd missed him.

"I can't seem to stay away, Christy. You ensnare me and I willingly go…" He stopped speaking to plunge his tongue into her mouth, seeking hers, commanding her heart, and pulling it out of her chest.

"I don't want you to stay away, Kyle. I want…" She stopped before she said something she'd regret.

His hands grasped her jaw as he searched her eyes. Christy's breasts rubbed against his hairless chest, nipples against nipples, and lazily moved one hand up and down his shaft while the other cupped his balls. His thumbs moved on her cheeks, then down to her lips as he bent and kissed her long and carefully, as if she were a China doll.

He picked her up with one arm under her knees and the other behind her shoulders. She buried her head in his neck, kissing him, biting him there. He placed her on the bed, then moved up to spread her legs and put his lips on her sex in one fluid movement. She offered no resistance, wanting him there. Her fingers dug into his thick brown hair and then moved behind his ears as his tongue pleasured her, licking her folds and sucking on her bud.

She asked to be found, and he found her, right there, between her legs, breathing life into her soul with his tongue and his hot breath.

Bending one knee and slipping her thigh in front of her, she turned to her belly to let him lap at her sex from the side and then behind. He placed two fingers deep inside her. She clutched the pillow and groaned into the fresh lavender linen, knowing he could see her face in profile. With her sighs and moans, Christy told him of her need and how beautifully he satisfied it.

She forced her rear up in the air, begging for penetration, and he pressed the crown of his cock at her opening. He slid inside her slowly so her body stretched and accepted his wide girth.

Bracing her arms in front of her, she placed her thighs outside his and arched her back up, then down as she impaled herself on him and ground into his groin He encased her back with his chest, whispering something in her ear and holding her breasts with his palms, letting the pillows of her flesh overflow between his fingers.

"I love making love to you, Christy."

Not exactly what she hoped to hear, but close. "Yes, Kyle. Oh…"

"Not possible"—he said between thrusts—"to stay away. Not possible."

She shuddered and exploded in a warm, fluttering orgasm that shook every cell in her body. At the same time, his spasms filled her in more ways than one.

ONLY A FEW minutes had passed, and Kyle was still embedded inside her where they'd collapsed on the bed.

"Thank you," Christy said as she turned to touch the side of his face with one hand, then trace over his lips. He bent and kissed her shoulder.

"I'm sorry I sent you away. I am so sorry."

Christy snuggled against his chest, her fingers lacing over his lips. "I'm glad you came back." Her hand reached down below and she found him nearly hard again.

"Oh, my," she whispered to his belly button.

KYLE LAY BACK, staring at the ceiling. Satisfied. This was the way it was supposed to feel. He'd finally found a woman who loved sex as much as he did.

Christy had fallen into a deep sleep, which surprised him. He loved the feel of her inhale and exhale, craved the sound of her gentle reverie.

He drifted off, thinking about his other teammates.

*Praise the Lord, Cooper would say.* He smiled as he recalled the time when Cooper had told him how hot it made women when he read them the Love Chapter from Psalms.

He'd asked the guys to call him when they heard back from Cooper's friend. Then he pictured Armando's house and hoped it was not part of a crime scene investigation. He wondered what the intruders were after.

*Probably guns.*

He was the only one who knew about the hiding place in the corner of Armando's bedroom—enough guns to start a small war. There'd be time to get his friend's gear out of there later. This break-in meant Armando hadn't given them what they wanted, unless they'd just found the guns. But Christy didn't say anything about the floor being ripped up, so hopefully Armando still lived. And Mia as well.

Christy had cuddled herself under his chin. She awoke and stretched, then began stroking his chest with those nails of hers, tracing over a few scars, most of them from surfing. A few jagged ridges were from knife wounds due to close encounters with some pretty sorry-assed bad guys, not all of whom had lived to tell their side of things.

He knew she waited for him to say something. Like it or not, she *was* involved, *wanted* to be involved. He hoped like hell she knew what she was doing. He sure didn't. He'd never felt this way about a new relationship.

"Thank you, Christy."

"For what?" She turned and gave him a crooked, wide-eyed smile.

"Thanks for the intel," he whispered to the top of her head. He got back the warm scent of lavender.

"Oh." She giggled. "No problem, sir. Anything else I can do for you?" She gripped his thigh between her legs.

A damned comedian, funny as hell. *Is this how life with her would be?* He studied her face, tilting up her chin, losing himself in the sparkle of her deep brown eyes. "No. I think you've done quite enough." He saw the beginnings of a lusty smile form on her lips and knew it wouldn't take long before he felt his own need growing. Again.

"Can I ask you what the message means? Or will I have to torture you to find out?" She kissed his left nipple and then licked it, swirling her tongue.

"Ah, not fair. Not sure this is in keeping with the Geneva Convention."

"Shall I beg?"

"Please, no! I'm not sure I can get it up any more. I mean, my mind's willing, but my body…"

She continued stroking him. "Please."

With those eyes of hers, who would be able to deny her?

*Hell, what would it hurt?* He'd be telling her all sorts of things in a minute if he weren't careful. "He said…" Kyle's voice grew husky and ragged, but he continued, "He was trying to tell me he's okay for now. But he's heavily guarded, and whoever has him doesn't mess around."

She tensed, and he knew he'd lost her again. He read her fear. She was afraid something would happen to him.

*Do I want to know this?*

"There are things you just should not know about. This is what my work is all about, Christy. All the time."

"Yes. I understand."

*But did she, really?*

"So you forgive me for breaking into your friend's house and listening to his personal messages?" she teased.

He chuckled, grateful for her humor. "No, I didn't say *that*." He paddled her rear in a mock spanking. "I'll have to punish you further, and…" He scanned her face again. "Make you tell me all your secrets." He kissed her wanton lips, murmuring to them, "And extracting how you cleverly wound me around your little finger so easily."

"You'd make me?"

"I could. I'm very good at interrogation," he whispered in her ear. He followed up with a kiss below her earlobe and felt the rumble of her moan.

"How would you get information from me? How would you *make* me tell you?"

"I'd improvise. Think of something." He rubbed his lips against hers, biting her lower lip.

"Improvise?" She arched to press her breasts against him.

"Use things at hand."

"How would you use these things?"

Kyle smiled. Her naïveté to the ways of the warrior community thrilled him. He stared into her lusty eyes. He wasn't quite sure what to say.

"I might have to use pantyhose," he said to her lips.

Christy's eyes drew wide and she arched again into him, rubbing her sex against his thigh. "You'd tie me up?" she said breathlessly.

Kyle started. *Was she asking for this?*

She sighed and whispered, "I want you to improvise. On my body. Make me tell you something."

"Ah." Kyle searched her face and then decided. He glanced at the floor beside the bed, reached over, and picked up the silk sash from her robe. He drew both her arms above her head while he kissed her underneath her jaw. Holding her wrists together with one hand, he wound the sash around them, binding them gently. Her lidded eyes told him of her pleasure. He wanted to kiss her all over her body.

He could feel her heart beating against him. He felt her moist arousal as he lazily fingered her bud and she moaned into his ear.

"Tell me, or I won't let you go," he said.

"I don't want to go."

"Yes you do. You want to squeeze your breasts. You want to pull me into you again," Kyle answered. He avoided her mound searching for his groin.

She started to move her arms down to encircle his neck and he stopped her.

"Bad girl. Tell me how you managed to capture my heart?"

"My name is Christy Nelson. I am a Realtor. That's all I'm going to reveal at this time."

"I think you'll reveal more," he said as he inserted two fingers into her wet sex.

"Ahh." She opened her eyes. "No. I won't tell." Her breathing was ragged. It looked like she was suppressing a smile.

"You must tell me." He pushed the head of his cock into the soft folds of her opening.

"Take me, Kyle. I am yours. All of me."

*God, I wish I could have you totally, Christy. What would that be like?* He realized he lived and died in her eyes. Could he have this forever?

"Tell me, Christy. Be a good girl and tell me how you manage to bewitch me so that all I think about is making love to you."

Had he ever said something even close to this before? Holy…

"I think of your hard places. I think of how I can wrap my softness against your hard body and make you need me. I try to get under your skin."

When he looked her in the eyes, tears had pooled there. If he put himself inside her, he would be lost forever. And that's what he wanted. He pressed his hand over her bound wrists and plunged into her.

"You have captured me again," he said as he stroked her insides. Her face was urgent. Her fingers curled into his and squeezed.

"You're a willing victim."

She sighed and gripped his thighs tighter with her knees, then opened herself wide again and let him plunge deeper.

"Yes, I am. Indeed, I am."

KYLE BASKED IN the scent of her spent body. Her breathing had calmed. Was she asleep?

Would it always be like this? With her the world was righted. He knew there wasn't anything this perfect in reality. But in the fantasy, everything seemed as it should be between them, which thrilled him.

And was so damned overdue.

And now so dangerous, because he'd formed another reason to live. Something he feared losing, like everything else in his life that meant anything.

Something had been lurking outside his consciousness, waiting for a dark moment to rush in. What?

And there it was again.

*Life isn't this perfect. Nothing lasts forever.* He remembered being a young boy of fourteen, like it was this morning. All the pain and uncertainty came flooding in.

*What have I done?*

CHRISTY HEARD KYLE'S heavy breathing and was thankful he'd fallen asleep. He tossed about, talking in his sleep. No sweet erotic dreams, like the ones she'd been having. His forehead creased and his lips pursed.

*Maybe he's just not used to sleeping with a woman.* She remembered the first few times she'd spent the night in a strange bed, in the arms of a lover. Every touch of Kyle's body heightened her hunger for him. This strong man with arms and shoulders that could hold the whole world, cared for her. Quiet and strong. Ever the gentleman, until she got him into bed, and then he consumed her. She'd never known a man who needed so much passion. He demanded her body perform for him and she would do it. Loved doing it. She even loved letting him bind her hands above her head while he pumped her silly.

Last time, he'd brought her to the brink of ecstasy so many times, then had held her still, only to fall into the crest of the wave of her passion. He rode that wave with her. Watching her. Attentive, but unyielding. She doubted she would ever be able to make love to a man again and not think of Kyle.

God, she hoped she didn't have to try.

She found the warm place beneath his chin and buried herself. Inhaled his musky scent and drifted off to oblivion. Tomorrow she'd worry about the future. Right now, her future lay in the warm body of this man, the one with whom she could easily spend the rest of her life.

# CHAPTER 11

**K**YLE WOKE UP with a start and couldn't get back to sleep. He sat in Christy's living room as the dark night became early morning. He usually loved this time of day. Everything was so quiet, peaceful. He could think better when it was like this.

He should have taken off last night, just left, but that wasn't the way to treat a lady, and Christy was that, with every luscious inch of her. Could a man be blamed if he wanted to spend just a little more time in her arms? Christy had obviously felt a connection. Hell, he'd felt the connection too. But that was before common sense took over and he realized he'd made a huge mistake. He had to face the music and fix it. It would be hard, but it was up to him to do the right thing.

He'd gone to see her at the realty office three days ago just to say he was sorry. But when he saw her fingertips touch the flowers he'd brought, he'd lost his head and asked her out to lunch. What did he do that for?

*You know better than to get involved. You don't do "relationships."* *You get in and get out before they get too attached.*

He shook his head. He was indeed a dumb ass. Was he still mourning the most important woman in his life? Could that be why he had such a hard time staying away from Christy? Was he that damaged, that out of control?

His mother died when he was fourteen. She had cancer. The disease had spread quickly and she was gone within weeks, despite the surgeries that tried to stem the tide. He'd told himself this meant she didn't suffer too much. At least, not until the end. But the speed with which the cancer overtook her didn't give young Kyle time to pull together his feelings and say a proper goodbye. It remained an unfinished chapter, an open wound.

Kyle knew he had been the light of her life. He remembered her laugh, how intently she would watch him and cheer at his soccer and baseball games. She was there when he was discouraged. Still, he felt somehow responsible for her cancer, and he would have done anything, even traded places with her to stop it.

He'd wanted for nothing, although it was clear his father resented having to work so hard and complaining about the expensive traveling tournaments, special camps, coaching, and expensive equipment. His mother ran interference, but young Kyle heard the arguments behind closed doors at night. She was devoted to him, almost at the cost of her failing marriage. Kyle's older sister, just one year his senior, was totally boy crazy and working on getting herself a fast ticket out of the hell that was their family.

He couldn't remember a single game his father went to—couldn't remember him ever being even slightly interested in what Kyle was doing. He would come home in a sullen mood and would say nothing at dinner except to pepper the conversation with his irritation, regardless of his wife's attempts at conversation. His father would drink wine until he fell asleep in front of the TV. After that, he'd go off to bed early. Some nights when Kyle stayed up to do his homework, he'd get a gentle kiss from his mother before she turned in for bed, but he'd hear her softly cry herself to sleep. It broke his heart.

Light was beginning to shimmer, a deep purple on the inlet. He liked the view of Coronado from this side of the island. It gave him a different perspective on his life in the Navy. He looked at the cold outlines of the destroyers in the early morning light and took strength from the cold, gray shadows they cast on the murky inlet.

The machines and hospital stays his mother had undergone scared him. He was afraid she would never open her eyes again each time he visited her, especially toward the end. She insisted she was getting better, but he could see that was a lie. He realized that nothing he could say or do could protect her, and she slipped away one evening while he was out of town at a soccer tournament. She'd made him promise to go. Told him she'd be stronger the next time he saw her.

She died alone. In the dark. He'd been told of her death on a cell phone call from his father. He'd been sitting on the second seat in a Suburban, driven by one of his teammate's moms, surrounded by seven other sweaty kids.

*The bastard couldn't even wait until I got home to tell me in person.*

That night Kyle didn't say a word to anybody. He stared out at the rest of the world going by, resentment making a home in his chest. How could everything go on just like nothing had happened? He knew he would never heal this loss. She'd been the only one who'd believed in him.

Things changed at home after his mother's death. There were no more camps or elite sports teams. Kyle focused on his studies and worked hard to bury the love for his dead mother and the ache of her leaving him. His father became even colder and more distant, and they rarely talked. Kyle hung out at the library or with friends who didn't play sports. It was a bitter year, and just as he was beginning to feel some hope for the future, circumstances conspired against him.

Kyle had met a nice girl, Judy Dobson, and had asked her to the prom. She was crazy for him, which annoyed Kyle sometimes. But she was a good girl—the pretty one everyone else overlooked because she wore huge, thick glasses. They were going to ride with his older sister and her current boyfriend, but at the last minute, his sister wanted to go alone with her date. Kyle suspected they were going to skip the dance altogether and get a motel room.

He and Judy had barely gotten to the dance when the police arrived, telling him his sister had been in a life-threatening car accident. Kyle spent the rest of the night in the emergency room, in his tux. A friend took Judy home. She'd wanted to stay, but Kyle wouldn't have it. He and his dad sat across from each other all evening, except for the times when his dad snuck out to the car to drink. They spoke not a word.

Near dawn they got the bad news. His sister was dead.

Kyle thought maybe his father would stop drinking, maybe start taking care of himself and pull things together. But that wasn't in the man's nature, and his father retreated further into his alcoholism.

And now Kyle hadn't talked to him in six years. He considered his dad dead.

At eighteen, the week after he'd graduated high school, Kyle reported to Indoc and joined the Navy, with an eye on trying out for the SEALs. His mom had wanted him to go to college on an athletic scholarship, but that wasn't in the cards. The Navy took him without any promises, and then he got his chance. One out of ten thousand was the odds of being allowed to try out for the Teams. But Kyle got his spot. The Navy became his new family, and it served him well.

Armando was in that famous class that almost was a complete wash-out. Out of the 190 men that started, only twelve graduated. Of the twelve, four were officers, which was unusual. He and Armando were the only ones without a college degree, but they scored higher than the rest academically. They were closer than brothers.

They would gladly die for each other. That got battle-tested during their first deployment in Iraq when they survived the battle of Fallujah. Their unit ran into more than 259 Tangos in a narrow street that wasn't anything more than an alleyway. They were being shot at from all sides, including above. After the mounted guns ran out of ammo, they used their personal assault weapons. And when those ran out they resorted to their sidearms as they scrambled to a safe spot until the extraction team could get them out. A few good men died that day. A record number of the enemy had been killed, and the SEALs would be up for some medals, which would be awarded in private. His friendship with Armando, forged in steel, would be with him forever.

So now he'd let this beautiful young thing into his world. She had no idea what she was getting into and deserved way more. What in the hell had he been thinking? He had to stay focused on finding Armando first. This had to remain his number one priority. Besides, his getting her involved in this mission was dangerous for her too.

How in the world could he have been so stupid?

CHRISTY AWOKE AND felt the bed cold behind her where a warm male chest had been. Being alone this morning, after yesterday's love making, scared her. She should have been able to start her new day in his arms, where she hoped she would remain until her last breath.

She sat up, naked and a little sore in wonderful places, still groggy from little sleep. Then she smelled coffee, and that made her feel better.

*He's still here.*

She rose and put on the flowered kimono-type robe her mother had left her and cinched the sash that brought back wonderful erotic memories. Fluffing up her hair, she looked in the mirror and yes, she looked like "the wreck of the Hesperus," as her mother would say. Mascara pooled under swollen lower eyelids, which covered faintly bloodshot eyes. Her stomach twitched, as if starved for food. But it wasn't that. She was in love. That new, wonderful feeling that came when she met someone special and the whole world became a possibility instead of an obstacle course.

And Kyle loved her too. He didn't say it, but she knew he did. Just remembering those kisses emblazoned on her flesh last night in the moonlight made her wet. God, she'd fallen hard for this guy. She was normally slower to make a judgment about dating someone, but here she'd hopped into bed with him several times in three days. This relationship had started off as a safe lunch, but had become so much more.

Half the time they were having unprotected sex. She was never this casual with her body. Was she being foolish? Was her unbridled passion going to get her heart broken again?

She hoped not, but it wasn't going to change one iota of the way she would play it out.

*God, it would hurt so bad, this one. He's so perfect for me.*

She put her hair up in a ponytail and stepped into her oversized ivory tumbled granite shower. It was what she loved best about this beautiful condo her mother had left her. She soaped off, used the shower wand to softly stimulate the swollen lips of her sex. It felt good to be exhausted, to have been covered with his hard body, have him breathing and groaning in her ear as he took her. He liked to make love with her hands above her head, the sash forming invisible handcuffs. He'd press her palms to his and wouldn't let her move except to wrap her legs around his slim waist and arch to receive him, to let him plunder her again and again. And whenever she'd opened her eyes, he was watching her, as if the look on her face was what fed him and made him the man he was.

*Am I up for a man like this? Can I be the woman he needs?*

She knew, remembering the first time they had been together, when he tripped her to the ground and immobilized her with her own pantyhose, that he was not going to be an easy man to love. He was complicated and secretive. Would she be able to keep him satisfied without getting herself hurt? Was she strong enough for this?

Drying off with the oversized fluffy white towel, she felt courage and hope for a beautiful new today. Maybe not tomorrow or the next day, but today she could be the woman he needed. Tomorrow would have to take care of itself. And she didn't want to ponder the "what ifs" any longer.

*Showtime.* She splashed on a little French cologne, brushed her hair back into a clip, donned her sexy silk robe, then put on light pink cherry lip gloss and a tiny bit of mascara. She could face anything after a shower. Well, almost anything.

When Christy walked into her living room and saw him out on the balcony, bent over her railing, fully dressed, sipping a mug of coffee and looking out over the inlet, she knew today was not going to be a continuation of yesterday's lazy bedtime caper. There was something hard about him she couldn't identify. His armor was in place and locked down.

God help her if he said they were moving too fast toward a relationship he wasn't ready for. Would she have to play the casual game, pretend it didn't matter? She'd heard all those excuses before, after the dinners and the dating, after the mating dance of a first kiss and the first fall into deep, dark, uncharted waters. Passion plays, all of them. Then came all the reasons why it wasn't the right time. Half the time, she was the one doing the leaving. And of the ones who had left her, if she were to be honest with herself, she was secretly happy for the ending.

But this one, the one with the strong back and straight shoulders, with that tight little ass so clearly delineated for her as he bent over and searched the water and harbor below like a hawk looking for prey, this one would hurt her.

Big time.

"Hi," she said in her best Marilyn Monroe voice. He turned to face her and she let the tie to her robe slip loose. She twirled the smooth silk with her fingers and saw the flame in his eyes, a slight flush of his cheeks perhaps at the memory of her hands bound above her head. The flowered silk parted and she stood like a deer in the forest, caught in a ray of sunlight, unable to move.

His gaze traveled down her body, focusing on the triangle at the juncture between her legs, and then worked back up to her lips. He smiled, as though he remembered pleasant things about the night before. But he was holding back. It would have warmed her heart if he'd grabbed her, just picked her up and made love to her anywhere. But his restraint was dominant over his desire. She saw just the faint flicker of something burning in his eyes when he swallowed.

"Good morning."

His words were soft, but efficient. And he didn't come to her.

"Can't a girl get a morning kiss?" She toyed with him enough to get a reaction, but not the one she was hoping for.

"Sure," he said, and kissed her on the cheek. Then he grabbed her hand and tugged her inside, closing the sliding glass door behind them. "We have to talk, Christy."

*So here it comes. The big talk. Is this the part where I want to throw myself over the balcony, where he can watch me die as he tells me he never meant to cause me pain?*

She wondered why she saw so much blood and gore. Or was it rubbing off him and onto her? Was this his legacy, what he would bring to her life? She inhaled and tried to steady her nerves, prepared to face whatever he was going to dish out.

"Am I allowed to have coffee first," she delivered in her most sultry voice, "or do you normally continue to keep your prisoners up, sleep deprived, and without the aid of caffeine?"

He came over to her, but she slipped away and quietly darted to the kitchen, padding in her bare feet with the ridiculous hot pink toenail polish. She felt like crying, realizing it was such a stupid color. The happy pink was out of place this morning.

He rounded the corner. "It's not what you think."

"Oh?" she said as she rummaged for some cream in the refrigerator. "You need a fill up or are you done with this pit stop?" She held up the pot after pouring coffee into her half and half.

"It isn't a pit stop and you know it."

"I see. Well then, sailor, suppose you tell me exactly what it is," she said as she looked over the top of the steaming mug, into his eyes that weren't afraid to stare right back at her.

"I'm not sure I can do this. Or, what I really mean is, I'm not sure I'm any good at this."

*So, he's not used to begging.* She knew he was trying hard to cover up something. She liked it better when his control waned.

"Oh, sure you can. Just say thanks for the hot sex, Christy. Maybe we can do it again some time. That sort of thing…"

She turned and took her next sip of coffee so he couldn't see the tears breaking free and running down her cheeks.

Christy heard the flinch and his instant reaction toward her. He slipped his arms around her waist, one hand sneaking inside the delicate silk with a soft brushing sound like leaves in the fall as he spooned her back into his stunning chest she hadn't had enough time to study, and whispered, "It isn't like that, and you know it." His voice was soft, but urgent.

His fingers massaged her breast as his tongue traced along the curve of her earlobe, driving her crazy for him again. In spite of it all. Even if it was going to be the last time she'd ever see him, if he asked, she would fuck him silly and make him think about her and wish he'd stayed.

Damn the man. It was going to hurt. Maybe this one would be lethal.

She set her coffee down on the countertop and turned to face him straight on. The side of her robe had brushed open and her naked body was against his fully clothed one. The next thing she knew, he was kissing her neck, then her mouth. She was unbuttoning his fly, finding his erection. She was a woman without pride, on a collision course with a man who was practiced at getting in and out without being noticed. Well, she'd make him pay. She'd make sure he never forgot how much she needed him and how good it felt to be inside her.

She nudged a toe behind a cabinet door and stepped up to sit on the counter while he dropped his pants to his ankles. She pulled his T-shirt off and spread her palms against his smooth, warm chest. She let her knees drop to the sides and he urgently impaled her. She lay back among the clean dishes and glasses, which she knocked to the side. He mounted the countertop and pressed down on her. Dishes were falling, breaking. A glass shattered as it hit the floor, but he didn't flinch and he certainly didn't have any intention of stopping. He rode her, obsessed with something raging inside him.

He brought both his thumbs to bear down on her nub and she thought she would go insane with pleasure.

"Oh, Kyle. I..." She bit her hand to keep from saying the words. She wouldn't tell him she loved him, because he wasn't going to tell her that either.

It was over quickly, except that she was still vibrating from the deep thrusting. He pressed his shaft against her insides and came in huge explosive grunts, as if his climax would never end. She was already rubbed raw and perhaps lightly bruised inside from his ministrations the night before. She quivered like a puddle in an earthquake.

"This is not a pit stop," he whispered as he bit her earlobe.

She wanted to believe him. Deep down inside, she thought that she could.

"But...?"

"I need this...maybe too much."

"Is that possible, Kyle?" She looked into his blue eyes and thought she could see his pure white soul. But it was terrorized by something dark that she could not see.

Another glass fell to the floor. She laughed at the fact that this was going to be their last time and he was breaking her things. He'd fucked her on the countertop, of all places. No one had ever done that. "That's one way to get out of doing dishes."

He pulled up his pants with one hand and carefully lifted her up off the counter, then brought her to the living room couch, saving her delicate feet from harm. But she was disappointed he did not bring her to bed. She'd been right. He was leaving, after all.

She sat snuggled in his lap, running her fingers over his chest, memorizing every bulging muscle, the size and feel of his nipples, the way his Adam's apple moved when he talked or swallowed, the size of his full lower lip that she traced with her index finger. He covered her mouth with his, then drew back and held her face in his palms.

"You are so…" he started. "I've never met anyone like you."

"Same here. I've never had so much fun in my kitchen before, either. You do this sort of thing often?" She could show her thick skin too.

She got an angry glare back.

"Are you going to walk away from this? Isn't there anything I can do to convince you to stay?" She had looked down at his chest as she'd asked the question, but he continued to hold her head between his hands and made her look at him.

He searched her eyes, and for a second she thought perhaps he would say something else, something she would like, but then again the control came back and his eyes died right along with her heart. It was no use. He dropped his hands and sighed.

"I said some things last night I shouldn't have."

"No," she said, turning her head from side to side, rubbing her forehead against his jaw. "No. Don't you dare say that. Not now." Tears began to form. Hot tears.

"I have no right to—"

"That's for damn sure. You have no damned right to come waltzing in, saying things you don't mean so you can get into my bed. Or in this case, on my kitchen counter."

It felt exhilarating to let the anger spread. It was stuffy in her condo.

He got up abruptly and fastened the top of his pants, leaving her disheveled, and her robe gaping. She quickly covered her body and wiped her eyes, hoping he couldn't see her tears.

"I'm going to clean up the mess in the kitchen," he said. He looked like he was ten years old and had just broken his mother's cookie jar.

"Don't be ridiculous. Who the hell are you? One minute I see glimpses of a man I could love, and the next, a cold, calculating—" She teared up again.

"I'm sorry."

"Leave. Just go."

It hurt to say it, but her pride and what was left of her self-esteem was at stake. Better if she sent him off.

"Christy. I really enjoyed our time together."

"But not enough to stay."

"There's no future here," he said, tapping his chest with his tattooed forearm, the one with the little three legged creature prints. He squinted his eyes.

"Guess not. Maybe someday when I'm not naked and just been given the goodbye fuck you could tell me what you meant to say but didn't."

"I can't promise that. I'm afraid this is all we have. I'm sorry."

"Will you stop saying you're sorry? I would have preferred, 'I can't,' before you screwed me."

He turned and walked out of her life.

She was in shock. She could still smell him in the air, on her skin. She could still feel the touch of his fingers and his thumbs as he'd played her, as he'd snagged her heart and then ripped it right out of her chest.

# CHAPTER 12

KYLE SPENT THE morning gathering equipment. He put things together to make small IEDs, bought and borrowed ammo, and purchased thin razor wire. He ran into Cooper, who was stocking up his medic kit. The tall SEAL held up a plastic tube.

"You wanna know what we use these for in Nebraska?"

Kyle had no idea. He welcomed any conversation as a distraction from the hollow cavern in his chest.

"Mom said her dad, when he got older, wouldn't want to come into the house when he had to pee if he was way down plowing his fields. Used to keep one o' these tucked into the brim of his hat."

Kyle wasn't sure where this was going. But he knew he was going to wince.

"Granddad's solution was to shove this thing up his unit and he'd spew like Yellowstone. Became the only way he could pee during the day."

Kyle frowned, worried his friend was perhaps on a bender. And Coop didn't do benders anymore.

"Not very sanitary, and it would hurt like hell," Kyle finally said. "Something wrong with just whipping it out and peeing on the ground? He enjoy the pain and irritation it must have caused?"

Cooper shrugged. "Damn straight. Exactly what I thought. Mom said he was always on penicillin. I think he had a low-level bladder infection and had to pee constantly. Happened all during my younger years until he died. All those farmers did in those days. They didn't go to a doctor, they went to their vet."

Kyle shook his head.

"And here I am, using these as chest compression tubes. The very same stuff. Goes to show how some things change and some things stay the same."

Cooper wandered off down the aisle, in search of something else. Kyle was in awe of how the farm boy knew so much about mechanical things, both gas-fired and human. Cooper just knew how things worked in every sense of the word.

*All machinery.*

And Kyle knew Cooper was probably an expert with the ladies, due to all this knowledge of working parts.

Then Kyle remembered about Christy. He got hard in spite of himself.

Damn. He felt bad about how he had treated her. But it had to be done. And she'd made it easy on him. She'd asked him to leave. He wasn't half sure he would have if she hadn't insisted on it.

But what a way to break it off. Fuck her on the countertop amongst the dishes.

*You are a goddamned dog. That's all there is to it. You're the same man as your father. Add a little alcohol, and hell, you are as mean and uncaring as your father.* He was glad she got away. He didn't want to make a woman as miserable as his father had made his mother.

He called Timmons, who had no news. The chief was near hysterical.

"You better get me something quick. I'm starting to smell here in this office. Hard to cover up shit like this."

"Copy that. Armando was alive yesterday, that's all we know. Coop has a friend at DOJ, off the record. He already found out Armando's cell is whacked. Gonna see if AT&T can give us the location of his last call. But I doubt it will be helpful. Too old now."

"I was afraid of that."

"But Timmons, we got Mia's cell. I think I'll have the locator on it today. Armando left a message on his answering machine yesterday afternoon from that number. Told us we've got three or four days. I'm thinking three."

"Damn it all. I'm going to go talk to my liaison with the local PD. Maybe they can help."

"Good idea. You can pull rank, and remind them to play nice."

"Well, they won't play so nice if this caper doesn't get solved right away."

"Roger that. Doing the best I can, under the circumstances. Not like we can break down doors and start laying traps."

"Fucking A. You need anything?" Timmons asked.

"A miracle."

COOPER AND FREDO were waiting for him at the Scupper. Gunny was on his way from the gym.

"Timmons is going to ask for some backup for us." Kyle's stare drilled a hole right through their heads. "We need to get this done before any of the locals catch wind of this."

The hard look he got back from Fredo and Coop told him they got the message. Their ability to move unfettered would be greatly curtailed if they had to ask for permission and wait for jurisdictional etiquette. It would be a cluster fuck, and might cost Armando his life.

Fredo swore, but Cooper just looked back at him, chewing on a toothpick like one of his family's Herefords in Nebraska chewing on a strand of hay. The farm boy took a slip of paper out of his vest pocket and pushed it with his long fingers across the greasy table with a squeaking sound. "Here's the address. That cell phone has been there two days now. The friendlies at DOJ are watching it for us."

"Thanks, Coop."

"My guy said someone's been nursing the battery. Turning it off and on. Trying to make it last and sending out a signal every few hours."

"That's got to be Armando."

"That's what I told him."

"Think your *Babemobile* is ready for a little undercover work?" Kyle dropped this bomb on Cooper, but again, the farm boy didn't flinch. Cooper lived in the converted and customized motor home at the ocean, but they'd never used it for a domestic mission like this one. Built to look just like an old fisherman's motor home, Coop had installed state-of-the-art surveillance equipment so he could monitor the whole area. It also contained arms stored in hidden compartments, and half a dozen drones he'd picked up overseas on the black market.

Cooper kept the beast clean and stocked with fresh flowers nearly every day. He'd told Kyle that he never knew when his walks on the beach would produce a young lady willing to share his bed for the evening. He didn't have far to go, so when the urge overtook them, he had a pleasure palace outfitted with candles, music, and clean scented sheets, not to mention the flowers, which the girls always loved. It sure was a damn sight cheaper than a motel room. Kyle halfway admired the boy for his frugality, which was legendary among the Teams.

"She's ready, boss."

Fredo chuckled and finished his beer. "I sure hope you changed the sheets…"

"I'm not sleeping with you, Mr. Beans-And-Tortillas-For-Breakfast-Lunch-And-Dinner." Cooper gave Fredo a twisted grin. "Besides," he said, showing off his straight, oversized white teeth that obviously had cost his parents a small fortune, "I'd rather smell the sheets than your sorry little ass. Little Miss Saturday Night likes Chanel No. 5, and it's growing on me."

Kyle watched as Fredo gave Coop a punch in the arm that almost sent the giant sprawling to the floor.

"Okay, gents. Showtime." Kyle was impatient to begin.

All three got up. Cooper dumped the last of his fries and some pack-ets of sugar and salt into a napkin and wadded the top closed. He never left a morsel on his plate, or anyone else's either.

"Supplies," Coop said to Fredo's frown.

Kyle felt like two people who inhabited the same body. One side heard and was entertained by the shit talk between two best friends who were closer than blood brothers. His other side was worried about what would happen at Christy's condo while they were off during surveillance. And he couldn't deny the fantasy of slipping his long frame against her warm supple backside and riding her all night long.

*Be safe, Christy. Be smart. Don't want to lose you.*

He wished he could be the last thing she saw at night and the first thing she saw in the morning, for however long he was given the oppor-tunity.

*What am I doing? Wake up, sailor.*

They found Cooper's wheels in the parking lot adjacent to the beach, amid trucks and vans loaded with surfboards and marine toys. The Navy gave the farm boy a sizeable housing allowance since he did what most of the Team guys did, choosing not to live on base except for specialized trainings. Instead of procuring an expensive apartment, he'd bought the smoking ten-year-old toy hauler, and chose to get around town on a bright red scooter he kept well secured in the rollup compartment at the rear. What would have been a problem to tinker with and maintain for the average guy was hardly a challenge for Coop, who spent most of his youth on his back fixing his father's tractors and trucks.

When Kyle followed Cooper's bony ass up the metal pull-down steps to the motor home, he noticed a new hand-painted sign to the right of the small front door curtain window: "Mi Casa Es Su Casa." Kyle chuckled and thumped the tiny daisy drawn below it on the painted aluminum frame. It was someone's calling card. From the style and lettering, Kyle recognized it as being done by Daisy, the buxom blonde from one of the tattoo parlors they frequented.

*Son of a bitch. He's nailing her.*

Sometimes Coop just outdid himself. Every Team guy who was single and half the married ones were trying to get into that young lady's pants. Leave it to Coop.

The small space did smell flowery. Fredo was swearing and holding his nose.

"Lose the air freshener, man. It's just gross, man."

"After an hour it'll smell like your pits, and then I'll have to wear a mask."

Kyle had to admit, the smell was a little obnoxious. "I can't believe they actually like it this way. You better open some windows or we're gonna pass out," he said.

Cooper opened a window over the kitchen sink. "That's all I'm doing, since it takes a boatload of gas to run the heater."

Fredo tossed the bouquet of flowers out onto the parking lot, then poured the remaining water on top.

"Hey, you owe me five bucks for those, Fredo," Cooper lashed out, grabbing back the vase.

"Got hay fever. Don't you ever listen? Asthma too. I wind up at the ER and you're gonna pay for it."

Kyle knew it wasn't true. No way the Navy would have cleared him for SEAL duty with asthma or a severe case of hay fever. Every cell of Fredo's body had been inspected and none had been found lacking.

Except for maybe some of his brain cells.

Cooper crawled over the dinette seat and inserted himself into the driver's console. The passenger seat door was wired shut, so Kyle followed Cooper's ass and dumped his bones into the passenger seat next to his teammate. Stuck to the dash were glued plastic dinosaurs and some of his favorite childhood toys like Skeletor, He-Man, and Conan.

The *Babemobile* spewed smoke out the back and coughed a few times before reaching a safe cruising speed of twenty-five miles an hour. By the time they got to Gunny's, a trail of more than a dozen cars were backed up behind. When they pulled up to the curb, Cooper got honked at and was given a generous serving of one-finger salutes.

Cooper looked as if he hadn't paid attention, but Kyle knew better.

Gunny was at his front door, locking up early.

"You ready to ride, Gunny?" Kyle said through the open window.

"You bet. Halfway thought you guys'd leave me behind."

"Nope. Need a chaperone for these two." Kyle tilted his head back as Gunny climbed aboard.

Gunny sat at the built-in dinette table with Fredo while Cooper punched the address into the GPS unit, then turned over the motor, which was reluctant to start. The machine backfired, sending two Team guys on the street horizontal on the sidewalk. With a slow rumble and another backfire, the beast took off on its secret military mission, the sun just setting in an orange puddle on the inlet.

They drove up the coast for nearly half an hour, heading north, and then turned inland.

Kyle got his sat phone out of the black duty bag he'd brought, along with his night vision goggles and other equipment. "Reception here is terrible, but I got it boosted." He showed the wire antennae running down the inside of his jacket. "The computer will track everything too." He pointed to the MAC plugged into the center console.

Coop was focused on driving, but nodded to the roadway, which had grown twisty. They were headed into small foothills.

"Coop, you're gonna have to talk to your friend when we get there."

Kyle got more nods.

Fredo looked worried. "So, Kyle, what are they looking for?"

"I'm thinking guns. Guns they can't buy on the street."

"But why take the girl?"

"I don't think they wanted her. I think they want something from Armando."

"Can't believe he'd let himself get caught like that."

"I think his sister told them about Armando. She's less than discreet. I'm being kind," Kyle said.

"Kid's had it rough, from what I hear," said Fredo. "Raped at fourteen. The dude woulda died, too, if the cops hadn't gotten there in time and stopped Mama Guzman. That woman's a pistol."

Cooper laughed. "Well, no wonder you're scared shitless about asking Mia out to dinner, Fredo."

"I never said that," Fredo's defensive tone gave him away. Kyle hadn't noticed this little soap opera. Knowing Fredo, the athletic SEAL had a personal reason to protect her from the lowlifes she'd been hanging around with. That would be like him. But only if her mama approved.

They drove for another few minutes in silence. Kyle thought out loud. "I think Armando didn't expect to meet anyone but Mia. Otherwise, he would have been more prepared." It was the only thing that did make sense in this scenario.

"Except that he didn't check in with you or Timmons at ProDev," Cooper yelled over the noise of the engine.

"Exactly. He knew I'd go look for him if he disappeared."

"I don't like it. Going after civilians," Fredo said.

"Don't have to. We can let you out right here, if you want. You're either in or out."

"No. I'm in. I just don't like it."

"They're dangerous, bad people," said Kyle. "They kidnap and terrorize innocents like some of the guys we saw overseas, except these guys do it for the money. No religious morals here."

Fredo nodded his head. "Yeah, and they expect to live about as long as the sand rebels do."

"Without the glory," Kyle added.

"Or the virgins." Cooper turned and grinned at them.

Kyle was thinking about Mia and what her mother had told him. Pregnant with the bad guy's baby. That made it more complicated. He hoped none of his Team would have to sacrifice their lives or sustain major injuries just to save Caesar's offspring.

*What a fucked up twist of fate that would be.*

The motor droned on with mind-numbing vibrations. Kyle lost track of time. They turned off the main road and onto a dirt trail that wound through a dense, unmarred forest of small saplings. A young branch slapped the side of the aluminum shell, sounding like a gunshot, sending all of them but Coop to their feet. Cooper allowed the beast to idle in a crawl. The hauler snaked through the foliage, which grew sparser.

Kyle leaned back and stared at the ceiling. It had gotten dark outside. He'd been lulled to near sleep by the bouncing and rocking of the clumsy vehicle.

"Coop, how come you know about all these places?" Fredo wanted to know.

"Boy Scouts. This was an old scout camp. I came every summer. That's how come I wanted to join the Navy. I saw those guys one day running down the beach and thought to myself, that's what I wanted to do."

"Yeah, being a SEAL is all beach and babes, right?" Fredo gave a smirk.

"Little did your parents know," Gunny added.

"Yeah, they freaked. Thought I'd get excited about the San Diego area and decide to go to college here. Maybe settle down. They always wanted to retire here. Farming is a hard life."

That was an understatement, Kyle thought, recalling some of Cooper's stories.

Fredo closed his eyes and tried to doze off. Kyle thought Gunny was in pain from the jostling around and couldn't fall asleep, so Kyle took advantage of a few minutes rest. It felt like he'd just closed his eyes when he heard a thump.

They had stopped.

"Okay. We're a click away." Cooper turned and faced the trio. "I'm gonna call Morris."

Cooper got out and slammed the door, rocking the aluminum frame, which startled Fredo fully awake. He looked in panic at Kyle, his hand instinctively reaching for his Benchmade knife.

"Coop's calling his friend," Kyle said.

Fredo seemed relieved, but stayed alert. Both of them looked outside the windows. No lights were visible anywhere.

"Black as hell out here," Fredo said.

"Black is beautiful," Kyle said. Using state-of-the-art night vision equipment would give them a real advantage.

Before Fredo could respond, Cooper was inside the cabin. "No change in the position of the cell phone. Battery still sending out signals." He looked down as he slipped the phone back into his pocket. "We gotta plan for the possibility that perhaps she's dead. That could be why the signal hasn't moved."

"Don't think so," Kyle said. "If Mia were dead, Armando would have done something to draw attention. He's being stealth because they're alive and he wants it to stay that way."

"He'd have taken out a bunch of the bad guys," Fredo added.

They pulled into an abandoned campground a few hundred feet from the turnoff. Small shacks were built around a half-acre open area with an old, crumbling stone fire pit built in the center.

They transferred their gear from their duty bags that had been stored below the couch cushions to backpacks.

"Okay, Gunny. You stay with the ship," Kyle announced.

"Not sure I can get into that seat," Gunny said as he pointed to the driver swivel chair that looked more like his dad's old La-Z-Boy. When Kyle was a boy, his dad wouldn't let anyone else sit in it. But then, after all the drool and vomit Kyle's mom had cleaned off the surface over the years, no one had wanted to.

Cooper was helpful. "No problemo, Gunny. You'll not have to drive it. But I'm leaving the keys, just in case. Just watch her for me a bit. I'd offer to load up some triple Xers on the CD player here, but the battery is acting wonky. Don't want to chance it."

"I don't watch the stuff anyway."

Kyle knew the only TV Gunny watched was the Military Channel, which ran 24/7 at the gym.

The three SEALs put on Kevlar vests and blacked their faces. They positioned their night goggles after killing all the lights. Cooper had obtained a 9mm SigSauer P225 for Kyle. Fredo and Cooper had their H&K "USC" .45.

"Gunny, if I hear you honk the horn twice, I'll know we can't return, got it? Need to know if we're walking into something," Kyle said to his older and unofficial fourth member of the Team.

"That I can do."

"That means you're on your own. And the first call you should make is to Timmons."

"Will do. But you come back soon, 'cause I'm fucking scared of the dark."

Everyone chuckled. Then it was down to business. Kyle and his team finished their preparations. No one spoke. The hauler was filled with sounds of zipping and Velcro being separated and smoothed over.

Gunny picked up a paperback book that had a near-naked man on the cover. "Shit, Coop. I didn't know you was gay."

Cooper grabbed the book, obviously embarrassed. His face was a shade of peach Kyle had never seen.

"It's a romance novel." He pointed to a woman standing behind the hunk on the cover. "See? Besides, it isn't mine. Someone left it behind."

"Uh huh. Sure," Fredo added.

THE PLAN WAS to go in quietly, now that darkness had fallen, and grab Armando and Mia, if she was there, and then get out before anyone found them. Kyle knew they had to avoid any big firefight. And they absolutely couldn't get captured.

They left the cab of the hauler and dove into the forest with less noise than an owl's wing flap. They jogged for nearly twenty minutes.

The trio traveled through low-lying brush, using their night vision goggles. Eyes of small animals and one pair of deer flashed before them as they kept to occasional outcroppings of rocks and tree stumps. The area had been forest at one time, but a recent fire had eliminated any semblance of the lush wilderness it had once been. Kyle could still smell the charred remains of scorched trees.

They came upon a clearing and a lighted cabin, with gray smoke barely visible snaking up from the chimney behind. Two black Suburbans were parked out front, along with Armando's Land Rover. There was no sign of the brown sedan. Kyle wasn't happy with this.

The front door to the cabin opened and a male figure stepped out, profiled by the warm yellow candlelight from inside. The man, with an AK-47 slung over his shoulder, scanned the darkness. He unzipped his pants and urinated. The three of them stayed very still, waiting until he finished his business. He went back inside and slammed the door shut. They heard the click of a lock as it was secured.

Kyle went around the back of the cabin as Fredo and Cooper waited in place, scanning for new arrivals. He pulled up his black facemask to cover every inch of exposed skin. Coupled with the goggles that covered his eyes, nothing of his skin showed in the dim light of a half moon beginning to travel above the horizon. His shadow crouched at the backside of the structure as he slowly looked through one window. He caught a glimpse of Armando, asleep, his hands in handcuffs, chained to a large metal hook drilled into a four-by-eight wooden beam. He'd been beaten; his usually handsome face was swollen around the eyes and cheeks. A bloody slit extended from his lower lip down to his chin. But

Kyle didn't see a puddle of blood anywhere on the floor or blood sprays splattered along the wall, which was what he'd been half expecting, and he was relieved.

A male figure entered the doorway to the room and Kyle ducked just in time to avoid looking into the man's eyes.

Kyle peered back into the window. The man was administering a shot to Armando. Kyle suspected it might be heroin, or something to keep Armando quiet or unable to plan an escape. He could see the disgusted expression on Armando's face as the drug took effect. His eyes opened just slightly wider, two little sparkling slits of dark pain. Armando's gaze connected with Kyle's and registered. Armando's smile was wide as he bobbed his head to the left to let Kyle know he saw him.

"You like this shit, don't you, hero boy?" The heavily accented man kicked Armando in the gut.

Armando retched, and then raised his head up with another wide grin. "Oh, yeah. I like it all right. I'm dreaming of peeling your skin off in strips and cooking it like bacon, man."

Armando got another kick in the gut for that one.

"Yum," Armando said, and then spat out blood onto the man's shoes.

Kyle figured Armando was going to get a fist and probably more kicks, but the phone rang, and the man went after it. Left alone, Armando nodded to his left twice in quick succession, indicating Mia was probably in the next room.

Kyle silently crept to the other window and saw Mia, her arms cuffed up over her head and her ankles spread and cuffed to the iron bed frame. She was covered with a dirty blanket. Her sleep was deep.

*God, hope they didn't drug her too.*

Kyle thought he heard a vehicle in the distance. He adjusted his goggles and scanned the forest, but couldn't detect a light source. He ran near soundlessly through the brush until he reached Cooper and Fredo.

"You hear that?" he asked.

"Yeah, sounded a ways off, though. Came from there," Coop whispered, nodding toward the motor home. Kyle recognized a slight waver in his buddy's voice. The last time he'd heard it they'd been lying on their bellies on a rooftop in Afghanistan.

Kyle knew if something happened to the motor home, they'd have to wing it in the woods. But they had gear and had been trained to improvise, to use what was around them. It would be a minor inconvenience for them, but might put Gunny in harm's way. But wasn't anything he could dwell on right now.

At least they weren't in the frozen tundra in Alaska, where they'd been trained.

Kyle began making a plan, assuming there were at least two bad guys in the house. Perhaps more in the woods. Definitely more coming. Though outnumbered, at least they had the element of surprise on their side. And so far, they didn't have anyone shooting at them.

Something whizzed through the night air. Three definite taps hit the tree right behind Fredo and splinters of pinewood flew in all directions. Kyle recognized silenced automatic fire.

# CHAPTER 13

C HRISTY HAD SPENT a restless morning cleaning her condo. Again.
*Twice in one week? I'm turning into my mother.*

But she knew she'd have to step outside her cocoon eventually and face the real world. She wouldn't be looking for anyone to take the SEALs place. Just something to distract her thoughts until her heart could heal.

If that was even possible.

She thought about calling Marla, but didn't need the questions she knew would come. She needed an intense workout, though, and Marla, the toughest of the personal training staff, would push her as hard as she wanted to go. And then ask all her questions.

*So be it.* Christy really didn't want to be alone. And maybe after the workout, she'd even think up some answers that might make some sense.

Marla agreed to meet her at the gym an hour before closing. She put off the trainer's sharp queries, promising to catch her up later.

She grabbed her keys, loaded her gym bag for later, and left it on her bed.

Though she knew it wasn't wise, she needed to go look for Kyle. He was probably occupied with searching for Armando, but she hoped for a chance encounter. Or perhaps word would get back to him she was looking for him again.

*Will this send him away permanently?* She decided it didn't matter.

Her hallway was deserted. Downstairs in the garage, it was deathly quiet. A pair of finches had traveled into the huge underground structure and made a nest. She heard the peeping of young life echoing faintly in the cold, gray cave of the bowels of her complex. It took away some of her apprehension.

*Why can't I relax?*

It wasn't as if she was in any danger. Kyle was the one who was doing all the exciting stuff. Christy was a Realtor. The only thing she had to do was land on her feet after a rocky first week at the company. Time would heal her jitters. If Patterson Realty wasn't going to start getting comfortable right away, she'd move on. She would try another office. Make another fresh start.

*Or I'll quit and go back home to San Francisco.*

Her Honda was still clean after last Sunday's bath. When she'd been ready to launch her career. Been dressed to the nines. Hopeful. All this had been just four little days ago, back when all things were possible. Before the guy with the three-legged tattoo had wound her pantyhose around her wrists and challenged her very existence.

As she exited past the lumbering automatic rolling grates of the garage, afternoon sunlight caught her like a blast from a furnace. Her eyes hurt from all the crying she'd done. One look into the rear view mirror told her it showed. The car had no forgiving light fixture like the one in the bathroom. Harsh sunlight showed every wrinkle, every bloodshot vessel in the whites of her eyes, every part of her puffy red eyelids. Crying and lack of sleep made her look ten years older, she thought.

*Come on, Christy. Get yourself together. Focus.*

Nothing looked familiar yet in San Diego. Every street was new. Every building, office, or restaurant was more eye candy. The colors of the bay, the clouds in the sky—everything was different from San Francisco, a city she knew so well. A city where she'd felt safe. Not like here, although San Diego was probably safer with all these hunky guys running up and down the beaches. The only constant was that she felt she didn't belong here yet.

Her Honda pulled up outside the sandwich shop Kyle had taken her to on the island as if she'd willed it that way. She'd traveled without being conscious of where she was driving. Over the Coronado bridge that always scared her just a little bit. She hadn't noticed.

*Why?*

Though Kyle was the biggest asshole she'd ever met, he was also a complicated package doing a hard job. She was collateral damage. Plain and simple.

The thought didn't help her as much as she wanted it to. She'd wanted to be more than collateral. That was the whole point. She wanted to be the center of someone's universe. And she knew with Kyle, that could never be. His duty, his job, would always come first.

*My own damn fault. That's right, Christy. You knew it would hurt. Well, babe, you were right.*

God, how she hated to be right, especially when she didn't listen to herself.

"Fuck it," she whispered as she exited the car and tweeted it locked.

The grill was hopping, with a full crowd. Too early for happy hour. She spotted a table full of America's finest, eating hamburgers and drinking shakes. She knew, just knew they were SEALs. They were all dressed casual, with their hair a little longer than regular military, and even a couple had moustaches. Their muscles were bulging and from what she could see, she figured that among the eight of them, there were probably fifty tattoos. She didn't want to stare.

But she did.

Almost on cue, all of them turned and quietly assessed her. They looked in her eyes, every one of them. She could tell they were scanning elsewhere, but wouldn't show it, with that damned peripheral vision Kyle used.

Did they know she'd been with Kyle here? *No way.* How in the heck could they tell?

She nodded in their direction, smiled, and took a flying leap of faith. Her legs automatically took her to their table's edge and she addressed them.

"Hi there, fellas."

"Afternoon, ma'am," one said. Several of them stood.

"No. Stay seated, but thank you."

"You like to join us?"

God, he was good looking. Dark, almond eyes and light, coffee-colored skin. They all were specimens. She smelled something familiar in their group.

*Confidence.*

"Well, I..."

"Sure she will, gents." Griz came over and handed her a menu. "I'm giving her this, but I already know she likes the fresh crab sandwich." He winked, and several of the men nodded.

*So that's how it's done.* Griz just let them know she'd been there with someone. Didn't matter who. Someone had claimed her.

*But do they know he's dumped me?*

It probably didn't matter. She could tell she was permanently off limits. And it wouldn't be the first time an ex-girlfriend...and *what in the hell are you thinking, Christy?*

*I'm no ex anything. I was a two-night stand. Nothing more.*

That did it. Her eyes stung because the tears were being dredged up all the way from her feet. She'd cried so much last night she was plain out of tears and hadn't recovered, probably wouldn't recover for days.

She shoved the menu against Griz's chest, chanced a quick glance into his puzzled eyes, and then took off. She ran. She ran down the sidewalk three blocks, hoping the wind would take the tears away before she felt them running down her cheeks.

And then she stopped.

*What am I doing?*

She'd run past her car. She saw water glistening on the inlet and she walked toward it, down to where the waves were lapping on the shore. The sand was warm under her feet. A couple of little kids were playing in the surf. The beach was dotted with visitors.

Christy turned to the left and saw a portion of the beach roped off in orange. Out in the bay several gray boat crews were bobbing up and down, their oars dipping deep into the murky water, held by muscled arms. It kept them from being pulled onto the rocks ahead of them on the shore. Another small crew of men ran in tandem down the beach, carrying a rubber boat over their heads, looking like ants under a bulky sausage. A lone man with a bright orange vest was shouting through a white bullhorn. He stood atop the large boulders of the breakwater.

She walked closer to the spectacle. A small crowd of tourists was standing outside the orange zone. As another crew passed them, someone shouted, "Smile, gentlemen. We got pretty girls ahead."

Half of the men didn't look up, but the handsome boat crew leader showed off his pearly whites to a couple of well-tanned lovelies in their all-too-skimpy bikinis, each holding up their iPhones to take pictures.

"Bet he won't be smiling tonight," someone said in the audience.

Another instructor with a bullhorn shouted behind one brave soul, who was limping.

"I said sandy. Good and sandy, mister."

The whole beach could hear him.

"Yessir."

"Don't yessir me. Get sandy, sailor."

"Yessir." The recruit did somersaults all the way to the edge of the surf, where he lay back and allowed the little slapping waves to cover him. He threw wet sand over his camis and boots that were laced up mid-calf. The young man looked up to see where his tormentor was.

"Did I say you could raise your head, sailor?"

The recruit put his stubbled head back onto the wet beach and continued to splash water and wet, sloppy sand on his own face.

Christy heard the bullhorn blurt out something toward the waiting boat crews on the water, and she watched as one crew cheered and began paddling in. Reaching the rocks, they dismounted, held their boat above their heads, and inched up, painfully slow, as one crab-like animal. They brought the precious boat up and over the rocks without damaging it. They cheered, as they must have been rewarded with something the instructor said. They ran the rest of the way to take their positions next to another crew, who was sitting on the edge of their boat, sunning themselves. Waiting.

*So this is what he did.*

She'd seen the TV programs. She was touched that this little routine of triumph and defeat was so openly visible for everyone to see. If someone failed today, some of the people they were supposed to defend were going to witness it.

*Have I ever faced that kind of reality?*

She had to say yes. She'd come during her mother's last days, taken a few days off from the lingerie shop in San Francisco. When her mother died, she felt totally alone.

The first few days after her mother's death, she didn't even cry. It wasn't until her mother's pastor stopped by to visit, as she was boxing up some of her mother's things she was taking to her brother or to donate that she'd collapsed against his chest and let loose. Was that all it took? Someone's big strong arms to hold her so she could free herself of the pent up grief and loneliness? Someone to help her feel what it was like to be truly alone?

After that, she'd taken a breather from packing, and for the next two days she'd walked down to the water's edge, watching the boats. She had watched the sun setting both nights. On the second evening, as the pink and orange sky turned purple, she'd decided she'd stay in San Diego. Something in the water called her.

She dialed Madame M and told her she wasn't coming back to the shop after all.

"Ah, ma chère, I feel a great adventure awaiting you. Is there a man, perhaps?"

"Hardly. Unless he's the doorman, or a driver for Goodwill."

"No romantic dinners by the water's edge?"

"No."

"Galleries. They have wonderful galleries. Not as great as here, of course."

Nothing was ever as good as it was in San Francisco. Madame squealed about every new yogurt shop or cupcake bakery that opened. It was their secret mission to visit all the new ones within the first week of their opening.

"And then there are the boys on the beach. The ones that run bare-chested."

"I've not even seen them."

"Then you must. In fact, I will never forgive you unless you do."

Christy knew Madame would be stressed and shorthanded with her absence. But while the women knew her customers, she knew her staff even better. There'd be nothing she could say to change Christy's mind.

Christy had intended to transition to work for a wealthy San Francis-co developer and customer of the shop. He'd been delighted when she told him she'd passed her test.

She called Tom Bergeron's office and told his secretary she was going to hang her new license somewhere else, and would be permanently relocating to San Diego. The secretary feigned disappointment, but Christy knew the older woman was secretly jealous of the attention the handsome owner paid to her. At least he did before his recent public spectacle of a wedding to the famous international supermodel. Married on the bay, on a full moonlit night. She'd watched the couple and hoped someday her wedding would be just as beautiful.

If she could only meet the right guy.

Mr. Simms was going to be the Realtor she had selected to sell her mother's condo, but when he offered her the job instead, she took it. And that was how she got here, on the beach. Watching some poor mother's son get wet and sandy.

Finding out where his limits were.

And where hers were, as well.

Christy left the beach and returned home. In her dusky-lit condo,

Christy made some client calls and then checked her emails. She checked her cell. Nothing from Kyle, of course. She fixed herself a salad and ate alone on the balcony, watching the sunset over the channel.

She wondered what he was doing. If he was safe. If he'd found Armando.

*Stop this. Not good for you.*

The orange sunset reminded her of that first night they'd shared together. His dark hair had a red streak to it in the sunlight. Even the hair on his thighs and calves had orange tips, like they were on fire. She'd looked down and touched him there at their joining, then had drawn her hands up over his flat abdomen, drifting over the smooth muscles that moved under his warm skin as he made love to her. His body had undulated close and then apart as he'd thrust slowly and completely in and then out, ministering to her, giving her something she'd never had.

She'd wanted to see it all. Wanted to watch what they looked like making love. Then she'd felt his gaze on her as she looked up to his face. He'd stopped. And as they'd shared the gaze between them in the quiet afternoon, he'd entered her deep and stayed there, and filled her.

Something had happened. She knew it did. Did he feel the same?

Her face was warmed as she stared out at the glistening water. If she thought very hard, she could still feel his lips on hers. Her body responded. She remembered what it felt like to touch his chest with her nipples and arch up to his warmth and see his pleasure in those blue eyes.

It was going to be another restless night. Maybe her workout would sweat it out of her.

*Maybe not.*

# CHAPTER 14

KYLE AND THE team took off, running toward the cabin to do a snatch and grab on Armando, but a rain of automatic gunfire from that direction stopped them. Caught between the cabin and their safe house on wheels, they elected to go off toward the road and lead their pursuers away from the van. Then they slipped back and waited.

"They've got some decent equipment," Fredo whispered.

"Ex-military?" Cooper asked.

Kyle nodded. Whoever was hunting them had night vision too, so their advantage of surprise and their equipment had been equalized. He decided the best method was to retreat and sneak back later. He wasn't sure who was lying in wait for them. Perhaps it had been a trap—one they'd walked right into.

Every few yards they stopped to listen. Nothing was moving. No animals, no sounds from anything. Just rustling wind. It chilled Kyle to the bone and worried him.

*"You don't worry about the animal sounds around you in the jungle. It's when there's no sound it's the most dangerous,"* Gunny had told him.

Cooper tapped him on the shoulder and pointed west. Kyle turned and saw two heavily armed men, wearing all black, running between rocks and trees, using them as cover. He motioned for Fredo and Cooper to split up. The three of them would come at the men from behind.

Fredo set off a small timed IED under a tent of charred branches, and then the three dispersed. In thirty seconds, the explosion echoed throughout the forest and up into the foothills above them. While the men were focused on the blast, Kyle and Cooper came up behind them and with quick jerks to their neck, rendered them unconscious. The team tied the pair up back-to-back and added strips of heavy military duct tape across their eyes and mouth, and then secured their wrists and ankles with zip ties.

The team waited for evidence of more gunmen, but all was silent. Coop injected something in the men to make sure they remained passed out.

"That buys us an hour," Coop told Kyle.

They returned to the clearing with the cabin. This time the brown sedan had just pulled up alongside one black Suburban, and two occupants jumped out. Armando's Land Rover was parked off in the bushes to the side.

Dust from the off-road trail was settling all around them. Another vehicle approached—a Jeep. Its engine whined, then sputtered to silence behind the Suburban. A single male occupant in police uniform, armed with an automatic strapped to his chest, got out of the Jeep and headed for the front door of the cabin. Kyle realized they were out-gunned, maybe three to one.

*Not bad odds, if there were no wounded.*

Heated voices came from within.

What Kyle and his team heard next froze them to the ground. A hail of bullets came from inside the house, along with a woman's scream.

Mia's emotional pleas were difficult to understand, but Kyle could hear the occasional "No." That meant the men were doing something horrible to her or Armando. After the expended rounds, her sobs pierced the otherwise silent and dark night.

Kyle's eyes filled with water as he drew on one horrifying thought: Armando might be dead.

Fredo and Cooper checked Kyle's expression before he quickly sent them off. Practiced at reading each other without words, the team made their way to cover the house, Kyle in the rear, Cooper up front, near the porch overhang, hidden behind a water tank, and Fredo on the side of the house, where he hopefully took up a vantage point by the living room window.

Kyle looked into the first bedroom and saw the two men kicking someone he thought was Armando at first. But he soon realized his buddy was handcuffed to the doorframe, looking more out of it than before. The man on the floor had been the one who had injected Armando with the junk. From the blood pooling around him, Kyle figured he'd been shot. The smoke from recent gunfire wafted through the room like incense. The man on the floor put up no resistance to the barrage of kicking and fists pummeling his body. Kyle knew the man was probably dead.

The policeman was at the doorway and swore when he saw the corpse.

"What the hell were you thinking, Caesar? You're gonna fuck us all," he shouted.

"He pumped Armando so full of junk he didn't even know Mia's name. And just now I caught him going down on Mia, the sick fuck. She's my woman. And Armando has told us nothing," Caesar answered. "I caught this guy yesterday with his hands all over her ass."

"The girl means nothing except for him," the dirty cop said, nodding to Armando who remained motionless, eyes closed. If he was awake, Kyle couldn't tell. Bloody drool was dripping down his chin and onto his stained white T-shirt. Maybe a bicep flinched in response to information about the man's attempts with Mia. Maybe. Kyle couldn't be sure.

Caesar was glaring at the policeman, keeping one hand on the knife strapped to his thigh.

"You gonna use that? You fucking dickhead. We're gonna have to torch this place. The squad will be here any minute with all that fucking gunfire. Can't leave evidence."

The cop gave instructions in English to two huge guys. The pair dashed off to the Suburban.

Caesar swore and left the room.

Kyle couldn't get Armando's attention, so he moved on. Mia was whimpering in the next room, sobbing uncontrollably. Her body jolted in rhythm with her sobs as she writhed on the dirty mattress, trying to dislodge herself from the restraints. She seemed beyond hope, naked and beside herself.

Caesar was wrapping her dirty flesh with an old quilt, trying to calm her sobs. She raised herself up as far as she could and spat at him, earning her a slap across the face that sent her back onto the dirty mattress, where she lay still. Kyle gripped the handle on his sidearm. If it weren't too dangerous, he'd put a bullet through the guy's skull, but it was too risky.

Caesar checked Mia's pulse and swore.

"We gotta go, Caesar. Cops are on their way," the other man said.

Kyle had every reason to avoid the cops as Caesar did.

"Give me a hand, Zario. I gotta get her unhooked."

"He says to leave her," Zario answered.

"What the fuck?"

"Leave her," Zario repeated.

Kyle could smell gasoline.

"No, man. She's carrying my kid. I can't leave her."

"So Caesar, you gonna think with your dick or with your brains? She's baggage, man." The cop had appeared at the doorway and shoved the other man away. He leveled his gun at Caesar. "You wanna die for her, hum? That what you're saying? 'Cause I'm not."

Kyle thought Caesar would make a run for the cop's throat. Caesar seemed to be seething with hatred, barely able to control the blind anger inside. There was no way both of them would be alive by morning.

"Give her a chance," Caesar said.

"No. We go. Now." The cop was smart enough to wait for Caesar to leave the room first. "Zario, go get the stuff."

Kyle joined Fredo on the side and watched as the men loaded Armando into the brown sedan's ample trunk. He saw Fredo write down the license plate number for both the vans.

Kyle briefly considered launching an attack against the bad guys, but he couldn't risk further injury to Armando and Mia.

Zario disappeared into the house for a minute, and then brought something out. Kyle saw a homemade IED that Zario set on the porch by the open front door. In a matter of seconds the place was going to blow, depending on the timer. Kyle motioned to Fredo to take cover behind a boulder. Fredo stood in his tracks and shook his head.

The jeep and brown sedan turned and took off down the dirt road, in the direction of Gunny and the van.

"I'm going in to get her."

"No. You stay put..." But Kyle doubted Fredo even heard him.

The explosion rocked the house, sending sparks into the forest, igniting trees like matchsticks.

Water from the tank adjacent to the building spilled all over the yard, partially putting out the resulting fire. Kyle hoped Coop had been safe behind the ruptured tank. Through the burning timbers he and Fredo found Mia, who was badly burned and bruised, and thankfully unconscious. She'd been covered with the thick quilt and curtains as well as other debris, which had probably saved her life.

They couldn't remove her shackles, but the bed frame was so rickety they could detach her, and so they brought her outside, slung in the bed sheets. She was breathing. Fredo poured water on a strip of cotton and wiped her face as Coop checked for further injuries. Fredo offered her a drink from his pack. She moaned and spit up blood.

"She's got something internal going on," Coop said. "We gotta get her to the hospital."

Sirens were getting closer.

Kyle nodded.

"We could leave her with them. They'd take her," Coop offered.

"Nah, can't risk it. Remember, she might be able to ID the cop."

Kyle pulled a folded tarp from his pack, and they placed it under the sheet to make a sturdy sling to carry her. They took off toward the van. It was slow going through the brush, and they alternated two at a time so one could concentrate on lookout and cover, but they ran as fast as they could. Thank God Mia was a little thing. It would have been faster to drape her over a shoulder, but Kyle couldn't risk exacerbating her internal injuries in doing so.

In the direction of the roadway came the sounds of other engines. Two RTVs were snarling and echoing off the rocks in the night air. They reminded Kyle of the sounds of chainsaws he'd wielded working the logging camp one summer between his last two years of high school. The sounds were getting closer.

The three men set Mia down under a small madrone and some brush. Kyle rigged a catch with lightweight razor wire from his pack. They wrapped it around two outcroppings of rocks. Someone was going to have to be bait, Kyle thought as he looked at his team. No one said a word, but Cooper ran up through the brush and conspicuously stepped on a fallen tree branch and fell, expelling a scream on purpose. Kyle and Fredo moved to either side of the rocks, the razor wire wound several times around the boulders between them. They hoped the person on the RTV would be attracted to their buddy like a fly to shit. Cooper would light up like a Christmas tree, but Kyle was hoping whoever was after them would miss seeing the wire.

Both RTVs came at Cooper's direction. He lay centered about thirty feet from the trap, holding his leg like he had twisted it. Just as he saw the headlights of the vehicles reflected on Coop's face, Kyle saw him check to make sure his flak vest was secured. Kyle checked the taut wire. Cooper flashed light in the two driver's direction, distracting them enough to miss the trap.

It worked.

The first RTV ran right into the razor thin wire, knocking the rider off. His limp body lay motionless where it fell. Kyle and Fredo kept the wire taut. The second rider tried to stop, and as he slowed, Fredo lurched at him, tackling him off the whining machine. Cooper went to switch off the first engine, but Kyle stopped him.

Fredo wrestled the other driver, who was considerably larger than the SEAL, and seemed well-trained.

*Probably ex-military.*

The man crashed against a boulder, and Kyle heard the familiar snap of a bone breaking. Fredo bounced up and immobilized the unconscious man with zip ties on his wrists and ankles. Kyle hogtied the other one, who still hadn't regained consciousness.

"He's got a busted shoulder. Bad break," Fredo said. "He'll be screaming his lungs out when he wakes up."

"Someone will find them. Let's get out of here."

They quietly covered up their footsteps and picked up Mia.

"Whoever is out there will be listening. They're gonna know if the drivers don't come back," said Coop.

Kyle answered him by sending off a few rounds of fire from the weapon he'd ripped from the bad guy's fingers. He tossed the other automatic to Coop. He signaled, and farm boy took one RTV, mounting it with glee.

"Always wanted one of these."

Kyle shook his head. "You and your toys." He turned to Fredo. "Can you handle Mia for a bit? I guess you've got five hundred yards or so to go."

"No problem, boss." Fredo held Mia's dead weight against his chest and took off. Kyle hopped onto the other coughing RTV. He and Coop zigzagged through the forest to distract any other snipers out there, giving time for Fredo to get the girl to the hauler.

A few minutes later they stopped and fired off a few more rounds. They headed back toward the hauler.

When they found Fredo hiding behind a large rock outcropping, they shut the motors off.

"Someone's pulled up. Heard maybe three trucks pass by," Fredo whispered.

"The Suburbans?" Kyle asked.

Fredo shook his head. "I think these are local law enforcement. Must have been running a roadblock or were headed out to the cabin They'll send a chopper too."

Mia started to moan. Cooper pulled her away from Fredo's chest to check her, but the SEAL possessively wouldn't let go.

"I got to check her, dumbass. She's not your girlfriend."

Fredo shot him a warning look. Coop knew he'd embarrassed the man. Had singed his pride. Fredo defiantly held Mia's hand during Kyle's examination. A thin trickle of blood poured out of her mouth.

"Keep her warm. Jeez, I hope we can get her in the van soon," Coop said.

"She gonna be okay?" Fredo asked.

"If she gets help. I can't tell what's going on inside, except for this." Kyle pointed to a thread of fresh red blood running down her bare leg.

Mia was losing her baby, Kyle thought.

Cooper looked at both teammates. "The body does what the body does."

"We'd better go the rest of the way on foot," Kyle changed the subject, not wanting to look in Fredo's eyes. They covered the RTVs with branches, Cooper taking one last long look before covering the red one. Then they moved out.

The forest was erupting with lights and sirens, and the smoke from the cottage fire had plumed up into the air about forty feet. Just before they came upon the toy hauler, they heard the horn honk. Twice.

"Shit," Kyle said under his breath.

# CHAPTER 15

BACK AT HER condo, Christy had decided to eat dinner, then sat at the dinette table, staring into space, until she dropped her fork. It clattered on the glass top, the sound bringing her abruptly back to reality. She'd been sitting there. In the dark. All alone. What was she looking for?

*Enough.*

Checking the time, she noted she'd be a few minutes late for her workout with Marla.

She took the last of her unfinished salad and water to the kitchen and dumped them in the sink. Her appetite was gone.

In her bedroom, she shed her clothes and put on her workout sweats. She still felt Kyle's kisses at the back of her neck, the touch of his fingers as he'd moved down her spine and kissed every vertebra. She'd never felt so worshiped. And so abandoned.

She tied her shoes and put her hair up in a scrunchie, then gave herself a good hard look in the mirror. Some of the puffiness around her eyes had calmed down.

She slung her gym bag over her right shoulder, grabbed her keys, and walked down the silent hall to the elevator for the second time today. The gym was on the top floor. It was going to close in an hour, so she'd have just enough time for a quick workout with Marla and maybe a sauna.

Then maybe she could sleep tonight, after all.

She didn't know why the hair at the back of her neck prickled as she walked toward the elevator. She couldn't remember a time when the condo had been so quiet. The art deco doors opened and she stepped in, then pushed the black up button for the gym and common area. The elevator rumbled, as if asking her if she wanted to change her mind at the last minute. Took forever. Were the lumbering doors always this slow?

*What am I afraid of?*

The gym was nearly empty. Marla wasn't there waiting for her, as she usually was. A new male employee with the Infineon's green polo shirt logo was wiping down the weight machines with a white towel, using a spray bottle of emerald green cleanser. He held the bottle up to Christy in a salute.

"Marla here?" she shouted.

He shrugged and held up his hands again as if he didn't understand.

"I'm going to do some cardio first, then I might come in here," Christy shouted out to him over the classic rock and roll. The music blaring throughout the gym was a little too loud, and it was irritating.

"Suit yourself," he shouted back. "We're open for another hour and twenty." His British accent bothered her. And she hadn't recalled the gym being open so late before.

*Why?* No one was here. She looked down the hallway of offices. Marla's door was closed, but a light shone under a crack at the bottom.

*Probably on the phone.*

Christy thought perhaps she'd take her sauna before a quick workout to relax, but didn't want to miss Marla. She headed for the cardio room. Her body flinched at every little creaking door, and at the sound of howling winds whipping around the glass corner windows that overlooked the dark sky. Lights twinkled on hanging streetlamps at sidewalk level below. Some of the boats in the inlet had strings of lights illuminating their masts.

She slung a towel around her neck, put on her headphones, plugged them into the elliptical machine and clicked the TV on the wall directly in front of her. Two other TV screens mutely flashed ads and programming down at the end of the room, playing to ghosts of workout patrons who had long since vanished.

She clicked through her choices until she found a movie channel and started playing an old Rambo film. Kyle's biceps weren't as big as Stallone's, but she liked them better. All alone in the cardio room, Christy became absorbed in the movie as she coursed through her three-and-a-half mile routine.

Until images of a fire in the Santa Nella forest flashed on the screen of the TV furthest from her. A reporter was in a helicopter as the overhead camera zoomed in on a burning cabin. She switched her channel changer to listen to the newscast on the screen right in front of her.

*"Police and fire crews are still trying to determine the cause of the blaze. The bodies of three men some half-mile away have been found, dead under what the coroner has called 'unusual circumstances.'"*

That got Christy's attention. But why did she suddenly feel like Kyle had something to do with this? Would she always wonder if Kyle was involved when she saw a news report about an unusual occurrence? Is this what came with the territory: feeling afraid to watch the news? And why did it make her fear her own surroundings?

She hated being afraid. When she was little, her biggest fear was of drowning. She'd developed this fear after she'd had a close call at a neighbor's pool. Although now a good swimmer, it had been a whole four days before she would jump into the pool with all the other youngsters during summertime swimming lessons after her near drowning. But once she got the knack of it, she became the fastest swimmer in the class.

She used to lock up Madame M's store at night in San Francisco dozens of times, and she wasn't as apprehensive then as she felt tonight.

This was something she'd have to fix. Being with Kyle was giving her the heebie-jeebies. And that wasn't good.

She switched back to her movie and completed her forty minutes. No one else came in during that time, which she thought was odd. Marla must have gotten involved in something else, probably left her a message she'd get later on her cell.

Someone was cleaning out the garbage in the weight room, but still there was no sign of the other staff or other patrons. Christy decided she'd take a sauna in hopes it would quiet her nerves.

In the changing room, she slipped off her workout pants and sports bra top, left her shoes underneath the clothes peg in her locker, wrapped herself in the oversized white fluffy towel, and stepped to the sauna area. Just outside the glass door she found a water bottle steeping in a bowl of half-melted ice cubes, along with a rolled-up washcloth. She grabbed them and stepped inside the warm moist enclosure.

She poured water on the artificial coals to create steam inside the chamber, spread her towel down on the cedar planks, lay on her back, and placed the ice-cold washcloth over her eyes. The wet heat soothed her bones. Her skin loved the moist womb of the sauna.

Raising her knees, she felt the little bruises left between her legs from her night of heavy lovemaking. She had the urge to place her own fingers there, but decided against it.

Someone walked past the door.

In pants.

*In the women's wet area?*

Christy sprung to the glass door, pressing against it, and peeked out, but she could not see anyone else. She threw the towel around her, opened the sauna door a crack, and then quickly made it to the dressing area, where she dressed. Without taking the time to put her shoes on, she ran out through the women's side lobby, clutching her shoes by the laces, and into the reception area next to the weight room. The phone was ringing, but no one was manning the desk. Through the glass wall that divided the reception area from the weight room, she could see the bottle of green spray and the towel the staff member had left on one of the padded benches. The garbage can in the corner was tipped over.

She hit the heavy glass doors of the gym and discovered they were locked. She turned the heavy metal lock, pushing on the door handle. She burst into the hallway, running to the elevator. As she stepped in, she heard the gym doors open. She pushed the down button multiple times as she heard the sound of footsteps running toward her.

Christy flattened her body against the right side of the elevator car as the doors slowly closed. She half expected someone's hand to separate the doors and come after her, but the elevator began its slow descent to the fourteenth floor. Once again, she was safe for now. But what awaited her at her condo? It took forever to get there, and luckily, the compartment hadn't stopped.

Again, the hallway was deserted. After checking both right and left, Christy dashed to her condo door and scanned the pad with her room card, which released the latch. She slammed the door behind her.

*Home.*

Any calm she'd achieved with her workout and the sauna had been shattered by the fear that someone was after her. Images of the last hour flipped through her mind. Sure, she'd exercised by herself before, especially late at night. She'd been the last one in the gym several times. Maybe this was just her crazy imagination.

Where was Marla? The other staff? Why was the garbage can turned over? And why wasn't anyone at the desk?

# CHAPTER 16

G UNNY HEARD THE explosion and knew nothing good was going to come of it. Then cars pulled up all around the van. He wasn't going to go for his piece, which was tucked in a plastic bowl and covered with a tea towel. There were too many of them. He heard the familiar clicking sounds of rifles and weapons being readied.

"Please step out of the vehicle with your hands up," the stern voice yelled. Bright light shone through the small portal of the front door. Gunny swore loudly so the men outside could hear him, and acted like he'd fallen, hitting the horn on the steering wheel to give the signal. As he slipped his pants down, leaving just his shorts in place, he swore again even louder and looked around, wondering if it would be the last time he'd see the cabin, then slowly pushed down on the door lever and stepped outside into the blinding light with his hands up.

He saw outlines of sheriff's hats and some baseball caps. No military, he was relieved to note. But then, the only military he was worried about would never let themselves be seen.

He placed the back of his arm against his forehead to shade his eyes.

"Turn around slowly," came the next command. Gunny lowered his hands and started to turn.

"Hands. Get your fucking hands in the air."

Gunny complied. But he turned his head as his wrists were jerked down by a uniformed officer and handcuffed together with two cuffs, due to Gunny's girth.

"You wanna tell me what I've done, officers? Is there a law against camping?"

As he turned back to face the light, he heard someone whisper, "That's Gunny."

So someone was military, or at least they hung out with military.

"You're no fuckin' camper. Where are your friends?" the officer asked.

"Back at the gym."

Someone in the crowd snickered and was silenced.

"Mind telling me what's going on?" Gunny persisted.

"There were two murders out this way we're investigating."

"Gents, do you mind? I'm not a well man. I'm standing here in my underwear. You caught me taking a piss, and then I was going to go back to bed and sleep off a hangover." He squinted and nodded at the array of lights. "I sure as hell didn't kill anybody. At least not tonight, anyways."

Gunny was glad he had thought to remove his pants down to his aloha shorts. Barefoot and bare chested. Hardly a threat.

"Fellas, I've had a bad day. I'm a little plastered, and no threat to anybody."

"That's for fucking sure." A smooth-shaven, handsome, square-jawed officer in a light tan uniform strode to up to Gunny and gave him a sniff. The officer waved and immediately half the lights cut out. "You don't smell like you've been on a bender, Gunny."

"I'm sorry, do I know you?"

"Not nearly as well as you're going to." The officer exhaled and stepped back, looking Gunny up and down. "You like pain, Gunny?"

Gunny tried to stand as straight as he could, but the cuffs hindered him. "I'm Gunnery Sergeant First Class Joseph Hoskins to you, sir."

The officer hit Gunny on the kneecap with his baton. Gunny went down like a sack of bricks, hitting his head in the gravel, which caused a gash on his forehead just above his right eye.

"Hold on, Warren. You got no cause to do that. He's a local and well known to have no ties to any drug dealing."

Gunny didn't recognize the voice, but the boots told him the man was not military, but local law.

"Well, he's in the wrong place at the wrong time," the lawman they called Warren noted.

"I'll admit that. But we might need his cooperation."

Red lights flared as a black Suburban pulled up. Two dark-clothed ATF uniformed officers got out and ran up. The three of them conferred, then broke. The two new men took Gunny into custody, pulling him up and placing him in the second seat of the Suburban.

"Can't I have my pants? Maybe some shoes?" he yelled from the open door.

"Sure, I'll get them." A minute later his clothes were placed on the bench seat next to Gunny, who was still handcuffed, but now seat belted in. Before the Suburban backed up, Gunny heard the special agent tell Warren to wait for someone to come back and claim the *Babemobile*.

"I already know who it belongs to," Warren said.

"So why didn't you tell me? This guy owns this rig?" the ATF officer asked.

"Nope. It belongs to Cooper, one of Kyle Lansdowne's friends. And Coop was seen driving it off the base tonight."

"We got to get back to the fire. Don't touch anything inside. If they don't come in an hour, see if you can secure it and get back to town."

"What if there's another homicide at the fire? I got jurisdiction."

The agent stepped to within three inches of Warren's face and chest. "And how the hell would you know there was another body at the fire?"

"That's no fire, and you know it. That was an explosion. Like a military explosion."

"Fine. You wanna go back to the fire with us? Okay by me. But in your position, I'd be pretty darn pleased with the opportunity to catch up on my sleep. This hits the press and tomorrow you won't have two minutes to yourself."

"I'll post a guard. But I think I could be more help to you at the scene. Who knows, maybe Gunny will start to feel talkative."


KYLE COULDN'T BELIEVE they were all leaving. All except one young deputy sheriff, who looked like he belonged in one of Cooper's scout troops. The kid was barely legal age and skinny as the saplings they'd been hiding behind.

After a quiet darkness descended on the area, Kyle got up behind the young lawman and whispered in his ear, "I don't want to hurt you. Just going to tie you up."

The kid tried to turn around, but Kyle had him in a choke hold.

"Nah, uh, uh. That'll get you into trouble. You're going to see my face soon enough, but not tonight, hear?"

The kid nodded.

"Good boy." Kyle patted his head. He had already secured the boy's wrists with a zip tie. "You remember when you used to play Pin the Tail?"

The boy nodded.

"Just like that. Although I trust you, I'm going to make sure you don't cheat." Kyle applied a black nylon tape across the boy's eyes. "Sorry, but it will pull out some eyebrows. Keep your eyes closed and it won't get your eyelashes. They don't grow back."

Kyle could feel the kid flinch at the thought of going through the rest of his courting life like a hairless freak. He sat the boy down next to a tree stump, then removed his service revolver and knife.

Cooper was going to say something, but Kyle put his finger to his lips. He brought his two rolled up fists together, then pointed to the van. Cooper climbed inside to jump the vehicle for their getaway.

Kyle and Fredo carefully lifted Mia into the back, placing her on the bed. Fredo looked down on her as though it were the first time he'd seen a naked girl. He found a clean sheet, placed it over her brown flesh, and patted her thigh.

"You're safe now, honey. You warm enough?"

She nodded, but was shaking and biting her lip. Fredo placed a blanket over her, and she smiled back up at him.

Kyle and Cooper ran back to where they'd left the RTVs.

Cooper was walking around the little toys, their shiny surfaces glistening in the moonlight. Kyle could tell he was admiring them. The Nebraska Team guy was a man who loved his toys and gadgets even more than his women, Kyle thought.

"We can't bring them."

"How about one?"

Kyle thought about it. He'd seen a steep drop around one of the curves Cooper had driven past on their way out. "Okay, one. But one we gotta dump and burn."

He knew it was going to break Cooper's heart to see a perfectly good vehicle ruined, but there was no way around it. They needed just a little time as well as the possibility of sending a message to Timmons for help, maybe draw off some of the heat. A fire would do that.

"I'll need a ravine, Coop. Something flashy," Kyle said.

"Got just the spot." Cooper started his RTV and took off. Kyle was glad his started right up because Cooper was already out of sight. He followed the filtered headlight he saw through the trees.

Coop revved up the RTV and sent it over the edge with a small explosive charge on it. When it hit the creek bottom it burst into a fireball, sending a long fiery tail up into the dark sky.

Kyle hopped on behind Cooper, and they hauled ass off toward the hauler.

*Time to get the fuck out of Dodge.*

Everything was quiet when they got back, except for the hauler's purring motor. They could hear Mia, inside, talking to Fredo. She was fully awake, but seemed to be in pain.

Cooper lowered the rear of his van and pulled the other RTV inside, then pushed the button to roll up the door. Kyle saw the look of appreciation on the farm boy's face.

"Thanks, boss. You let me have the red one."

"Sure hope it was the right choice." Kyle laughed as they ran to the door.

"Don't matter," Coop said as he resumed his driver duties. "It was a steal."

The hauler came to life, and they motored out of the forest without revving the engine. They had parked on a slight knoll, so they were able to slide down the hill quietly and drive away to safety.

Kyle observed Mia's skin began to peel and bubble from the bomb and heat of the fire.

"Coop. I need you to look at her. She's blistering and starting to shiver. I think it's shock," Kyle shouted up the aisle to Cooper. They switched places just before they hit the main road. To the right were some distant lights. Kyle donned his night vision goggles, killed the hauler's headlights, and turned left, back toward the coast. With the goggles, he had no trouble following the road and saw every raccoon, deer, and possum along the way.

A half hour later, they pulled up to San Diego General Hospital emergency room. Kyle ran inside, then returned, followed by two attendants with a gurney. Mia was carefully unloaded to the gurney and taken inside.

"We gotta split. Can't have us here like sitting ducks," Kyle said. "I'll call her mom and get her over here."

The horizon was beginning to glow, indicating sunrise was a couple of hours away, as the three Team guys drove toward Coronado. Kyle started to feel the weight of their nearly twenty-four-hour shift. But it was a momentary lull. He'd learned in his training he could stay up for as many as three or four days in a row with just a couple of catnaps in between. Trick was to push through the low-energy phase until he got his second wind back. And it would come back. It always did. He would need it today.

Kyle dialed Mama Guzman on the phone while Coop drove the *Babemobile* to where Fredo's car was parked along the strip. He'd left it in the two-hour parking in front of Jimmy's Bar and Grill. Sure enough, Fredo had earned a ticket, just like they'd planned. Fredo and Kyle got into Fredo's car and headed back to base, Cooper tight on their tail in the hauler. At the base, while Cooper waited in the van down the block, Fredo and Kyle drove Fredo's car past the guard shack to check who was on duty.

They were in luck. Carlisle wasn't around anywhere. They checked through, drove to the parking area, and waited for Coop, who passed through the guard gate without incident and parked the van where he usually did, then secured it. He wore Fredo and Kyle's duty bags on him as if he were hauling a couple of spare oars on his back. Behind the locked and guarded gate, local officials would have to maneuver through the minefield of the Navy's paperwork to get permission to search the vehicle. And Timmons could perhaps run interference, delaying the process further.

There wouldn't be any evidence of foul play since Cooper had sent the bloody sheets with Mia to the emergency room. Kyle figured nothing else there would tie them to the firefight or rescue.

They stopped near the beach at a breakfast café that catered to surfers and an occasional Team guy still up from a night of raising hell. The sunlight shining on the water hurt Kyle's eyes. He wanted a shower. He wanted to be tucked in and warmed by Christy's smooth flesh.

God, it had been hours since he'd thought about Christy. And he couldn't help it now. This was the quiet before a shit-kicking storm that was about to come down on all of them. But one look from her, one kiss, would sure feel nice. She was good for *him*. Just that he was bad news for *her*.

And that was exactly why he needed to stay away.

He dug into his Mickey Mouse pancakes, delivered with a smirk by the waitress named Dottie, who could have been their grandmother. Fredo and Coop took turns punching him in the arm.

"Glad you're back to your old self," Cooper said. The cook had learned long ago Kyle loved pancakes with mouse ears and chocolate chips. And four extra mini pitchers of syrup. He ate lots of chocolate and sweets when he was stressed.

Fredo was having huevos rancheros, while Cooper stuck with his usual: oatmeal and a bacon and egg scramble.

The coffee was thick like oil, but it tasted good, and they knew the caffeine would keep them awake until noon. That and the sugar rush.

"You gotta call Timmons, man," Fredo said.

"I intend to."

"He's probably worn a hole in that floor by now."

Kyle nodded and considered Fredo's statement. "Hope he hasn't gotten any flack from upstairs. We aren't the most popular team around, you know."

"Wonder how Gunny's holding up," Cooper said, hanging his jaw in a frown. He motioned toward the last pitcher of syrup which had been only half drained.

Kyle nodded. "Best thing for him is to learn we made it out alive," Kyle said.

"I'll do that," Fredo eagerly volunteered.

"Fredo, you and Gunny mind meld or something? Where the hell are you going to find him?"

Fredo stretched and then rolled his head, setting off several loud cracks from the back of his neck. "I'm feeling the need for a workout, boys. They'll know down at the gym."

"Without him, it'll be closed."

"Nah, he'll ask someone to open it for him. He won't let the boys miss a day of PT. He lives for that shit."

Fredo signed the "loser" signal with his thumb and index finger attached to his forehead, then got up and left the café. Cooper was scooping the last of Kyle's maple syrup into his yogurt with a knife.

Cooper looked up at Kyle and said, "Can't give you a lift anywhere, unless you want to ride with me on the scooter."

"No worries. I'm walking, not going far."

Kyle looked out at the water. He'd have liked to spend the day in the warm sand with Christy, holding hands and anything else he could get away with holding. Kissing her and making her blush, making her moan.

He'd bring her here. Watch the wind in her hair and wipe the sleep out of her eyes. She'd look beautiful in that crazy-tired way. They'd have explored each other's bodies all night and not tired of it. They'd feed each other as if they had a million golden days like this left. As if their pasts didn't matter. As if everything was in the future.

Cooper's clicking fingers brought him back.

"Fredo's right, boss. You're dreamin' all the time now. She that special?"

"Yeah, she is. More than I deserve." Kyle took his last huge bite of pancake that dripped with syrup. It was almost too much to swallow at once. "And I treated her like shit."

Cooper's blue eyes studied Kyle's face. Kyle could feel the examination, the evaluation going on. Did he look like a fuckup now to this loyal Team member? Did Coop doubt Kyle had the stones to see this mission through? Now that he might have something else to live for?

No. Cooper still believed in him. Probably more than he did.

But now it was time for work. "I better call Timmons," Kyle said.

AFTER KYLE'S BUDDIES took off, he called his chief.

"Kyle, I got incoming from all directions," Timmons said. "They've got three fucking bodies and even the Feds screaming at me, telling me I got a rogue killer on my hands. Tell me something I'm not going to have to resign over."

"Only one body that I know of. He was killed by his own men. Who are the other two?"

"Two shot in the head, out in the forest. One in the house, burned all to hell. Can't make out ID yet."

*So they offed their own gunmen. That would cost them some loyalty, if anyone left had any balls at all.* Leaving a man behind was bad enough. Killing your own men to set someone else up, unthinkable in the SEAL community. A desperate act.

"Timmons, there's a dirty cop involved. You need to be very careful who you level with."

"Shit, Kyle. Don't fuckin' tell me who I can and can't talk to. Where the hell is Armando?"

"I don't know."

Timmons swore, then Kyle heard a crash and shatter. Timmons probably had kicked the frog statue the Team had spent $300 for last year at Christmas.

"Mia is safe, sir."

"Mia? Armando's sister?"

"The same. She was in the explosion. Not in real good shape. But we got her to the ER and I called her mom."

"Good work, son."

"Gunny's been arrested."

"Fuck me. He's on his own. Nothing I can do about that. How did that happen?"

"We went in for Armando and left Gunny with the van. The ATF took him. Not that I like it, but I think he's safe in their custody. Can you find out where he's being held?"

"I'll try."

"The dead guys. Can you find out who they are, Timmons?" He gave his chief the license plate numbers from the Suburbans.

There was silence on the other end of the line. "Have to be careful," Timmons finally said. "You don't want anything to get through to Carlisle, right?"

"Carlisle? What's he got to do with this?" Kyle couldn't imagine the guard would be anywhere near anything dangerous. And this situation was fucking dangerous.

"Got himself assigned to the local squad as the Navy liaison. I'm supposed to go through him, can you imagine it? That asshole? Fancies himself as a policeman some day. He's making real nice with the County dudes."

"I'll bet. Can just see him busting sailors' chops and getting paid for it."

"I'd like to find him dirty, Kyle. He smells dirty. We could get him bounced. He has been a pain in my side for years. And for every one of my guys. Especially my guys."

"What's the story?"

"Not today. Someday I'll tell you. So, what's the plan?"

"I gotta get back to my Hummer." But then Kyle thought about the night before and of the man shot in the cabin. "The dirty cop's name is Warren something. I'm thinking now he shot that dude with an MP5. I think these guys are hooked up with some ex-military. They've got equipment."

"This Warren shot the one in the fire?"

"Yeah."

"How does Armando look?"

"He's messed up. They injected him with heroin, I think. And beat him pretty bad."

"Wonder what the hell they want."

"I'm guessing his cooperation. You know they're recruiting from the Special Forces. Recruiting for gang members to help run drugs, train the bad guys, get the special equipment. With Armani's history..."

"Yes I thought about that. Last time he was busted for being drunk in public, it nearly cost him his position on the Teams."

"And I'm glad for my sake you went to bat for him."

"You think his past has caught up to him?"

"Nope. I think it's for Mia. Armando is solid as a rock. But he'd do anything for his family."

"That should worry you."

"It does, but he'd sacrifice rather than cave in to them. If he had a choice, I mean."

"Cocky as hell, right to the last, huh?"

"I'm guessing these guys know him. Trying to turn him. Fredo told me a little about it in Afghanistan this last tour."

"Shit, Kyle. This is sounding worse by the minute."

"Just what they do, Chief. They hit guys in their weak spot."

"No way any Team guys would do that."

"They're recruiting kids that have a beef with the military. Their way of getting even. Fredo says they don't even care if the guys don't speak Spanish. They want the military training."

"What kind of a fucking world is it coming to?"

Kyle thought about the question and then answered Timmons. "I can't stop them all. But we're going to stop these bastards. No way they're going to take Armando. He'd rather die than be used by those guys."

"Then you better hope they don't tell him his sister's safe."

Kyle knew either way would be bad news. It didn't matter whether Mia was dead or safe. If Armando found out, he'd not worry one whit about his own safety and might do something stupid.

*Unless I can get there first.*

# CHAPTER 17

I N BED, CHRISTY opened her eyes and took stock of her room, of the sounds around her, and of the smells.

*No coffee.*

So the dreams about Kyle last night had been just that. Dreams. She'd gone to bed scared to death, but sleep came crawling, and with it the erotic dreams. Things they had done, things she wanted to do. Maybe if she fell back asleep, the dreams would all come back. She could be in his arms. He'd be kissing her.

She rolled her naked body to her side and hugged the pillow he'd slept on, needing just a hint of the man she knew she craved. The man she probably loved. The man she might never see again.

*Fatal love.* She knew it was a really bad idea to cling to something she could never have again.

She closed her eyes and willed the sun to go back down. Willed the world to swing back and replay Wednesday night. Every glorious detail of it. Every kiss. Every stroke.

*Damn.* Sleep was lost to her. Sunk to the bottom of the ocean like a lead anchor.

Several times in the night she'd awaken, having heard some sound. She'd hoped he'd somehow returned and would slide that wonderful hard body of his against her backside and let her melt into his arms as they pulled her to him. She could feel his kisses on her neck and shoulders, could feel him roll her over and spread her legs for him, could feel him coax her sex to make love to his fingers while he watched, until she was close to a climax, until she wanted him so badly she could not stand another minute without his shaft ramming inside her to the hilt. In her fantasy she knew he wouldn't do it just yet. While she was spiraling into oblivion, he'd bend down and lap her juices, kiss the pink lips of her sex, and beg her to give his tongue entry.

And then he'd climb her and ride her hard, watching her, bending to kiss her neck and whisper in her ear, take the moans from her mouth with his own. He'd call her name, and she'd listen for the three little words he'd not said yet.

*I am your willing prisoner, Kyle. Give me those little words and I'd gladly give you my life too.*

She opened her eyes. Her wet fingers remained between her legs as she gently massaged herself there, and then stopped.

*I'm being stupid. I'm lost in some fantasy.* Truth was, Kyle didn't want anything more to do with her. She was a pit stop fuck on his highway to heroism. Why, she wondered, had she made an emotional investment with this man? Would it ruin her? Or would she recover?

And she knew it didn't matter. She was going for broke. Whatever it took. She had no way to stop it.

*Please come back to me. Give me another chance. I can handle it, handle whatever you can give me.*

The room didn't answer. Sunlight was a stubborn friend, unrelenting, unforgiving, and invading everything about the place. There would be no going back to bed.

*Maybe he'll show up this morning!* The lingering worries from last night seemed like a distant memory. Things were much better, much safer in the light of day. She'd been ridiculous. Her imagination had gotten the better of her, she decided.

She bounded out of bed, ready to start a new mission, then ran naked down the hallway to the bathroom and turned on the hot steam shower. She shampooed, soaped, and shaved everywhere, working quickly as if he would arrive any minute. But she was thorough. She wouldn't miss a hair or forget to wash a crevice or cave. The lavender conditioner sluiced down her skin, over her pert nipples, and made purple ribbons down her smooth legs and over those damned pink toes.

When she stepped out of the shower, she thought she heard a tapping sound. She dabbed her face with the fluffy peach-colored towel and listened. She heard the sound again, so threw on her old terrycloth robe that hung at the bathroom door hook and stepped to the hallway, rubbing her wet hair with the towel, and listened. Someone was tapping on her door.

Dashing to her bedroom, Christy put her pajama bottoms on and an oversized sweatshirt. Excitement brewed as she was sure it was Kyle. She wasn't going to check the peephole, just open the door wide and kiss him to oblivion.

*Thank God. He's come to apologize.*

"San Diego PD. Please open up."

Her heart raced, and her mouth became parched. This wasn't a very good sign. What had happened? She was going to say something, but all she could do was wheeze.

*I'm having a panic attack!*

"Just a minute. I'm coming," she managed to call out weakly.

She opened the door to greet four officers—three men and a woman.

"We need to come in, ma'am," the eldest of the males commanded as he held up his badge.

"Sure." She stepped aside and the four burst into her condo hallway, and then began a casual visual search of her living room and kitchen area. Before closing her door, Christy took a quick peek out toward the elevators and saw her neighbors, an elderly African-American couple wearing their slippers, standing just outside their door two units down. The man was in a robe, holding a drink in one hand and the paper in the other.

She waved to them both, having just met them a week ago. Mr. and Mrs. Jefferson. They didn't move, but Mr. Jefferson shouted down to her, "They came here first."

"Everything's okay," Christy replied. "Don't worry. Another mistake." She shrugged and that seemed to satisfy the couple, who nodded and went inside.

The older officer flew past her and into the hallway. He turned back to her. "Who are you talking to?"

"The neighbors you terrorized." She enjoyed the words.

It wasn't fair to take her anger out on the police, but since Kyle was MIA, she couldn't scream at him.

*Maybe he joined his friend. Two missing SEALs now.*

"That kind of language is not smart, missy. I need you to get back inside. Now." He grabbed her arm firmly but without violence, and wheeled her inside, slamming the door behind him.

Christy yanked herself free. This picture was all wrong.

"He's not here, sir," the policewoman said what was obvious.

"Who?" Christy asked, pouting.

"You know damned well who, young lady. Your boyfriend, that's who." The older officer was annoyed.

She snorted. The situation would be funny if it wasn't so sad. *Boyfriend?* "He's not my boyfriend."

He leaned his tall frame into her bedroom, eyeing the tussled sheets.

Christy's cheeks flamed and she looked down at her bare toes with the bright pink polish. Her eyes began to well up with tears. Damn, she was going to have to change the polish. Every time she looked at her toes now, she cried.

She steeled herself, looking straight into the woman officer's face, letting her tears spill over and trace down her cheeks. "It was a goodbye fuck."

The woman officer's eyes grew round and she gave a hint of a nod. Christy saw traces of some pain on her face. But immediately a mask developed and the woman looked away.

"So, where did he go?" The senior man had graying sandy blond hair and clear blue eyes. Despite his age, he looked to be in great shape. Well defined muscles and a proud carriage. More military than police. Christy wasn't done testing the man.

"Out," she answered.

The lead man looked up to the ceiling and shook his head, murmuring something. He sighed and gestured for her to sit on the leather chair she still thought of as Kyle's.

"I'm Sergeant Mayfield, and these are officers Jones, Thiessen, and Woodward."

The woman was named Woodward, Christy noted. Christy crossed her arms and legs as she sat, not about to offer them coffee, tea, or water. They'd have to beg for it. And even then, she'd think about it.

Once everyone was seated, Sergeant Mayfield began. "We are looking for a man named Kyle Lansdowne. We know that he spent some time here."

"Yes. Is it a crime to date?"

"Look, I've reminded you before about your attitude. If you cooperate with us, there's no need for you to get mixed up in this mess."

"And I should believe you why?" Christy fluffed her drying hair.

"Unless you'd prefer to answer questions downtown. And of course, if you refuse, we could hold you."

"What questions? I don't know anything. I meet a cute guy, he came over here and we...you know..." She looked at the female cop, who immediately averted her gaze. "We had a good time. I'm single. But I don't know anything about him."

"Except you know what he does for a living," Mayfield persisted.

"Yes. He told me that."

"And why?"

Christy thought about their first meeting, and no way was she going to tell them.

"He returned some signs I had left at an open house. And he asked me out. Simple as that." She measured Mayfield's expression and found a hint of kindness there, not the bravado he was trying hard to portray. She addressed his ramrod chest. "Don't you tell a girl what *you* do for a living?"

The three younger officers looked briefly to their sergeant, then away. One tapped his foot. Woodward looked out the sliding glass doors to nothing but blue sky, and the third one examined his fingernails.

Christy could see she'd wounded the older man in some way. He was probably a lot like Kyle. A loner, except for his brothers in blue.

Mayfield cleared his throat. "I want to know everything he told you. Start to finish. From the top, missy." The look he delivered told her he could be nice, but only for so long. She'd better comply. She sighed, watching him pull out a notepad from his vest pocket.

"He's looking for his buddy, his teammate. He's gone missing, and Kyle thinks it isn't voluntary. That's all I know."

"Where is he looking for him?"

"I'm sure I don't know."

"Who does he think has his friend?"

"I don't know. He hasn't said, and I don't think he knows, either."

"Why does he think the guy has been taken against his will?"

Christy had to think about what Kyle had told her. "Armando is his friend from the Teams..." She could see Mayfield picked up on her words right away. "Armando's sister is in some kind of trouble, and Kyle thinks Armando went to find her."

She watched as he scratched notes in his notepad.

"These aren't the bad guys here," Christy continued. "Except for the fact that they are known for their one night stands. But in my case it was two, thank you very much." She placed her palm against her heart and closed her eyes. She'd seen by their squirming none of the officers wanted to be there. "I doubt he'll ever come back here again, so you're wasting your time questioning me. The bad guys are the ones messing with Armando's sister."

"No, missy, I'm afraid I can't agree with you entirely," Mayfield said.

"How so?" she asked.

"We're not in Afghanistan. We're in the U S of A, and *here*, *we* take care of the bad guys. Kyle and his SEAL buddies don't get to act on their own just because they think it's a good idea. They're not supposed to interfere with local authority. They're supposed to cooperate."

The argument was valid. No one said a word. Christy didn't want to look at any of them. But that same question had gnawed a hole in her stomach.

Mayfield flipped out a business card and passed it to her between two fingers.

"And now we got three dead bodies. Men brutally murdered. I think Kyle had something to do with those murders. That makes him one of the bad guys."


AN HOUR LATER, Christy nearly jumped out of her skin when she heard her cell ring. She didn't recognize the number at all.

"Hello?"

"Christy? Everything okay?"

Kyle's voice sounded far away. She worked to stay cold to him.

*Self preservation.*

"I think it's a good idea if you leave me alone." It was true, but so painful to deliver.

"I'd have to agree with you there. But things have escalated and I just want you to be very careful. We're dealing with some people who have already killed. I don't want you anywhere near them."

"I would have liked a nice talk like this yesterday morning. Seeing as how you're so concerned for my welfare. But the slam, bam thank you ma'am thing…"

"No. That's not me."

"Oh, really? You have a multiple personality disorder? One minute you're fucking my brains out and the next…"

*Careful, Christy. Don't say something you'll regret.*

"Look, I'm sorry about how all this happened," he said.

Christy lost it. "You know what, Kyle?" Here. It. Comes. *Don't do this, Christy!* "I'd say as a lover, you're probably an eight, eight and a half…" *You're such a bad liar.* "But as a hero, and I thought all you SEAL guys were heroes, you're a fucking zero." She hung up.

She counted to ten. No return call. She took the battery out of her phone so she wouldn't know if he tried to call her back. She ran for the shower, stepped in, and turned on the warm water, drenching her pajama bottoms and sweatshirt.

*THIS IS FOR the best.* Kyle wanted to call Christy back—heck, he wanted to do way more—but he knew this mission was probably not going to have a happy ending. He needed to walk away from Christy. Better to involve only those people who had fully signed on for that kind of danger. Let Christy live with the illusion that life was fair and filled with good people. Sure, she'd be nursing a broken heart for a while, but that was being kind, he told himself.

*Just focus on the mission. Don't let it get complicated.* Then throw everything into his workup for the next deployment.

*If they don't boot my sorry ass outta the Navy.*

And that would depend on whether or not this mission succeeded.

# CHAPTER 18

**M**AYFIELD WAS FILLING out reports from the interview with Christy Nelson that morning. She hadn't been much help, and her attitude had been irritating at first. But he understood her motivation to protect a man she clearly trusted. He couldn't fault her for being loyal. And more important, he knew she was honest. He'd believed her story about her SEAL. He'd known a few SEALs, even tried the BUD/S course during his ten-year stint in the Navy. But since he wanted to fly jets, he wasn't too disappointed when he washed out. In the end, he'd had to give up flying, too, due to his eyesight.

The SEALs he'd met socially, in the Navy and through his line of work, stuck together and usually cleaned up their own messes. This was all too public and out of control. Something was wrong with the picture. It was starting to smell, too, as the body count was increasing.

This investigation was just not making sense and was going in circles. He'd watched the news report this morning about the late night fire, and it really worried him. That's probably what prompted the call, before he could finish breakfast. He was asked to bring lots of backup and to be armed.

No, the deeper he investigated, the more things didn't add up.

The task force, made up of members of the ATF, SDPD, and the San Diego Sheriff's Department, plus a Naval Officer he'd never met before, had three murders to investigate now, and for some reason, he felt there would be more. That was definitely not going in the right direction. His superiors were screaming at everyone, indiscriminately, while publicly and on camera telling the media they had utmost faith in their men and women and that the perps would be caught. The public was now aware of the Navy angle. He wondered how they had gotten wind of that particular fact. Feeling in the San Diego area ran either hot or cold for sailors. Not much left in the middle. He didn't want those emotions tainting his investigation.

He looked up to see Sherriff's Deputy Warren Hilber stride through the office doors and glamour the staffers and officers as if he were a vampire at a sweet sixteen ball. Mayfield didn't like him and he sure as hell didn't trust him. Hilber's sidekick of recent was that jerk-off from the Navy, Carlisle with a big fat III after his name, the one who wanted to join his force some day. Mayfield would never allow either the deputy or the Navy tin cop anywhere near his squad if he could help it.

Only, he wasn't sure he could help it.

He knew they were coming in to see him. Every time he talked with Hilber, he felt like punching his lights out, effectively ending his own career. Something dirty about the man.

Warren knocked on Mayfield's opened doorframe. And then he smiled.

*Shit. Let the games begin.*

"Come on in, fellas. You guys off today?"

"No sir, we're just getting revved up. Got real close to catching that rogue SEAL and his merry band of men last night." Warren was eager.

"Don't tell me he got away." Mayfield leaned back in his chair.

*Now why does this make me a little happy?*

He laced his fingers behind his head. He needed a haircut. And now, at the stench these two gave off, he needed a shower.

The smile was wiped off Warren's face like cold cream wiped off a whore's red lipstick. Warren was sizing him up, and Mayfield could tell he wasn't intimidated in the slightest. This made Warren and his Petty Officer Carlisle the III dangerous. And desperate.

"This time. But we arrested an accomplice," Warren Hilber said.

"And who would that be?" Mayfield asked.

"Sergeant Wilbur Hoskins, retired."

"Gunny. You got Gunny. Good job, boys. I hear women halfway around the world have been looking for that son of a bitch for years." Everyone in San Diego knew about Gunny and his legendary gym. He wasn't much as a husband, preferred his wives to not speak English, but he was still a hell of a guy and a rock in the community. Mayfield wished he were a cigar smoker. He'd have lit one up in celebration and laughed these two out of his office.

Carlisle piped up, "Detective Mayfield, I got it on good authority Gunny is aiding and abetting these criminals, these rogue SEALs."

"Well, Carlisle," Mayfield said, as he stood up and looked out the window, showing his profile to both men standing before him. He knew it wasn't lost on them that Mayfield was almost a foot taller than either of them. He intended for them to squirm a bit. He looked down on Carlisle as he finished his sentence. "I've never heard Gunny pick a fight in the twenty years since I've known him. In fact, he's the one the guys call to stop the fights, or to come clean up the pieces. But aiding and abetting? That's a stretch, don't you think?"

He finished, looking out the window. When he turned, Warren was peering down at his report. Mayfield sat down and put a file over it. A slight frown fell over the deputy's face.

Warren and Carlisle looked at each other. Mayfield continued his lecture. "Fellas, it's like firing the school janitor if the students' test scores drop."

Mayfield could see it got to Warren, who was trying to make nice, with a wolfish grin that was all mouth and no eyes. Lots of attitude oozing through.

"Sir, I understand he isn't the primary target. But I think we can use him as bait. Lansdowne will have to surface. He'll contact Gunny. The Feds are releasing him this afternoon, just holding him as long as they can. Everyone Kyle knows should be under surveillance."

"Well, we've talked to the girlfriend, and I don't think she knows anything either, Warren," Mayfield said. At the expression on Carlisle's face, he wished he hadn't revealed so much, and Hilber had been way too interested in that report lying on his desk.

"That where he was last seen, at her place?" Warren asked.

"Yes. Nearby." He didn't want to give the girl's location, specifically. He hoped Hilber hadn't read it on the report sheet. His antenna was beginning to trace.

"He's going to want to go back," Carlisle said. "He's a real ladies man."

So Carlisle thought he was aiding the investigation and was trying to earn his stripes, a way to get on the police force somehow. Mayfield saw his hatred of the young SEAL as plain as the tattoo of an anchor he wouldn't let his wife get years ago.

"And just what are you talking about, sailor?"

That actually made Carlisle blush. Warren kicked him in the shin and saw the man start.

His words directed more at Hilber, the Navy man tried to explain further. "They all do this, hang around the ladies. Drinking and raising hell. No sense of decency. I've had him cited for service unbecoming for years. The Navy's just looking for an excuse to boot his sorry ass outta here."

Mayfield wondered what in the stars was out there to get young Lansdowne in the crosshairs of so many assholes. Why were these two so anxious to bust him? Why was he in the middle of shit between the Feds and the Navy?

All he had to do was put in another five years and collect a good retirement. He needed all this controversy like he needed another ulcer. Or another girlfriend.

*Maria, I'm so sorry you had to hear that.* He spoke to his beloved dead wife, only gone ten months now. Mayfield felt she saw everything that rattled around in his brain, including his need for some recreational female companionship.

"We've got some work to do, sir. And I can see you're busy and got your hands full with the press. We'll get out of your hair." Warren gave a bitter smile and dragged Carlisle out through Mayfield's door.

*A pair of regulation assholes.*

Mayfield had the sense that if he didn't solve this case soon, there would be further violence. Something that wouldn't reflect well on the Department or the Navy. Something that could affect his retirement.

Big time.

# CHAPTER 19

KYLE WAS TEMPORARILY holed up at Fredo's apartment, trying to stay out of sight. He'd sent Fredo to go check on Gunny, who had sustained some injury and was being held overnight at the hospital. A morning paper had been delivered, so Kyle was reading an article about the explosion at the cabin and the purported murders. He knew they were murders. He didn't like the fact that members of a SEAL Team were implicated. Although the article didn't mention him or his team by name, he knew it was only time before he was found to be a link. If the local authorities knew about the SEAL connection, they'd get to him sooner or later.

His cell rang.

"Gunny's pissed he has to stay longer. They're not going to release him today like they promised," Fredo squawked on the phone.

Kyle nodded. He'd guessed as much. "How long?"

"They're running tests. Doesn't know."

"And so that means we break him out, right?"

"Damn fuckin' straight. He said tonight, when they change shifts."

"He hooked up to anything?"

"Heart monitors, things that drive him crazy. He tries to take them off and then the nurses come running in, thinking he's having a heart attack. Has nothing to do with what they did to him last night. They've found something else."

"If Cooper says he's okay, then we take him. Tell him that, Fredo. I'm not taking him if it's going to risk his life."

"Roger that. I'll tell him. Not that it would make any difference."

"Not going to happen. Don't care how much he begs. I'm not going to have his death on my conscience."

It was one thing to have the deaths on his hands of the good men he led into battle, but then they'd signed up and knew the risk. Another thing entirely to have a civilian suffer. Someone who'd already paid his debt to his nation. Who'd earned his retirement.

Fredo had obtained Gunny's truck keys. They made plans to meet up with Coop, and the three of them would go to Armando's to retrieve his stash of weapons. No need having that potential discovery adding thickness to the goo they were already in. But first, Kyle had a number of things to do before they carried out Gunny's mission of mercy.

He called Cooper.

"Did Fredo say whether or not he is under house arrest?" Coop asked.

"Nope. I'm guessing yes, but really depends on who."

Cooper whistled. "That's a fact."

"Fredo will follow in his car. I'm going to get the beater. Pick you up in about twenty?" Kyle asked his medic.

"Roger that." Cooper hung up.

IT SURPRISED KYLE there wasn't anyone guarding Armando's house, or at least no guards that they could see. He doubted the guys who had trashed the house earlier in the week would resort to anything complicated, as far as surveillance went. That meant this wasn't an organized unit.

They parked both vehicles on the block behind and made short work of slipping along the side of a house that was vacant and for sale, then over the rear fence to Armando's rear yard. They disabled the slider lock and stopped inside the kitchen, listening for anything.

Deathly silence greeted them. The mess all over the house was just as Christy had described. Coop and Fredo were swearing. With their gloved hands, they began picking up some of Armando's broken picture frames and things that might have been important to the man in happier times.

"Don't get your aprons on yet, ladies," Kyle said. It earned him the finger from Fredo, whose idea of housework was moving to another apartment rather than cleaning.

Kyle made it back to Armando's bedroom with images of that day he'd been naked on the bed when Christy found him. That was barely a week ago, but how things had changed.

*No time for those thoughts.*

He sprung to the corner, relieved nothing looked disturbed, and peeled back the blue carpeting, revealing a square cutout with a metal loop handle embedded in the plywood underlayment. He opened the two-foot-wide hatch and flashed his penlight into the cubbyhole, revealing black powder-coated weapons and boxes of ammo. Fredo and Cooper were right behind him as he carefully extracted the weapons, including an .88 Karl Gustav rocket launcher. One at a time, amid admiring whistles and profanity from the two Team guys, they reverently lay everything on the bed. Enough fire power to start a revolution.

*Start one. But couldn't finish the job without help.*

In Armando's closet was an empty duty bag. They loaded the equipment, except for the Karl Gustav, which had to be wrapped in a camouflaged laundry bag, and then carefully put back the hatch opening and carpeting.

Kyle searched the street through the closed living room curtains and didn't see anything of interest. All of the sudden, a San Diego police car cruised by, but the two occupants were not slowing down and kept looking straight ahead. He took it to mean a random coincidence.

In the hot afternoon sun, they silently made their way alongside Armando's pool. Kyle noticed the buildup of leaves had gotten worse. Once over the fence, they checked the street again and found nothing that interested them, so they remounted their vehicles, Kyle stashing the bag of weapons under the rear seat in Gunny's truck. The launcher was precariously laid on the floor behind and he threw a windbreaker over the protruding tip.

Except for the grinding of gears and the lugging of an overworked motor, they left the neighborhood quietly.

They stopped by Kyle's Hummer that he'd left in an alleyway behind a local warehouse for lease. There were no windows from which anyone could watch them transfer Armando's firepower into the Hummer. Kyle wasn't comfortable with letting them out of his sight, and stored his own gear there all the time. With two locking steel boxes bolted to the frame beneath the second seats, unless they were looking, there'd be no way to find them. The Gustav was another problem, and they had to resort to keeping it wrapped, lying on Fredo's rear seat, fully covered.

They parked Fredo's car in the garage at his apartment complex, unloading the CG and stashing it in Fredo's locked gun locker. They took Gunny's beater over to the base. Cruising past the guard gate on their way down the strand, they could see that Cooper's motor home seemed untouched.

"If they was looking, they'd have everything out all over the tarmac," Cooper said to Kyle.

"I don't think Carlisle has seen it back in the lot. But he will."

"Yup," the farm boy replied.

Kyle's thoughts drifted Christy's way. He wished he could clean up things with her. Maybe he would give her a call later.

*Maybe not such a good idea.* He shelved that pleasant thought for now.

COOPER WAS TO go into the hospital first. He wore a white lab coat and stethoscope around his neck, and was using his military nametag from his rotation at the burn unit in Texas. He wasn't going to say he was a doctor, but his height and confident good looks, Kyle knew, would help give him the air of authority. Kyle wanted him to look like he belonged strolling down the corridor.

Kyle and Fredo watched him go, then they turned into one of the housekeeping closets and were in luck to find several stacks of scrubs. They picked ones big enough to go over their clothes. Fredo found a box of paper caps, along with some foot dusters. Kyle couldn't help but whisper, "I'll have two tacos please, amigo."

"Yeah, you get the one I spit in, man." At Kyle's chuckle, Fredo added, "They do that, man. Got a cousin who works at a hospital in LA. You wouldn't believe what they put in the food sometimes."

"Confirms my thoughts about hospital food."

They walked down a deserted hallway, looking for signs of a police presence. Luckily, Gunny was on the first floor, just around the corner.

Fredo stopped Kyle as they passed by a room with an opened door. He pulled out a wheelchair that was collapsed just inside the doorframe. "The nurse's station is at the end of the hall before the turn. We gotta go one at a time. Here," he told Kyle. Fredo handed his LPO a tall plastic garbage can on wheels. "You take this and walk up and down the hall while I go toward the room. If anyone comes, pretend you're changing the plastic liner."

"Fredo?"

"Uh huh, boss?"

"How much time you spend in hospitals?"

"Don't ask. More than your average Mexican."

Kyle would leave it at that. Although they shared personal details of their past, there were some things that would be left unsaid. It wasn't helpful to say too much. Those who felt the need to spill their guts never made it through the training.

Fredo made easy work leering at the nurses as he walked past the station. He had a way of making women turn away from him as he focused on their body parts, on purpose this time. He rounded the corner and Kyle didn't hear a flutter.

Within five minutes, Gunny was grinning from ear to ear, seated in the wheelchair, followed by his personal physician with a metal clipboard, and pushed by a Mexican orderly. Cooper nodded to the ladies.

"Taking him to X-ray."

"Hold it. You mean that way," Kyle heard.

"Nope, going to take him by the service elevator. Hallway's jammed up there," Cooper answered without stopping.

Kyle abandoned the garbage can and pushed the automatic doors open to go get the truck. He pulled up and Fredo immediately helped Gunny into the rear seat, while Cooper argued with a very large, belligerent head nurse who seemed to know the picture was all wrong. She was pointing at his nametag, saying, "If that's even your real name."

Cooper barely had time to step inside the truck before they sped off in a cloud of dark gray smoke, leaving a bevy of white uniforms behind.

"Sorry, Gunny. But sure as shit they've got your license plates."

"Hey, you hear me complaining? I'm so fucking glad to be out of that house of pain and death. That was a close one."

"You feeling up to this?"

"You kiddin'? All I need is a pair of pants."

Kyle hadn't noticed Gunny was in his shorts, having tossed the hospital gown.

Fredo added, "And man, a T-shirt, too. No way I'm gonna stare at those tits of yours, Gunny."

"Your fuckin' body will do the same, Don Juan." He sighed. "I got extra clothes at the gym. I'll quickly grab them."

"So why were they keeping you?" Fredo asked.

Kyle exchanged a look with Gunny through the rear view mirror.

"Something," Gunny began. "They found something they didn't

like."

No one said a word. It was Gunny's information to share, if he wanted, and Kyle knew he didn't want to.

"You know how it is, fellas. The mind is willing but the body has other plans."

Coop and Fredo nodded while Kyle shared another look with Gunny in the mirror but kept his mouth shut.

"So, after I get dressed, where are we going? Where are they keeping Armando?" Gunny asked.

Kyle had no idea.

# CHAPTER 20

C HRISTY HAD JUST returned from the gym. She'd asked for Marla, but no one had seen her all day. The light under the trainer's locked office door had been turned off, however.

So was everything else just part of Christy's active imagination? Being in the gym in the middle of the afternoon didn't scare her at all, but she was going stir crazy seeking answers to all her questions about the news reports of last night and today.

She was missing her extra passkey, and it bothered her. She looked through her gym bag and all her sweats, but came up short.

She needed a couple of things at the store, but she liked the safety of her place.

Still in her workout gear, she made herself a turkey sandwich and checked her emails. There were a couple of property searches she completed and sent off to clients. Then she updated her database for search matches against new listings. She heard another tap on her front door.

*Now what?*

Through the peephole, Christy saw two men in different colored uniforms. The blue Navy camis didn't catch her eye, but the gold badge did, so she slipped on an oversized sweatshirt to hide her skimpy workout wear. Opening the door, she hoped they'd have news about Kyle.

He was barely taller than Christy, dressed in a wrinkled sandy-colored shirt and matching pants with a beige stripe—the uniform of the local Sheriff's Department. He looked as though he was coming down with the flu. His eyes were rheumy and red. Or maybe he was a drinker. His holstered gun was snapped in place. He held a small sheaf of papers in his right hand. Healthy and freshly rested, he might have been a handsome man, if she liked short ones, but there was something about the way he looked at her she did not care for. Sort of feral, predatory.

But then, she didn't like the way most men looked at her. Especially now, in her exercise pants that hugged her ass like a second skin.

"Ma'am. Sorry to bother you," the deputy said. Regular Navy looked directly at her rack. She knew those kinds of guys couldn't help themselves. Gentlemen who knew it was inappropriate and didn't care were the truly scary ones. This guy had a gun too.

*This is definitely about Kyle.*

"I'm Deputy Sheriff Warren Hilber, and this is Petty Officer Carlisle."

Christy didn't want to look at the Navy guy any more than she had to. But she wouldn't trust turning her back on him, either. "I would like to get dressed first, if you don't mind." She pulled at the sweatshirt and pointed to her black yoga pants.

"Of course, we'll just wait…" He started to walk past her into the hallway, but Christy put a palm to his chest before he could take more than a step.

"You'll wait outside, or I'll call security." She wrinkled up her nose and whispered, "They have guns too, but you're probably a better shot."

She slammed the door in their faces. And locked it.

*Jerks! First the SDPD and now the Sheriff's Department and the Navy. Who's next? The fucking FBI?*

"Give me two minutes, 'kay?" she said through the metal door.

There was no answer, so she dashed to the bedroom and quickly slipped on a pair of tan khakis and put back on the light yellow oversized sweatshirt. She brushed out her wet hair and pulled it in a scrunchie. She decided against makeup. No body-enhancing underwear either. No reason to encourage either of them, but especially the one called Carlisle. In her bare feet, she unlocked and opened her front door, greeting them with as much of a smile as she could muster.

She was regarded carefully. She could see Warren was the smarter one, and for now, the leader. She stepped aside and they both walked past her. She leaned out into the hallway and found Mr. Jefferson standing, a puzzled expression on his face.

She waved to him, but he just stared back at her. He was still wearing slippers. She quietly closed her door.

"Please," she said as she motioned to her couch, where they both sat side by side. She took up a position in Kyle's leather chair and assumed the pose she'd taken when she'd talked to Mayfield this morning.

"I've answered all the San Diego police's questions this morning. I know nothing about all the murders on TV, if that's what you're here about."

"You're Kyle's girlfriend, then," Warren said, his lips slanted at an angle while he examined a piece of lint on his starched but wrinkled pants. His shoes were dusty too. Christy knew he'd been to somewhere probably Kyle had been. And that place wasn't in town.

"Right now, I'm not quite sure what I am. Why don't *you* tell *me*?" she asked them.

"Well, you could be an accomplice, perhaps an unwitting accomplice. If you help him in any way or impede our investigation, you'll be charged just like the rest of them."

"Them?" she asked.

"I'm sure you know he leads Teams for a living," Hilber began. "Special teams that do things most people would find offensive. And dangerous." He smiled and she got the chills. "We'd be grateful for your help. Thought perhaps we could strike a little deal with you."

The brittle smile across his face didn't seem natural to him. He didn't seem very practiced at making it look sincere.

"A deal? Why would I be interested in a deal, or even need one?"

"Well, right now there's a shoot to kill order, since your man here is armed and dangerous. If you help us catch him, I'll do my best to bring him in alive."

"Surely you are joking."

"I'm afraid not, ma'am."

Carlisle inserted himself in the conversation, apparently having waited long enough. "You may not know this, but Kyle is about to be booted from the Navy. I've been watching him for a couple of years now. I have reams of violations he's been written up for. He's coming unhinged. Very unstable."

She dismissed his comment as if it were the sound of a garbage truck.

He continued, "I've seen things he's done you don't know about. You're lucky to be alive. He's a dangerous man."

*He is dangerous. His kisses are dangerous. The way he loves me with total abandon is dangerous. It's dangerous how much I need him even now.*

Warren said, "He's a real smooth one. The ladies love him, and—h" he waited until she looked up at him "—he's loved a good many of them in return." He winked, stopping to watch perhaps a flicker of pain cross her face? Christy hoped she'd properly masked it.

The idea that those tattooed arms would ever hold another woman was a nightmare she did not want to endure. But worse was seeing the satisfied look on Warren's face when he realized he'd hit pay dirt. He'd gotten to her. And she knew it was probably all BS anyway, but it got to her, nonetheless.

Warren shook his head. "You know as well as I do, he's married to the SEALs. They are his family. You're baggage." Warren skewered her with a direct stare she couldn't escape. "Only a matter of time before he takes out the garbage. No offense, ma'am."

Again he had misjudged her.

"You're wrong."

"Am I?"

She worked on her composure. This man knew right where to hit her, where it hurt the most. She sucked it in and continued. "He's looking for his friend who's been kidnapped."

"Kidnapped? You believe that?" Warren looked at Carlisle and they chuckled and shook their heads, as if it were some private joke.

"I'd say more like he wanted in on Armando's golden goose. Armando's dirty. Running drugs and guns for a gang here we've been tracking for some time."

Christy's cell rang from the kitchen, sending her leaping to her feet to retrieve it. Before she could get there, Hilber picked it up off the kitchen counter. He looked at the display, then frowned and tilted his head to the side.

"Wayne Somerville? You holding out on Kyle?" he asked, handing her the phone. Even the beefy Realtor she loathed was a welcome distraction.

"H-hello?"

"Hey, Christy, you all right? I've been worried about you. Everyone here at the office is curious as hell…"

"I'm fine." She closed her eyes and wished she could will it so.

*Wish I were on someone else's radar.*

"Well, that's good to hear. I'll tell everyone."

"Do that."

"Hey, Christy, I wanted to apologize for, well for getting you into this mess you're in. It was an honest accident, giving you the wrong address, but I'm real sorry…and I…"

She needed to prolong the call. Anything to keep her away from the two men in her condo. Hilber and the other one were scanning her living room. She felt undressed.

"I don't know what you're talking about, Wayne," she said into the phone, but she didn't take her eyes off the two men.

Warren began to pace back and forth. He seemed nervous about something because he kept checking his watch.

"I been reading the papers, and, well, I think this guy who attacked you is the one running around killing people. You should have some protection."

Then she understood the purpose of Wayne's call. This was his not too smooth way of inviting himself over for a cuddle and whatever else he could get away with. "Well, Wayne, right now I have protection from Deputy Sheriff Warren Hilber and Petty Officer Carlisle. They're standing right here in my condo, talking to me." She decided it was a good idea to let someone else know about the two jackals in her home.

Hilber winced as Carlisle looked on sheepishly.

Christy had an idea. "I actually think you could tell the whole office these guys are here to protect me right now. Please tell Simms too. I don't want any of you guys to worry."

"Oh, that's good, Christy. Do you need anything? Simms says you're taking a few days off."

"That's right. The stress has been almost too much. Had a bit of a rocky start and all." She looked at Warren. "But I'll tell you what, could you come over in, oh, say an hour? I need a couple of things from my desk."

"Sure. Happy to help. In any way," he lowered his voice and her stomach turned.

"I have two buyer files I'm working on. They're inside my middle drawer. Could you bring them over?" The files wouldn't be too hard to find. They were the only two in her desk.

She didn't look at Warren but saw him flinch.

"Maybe I'll detain these two nice gentlemen so you can see for yourself how well taken care of I am. I think one of them is looking to buy a new home. And I'm going to be tied up for a few days."

Carlisle was looking up at Warren with a pained expression, holding his hands out, palms up, and shrugging.

"Sure. Sure I could do that, Christy. Anything else?"

"Ask Simms to call me later tonight, okay? I have some questions."

"Yeah. I'll be over in about an hour, maybe less, if it's okay."

"Fine by me." She paused, sucked in her gut and said, "Come over as soon as you like. Thanks, Wayne. That's real sweet."

She couldn't help but gloat when she hung up the phone.

"Well, officers. I need to get this questioning over with so I can get ready to receive company. You're welcome to stay, of course. We were discussing cooperation."

"If Kyle calls you, we want you to let us know," Hilber blurted out.

"Gee, I would have thought you'd have gotten a wiretap by now."

"The man can't be trusted, miss. Do yourself and everyone else a favor. Don't let him con you like he's done others," Carlisle said without expression. "You're in way over your head. Don't risk it for a little…a little…fun." His right eye flinched when he said this.

"Well, suppose you leave me your cards so I'll have your numbers handy." She looked back and forth between the two men. Carlisle turned to face Warren just a little too quickly.

Warren patted down his breast pocket and then the seat of his pants. "I'm fresh out of cards, miss."

Christy took one of hers out from a box next to her chair. Flipping it over, she handed it to Warren, with a pen. "Why don't you just write your contact information here? Do you check emails?"

"Yes, I do," he said, with a lopsided smile, looking up to her looming over him. She didn't trust the man. It was more than the creep factor she had with that dog Wayne. This man was pure cold evil. With authority and a gun.

He wrote his phone number and email address neatly on the card and handed it back to her. Again, his cold stare chilled her.

"Now your turn." She presented the pen and card to Carlisle, who leaned back so as not to touch it.

"It would be better if you just contact Warren. He's lead on this," he said, his eyes not returning her gaze.

"Um hum. Just give me your contact info anyway. Humor me," Christy insisted, her head cocked at an angle. She smiled to let him know she knew he was struggling and was asking anyway.

"I'm sorry, ma'am. That's classified."

"Then next time, you can stay outside, sailor." She put the card and pen on her kitchen countertop next to the stove. Warren was fidgeting, looking unhappy.

"If you will excuse me." She motioned to her front door.

The two men exited. Warren turned before he closed the door behind him. "We're going to catch him and all his team members. Even you can't deny that a rogue SEAL with a boatload of guns and explosives stashed everywhere is a danger to the good people of San Diego County. Way too dangerous for you to be playing with. You don't want to get scooped up in this net. Trust me, you don't."

*I already am. Nothing I can do about that now. Only person who can pull me off is the guy with the three-toed creature tattoo.*

THE SECURITY DESK downstairs in the Infinity office rang her phone about a half hour later.

"We got a Wayne Somerville down here. Says he has an appointment with you," Jerry's usual friendly voice was stiff and oddly cold.

"Sure, send him up."

Jerry didn't say anything before he hung up. She was going to thank him but got a dial tone in her ear.

When she heard the ping of the elevator, she opened her door and watched as Wayne lumbered down the hallway in a suit that looked a size or two too small and that showed off his midsection girth. The difference between the layer of blubbery fat jiggling as he moved and Kyle's measured strides and chiseled abs was laughable, but she held it in and risked him thinking she was glad to see him.

But in a way, she was. She'd been surrounded by men the last twenty-four hours, and there was only one man she wanted to see.

She smiled and said, "Thanks, Wayne," as he handed her the files. "I really appreciate this."

"No problem. I was going to bring you some flowers too, but thought it would, you know, remind you of the incident and of that bad guy."

She knew he was making excuses for being cheap. Why bring flowers if you weren't sure it was going to pay off?

"How thoughtful. Thanks again. You want to come in?"

"Sure." Wayne's eyes bugged out of his head, growing to saucer size.

"You want some coffee?"

"Sure, Christy. Thanks," Wayne said as he poked his head in her bedroom doorway, and then did a 360 in her living room. "This place is really nice. I've sold a couple of units here, but I think this one is way better."

"Yeah, my mom left it to me." She started grinding coffee beans.

"Free and clear?" He whirled around to look at her.

She was offended, of course, that he wanted to know how well off she was, but today she felt generous and had already dished out her quota of frost this morning. And Wayne didn't really deserve the sharp end of her patience.

"Yes. I have no mortgage." She smiled to the brewing coffee—that pleasant smell she'd loved while lying in her bed when she knew Kyle was in the next room, waiting for her to awaken.

"Wow. That's nice. Wish I had a rich relative." Envy lurked like a snake between his words.

"She wasn't rich. It was the only thing she had, and she'd saved her whole life to buy the place. Used some money she got when my dad passed away."

"Oh. Good for her," he said distractedly as she handed him his mug. He peered down into the creamy brew. "Thanks for the cream."

"Two lumps of sugar too."

"You remembered. That means a lot to me, Christy," he said as he lowered his voice, his gaze lowering to her chest.

"Funny how I remember little details like that." She sat on Kyle's chair. "Have a seat."

Wayne repositioned the pillows so his hefty frame would fit on the couch and then sat, leaving little space for another person.

"Who was your mom's Realtor?"

"She bought it from the builder. A grand opening special, I think."

"Jeez. Talk about timing. Good for her...and for you too."

She was letting his lack of transparency amuse her this morning, a morning without very much good news.

He sipped his coffee and put it on the table in front of him. Leaning forward, he pressed his palms together. "I'm sorry we got off to a difficult start. I was hoping we could be...friends." He had blushed, and Christy thought it looked more like unwelcomed sunburn.

*Everyone wants to help me. Do I look that helpless?*

Yes. She decided she did. Damn it. That was going to have to change.

"I suddenly have lots of people offering to help me."

"Oh, yeah? Who?"

He was probably wondering if another Realtor was in the picture.

"Well, there's the local police, and the San Diego County Sheriff's Department, and some Naval policeman or something. Forgot what they call him."

"MA. Navy term for MP. Wonder why all of them are so interested. I mean, I can see why they'd be interested in you, but…"

"The triple homicide."

"You were unlucky. I'm sure they'll figure it out soon enough." Wayne frowned and added, "They think he'll continue to strike until he gets caught. Death by cop sort of thing, I guess."

This worried her.

"Just how well do you know this guy, Christy?" He squinted his eyes and waited for her answer.

"We're friends."

"Be careful. You're playing with fire, Christy."

*Tell me about it.*

# CHAPTER 21

I T WASN'T WISE, but Kyle knew he would call her. He wasn't even sure which was more important, his worry over her safety or his need to talk to her for his own personal reasons. And it didn't matter.

She picked it up on the first ring.

"Christy's house of good times."

Kyle didn't quite know what to say. He heard the bitterness in her voice, but something else.

*Pain.*

He remembered himself, and his reason—at least the reason he'd given himself—for calling. "Christy, I apologize for my behavior."

"You seem to be repeating your sorry routine an awful lot, sailor. I'd say you're pretty practiced at it. Impressive."

"Actually, I'm not. I don't usually have to."

"Well, you don't have to now."

"What I mean is, I don't usually get involved."

Now it was Christy's turn to pause. "Is that what we are? Involved?"

"Yes." There. He'd whispered it. Had she heard? "I told you before, this wasn't a pit stop. You're a nice lady. You deserve more than I can give right now."

"So exactly what is *this* thing between us that you won't describe—this thing that isn't what you can give me right now?"

"I care about what happens to you."

"Get in line."

"Excuse me?"

"Let's see. Where do I begin? I get scared out of my gourd at the gym last night with some strange guy walking past my sauna door when I'm lying there buck naked. I decide maybe I'm being foolish, but no, the San

Diego PD is here this morning asking questions about some fire and a triple murder, thinking you're involved. *He* wants to help. A deputy sheriff stops by with one of your Navy buddies…"

"The Sheriff's Department was there?" This wasn't a good sign. But what did he expect?

"Yessir."

He'd been a dumbass. Stupid. Why hadn't he thought about Christy being questioned?

"Can I come over and talk to you?"

He heard her sigh into the phone, clouding the reception.

"Which Kyle is it who is coming over? The one who screwed me on the countertop and said he wasn't ready for this, or the one who just wants to talk?"

"I promise. Just talk." It wasn't much, but he'd take it. If she'd let him.


WHILE WAITING FOR him to arrive, Christy wished the chatter in her head would stop. Her pulse had quickened. She was beginning to sweat again and knew she didn't have time for another shower. In spite of what she told herself, she'd put on makeup, just a little of Madame's perfume, the cherry lip gloss, a little mascara. She brushed out her hair, and then she heard him, the relentless tap tap tap on her door like the beating of her heart.

*Bad sign, girl. Here you go again.*

Kyle had arrived at her door so fast she'd barely had time to finish getting on decent clothes.

*Damn.* Even his knock was sexy. She inhaled a big gulp of air and opened the door.

She was doomed. He stood, leaning against the doorframe, one forearm resting against the trim, his hips at an angle, his smile at an opposite angle. And the crease at the side of his lip. On the left. Did he know?

Did it matter?

*Oh, hell no.*

His hard chest was against her, his arms tight around her waist. The force of his lips as he kissed her instilled courage and resolve. She'd been ridiculous, of course, but she was so far over the edge for this man, even if he had done what they said he'd done…

*Christy, what in the world are you doing? The guy could be a cold-blooded killer.*

"Where's that little talk we were going to have?" she said to his hungry mouth. God, she needed that mouth on her right now. She stepped on tiptoes and pressed her lips hard against his. His tongue plunged in deep. His hands found her chest and snaked under her bra, squeezing her breasts. Was that her moan she heard, or his?

He stopped, dropped her from his arms, and looked to the floor. He took a step backward into the opened door to the hallway.

"I'm s…"

She couldn't stand to hear another "I'm sorry" from the man.

"Oh, shut up and fuck me," she said as she slammed into his chest, pushing the door closed. His expression turned from apology to fire.

She leaned into him, wrapping her arms up and around his neck. She liked the feeling of relying on his strength, how hard he was, how sure of himself. How his hands found their way to her, wanting flesh. He picked her up and brought her to the bedroom.

At the foot of the bed, he set her down and kneeled. He shed her pants, then stood and pulled off her pink T-shirt. He looked at her breasts as his hands cupped around them, thumbs rubbing over her nipples through the silky peach satin lace of the bra. She loved how he always seemed to be seeing her for the first time. He smiled and said, "I love your body, Christy. I thank God every time I get to hold you."

*But do you love me, Kyle? Tell me.*

He kissed her. Christy's hands smoothed over the ripples in his chest, touching the scars and kissing every one of them. Her hands traveled around the backside of his waist and down further to his butt cheeks and she pulled him to her. She ground her pelvis against his hardened shaft, undid his button fly, and slid his pants down. She took hold of the length of him and squeezed, then reached to find his balls and squeezed them as well.

He kicked off his shoes and stepped out of his jeans as she came to her knees. She took him inside her mouth, massaging his sac. His precum relaxed her. His musky scent made her cream between her legs as she worked his shaft, sucking, licking, and inhaling him.

He was beginning to jerk and Christy could tell his climax was close, so she stopped and looked up at him, kneading his cock in the palm of her right hand.

He quickly picked her up and placed her back on the bed. She moved aside several pillows to prop her head. He pulled one of the pillows away and shoved it beneath her hips, raising her sex to him, giving him a deep angle for penetration. God, she needed him inside her. Deep inside her.

She knew he was rock hard and ready to spurt, but he spread her knees and watched his fingers move in and out of the lips of her sex. Then he bent and kissed her there, lapping her juices, rubbing a thumb over her nub and sending little sharp spasms up her back and down both legs. Her whole world lay open to him, to his slick tongue that pushed in and out of her opening, his hot breath on her waiting womb.

She moaned as delicious ripples of pleasure overtook her. Kyle covered her now, kissing her lips and face.

"I need you. Oh God, I need you," she whispered. Her sex felt vacant, wanting.

Kyle's cock teased at her opening, and then he thrust deep inside, the angle set up by the pillow forcing him against her soft tissues. It sent her muscles into contractions as she tightly held him, refusing to release him as he pulled back before plunging in again. She grabbed the pillow at her side, arched, and cried out. Her body jerked, consumed with the magic of his slow and deliberate motions. His back muscles worked in tandem with the tensed muscles of his ass. She felt his cheeks go soft and then flex and as he ground against her, as he filled her and demanded more.

She vaguely remembered being scared. But not now. Now she was being pleasured by the man she loved, would always love. She dug her heels into the bed and raised her pelvis as he plunged in and out, deep.

A few strokes later, he turned her body to the side by rolling over one thigh. She tried to raise a knee, and he smiled and stopped her. He wanted the deeper penetration as he kissed the sides of her face.

Still inside her, he pumped her from behind as he spooned himself to the backs of her thighs, her back. He pulled her down onto his shaft. The pillow was between her knees as she pushed her rear against him, allowing him deep. He kissed her neck, found her ear, and whispered, "Need you, Christy. I…" But he stopped. He didn't say it.

And it was all right that he needed her. A man who didn't need anything or anyone and he now needed her. And that was going to have to be enough for now.

"I'm yours, Kyle, all of me."

That seemed to drive him crazy. Her body responded, exploding in her own pleasure, clenching down on him. He lurched inside her and she heard the familiar groans of his passion as he filled her with his sperm. She drew him in, accepting every drop, until he fell against her back with an exhausted sigh.

He stayed inside her as they rested. His hands caressed her nipples and breasts while he kissed her shoulder and down her spine, one vertebra at a time.

"I love this," she said. Then she turned her head. He saw it there, she knew it. He saw what she wanted to say, but wouldn't until he did.

"Anything is possible, Christy. Anything." He buried his head at the nape of her neck and pulled her against his chest and held her tight, but didn't look at her.

A minute later, she heard him snore, sound asleep. For some strange reason, the idea that he was so relaxed that he could fall asleep thrilled her. He was totally vulnerable, totally at risk to her. He had bared his soul. The words would come. She knew they would.

A HALF HOUR later, she pulled the blanket over them so Kyle would sleep longer, but he jerked awake. He'd fallen asleep inside her and began to pump her from behind again.

"Hmm. I've missed this so much." She leaned back into him.

"Me too," he whispered. "Sometimes I think about you, like this, and I can't concentrate." He thrust up into her.

"God, that feels so good."

He continued. He propped himself up on his arms, letting his groin have its way with her. She rose to receive him. "Yes," he said.

"I just want all this…agh…past…to be over with, so we can get on with our lives," she whispered between his kisses.

"Me, too." He rubbed his lips against her neck, tipped her head back, and kissed her under her chin. He pulled her lower torso to him, his fingers finding the spot between her legs as he touched their joining. She matched his hands with hers and they touched together, lacing fingers. It was more than sex. Way more than sex. For the first time in her life, she was making love to the man she loved with all her heart.

His hot kisses made her cheeks and chest flush. Her insides began to glow with fire. She was going to explode.

He held her as her body jerked. "Yes," he said as she gave him her climax. He held her tight, pressing with his fingers, pulling with his forearms.

She was spent at last. He continued kissing her until the very end, when he thrust, arched up, and groaned.

She turned to face him. He touched her face, fingers brushing over her lips, thumbs smoothing over her cheekbones. He planted another gentle kiss under her chin. His warm blue eyes searched hers.

She saw he wanted to say something. She wasn't going to ask. When he did speak, it wasn't exactly what she was expecting.

"You may never know where I am or what I'm doing. I won't always be here to help you with the nerves. And you've got to get used to the fact I might not come back."

That filled her eyes with tears. "No, Kyle, I can never get used to that idea. That just isn't something that is going to happen."

He smiled down on her. "Well, then, hold on to that thought. It'll be my homing beacon. Just remember how nice it is when we're together. I have no right to ask for anything else."

Her heart was aching. If there ever was a time she wanted to hear that he loved her, it was now. She knew he cared. But she wanted to hear it. She was looking for the man who could tell her he loved her. He wasn't there yet. But she would wait. She'd do it. She'd try.


HE HELD HER hand as they meandered down to the marina and the Salty Dog restaurant. He sat next to her so his thigh could be pressed against hers, and he took every opportunity he could to inhale the wonderful warm scent of her. His left arm encircled her waist while he tried to eat with his right hand.

She was looking out over the boats, her brown eyes sparkling. Her face was flushed, hair with that just-fucked look that made him hot for her all over again. The whole afternoon had been one turn-on after another.

*Did she feel as good as he did? Did she feel the connection, the mating that could be for life, if there ever was such a thing possible?*

He told himself the answer was yes. As incredible as it was, he believed it had finally happened to him.

She turned, and her eyes were hungry as she leaned into him. She pressed the nipples of her breasts against his chest and softly kissed him.

She was telling him the space between her legs needed to be filled again, that she needed his tongue there and then needed to be filled with his aching erection. She didn't have to say it. She was ready to go home and give herself to him all over again, all night long. She didn't have to say it. He could feel it hitting his face and chest like a blast furnace.

After they finished their chowders, she led him down the walkway by the boats and out along the promenade. Bells in the distance, a foghorn and lapping water, were all familiar sounds of this place that had molded him, had made him a man among men. These things sang to him. The familiar chilly saltwater mist heightened the warm feel of Christy's velvet smooth lips on his neck, working their way down his chest, as they sat on a bench overlooking the water. She unzipped his pants and felt inside to grab him. She squeezed her fingers over his shaft, up and down, ending with her thumb rubbing a drop of precum over his crown. She straddled him, slipped aside her unnecessary panties, and impaled herself on his cock.

God, he loved how much she needed him.

Her elbows squeezed her breasts together, pressing the firm mounds against his pecs. Her warm ass was a handful in each palm. He lifted her to rub a thumb over her nub as she rode him, and gasped with an "oh" from the sudden jolt of pleasure. He could watch her do that all night. He would surprise her, take her in his mouth, and push his way inside her from behind and deep, from the side at an angle. He wasn't going to stop until his body gave out. He'd trained well for this mission, and he wasn't going to end his pleasuring her until she was unable to walk, and then some.

She was riding him deep, her back arching as he lifted her and pulled her down onto him. He ground against her in the darkness, and then let her free only to have her sheath him again. He felt her thighs rub against his jeans as she moaned and fluttered her eyes. He started spurting first, and then she shivered and came on top of him. He wanted to reach inside deep, press against her womb as she rubbed it over the head of his cock and jumped with every little spasm.

"God, I could just sit here all night," she whispered. She lowered her lips to his and ground her pelvis.

"I wish you would. I'm a polar bear."

"You can keep me warm, then. I don't like the cold."

"Yes," he said as he moved against her. He was fully spent. "I can do that. Give me an hour and I can keep you warm all night long."

"Kyle, I feel like I've known you my whole life."

*Me, too.*

She leaned into his space and he held her tight, encircling her back and shoulders with his arms. He fell into the rhythm of her breathing and felt the tiny flutter of her heart against his chest. She had fallen asleep. He loved the feel of her warm breath against his neck. She murmured something.

"Are you warm enough?" he whispered.

She nodded and then looked at him. Her hair was messed up and covering her face. He smoothed it to the sides.

"I was having a wonderful dream just now," she said.

"God, I *hope* it was me you were dreaming about." He smiled and was rewarded with a smile in kind. He started to say something perhaps he shouldn't, but he couldn't stop himself.

"Christy, I…"

"Shhh." She put a finger to his lips. Her eyes sparkled with the reflection of lights from downtown behind him. "Don't tell me the bad news. Tell me how right this feels. Tell me you won't ever go."

"No bad news," he said, touching his forehead to hers. "It's all good here. All of it. I want it all, Christy. I want all of you."

*And there. He'd said it.*

She leaned back and searched his eyes. He had put himself out to her, and for the first time, he felt totally at a woman's mercy. She could end his life with a word. With a frown.

Tears formed in her eyes. She nodded. "Me, too, Kyle. Me, too."

Nothing more needed to be said. A perfect moment, a perfect evening.

# CHAPTER 22

I N THE MORNING, Christy got up first. Kyle knew he had to get going.
But hell, he'd be back. She'd tried to let him sleep, but the sounds of
her doing things in the kitchen and the smell of fresh coffee kept him
awake. He heard her take a shower, thought about the texture of her silky
skin as he massaged warm steamy bubbles over every delicious part of
her. But as nice as the vision was, he had a job to do and needed time to
think.

The waiting was getting harder. And, damn, so was he.

*Not again.*

She finished getting dressed and puttering in the kitchen. He pretended to be asleep when she climbed back into bed with a steaming mug
of coffee for him.

She might have known him better by now. He wasn't at all interested
in the coffee.

He took the mug from her fingers, took a sip, and watched the need
in her eyes fan his own desire. Oh, the things he was going to do to her
this morning. There'd be time later for their little talk.


KYLE STARED AT rays of sunlight that filtered through a palm tree outside,
making patterns on the ceiling.

*Armando? Where the fuck are you?*

"Kyle." Christy was awake and had been watching him think. "There
was a report on the news about a fire in the Santa Nella forest. You know
anything about that? About a couple of dead guys?"

"Had nothing to do with us."

She sighed. "I want to believe you."

He thought about that. Good that she trusted him. But should she? He knew the pause told her things. Things she didn't like. He sat up, eased off the bed, and pulled on his boxers. If he stayed in bed with her a minute longer, they'd be into another lovemaking session. A long one.

She donned her robe and followed him into the kitchen. He could feel the questions mulling around in her head. Questions he wasn't ready to answer yet. There were no answers in the refrigerator.

She handed him the yogurt mixture he was looking for.

He thanked her. "I can't tell you things because it's safer if you don't know. You must promise me you'll not go anywhere for a few days."

"But I will have work. I told them I'm taking a couple of days off, but I can't afford not to work, Kyle."

"Exactly. Stay in place for now. Work on the computer from home. *Live*." He stepped to her, slipping a hand under her robe. "God, I love this robe."

"I love the tie," she whispered, pressing her breasts against his bare chest.

Kyle leaned down and kissed her softly on the lips. He felt her breath catch as he eased one hand down to her rear. "I do, too." He couldn't get enough of her.

"I promise to wear it 24/7 then." She kissed him again. She pulled back and smiled. She handed him fresh coffee, then tiptoed to whisper in his ear, "And nothing else."

His one free hand roamed her backside, then felt her wetness and her need. "Wish I could do this all day, but I can't." Her lips were soft and hard to tear away from.

"Well, sailor, I'm totally at your beck and call. You can come here morning, noon, and night. I'll just be waiting here, in this robe." She fingered the tie. The silk robe parted so he could see the little triangle at the apex of her thighs he loved looking at. That place he could lose himself in.

It almost worked.

She fluffed her hair and licked her lips. She hadn't given up. But damn, he had to.

Kyle didn't try to cover up how she made him feel. And how he hated to go. But the urgency of finding Armando crept back in. He was tired of waiting. He knew his buddy would send another sign. And he would have to be ready to go.

Somehow.

With regret, he dressed in two minutes. She'd made him a turkey sandwich, tucking it and an apple in a brown paper bag she handed him. He'd finished off his coffee and the granola yogurt mixture.

"So, when?" she asked as she fingered his T-shirt that ribbed at his neck. He could still feel her pert nipples through her robe through his tee.

"Can't say. But I'll call you."

She nodded.

"Christy, you have to be very careful. Watch everything. Notice everything. I don't want something to happen to you while I'm gone."

She nodded again. "Promise." She cocked her head to the side and smiled. "But I like being punished when I'm a bad girl." She held up the silk tie.

Her eyes stopped sparkling when she saw his serious expression. Kyle saw she was waiting for her dose of medicine.

"Honey, I don't want you anywhere close to danger. You've got to stay away from Armando's house, maybe even me for a while. They could be following me. And now, they could be following you."

"How do you know this?"

"Well, look at all the attention you've attracted already."

She nodded. "Because of you."

"They want something from him, and yes, maybe from me, too."

"I don't understand."

"If they'd wanted to kill him, they would have. We'd already have found his body by now. Those guys always leave a calling card like a neon sign for anyone else to read. There's something else they want."

"What?"

"I can't say. Please, it's not that I don't want to tell you, but I need to keep you out of this."

"Do I have to stay physically right here?"

"With the gates and guards, this is probably the safest place to be."

"How about the gym?"

"I'd say no."

"But it's inside the complex…"

"Christy, someone could have gotten a temporary pass key. You were right about that place. I can't defend you if you're not right here."

"I'm sure it was my imagination. This place is tougher than Fort Knox to get into."

"I got in without any trouble."

Her eyes grew wide. "How?"

He pulled out a spare scan key from his pocket. "I took the Realtor's key she left in the door when she was distracted with your shameful behavior."

"That's where my other card went. She must have mine."

"Promise me you won't go anywhere for a few days." He leaned in close, next to the side of her head, and said softly in her ear, "Please? Just for a little while longer. When this is all over…"

His cell phone chirped.

"Hey, Fredo. What's up?"

"Not good. Not good at all. They want you for questioning." Fredo's voice was calm, measured, but laced with tension. It brought reality back like a cold wave.

"What about the help from locals?" Kyle asked.

"Not even on the horizon until you answer their questions about the bodies."

"They really think a bunch of SEALs would off some local muscle? Besides, those thugs who took Armani used to be military. I'm sure of it."

"Who the hell knows?"

Kyle scanned his choices.

"So what now?" Fredo asked.

"Well, I'm not about to oblige them. I'm not going anywhere near a police station."

"Thought you'd say that, boss."

Kyle felt his choices drying up by the minute. *Armani, anytime now. Another message would be great.*

"Boss, something new. Coop got intel from his Fed connection there's a gang working with some Special Operators, bringing in some illegals, drugs, and guns. There's a hint that there's some official coopera-tion for protection."

"Not possible it could be Team guys."

"You and I know it and Cooper knows it. Timmons is shit-kicking mad and says you gotta comply. It's bullshit, man, but hey, the locals are working with the Navy regulars. Having some jurisdictional catfight I'd actually like to see."

Kyle thought about the thorn in his side: Carlisle. He could smell the ill intentions of this cretin from miles away. And Carlisle wasn't stupid, either. He'd heap it on, for sure. Tell them what a fuck-up Kyle was. How many reprimands and citations Kyle had been issued. How Kyle was such a loose cannon. Yeah, he could see that happening.

"Only one thing to do, then."

"Yup," Fredo agreed.

"Meet me at the Scupper in a half hour."

"How you gonna get there?" Fredo asked.

"Fly. What do you mean?"

"They impounded your Hummer, Kyle. Found all your gear, filled with enough guns to worry the locals. Shoulda brought 'em with you, bro."

"I was entertaining a…" Kyle looked over at Christy. Her body spilled out from the silk robe she'd neglected to secure. She was watching him, her smile as missing as water in the Sahara.

"Well, it's not looking good, man. Maybe they know about her too. You better think about that, man." Fredo's staccato burst of words hit Kyle. Square in the middle of his gut. Christy said there'd been *two* sets of officers, regular SDPD and a deputy sheriff.

*Damn. How did this happen?*

"You gotta get out of there, Kyle, before they come in and get you. Get you both."

"Thanks. I'm on my way." He was about to hang up when he thought of something. "You bring the razor wire back, or was that in my bag?" Although he knew he'd wiped the metal down as best he could, he didn't recall putting it anywhere. It wouldn't be good to have blood in his bag match the bodies.

"Dude, you don't remember that?" Fredo sounded irritated with him.

"No, I don't. I think I stuck it in my bag."

"Then the cops have it. You're in some sorry shit, man. You better get your ass over here."

Kyle hung up and wanted to throw a chair through the window. How could he have been so fucking stupid? And it would be only a matter of time before the cops came for Christy too. His prints and hair were all over this place.

Christy came up behind him and leaned into his back, wrapping her arms around his waist. He stiffened. She jerked in response and abruptly stopped stroking his chest. He grabbed her hand before it could start to travel again down to his groin. He turned around to face her. There was going to be no easy way to tell her the bad news and he had no time to do it properly.

"I screwed up, Christy. They want me for questioning." He saw her eyebrows rise up into little tents, saw creases form in her forehead. She cocked her head, and then shook it from side to side.

"Just level with me. Tell me what's going on."

He could see the beg on her face, the urgent plea to become part of his life. *All* of his life.

"I can't. I can't get you involved."

"But I *am* involved, Kyle. Can't you see that?"

He walked to the sliding glass door, but didn't go out on the veranda. He spotted two police cars with lights flashing down below. Several others were approaching, with sirens wailing.

"I gotta go now. The guys are waiting."

Kyle picked up his keys and jacket, turning to face her. He placed his palms on either side of her face. "I'll call you. Stay here. Don't go out."

"What if the police…"

"Obey the police, but no one else, you got it? I'll try to call you on your cell. And don't talk about me to anyone. Anyone. Only the San Diego PD."

He was out the door and on the fire escape when he heard the elevator doors ping open in the background. He ran down the stairs all the way to the street level.

Kyle burst into a lobby full of police. Outside the building, police cars had been parked at odd angles, as more were expected to arrive. A crowd was gathering, along with a news crew. A white coronor's van was parked nearby, its doors open. Something awful had happened, and Kyle knew there was a dead body somewhere in the building. Although he wished he could stay, he knew leaving was the best thing he could do to protect Christy.

# CHAPTER 23

KYLE RAN A full mile and then hailed a cab to the island, headed for the Scupper. Once there, he found the SEAL bar dotted with tourists, taking pictures of all the SEAL memorabilia and of themselves in front of Team insignias. Later on the joint would fill up, like any good meat market, revving up to go on until the wee hours of the morning. Weekends were when the locals liked to think they could safely mingle with his crowd. The wanna-bes. Truth was, most of the real Team guys would never be caught there on Friday or Saturday nights, except when they needed an emergency pickup to push something out of their minds. Kyle had done it a time or two. Amazing what an anonymous night of sex could do. And the girl usually liked it, as well.

He scanned the room, catching a few long, lusty looks from several of the female population and "man up" gazes from some of the guys, but he didn't catch the eye of anyone familiar. He heard a whistle over the din, and then saw Cooper, his lanky frame towering a good foot above everyone else, near the exit sign in back.

"We were beginning to get worried," Cooper said as he backed through the rear door, ducking.

Kyle shook his shoulders and checked the sky. It was refreshing to be outside again. Even the brief crowd of innocents made him nervous now. Being in the Scupper felt more like spending time in a jail cell. And maybe that's because he worried he'd be landing there very soon. Until the Hummer had been hauled off, at Christy's condo, no less, he'd thought they were close to ending the caper. Mia was safe. All they had to do was find Armando. Now a whole new chapter had erupted. Things were spiraling out of control.

*Think, dammit.*

Kyle saw Fredo and Cooper leaning against the block wall of the vacant warehouse behind the Scupper, watching him, arms and legs crossed in an exact mirror image of each other.

"Dude. You have shit for brains, man," Fredo began. "Never seen you so spaced. Whatever she did to you, carve it out right now. No place for it here, or you're gonna get us all killed."

Fredo spoke the truth. It wasn't fair these two would suffer for his lack of judgment. They had to have their wits about them, like they did on the job overseas.

"Let me just say one thing—"

"Shut up. Let's get going," Cooper said as he punched Kyle's arm. "What's the plan?"

*Plan? What fucking plan?* How could he plan when he didn't know what the fuck he was doing? He'd spent the last twenty-four hours dreaming of a life he could never have. For the first time in his career, he had no plan.

*Well then, make one up, asshole.* He knew if he could just get into action, readjust his course, it would be easier to correct any mistake he'd made.

"First, I got to tell you something's gone wrong at Christy's condo. I passed a flock of black and whites." He scanned Fredo and Cooper. "And the coroner is there."

Fredo whistled. "Your lady know about it?" he asked.

"Not when I left her. But I'm betting they'll make sure she's fully clued in."

Both of them stood with their legs wide, arms folded on their chests. Watching him. They wouldn't ask and he wasn't going to tell them what they wanted to know. Just like he wasn't going to tell Christy what was really going on, either.

"If it goes bad, I want you guys to know I'll take the fall, and I'll say I acted alone. I don't want you two or Gunny mixed up in this."

"That's the most ridiculous fucking thing I've heard you say," said a voice from behind him. Gunny joined Fredo and Cooper, and now all three regarded Kyle with suspicion.

"Gunny, you shouldn't be here." Kyle didn't need another innocent's blood on his hands.

"Shut up. You're wasting time," Gunny barked back. "Cooper asked you already. What's the plan, boss?" Gunny's eyes looked surprisingly clear and blue.

# CHAPTER 24

**C**HRISTY LEANED AGAINST the door she'd just shut and closed her eyes, reliving the sight of Kyle jumping into the stairway.

*He's gone.*

When the knock came at her door, she almost opened it without checking, hoping Kyle had changed his mind. Through the peephole, she saw Sergeant Mayfield's large frame, along with the woman officer, Woodward.

She cinched her robe, put on her game face, and opened the door.

"Morning, ma'am." Mayfield was all smiles today. A little apologetic, she thought.

"Sergeant. You two like to come in?"

"Yes, ma'am," he said as he passed her. The creak of leather from his belt and all the equipment he wore sent a shiver up her spine. Woodward whispered a curt "thank you" as she passed by. Christy could smell cigarettes on her clothes.

"I made coffee a bit ago. Let me go make some more…"

"That won't be necessary, Ms. Nelson." Mayfield looked ridiculous, armed to the teeth, in the middle of her living room. His flack vest looked uncomfortable, with his arms and legs protruding from under the heavy layer like the parts of a turtle protruding from under its shell. Unnecessary protection. He didn't seem happy to be there.

"All right." She joined them and motioned for them to sit down, which they both ignored. "Okay then, would you please tell me what this is all about?"

Mayfield took out the little book from his vest pocket and flipped through white lined pages. "You know a Marla Cunningham?"

Christy found Kyle's chair and sat. Her stomach felt vacant. Her heart pounded. Little black dots began swirling around, clouding her eyesight.

"I can see you do." Mayfield was stern. Suddenly unfriendly.

"She's my trainer," Christy said as she looked up to his face. She felt all the blood rush from her cheeks.

"When was the last time you saw her?"

Christy had to think. It had been after the open house. "Sunday night. I took a spinning class from her."

"Seems that she called into a crisis hotline to report a possible attack."

"When?"

"Two days ago."

"Oh."

"You know about anyone who had a thing for Ms. Cunningham?"

"No. We never talked about *her* personal life. Just about mine."

"And so now I gotta ask you about yours. Your SEAL boyfriend…"

"Look, he's not…" But she was lying now. Kyle had said cooperate with the police. "What does *my* personal life have to do with…just what exactly are you saying? Is something wrong with Marla?"

Did she want to hear this?

"She's been found dead."

Christy's chest caved. She couldn't find the air to fill her lungs. Black spots played checkers before her eyes, obscuring the large officer and the lady.

*Dead?*

She pulled herself back together. They had not offered condolences. Both of them were watching her. She wrapped her arms around her torso to stop the shaking and the buzzing in her head that was like a dentist's drill.

"Where?"

"And what difference would *that* make?" Mayfield was cool as he frowned. Woodward was checking out Christy's pink toes.

"Well, I was supposed to meet her at the gym Thursday night. She never showed."

Mayfield and Woodward looked at each other.

"She was found in her office," Mayfield answered.

Now Christy remembered the light under the office door. Poor Marla might have been fighting off her attacker at that very moment. Christy could have helped her. But instead she'd run. Run to safety. And now her friend was dead. She had to ask the question. "And why do you think Kyle is involved?"

"I can't say, exactly, due to the investigation." Mayfield put his forefinger into his collar and stretched it loose. "Seems Marla kept a journal of her activities and sessions at the club. Her entry for Sunday night was interesting in light of what we found today."

Christy looked at the woman, who was having difficulty keeping eye contact. This was going to be bad.

"She wrote that you'd had an altercation yourself. That a crazy showed up and restrained you, and then let you go."

"It was a misunderstanding," Christy said, the defiance in her voice putting a chill in the room.

Woodward shot her a look that told her the officer had heard it before and hadn't believed it then, either.

"We're thinking it was the same person." Mayfield let it sink in. Christy was starting to get sick to her stomach.

"Why?" She had to force herself to ask it. This was not going to be something she really wanted to know.

"The method of restraint. The man who killed Marla used pantyhose."

# CHAPTER 25

MAYFIELD WAS SURPRISED to see Deputy Hilber at the crime scene, since it wasn't the sheriff's jurisdiction. The little prick from the Navy was dutifully at Hilber's side. Mayfield hoped like hell the man never applied to work in his department, and he made a note in his book to check the test roster to see if he'd qualified for consideration. Had to be some way to lose Carlisle's application, if he was stupid enough to have submitted one.

"I imagine this is a little different than checking cars at the guard shack on base, sailor." Mayfield had years of practice looking stern. The young MA might not pick up on the twinkle in his eye.

"Fascinating, sir, watching them work," Carlisle said, scanning the crew from the coroner's office, the photographer, and the forensic team. "Just like on TV."

Mayfield made a mental note this time. The guy was digging the gore and the details of a murder.

Hilber was another story. He was admiring the angle of broken fingers protruding up from the body of Marla Cunningham, whose hands were secured in place by a pair of black pantyhose. He noticed the pantyhose were tied in a bow.

*Calling card.*

This was someone who was begging them to chase after him. Well, Mayfield might just have to comply.

The coroner's assistant came over and asked Mayfield to step aside so she could take another picture of the hands. She must've seen the same thing Mayfield did.

"These were tied together after death, am I right?" Mayfield whispered to her.

She nodded and clicked the camera, which set off a bright flash.

"I know you can't say anything officially, but how long has she been dead? Guess."

"More than a day, probably two." She pointed to the excrement and fluids leaking all over Marla's desk chair, which had formed in a puddle on the floor. Marla's purple lips and chalky white skin were ghastly enough, but the white coating over her eyes was something right out of a horror film. If the perp had known her, he would have closed her eyes. With no apparent mutilation other than the fingers, it appeared this wasn't personal. And too many clues had been left to be professional.

Marla had been chosen because she'd had information. Information on Christy.

Woodward stood next to him, a handkerchief over her mouth and nose. Mayfield watched her bring out a small brown bottle with a lavender label that read *Clarity*. He'd seen several of the officers with this womanly brand of smelling salts around at the station.

"Who found her, sir?" Woodward asked through the hankie.

"The manager, when he opened this morning. I'm guessing the smell probably tipped him off."

"She died the night she made the call?"

"April here thinks so. More than twenty-four hours ago, and that was the last anyone heard from her."

He collared the coroner's assistant again. "Can I see the journal?"

The book had been wrapped in an oversized clear evidence bag, left open on the same page it had been opened to when it had been found on the desk. Mayfield put on gloves and carefully removed it.

The assistant frowned.

Hilber had lost interest in chatting up a female reporter. "What's this?" he asked, looking at the journal.

"The lady's notebook."

Hilber blanched, then furrowed his brow. "She able to name her attacker?"

"In a manner of speaking." Mayfield showed him the passage.

"*Raised security concerns today on deaf ears. Now they've gone and hired a new janitor and not told us…,*" Hilber recited.

"No. That's Thursday's entry, which she didn't finish. Look at the one for Sunday."

"*Christy Nelson has been attacked today by a crazed psycho who tied her up with her pantyhose. I tried to get her to call the police, but she seems to think there is an explanation for it. Though this happened off site, I'm going to bring it up at the next staff meeting, without naming names. Security has been lax lately."*

Hilber beamed after he read it. "You're right. All we need to do now is find the guy who attacked Christy. This lady was directing us right to the guy."

Mayfield watched Hilber's back as the man chuckled his way out to the hallway, too happy with this finding. And a long way from his jurisdiction.

He looked for the Navy guy and didn't see him anywhere.

The sergeant flipped through the day planner's address and phone numbers carefully. He found a listing for Christy Nelson, including her cell phone number and email. And her condo number: 14J. Checking back on the monthly calendar, he saw her name in the box for Thursday. And it wasn't crossed out.

He looked back at the journal entry. Would Marla have had the strength to get the book, open it up, and leave it perfectly centered on her desk, just before she died? And after the torture she'd been through, with the broken fingers, which was a specialty of the local youth gangs, would she have had the presence of mind to do this?

He thought not. More than likely it was the recipe the killer needed to stage it to look like the other attack.

Biggest question in Mayfield's mind was why Hilber was so pleased with it.

"Make sure I get prints on this," he said to the assistant as he placed the book back in a new evidence bag she handed him.

The attractive coroner's assistant stood a little close beside him, holding out her clipboard so he could deposit the cellophane wrapped package on top. He'd known she had the hots for him, but he pretended to not pay attention. God, why were women always trying to ease his pain? And they were younger women too. Still, her perfume was a welcome reprieve to the dastardly smell of rotting flesh and bodily fluids released after death.

"I can get you a copy of the report tomorrow morning, unless you need a phone interview."

"Thanks, April. I appreciate that." He did. But he didn't look her way. Wasn't fair to give her hope. Her eyes on his face and chest were soft and dewy. And dangerous. At least the part he could see. He smiled and whispered, "Thanks," to the floor.

He motioned Woodward to leave with him. They stepped out into the hallway just as Hilber ducked into the elevator. He'd just hung up his cell phone. He didn't hold the doors for them, pretending to try to push the buttons a little too late. It was a complete act. Mayfield could see Hilber shrug as the elevator doors closed and left him and Woodward standing in the hallway.

He cursed and heard Woodward giggle at his side.

"Sir, if it makes it any better, I can't stand the guy either. I mean, why is he even here?" she said.

He appreciated her sentiment.

"Probably because he's got the Feds convinced it has something to do with his murders in the Santa Nella forest. And I'm sure they are linked. Just not sure how Hilber's putting the pieces together."

"Understood, sir. So can I ask?"

"You honestly think I know?" He was pleased she thought so, but everything was swimming around and he didn't know where it landed.

"Yes. I think your instincts are the best I've ever seen. That's why I'm here. To learn, sir. If I became half the cop you are, I'd consider myself lucky."

"I thank you." He looked down at the top of her head. He'd never noticed how pretty her hair was—and what the hell was he doing? How easily a woman could get to him, still.

"I want the trash searched. Probably won't be in the gym area, but I'm guessing there's a cardboard or plastic wrapper for those pantyhose, and if I'm not mistaken, they would be a medium, the size Marla would wear. I don't know about the black, but maybe she liked the color. Someone would know. Ask her friends at the gym. They might have seen her dress up to go out. Most women would have a pair of flesh-toned hose around."

"Very good, sir. Consider it done. How about the girl? Christy. Should I ask her?"

"Nah, I'd leave her alone for now. She's spooked out of her gourd. I need her cooperative."

IN THE EARLY afternoon, Mayfield got a call from Woodward. They'd found a trash bag in the back of the complex. It contained a cellophane wrapper with one pair of black pantyhose remaining, size medium. It had been a two-pack.

And there were dustable prints all over it.

HILBER DROPPED BY Mayfield's office, without his buddy this time.

"You guys done with the Hummer yet?" Hilber looked as though he was trying to whistle or do something to look as if he wasn't as interested as he clearly was.

"Haven't heard back from forensics. Should be soon, though. Maybe tomorrow morning."

"And I'm guessing no one's called about it?"

"You mean called to claim it?"

"Yup." Hilber checked his fingernails as he leaned into the door-frame.

"That's a Roger that," Mayfield returned.

"All his equipment still logged in?"

"Everything I was given." Mayfield wondered why Warren was concerned about the guns and shit.

"Got the coroner's or crime scene reports yet?"

Mayfield wasn't going to tell him about the pantyhose wrapper they'd found. He leaned into his desk, throwing down a pen. "Hilber, suppose I refrain from asking you what the hell you're doing over here, sticking your nose into *my* business? How about you quit interfering? You'll get your goddamned report soon enough."

The cold blue stare Mayfield got froze his bones. Given the chance, this man would put a bullet in the back of his head rather than get caught.

"How did you boys in the Sherriff's Department manage to get the impound order?" Mayfield asked.

"Jurisdictional hospitality. You scratch my back, I scratch yours." Hilber had leaned back. Mayfield didn't like the man's sneer.

"Who signed it?" Mayfield wanted to know who Warren's accomplice was. He could check the records, of course, but he wanted to see the man spew it out.

"Carpenter."

Now there was another man Mayfield didn't trust. Carpenter was known to be a little heavy-handed, especially with the swabs, but he was hell on wheels with the ladies too.

He was beginning to understand the real enemy in this game.

# CHAPTER 26

T HE LITTLE TEAM was driving through a seedy part of San Diego. Fredo had given Gunny the directions to his informant's neighborhood.

"Not sure it's a good idea to be seen talking to him. Might make him shy," Fredo said.

"So call him," Cooper squawked.

"Oh, yes. Let me just call 4-1-1 and see if AT&T has the numbers to the Gang Information Directory."

"Think we'd better drop you off a few blocks away," Kyle offered.

"That's what I was thinkin'," Fredo replied.

"You wired, Fredo?" Gunny asked.

"Got my Invisio right here." He flicked his finger hard on his right ear. Coop jumped in his seat, swearing. "And Coop has the earphones, as you can see."

Cooper bore an expression as if he were going to eat the earphones or throw them out of the window.

"Ladies, please," Kyle pleaded.

They passed over several railroad tracks filled with rail cars spray-painted with colorful gang graffiti artwork. A local news crew had done a series on street art. Some of the members were talented and could have made a living as artists if the drug money wasn't so lucrative.

Surrounding buildings were in a sorry state. Everywhere there was rubble: broken bottles, broken windows. In spite of it all, a small group of five and six-year-old boys was trying to play soccer in one of the alleyways they passed. Laundry hung between windows. Dogs were barking inside apartments that had bars over the windows, many of which were boarded up or coated with tinfoil. It reminded Kyle of some of the killing zones in Afghanistan, except without all the incessant sandy dust that seemed to blow right through him. Kids played soccer there too.

But there were not many dogs. People had goats, but those weren't pets.

Gunny parked the beater where Fredo indicated. Fredo exited the truck and wandered through the rubble that was the sidewalk.

Cooper slouched back in the seat, donning his baseball cap, which covered the earphones. Kyle used a small set of binoculars he'd fished out of his pocket. Without his usual uniform, including his bulletproof vest, he felt hairless and naked. He didn't like the feeling one bit.

"You got me?" The small radio speaker squawked. Cooper was hearing it in stereo and recording it.

"Yeah, you little spic. You know there's a hole in your jeans right where your butthole is?"

Cooper and Fredo had a routine that kept them from getting nervous.

"Musta been that quickie last night." Fredo exaggerated his hip swing.

"Nah, I think it was your farts, Taco Man."

"Well, even rotting goats smell better than yours. Too many vitamins."

"I'm going to break Gunny's record. I'll be getting it up when you can't see yours."

"Okay, ladies. We got incoming," Fredo whispered.

Fredo spewed off Spanish slang no one could follow. The guy could talk faster than an automatic. He spliced in some English, and as the other speaker followed suit, they continued in English.

"Yo. I got some Franklins here for you. Thought you might want a little party. Thought I'd make a donation to your college fund, or an investment in your future," Fredo said.

"What'd you have in mind?" the male voice asked. "Minding the girls, Fredo?"

"Nah. I got that covered. Too much, as a matter of fact."

"Ain't no such thing."

"I hear you. Okay, now for the reason I'm here. Word has it you got some information, and I'm buyin."

"Didn't take you for a buyer."

"Information."

"No ladies, man? We gots the best."

"I'm saving money for a little chiquita I knocked up in LA. You feel me?"

"Shit, Fredo. It's free. They got a free clinic here."

"No free clinic. She's not legal. And I'm having this baby."

"You're having it. Thought the lady did all that."

"You know what I mean. Trying to get respectable. Make an honest woman of her."

"Get in line. They don't even ask, if you want to go the other way."

"I'm not doin' it that way. Don't want any complications. And I love the chiquita."

There was silence for a minute. Fredo pushed, "Hey, sorry man, if you're not comfortable with this. I'll just move on. What was I thinking?"

"No, it's cool. Who're you lookin' for?"

"Calls himself Caesar. Runs girls, and guns too, I hear. I need to find him, man."

"I don't know no Caesar."

"Right. And I'm not Mexican. How much?"

"Three, maybe four."

"How about one to start and then if you got more, you get more."

"Okay. He works out of his bar, the Los Ladies."

They could hear Fredo peeling off a bill and handing it to the informant. "Here's a Franklin. What else you got?"

"I'm not too comfortable with anything else. There's a guy you might want to talk to."

"He buying?"

"Maybe. He works out of Los Ladies."

Kyle rolled his eyes as he looked at Cooper. The topless bar that specialized in bathroom sex, forged papers, and drug deals. Quite the place.

"I've been there a time or two."

"But you don't ask for Caesar. You ask for his woman, Mia."

The team heard Fredo stutter. "Mia, is it? Sure, I'll ask for her."

Kyle heard the banter in Spanish and a slapping handshake. They heard the familiar crinkle of paper.

*Makes two hundred.*

Fredo questioned the male. "Hey, when was the last time you saw Caesar and this Mia?"

"Haven't seen Caesar for a few days. I've only seen Mia at the Ladies.

She dances there sometimes."

"Uh huh." They could hear Fredo breathing fast.

"He's been flashing around some green. Had a very successful few days, I'd say."

"So if he wasn't at the Ladies, where would he be? I'm kinda in a hurry."

"That's an expensive question."

"How much?"

"Another two at least."

Fredo sighed, breathing heavy into the microphone. He lowered his voice and, in a whisper, added, "Okay, this better be good. I got three hundred here. Where does the dude live?"

"He lives with his mama, and don't the fuck tell him I told you. The yellow house on Greenwich."

"I know it," Fredo said. Kyle did, too. It was a block away from Armando's mother's home.

"If you boys are smart you'd get in on this. Gonna get yourself rich, man."

"What do you mean?"

"I just thought you were going to sell something to Caesar. He's buying. Big time."

"I considered it."

"I'll bet you did. Hell of a lot more than Uncle Sam pays. You military types are sitting on a gold mine. Caesar buys the stuff cheap too. Sells it back to the gangs and makes a buttload of green."

"It's a good business model."

"Might as well secure your retirement. War's going to be over soon. You guys will be out of a job."

*Not in your dreams, dickwad.* Kyle was amazed how naïve people were, even gang-bangers.

"That's for sure." Fredo played along.

"Thanks, man. Be safe."

Kyle was worried he'd already asked too many questions. Now that they knew where Caesar was, finding Armando might not be hard. He hoped. He heard Fredo whistle as he walked back and came into view. Kyle covered him with his sidearm just in case. The informant did not accompany him.

"Gunny, get in the passenger seat. Now," Kyle barked. Gunny's frame barely made it by the time Fredo opened the driver's side door and got in.

Fredo fired up the beater, which backfired. They turned around and went back the way they'd come in.

"They're buying guns and shit all right," Fredo said in disgust. Everyone was quiet for what they knew was coming. "And they're using Mia." Fredo turned and looked at Kyle over the back of the seat. "You think she's back there already?"

"Fredo, she made her bed." Kyle said the obvious.

"The woman's like a cat with nine lives, and wasting all of them. All at once."

"Some people do that." Kyle added, "Can't help those who don't care."

Cooper was carefully winding the wires of the headset around a white plastic cone. He positioned them inside a small case that held the miniature recorder. He leaned against the window. "So what's up now, boss?"

"I gotta make a couple of calls."


KYLE HAD BEEN places that had scared him shitless. This was even more frightening. He dialed Christy, who picked up on the second ring.

"Hi there," he said.

"Kyle! Oh, my God, are you okay?"

"I'm fine." He hoped he didn't sound as nervous as he felt.

"I was worried. I still am."

He had to be careful. "I told you not to worry. I said I'd call you."

She was sniffling on her end of the line. He heard the strain in her voice as she tried to settle herself. "When can I see you?" she whispered. Her need poured all over him.

He inhaled. This was more difficult than he'd thought. Thank God he had enough sense not to go over to her condo. "Better for you if I stay away. Just didn't want you to worry."

"But the police, the sheriff, and even the Navy—everyone's been saying some...very disturbing things. I'm..."

"Don't believe them."

"But you said to cooperate with the police."

"Look, Christy, things got kind of crazy. I'm afraid I've made a terrible mistake getting you involved."

"Kyle, don't..."

"I wasn't using my head." He could do this. He told himself it was better if she got hurt now. Maybe it would send her back to San Francisco. Best place for her. Safest place right now.

"Don't say that. You know I don't feel the same way about this. I *want* to be involved."

There was no easy way out of the box he'd put himself into. Only one right thing to do, and damn, it was going to hurt her in the short run. But way better for her in the long run.

"Christy," he began, "you've got to just forget about all this. I've changed my mind about us."

The deafening silence on the other end of the phone gave him the shivers.

He continued, "I need to focus on finding Armando before it's too late."

The phone went dead.

# CHAPTER 27

NEXT MORNING, CHRISTY tried to focus on anything other than Kyle. She cleaned her condo thoroughly, even scrubbing her toilet. She cleaned her oven, which had hardly been used over the past few weeks. She tried to read one of her romance novels, and threw it across the room when she came to a love scene. She cranked some Candy Dulfer sax music up until she got a call from downstairs telling her to lessen the volume, and even kneeled on the floor and gave in to the need to just sob, to get it all out. She knew that, in time, it would get better. Everything got better in time. But today she had to occupy herself with awful things she hated doing. Just get through today.

To her amazement, she started to feel better as the Sunday morning dribbled away.

But then she got stir crazy. How long would she be confined to her apartment now that Kyle had given her the brush-off yesterday? Just because he said so, was she really now no longer involved? It sure seemed to her that the SDPD or the Sheriff's Department would still be interested in what little information she had. She had taken the call with Simms last night and had told him what had happened with the authorities and that she was done with the Navy guy. She said she would be back at work soon. He told her to take as much time as she needed and that he was sorry.

Sorry didn't begin to describe how she looked, she realized, as she washed her hands in her bathroom lavie and re-tied up her hair. She thought she had aged ten years since last she'd last examined her face. But again, she knew it would get better.

Maybe she should leave San Diego. Would she ever see a Navy jet or a ship or those well-developed bodies running down the beach and not think of him? Wouldn't it be easier to just get away from any memory of him?

But no, she wasn't made of that kind of stock. She had never been a quitter. San Francisco was a one-way street going nowhere. Her mother had given her a ticket to paradise. She'd just have to find it alone, and not in the arms of the most handsome, wonderful guy she had ever met.

*There must be someone else out there for me. I thought it was Kyle.*

But no. It wouldn't be Kyle. Not now. And this time, even if he did come back to her, she'd have to say no and mean it.

Though he was the bastard who broke her heart, she still couldn't see him as a rogue killer, like the cops said.

*No, couldn't be. I just can't go there.* For as much pain as she was feeling, she just couldn't see him killing for sport or profit. She couldn't see him killing at all. He was dangerous, yes. Dangerous in all the ways—and *here it comes again.* A flood of tears sprang up and she gasped.

*Damn.* Her mother would be furious with her. Look how she was treating her mom's gift.

Maybe she knew this would happen. Maybe she had even caused it, thinking how much it would hurt if he left. And now he had, and so it hurt. But she knew she'd survive.

Somehow.

Her phone rang.

"Hello?"

"Cherie?" Madame M's voice cheerily greeted her on the other end of the line.

"Madame! How wonderful to hear from you. How have you been?"

"Oh, très bien. Very well. Business has begun to pick up. I'm flush with customers."

Christy had a brief moment of regret for having left the woman behind. She was like a second mother to her. And now the closest thing to a mother she would have for the rest of her life.

"Christy? You are well?"

"Yes. Yes, Madame. I'm very well. My mother's place is just perfect for me. I'm enjoying real estate," she lied. "I'm still, you know, getting settled, but it's coming along."

"Oh, that's too bad."

"Excuse me?"

"Well, I was hoping you could come up here and help me for a bit."

"Oh, Madame, I can't." Then Christy thought about it.

*Why not? Kyle has just turned me out to pasture. Why shouldn't I get away from all this? If it gets worse, a little break would do me good. If it improves, well, it sure as hell wouldn't have anything to do with her. So why not?*

"Cherie, I have to go in for some surgery. I have no one here who knows our shop like you do. You should know I've not really been able to replace you…"

"Madame, that's nice of you to say, but…"

"It's true. You know my customers, you know the business. My reps still ask about you."

Christy was silent, collecting her thoughts, remembering the happy days there, those days sandwiched between the lonely ones when she knew there was more to life than catering to a bunch of rich men who bought beautiful lingerie for the women in their lives.

"Is this surgery serious?"

"Non, ma chère! Just a little female work."

Approaching sixty years of age, Madame M was the most striking older women Christy knew. How she managed to stay single after the death of her young husband, years ago, was a mystery to Christy. Madame M had offers for dates and expensive travel with eligible, wealthy men whom she turned down frequently.

"I'm holding out for a duke, a prince, or perhaps a king!" she would tell Christy. And they would laugh. Madame would ask her sometimes, "And you? Who are you waiting for?"

Well, she knew the answer to that one. She didn't expect it would hurt this much, though.

"How long will you be out?" Christy asked, not wanting to know the answer.

"Not long. About two weeks. First week I will be in hospital. Next week I must be home and then I can go back, although the doctors want me to be off for a month. Mon Dieu! I can't be gone that long."

"Do you have anyone in training now?"

"Yes, I have two very nice girls. But they are young, ma chère. Very young."

*And what am I at twenty-six? Am I old now?*

"They work for me while going to college. Neither one of them wants to go into the business."

"Ah. I see."

"Cherìe," Madame M began softly, "have you ever thought about returning to San Francisco?"

"Not really." Christy's stomach clenched up. She knew there was an offer coming she would have difficulty declining, but also knew she would.

"Would you consider coming to help out while I am infirmed, and then possibly taking over the shop some day? I would be happy to give it to you, if it became too much for me to handle. I am not a young woman any longer, you know."

That told Christy the "surgery" was more serious than she was letting on. But she had to be honest.

"Madame, there is no future for me there. I wanted a fresh start."

"I understand. I think the difference between an older woman and a younger one is an older one knows how to think practically. Young ones always go looking for love and think that will save them. The cost is too great, cherìe. Take it from me."

Christy knew exactly what Madame as saying.

"There are lots of attractive, older men who frequent my shop, and several of them ask about you. I think even one or two have come in just to see you. They could make your life comfortable and aren't so bad to look at, either. Money can heal a lot of loneliness."

*But not for me. There isn't enough money in the world to heal my wound. I have to do this myself.*

"Have I offended, ma chère?"

"No, Madame. I take no offense. I just am not interested. Can I think about this for a day or so? When is your surgery?"

"Two days. Not to worry, I have already begun to tell people the store will close for two weeks. Perhaps this is why I have been so busy lately." Madame giggled like a little girl.

Christy saw another phone call was coming in. "Madame, I must go. I'll think seriously about it and then will call you back later tonight. Is that all right?"

"Call me tomorrow?"

Christy pushed the button for the next call, but had just missed it. She hit redial. A crusty voice answered on the other end.

"Security."

"Jerry, is that you?" Christy asked.

"Oh, yes. This is Ms. Nelson?"

"Jerry, it's Christy. Is there something wrong?"

He cleared his throat. "Uh, Ms. Nelson," he started, ignoring her comment, "we've gotten some complaints, and the Co-op Association has asked me to call you about it."

"Complaints? Complaints about me?"

"Yes, ma'am."

"I'm sorry, I don't understand. What complaints?"

"You know about Marla?"

"Yes, the police were here today."

"Seems there's a sort of criminal element hanging around here since you moved in."

Christy felt like throwing the phone through the opened sliding glass door to shatter on the ground below.

"I had a chance encounter with someone…I met a man who…" Everything she started to say was wrong. "The police and the Sheriff's Department have questioned me about someone I met quite by accident." She remembered the feel of Kyle's hard body against hers as he immobilized her knees, her wrists. The smell of his faint cologne, the way his kisses tasted, the words he whispered in her ears—everything came flooding back to her.

"See, Ms. Nelson…"

"Christy. Please, Jerry, are you interrogating me too? You know who I am, what I'm about."

"Look, I need this job. They just want me to deliver a message. They're going to take a vote. I have no say in the matter. Some of the older folks are staying elsewhere. They're afraid to even return back here."

"I see. But this isn't anything I've caused."

"The police have been asking questions about you everywhere. It makes folks uncomfortable."

"Jerry, you know me."

"Like I said, I have no say so here. It's up to the Association, and they have the right to ask someone to leave if that person is attracting a criminal element." He sighed and then gave her the punch she was expecting. "They're going to vote in two days. I'm supposed to let you know they will probably be asking you to leave and that you should prepare yourself accordingly."

"They can do that?"

"Come on, Ch…er… Ms. Nelson. You know they can. Or they can make it expensive for you if you fight them. You're a Realtor. You know the CC&R's."

"But what would I do? Can they force me to sell?"

"No, but they can bar you from living here."

And there it was. Suddenly the place Kyle thought she was safest at had turned out to be the place she had to leave—*might* have to leave.

That made Madame M's offer more attractive. Only question was, would she be able to come back here? Some day?

# CHAPTER 28

SERGEANT MAYFIELD LOOKED at the flashing line on his phone that indicated he had voicemail. He hated voicemail. Reminded him of how he'd spent most of his days behind a desk. Maria would have liked the fact he was now out of harm's way more often than not, but there was that part of him the Navy hadn't drilled out of him, about wanting to be where the action was. That's why he'd wanted to fly jets, but he couldn't pass the vision tests.

He'd gone to BUD/S too, but didn't make it past Hell Week. He wondered how his life would have changed if he could have stuck with it. But he'd had a good life, even though he and Maria had never had kids. Although his current work wasn't the SEALs, he took some pride in seeing to it that young recruits turned out to be fine cops. Honest cops. And he'd seen a few of the other kind, dirty cops, where just one or two bad apples could demoralize a whole battalion. Never thought he'd have to look over his shoulder, but he learned he had to be careful. Everywhere.

Having the desk job gave him the occasional chance to right a wrong that had been done, either by one of his own or a member of the public, or on behalf of someone who'd been victimized by the system. He didn't know why, but he felt Kyle Lansdowne wasn't one of the bad guys. Christy Nelson believed in the Team guy. Mayfield saw it in her body language, as well as in her eyes. And those eyes were not the naïve doe eyes of someone with nothing upstairs. This girl was quality. Someone he knew Maria would have wanted him to find. Not this young, of course, but someone who had the same strength.

So it was a pleasant coincidence that the voicemail message was from Miss Nelson herself.

"*I'm going to leave San Diego for a couple of weeks. I can still be reached on my cell.*" There was a pause. He could tell she didn't want to leave the message. And it wasn't really for him.

"*You never told me I had to check in with you, but you seemed the only one I could trust.*"

Mayfield wondered what was up with that. Whom else had she talked to? He'd have to ask Jones, Theissen, and Woodward if they'd done a second round of questioning. He doubted it, though.

"*A friend of mine is sick in San Francisco, and I'm going to go there and run her shop while she's recovering. I'll be staying at a little cottage at 484 Stanyan Street. My cell is the best way to reach me, though.*" She left her cell number and hung up.

He smiled. San Francisco brought wonderful memories of the honeymoon he and Maria had there, back in the late eighties. He could have lived there, but Maria didn't want to be far from her family in Mexico. Even after many of them came to the States or had died, his career was in full swing in San Diego, and then *he* was the one who didn't want to move.

He marked down Christy's new address on his vest pocket notebook, then programmed her number into his cell in case she called back. He didn't want to leave a written copy of that around. For some reason, he felt protective of her.

The second voicemail was from a Chief Petty Officer Timmons, Kyle's boss.

"*Got a couple of things I need to discuss, off the record. If you don't mind calling me back on my cell…*"

Now that was interesting, he thought. He knew he was about to find out for sure whether Kyle was a good guy or a bad guy.

THEY'D AGREED TO meet at Jimmy's. Mayfield knew it well, although not entirely on nostalgic terms like some of its patrons. He'd done his share of arrests for drunk and disorderly conduct, but mostly he'd cleaned up the civilian garbage and let the Navy take care of theirs. But there was always some guy who thought he was better and stronger than a soft-spoken SEAL who shied away from local conflict. All the same, there was a limit, Mayfield knew. And once that line was crossed, well, someone would go to the hospital, and it usually wasn't the swab.

That's why this situation bothered him so much. Bodies. Not your normal Navy incident. So Mr. Lansdowne was either a very misunderstood guy or one hell of a bad dude. Either way, this was messy. Too messy for a guy who needed his pension to retire on in five years.

But, he'd always taken the high road. And Maria had often reminded him why she'd married him: he always did the right thing, even if it wasn't always the smartest in terms of his career advancement. True to her word, her last words to him were, "I love you. I will miss you May Day." She knew he loved to hear her call him this. Her private name for him, stemming back to the first time she'd seen him. She'd told him she knew instantly her life would never be the same afterwards.

*God, I miss you too, Maria.* But he'd promised her he wouldn't mope around. He wished they'd had children. She was insistent it was something wrong with her, but he had his doubts. He'd figured it was something related to his Navy service. She never once complained about being "unfulfilled" like other women would say on TV. If it was a burden to her, she carried it alone.

But he wished something of her remained. Just something.

Soft rock and roll was playing on a radio back in a dark corner. Posters and pictures of Teams on the beach and in Africa, original artwork, and T-shirts signed by Teams all adorned the lower part of the walls. Above all the memorabilia and posters, now occupying both sides of the narrow bar, were row upon row of flags with pictures underneath them. "Fallen Heroes," the sign read. As he studied the faces in the mostly black and white photos, he noted how good looking almost every single one of those men were. And how young. Heck, they looked like kids he'd played football with in high school. Kids he could have had.

But that was because he was in his fifties, and war was a young man's sport. And these young, brave men had given their lives so he could have a desk job in the sunny warm weather of San Diego, so he could finish out his life in comfort and retire to contemplate the death of his wife. So he could have a future he wasn't exactly sure he wanted anymore. But because they gave up theirs, he would do the best he could.

Timmons looked like he sounded on the phone, gnarly and mostly grumpy, with a ruddy pockmarked complexion and beefy hands with sausage fingers. His biceps and shoulders hovered like the guns they were, perched over rock-hard abs. He didn't seem to be the kind of man you wanted to be around when he wasn't having a good day. Mayfield shook hands with him and realized that, under different circumstances, they could have been brothers. Mayfield's fingers got crushed in the vise grip Timmons delivered without flinching or straining a muscle.

"Thanks for coming, Mayfield," Timmons said while he hailed the waitress. "I know you're busy, so I'll buy you a burger and a beer if you'll share one with me."

"No thanks. I had a peanut butter and jelly sandwich at my desk. And I don't drink on duty." Mayfield studied the bluish purple bags under Timmons's eyes.

"We gotta talk," Timmons said after he ordered a cheeseburger and fries to go with the beer he had started. He nodded to two muscled young men who walked in and took up a seat at the bar to watch a game on the big-screen monitor.

"I've never had a SEAL turn rogue. I've trained some crazy-assed men, though."

Mayfield nodded and sipped on a diet Coke the waitress brought.

"Despite what the papers have said, I don't think there's been more than a handful. Certainly nothing like any of the other branches," Mayfield replied.

"None of these special ops guys go evil, but they do get snagged with money problems occasionally. Compromised, but not often. I worry about the ones who almost get through the training and then quit. Not because they can't do it—they quit sometimes because they decide they don't want to. And there's no shame in that. There are a few where the training just picks a scab, opens up an old wound, and they are so filled with hate they can't function and are never the same. We get only a few a year. And it's the part of the training I don't care for. Letting those young guys loose on society."

"Those guys become my problem," Mayfield said.

"I'm sure they do."

"So you called me over this afternoon to apologize?"

Timmons chuckled and cocked his head, as if regarding Mayfield's casual demeanor. "I met you once before, you know?"

"Sorry. Don't remember."

"You'd come by to pick your wife up at the hospital where my kid was. Your wife took real good care of my Cassie when she fell from a horse and broke her arm."

That had been another irony. Maria had worked as a nurse on the children's ward. It was difficult for her when she lost one of her charges, Mayfield thought, almost as bad as losing one of her own. He didn't remember meeting Timmons.

"I'm sure she did a great job. She was known for it."

Timmons looked up at him quickly. "Was?"

"She died almost a year ago."

"I'm sorry to hear that."

"Don't be. Got almost thirty years with her. I'm the lucky one."

Timmons mumbled something before he took another sip of his beer. Mayfield got the impression his marriage wasn't as special. But the man had a kid. And that was something he could take pride in. And live for.

"We could sit here and reminisce, but there are people after someone you and I both know will need help if he's to get out of this jam," said Mayfield.

"So you believe Kyle." It was more of a statement than a question.

"Never met him. But I saw his lady. She's a nice package. Perfect for him."

"And I've never met *her*. I'm sorry to say he's had to distance himself from her," Timmons said flatly.

"I know about it. She told me the same."

Mayfield looked at the walls around them, the history of the lives lost and lives lived to the maximum, the rush of history and years of joy, years of pain. There they were, two men with very different tastes, needs, and desires, on two different career paths. But both with the same focus.

To get Kyle out of this mess. And find his Team buddy.

And like members of his team years ago when he was running little boats down the beach, Mayfield knew the team he and Timmons had set up today was dependent on both of them giving their all for the cause.

And that would be the only way any of them would survive.

# CHAPTER 29

T HE DRIVE FROM San Diego to San Francisco was easy, especially since Christy decided to break the monotony of the nine-hour trek by listening to a book on tape. It was a steamy romance by one of her favorite authors. She was in tears when she pulled up for gas mid-way, as she had just listened to a breakup scene. She knew the reason the story had affected her more than it might have ordinarily. Kyle was probably history, a not-too-pleasant part of her past, when he should have been the best part of her future.

She couldn't stop herself from missing him and felt her wound get deeper the more she thought about it.

Four hours later, when she arrived in San Francisco at the huge house on Stanyan Street, she felt a part of her had arrived home. Tom Bergeron kept this place for clients he entertained who came from outside the country. He'd agreed to let Christy stay there until she got herself settled—whatever that meant.

Tom was one of the handsomest older men she had ever met. He frequented Madame M's shop, which had become kind of a liaison between eligible men and the young ladies looking for them. That was part of the service Madame loved: being a matchmaker. Everyone on the Peninsula knew Madame liked to keep her customers paired with partners who liked expensive lingerie and a healthy sex life. It was, after all, good for business.

Tom was in his mid-fifties, had graying hair, a trim physique, and a nice, soft-spoken, well-educated style. He could afford the finer things in life. He'd made no secret he liked Christy, but he had just married a former model and had a lavish yacht wedding on the San Francisco Bay. Over the three years Christy had worked at the shop, she would hold up little frilly things he bought for some of his gorgeous, high-profile girlfriends, and later, his beautiful wife. But he always flirted with Christy, making her blush. She actually enjoyed it.

"You're a good girl, Christy. I hope you find someone who will treat you like the lady you are," he'd said one day as she wrapped a lacy purple bra and thong set in matching purple tissue. When she'd looked up into his cool blue eyes, she'd known he would be someone she might have broken the rules for. Maybe marrying an older man could work, she'd thought that day.

But then she'd realized that was folly. She wanted a family.

Since Tom was now happily married, staying at his cottage behind the main house on Stanyan Street didn't pose a problem for her. Though she didn't need it, the thought of having a protector was a pleasant one. She trusted Tom.

She parked her red Honda on the street, the hood pointing downhill, the tires curbed. She removed her bag, then walked up the brick and cobblestone steps alongside the driveway and rang the doorbell at the main house. The front porch was the size of her condo's kitchen; its large columns and half-walled wooden railings allowed an expansive view of the bay below.

Tom came to the front door, barefoot and in jeans and a light blue shirt, which was buttoned a little low, Christy thought. He had a glass of red wine in his hand. As he opened the large glass and metal sculptured door, she heard jazz coming from inside and caught the faint smell of fresh soap.

"Christy. Lovely to see you again." He took her hand and kissed it tenderly.

Her back was ramrod straight as her knees buckled from his attentiveness. She was conscious of his breathing, the tanned skin with a light dusting of hair on his well-formed chest.

"Thank you, Tom. I appreciate this."

"Please," he said as he gestured to the rest of his kingdom. He grabbed her bag as she passed him.

He collected grandfather clocks, and the incessant clicking of small metal pieces inside massive wooden chests was both stimulating and reassuring. Measured. Organized. Tom had an attention to detail unlike any other man she had ever met.

Except one.

Across thick deep burgundy carpeting, she walked down the walnut-paneled hallway and into the kitchen at the rear, which overlooked a peaceful garden with a running water fountain. The music, the bubbling water, the smell of basil and tomato coming from the stove, all felt like a stage had been set. And so she asked.

"Where is Johanna?"

Tom's back was turned as he got down two plates from his upper cabinet without asking Christy if she wanted supper. He was going to make it for her anyway. "Gone," he said to the cabinet.

"Gone?" she asked.

"She's left me, Christy."

"I'm so sorry, Tom."

"Don't be." He looked up and smiled. "She was not wife material."

Maybe Christy's radar was set higher than normal, but there was something else behind his eyes that he did not say.

Christy stumbled on a couple of responses she couldn't finish.

Tom interrupted her. "She neglected to tell me she intended to keep one or two of her close girlfriends, and I didn't want to share."

"Girlfriends? You mean boyfriends, right?"

"No. You heard me right. Guess I didn't do a very good job qualifying." Tom sighed. "Remember when I taught you about qualifying being the most important part of the sales process?"

Had she asked the right questions of Kyle when she'd had the chance? The vision of Kyle's tattooed arms holding another woman's body loomed large and she felt her stomach lurch as tears painfully forced their way to her eyes.

Tom was perceptive. In an instant he was in front of her, holding her face between his massive warm hands, wiping her tears away with his thumbs. "Madame M has told me about your SEAL, Christy. Perhaps…" His hands were trembling slightly. He licked his lips and continued. "Perhaps we could heal each other…" He bent to kiss her in what she knew would be a tender kiss, but she just couldn't do it. She turned away from him and broke free.

"Sorry. If…if…Madame…," she began.

"No. That was me, just being a man seeing a beautiful woman in pain. I want to help." He went back to the plates, turned, and said softly, his eyes downturned, "Forgive me."

God, there was nothing to forgive! Was she nuts?

"Thank you, but your apology is not needed. I'm overly sensitive right now. But I'll land on my feet eventually. I always do." She gave a brittle, victorious smile he didn't buy, and watched him dish up a tossed green salad next to a red pasta dish.

"Come. We'll eat, have a glass of wine, and then I'll take you to the cottage so you can take a hot bath and fall asleep, okay?"

Of course she was okay with that. Who wouldn't be?

They ate at the formal dining room with large picture windows, over-looking the sight of the city at dusk. It was unusually fogless. Lights began to twinkle as the sky overhead turned deep turquoise.

The food was perfect. The wine was perfect. The man sitting before her was perfect, except he wasn't Kyle. She wondered why she couldn't just lose herself in the moment, let Tom care for her, heal her, as he had said. But she couldn't.

"So, how is your real estate career going?" he asked as he looked at her lips from across the table.

"Good. I was just holding my first open house—well, it was actually sort of a fiasco—I mean..." She couldn't finish. "Oh, I've just been making all the mistakes a newbie agent makes."

"Then you are learning, if you know they are mistakes."

"It is a cutthroat business. People are only too kind to let you know when you've screwed up," she finally said.

"I understand completely. When I was actively selling, I knew how those offices could be. Can't say I miss it."

"Once I build a little confidence, I'll be okay. I'm just not sure what I'm doing yet. I don't want to waste someone else's money."

"Yes. I used to tell people I'd made all the mistakes with my own money first, so I ought to be good with theirs."

Christy laughed.

"You have a condo, Madame M tells me."

"Yes. My mother left it to me. It's a nice place, overlooking the water, the boats, Coronado Island."

"And you will think of your SEAL friend when you look at the is-land?"

Christy blushed and looked down at her lap. Her fingers smoothed over crease lines of the ironed linen monogrammed napkin that matched the tablecloth. Her fingers couldn't stop the little tenting of the fold. She felt the heat from her body radiating through to her palm. She looked up and Tom was studying her, his head slightly tilted. Handsome, available. Waiting for her move. She smiled as she thought of Madame M's favorite saying, so repeated it to him.

"Better to have loved and lost than never to have loved at all."

At first he didn't react, but after noticing an extra flutter of his eyelids, she could see she had speared him in a most delicate place. Where he hurt. He inhaled and raised his crystal wine glass to her.

"To our broken hearts, then."

IT WOULD HAVE been easy to fall into the rhythm of this household, she thought as she walked into the two-story living room with her glass of port. The antiques, the clicking of the well-timed clocks, the sounds of foghorns over the bay, the glistening lights of the bridges and water at moonlight were pleasant details of a life she could have. What was there not to love about the man who stood behind her, but just far enough away so as not to intrude? She could feel his heat, feel his desire, and knew she could heal him at the cost of herself.

But that is what this relationship with Tom would be, sacrificing herself for something that didn't make her whole. She'd always had her standards. But now she had a taste of what her life could be like, and this wasn't it. She could pass all this up for a picnic on a park bench or a ride in a rusty rowboat powered by arms she longed for to hold her. For a cup of chowder or sandwich at a bar that held pictures of fallen heroes on its walls.

"I'm tired. I'd like to turn in," she said.

His grave response was, "Yes."

He followed behind, carrying her bag as she walked the brick path to the cottage. The fire was lit. Through open French doors, she couldn't help but notice the bed had a centered view of the flames. She heard her bag drop to the floor. His hand was on her shoulder, and he turned her, but did not step closer.

"If you change your mind, I will leave the back door open, Christy," he said softly. He bent, held her face between his hands, and kissed both cheeks. "Goodnight."

And he was gone.

Her fingers fumbled as she placed her bag on the bed and started to unzip it. She removed her toiletry kit, and then hooked it on a custom gargoyle loop above the white marble vanity top in the adjoining bath. She poured a generous portion of lavender bath gel into the two-person tub and turned on the water. She stripped off her traveling clothes, then walked naked to her bag and took out her sets of black pants and stretchy tops like Madame M liked her to wear and hung them up. She put her hair up in a ponytail and stepped into the warm bath water, and melted.

The full moon hung heavy over the arched window as she lay her head back against the cool marble. It was the same moon Kyle would see.

If he looked up.

# CHAPTER 30

KYLE BROUGHT THE Karl Gustav and its deadly ammunition to Gunny's gym to stash in an old bank safe he kept there. They were running out of places to stay. Coop's motor home was under surveillance, Gunny's truck was going to be impounded sooner or later, and Gunny was a fugitive from the hospital, thanks to the trio. They were running out of time.

Fredo's apartment was in a low-rent district down the strand, under the freeway. They sat out on his veranda amid the deafening sound of cars while they ate pizza Fredo had ordered. Kyle looked up and noticed the full moon in the cloudless sky. He couldn't help but think of her. And wondered what she was doing right now.

"I guess Mia's going to be okay," Fredo started in.

"Yeah? How'd you find that out?" Cooper said.

"Stopped by today. She looks good, man."

Kyle smiled. He was sure Fredo was recalling what Mia had looked like naked, even though she'd been suffering from the burns of the explosion. Fredo was smitten. No doubt about it.

"I'm sure she appreciated the company. How was Mama?" Kyle said to Fredo's smirk.

"They were arguing something fierce when I walked in. Cops were interested in her too, until she told them I was her cousin."

"Kissing cousins, I'd say," Cooper continued.

Fredo threw his wadded napkin in Cooper's face.

"Gunny, you want some pizza? Better hurry up, or it'll all be gone," Kyle shouted over the traffic din through the opened sliding glass door. The older man had locked himself in the bathroom and was coughing.

Gunny's hacking and coughing continued, accelerating.

"He's not too well," Fredo announced.

"I think we should take him home. I don't want him to drive," Kyle said.

"I heard that," Gunny said as he approached. "You boys are going to nursemaid me to death. I'm fine. I think we need to start focusing on Armando."

Kyle told them about the conversation he'd had with Timmons after Detective Mayfield's meeting. "They think he's still alive, but the gang will step up the play. They haven't gotten what they want yet."

"What does Timmons think they want?" Fredo asked Kyle.

"Not what. Who. He thinks they want me."

"That explains why Carlisle is so interested," Coop added.

"You think they trashed Armando's house for the guns?" Gunny asked.

"Absolutely. And I think they want more. Think I'll trade them guns for Armando."

"He'd never let that happen," said Fredo.

"And that's why we have to get to him first."

Kyle's cell phone rang. He didn't recognize the number. "Hello?"

"Kyle Lansdowne?"

"Yes."

"This is Detective Mayfield of the San Diego Police Department. I've spent most of the morning working on a case I think you're involved in. There's been a murder in the gym at the Infinity Building."

Kyle's stomach churned. He stood quickly. "Who?" He didn't want to know, but he had to find out. He noticed Cooper and Fredo had locked eyes with him.

"Not her," Mayfield said. "The deceased is a trainer, name's Marla. You know her?"

"No."

"I think she was a friend of Ms. Christy Nelson. I'm sure you know her."

"Yes. Yes, I do."

"Look, Mr. Lansdowne, I've spoken to Timmons. We're all on the same team here, but I got people all over my ass. This is the fourth body to show up, and you are the prime suspect."

Kyle took a big breath and then exhaled. He didn't know what to say. Cooper and Fredo were still on alert.

"But I'm not buying it, son," Mayfield continued.

Kyle was relieved. "Thank you, sir. So what's your theory?"

"Rather feels like flushing a rabbit out of a briar patch. They're trying to scare her, make her do something stupid. I think they're hoping she'll go find you."

"Ain't going to happen," Kyle said.

"Come again?"

Kyle looked at his buds and then answered Mayfield. "They won't find me through her. We broke it off."

"You know that, Timmons knows that and told me the same. But they don't."

"I thought her condo at the Infinity was the safest place for her."

"I'd normally agree. But these guys aren't amateurs. And they don't care how much publicity they stir up or who they hurt."

"Why are you calling me?" Kyle wasn't sure he could do anything to help. "You know I shouldn't go near her. Even with the murder, I still think that building is the safest place for her."

"Yeah. Except she isn't here."

Kyle swore under his breath. No one else said a word or made a sound.

"Where is she?"

"I'm not going to say. Not sure it's safe. Besides, you just said you shouldn't be anywhere near her. Let's just keep it that way."

"So what are you proposing?"

"You need to get yourself caught. You gotta be the bait."

"No way."

"They're going to find you, Kyle."

"Not unless I find them first."

"Son, you are thinking with the wrong part of your anatomy. If they don't find you, they'll get her, and if that fails, they'll kill her and your buddy too. She's safe right now, but I'd say you've got about twenty-four hours. That's it."

"Where is she?"

"Not telling."

"She in San Diego?"

"She's not at her condo, if that's what you mean. Someone has been, though. The place is a mess."

Kyle looked at Fredo and Cooper. Both SEALs were watching his face. Ready for anything.

"Look, Kyle. You've got to stop thinking about rescue here. Leave that to us. That's why I'm not telling you. You need to get yourself caught so we can track you. Can you do that, son?

"I'm not sure."

"Well, get sure. Find a way. I got no other way to do it."

Kyle knew he needed to find Christy. If they couldn't find him, they'd go after her. Mayfield was wrong. Christy was the bait. And he wasn't anywhere around her now.

That was going to have to change. Nothing he could do tonight. He'd go see Simms in the morning. If he couldn't get Christy's location from Mayfield, Christy might have told her employer.

Gunny's lumpy couch was going to be home tonight. As he stretched out, he stood up and looked at the almost full moon, bathing everything in a chalky highlight that glowed. Blue-white flashes from the television inside Gunny's added strobes of light to the outside porch. He knew she must have gone to San Francisco.

But where?

IN THE MORNING, Kyle woke up with a sore back. Gunny was sawing logs and had fallen asleep in the recliner with all his clothes on. They had stayed up to watch some wrestling show on late night TV since Kyle couldn't sleep.

He left a note for Gunny and took the beater off the island into San Diego, pulling up to the Patterson Realty office at eight-thirty. In the parking lot across the street he sat and watched, noting Simms was the first to arrive and was checking his watch. Kyle slipped in behind the man, causing Simms to jump as Kyle addressed him.

"Hello, Mr. Simms. I'm looking for Christy."

Simms scurried backward until he slammed himself up against the reception countertop.

"Look, I won't tell a soul you were here. Please, I have a family…"

Kyle swore. "I'm not here to cause any problems for you. I want to protect Christy. She's in danger."

"That's because of you."

"No, that's because some people are trying to mess with me. But I think they'll go after her next."

"Look, I don't know anything."

Kyle stepped closer to the man, who looked like he was going to pee in his pants. "I think you do. I think you know exactly where she is. She has no idea she's in danger."

"Well, why don't you call her then, if…if she'll take your call?"

"I'd like to do that from your phone, if I may." He directed Mr. Simms to go down the hallway, following behind.

"My phone? Here?" Simms asked at the entrance to his office.

"Yes."

"So she'll think it's me?"

"Yes."

"She said you two had broken up. She wouldn't be seeing you any-more."

"That's true."

"You'd better leave all this to the police. They're after you, you know. Came in here with questions."

"I'll bet."

They could hear one of the secretaries arriving. She busied herself, humming a tune, and began brewing coffee and turning on lights. She stopped short when she saw Kyle's hulking frame leaning against the doorway of the manager's office.

"Morning, ma'am."

She blushed, flustered and muttering something to herself, and then headed in the opposite direction.

"I'm not here to hurt anybody," Kyle repeated.

Simms pushed his phone across the desk so that the keypad faced Kyle. He had her cell number memorized. He dialed, heard the familiar ring. When he heard the recording of her voice, his throat became parched. He hung up right after the beep, not leaving a message.

"She'll call you back. Ask her where she's staying. I'm going to call you later and you're going to give me that address, Simms."

Simms frowned.

"For her own safety, you'll give me her address. I swear to you I would never hurt her."

Simms fell back into his chair, resigned. "Give me your number. I'll call you the instant I hear from her."

"Thank you." Kyle wrote his published cell number on a slip of memo paper. "I don't usually answer this, so leave me a message. If you get a call from me, it won't look like any number you're used to."

"Got it."

If he couldn't get it from Simms, he'd have to try to convince Sergeant Mayfield. But he wanted to stay clear of the locals. Now the hard part was starting. The waiting.

# CHAPTER 31

S IMMS WAS RELIEVED the SEAL was out of his office. He waited until he saw the soldier exit the parking lot in an old green truck with red Forest Service logos. He locked the front door.

"Stacey, I'm calling the police. Let in only people you know."

"And the police," she quipped.

He didn't have time for her backhanded challenge today, but made a note to talk to her about her attitude. He went straight to his office and picked up the phone. He fumbled a card from his middle desk drawer and dialed.

"Yeah?"

"This Deputy Hilber?"

"Who's this?" The deputy said without confirming.

"This is Carl Simms. I'm manager at the Patterson Realty office in San Diego. You asked me to call you if I heard from Kyle Lansdowne."

"Yes. So I take it you have?"

"He was just here."

"Where's that exactly?"

"Here. In my office. I'm the *manager* at Patterson…"

"Yes, yes," Hilber interrupted. "I *got* it now. Okay, what did he want?"

"He wanted to know where Christy was."

There was silence on the other end of the line. Then Simms heard a woman's voice in the background and the sound of what could be rustling sheets. He continued, "I'm sorry if I woke you up, sir. I get into the office early and…"

A hand muffled the phone, but Simms could hear the deputy swearing at someone, and a woman giggling in response.

*Probably caught him having sex with his wife.*

"No problem, Simms. I'm all ears now. So, he asked about... Ouch! God dammit. Fucking stop that." Hilber lowered his voice and said, "Excuse me," to Simms. "Having a little problem here on the home front, if you catch my drift."

Simms got quiet. Maybe he shouldn't have called. He'd never spoken to his wife like that. Ever.

"Officer Hilber, Lansdowne doesn't know where Christy is. Neither do I, but I can find out, and he wants me to. Didn't want to call from his own phone. Used mine here at the office. That sound fishy to you?"

"Absolutely. Do you have the number he called?"

Simms pushed down on the silver button at the middle of the headset. A phone number displayed in red digital numbers. He recognized it as Christy's cell. He gave it to the deputy.

"Good. This helps. When you find out her location, let us know first, okay? We need to give her some protection before he gets to her. It also would be a great way to catch him."

"You think he would harm her?"

"Look Simms, he's already killed four. He has the taste of blood in his mouth. He'll do it again."

"But I think he cares about this woman."

"I'd say more like he's obsessed. And maybe he's trying to cover his tracks. God only knows what info she has on him. Look, Simms, I don't think I have to tell you that these men are trained dogs. They are trained not to care about anything or anyone in order to do their jobs. But this isn't fucking Afghanistan."

It was partially true, Simms thought. But he'd never seen a SEAL member hurt a civilian. There were some stories about it, though, especially among the haters in the San Diego community. There were always a few of those.

"Anything else?" Hilber sounded impatient.

"No, sir. Just trying to be a good citizen," Simms answered. "What do I tell him when he calls?"

"Don't give the address to him when you get it. Don't call him back. Just call me."

"Oh. What happens if he comes back over here?"

"Call the locals. Geez, Simms, use your fuckin' head. Look, I gotta go. You got more questions than a schoolgirl on her first date."

"Just trying to cooperate fully, as you asked."

"Well, we thank you for that. Talk to you soon, then—oh, say, did you happen to notice what car he was driving?"

"Truck. Green truck with a red official logo on the door. Never seen it before today."


SIMMS GLANCED OVER contracts he was supposed to review this morning. He couldn't concentrate and had to read over everything twice. He'd wasted five minutes. He was seeing letters and numbers, but none of it was making any sense. Like this situation with Christy.

The secretary appeared at his doorway.

"There's a crowd outside the front door. They're wondering if we're going out of business."

"I told you to let in people you knew. Christ, I don't want to lock out my own agents."

Simms was irritated. He needed this little wrinkle like he needed the mumps. He made a mental note to fire Stacey at his first opportunity. After all this crap with Christy was over.

Stacey was still looking down at her shoes.

"Well, go ahead and let them in, or is there something else?"

"I want a word with you later, Mr. Simms."

*Fine. Leave me alone.* He grinned. "I'd be happy to speak with you after I return a few phone calls and review these contracts." He pointed to a stack about a foot high, all files he was supposed to review and sign off on.

He heard her heels *clickity-clack* down the tiled hallway and then heard the turn of the lock on the Patterson Realty front door.

Simms poured himself into the contracts again.

Christy was such a levelheaded lady, he thought. Not one to pick some loser rogue military guy. She seemed to be able to slice through people nicely without them knowing they'd been outmatched. Wayne Somerville had discovered that. Yet, she did it in such a way that Wayne was only too willing to come to her beck and call the instant she request-ed it. There was talent there, strength of personality and something else sorely lacking in his profession: she cared about people.

The phone rang and it startled him.

"Mr. Simms, this is Christy. You called me this morning when I was in the shower. Your message didn't record."

Of course she would assume it was an error, not a trap. Her basic faith in human nature was key to who she was.

"Christy, I gotta have your address, since you're not sure how long you'll be gone. I could use the address of the shop, if you want." Simms felt like a complete jerk.

"No. No, I don't want Madame M to get mixed up in this, and somehow that will happen if I start giving her address out. I'm staying at 484 Stanyan Street. I think the zip is 94117."

"Great. Thanks. I'll keep it in my file here in case I need it. So how long do you think you'll be, or do you know yet?" He asked this for his own sake of mind.

"Haven't talked to Madame M this morning. She's supposed to pick me up for breakfast."

"Oh, great. So you are okay?"

"Yes." She paused. Would she feel obligated to further explain? Something else was there, in the tone of her voice, as she continued, "I think the change of pace will be good for me right now."

"Much as I wish you were back here, I have to agree with you," Simms said. "You need any help on any of your work?"

"No. I gave Wayne my two buyer leads, but would you check on him? I'm thinking he won't be the exact fit for those clients. He's so different than I am, you know."

*Tell me about it.*

"Christy, why didn't you call me? I could have helped."

"Fact is, those two guys from the Sheriff's Department, well one from the sheriff's office and one Navy guy, surprised me. Just showed up on their own without announcing themselves. I just felt a little uncomfortable with them, being alone."

"So you called Wayne? Not me?"

Christy gave a nervous laugh. "He called me." Her voice faded on the other end of the line, then returned. "I asked Wayne to come over, sort of for protection. I knew he'd come right away. And I know how busy you are…"

"No problem. Just call me instead, okay?"

"Thank you. It's nice to know I have people around me I can trust."

Simms had a sharp pain in his gut. Felt like a hot poker of regret. And shame. He didn't want to tell her about Kyle, but felt he should.

"Christy, I haven't been entirely honest with you. Your Navy guy made that call."

"What?"

"He came by this morning, telling me you were in danger."

"And?"

"He demanded to know where you were."

Cold silence.

"Mr. Simms, I have to go. But please, please do not tell him where I'm staying."

"Don't worry. I won't. You can count on that."

"Don't even tell him I'm in San Francisco, or he'd figure it out."

"Right."

"Thanks for telling me. Keep the address private. Tell no one."

"I won't," he lied.

"Thanks for looking out for me. I appreciate it." She hung up.

Simms tapped the pad that had her address written on it. He had a choice to make and neither option facing him was good. One got him more involved and perhaps put Christy in danger. The other allowed someone he clearly didn't trust to have information he wasn't sure should be given out. He'd always believed in law enforcement. Maybe this sheriff was just a quirky guy with some unusual habits. Maybe that was what he was picking up from the man.

But one thing was for sure. He didn't want to mess with the Sheriff's Department. And the Navy should be taking care of their own. He dialed Warren Hilber.

"Got the address." He gave it to Hilber and got a curt thank you. Before the phone went dead, Simms knew he'd made a big mistake.

# CHAPTER 32

C HRISTY DRESSED AND waited. She'd decided to wear her new black stretch pants and a new pair of patent leather, four-inch spiked heels. When she used to work at the little shop, walking all day on tiptoes had made her top heavy and she had to press out her chest to keep her balance. By the end of the day her calves would ache, but she loved the way they felt.

She recalled what Madame M had said when she first told her of the shoes requirement. "I like the high heels because it simulates a woman's legs in orgasm. It brings sexual tension, and sexual tension is good for lingerie sales."

At first, it made Christy blush. But she eventually got comfortable with the look and feel of the shoes.

Madame was right about the impact it had on shop sales. The male customers didn't seem to mind when she accidentally bumped her chest against them.

To complete today's outfit, she wore a red stretch oversized top that showed off her soft ample bosom and matched the color of her flaming red lipstick.

She observed Tom's kitchen door was open, revealing a shiny inner screen door.

*Inviting.* Welcoming her to come into his house. She hadn't taken him up on his offer of last night.

Her cell phone chirped.

"Hello?"

"Cheríe, are you up? Refreshed?"

"Yes ma'am. Been up for awhile now."

Madame giggled. "I am so glad you are in town. You have spent some quality time with Mr. Bergeron?"

"Yes. He cooked me dinner last night. I was tired and turned in early afterward."

Madame giggled again.

"Alone. I went to bed alone." Christy didn't want to offend her former boss, but she needed to make it clear where she stood. "You didn't tell me about his divorce."

"Oui. I thought he should be the one to tell you, if he wished. And I see he has."

"Yes."

"C'est bien. I will be over in about twenty minutes. Tom told me he is cooking breakfast for us, if that is all right with you. I am running a little late, and a restaurant trip would make us even later."

"Fine." But Christy couldn't deny the knot in her stomach.

She walked across the brick patio that gurgled with water sounds from two fountains. Bright multi-colored lilies stood at attention along the path and gave off a heady aroma. She stopped and inhaled the glorious scent, filling her head with toxic thoughts of Kyle and how much she missed his hard flesh next to hers. How much she missed his kisses. How much she missed the way he used her body to bring them both such pleasure.

She opened the screen door and stepped into a kitchen filled with cooking smells and the light lacing of jazz in the background. Tom was in faded blue jeans with another blue shirt, buttoned low. But he had a flowered apron on, and that made her chuckle. He turned and flashed her a smile right out of GQ, holding a green spatula in his right hand.

"Wow. You are a vision, Christy. I'm...I'm speechless." He took a long, lingering look down the entire length of her body and back up, his eyes hungry. She hadn't dressed for him, but for Madame M's customers. But she liked it that he found her attractive. She couldn't help it. He wasn't bad to look at either.

She smiled, which pleased him.

"Thanks for cooking breakfast for us. Madame M just called. She's on her way now."

"Yes, I know. She called me too." He remained fixed in place, the utensil held like the Statue of Liberty's torch.

Christy cocked her head. "You guys are conspiring. I can tell."

He set down his spatula and stood in front of her. She could feel his body's heat. "It's a deadly game. I needed her help."

"You?" she asked, stepping back to a cool distance.

He looked at his feet and slid his palms into his front pockets, then shrugged his shoulders. "I had hoped you would come see me last night." He raised his blue eyes to hers. They watered. He licked his lips and focused on hers. She wished now she was wearing pink, not red.

"Tom." Christy stopped. Her words were going to come out harsh, and that wasn't what she wanted. "Look, I thought I made myself perfectly clear last night. I'm not interested in a relationship right now."

"But we already have one."

She looked down.

*I've used this line. Places reversed.*

She looked back up at him and studied his kind face. She could have loved him, at another time and place. But not now. Not after meeting Kyle.

"Yes, and I'd very much like to keep that friendship, if that is possible. I'm grateful for your generosity, Tom, for letting me stay here. But let's not get carried away."

It was hard to look at him. His tanned and lean body came close again. He held her face in his hands as he bent down. She was afraid he would kiss her, and she knew she would break away. Could he feel how her spine went stiff?

"I'm sorry, Tom." She placed her hands over his. She tried to reflect back to him the kindness she saw in his eyes. Without the need.

He pulled her body to his chest and embraced her. "Not to worry, Christy. Just know that I am here." He kissed the top of her head, and whispered, "But just give me a chance to make you happy."

She nodded to his chest. But these were not the arms she wanted to be enveloped in.

*Will I ever be able to forget him?*

They dropped their arms and the awkward silence forced them both to smile. Something was smoking on the stove. He ran to the smoking pan of bacon, which was spattering all over the stovetop. He reached up and turned up the six-foot stainless steel commercial hood fan.

"I know this isn't good for you. But I love bacon for breakfast sometimes," he said.

"Yes, thank you. I'm somewhat of an expert on things that are bad for me."

With the smoke under control, Tom fired up his espresso maker, busying himself with making her a cappuccino. He delivered the little cup and saucer filled with foamed half-and-half and garnished with a little nutmeg—just the way she liked it. And he smiled as she took it.

"Thank you. This is perfect."

"I am a student of what a beautiful woman desires." His voice was low and raspy.

Where had he learned she loved cappuccinos? She slipped by him and planted herself at the eating bar. The espresso drink was indeed as perfect as it looked. He'd even sculpted a heart into the creamy foam on top.

*Why couldn't this be Kyle in the kitchen? Why couldn't we be here, thinking about what we could do today? We could go to Chinatown. Walk along the piers. Eat oysters and warmed olives. Sip wine and watch the Marin Ferry go and come.*

Tom turned and she could feel his eyes on her, though her gaze had traveled out the windows toward the bay watching all the little sailboats already out on the dark blue water.

"It's going to be a lovely day. No fog," she said as she sighed.

"I ordered it special," he answered. "There isn't anything I wouldn't do to make you happy."

Christy sipped her cappuccino. "You don't make it easy, Tom."

"Nor do you. I look at you, and, well…I think to myself…"

"Are you sure it isn't just loneliness, Tom?"

"Does it matter?"

*Oh, yes. It matters.*

Christy couldn't answer him. She now knew it was not a good idea to stay here. Tom was not picking up the message like she'd hoped. She stood and walked with her cappuccino to peer out the front living room windows. She heard the slam of a car door down below. Madame M's driver in the black Lincoln was rounding the rear. He stopped, got out, and then opened up the passenger door. Christy noted how frail the older woman was as she extricated herself from the rear seat, refusing assistance from the driver.

Madame M sighed and looked up at the long bank of crisscrossed stairs leading to Tom's front door. Her initial expression of concern changed when she saw Christy's face. Her mask, that impenetrable face of steel, came back, and she took to the first few steps like she was a triathlete. But she soon tired. Eventually she made it to the top, even accepting the driver's assistance.

They ate spinach and mushroom omelets, buttered cranberry-orange scones, and drank more cappuccino and fresh orange juice. Though Madame M was several years older than Tom, the banter between the two was passionate, with all statements taking on a double entendre. They continued with their sexy word play all during the breakfast. Christy found it lightened her mood, took her mind off all the problems that were looming on the horizon. She imagined Madame M had been quite the tease as a younger woman and wondered why she spent so much of her life alone. She'd have been a great partner.

They were ready to leave. Madame M had checked to make sure her driver hadn't left.

"Tom, could I trouble you for another cappuccino for the road, for Carlo?"

"No problem. Christy, you want to take one, too?"

"No thanks, I've had plenty."

Tom prepared Madame's espresso drink in a white mug, without the nutmeg sprinkles, and handed it to the older woman with a bag containing the remaining orange scone.

"Just send the cup home with Christy tonight," he said.

"Oui, *certainement.*"

Christy found it difficult to look into Tom's blue eyes knowing he would be again asking her to share his bed this evening. And again she'd have to turn him down.

"What time will you return?" he asked, right on cue.

"Oh, well, perhaps six or seven, what do you think, cheríe?" Madame asked. "You want to go to dinner afterwards?"

"No, I'll just pick something up on my way home," Christy said.

"I was hoping to be prepared. I wanted to cook for Christy again. I've bought everything I need."

"I will have Carlo deliver her promptly at six, then. That settles it."

Christy knew Tom was watching her as she stepped out the front door behind Madame M. She hadn't said goodbye to the man she was going to have to turn down tonight. And this time, she'd have to take the gloves off, to make sure he understood there wasn't going to be a sexual relationship brewing.

ON THE WAY to the shop, Madame M leaned against Christy's frame. They were seated together in the back of the black car. Familiar buildings flashed by the window. Christy hadn't realized she missed the city so much.

"I don't understand you, my dear. You could do much worse than Tom. And I think he likes you."

"You think?" Christy frowned. "I don't want to involve him."

"You already have, cheríe. I can smell a man in love a block away."

"I'm not ready for all that."

"Then tell him to wait. Give him one sign, a little hope, and I think he'll wait. But someone is going to land a very nice future with a handsome billionaire."

At Christy's surprised expression, Madame M continued, "Oh yes, he's now a billionaire. It was in Baron's. One of the top 100 in the U.S. now."

"Good for him." It mattered little to her. "I'm sure his ex wives would be grateful."

"Ah, cheríe, that's not kind. He has only one ex, as you know. And she, well, she..."

"He told me about her."

"He has no children. I understand he wants them now. That means he will be looking for a younger woman."

"Please, Madame M. Don't do this anymore. I'm here to help you."

THEY SPENT THE morning going over shop procedures. Traffic was very light. Christy found herself back in the rhythm of the little place on Maiden Lane, with its exotic French Lavender fragrance, the Piaf music playing softly in the background, and Madame M's murmurs in French as she sorted, checked off lists of orders, and poured her arthritic hands over the lacy fabric of pretty things.

Christy found a new boxed Parisian couture bra and panty set made of light rose-colored gossamer and embroidered in tiny white and light pink flowers that was exactly her size. The retail price was over three hundred dollars for the pair. Madame M caught her drooling over them.

"Take them. Just wear them for something special." She pushed the box into Christy's chest. "I insist."

"You mustn't spoil me this way, Madame."

"Now, my dear, you must learn to say thank you. That is all I require." Madame had her hands on her tiny hips, tapping the floor with the black toe of her ballet slipper.

The door behind Christy tinkled as someone with heavy footsteps walked in.

# CHAPTER 33

KYLE CALLED SIMMS four times. As one hour turned into two, it became clear to him the man was ignoring him. He jumped in the truck and headed for Patterson Realty.

The receptionist gave him a squinting frown like the vice principal at his school had all those years ago when Kyle and his buddy Marc tried to skip class. They liked to hang out behind the gym and watch the girl's volleyball team practice. Marc was dating the captain, a long-legged giraffe of a girl who was about two inches taller than him. Kyle loved looking at the black spandex and blond pigtail of his favorite girl. Way more important than History or English.

"I'm Kyle Lansdowne. I've left like several messages for Mr. Simms, and I know his car is here. Can I see him?" He tried to soften her sharp inspection with a killer smile that usually worked. But the woman was hardened. Not exactly unattractive, but damaged somehow.

"No. He's asked not to be disturbed."

Just then Wayne Somerville came into the lobby, carrying an over-stuffed briefcase and a load of manila files. His white shirt was overstretched across his chest. It wasn't as big as his fleshy belly. One of the fake pearl buttons was about to pop at any moment.

"Hey there, Wayne. Remember me?" Kyle was watching the receptionist out of the corner of his eye. He needed to have an excuse to be here, to talk to Simms.

The startled look on Wayne's face told him Wayne had remembered the encounter days before. Kyle continued, "Christy was showing me condos, and all of a sudden she's disappeared."

"Uh huh," Wayne said, juggling the files under his left arm. He leaned back and briefly looked at the receptionist standing at Kyle's back.

Kyle continued, "Don't know what the protocol is, but I got a bonus coming, and if she's not available, I was wondering…"

Simms entered the lobby area. "Stacey, I'm going to step out for some…" He stopped in his tracks at the sight of Kyle, and uttered a soft, "Oh."

Wayne was quick on his feet and launched into his salesman persona. "It's okay, Carl, he and I were just talking about real estate things. I got it." Wayne winked at his manager. "Kyle, let me put these down at my desk and we'll…"

"Just one second, Wayne. I need to talk to your manager first. Give me a card. I'll call you later on, if that works for you." Kyle could see Somerville's blood pressure was rising. A fat vein pulsed at the side of his thick, deep, pink neck. "I promise. I will call you later on." He didn't think Wayne was dishonest. Just gutless.

Wayne glared at his manager, then nodded. Repositioning his files, he produced a card from his shirt pocket and handed it to Kyle.

Kyle put the dog-eared card in his back pocket and turned to Simms, ignoring Somerville. With a firm hand on the manager's shoulder, indicating he wouldn't take no for an answer, he said, "I'll buy you a sandwich and we can talk." He leaned into Simms' personal space and whispered, "You got the address?"

"Not yet."

Kyle knew it was a complete lie. "Hear me out, first. It's a matter of life and death," Kyle whispered.

Simms turned and glared at the receptionist. "Hold down the fort for a half hour. I'll be right back."

The lack of response from the receptionist made the room seem small. Kyle pushed Simms out the door and toward his truck.

Once outside, Simms backed up and put his palms out toward Kyle, distancing him from the SEAL. "Look, fella. I don't want any trouble. I've already talked to the authorities."

"No trouble. Not here to make any trouble for you or anyone," Kyle whispered. He opened the driver door to the bench seat of Gunny's truck. "Get in. Now."

Simms hesitantly looked around first, then climbed into the cab and scooted over to the passenger side. His brown Oxfords were nicely polished but didn't match his grey suit, Kyle thought. The flesh appearing over the tops of his socks was pasty white.

He took Simms to a Burger Palace and paid for their order. He sat across the man and dipped fries into a little white paper cup of catsup.

"The fries are the best here."

"Um..."

"So why won't you give me Christy's address? I know she called you."

"How do you know that?"

"You just told me."

Simms muttered, shook his head, and looked to the left.

"She is in danger. She trusts some very bad guys."

"No doubt. I think I'm sitting across from one."

"Come on, Simms. If you really thought that, you wouldn't be here."

"I have a healthy respect for your profession. But I've been told..."

"Who told you about me? Besides Christy." Kyle couldn't help but blush.

"Well, let's see. I got a visit from a Deputy Hilber and some other Navy MP guy with an unpleasant demeanor. I've received a couple of calls from the San Diego PD I haven't returned. There's you. And of course Christy."

"Look, I don't know how to make you believe this, but she really is in danger. I'm trying to protect her."

"That's what the sheriff's deputy said too."

"Yeah, and he's dirty."

"And that's what he says about you."

"Not a chance in hell. This guy actually killed one of his own men. I saw it."

"So why aren't the cops out looking for him instead of you?"

"I don't have all the answers. But the only reason they want Christy is to get to me. They're not really interested in arresting me."

Kyle and Simms shared a look. Kyle could see Simms was thinking over his words.

The two men ate in silence. Kyle wiped his mouth and fingers on the thin white napkin. He took out a small notebook from his vest pocket, wrote a number on it, along with a name. He tore the perforated page off and slipped it across the table to Simms with one finger.

"Call him. He's my Chief. He'll vouch for me."

Simms took the paper, but shook his head as he slipped it into his wallet.

"You gotta hurry up, though," Kyle continued. "We are running out of time." Kyle saw fear written in the man's eyes. A second later it was gone.

"Take me back to the office. Now." Simms's burger and fries were half eaten.

"WHERE THE HELL you been, Kyle?" Timmons barked into the receiver.

"Talked to you yesterday, sir."

"I got people all over the place looking for you. This is no good, son. You any closer to finding Armando? I'm going to have to pull rank here to keep myself out of the wringer now."

"Sorry to hear that. Look. I think this Deputy Hilber guy is after Christy now. Her manager, a Mr. Simms, won't give me her address, but I understand this guy has been snooping around, looking for her. Saying he's trying to protect her from me, of all people."

"That's becoming a common thought every time another body turns up."

"I asked him to call you, sir. Did he?"

"Hilber?"

"No. Simms."

"Nope."

"Shit. I gotta find her before Hilber does."

"Well, what about Armando?"

"He's trained. He's going to have to go it alone for now. He'd be onboard with protecting an innocent."

"This is ill advised. Never should have gotten her involved in the first place, Kyle. What were you thinking?"

"You know what I was thinking, sir."

"I don't like it when the public gets involved. You should just concentrate on Armando, son. I thought I'd made myself clear about that."

"Timmons, I'm the reason she's in danger. I can't just walk away and pretend it doesn't matter if she gets hurt."

Kyle felt tightness in his chest. His voice waivered, his eyes felt like they were suddenly filled with sandpaper. He inhaled trying to calm his insides. It worked.

"Goddamn it. You guys are all alike. Thinking with your small head. Don't go bringing that shit down on me too, Kyle. I can protect you only so far."

"Understood. If it comes to that, I'll take the fall. All of it." It was what he'd told his team. Timmons didn't jump in and offer to share the burden, but that wouldn't be fair anyway. "We need to get that address. I'm not going to beat it out of him. But if we don't, Timmons, I know she'll get hurt. These guys don't care about anything. Pure rogue." Then Kyle remembered the call from Sergeant Mayfield. "There's this SDPD guy, Mayfield."

"I met him. I think he's okay. Why, is he in on this thing?"

"No. I think he's clean. Did me a favor and called me about the murder…"

"Another murder?"

"In Christy's condo complex yesterday. A trainer in the gym."

"Okay. He call you again?"

"No, but he told me he has the address where Christy is staying."

"I'll get it, then. I know the sonofabitch."

Kyle wondered what Timmons had up his sleeve. He only hoped he'd get to Christy in time.

KYLE MET UP with Fredo and Cooper at Fredo's apartment. They were arguing over how many dryer sheets Fredo was using. Kyle knew that meant they were using Coop's box of fabric softener, since he doubted Fredo even used the stuff.

"You know what the problem of living with you is?" Fredo was standing close to Coop, head leaned back to all six-foot-four of a towering farm boy in front of him.

Coop stood his ground. "No, but you're gonna fuckin' tell me. So hurry up and get it over with so we can get your panties washed."

Kyle knew they would shout, yell, and curse. But neither one would touch the other. Not in anger. Jesting, joking, yes. But you don't touch a SEAL in anger. Then you'd deserve everything you got.

"You're wired up so tight," Fredo said. "You'd have a heart attack if you won the lottery. Who gives a shit if I use one or three dryer sheets? You fuckin' offered, man. So I grabbed a handful."

"They cost one point four cents a sheet."

"Incredible. You're never getting married, man."

"Don't plan on it, Frodo. But at least I smell good."

That nearly earned Coop a punch. Kyle stepped in between them.

"Hold on, ladies. Are we really arguing about laundry?" Kyle said, looking from one set of dull blue eyes to another set of dark squinting eyes.

Fredo swore and left the room. Kyle heard the dryer door open. He came back with a fistful of sheets, more than three, and thrust them at Cooper's chest.

"Here. I don't want your fucking jasmine breeze sheets. I'll pay you back next week. All five cents of it."

Coop took the white squares and did count them, which got Kyle laughing inside. To Fredo's back, Cooper whispered, "Five. You took five."

"We go shopping. He gets the two-day-old meat and the no-name stuff from the little Super Saver. He even buys bruised bananas in a bag. That's sick, man." Fredo began to curse in Spanish.

Kyle knew they were nervous. All of them. The waiting was killing them.

Kyle spoke to break the stalemate. "I got Timmons getting Christy's address. She's not at her apartment. I'm guessing she's in San Francisco."

"Frisco, huh. We going to Frisco?" Fredo asked.

"Not *we,* just me."

"Like hell you are. And Gunny won't like it either."

"First I got to get an address. The sheriff we saw at the cabin is after her. I think he's already on his way."

# CHAPTER 34

TIMMONS CAUGHT THEM a ride on a Navy transport plane to Moffett Field. Gunny couldn't fit into any of the cami shirts they had, so they let him go out of his uniform disguise, which raised some eyebrows. After landing in Mountain View, the foursome hitched a ride to a rental car agency on El Camino Real. They got caught in commuter traffic to the city.

They arrived at the house on Stanyan Street at seven o'clock. Timmons had told him Christy was staying in a cottage behind the main house. As he looked up the tower of stairs to the side of the big Victorian, he couldn't see the cottage. But he noticed the front door of the main house was wide open.

And gray smoke was coming from the rear. Kyle's blood pressure rose.

They quickly parked their rented Tahoe on the street. The three Team guys quietly checked their surroundings as they donned their backpacks. Kyle slung a bag with some additional firepower over his shoulder and checked the deep turquoise sky. Clear as a bell. There was a distant siren, but it could be going somewhere else. No one in the neighborhood stirred. There was little traffic.

Gunny stayed in the Tahoe as lookout, while Kyle, Cooper, and Fredo quickly climbed the front steps to the Victorian. Kyle silently dropped his bag on the porch. Everyone unholstered their sidearms. On Kyle's mark, all three breached the open doorway, fanning out in three directions. Cooper went right, Fredo left. Kyle went straight back to the source of the fire in the back.

A few moments later, they gathered back in the kitchen. Someone had left meat in a pan, and it had burned until the pan itself was red hot.

The back door was open, so most the smoke had gone out that way. It made an excellent calling card. Kyle had shut off the gas to the expensive commercial range. He didn't want to alert anyone still in the house to their presence, so didn't turn on the fan.

Next, they mounted the stairs without a sound, Kyle leading the way. They heard labored breathing and shallow coughing. And then came a faint cry, "Help."

They were in the master bedroom. There were two bodies on the bed. An older man had been shot in the chest, and was having trouble breathing. Kyle thought it might have been a direct hit near his heart, but noticed the blood had pooled left and the gunshot was luckily on the right. The frail woman next to him looked like she could be his mother. She was clearly dead. Her shocked expression was permanently etched on her face. The back of her head was wet and soppy with dark blood. They'd punched her in the nose before they'd killed her. A trickle of blood ran down the side of her mouth, onto the flowered bedspread.

"Didn't even tie her up," Fredo said, and then he swore. "She was no threat to anybody." Kyle knew it made Fredo sick to his stomach to see the elderly, especially women, abused. Kyle pointed down the hall, asking for Fredo to check out the rest of the floor.

Stripping away the man's shirt, Coop applied an occlusive dressing to the wound with chest seals.

"Come on, buddy, don't give out on me now." Coop coaxed him to stay conscious. The man's large eyes stared back, gasping for breath. The SEAL medic dug for his blow out kit, and then applied needle decompression to the right of the man's sternum, which relieved the man's breathing almost immediately. A hissing sound came from the 14-gauge needle. Coop re-checked the man's blood pressure.

"Coop?" Kyle asked. He needed a quick assessment.

"Pretty bad, but if he gets to the hospital, he'll be okay. I've stopped the bleeding for now, given some relief so his lungs don't collapse, but this is only temporary. He's bleeding on the inside and he's in a lot of pain, and weak. Don't think the bullet hit any other organ but the lung. We need an EMT. Can't risk moving him with this chest tube."

Fredo had returned. "All clear. You want me to call it in?" he asked.

Kyle gave a nod and Fredo dashed from the room.

"Don't touch anything except the phone, Fredo," Kyle said to his back. He looked down at their patient. His chest rose and fell, the tube hissing with each breath. "Can he talk?"

"Not sure. We can try." Cooper moved the man's head from side to side. "Hey, buddy, help's on the way. You gotta try staying awake. Can you do that for me?"

The man nodded his head. Sweat covered his forehead, but his color was coming back.

"Who did this to you?" Kyle asked.

The man's eyes opened halfway. He scanned the two faces in front of him and then focused on Kyle. "You're Christy's SEAL, aren't you?"

Kyle winced. God, he wished he were. "Where is she?" he asked.

"They took her."

"They?"

"Three guys. One was in uniform."

"Military?"

"No, khaki." He coughed and spit blood.

"Shit," Cooper said. He shook his head, looking at Kyle. "No more talking."

"They left you a note..." The man was fighting for every word. He raised a bloody finger and pointed to the bureau. His arm collapsed back onto the bed.

Fredo returned. "They're on their way. Someone else had already reported the smoke."

"She..." The man was struggling to say something to Kyle.

"Don't. Don't talk right now. The paramedics are on their way. Save your energy," Coop said tenderly as he brushed back the graying hair from his forehead and checked the man's eyes.

"She loves you." He wouldn't stop staring at Kyle. "Please. You must save her."

"Let's get the hell out of here. Nothing more we can do for him," Cooper said. He punched Kyle in the arm, which brought the SEAL back to reality. The man's body had gone limp again.

On the way out, Kyle picked up the envelope with his name written on it in Christy's handwriting. He looked at the man on the bed and said a little prayer for him.

A small explosion downstairs in the kitchen caught them all off guard.

This was not a good sign.

"Must've set a timed IED," Fredo said from behind as they were jumping down the stairs. Kyle was worried more timed devices were set. Was this a trap?

Gunny had the Tahoe running as the trio slid down along the stair railing, avoiding the stairs themselves. Sirens were coming from the bottom of the hill. They could see the red lights flashing. The big behemoth fire truck had to come up slow, honking and almost coming to a complete stop at each intersection along the way. Luckily, there were lots of intersections, even though the signs made cross traffic stop before proceeding across Stanyan. It gave Kyle and the crew barely enough time to get into the SUV.

Gunny stepped on the gas and almost killed the engine. Everyone else slid down in their seats, ducking under the lid of their caps, and waited. At last, the sputtering truck, romanced by the steady stream of filthy diatribes from Gunny, lumbered up one block. Gunny turned, but continued to swear at the vehicle, telling it that it lacked a soul, that its newness was its flaw. He extolled the virtues of his old but reliable truck back home.

"No special gas. Turns over every time. It'll be running circles around you while you're on your way to the junkyard."

They were headed down toward the bay, and then followed the meandering side street around a neighborhood dog park and then back down to 19th Avenue.

When Kyle was sure they weren't being followed, he sat up and others took his cue, doing the same.

"You gonna open that love letter, Kyle?" Fredo wanted to know.

Kyle's palm smoothed over the script on the outside of the cream-colored vellum. He would have put it to his nose, if he'd been alone.

His tongue flicked at his upper right lip as he carefully slit the letter open with his utility knife. He felt as if he were violating her, so he did it carefully. The quiet purr of the three-fifty V8 engine was the only noise Kyle heard. He didn't even hear his own breath as he unfolded the stiff paper.

*Kyle,*

*I'm writing this at the request of the Scorpion Kings. Caesar asks, commander to commander, that you meet him, or he says he will do things to me that will make it impossible to identify my body, except through DNA. (His words).*

> *He's left you a note in a Taco Bell bag in a garbage can at the corner of 19th Avenue and Kearney, just outside Starbucks.*
> *You'll be watched, so come alone and no one will get hurt.*
>
> *Christy—*

He was holding evidence in his hands. Evidence he was bad for all the women in his life. Evidence that yet another person was going to pay the price for his lack of judgment. Because he couldn't get a grip on himself and just stay the hell away. He'd known getting involved with Christy was a mistake from the beginning. And now, because of his lack of control, his animal need, others were suffering. It was the heaviest burden he'd ever had to bear.

He vowed when all of this was done, he'd stay as far away from Christy as he possibly could. Maybe he'd request one of the East Coast Teams. Yeah. But then he'd be leaving Fredo and Cooper. He could do it. And maybe they could go together. But he had to get away from her.

He imagined how she was feeling right now. Scared to death. And his involvement with her had caused all this. He folded the letter without saying anything and tapped it against his other palm, looking out the windshield at pedestrians in the crosswalk as the vehicle stopped at a red light. It was an unusually warm San Francisco night.

They were sitting ducks, he thought. They had the all the firepower in the world, but were not able to use it. Even though there was always collateral damage, it was different here. These people he watched didn't sign on for this. The gangly kids and couples and seniors walking their dogs this night were the ones he was supposed to be fighting to protect.

The truck lurched forward, Kyle almost hitting his head against the windshield. When he turned to look at Gunny, he saw a pair of red, rheumy eyes staring back at him.

"You gonna leave me here holding my dick, or are we gonna go get these guys?"

"Keep your hands on the steering wheel, Gunny," Fredo shouted. "That ain't nothin' I wanna see in my lifetime."

Gunny ignored the insult and kept his gaze on Kyle. "Any day now. What'd they want?"

"I'm supposed to go pick up a note in a garbage can on 19th Avenue." Kyle turned to Fredo and Cooper. "By the Starbucks."

Cooper had his gloved hand outstretched. Kyle gave him the note.

Fredo was whistling from the back seat. "No way you're going alone."

"Have to."

"No fuckin' way, Kyle," Fredo insisted. "I'll set you up with a wire. You'll read their note out loud and we'll be a block away, hearing every word."

"First I call Timmons," Kyle said.

KYLE WAS SURPRISED to find Timmons in the office this late. He knew some brass were in the office with him, because his chief addressed him as Adele and said he was sorry the dinner plans he had with he and his wife were canceled. "That's real sad about your mom. Hope your family can be of some comfort to you. Be safe, okay? We can reschedule for next week."

"You got big timers there?" Kyle asked.

"Don't worry about me, honey. You just go be with your family in this time of crisis and I'll call you later."

Timmons hung up.

Kyle let the team know about the call. It was the closest to a green light he was going to get from the US Navy.

FREDO HAD KYLE fitted with a small Invisio earpiece with a microphone, so they could talk back and forth. The thing was so small, he didn't like to use it on missions because occasionally it would get lodged into his ear too far and hurt like a son of a gun pulling it out. It also made him a bit hard of hearing, and he had to be careful not to talk too loud when under cover. But in this case, this small earpiece was way safer.

Fredo had fashioned portable mikes mounted behind cheap, American flag pins he'd bought at a souvenir store on Coronado. He pinned one to Kyle's chest on the right side so Kyle's heartbeat wouldn't interfere with the reception. They were that good.

"This one is bait. They find it and think they've got the device, you feel me?" Fredo said.

Kyle nodded.

Fredo had gotten written up for pinning one of Carlisle's flunkies. The whole team listened and recorded the young MA banging a pro for fifty bucks. CDs of the incident earned Fredo enough to pay for all the equipment. But he got a letter in his file. The young MA got himself transferred to a ship, he'd been so hounded by Team guys.

"How many of these did you make?" Kyle asked as he tapped on the flag.

Coop jumped violently out of his seat, hitting his head on the roof of the truck. He pulled off his headset. "Shit, shit, shit. That thing is strong."

Fredo frowned and looked back at Coop as if to tell him to grow up, but didn't. He focused back on Kyle.

"If you need to, you put this thing in under your collar, or your breast pocket if you don't have time."

They dropped Kyle off at the corner, and he took a taxi the rest of the way to the Starbucks. He'd instructed the boys to stay several blocks behind, turn right before Kearney and park within view of the garbage can. Kyle asked the cab to wait, figuring he'd need transportation.

He fished through wrappers and wet semi-empty coffee cups. He found the bag down about a foot into the trash and pulled it out, earning him a scowl from an older, nearly hairless Chinese barber who watched him through the plate glass window of his shop.

When he opened the bag, he found another note, but this time it was written on a yellow Post-It.

"Keep the bag for prints," he heard in his earpiece.

"Go to the rear entrance of the Shoe Barn at 16th and Harrison." He turned the note over. "Nothing else."

Kyle gave the directions to the driver, a portly black man, who chewed on a toothpick. He folded and stuffed the Taco Bell bag into his backpack.

They arrived at the Shoe Barn, but the huge building, taking up a full city block, was boarded up. Half its windows were broken and replaced with plywood. However, some gaping holes remained. From the row of street people sitting out front with shopping carts filled with belongings and sleeping bags, Kyle realized this place was probably a makeshift hotel of sorts.

*Was Christy held in this grimy warehouse with the drunks and filth?*

Kyle instructed the driver to go around to the backside of the large building, where they found rollup garage doors spray-painted with gang graffiti and one metal exterior door.

"Look man, I don't want no trouble. This is a dangerous neighbor-hood," the cabbie said.

"No trouble. I'm supposed to meet someone here. But they might have left another note. Gotta be sure I don't need another ride."

The driver harrumphed and put the cab in park, shaking his head. As Kyle started to get out, the driver called to him through the opened driver's side window. "Hey, dude. How about I get paid for the two fares *now*." His palm was outstretched.

Kyle scanned the empty storage yard, pulled out his wallet, and handed the driver a couple of twenties. "Wait. If I don't come out in five minutes, you can take off," Kyle said.

As soon as he was paid, the cabbie revved the engine, his tires spinning loose gravel all over Kyle. The cabbie took off like his life depended on it.

"Fuck. Hope you guys are nearby. My driver just bailed on me. I'm behind the building." He inhaled, not getting a response in his ear. "I'm going in."

Still nothing. As he touched the silver knob of the door, he heard the crackle in his ear. "We're here."

The door was unlocked. Kyle stepped into a darkened expanse. Pigeons fluttered in the filtered light between a couple of dangling fluorescent fixtures. He heard water dripping somewhere, then the sound of a chair sliding on concrete. He heard footsteps as he unclipped his side arm, but didn't unholster it.

"Well, well, well. We meet at last." The figure of a man appeared from the dark shadows in front of him, and said, "If you value your life, you'll give me that weapon."

# CHAPTER 35

K YLE WAITED UNTIL the man stepped into the light created by a four-bulb fluorescent fixture that fluttered on one bulb. He was shorter than Kyle by several inches, with a buzz cut and a deep scar over his left eye that extended into a lopsided cavern in his cheek, as if a bullet had been dug out with a spoon. It was a prison wound. His neck and exposed forearms were covered in ink. Blurry and milky tattoos. Not many of them professional.

*Junkyard dog.*

The man's upper torso was as hard as any of Kyle's SEAL Team members, but the leathery skin was scarred and pockmarked. His arms were longer than the rest of him proportionally. Well developed guns, connected to gnarly fingers. He held a semiautomatic that Kyle recognized as an FN 5.7, which could hold 20 armor-piercing rounds. Across his chest was an AK-47 strap.

The guy was connected. And armed for bloody battle.

"Allow me to introduce myself. I'm Caesar Rodriguez." A muscled forearm covered with tats of naked women extended, palm up. He wiggled his fingers, indicating he wanted Kyle's gun.

Kyle gave it to him. Caesar looked to his left and a young boy popped out of the shadows, grabbed the gun, and ran into the safety of darkness.

"Now I will shake your hand," Caesar said, "for saving my brother's life."

*Brother?*

"Excuse me?" Kyle asked. He stepped back and heard the sounds of safeties being released.

"Stop right there, amigo."

Kyle did as he was told and froze in place. He was listening, searching for any small movement. He counted three, maybe four other breathing patterns.

"Any friend to my brother is a friend to me." Caesar extended his hand again, palm up. "We will finish the formalities, like two soldiers on the battlefield, then we will talk and determine if we are enemies."

Kyle shook his hand, which was hard as a piece of wood, callused and scratchy. This was a man who was used to fighting barehanded, without the use of the military-issue gloves.

*Big box taught.*

"And here I thought you cared for the girl." Kyle could see a flicker of panic in Caesar's eyes. "We got her some place safe. Not sure about the baby, though."

Caesar withdrew his hand and grimaced in spite of himself. He was missing several upper teeth. The gaping smile chilled Kyle. The man had no soul. That meant he had no limits.

"So who is your brother?" Kyle asked as he dropped his arm down by his side, resisting the temptation to wipe his hand on his pants.

"Blood brother, really. Armando Guzman. I believe you know him, yes?"

The creature was enjoying this too much, Kyle thought. His time would come. It dawned on him that's why Armando was probably still alive. And why they'd killed the guy who'd overdosed Armando on heroin. This thug and Armando were childhood friends. Kyle had been told about them, how Armando had fought his way out of the street and eventually joined the Navy after he relocated his mom and sister. Pieces were clicking into place as a familiar face walked around Caesar, holding two white zip ties in his right hand.

"We use these too, asshole," Deputy Hilber whispered to the side of Kyle's face. Before he could secure Kyle's wrists, Caesar bid him to stop. Hilber definitely looked disappointed, but obeyed.

"When you say *we,* you mean the San Diego Sheriff's Office, or your vast criminal enterprise here in San Francisco," Kyle said with mock respect.

"You'll see," Hilber said, pulling Kyle by the shirt.

"No need for that," Caesar interjected. "Get your filthy hands off my guest."

"Well, he's not *my* guest. I'd just as soon see these guys disappear." Hilber sneered at his ally, who spat on his shoes and got a face full of hatred for his efforts.

*An unholy alliance. Divide and conquer.* Kyle saw the power struggle already, and wondered who the warriors in the background were loyal to.

His eyes were getting used to the dark now. He glanced around and found a couple of dirty mattresses on the floor, some blankets drying on a clothesline, an ice chest, and a hospital gurney with the unmistakable body of Armando strapped to it, an IV inserted into his arm. Armando's eyes were closed.

"That Armando over there?" he asked his captors.

Caesar nodded, studying him. "Your brother too. More recent war. Now I hope we can all be friends."

Hilber swore.

"You proud of the fact that you kidnapped your own best friend?"

The man didn't move a muscle, but his mouth turned down in a sneer. He stared into Kyle's eyes without moving back and forth. Thinking. "Thank you, amigo, for understanding our connection. But no, I'm not proud of it."

Caesar motioned to have Kyle walk over. "I do what I must to be valuable to the organization." He placed his palm against his chest and bowed. "Please. You will confirm now that he is still alive. Everything you do next will ensure he stays that way."

Kyle looked at his Team buddy, sleeping soundly. But he noticed the left side of Armando's mouth twitching, which was the sign he was looking for. That meant he was fully awake, listening, and uninjured enough to fight. Armando's wrists were bound with zip ties, but Kyle saw Armando had already moved the flaps back and forth to break them with a sudden jerk.

"Has he suffered injuries? How'd you get him to sleep?"

"You saw it, Mr. SEAL man. We give him heroin." Caesar glanced over Armando's body. "He likes it now, man. Don't you, little Paco?" Caesar jammed his fist into Armando's thigh, but the SEAL didn't move. Kyle saw Armando's jaw tense, sending a flash to his temple, but the movement was so slight, he doubted anyone else saw it. But he sure as hell knew that grimace. He'd seen it before when Armando had caught a bullet in his back while he was bending over to pick Kyle up when Kyle had been wounded. Armando had got the wound looked at only after Kyle was safely in the arms of the medic.

"And what makes you think I would help you with all this, whatever it is?" Kyle spoke quickly to hopefully keep from earning Armando another blow.

"Come, my friend of my friend. We will talk like two generals." Caesar motioned to two dirty leather recliners on the cold oily warehouse floor, one losing its stuffing.

Kyle complied. He chose the chair facing Armando and noticed his buddy rolled his head slightly in his direction and smiled.

"We want to procure some equipment. Guns and shit like that. Armor. All that crazy shit you guys get to use every day."

"So you can use them against innocents?" Kyle asked, meeting Caesar's gaze head-on.

"Nah, mostly against people who have made promises they haven't kept. Officials that don't play nice. Other organizations who want a piece of our action. Sticking their noses where they don't fucking belong. We run a very efficient and profitable business here. It feeds people. Women and children too. It's *our* Stimulus Package. We require your services."

"You've got my gun. I presume you unloaded something from Armando too. You don't want a fight with our kind."

"On the contrary. I *like* your kind. I *respect* your kind." Caesar gave a quick look to Hilber, who squinted in reply. Kyle could tell the men hated each other. And the only reason Hilber was behaving himself was because they were on Caesar's turf. Not the other way around.

Caesar leaned forward, elbows on his knees.

"You see, I have two things you want. One perhaps more than the other. I'm not interested in just a couple of things here and there—I want to establish an enterprise that will make you and your friend, if he cooperates, very rich men. I want enough so that I feel protected. So my friends can do business in the manner to which they are accustomed."

"Selling drugs."

"I give my customers what they want."

"You steal their futures, their youth."

"They're bored. They willingly give it up. Lotta sick people around these days, you know? We don't bother anyone else unless they interfere, my friend. It reduces our overhead when we don't have to pay so much for protection." He nodded to Hilber, who crossed his chest with his folded arms.

"And you think I will do this because you have Armando here."

Caesar stood up and motioned for Kyle to follow him.

"I am going to ask much of you, I agree. This is a serious commitment you are going to have to make. But then, there is much at stake." He walked over to the rose-colored blanket draped over a white nylon cord and pulled it back with his heavily inked fingers.

Christy was tied to a chair. Her hair was tussled, eye makeup running down her cheeks, but other than that, she looked unharmed. She actually looked wonderful. Kyle couldn't believe how good it felt to see her. Alive and breathing.

Her eyes looked big and scared above the red bandana tied across her mouth a little too tight. Her eyes got even bigger when she saw Kyle.

Caesar walked over to her. "I believe you know this woman in, shall we say, the carnal way?" He smiled and slipped his hand under the hem of her red top and fondled her breast. Christy closed her eyes and suffered in silence. She didn't flinch. Kyle knew she wouldn't show her fear or her humiliation.

"May I speak with her?"

"Sure, sure." Caesar continued to fondle her, but motioned for Kyle to step closer.

Kyle could have killed him right then and there. The foul-breathed cretin leaned in and whispered in his ear, "Are her thighs as creamy? She has the smoothest skin." He brushed the fingers of his hand against her cheek, wiping the tears that had spilled down in rivulets, had dripped off her chin. Caesar touched the shiny droplets like they were diamonds. "Too perfect. Maybe I should take a bite, so you can remember me later when I let you fuck her and I get to watch."

Kyle's hands made fists.

"Watch it there, cowboy." Hilber reminded him he was still at his back. And a gun was trained at his head.

Kyle extended his hands to the side, watched Caesar nod at him, giving him the green light to speak to Christy. He knelt in front of her. He would do anything to protect her. When he put his hand on her knee, she jumped and opened her eyes. He gave her warm flesh a little squeeze, hoping it reassured her. She couldn't hide the terror trembling inside her.

"I'm sorry for this, Christy. I'm going to do everything I can to keep you safe. Whatever they ask, I will do it. Please don't worry. Just stay the course."

He thought about Mayfield's suggestion: "Become the bait." Yeah, he could do that.

Christy's face was still beautiful, despite the panic he read in her eyes and the dried tears that ran black down her cheeks. She needed him, clung to him, and, yes, wanted him. She'd been strong, holding out so as not to show emotion, but this touch on her knee opened the floodgates. Her lower lip quivered beneath the dirty bandana, but there was no sobbing.

"May I?" Kyle asked his captor, holding up the palm with teeth marks, now healing, as if to touch her face in a tender caress.

Caesar shrugged.

Kyle quickly lunged, grabbed Caesar's forearm, and from kneeling position, twisted it, and heard a loud crack as the two bones shattered. He jammed the broken bones up through the man's elbow joint and heard the scream. It echoed for several seconds throughout the warehouse.

Kyle felt the gun butt to his head the instant he saw Christy's horrified expression, and then blackness.

FREDO SAT UP. "Holy shit. He just brought hell down on all of them."

He explained what he'd heard to Cooper and Gunny. They had positioned themselves up the block so they could watch the back door with night-vision binoculars. The large warehouse/store complex was in a swale between two residential streets.

"I'm calling Timmons," Cooper said as he got out his cell. Gunny was on his phone as well.

Fredo tried to make out muffled talking, but Kyle had apparently landed face-down and the flag microphone was buried beneath his body, the Invisio slammed against the floor. One thing was for sure, whoever Caesar was, Fredo doubted the man would ever be the same. He could hear him screaming even without the microphone. It spooked several of the homeless guys leaning up against the wall and sleeping on the ground outside the compound.

Fredo hoped Kyle had broken some body part that would permanently cripple the dude. From the screams, whatever Kyle had done, didn't sound like this type of injury could go untreated for long. Caesar would have to go to a hospital, and soon. And that would mean one less bad guy. For now.

A dark van with blackened windows pulled up, and five heavy-set ex-military types got out and entered the warehouse door.

"Coop, Gunny. Get your asses over here," Fredo said.

He directed them to leave immediately. Neither wanted to. "Look, when they find the mike, they're going to be all over here."

"I'm staying. Gunny, you go," Cooper commanded.

Gunny looked between the two SEALs. "I'll be back in an hour. I've got some friends here, if there's time. Text me if it gets...if you can."

"Fredo will protect me," Coop said, throwing an arm around Fredo's neck. Gunny was given the keys and left.

"Shh!" Fredo whispered, throwing off Cooper's arm and scowling. "Something's happening." Coop pulled down his goggles and watched.

Fredo heard muffled scraping noises through the little microphone. He guessed it was from dragging Kyle's body across the floor. He thought he heard a faint, "left," from Kyle, but wasn't sure. That would mean that he was alive, and so was everyone else.

Fredo and Coop watched the five goons load a groggy, half-dead Armando into the back of the van. A second black SUV pulled up and two more characters got out and ran inside the compound. Next came Deputy Hilber. He stood out like a white worm with his khaki uniform that almost glowed in the night-vision goggles. He held the girl by the hair. She had her hands tied in front of her and was walking on tiptoes in ridiculous high heels that seemed way out of place. She was trying to wrench her head around to look at something. Fredo saw Kyle being dragged under both arms toward the other van.

Hilber pushed the girl into the SUV and came back to Kyle and bent over. Fredo listened as the microphone on the American flag was plucked from Kyle's shirt. Hilber scanned the surrounding buildings and streets, briefly hesitating over their position. He dropped the mike and Fredo heard the crackle, followed by silence as Hilber ground the thing into the asphalt.

"Flag Audio's gone."

Coop nodded, watching the same thing. "His Invisio still working?"

"Yessir, for now."

"But knowing you, there's another backup."

"Fuckin' A. We can track him."

The men loaded Kyle in the second van as Hilber barked orders to two men, who took off running as if it were a marathon. The vans left. The two men were headed right toward their location. Fredo recognized how quickly they tackled the incline, their speed most likely a result of years of military training.

"I'm itching for a burger," Fredo whispered while watching the ex-military types disappear into the neighborhood below. He presumed they were making their way up the hill and would be there within minutes. "Wonder if they got a decent place here, or if it's all tofu and grilled veggies."

Coop shrugged, then stowed his goggles, lifted the collar up on his jacket, and replaced his black cap with a Giants baseball cap he'd lifted from their ride. "I don't care, as long as you're paying."

To the average citizen, they would look like an ordinary pair of Joes on their way home from a late night shift. They ducked into the shadows along a back alleyway and disappeared.


GUNNY RETURNED AN hour later, as he'd promised, to the now-deserted spot and texted Fredo and Cooper, who were eating tacos at a canteen truck nearby. Fredo gave Gunny the address and five minutes later the Tahoe pulled up. It was filled with overweight, silver-haired guys who all looked just like Gunny.

"Whoa, we having a family gathering here?" Fredo barked. "Sure you got room for a little Mexican?"

Gunny introduced them to his friends, who were mostly retired police and firemen. Men he'd served with in Korea and Viet Nam. It wasn't lost on Fredo that these guys were looking for one last good fight. He could tell they missed the hunt.

He shook his head. "Hate involving innocents," he whispered to Coop, who just shrugged.

Coop leaned toward him and, out of earshot of the big guys in the front seats and said, "They're far from innocent. They heeded the call when you were in diapers, amigo."

*Ain't that a fact?* Fredo still didn't like it.

# CHAPTER 36

MAYFIELD DECIDED IT was his turn to call the meeting with Timmons. He'd heard nothing from Kyle or Christy, though he'd placed a call to her. There also had been no answer at the house on Stanyan Street, which worried him too. Hilber wasn't available, and the office said he'd taken a couple days leave.

*Sure he was. In the middle of a quadruple homicide?*

Maybe he'd waited too long, he thought. Things had started coming unraveled and he was getting more and more uncomfortable with circumstances by the hour.

"This isn't an official meet and greet," he said to Timmons, on the phone.

"So then that means shots at Jimmy's."

Mayfield looked at his watch. Christ, it was nearly ten. Way too late for a meeting, but never the right time for shots.

"Can you be there in a half hour?" Mayfield asked.

"I'm here now."

He could hear the crowd in the background. It was Sunday, so it would be tamer than usual. "Okay. I'll be there as soon as I can."

"Take your time, man. I'm expecting a call from Fredo and the team at any time. I assume that's who you're gonna want to talk about."

"Yup."

"You coming alone?" Timmons asked.

"Of course."

"Then I'll wiggle out of my friends."

"I appreciate that." The last thing Mayfield wanted was a public viewing. Here he was conspiring with the Navy against one of his own. But that was what he was about to do.

Or he'd be on his way to no retirement at that little fishing village in Mexico, where he'd live until the ammo gave out. Forget about the pension.

The patio outside Jimmy's was warm, but a blazing fire pit at the center threw off a pleasant glow and heat that felt real good. Mayfield couldn't get the cold chill off the back of his neck that persisted in spite of the fire and the warm night air. Timmons was watching him from a table in the dark corner. The guy was so still, Mayfield almost walked right past him.

Cars slowly tooled past. An elderly couple in matching workout clothes walked their little white dog. The dog obviously thought he was leading.

Maybe he was, Mayfield thought. Not sure why it tickled him, but it did.

He sat in front of Timmons and in an instant was met by a young nubile thing with a low-cut white cotton smock shirt over an impossibly short skirt. She kneeled in front of him and he couldn't help but take a quick glance. Just a quick one. She had a wonderful rack. He murmured a forgiveness prayer to Maria.

"Sir? You want a beer, or something else?"

The something else came to mind, and Timmons grinned, picking up his drift somehow.

"Diet Coke."

"Coming right up." She rose and he had to follow those tanned long legs to the bar.

"How long's it been, Mayfield?"

Mayfield checked out his unmanicured fingernails, wiggled his fingers, which moved the little heart tattoo with "Maria" written in the center, emblazoned on his forearm, and answered, "I had a Coke for lunch."

Timmons was well on his way to being indecent in public. He tossed back another shot and winced like it was mouthwash, the kind that burned all the way down to your butt. He peered over at Mayfield in what looked like a challenge. He could see the officer wasn't having a good day.

And that probably meant Mayfield's day was shit too. But what the hell. He leaned in and asked, "I got a dead guy burnt to a crisp in a cabin we haven't been able to ID yet and two dead ex-deputies in the Palos Vega forest, and a dead personal trainer at one of our most exclusive condo complexes." He looked right and left, then behind him, then whispered and leaned further across the table. "Something's seriously out of whack. Everyone around this Lansdowne character is dying. And violently. Only a matter of time before one of your Team guys gets it too."

"You've got more to think about."

"Excuse me?" Mayfield knew he wasn't going to like the explanation.

"You've also—well, not you, but San Francisco—has a dead shopkeeper and a celebrity billionaire shot in the chest, almost dead. And a dirty cop. Name's Hilber."

Timmons stopped. Then it hit Mayfield. Hilber had gone too far and now the Navy was getting a whiff of his stink. But this caper was long beyond anyone's control now. Least of all his.

"Just thought you ought to know," Timmons added helpfully. Mayfield could see why the man was on the drunker side of conscious.

"And now I'm missing *two* of mine," Timmons added, holding up his fingers in the V sign.

Mayfield could see his retirement package going through a paper shredder. Shoot, at this rate, he'd have to hitchhike to San Felipe, carrying everything he owned on his back. This was a cluster fuck extraordinaire.

"I shouldn't have trusted your SEALs."

"Oh, yeah? Well, I understand you told Kyle to *be the bait?*"

The man was right. It was partially his fault too. "And so that's what's happened?"

"Yup. They've got Kyle. As far as I know, everyone's alive. Point is, we can't really go in there. We know where they are, but we have to let the locals do it."

"I can ask for a certain amount of cooperation from several departments, but that's only going to go so far. Pretty soon, they're going to link everything to Lansdowne, make him out as the one running the operation. And, as the man-hours keep ratcheting up in this time of economic crisis, they'll just come in blasting and sort it out later. You get my meaning?"

Timmons nodded.

"Someone's connected the dots real good. Got ATF, maybe the FBI on it too. This is becoming one giant fucking pile of shit, Timmons, and you know who is right in the middle of it."

"Warren Hilber," Timmons said.

Mayfield was going to swear loudly, but the nice young thing with the silky thighs brought his diet Coke, with a lime wedge on the lip for good measure.

*Perfect.*

He saluted her and took a long drag. Then he squeezed the lime over the top and took another. It seemed to ease his belly some, but not enough. "I don't even want to fucking answer my phone anymore." He took several ice cubes and ground them down quickly with his molars.

Timmons was nodding, staring at his empty glass. The girl hadn't asked him if he wanted another. That meant she could count pretty good, Mayfield thought.

"So, Timmons, tell me something that'll make me fucking feel better."

Timmons smiled lopsided and speared him in the eyes with a stare Mayfield knew was only the precursor to something bad. Really bad.

"Kyle and the team didn't get there in time." Timmons said.

"And?"

"Used her as bait, and now they have Kyle too, just like you instructed."

"Okay. Get to the point."

"They saved the billionaire's life. We have to get that word out there. But I've asked the two other members of Kyle's team to come in.

"And?"

"They refused."

Mayfield wanted to strangle the man, except they were on the same team and he was having his own share of problems. Of course, this news might convince a couple of his superiors that Kyle was more victim than perp, but it was a risk. He knew he'd waited too long to get additional help. He just thought these guys could handle it on their own. But the operation was exploding out of control.

"The one who is behind it all is Caesar Rodriguez, of the Scorpions. They—"

"I know who they are. They run guns and provide protection for the big Mexican gangs from San Diego. Got safe houses all the way from here to the border." Mayfield waved off down the strand. "Word has it, they use ex-military."

"No doubt," Timmons said, frowning. "Our training's the best." He sat back and looked into the night air, as if he were thinking about what to say. "We try to weed them out, but I'd be the first one to admit, we don't get them all."

"And the dropouts, the DORs?"

"Them too. They get just enough training to be dangerous, but we try to get into their heads right away and weed out the nut jobs."

"Or the ones with a higher calling."

"You know the drill. You were there."

That he was. Mayfield could remember the wet and sandy evenings, the chafing, the blood running down his leg under his uniform that Saturday after they'd passed Hell Week. He hadn't bothered to take off his clothes and had showered in the warm water, shampooed his face, and fallen asleep soaking wet on the cheap motel room bed. He'd woken up twelve hours later and was starving. They all ate together at a café that overlooked the ocean they had spent six excruciating days in. All thirty of them, less than a quarter of the original class, had walked as if they were crab-like creatures from the black lagoon. And when he finally had taken off his shoes, his feet had been green.

"How'd Caesar get to your guys?" Mayfield finally asked as he ground down another few ice chips.

"Childhood friend. Someone who knows the family. Got mixed up with Armando's sister off and on for years."

Timmons held his glass up and it was taken within seconds.

"I think your sheriff is there, in San Francisco," Timmons said.

"Good. I'll throw some shit his way. That I *can* do."

"And Kyle injured Caesar. He's probably going to need medical attention, from the sound of it."

"So we check the ERs. What kind of injury?"

"Fredo says he thinks an arm thing. The guy was screaming and passing out from the pain."

The girl brought two glasses. "Another?" she asked Mayfield.

"Sure." He was thinking about whom he could call to get the heat on Hilber, who was probably getting fairly desperate by now. "You know where they are?"

Timmons hesitated, and then tossed down the first of his two new drinks. "Yup. Know right where they all are. Kyle's painted."

"Painted?"

"We have a locator on him."

Mayfield understood. "Anything else I should know about?"

"Nope." Timmons grinned. "Well, if I told you, I'd have to kill you."

They both laughed at that one.

"You guys have some toys, I'll grant you that. Shoot, if we had your budget…"

"You'd catch more bad guys. I completely agree."

"Sometimes I think that's why I tried out for the SEALs," Mayfield said.

"Yup. Heard that one too."

Timmons was having a good time playing cat and mouse with him. Mayfield had to ask the question. "Your guys aren't actually thinking of going in there and getting him? Them, I mean?"

Timmons cocked his head and thought about it a minute. "Can't honestly say. I hope not, for the sake of their careers. Hell, for mine too. And you guys will never convince everyone in San Diego and San Francisco, as well as the Feds, in time, either."

"We're fucked." Mayfield knew it. No way this was going to work out, unless…

"I'd put my money on my SEALs. Everything we need is inside that warehouse, or wherever the hell they are. The Scorpion King has no idea what or who they are dealing with."

"If he's still alive," Mayfield said.

"Oh, he's still alive. They both are. Trust me, if either one or both of them goes out, you and everyone else will know it."

# CHAPTER 37

C HRISTY HAD BEEN placed on a blanket on the carpeted floor, but she still woke up stiff from the few hours' sleep she'd been able to snatch. She didn't recognize her surroundings. It was an apartment of sorts. She heard traffic and the ring of a cable car, so she knew she was still in San Francisco.

In a cruel twist of fate, she was on her side, nearly touching Kyle's sleeping form, the one person in the world she wanted to be sleeping next to. But he was hog-tied and her hands ached from the zip ties at her wrists in front of her. All night long she kept forgetting where she was and would try to force her arms apart, to adjust to a more comfortable position, but then realization of her situation would dawn and she'd quickly remember comfort and movement was useless.

She had to pee, though it had been hours, nearly twenty now, since she'd eaten or had anything to drink. That told her there was no real concern for her safety or her health.

No smell of coffee. No warm bed smelling of fresh lovemaking. No warm shower and lavender shower gel. No warm scent at the back of Kyle's neck that she could bury her nose in. No touch of his solid ass as he came alive to the caress of her thighs. No holding the man who was a god—perhaps too much of a god. Was it possible to love someone, to need someone so much? Was it a good thing or a very bad thing?

Death stared her in the face. Kyle looked at peace in his sleep.

What if Kyle died? What if she had to watch that? What if she died? On the scale in her soul, she knew her life wasn't worth half of his. This was the man who had touched her on the knee last night and told her everything would be all right. And she had believed him. He'd wanted to take the burden and the pain from her. She vowed if there were a chance, even if it meant sacrificing herself, she would provide a distraction. Somehow she would help set him free. That was the only thing she would focus on today.

What had he said before he'd been beaten? *Stay the course.* Not *have a nice life,* or *don't worry.* Those would have been useless words. Unrealistic words. No. He'd asked her to endure. Not give up. Not to think about it. Just go on.

She knew it all would happen today. There wouldn't be a long few days of torture. All she had to do was get through this next day, because she was certain there wouldn't be another one.

*Time is of the essence.* Just like what she'd learned in her real estate classes.

Madame M had had no time to prepare for her end of days, although Christy suspected the woman had not been entirely truthful with her. Christy had watched in horror as Madame was beaten and then shot. Caesar had put the gun to Tom's chest and got Christy to write the note to Kyle, creating the snare that would entrap him. And then the devil shot Tom anyway. Just for spite.

*It's all my fault.*

Tom? She'd heard the shot. Was he gone too? Her thoughts wandered. She allowed herself to explore what could have been her future. Could she have changed the course of his involvement in this drama? She said a prayer for him. God, she hoped he was alive. He didn't deserve this fate. It was hers. It wasn't his.

*Forgive me, Tom.* She had never meant to hurt him. Never meant to hurt Madame. And Marla. Was Kyle going to be next? Was everyone who cared about her going to die?

Tears flowed down her cheeks as she fluttered her eyelids so the blurriness of Kyle's handsome face wasn't lost to her. She would need that strong jaw line, those blue eyes that made her feel like some great Amazon warrior princess at his side. With this man, she could overcome anything. All he had to do was love her and she would be healed. She was everything she needed to be. She had everything she wanted to have. Even if it was for a day.

All she needed to do now was save him. Somehow. And today was the day it would have to happen.

Kyle stirred. A beam of early morning light had crossed the side of his face. The black stubble on his cheeks glistened, the hairs at his neckline rose and fell with his steady breathing. He wasn't like anyone else she had ever met. His body was a lean killing machine, but his heart was as full and tender as a child's. Full of life. Full of love. Full of hope— not just for her, but for a nation she knew needed him. A nation that would never be able to thank him the way he deserved. Who would never understand the heart of the man. The heart and dedication of a warrior. Being a SEAL was his true calling and always would be.

Another wave of tears shielded the view of him. He nestled his head against the floor and arched his back. His chest expanded and rose. Her fingers and lips had explored the length of that chest not nearly enough times. She hadn't heard his steady heartbeat enough. She needed to lay her ear against his breast and listen to life as it was meant to be. Until it was all over, the memory of those glorious moments in his arms would be all she would have.

And though it wouldn't be nearly enough, it would have to do.

It was all she had, after all.

And for right now he was lying next to her, in the morning, with the sun on his chest. And he was alive.

She fell to sleep dreaming of a life that could have been.

# CHAPTER 38

KYLE WOKE TO a splitting headache. He felt like he was wearing a hatchet lodged in his forehead, right between his eyes. Eyes that refused to focus.

But when the fuzzy red spots in front of him cleared, he saw Christy's luscious shape. Her cherry red top was half slung over one shoulder and smudged. She was on her side, facing him, her hands bloody from struggling with the zip ties. But right now they lay relaxed and in repose. Like she was praying.

He looked at her strong arched eyebrows and her long smooth nose, ending with just a slight upturn guarding full rose-colored lips. A little of her red lipstick remained. He remembered everything about those lips.

He had no right to be thinking about them right now. Cooper and Fredo were right—those kinds of thoughts could get a good Team guy killed. That wasn't the hard part, he thought. He didn't want to make Armando and Christy sacrifice for his mistakes. That just wasn't going to happen.

Soft blond curls hugged the dark canyon along her neck. Her shiny shoulder, transected by a red satin bra strap, rose and fell with her even breathing. They hadn't beaten her, thank God. Her black, form-fitting pants hugged those long legs of hers, with one crossed over the other. His gaze followed down to her ankles with just a couple of blue veins visible at the top of her foot.

And then there were those heels.

They were still shiny, as if she'd been protecting them. Probably expensive, he thought. He fantasized what those bare legs would look like with the patent leather, spiked heels wrapped around his waist or flat up against the wall as he sunk himself deep inside her.

Not helpful, these thoughts. Dangerous. His package was coming to life. Oblivious to danger. Maybe because of the danger. What kind of thinking was that? It was gallows humor, for sure.

She was trying to turn over in her sleep. She arched her spine just enough so he could see the outline of her breasts under the top, the hint of shadow he could remember that played between her nipples those times when he buried his head there, those times when he tasted this gentle woman who had the heart of a lion in a siren's body.

Knowing her, it was the first time he'd found someone who could take everything he could dish out. All of it. All the lovemaking, all the moodiness and distances he had to maintain to keep sight of the mission, all of who he was. She was his equal in every respect, and perhaps superior to him in many. If it took every ounce of courage and life force, he would make sure she survived.

Maybe if he didn't survive and Armando did, his buddy would take care of her, protect her, and learn to cherish her like he had. Christy deserved someone in her life who would bring her a deep love that would rock her to her core, not something casual and brittle. Something deep, everlasting. Something worthy of her courage and strength.

*If it can't be me, let it be someone like Armando.*

Kyle did feel the pangs of regret and jealousy. Had he mentally agreed to give her up? Well, if he died saving her life, that is what he would do. She was worth it, after all.

He scanned as much of the room as he could see. And he listened. Hispanic music was playing outside on the street somewhere. The sound of traffic came from below, which meant they were in an urban neighborhood, most likely on a second or third floor. He could hear morning delivery trucks. An occasional car swished by. Doors slammed and motors revved, and then he heard the telltale ring of a cable car nearby.

He was in San Francisco. People were coming and going about their lives.

A cheap dresser with pictures stuck into the mirror frame was on the opposite side of the room. He could feel fabric and the metal band of a bed frame behind him. Someone was snoring on the bed. He hoped it was Armando, but after listening to the rhythmic snoring, he realized the pattern wasn't familiar. So one of his captors was with them.

Where was Armando?

He heard a door slam shut downstairs and footsteps get closer. They were heavy, like combat boots on wooden steps, two—no, three sets of boots. And whoever it was, they were big men. Like the ex-military types he'd seen at the warehouse.

So it was all starting now. He checked his heartbeat. No evidence he'd been drugged. But he had a dull ache at what probably was a big knob at the back of his head where he was sure he'd been gun-butted. Hilber's love tap, he thought. Kyle squeezed his fists and released them twice. Time for dealing with Hilber was soon approaching.

He wiggled the flap on his zip ties, twisting his wrists so a finger could move the flap back and forth like they'd been shown in captor training. In a few seconds the plastic failed, and his hands were free. Quietly, he rose up and took a quick peek at the bed. Sure enough, one huge guy dwarfed the bare twin mattress. He was fully clothed and a 9mm was laced in his limp fingers. It was too much of a risk to go for the gun.

Kyle worked the tie on his ankles and saw Christy's eyes open. He put a finger to his lips and she smiled. God, he would have to stretch, but he would kiss those lips. Slowly, quietly, he arched, lifting his torso in a one-armed pushup so he wouldn't drag over the carpet and make a sound.

She kept her eyes open when he kissed her.

"I won't let anything happen to you," he whispered. She nodded and looked at his lips again. When he kissed her again, she tried to arch her chest to his. Her sweet breath and kisses were furtive, desperate, strained at having to be kept quiet. Like she didn't think she'd ever get another kiss. He could feel the moan in her chest she wouldn't reveal. He smelled the perfume in her hair as her pulse points released her scent to him. She was his woman in every sense of the word. The better half of him. The half he would save. Even if the other half had to die.

# CHAPTER 39

B Y NINE O'CLOCK in the morning, Mayfield made the calls to the IA Department at the San Diego sheriff's office, promising a full written report on Deputy Hilber and his involvement in the gang's swath of violence. As a courtesy, he also called the sheriff, who said he'd had his own suspicions about Hilber's extracurricular activities. There'd been rumors, he told Mayfield.

*A politician's answer.*

For jurisdictional harmony, Mayfield bought the story, for now. He didn't need another enemy just at this moment in his career. He knew the elected man was going to do everything possible to keep the dirty cop angle minimized.

Mayfield also alerted his chief, who pulled in the commissioner. One thing going for them was that it didn't look like any regular SDPD units were involved. And that was one hell of a good thing. At least the war was only on two fronts. Not like what Kyle and those poor bastards in the Navy had on their hands in Iraq and Afghanistan.

*Arab Spring, my ass.*

All he had to worry about now were the drug gangs and the rogue deputy's protection racket. He knew what they were after. And he knew they'd never succeed. He may not have trusted Kyle with his daughter, if he had one, but he knew the young man would rather die than resort to a life of crime and violence in the private sector. No guns for hire with this lot.

He believed Timmons's assessment that the two SEALs were still alive. No big explosions, shootouts, or vehicles bursting into flames had been reported. And it had been two days without another dead body turning up. Thank God for small favors.

He had no choice but to trust the men Timmons trusted. He wondered how Timmons was managing to keep the brass off his back.

*Not my war. It's his.*

Whatever private hell Hilber had created, the man wasn't going to be able to hide behind the badge anymore. Even if he survived, his days of running protection for the San Diego gangs were over. At least now the public could breathe a little easier.

Until the gangs found someone else. Hell, they probably had several eager candidates already lining up. Someone who needed money. Someone who felt they deserved a little extra special retirement package in exchange for their years of faithful service. The money was enough to tempt a saint.

Mayfield sometimes wished he felt the same way. Maybe life would be easier. Just sell out. But no, that would never happen. The system wasn't perfect. Lots of holes in it. But it was the only one around that made any sense, and, in general, the system improved the lives of the public. And they were his real bosses. Not the brass or the guys who signed his paycheck. He worked for those couples in the matching leisure suits out walking their dogs on a balmy San Diego night. The little people. The people who had families, went to work, paid their mortgages, and sent their kids to college.

He thought maybe Maria would like it if he went back to church. Maybe he'd get to spend more time with her there. He chuckled. She'd scold him. He'd been having some thoughts lately. And admitted for the first time, perhaps he was lonely after all.

*No replacing you, Maria. Just saying a man has needs.*

Maybe if he went to church and asked for help, she'd put her head together with Jesus and they'd find someone good for him.

*Nah. Not going to happen.*

He knew as sure as he was alive today that if he ever did that, he wouldn't be able to hear Maria scolding him any longer. Like she'd be gone forever.

And he wasn't ready for that. Not yet.

Mayfield called the SFPD's Office of Special Affairs, the ones who handled jurisdictional cooperation, and told them about Caesar and his injury. They promised to alert ERs in the San Francisco Bay Area. He knew SFPD would get Caesar. And he didn't mind that they would get credit for the collar. There was a need for San Francisco to show some toughness on crime, and this gave them that opportunity on a silver platter. Mayfield didn't need the medal.

He didn't even take joy knowing the DEA and ATF would send out hunting parties, rounding up gang members, weeding out their support system and wiping the slate clean for a time. He never really liked manhunts. Probably was a good thing he'd never made it through the SEAL program to earn a Trident.

Mayfield wondered how long it would be before Hilber would lose control over those gang members. He couldn't ever recall hearing Hilber speak Spanish. That was a real handicap. And if Hilber was no longer a deputy, he might be more of a liability, more of a loose end to the gangs than he'd ever figured he'd be.

Could be, sooner or later, Hilber would find himself a nice watery grave, if the gangs even bothered to find a grave at all. With Caesar out of the picture for a while, someone else no doubt would soon step up to fill his shoes. The new guy would need to do some housecleaning. And that would be bad news for the soon-to-be ex-deputy.

But it was also true that if Kyle and Armando wouldn't cooperate, they'd be loose ends as well. Mayfield knew from experience that the real leadership was in Mexico, hiding in plain sight, probably running operations right out of some territorial police captain's office, one or two steps from a prison term himself. Maybe even paid for by US anti-drug task force money.

*Crime finds a way.* It doesn't really pay, but for a time, crime always looks as if it's winning.

He checked his watch. Only nine-thirty. Today was going to be a big day, if his instincts were right. He decided it was time to do a little research in the field to help set up the next phase of hunting down the bad guys and putting them behind bars. That was his job, after all.


FELICIA GUZMAN WAS hanging laundry in her backyard when Sergeant Mayfield drove up in his patrol car. He saw her flowered dress and the braid wound up on top of her head, just like how Maria used to wear her hair. The sight almost took him back a step.

The house was painted bright yellow. Way too bright. An explosion of huge bursting dahlias and fragrant columns of pink and blue flowers grew all along the front of the stucco house. In front of the tall stalks was a profusion of low bedding flowers. In contrast to the rest of the neighborhood, Mrs. Guzman's house looked like the Fourth of July and Christmas all at once, only without the flags and twinkle lights. No way you could drive down the street and miss it.

The dark little woman wiped her hands on her apron and prepared to greet him. He could see she was steeling herself for some bad news. Didn't she know if bad news was being delivered, the Navy would be the ones to call and not some lowly San Diego police sergeant?

"Ma'am." He wore his badge on his uniform and she was staring at it. "I'm Sergeant Mayfield from the San Diego Police Department."

"You have some news about my son?"

She had a lined face that was full of character and resolution. The way she stared back at Mayfield almost made him embarrassed for some reason. Her large nut-brown eyes were soft but demanding. He didn't see any trace of the fear and concern he knew she felt.

A young, twenty-something woman came dashing down the front steps. She had a gauze pad taped to her forehead. She was stunning in every sense of the word. A total knockout. Her long dark hair and tanned limbs nearly took his breath away. She was a taller, younger, and thinner version of her mother. The mother was quite stunning as well.

"Mom. I'm going down to Gina's place for a couple of hours. She wants to help me pick out some clothes for the baby. We might go shopping, but I'll be home before dinner. You want me to get you anything?"

"No. Mia, I don't like you leaving the house." She frowned and addressed Mayfield. "Mia, this is Sergeant—I'm sorry, I don't remember your name..."

"Mayfield."

"Nice to meet you," Mia said as she extended her hand.

He saw the same strength her mother showed, but also saw defiance, especially directed at his uniform. What could be so attractive about the low-lives like Caesar when she had a home and a mother like this little woman standing next to her?

Mayfield shook her soft hand, very tentatively placed.

"You will stay home today, Mia. Have you no respect for your brother? Now go back inside. I need to discuss some things with the sergeant here."

"Oh, Mama. They probably think I'm in the hospital. Besides, if they were looking for me, they would never expect me to be with Gina."

Felicia Guzman dropped her gaze. "Mia, I am not happy about this. It isn't safe."

"You worry too much. He'll..." Mia looked up at Mayfield.

He blurted out, "I know about your brother. That's why I'm here."

Mia took her mother by the shoulders and leveled a gaze at her that translated to a rejection of Felicia's demand.

"He's going to be okay. You'll see. Armando always finds a way."

After Mia gave her mother a peck on her cheek, they both watched Felicia's daughter saunter out to her car.

"Armando's sister. You've met my son?"

"No. I have not. Heard a lot of good things about him, though."

"That's good. He's good to his mama." She pulled a pair of clippers out from her apron and began to deadhead a rose bush. "You have news, then, about my son?" she said to the bush.

"Not really. You'll have to be talking to the Navy about that. All I know is that he's still being held, but we believe he is alive."

She put her palm to her throat and closed her eyes. "Thank God." She crossed herself. "And Kyle Lansdowne? Is he safe?"

"Not quite. They are together. And the girl too."

"What girl?" She was alarmed.

Mayfield looked down the street and saw he was attracting some attention. "Would you mind if I grabbed a glass of water and discussed this with you inside? I have some questions I need to ask, in private."

"Oh, pardon my manners. Of course. Come."

Mayfield followed her inside, and it felt like he was going back in time to the early days of his marriage with Maria. When she had felt better. When she filled his life with sunshine and joy.

When she grew big showy dahlias just like Felicia Guzman's.

# CHAPTER 40

**K**YLE HEARD AN argument going on in the next room, and it was getting louder. He was expecting the staccato of gunfire at any moment. He pulled a thin razor wire from the flap in his belt and cut Christy's ties. She rubbed her wrists together, showing him with her eyes how grateful she was. He motioned for her to stay down and she nodded. He was on his feet and had garroted the sleeping thug with the razor wire.

He checked the man's weapon to make sure it was operational. He found two clips he knew he'd need, and then rolled the body toward the wall, dumping a pillow on the man's head to hide the blood. He checked for an additional weapon and found one stowed in his groin. Kyle tucked it in the front of his pants under his shirt. He lifted a limp arm over the top to make it look like the guy had fallen into a deep sleep.

When Kyle turned around, Christy was watching him from the floor. She'd just seen him kill a man. He saw the twins: fear and acceptance. But there was more.

Admiration.

Not what he needed, but what she wanted to show.

He helped Christy up so she wouldn't stumble, but she did, and into his chest. He felt her breasts press against him and the brush of her hair under his chin. With his free hand, he clutched the back of her head and sunk a deep kiss, feeling her arms go up and around his neck. Her body went limp in his embrace.

But this was folly. He pulled her away and asked her with his eyes if she was ready.

Christy nodded.

*That's my girl.*

Kyle debated whether or not he should arm Christy with the 9mm and decided not to. He motioned for her to stay in the corner. A sliding closet door was opened, but not wide enough for her to slip into. He shook his finger at it so she wouldn't consider trying to enter. She crouched down in the corner, the shiny patent leather pumps dangerously delicious, even now. She looked like cat woman. He wanted to fuck her so bad it really did hurt. His package was rubbing against the blue steel of the weapon.

"How many?" he mouthed to her.

She looked up to the right, and then leveled back at him. She held up six fingers, then pointed to the man on the bed and turned a finger down. Five.

"Armando?" he whispered.

The arguing in Spanish stopped abruptly and Kyle tensed, then leaned flat against the doorframe. Christy pointed through the wall to the next room.

Armando was next door.

The Spanish conversations resumed, but the voices were calmer now. Kyle heard four distinct voices and the rustling of bags. He guessed the three returning boots had brought breakfast. And they'd want to share it with the dead guy.

Something was said in Spanish outside the door. Kyle and Christy waited.

The door burst open. Kyle let the gunman enter the room fully before he pushed the door closed, twisted the man's neck, breaking it instantly, keeping his palm over the man's mouth to muffle any sound.

Now Christy had seen him kill two men. In less than five minutes. He glanced in her direction and was thankful to see her staring at the floor. Killing was not something he was proud of, but if the odds were down to four versus two, not counting Christy, they had a damned good chance. If Armando was in any shape to fight.

The absence of the two gunmen was getting attention from the other room. The door was kicked open and then the room was sprayed with automatic gunfire, splinters of wood flying like a wood chipper. Someone breached the doorway and caught Kyle's rounds across the chest. Kyle hadn't been sure until that moment whether or not the ammo was hollow point, and thank God it was. The body, encased in a flak vest, crumbled to the ground.

The other two gunmen fanned out in opposite directions on the other side of the door, disappearing into the shadows of the hallway. Kyle hoped Armando was awake and ready. He kicked the door in with the heel of his boot and stepped into the living room, his weapon trained on anything that moved. Armando stepped up next to him. His teammate was weaving.

Kyle went to fish out his other 9mm, but Armando held up the captor's weapon.

"You okay?"

"Fucked, man, but I can do this blindfolded."

It felt good to hear Armando's voice after all this time.

Another hail of automatic rounds pierced the air, sending little explosions along the walls, shattering the window glass. Armando and Kyle pressed themselves to the floor until the firestorm subsided, then leapt through the doorway and swung an arc of fire across the room, cutting one man down but pinning the other one behind the kitchen counter. Armando was going to blast through the cabinets.

But that wasn't the real problem.

"Hey, asshole," came the familiar voice of Deputy Hilber behind Kyle.

Kyle turned and saw Hilber in his shorts and a T-shirt, barefoot, gingerly stepping across debris from the gunfight. He had Christy in a chokehold and had an automatic aimed at her temple. She was barely able to keep upright, Kyle saw. Her feet were slipping on pieces of door, furniture, and sheetrock as she and Hilber made their shaky path from the doorway into the living room.

Kyle and Armando lowered their weapons, but didn't let them drop.

"Aquí, aquí," Hilber said to the gunman behind the counter, pointing to Armando and Kyle with his forehead.

The two SEALs were disarmed. Kyle's gaze flew back and forth between Christy and Hilber. He and Armando spread out from each other, then slowly raised their hands and placed them behind their heads as they'd been instructed. They continued to turn toward Hilber and spread apart further. Kyle was slightly forward. Armando was closer to the other gunman, backing into the kitchen area.

"Not so fast, gentlemen. Stop right there." Hilber was having a hard time with Christy's balance. She was leaning into him, trying to get her footing on the uneven floor.

Christy's eyes were not wild and unfocused. She was trying to tell him something, but Kyle couldn't get it.

He looked at Armando, who twitched the left side of his lip. The gunman in the corner looked like he was about to pee in his pants. He was mumbling something Kyle couldn't understand, but Armando whispered a terse sentence back at him in Spanish, which made the man flinch and aim his weapon on him.

"I said knock it off, *a-mee-gos*. Or she gets it. *Com-pren-day*?" Hilber shouted. He looked ridiculous in his shorts. His one eye had taken a blow and was nearly swollen shut, but his good eye was darting all over the room, looking for danger in every corner. "Ever try talking to a bunch of Mexicans without their leader? No offense." He nodded to Armando.

"I'm Puerto Rican," Armando shot back.

Christy was still having difficulty balancing. Kyle watched her feet and ankles twisting over the debris.

"Will you fucking stop with the wiggling?" Hilber screamed at her and bent her backward. Kyle knew Hilber was past his breaking point and was highly dangerous. A sudden jerk could set his trigger finger askew and Christy's head would explode.

Christy's expression got wide, she was damn scared. Her gaze clung to him like he was her lifeline. She wouldn't take her eyes off him.

She glanced down quickly and then right back up to Kyle's face in a deliberate attempt to send him a message. That's when it hit him. He watched in slow motion as she fumbled to balance herself on one foot. One long black leg bent at the knee and rose up slowly. He knew what was coming next. He hoped Armando was ready because they were going to go on her mark.

Christy jammed her heel back into the fleshy portion on the inside of Hilber's right thigh. At least three inches of the deadly weapon ripped and tore away at his skin. The deputy screamed. Blood spurted across the room from Hilber's severed femoral artery.

Armando hit the other gunman with a roundhouse kick to the nose. The man's weapons clattered to the ground like pickup sticks. He was dead before he landed on top.

The outside door burst open and a herd of hefty gray-hairs stormed in like elephants in musth. Guns drawn. Flack jackets flapping, unable to be fastened at the sides. Kyle was going to train his weapon on them when he heard Fredo's voice. "Hold it, Kyle. Friendlies."

Kyle was never so happy to see a bunch of overweight retirees in his life, even though one of them swore at having missed the chance to fire a weapon.

Cooper looked between Kyle, Armando, and Christy, and then kneeled to examine Hilber, who was trying to stop the bleeding by holding onto his thigh, but to no avail.

Gunny was there too. "Let the sonofabitch bleed out," he said to Cooper's arched back.

"Can't do that," Cooper answered. He quickly fashioned a tourniquet from his medic kit and the spurting stopped in mere seconds.

Christy stood in the middle of the carnage, still trying to get her balance. Her dainty pink toes were exposed on her right foot, her left still wore the stiletto. Kyle swept her up in his arms and took her to a corner, where he consumed every inch of her body he could touch with kisses.

Sirens were blaring outside as the younger version of the elephant squad arrived in full battle gear. Everyone silently began checking the dead, whispering among themselves. There was a lot of nodding of heads as whispers were passed around from man to man.

Kyle and Armando shook every hand that was outstretched. Armando made some comment about it feeling like an election, with the slapping on the back and the "Well done, sons," going around.

"Privilege, kid."

"It's an honor."

"Glad we could help out."

"Nothin' else to do," was Gunny's response.

Kyle grabbed the man and gave him a bear hug. The four Team brothers locked shoulders in a circle and looked to each other without uttering a word.

*Damn good to be alive.*

Just as quickly as the circle formed, they dropped their arms and stepped away, all of them focused on a spot behind Kyle's back. Kyle turned and saw Christy come up to the group. She slipped into the circle next to Kyle and wrapped her arms around his waist. And they let her stand there.

Just like one of the guys. Kyle was so proud of her.

"Now you're an honorary member of SEAL Team 3," Kyle said.

She threw her head back and giggled. "Yes! Accidentally."

# CHAPTER 41

CHRISTY STUDIED THEIR faces. These were her new brothers. She was not their equal in any way, but these were brothers who would have sacrificed their lives for her. It was a family of brothers unlike any other family she had ever known or had heard about.

"Thank you?" Her expression came out like a question and she cursed to herself. "I really don't know exactly what to say. I'm so grateful to all of you."

"Oh, it's okay, missy," Fredo said. "Kyle has that effect on women all the time, don't you, studly?" Fredo winked at Kyle and got the finger for it.

"Sorry," Kyle whispered to the top of her head.

She answered him by clutching his body closer to hers. He chuckled and looked back down into her eyes. Their shared reverie was interrupted by groans coming from the other SEALs. But Gunny was grinning like he'd found a million dollars. Kyle shrugged.

Fredo announced they were getting out of the battle zone.

Kyle pulled Christy alongside him as they walked past the squads. There were smiles all around.

Christy heard Fredo shout out, "Kyle, for Chrissakes, would you two get a room?"

More bitching and comments bounced off the walls. The four SEALs had their swagger back. Christy knew tonight they'd be celebrating—without Kyle, of course. She had plans of her own.

They loaded up in the Tahoe, Kyle pulling Christy into the third seat for some privacy. Christy felt her skin tingle as his thigh brushed against hers. He slipped his hand under her top and squeezed her breasts one at a time.

"Satin. Red satin," he whispered.

"What? What are you talking about?" she asked. But he covered her mouth and flicked his tongue over her teeth.

When he pulled away, he whispered, "You once asked me what kind of underwear I liked. I like you in red satin." One hand was finding its way down the front of her pants. She closed her eyes when his fingers rubbed over her nub and sought entry along the lacy opening at the top of her thigh.

When she opened her eyes, Fredo's chin was resting on his two fists stacked on the back of the second seat. He had a very intimate view of what Kyle was doing, and wasn't afraid to watch. Kyle hadn't seen him.

Yet.

"Do your nipples get hard when he does that? I've just always wanted to know, from a woman's perspective," Fredo asked with a clinical air. The Team guys burst into laughter.

Kyle raised his head and pushed Fredo so hard he almost slid off the bench seat.

Christy watched Kyle lean back, stretch, and look up to the headliner of the van. "We've got all night," she whispered to the side of his face. "And your presence is required the whole time." She smiled and saw her smile returned.

Gunny and Kyle shared a conspiratorial wink via the rear view mirror. They had something up their sleeve.

And Christy could hardly wait.

"Don't know what it is, fellas. He gets kidnapped, he gets us running all over California looking for him, and he gets the girl. Armando, you got kidnapped and beat up real good too. Where's your woman?" Fredo was merciless.

Armando flashed a big white smile behind to Kyle. They hand slapped their greeting.

"Yeah, thanks, man." Armando cocked his head. "I'm hoping Kyle will introduce me here to her cute sister."

The others chimed in, complaining about the lack of an introduction.

"Christy, this is the group. Fellas, this is Christy." Kyle pointed. "This one is Cooper. We call him Coop. He hangs out at the beach a lot when we're home."

Christy nodded her head to Cooper.

"He brings his bedroom with him so he's always ready," Fredo added.

More laughter. Christy didn't understand the statement and squinted.

"I'll explain it to you later, baby," Kyle said and kissed the side of her face. "This one, of course, is Armando. Saved my bones in BUD/S. Strongest swimmer on the team too. And, as he's already told you, he's from Puerto Rico."

"Nice to meet you, Armando," she said.

"Nah, man. The pleasure is all mine."

Armando could have easily been a cover model, or soap opera star, once his black and blue parts healed. His quiet demeanor and brilliant smile probably stole hearts on a regular basis, she thought.

"Wish I had a sister. But sadly, I'm the only one," she said.

"That you are, my dear. That you are." Kyle planted a long, languid kiss up the side of her neck, ending the kiss in her ear. "And I'm going to kiss every inch of you tonight," he whispered, but his words weren't exactly out of earshot.

She felt her cheeks flush as she watched the envious faces of Cooper, Armando, and Fredo. Even Gunny was watching in the mirror again.

The space between her legs ached and she was so ready to let Kyle do whatever it was he had in mind. As often as he had it in mind. "I'm going to hold you to that promise," she said as she winked at Armando. She tapped Kyle's lower lip with her forefinger and he sucked it into his mouth.

"So I'm the invisible Mexican now?" Fredo shouted. "No respect. This discrimination thing sucks, man. Really sucks."

"Christy, this is Fredo."

Fredo took her hand and, just like in a historical romance, brought it to his lips. "Alphonso Manuel Esquidido Chavez, mi lady."

"Whoa. Alphonso?" Cooper teased. "All this time I never knew that was your fuckin' name, man."

"You didn't ask nice," Fredo answered.

Everyone left Christy and Kyle alone again.

"What's the plan?" she whispered to Kyle's lips.

"Shower and bed. In that order."

"And then?"

"We'll see. We'll have to talk, Christy." He drew her to his chest. She could hear his heartbeat, at last.

# CHAPTER 42

G UNNY DROPPED THEM off at a boutique hotel near the Ferry Building. The rest of the guys were staying elsewhere. Disappearing, Christy thought.

The familiar ache in her stomach came back, just like the first night she and Kyle had stayed up nearly the whole night. Talking. Kissing. Making love. Until they both had fallen asleep, exhausted, entangled in sheets. Entangled in each other's legs and arms.

At breakfast that first morning, she'd known her body was tired and that she had gotten so little sleep. But she'd willed herself to enjoy every minute in his presence. Just like today. She urgently needed a hot shower and then to feel Kyle's hard body on hers.

She walked barefoot onto the plush flower patterned carpet of the hotel lobby, holding her remaining patent leather stiletto. It garnered some worried looks, but she was beyond caring. She wondered why she'd even brought the darned thing along. Kyle had his backpack and duffel bag slung over his right shoulder.

Gunny had made the arrangements, Kyle told her. He was very tight-lipped about what he knew, if anything. The front desk clerk asked if they needed help with their luggage and they both laughed. If the clerk only knew what the bags contained: enough firepower to start a war. Arm in arm, they walked down the hallway to the elevators. Kyle was deliberately slow and Christy found herself dragging him a slight bit. He wasn't hesitant in any way. He was teasing her, looking at her with that crooked grin that hinted of things to come.

She walked backward, towing him, watching the way his beautiful body moved lithely at her command. At her beck and call. She blushed as she thought about what they would be doing shortly. Loving Kyle

Lansdowne was way more than sex.

It was an art form.

"Remember that elevator ride from the model that first day?" she asked as she punched the elevator call button. The doors opened immediately.

Once inside, Kyle inserted the gold plastic room card above the bank of numbers on the elevator menu, and immediately the doors closed. "Of course I do." His eyes swept up her body. He owned her. She wanted him to see it, and he did. He stepped to her and pressed her back against the walls of the humming elevator box, clutching her hands above her head, rubbing his erection against her thigh. They kissed, Kyle teasing her lips open, his need mingling with hers.

The doors pinged open and they found themselves in a mini anteroom. Its large windows framed breathtaking views of the pier and the San Francisco Bay. The glassy sparkle of cities across the bay shot up from the horizon like copper crystals.

Only one set of double doors lead off of this reception area. Kyle put his key in the slot. Christy heard it click, and the doors were opened to a warm room done in peach tones with equally stunning views of the bay, the bridges, and beyond. On one end, a mirror hung above a gas-fired fireplace, fully flaming. On the other side, sitting atop a raised dais, was the largest bed Christy had ever seen. It was covered in a thick comforter of shiny rose pink satin and lace, littered with red rose petals and a smattering of multicolored silk pillows.

"Did you..." She couldn't get the question finished. His mouth was covering hers again, and she melted into his arms.

Kyle's hands found her flesh underneath her red top. He kneeled in front of her and pushed up the fabric to kiss her lower abdomen. His fingers kneaded her vertebrae at the back of her waist and then smoothed over her ass, finishing with a squeeze. He hugged her body, kissing and licking her belly button, making a wet trail with his tongue that went lower. He slid his palms down over her hips, hooking her black pants and panties along the way as he peeled her clothes down to her ankles.

She removed her top, tossing it aside, and stood before him, wearing only the expensive satin bra. She pulled his shirt up and over his shoulders and head. His fingers found the empty spot between her legs that needed to be filled. He slowly caressed the lips of her sex. Looking up into her eyes, he pressed two fingers inside her.

Christy melted, enjoying the sensation of being impaled by his fingers, which moved in a gentle rhythm. Practiced. Confident. Fingers she wanted all over her body.

She knelt down and joined him, leaning forward. She felt his chest against hers as flesh met flesh again. He hugged her tight, pressing her breasts against him.

Kyle's belt was undone. She quickly slid his pants down to his knees and placed her palms on his shaft, lacing his length with her fingers. They held each other while blending in a deep kiss that sent her spine tingling. His stiff cock got in the way.

"Will you bathe me?" she asked.

"With pleasure."

Kyle stood, bringing her up with him, and stepped out of his pants. They leaned against each other, fully naked. The honest look in his eyes told her she would remember this afternoon forever. There was nothing to run from anymore, and everything to savor and walk toward.

The bathroom was done in rich chocolate brown marble. Floors, walls, the massive roman tub and stall shower with dual heads were covered in the heavily veined stone. She entered the shower and turned on one spigot. Kyle took the other.

Under the warm water cascading over her body, she watched his muscled torso and his strong and thickly muscled thighs move under the steamy spray. His forearm with the little three-legged tattoo flexed as he poured shower gel into the palm of his hand and smoothed it down over his torso, and then lower to massage his thighs. He handed the plastic tube of gel to her.

She touched the tattoo. "What is this?"

"It's the footprints of a tree frog. Everyone on the Team has them."

She bent and kissed each footprint, one by one. Then she reached up and covered his mouth with hers. "I thought you were a SEAL." She fed from his mouth. His hands massaged her rear. His groan was delicious and made her spine tingle.

"We are. It's just what we do," he whispered in return.

"Well, sailor. What else do you do?"

"I do it all. Anything you like. For as long as you like."

She leaned back. His eyes roved over her hands as she massaged the soapy bubbled mixture over her breasts. She squeezed them together, then flicked her nipples. He licked his lips as his full erection lurched. Her hands traveled up around her neck, over her shoulders and down each arm, one at a time. She applied another generous dollop to her palm and rubbed her thighs with the gel, and then let her fingers play in and over her sex.

He was completely still as he watched her sluice her body with warm rinse water. She poured shampoo in the palm of her right hand and worked the suds through her scalp. He was fixated on her breasts that rose, her elbows above her head. She closed her eyes and let the warm spray cover her crown, working all the shampoo out of her hair. Kyle's hands were at her knees, gently prodding them to part. She looked down and saw he had kneeled, his mouth enveloped her sex, sucking and licking her slick petals. His hot tongue sliced a wedge between her lips and then found its way inside.

Her fingers curled in his hair as he ministered to her sex, lighting her whole body on fire. One of Kyle's palms was gently grazing her right thigh. The other hand pushed her lower torso onto his tongue, which swirled around her nub. She jumped with the burst of sensation. She felt his teeth rub against the flesh of her sex, pushing against her pubic bone. He pulled back, spread her lips with his fingers, and looked at her there.

When their eyes met, she saw the deep hunger he had for her. She cupped her hands under his jaw and drew him up to kiss him, giving him her tongue, tasting the juices of her own body on his lips.

He broke free. "God, Christy," he whispered in her ear. "I can't get enough of you. I don't want this to ever end."

She touched his cock, then wrapped her fingers around it and squeezed. She rubbed the lips of her sex against his thigh as their passion bloomed. He kissed the side of her neck, from the hollow of her shoulder to a place just under her ear.

She could spend eternity with him in the shower, until their skin withered away and their bones creaked. But she was listening for three little words. And she wasn't going to give up until she heard them.

"Tell me again." She smiled and squeezed his left nipple.

"I don't ever want this to end."

"Nor do I. Tell me again."

Kyle halted his massaging. With the warm water coursing down between both their bodies, he looked into her eyes. He pressed his hands over her cheeks, clutching her head, rubbing his thumbs over her lips. He pulled her to his mouth and kissed her tenderly. And then he looked at her again.

"I love you."

And there it was.

Her eyes filled with tears.

He kissed one eye, and then the other. "I love you, Christy," he whispered again. "I love you."

"And I have loved you, Kyle Lansdowne, ever since you tied me up and lay on top of me. I belonged to you that first day and always will."

CHRISTY DRIED OFF first, then ran to the bed and fell back among the rose petals. The plush satin coverlet was delicious under her warm, steamy flesh. She propped her head up with a light green pillow, put another under her rear, and raised one knee.

Kyle was there with something in his right hand. His fingers wrapped around her ankle as he raised her leg into the air. He kneeled on the bed and placed the black stiletto on her foot. He traced from her ankle down the inside of her leg until the finger teased the outsides of her lips. She needed that finger plunged deep inside her, but he smiled and rimmed her opening and around her nub in a figure-eight motion.

Christy was dripping wet. She could feel her internal muscles working in vain to try to draw his digit in. With his left hand and finger strategically left between her legs, he turned and kissed her ankle, holding her stiletto-clad foot around the ankle with a hand.

He kissed her twice on the backside of her knee, then once on the front. He guided her leg to bend over his shoulder. Christy was careful not to hurt him with the pointed tip, but then she forgot about it when he inserted his finger a mere half-inch. She was insane with desire for more.

Her pleading look generated a smile and he inserted another finger into her wet opening. He kissed her thigh, then lower toward her sex, and just before his tongue touched her lips, his two fingers slid easily to the hilt. She arched, presenting herself to him. She needed to be tasted. Needed him inside her.

Christy writhed on the bed as he played with her, as he slid the surface of his tongue up and down her opening, around her folds, and tasted her. Every time she opened her eyes he was looking at her, needing to see her passion.

"I need you inside me, please."

"Yes. Soon, Christy. I need to make sure you are ready."

"I'm ready now."

"Yes, soon. Before exertion you must loosen and warm your body up."

"I'm loose. I'm warm. Trust me, Kyle, I'm ready."

"Are you sure?" He plunged his tongue deeper.

"God, yes!" She grabbed pillows and squeezed them to her chest.

"No, no. You don't get to cover up. I must see those. I may need to taste them, too." He pulled the pillows away and shoved them under her rear. Her pelvis was now lifted off the bed. She clutched the satin coverlet at her sides, drunk with need.

"And something else," he whispered as he kissed her belly button. He climbed up over to the head of the bed. Under one of the satin pillows was a one-inch wide red satin ribbon. He held it up in front of her face, waving it back and forth.

"What are you doing?" she asked.

He smirked, grabbed hold of both her hands with one of his, and lay them gently up over her head. He wound the red ribbon around her wrists in a loose figure eight. Christy felt like she was going to explode inside.

"Please. Please," she begged.

"Yes. You like this?"

"Yes. I belong to you. All yours. Please, Kyle. Make love to me."

"Yes, you are mine. You always will be mine."

"Please. Fill me. I need you."

"Yes."

"I love you, Kyle. Please love me. Please never leave me again."

Kyle climbed over her body, holding his muscled torso with one hand over her, barely touching her flesh. With his other hand he placed her other knee over his shoulder. With her pelvis angled to meet him, he placed the head of his penis at her opening and smiled as she gasped.

"I have no protection."

"You are my protection."

"Are you sure?"

"Completely. You are my protection, Kyle. You are all I need, all I ever will need."

"And you are mine." With that, he thrust deep inside her.

He rocked gently at first, with back and forth motions that sent jolts of pleasure all over her body, radiating from between her legs. She saw his tanned, handsome face, the square jaw and full lips now forming a smile. Her fingers struggled and he gripped her wrists and the ribbon firmly as he plunged in deeper holding her in place, restraining her body, possessing her in every way possible.

"Love you," she whispered.

"Love you," he repeated.

He changed angles, rolling her to the side, repositioning her leg as he fucked her harder. She felt a long orgasm growing and wanted to match his, but couldn't wait. All of a sudden, spasms rocked her body. Her eyes fluttered closed as she arched her back. He used the new angle to plunge in deeper, which was exactly what she wanted, needed. She moaned as he filled her, as he rubbed his thighs against hers, as he pressed a thumb into her nub and watched her lurch.

Everything he did heightened her pleasure. Her orgasm was beginning to fade as he continued to pump her, then he'd stop, change a leg, or an angle and show her a spot he'd missed that sent her over the edge again.

He flipped her over on her belly with one arm as she presented herself to him, her hands out front, bound in the red ribbon.

She begged, "Please."

He first kissed the quivering lips, red-hot and still filled with need. Balancing himself on one knee and arm, he placed himself at her opening. She backed toward him.

He backed away. She turned to look at his eyes. She raised her rear up, over his erect penis, rubbed herself over his head, and laved herself against the delicious feel of his shaft.

And then she pushed herself onto him, moving up and down, back and forth, showing him how much she loved him there. She watched his face as he looked at the place where they joined. She wished she could see where they mated. She wished she could see him thrusting in and out of her.

He stuffed two pillows under her belly, then put two powerful hands on her shoulders and pulled her back onto his length. His movements became frenzied and again her insides began to explode. She moaned as the wave of contractions clamped down on him, milking him, driving him deeper. Just as she was losing the last ounce of control she felt the bonds of her ribbons loosen. All at once he shuddered, and then he moaned as his own spasms matched hers.

She wanted every drop of him.

She would take him all.

Forever. She would never give up loving him.

No matter what.

# CHAPTER 43

KYLE FELT LIKE he was floating on a cloud. He wasn't used to it. He'd given himself permission to go over the edge with Christy, to let his guard down. And he knew she would gladly give him anything he asked.

He snuggled against her soft backside as she slept. He'd wrapped them both in the satin spread. Rose petals had gotten caught in her hair when he'd eased the silky surface over her body.

She had tied the satin ribbon around her neck in a bow.

She was smiling in her sleep. Oblivious to the world. Lost in a dream state of her own making. He hoped she was dreaming about him. He was sure daydreaming about her. In fact, he'd gotten hard again mere minutes after he heard her fall off into a deep sleep. He decided if she moved a muscle in his direction, he'd have his lovely way with her again. Her fingers would find him. Her legs would rub against his thighs and send him soaring.

He'd untie the ribbon and watch her come.

He'd never told a woman he loved her. But he'd told Christy several times this evening. And he couldn't wait to do it again. He kissed the back of her neck and pulled her into his chest again.

*Please wake so I can have you again.*

TWO HOURS LATER, twilight had turned to darkness. Kyle was starved. Christy was now resting on his chest. After the second lovemaking, he had finally fallen asleep. And now he was enveloped in the scent of the lavender gel shampoo that lingered in her still-damp hair. The pillows were all over the room. He looked down her body, draped over his. She'd tucked his thigh between both of hers, as if she was making sure he wasn't going to leave.

No, he would never leave her. If she asked him, he would leave the SEALs. He never thought he'd say that. It would be a difficult choice. But his place was at her side now. Perhaps his days of running into and through trouble were over. Maybe he could join the ranks of the good cops like Mayfield. There was honor in that. Leave the Teams for the younger ones coming up from BUD/S. Give them a chance to show what they're made of.

It was strange to even think about leaving the Navy, though. He'd never thought anything but the Navy was his family. But now there was Christy. And she was his life. She had to be a part of his life, for however long that was. And women didn't like to be second best to anything. Not the military, not to duty, not to honor. They had to come first. And then there might be kids. Kids need a dad. Not some father who was vacant like his dad had been. He wouldn't do that to a kid.

Especially not his kid.

There she was again. Arching her body against him, squeezing his thigh high up against her wet sex. The little things she did to show him she was interested were such an unexpected thrill. He looked forward to learning all about the ways it would take to turn her on, keep her satisfied, and keep her wanting more. And the more he gave, the more he wanted to give.

And the more he had something to lose.

There were those fingers again, strumming the flesh around his left nipple. If he opened his eyes, she'd be kissing him in seconds. He'd be spilling his seed inside her in no time. It was just about the only thing he could think about.

"I know you're awake, Kyle," she whispered.

He let his lips tell her she was right as he allowed a smile to form. Sure enough, she was up and over him. She'd migrated her knee to over his lower abdomen, grazing his shaft that was standing at full attention. He loved the chance encounter with her soft flesh, no matter how brief.

He watched her wrap the satin ribbon around his left wrist. She was on her way to obtaining his other one.

"So you don't want me to use my hands, then?" he said as he watched his words register. While she considered her options.

She halted, and then removed the ribbon and tossed it off the bed.

She lowered herself on his legs and licked the length of his shaft. She sucked hard, and then licked the long length of him. Was this round three or four?

Did it matter?

He lay there and enjoyed her wanting to pleasure him. After only a few minutes, he was hard as a rock and about to come in her mouth as she moved up and down his length. He loved watching her mouth work him over. She flashed her big brown eyes up at him.

*Ah, delicious.* She was a wonder, all right. Long curls falling all over his thighs, those honest eyes that begged him to fuck her. Well, he'd deliver on that request as many times as she asked it of him. Happy to oblige, in fact.

She mounted him, slowly settling down on his cock, and was arching backward, holding her breasts, tweaking her nipples. Her eyes flashed open when he raised his pelvis up, placing a couple of pillows under his butt. It gave her a higher mount so she could ride him. And ride him she did.

He pushed himself deep inside her and she quivered, moaned. She held her hair up with her hands, letting it fall partially over her eyes as she looked at him. She turned in profile. He followed the line of her perfect torso and filled his hands with soft pillows of flesh. She licked her lips slowly and he lost it. Next thing he knew he was shooting inside her like a seventeen-year-old.

The woman was going to wear him out.

And he was going to love every minute of it.

CHRISTY LAY NEXT to Kyle. Both stared at the ceiling. She was enjoying the sounds of his heavy breathing. He laced his fingers through hers and kissed her hand.

"Are you hungry?" he asked.

Christy hadn't thought about it until just then, but she was. "Famished. Let's go walk some place close by."

"I was hoping you'd say that." He turned his head. She felt his stare on the side of her face. He raised himself up on one arm, outlining her nipples with a forefinger. He kissed her first on one side, and then the other. She couldn't escape those blue eyes softly bearing down on hers. "Christy, I'm thinking about leaving the Navy when my time is up this fall."

"Why?" His statement surprised her.

"Maybe it's time I grow up. I've been blowing things up, snatching and grabbing bad guys. Playing with really cool gear for ten years now. Can't do that forever." He was watching her reaction.

"But it's who you are, Kyle. Don't you love what you do?"

"Absolutely." He lay back on the bed and sighed. They lay in silence, Kyle's warm thigh against hers, as if they'd been doing this for years. As if it were a routine, the talking and then the lovemaking, and then the talking and then...it felt like life as it was supposed to be.

"Don't do it for me," she said finally. "I don't want to be the one responsible for taking you away from something that means so much. I love you for who you are. And who you are, right now at least, is a SEAL. You were born to be one. I want you to do what you love. And I'll be here when you come home."

She turned her head and saw he'd been watching her. Something deep in his eyes held her. It was devotion. She'd never seen anyone look at her that way before.

"If it wasn't for me, what would you do?" she asked.

"I'd stay in."

"Then that's what you should—no, that's what I *want* you to do."

THEY WALKED THROUGH the shops at Ferry Plaza, tasting wine, olive oil, and homemade chocolates along the way. Her feet were cold in the flip-flops he'd bought her in the lobby shop. Christy wanted to go to the oyster bar overlooking the Marin Ferry. They stayed inside and watched the twinkle of lights from the Bay Bridge reflected in the choppy waters of the Bay. She ordered a plate with three local varieties of oysters. They came smothered in garlic and simmering in butter.

Fog was beginning to roll in on the bay, covering the tips of the bridge arching high overhead, but the pier was still clear, and would be for another hour.

"Oysters are supposed to help your stamina," Christy said.

"You find something wrong with my stamina?" Kyle asked. He had butter and a piece of garlic stuck to his upper lip. She kissed it off.

"No. Not at all." She laughed. "I think perhaps *I* need it."

He curled his forefinger, motioning her to lean closer to him. "You are perfect just the way you are." He kissed her.

Christy glowed inside. The man could charm the pants off a…an oyster.

"So you like oysters?" she continued.

"I like eating anything around you. Everything tastes great."

With his fingers, he placed a stray lock of hair behind her left ear, and then held up her chin for another long kiss. His palm slid down her arm, over the fabric of her oversized San Francisco souvenir sweatshirt that matched his.

"And everything is good around you," he said in a raspy, dead-sexy bedroom voice.

She turned her stool and let his knee hit her pubic bone. She locked him there. "You know what I'm thinking?" she asked.

"I'm afraid to ask."

"Well, you've had your fortification. So, how many more times can we do it before midnight?"

"I should be good for one or two…but first I wanna have a little talk with you."

His face got serious. Christy held her breath. Every time there was a "serious" talk before, it had been bad news. Now what? Had their earlier discussion set off a chain of events that was now going to hurt?

Kyle fished something out of his San Francisco sweatshirt pocket.

He got down on one knee, and in front of the whole group of oyster-loving, beer drinking customers, held her left hand and said, "Christy Nelson. Would you marry me?"

Did he just ask me to marry him? She hadn't allowed herself to long for a proposal of marriage. She'd been planning on enjoying what was to come as long as he was there by her side.

"Absolutely," she answered. She couldn't believe it.

He put the ring on her finger.

The crowd took note of the proposal and burst into spontaneous clapping.

She looked at the costume jewelry ring he must have purchased at the hotel. It was the most beautiful stone she had ever seen, and it mattered not one whit that it wasn't real.

Her man was.

If you enjoyed Accidental SEAL, Book 1 of the SEAL Brotherhood Series, and want to continue in the original series that launched Sharon's career, you can continue with Fallen SEAL Legacy, book 2.

Or, if you want to read the first four books in this series, why don't you pick up, the Ultimate SEAL Collection #1, or the Ultimate SEAL Collection #2, and you will have all 9 of these fantastic romantic suspense reads, all with a different couple from SEAL Team 3. You can read all about them here. All of these books, either the singles, or the bundles, are available on Audible as well.

Sharon's new series, SEAL Brotherhood: Legacy, is a re-visit with those first four couples in the SEAL Brotherhood Series, starting with Kyle and Christy. You can get the first book in this new series, Watery Grave, which is presently available wide on all retailers, now!

And now, hold on to your heart, one of my most favorite characters, T.J. Talbot, is about to take the stage in **SEAL's Promise**. For some reason, I've never gotten over how T.J. lovingly came into my life and stole my heart. I hope you'll enjoy this beautiful story that had me crying more times than not, while writing. It was my way of healing after hearing of the death of a SEAL Team member, who was close to members of my family. T.J. figures prominently, like Kyle, in all my SEAL books.

# SEAL'S PROMISE

## Bad Boys of SEAL Team 3
## Book 1

## SHARON HAMILTON

# CHAPTER 1

T.J. TALBOT LIKED weddings because he could always enjoy generous helpings of his two favorite things: alcohol and young lovelies.

Whenever a buddy got sweet on a girl and was contemplating 'walking the plank', as he liked to call it, T.J. was only too happy to help him celebrate. He never did mind the cost of the tux rental, the dinners and bachelor parties he had to spring for. It was all a means to an end. And his end was usually hooking up with someone and getting it on.

That was why he usually went to weddings stag. He'd sometimes promise to meet this or that lovely there, but usually he would go alone and play the field. Playing the field was much better for everyone involved.

He didn't think of himself as a one-woman guy. He doubted anyone would be able to satisfy his appetites, especially his appetites in the bedroom. Experimentation was the norm for him. He didn't want anyone crying to him after the fact, so he was careful. Yes, it did occasionally mean he went home alone. Far better to do that than to go home with a woman you had to console or peel off your skin the next day.

Tonight he had his eye on one of the bride's best friends, Cindy. She had a funny little laugh, and he liked the way her tits jiggled whenever she did it. Her big blue eyes struck him right away as being interested in whatever he could dish out.

He always liked it when he could surprise a girl, help her learn new things about her sexual nature, and Cindy seemed like the perfect type, all spunky and full of sexual tension. He was going to pace himself, make sure he stayed in her line of sight a lot, and hope she'd chase him. He didn't like it that way ... unless he orchestrated it. Hell, he'd almost forgotten to line up with the other groomsmen he was thinking so hard about where he could take her for a bit of minor relief until he could have an all-nighter with her.

Four other SEALs were in the wedding party, and he had to admit they'd make a wedding portrait which would look good on the cover of any bridal magazine, except for their dark glasses. Only Frankie, the groom, posed without shades. Shannon had wanted them all without the shades, but T.J. smiled at her and put his back on in open defiance, and the others followed his lead.

She'd flounced off in a huff, a flurry of white cream puff material, and her perfume that made him sneeze. He knew about that hellcat streak she had. He angled his head to the side and intently studied her as she marched off to whatever mythical place brides hide when they go crazy. Even he had to admit that.

Frankie was white as a sheet as they gathered. "I wanna pray first," he'd said to his best buddies. Tyler was there, of course, and Kyle. Ollie and Rory were as well. But T.J. was Frankie's best friend, and that meant he had to be best man.

"Fuckin' going to need a lot more than fuckin' prayin'. Gonna need a miracle, Frankie. Shannon's had the evil eye on me all morning…yesterday, too, and that means I don't think you're getting any tonight, not that you haven't—"

"Fuck's sake, T.J. It's my fuckin' wedding and has nothing to do with how my bride looks at you. Get that fuckin' thought out of your head."

"I was just sayin'—"

"Not what you're sayin' I have a problem with. It's what you're *thinking*." Frankie was so nervous he was seeing conspiracies behind every plant, guest and bouquet.

"Just be glad we didn't send you to Alaska," Tyler said, making it worse. Last year, one of the young recruits was honored with time off from BUD/S to get married—a request which was almost never granted. The boys thought it necessary to save him from his quickie wedding in Las Vegas, and so they got him stinking drunk and put him on a plane to Alaska so he missed his own wedding. They incurred extra wet and sandy for that one, and the toilets were cleaned so many times you could eat out of them.

This had worried Shannon, and worried her mother even more. Mrs. "I Want Moore" was one of the hottest women T.J. had ever seen, a toned marathon runner in her fifties. He had never before had fantasies about the mother of the bride. Mrs. Moore was twenty-five years his senior, but he knew she could clean his clock. He'd enjoy chasing her around a few places.

Turning to face Frankie again, he felt a tad sheepish about his lusty thoughts. He wiped his mind clean and decided to concentrate harder on Frankie's day. His buddy was so crazy in love with Shannon, he needed extra protection to keep him from stepping out in front of traffic, or bumping into caterers, which he'd already managed to do several times today.

"Come on, Frankie. Lighten up." T.J. slapped his cheeks to redden them up. "You need to stop looking like a dead man if you're really gonna do this."

"Yup. I'm doing this," Frankie said to the auditorium full of people, the organ music now swelling up to the rafters. "I'm fuckin' doing this."

T.J. had a hunch he was looking for his courage and had come up short. He glanced down the hallway. Cindy was leaning against the wall right outside the bride's dressing room, keeping guard, but also giving him the long vacant look he knew only too well. He unabashedly scanned her entire body and let her see he couldn't wait to get her naked.

She abruptly turned, blushing.

*Perfect.*

Several minutes later, T.J. thought he might have to prop Frankie up he was so pale. "You okay?"

"Fuck you," Frankie whispered a little too loudly. Mrs. Moore in the front pew frowned. Her eyes swept over the row of SEALs, but zeroed back in on T.J.'s face with an admonition he couldn't mistake. Merely the little tilt of her chin down and the knotted brow told him he was on probation. Didn't help he'd given Frankie more tequila than he usually drank in a whole month. Frankie was spacing out and losing track of where they were and what they had to do next. T.J. had never seen him so fuckin' scared. Even in firefights overseas.

So he'd screwed up, been a bad influence on the groom. *So what else is new?* With a past of foster care home rejections and "repositioning" he was used to being on probation. It felt normal. Not until he got into BUD/S did he feel like he'd found home. A real home. Guys who finally shared his intensity for life and irreverence for batshit rules that everyone else thought applied to him. The SEAL's ethos was the only set of rules he wanted to live by. And the beginning pretty much said it all:

*In times of war or uncertainty there is a special breed of warrior ready to answer our Nation's call. A common man with uncommon desire to succeed.*

*...I am that man.*

He didn't have to be a perfect man, and hell, there were very few on the Teams. He was good enough. He'd never be perfect anyway, and who would want to be? No, he was that guy who wouldn't give up. That was all it was. Not ringing the bell. No matter what.

He thought about it while he watched Shannon's white dress fill the aisle as she began her stately walk along the burgundy carpet to her willing but completely shitfaced groom. Her father was proud, as any father would be, to have such a radiant daughter, pink and soft in all the right places. She possessed the steady gait of a fearless warrior princess, and the purposeful way she advanced, like she was intent on a plan she was going to fully execute, was just like any SEAL. Her eyes nailed Frankie, who didn't have a clue what he was getting himself into.

That made T.J. smile and check out his shoes. She was the kind of woman who would call the shots, run the household, run Frankie, manage the hell out of his schedule and get her future soccer players up on time and off to everything moms did with a house full of hellions. He saw lots of them in their future for some reason. Kids with snotty noses and hair a bit too long. Band-Aids and skinned knees. All the things he never had as a child.

But he'd watched those kids play through chain-link fences. Watched their parents cheer. Watched the juice breaks and the encouragement he never got from a single coach or foster mom. He was never noticed. Never special.

And that was just fine.

# CHAPTER 2

S HANNON FELT THE pressure of everyone's eyes on her back. She tried not to think about her maid of honor, Cindy, who had pummeled her with questions about the mysterious, bad-boy best man she hated, T.J. Talbot.

That man had done his best to break them up, Shannon thought, and now was working hard to ruin her wedding. He'd exposed Frankie to the seedier side of life. Nothing they experimented with in the bedroom had ever been Frankie's idea. It was always something T.J. had described to him.

*Fuck T.J.*

Yet, she knew that by marrying Frankie, tradition said she was, in fact, marrying all the SEALs on Team 3.

*To hell with that!*

Thank God she'd never have to sleep with any of the rest of them. Knowing they were so possessive about each other, made her a little bit jealous.

Frankie was listing to one side. T.J.'s strong arm propped him up, which was the biggest fuckbomb of all time.

*Stop it, Shannon.* She'd picked up their language, their mannerisms, as if they'd been wet paint and she was rolling through them naked. She not only thought in swear words, she was starting to say them. They rolled off her tongue as though she'd always talked and thought that way.

Yeah, and that was T.J.'s fault, too.

She could see the little Cheshire cat smile he was giving her, not that she would give him the satisfaction of knowing he was even a piece of cat litter stuck on the bottom of her shoe. Frankie was going to be all hers. She'd extricate him from his Brotherhood and give him back to them when she was good and ready. Screw the wives who told her she would always come second when it came to the Brotherhood. They didn't know their men. She didn't want a normal plain vanilla relationship with Frankie. He was fuckin' addicted to her, and that was exactly the way she liked it.

*There you go again. On your wedding day, and before you get to the altar and kiss your betrothed, you've sworn—what? Maybe three or four times? And had unclean thoughts?*

Yeah, even ladies in white wedding dresses had dirty thoughts.

She knew that was normal.

*Come on, Frankie. Stand up straight.* She saw the glassy eyes and knew T.J. had caused it. Her Frankie was drunker than he had a right to be. From the unearthly glow in his blue eyes it was probably tequila, which he couldn't hold well at all.

Not like she could. Oh yes, there was that song about dropping your clothes for margaritas. That was her. But Frankie was having a hard time standing up, let alone being conscious for the wedding. And it wasn't because all the blood had rushed to his groin, either. That would have been funny. She'd have been happy about that one.

She shot a quick *fuck-why-did-you-do-that?* look at T.J. His smile broadened, and she saw him move his arm when she stood about a foot away from the man she'd chosen for the rest of her life.

The moment T.J. released his hold on Frankie, the groom fell, almost toppling her as well. Her veil was ripped from her hair, her bodice pulled down—maybe too far down for a second or two. And accompanied by the screams of everyone, especially the two mothers in the front pew of the church. Frankie did a face-plant onto what was luckily plush carpeting.

She adjusted the detachable beaded bodice to make sure she was decent first, and then had difficulty turning in Frankie's direction, thanks to her long dress of chiffon and layers of voile. Feeling like her feet were stuck in mud, she turned slowly. T.J. was leaning down to get Frankie, and she caught a hint of his aftershave, nearly brushing her lips across his cheekbone as he stood.

Three big SEALs helped Frankie up. His face bright red, sweat pouring down his forehead, and his shame preceded what Shannon knew would be a huge bender, perhaps one that would eclipse their wedding night. He'd messed up her wedding. He'd tried so hard not to. He'd told her every day he hoped everything came off the way she wanted. Perfect. Like she was perfect, he'd said. Did he suffer from premonitions?

*Fuck perfect.*

So…there was her fifth swear word and unclean thought. She had another one as she grabbed his arm and hoisted him to her side, which made a few people in the audience titter. T.J. was chuckling just loud enough for her to hear that too.

*This is not happening.* She knew she would wake up any minute. This must be the nightmare wedding from a bad movie. This wasn't *her* wedding day. The day she'd dreamt about her whole life. The one where she'd be the star of the show.

After the vows were said and the rings exchanged, the two of them walked down the aisle, both relieved to have survived the ceremony without further bloodshed. Frankie led her straight to the bar, which she thought was a great idea.

He'd stopped to tell someone in the last row he wasn't even drunk, which was such an obvious lie. It was a classless further slight to her not-so-perfect wedding. Like maybe God was responsible for all this.

It could be her fault, scaring the shit out of him and making him need to get so drunk he passed out. It would be a cold day in hell before she'd admit it publicly, though. She knew Frankie was scared to death to displease her. In her heart of hearts, she knew she was fully responsible. But no one would ever know.

No one. Ever.

What she loved about Frankie was his soft heart and how easy-going he was. That, and the fact that she would be the center of his universe, regardless of what her girlfriends warned her about the Brotherhood. He would be a kind and devoted husband and some day father. She could count on him to be there for her. She loved exciting and surprising him. He would support her in everything she wanted to do without question.

T.J. came up behind her. She could smell him before he put his palm on her shoulder, matching the other palm on Frankie's shoulder while they stood waiting to get poison into their systems quick. The bartender had dropped the first glass he'd filled with ice for her Tom Collins, so the jitters were spreading. But not to T.J. He was rock-solid, steady and undistracted, and she hated every muscle and sinew of his body. Every drop of his blood. Every cell. She hated all of him for being so calm and light-hearted about her disaster of a wedding.

Not that he'd ever know. She did her best to give him a triumphant, smile. Then she took Frankie's double scotch and downed it before he could get his hands on it. With the liquor on her lips and a glow spreading down her chest, she didn't care how they looked at her. She was a bride on a mission. Her day. Her time, and they better fucking play her game or she'd take them both on.

T.J. gave her an appreciative return glance. Frankie was still trying to figure out what had happened as he told the confused bartender to give him the scotch he didn't get the first time.

"Okay. I'm good. Good now. Time to face my audience," she said and wafted off as if she was wearing a dress of white potato chips. She'd deal with Frankie after he found the courage to look at her. Until then, she didn't want to be anywhere near him or his fuckin' devil of a best friend.

Okay, so that was number six.


T.J. WAS ENRAPTURED. The bride was storming across the wooden floor of the fellowship hall, bloody entrails of his heart guts, if there was such a thing, caught in the hem of her dress. No woman had ever made him feel that way before. He was completely powerless to focus on anything else until she was out of sight.

"Glad that's fuckin' over," Frankie said with a croak, and then coughed.

That brought T.J. to life, but he found it hard to talk.

"I'm never going through that again. Something happens to her, someone else wants to have a big wedding, the answer is no, and if that means I stay a bachelor my whole life, so be it," Frankie said.

"You're not a fuckin' bachelor. Too late for that, man. You'd be a widower. Not a bachelor."

"Whatever the fuck they call it."

"You know, Frankie, I wonder if you realize what you've just done?"

"I don't catch your drift."

"You've committed yourself to one woman. You really sure this is a good thing?"

*Now, why are you even talking about that? Oh yeah, to cover up the fact that the bride is the object of your fantasies. Right now that fantasy involves a number of very unholy images. And you're standing next to the only man on the planet who has any right to have such fantasies. This is the guy you'd lay your life down for without a second thought...Oh, thank God, there is Miss Fresh Face walking through the door and aiming for me, just in time.*

"Hi, T.J. I thought I'd find you hanging around the bar," Cindy said.

God, she was a welcome sight. She was the drink of water that wouldn't save his life, but would definitely make the next few minutes possible. He was almost ready to ask her if she would suck his dick and be quick about it.

"Cindy, you're lookin' mighty fine," Frankie said, eyeing her. "I was getting a lecture from my best man, asking if I knew what kind of shit I was getting myself into, and you walk back into the room, and now we can talk about something really important."

Cindy giggled. She stood on tiptoes and gave Frankie a lip-lock. "And don't you forget it. I'd have spent my life with you, Frankie, and you wouldn't have had to walk down any aisle or dress up like a penguin." She whispered soft things to Frankie, and T.J. could see he liked it.

Until Shannon showed up. Of course, Shannon would blame T.J. If she'd look at him, that is. She was shooting daggers at Cindy. Frankie removed his palm from Cindy's ass and was, once again, red in the face.

This was not turning out to be one of Frankie's better days.

# CHAPTER 3

I T WAS DAYS before T.J. could get Frankie away to enjoy a beer at the Scupper.

"You ever think about settling down?"

T.J. returned a glare he knew Frankie would feel deep in his gut. "Don't ever ask me that fuckin' question again, Frankie." He watched some lovelies who strutted in with unbelievably tight cutoff jeans and knotted tee shirts that showed a good portion of smooth, flat abdomen—just his favorite kind of eye candy. All the girls who wanted to make it with a SEAL did this on Friday and Saturday nights. One of them snagged T.J.'s appreciative smile and gave him a wink.

*Perfect.*

Frankie watched where T.J. had focused and shook his head. "I don't know where you get all the energy, Talbot. Keeping stories straight, promising to call them and then—"

"What stories? Why the hell would you tell them stories? It goes like this, Frankie, 'Hon, you wanna screw?' Doesn't involve a lot of talking, Frankie. And then if they want to talk too much, you kiss them until they shut up."

Frankie giggled like he always did when T.J. revealed some of his philosophy on women and the other finer things in life. "I always let them talk." Frankie shrugged his shoulders. "I'm interested in what they have to say. Don't you want to know them a little bit first, T.J.?"

"Well, that tells me you're not a very good kisser."

"Fuck you, T.J. How do you know how I kiss? Shannon thinks I kiss real good. She loves it."

"I'll bet."

"I'm not shitting you, man. We get it on, T.J. You should try it. Staying monogamous. Sexy as hell knowing someone is waiting for me at home, and I get to fondle her all night long. And she'll still want to be there in the morning."

"Not for me."

"But I love her, T.J. You'd do it too if you married someone like my Shannon."

T.J. shook his head and raised a finger. "No. Never like Shannon. I'd have to work too hard."

"That's what you do when you love somebody, T.J. Shannon and I have a perfect love. I've never wanted to be so devoted to anyone, well, except for you, of course—"

"Shut the fuck up. Trying to make me jealous? I don't go for guys, Frankie."

"Yeah, but I love you, man. I wish you could have what Shannon and I have."

"You mean you do whatever she wants and have no will of your own."

"No, see, that's what you got wrong. I *want* to please her. She gets so excited sometimes, like a little girl. I feel so lucky every time I look at her. This beautiful, smart, sexy woman is mine and mine alone. I tell you, T.J., you're missing something. One night stands are boring, man. This is where it's at."

"Good for you, asshole." T.J. raised his beer, "To love, then."

"And family," Frankie added.

T.J. nearly spit out his beer "Family? You're not seriously gonna make me drink to family, are you? You remember who you're talking to?"

"Not *your* family, T.J. My family. I'm going to have a baby. Shannon and I made a baby together."

T.J. wanted to slap him. His insides turned to molten lead. He bit down so hard, grinding his molars he almost bit his own tongue. Procreation was a dirty word. He was halfway convinced he'd go get himself fixed so he never had to deal with that situation. His biggest fear was getting a girl pregnant, perhaps creating another fatherless soul, or having to marry someone you really didn't want to just to do the right thing.

And now Frankie was willingly walking into that buzz saw.

"I can't believe it. You ready to be a father, Frankie?"

"Hell yeah. And you know what? You're about to be a godfather."

"Not me."

"Yes, Shannon and I talked about it, and you're going to be the baby's godfather. We want you to do us this honor."

"You sure Shannon okayed this?" T.J. wanted to say no, but he knew it would hurt Frankie perhaps more than anything else he could do or say.

"She knows you're like a brother, T.J. She knows you would do anything for me, even die for me, you know? Who else could be that baby's godfather?"

"Anyone but me." T.J. had said, but in the end he'd agreed. He remembered the wedding and how nervous Frankie had been, so worried about ruining Shannon's perfect day. And now he was going to be a father.

But he knew Frankie, unlike T.J.'s own father, would never abandon his child. Frankie would be there to make sure that child had everything possible. And he'd do it out of love. He wouldn't farm an infant to some hellhole in another state, allowing him to be raised by sadists and mean women and their asshole husbands. Or raised in an institution like juvenile hall. Left like a leaf floating on the current of a river of no return. Nobody could call himself a man and do that to a child. Unforgiveable.


SIX MONTHS LATER, T.J. was thinking about Frankie's wedding day while he and the rest of SEAL Team 3 sat in a bombed-out building, waiting for nightfall so they could proceed to the rendezvous. The target hadn't been where they were told he would be.

In fact, this was the third time in as many days that the intel had been inaccurate, which wasn't a good sign. Each day, they were sent further out into the rural parts of the city of Goan. There hadn't been a shot fired, but the eyes of the people they'd seen were hard.

T.J. had tried warming up to their new interpreter. Not everyone on the team trusted him. He was no Jackie Daniels, the interpreter they'd used during their last deployment, who had literally saved their lives. This guy was shifty, didn't look him in the eyes when T.J. spoke to him, and that spooked the hell out of him. The terp was edgier than he'd seen kids on speed in juvie.

The unease was beginning to rub off, even before the terp told him in clipped English. "Something's not good here."

*Well if that wasn't the fuckin' understatement of the year.* "So tell me the *good* news, Sherlock." T.J. preferred using the name more similar to his Pashtu common name, a word no one, even the few of them well-schooled on the language, could pronounce. He was hoping for something slightly positive to compensate for the hairs standing out on the back of his neck, the ache he was getting in his shoulders from crouching quickly to take cover. The terp was doing it ten times more, eyeing corners and turning around to check for follows.

"No good news, boss. All bad here. Must be very, very careful."

T.J. heard several of their platoon swear openly and wished not so many had heard him. He decided to lessen the load on Frankie, who had been uncommonly quiet, as if he had a premonition. He'd thought Frankie was scared the day he married Shannon. That was a joke now.

"You remember that day when you passed out, Frankie? Your face is at least as red as that day."

"That's because it's fuckin' hot, man. Can't wait for midnight."

"I think it was because of all the tequila we drank. And everyone in their Sunday finest."

"That was a fuckin' nightmare of a day, except for the fact I married the girl of my dreams."

"That you did, my man." T.J. leaned to the left to peer out of the hole in the rubble. He couldn't shake the uneasy feeling about this place. He didn't like the howling wind, the way everyone avoided being anywhere close to them, like they were lepers. Sand was getting into everything. He was getting a huge blister where one of his socks had a hole, his boots unforgiving.

An RPG hit barely six feet from them, exploding out a cloud of rubble, sending all of them into the air. While pebbles and body parts rained down on them, T.J. saw they'd lost at least two men—and Frankie was hit. He checked himself and discovered he still had twenty and didn't hurt anywhere, and then he went to tend Frankie. He'd landed on his back, blood pouring from his mouth. T.J.'s gut tightened but he worked to hide the concern he felt for his best friend.

"Shit, Frankie. You bite your tongue?"

"No, man. Got hit in the back. Can't feel my legs, T.J. What the fuck?" Frankie brought his hands out from behind him. He'd been sitting on them. His fingers were dripping with his own blood.

T.J. rolled Frankie to the side, far enough to see a metal piece imbedded in Frankie's lower spine. The blood was bubbling, watered down by what T.J. assumed was spinal fluid. Fredo was radioing for extraction. T.J. swung around so he could hold Frankie's head up slightly while he checked for combatants.

"Got Marines on their way, gents," Kyle yelled out over the cries of their CIA embed, who had been hit as well. T.J. shared a look with his LPO, something he knew Kyle had seen many times before. His Team leader's tight jaw and unwavering eye contact commanded him he'd better hold it together for Frankie. That's when he understood Kyle knew Frankie wasn't going to make it, but they had to convince Frankie he would.

*Sonofabitch.* He took a deep breath and barked, "Frankie, getting you home. Bird is coming now. Hang tight. I'm going to go see if I can help out some of the others."

"No. Don't go. I don't want to die alone, man."

"Frankie, you're not going to die."

"T.J., you're a fuckin' bad liar. Always have been."

"Shut up, Frankie. I gotta stop the sound effects or they'll know right where to send the next one, and we'll all buy it."

"Trust me, they know. They're looking to get themselves a turkey. Why mess with a sparrow?"

T.J. knew Frankie was telling the truth. It still sucked.

It was happening more and more, light injuries requiring evacuation, and then the combatants went after the helo and got everyone. Of course, that was if the SEALs or a sniper on the chopper didn't pick them off first. But fifty percent of the time it worked, which was much worse than it used to be.

"T.J., please hang here for a minute while I finish this mission." Frankie's eyes were kind, tears running down his cheeks. "If there was ever anyone in the whole world I would want to take care of my Shannon, could ever see her fuckin' besides me, it would be you."

"Frankie, stop it. I'm not going to fuck Shannon."

"Your loss, you dumb shit. She's going to be a widow, and someone needs to watch over her and the baby. I want you to raise my little girl, T.J. I want you to beat up the first asshole who tries to get in her pants. I want you to hold Shannon's hand while she's in labor. And I'll be right there with you, man. Just not in this body."

"Frankie, stop it. This isn't helping your situation." T.J. could hear the chopper approaching, but he knew it wasn't what Frankie needed right now. Frankie needed a miracle, and T.J. couldn't do anything but watch his friend die. He wanted to hug the big dufus who he'd joked and played around with, slap him in the face and tell him to wake up, that the play was too realistic and was creeping him out. Take the man for a beer and laugh about scaring each other. He wanted to be anywhere but here, doing this thing right now, and not being able to say the things he'd never gotten to say to Frankie. Because if he lost it, Frankie would too. "Hear that? That's the sound of home, and apple pie, and you getting well and telling her all those things yourself."

"Love you, man. Do it, T.J. You promised. You're our little girl's godfather, man. You promised, man." Frankie's lethargic gaze showed nothing but love. T.J. never had a real brother, that he knew of, and now he was losing the only man in the world who had been more than a real brother to him.

"Do what?"

"*Promise* me. Promise me you'll take care of Shannon and the kid."

"Fuck me."

"*Do it,* goddamn you!"

T.J. nodded, gripping Frankie's hand, which didn't grip back. His blue eyes were as glazed as they had been on his wedding day. Except this time he wasn't going to wake up. He was already on his way to his next mission—in heaven.

# CHAPTER 4

S HANNON WASN'T SUPPOSED to, but she was painting the baby's room. They'd been told the little one, due in three months, would be a girl. Frankie had been thrilled, and it warmed Shannon, remembering that Skype call that day when she relayed the news. She'd chosen the name Courtney, and hoped Frankie would like it as much as she did. He hadn't called her last night at their scheduled time. But that wasn't unusual.

The baby was getting very active, so she made a mental note not to hobble up and down the ladder so much. Although she was steady on her feet, she didn't want to risk a fall.

The doorbell rang and she put down her light pink roller of paint, wiped her hands on an old paint-smudged hand towel and barefooted it over to the front door. Standing with the backdrop of a sunny, blue-sky San Diego day were a man and a woman in white Navy uniforms. The officer removed his hat and tucked it under his arm.

With a lump in her throat and heart pounding, she barely heard the news, delivered with unwavering eyes filled with compassion. It was a difficult job for them, she could see. It wasn't a job she'd want, or be able to do as well as they did. But she was thankful they were polished and professional.

She inhaled at first, ready to explode with tears on the exhale, but there was the baby to think of. Any upset she was feeling would affect Courtney, and that was, thankfully, her primary concern.

She thought about Frankie, the way he didn't like sand in his eyes, never told any of his buddies he hated the beach, the worst part of the wet and sandy they all had to endure during BUD/S. And yet, that's where he died, in a sand hole somewhere far away from her and her loving arms.

Her eyes stung and her lower lip quivered. The hole in her chest seemed bottomless, but as she let her breath out and mentally calmed herself she slowly came back to present day, this day she would always remember, and asked if they'd like to come in for a glass of water. They accepted, and entered her little bungalow. She puttered around in her bare feet, getting three tall glasses of ice water, filled to the brim with ice as she was lately fond of doing so she could crunch the tension of Frankie's deployment between her molars.

They did look a little uncomfortable. They answered questions, but didn't volunteer anything. She knew they'd done this many times before. The questions were probably the same, *How did he die? Did he suffer? Was he alone when he died? Who was with him?*

The answer to that last one was like a slap across the face.

"We understand your husband's best friend, Special Operator T.J. Talbot, was with him when he died."

"I'm sorry, but I'm Frankie's best friend. No one loves him as much as I do." She wasn't going to start using the past tense until she had to.

"Yes, ma'am," the gentleman said. "We understand that. However, SO Talbot was with him at the end. He did not die alone, ma'am."

The baby started kicking again, and she worried that her emotions had pumped adrenaline into her daughter's system. She took a long drink of water and closed her eyes, willing calm. If she weren't pregnant she'd be moaning and huddled in a heap on the ground, pouring her heart out. But with little Courtney in her belly, she wasn't going to take that chance. Somehow, it wasn't what she wanted to do, anyway. Her daughter was a strong reminder that life went on. It sucked, but it went on.

Just not with Frankie.

They rose to go when the conversation dwindled off into nowhere, and she began paying more attention to the pink nail polish on her toes. She was wearing pink every day now. Pink pajamas, the ones she could still wear, pink bed sheets (until Frankie came home), pink nail polish, and she even managed to put a hot pink extension in the side of her hair as if a little bit of Courtney was coming through.

The woman gave her a card to the Navy counseling group. Shannon already knew she'd go see Libby's dad, who had helped a lot of the SEALs with their emotional issues, not to mention the marital strains they experienced. And death. They'd all lost someone they loved. There wasn't anyone in the community who didn't know someone who hadn't come home. Today it was her turn.

"Mom. He's gone," she said into the phone before the Navy messengers of death had pulled from the curb outside, escaping to do another mission.

"What do you mean gone? I thought he was—Oh, my God, Shannon. No!" her mother said in a voice strained and brittle.

"Yes. They just left."

"I'll be on the next plane."

"No thanks, Mom. Give me a day or two, please. I've got friends here who can help. You come out soon, though. Give me time to be alone, but please don't think I don't appreciate what you want to do. I do. I need to do this first part alone and with a few of the other wives here. You have Dad."

"Don't be ridiculous. It's what a mother does. I'm still coming."

"No. Really. I need to be alone."


SHANNON KNEW HER mother was a little hurt, but would recover. Next she called Frankie's parents, who were out. She left a message without saying it was bad news. Only that she needed to talk to them right away. Important. Involving Frankie. It was the last phone call she had to make.

She put the glasses—the ice cubes hadn't melted yet—into the dishwasher, added soap and turned it on. The paint towels she tossed into the washing machine. She rinsed out the brush roller, the paint in the sink looking like the strawberry-flavored milk she'd loved so much as a child. She tapped the lid onto the paint can. Arched back to give herself a good reverse stretch and looked at the pink glow in the room, the walls she would finish soon, but probably not tomorrow.

Tomorrow she'd go get that white crib she liked with the dust ruffle in pink camo. She'd put up pictures of animals and buy fuzzy teddy bears and maybe a frilly dress or two. A headband with a bow on it. Some pink ruffled socks and Mary Janes.

The phone rang in the late afternoon, waking her. Gloria, Frankie's mom, was calling.

"We've been notified as well. I'm so sorry, Shannon. I can only imagine what you must be feeling."

"Oh, Gloria. He was your boy. I can't imagine how it must feel to lose the boy you raised, the boy who turned out to be a fine and loving man." She wiped the tears from her eyes, giving Gloria time to compose herself.

"We'll get through this, Shannon. We'll do it together. Your baby will want for nothing, sweetheart. Of that you can be sure."

"I know it, Mom." Using the term "Mom" must have touched Gloria, and she sobbed, handing the phone over to Shannon's father-in-law.

"Hey, sweetheart. Only thing I'm thinking about is that Frankie was doing what he always wanted to do. And doing it with the guys he loved so much, his brothers, Shannon. God help me, I'd rather go out that way. Not stuck in a nursing home that smells of piss or alone in a hospital ward. They told us T.J. held him at the very end."

*There was T.J. again, inserting himself in her life.* Her second thought was more compassionate as she realized he was grieving, too. How would he show his grief? How would he deal with it? He had no family, at least no one who wanted him, anyhow. Which was one of the things Frankie could never understand. How anyone could throw away a little boy's life like that?

T.J. was hard as nails because he'd had to leave behind his childhood before he was old enough to know how else to deal with it. She had to admit she felt a tinge of sorrow for him. A carefully guarded tinge, wrapped in camo duct tape. Something private, dark and never to be revealed to anyone.

They said their good-byes and she returned to face the house again, where she and Frankie had been so happy. There was still so much to look forward to, but all those bright sunny days now seemed like a burden. Everything she'd planned for her and Frankie was suddenly over. Why hadn't she thought about that before? It just never occurred to her that he wouldn't come home. Things like that always happened to other people, not to her.

It still felt like Frankie would walk in any minute, telling her it had been a joke, T.J.'s idea of funny. But no, even T.J. wouldn't play this trick on her. The walls were bare and unfinished. The room smelled of paint, but had a nice warm feel to it, although empty.

But her belly, unlike her heart, was full of life.

It wasn't fair. But that was the way it was.

# CHAPTER 5

T.J. PROCESSED OUT Frankie's things and signed the paperwork, taking ownership of his buddy's personal property. Part of him was angry with Frankie for leaving him with all his shit to have to deal with. He cursed under his breath at what an asshole he was to have even that thought.

Wasn't like Frankie had rejected him, like had happened to him so many times over the years. Frankie had touched a part of him that had been vacant and hollow and had filled it with admiration, respect, and trust.

He remembered those days in the group homes when a couple would come by to look at the "older" orphans, and they were made to shower and dress up in the one set of pants and shirt and tight black shoes handed down from some more fortunate boarder at the home. He'd stand in line like all the other boys, looking at them. Probably smirking. Which is why he was never chosen. He saw the other boys react, trying to look sweet and adoptable. And even though a tiny part of him felt the same way, he knew he showed that he didn't care, because that's what he told himself.

Screw them all. If your own parents didn't want you, who cared about anyone else?

Nah, it wasn't fair to blame Frankie for that, but T.J.'s anger still wasn't satisfied. Besides, Frankie made the request he was forced to honor, giving him such a fuckin' impossible task, to bring these things that had been important to Frankie, and hand them over to Shannon, who hated the ground T.J. walked on. Might even blame him for being the one who came back. Like T.J. had used up the quota of survivors for the day, thus abandoning his friend.

And he knew exactly how she felt. He felt the same way. He blamed himself for living, blamed himself for causing so much worry on the part of Frankie's widow. He blamed himself for not trusting his sixth sense over there—that funny feeling he got that said things were all fucked up. He'd kept that knowledge to himself this time. Why? Usually he told his LPO about situations he thought were extra dangerous.

But it was as if he had that force of will, he could make sure it wasn't their time. Like so many other close calls, they would always somehow emerge unscathed.

Except on that last deployment he knew deep down it wasn't the truth. They'd been one step behind. Perhaps trying to do a job the Marines should have been doing, not the SEALs. Not that the Marines were expendable, but the SEALs were supposed to do surgical strikes with good intel. He hoped some asshole's head rolled over that one. He hoped never to have to face the man who was responsible for the decision to go in on the third day and not have them pull out. None of them had liked it one bit.

So maybe that's why he didn't say anything now. Why none of them did. The other side had figured out how to kill more SEALs, and now was using that knowledge as a strategy. You wanted to go in confident when it came to high-risk missions. With enough practice and training, things could go wrong and they would still work out. But this one had seemed from the get-go like the wrong fuckin' TV program on the wrong fuckin' channel. Nothing had been right about it. And a man—Frankie Benson— his best friend, and a man who had everything in the world to live for, was gone.

It wasn't fair, but then death was indiscriminate. He knew that, but it didn't make it any easier to take. Frankie was the one who'd gotten the pretty girl, the good grades, made his parents proud, dutifully knocked up his wife right away, which was the way it was supposed to be done.

T.J., on the other hand, had broken a lot of hearts—foster parents and girls he'd known, teachers who'd believed in him, employers, coaches whose teams he'd had to walk off of because he had to work, or because his grades made him ineligible—he broke everyone's heart, and more than once too. He wasn't any better at the second chances than he was at the first. He was the one who should have bought the farm. Not fuckin' Frankie.

Everything fit into his buddy's duffel and one shoebox. That box had a collection of letters from Shannon. Frankie had read some of them to the guys. God, the lady could write damned sexy things, and everyone got revved up whenever Frankie got a love letter. He'd sit down as soon as those letters came, glued to the paper, that silly, shit-eating grin on his face, pink cheeks like the bottom of the daughter he'd never see, half embarrassed, but incredibly grateful for his life. That was the thing that separated them. Frankie was grateful for his life. T.J. was out to grab as much of it as he could before the bell rang.

T.J. had stitches in his thigh, on his forearm, and a couple of stitches on his left butt cheek he wasn't sure he really needed but was given anyway by an overzealous corpsman. That was the part that itched like hell, and he was halfway of a mind to rip them out with surgical scissors. They were damned annoying, and he hoped they didn't leave a scar he'd forever have to explain.

He swung the duffel over his right shoulder, cradling the shoebox in his left hand while he made his way to the pickup. He tossed the duffel in the second seat of the 4-door truck, and set the shoebox beside him on the bench seat in front.

Looking down, he pretended Frankie was inside that box, maybe done up in miniature like that movie he'd seen as a kid about the guy named Tom Thumb.

"You're gonna have to help me here, Frankie. Shannon doesn't want to see the likes of me. I can't just show up without calling first, but I did sign a paper saying I'd return your stuff to her, so send me a sign, would you? I'm in need of assistance."

He pretended Frankie said something nasty, which he most certainly would have, if the man had been alive.

*Fuck!* He punched his steering wheel and then pressed his forehead to the top of it, gently banging it against the black leather padding.

*This is totally messed up.*

In the silence of the truck cab, he thought he heard Frankie laughing at him. *Big, tough SEAL, afraid to talk to a woman.* But she was Frankie's woman, and she was six months pregnant. The facts were stacked against him. She was fragile, so he couldn't tell her off if she took it out on him, which he was sure she would. She'd lost her husband, so she didn't deserve to be treated in any way other than like the lady she most certainly was, so why did he have to be the one to take Frankie's stuff to her? She hated T.J. with everything in her soul because of all the shit he had caused her and her dead husband.

Maybe he should get Lansdowne to have one of the other Team guys return Frankie's belongings. Would it have been any easier to give it to Frankie's parents? That he could probably have done without any trouble at all, but Shannon? Shannon didn't deserve this.

He dialed her number and hoped like hell she wasn't home.

But he wasn't that lucky.

"Hey, Shannon. How're you holding up?" His voice was raspy, and it cracked like a boy of seventeen.

"How do you suppose I'm holding up, T.J.? You calling to say you're sorry or to give me a hard time?"

Her abruptness was her method of keeping her distance from everyone. He'd heard the other wives talk about how they had trouble getting close to her.

"No, even I wouldn't do that."

"Well, the day is young. Give it time. I'm sure you'll figure out a way to be an asshole before you go to bed."

That unfair statement pulled the plug on his anger. It was like the girls in grammar school who would call him names because they knew he wasn't allowed to push them back. Why was it okay for a girl to use verbal violence, but he wasn't allowed to protect himself by making them hurt in return? Some therapist's idea of the right order of the world. Probably a jerk who didn't know his ass from an anthill.

"You're entitled to your opinion. I might add that Frankie didn't share that opinion of me, not that it should make a fuck's difference to you." He was satisfied he'd delivered a slap and not a full-on blow to the chops.

"It doesn't mean shit to me, T.J." She breathed heavily into the phone. "Okay, look, I'm not at my best, so what is it you called about? You must have something in mind."

"I have a box of his things, and the Navy wants me to deliver it to you."

"I'll be gone tomorrow afternoon. Why don't you drop it by the house then, any time after twelve. It should be safe on the porch for a couple of hours until I get home."

"I could meet you where you're going."

"Seriously, T.J. I don't want you anywhere near my OB. I don't want to be reminded that all my husband's things are being handed over to me for their safekeeping or whatever. I'd like not to burst into tears in front of a waiting room filled with a bunch of emotional mothers-to-be and their husbands."

"I get your drift."

"You can leave it on the rocking chair on the front porch."

"I'll do that, then."

"Okay, we're done?"

"I think so."

"Good. Thanks for dropping the stuff off. Should I leave anything for you? Anything in there you want for yourself?"

"God, Shannon, I haven't even looked at anything much. I know about a few letters of yours in there. That's about it."

"No selfies in there?"

"Um, Frankie never took pictures of himself."

"No, asshole. I sent him a few naked selfies. I want those back."

*Oh, those.* He'd completely forgotten what fun they'd had with Shannon's selfies. Truth was, some of the guys would sneak them from under Frankie's bed and pass them around quarters while he was taking a shower. The last round had happened so fast, and then they were traveling, so T.J. still had the picture of Shannon in his shaving kit and hadn't had the heart to tell Frankie.

He certainly wasn't going to tell Shannon now.

THE NEXT DAY, the streets of San Diego were as charming as they always were, sunny, filled with light peach and white houses, green gardens and palm trees reaching up into a bright blue, cloudless sky. He usually reveled in the gentle weather, but today he felt almost resentful about it, as if it wasn't right there were so many happy people living in such a happy place when Frankie was dead.

Frankie and Shannon's house was small, which wasn't unusual, since it was an expensive neighborhood. Even a little one was ungodly expensive. They were able to buy it with the deployment bonus he earned, saying he doubted they'd be able to buy anything larger until they moved to the East Coast.

They'd lived here only a few months, but already the colors were crisper, brighter. Maybe someone had painted the outside. The front steps looked like they'd been painted red so recently he was worried that maybe he shouldn't walk on them yet.

As Shannon had told him, there was a white wicker rocker on the little concrete porch, obscured by a delicate metal handrail with boxwood bushes planted in a row in front. The trimmed hedge also bracketed the walkway to the porch.

He swung the duffel bag down on the far side of the chair, so it wouldn't be seen from the street, and placed the box on the seat. He looked inside at the living room through the small glass window embedded in the massive Craftsman-style front door and was satisfied no one was home.

Walking back to his truck, he checked his cell phone for the time. It was one o'clock. He told himself she'd be along anytime now, and he should get going, but he couldn't leave Frankie up there in that box alone and unable to defend himself should a complete stranger decide they wanted the worthless contents of the box.

He sat back and waited. As usually happened, when he thought about Frankie and Shannon, he remembered their wedding day. It had been a pretty incredible day, certainly memorable. As weddings went, he thought it was perfect. It was so much better when things didn't run on time, and all the unexpected things in life showed up at the wrong moments. He lived for those times.

And Shannon had been all tousled and white, delicate and sweet, like the buttery vanilla frosting on the wedding cake. After the ceremony, Frankie had been on serious probation, so was careful when he placed the cake in her mouth, but she still got a blob of frosting on the right corner of her lips. Frankie had kissed it off. The guy was enraptured. It had been good to see. It had been a good day, despite what Shannon might think. His buddy had the sendoff he deserved and the beginnings of a life he'd earned because he was such a good guy. One of the good guys.

It had always made T.J. feel like a better person when he hung around Frankie. He'd never told him that, and this he regretted. Maybe someday he'd tell Frankie's daughter. Probably would never tell Shannon.

An hour went by. He was surprised at himself for being patient, waiting. He didn't mind it. Was going to be his last time with Frankie, in a way. That box was up there, like Frankie was in heaven, and he, T.J., was here sitting in the front seat of a truck. Waiting for what? Well, to be honest, he was waiting for the rest of his life, and eventually for the end of it.

But he knew it wouldn't be for a while. Another one of his sixth senses.

He thought about the promise he'd made Frankie. Wasn't like he'd agreed to go chase Shannon and get her to marry him, which would be the biggest mistake of both their lives. But he'd find a way to secretly help the little girl, and yeah, he'd kick the first guy who tried to get fresh with her. Would be creepy for the kid, though, having an old, gnarled SEAL shadowing her while she was trying to survive high school. Have this dark shadow around every corner, ready to pop out and defend her. She probably wouldn't like that. And in another sixteen or seventeen years his capacity for stealth would be seriously compromised. Hell, he might even be using a cane, like Tyler had to occasionally.

He was sharing this chuckle with Frankie, really feeling him sitting in the box with the little mouse chuckle Tom Thumb would have given him, when Shannon arrived. Before she drove into the garage, she rolled down her window, and he did the same. They were heading in different directions.

"Left everything on the porch. Just wanted to make sure no one messed with it," he said in his softest, most compassionate tone. She did a quick inhale and ripped her eyes from his face, looking out through her dirty windshield.

"Thank you," she said over the top of her steering wheel. But she didn't gun it, like he'd expected. She was thinking, and then she tilted her head. "You want to come in for a drink?" she said, still looking straight ahead.

"I don't think so, Shannon. You'd probably prefer to be alone, and I only came to bring you his things." That got her to look at him, and he could see the red puffiness around her eyes. Part of him wanted to say he was sorry, but that would have earned him a rebuff. She kept watching him, like she expected Frankie to materialize if she stared at him long enough.

It gave him the creeps, so he looked down at his hands in his lap. "Well, I'll be going, then."

As he drove away, he heard her say, faintly, "Thank you."

But it was probably his imagination.

# CHAPTER 6

I T WAS JUST your basic plain brown box. Didn't identify itself as military, except for the sticker on the front. When she picked it up, it was very light. Much lighter than a box holding all the personal effects of a man, her husband, the father of the baby she was carrying should be. She'd expected it to be heavy, like lead or gold bricks. Because the stuff of a man's life was heavy, dense, not simple and lightweight. Not something that could be tipped over to blown away in a gentle wind. It should be heavy enough that, if you threw it, the box would go straight to the bottom of the ocean.

She set the box on the coffee table Frankie's dad had made years ago, when he'd gotten his woodworking tools. She went back outside and got the duffel, which was heavy.

*Laundry.*

Probably dirty laundry, she thought, like he always lugged home in this same bag she'd seen dozens of times. He'd walk into the house with the Cheshire cat grin and the gentle eagerness she loved about her Frankie, even though he was a piece of work. She suddenly wished she hadn't been so hard on him. On those days, soon as he got home, all he wanted to do was take her to the bedroom, and she usually held out for getting her "stuff" done. Today, her "stuff" wasn't that important.

She sat on the edge of the couch with the duffel bag propped between her knees. This was going to be hard. She'd always been a self-starter. Could handle any crisis, even when everyone else was freaking out. Right now she felt on the edge instead of in the eye of the storm. Things were buffeting and blowing around her, and she wished she could dance in the wind. She wished she could be scared, wished she could be angry, anything but morose. Dead. She felt dead.

Little Courtney stirred, reminding her that she was soon to be a mother. She'd throw everything into raising her. Everything. Her life depended on it. It was the one thing left she'd accomplished with Frankie, one thing they'd shared that would hopefully outlive them both. Courtney would be the best of him and the best of her. It was a miracle the way it had happened. She wanted this baby more than life itself.

She picked up the duffel and lugged it to the laundry room. Near the top his pork pie was laid to rest on Frankie's neatly folded and ironed shirts with his dress uniform underneath. She took the uniform into their bedroom, setting it, the shirts, and the hat on the bed, like he was going to put them on as soon as he got back from wherever he'd been.

Back in the laundry room, she pulled out camo shirts that hadn't been well laundered. Holding them up to her nose to determine if they were clean or not, she was filled with the glorious man-scent that was uniquely Frankie's, and she lost it.

She ran down the hallway to the bedroom. Crashing down onto the mattress, she held the shirt to her chest and cried like she hadn't been able to do before. She let it fly. She told little Courtney it would be over soon and not to worry.

"Some day you'll understand, sweetheart." She closed her eyes and she saw him bending over her, leaning into her body with his hips, reaching for her lips to kiss while he ground into her. He was always tender, caring more about what she was feeling than himself. Unselfish.

*"Love you, Shannon, baby doll."*

He'd been the only man ever to call her baby doll. "Love you too, Frankie," she whispered, keeping her eyes closed. "Missing you, baby."

Of course, the sobs involuntarily spasming her chest made it impossible to hear his response.

"I'm trying, Frankie. How am I going to do this without you?"

She thought maybe she heard him answer, *"Don't miss me, baby, love me."*

"I do, Frankie. Trust me, if you ever doubted me, I do" A new wave of tears began when she couldn't remember if she told him she loved him during the last Skype call. She wished she'd told him more often. "Courtney will be my witness. I do love you still. You won't ever be gone for me, baby."

She saw his smiling face as she fell asleep.

OVER THE NEXT few days, Shannon made herself busy by finishing up Courtney's room, finally removing the newspaper and tape from the window. She'd found the crib she wanted on sale and bought it. They were out of the pink camo sheets, bumper and curtains, so she ordered them. The changing table would arrive next week, so she'd paid for that as well.

The doctor had wanted her to come in to discuss some lab work that was spilling outside the ranges of normal. He made some changes to her diet and recommended she drink more water. She hadn't planned to tell him about Frankie's death until he began to stress the importance of having father at the visits.

"I'm a widow as of a few days ago, doc. I'm afraid I'll be bringing my mom at the end. And probably my mother-in-law."

He was moved, of course. With added concern, he asked, "You sleeping well, Shannon?"

"Yessir. I've been fine. Feeling the energy I was hoping I'd feel at this point. Reading my books. Getting the room ready before I get too big."

"Take it easy too. Don't push yourself. You've gone through a terrible experience, one which affects people's bodies in different ways. Get more rest than you think you need. Spend more time with friends. Don't be alone, Shannon."

"I hear you. Not quite yet, but I'll come out of my cave sooner or later. Don't worry about me." All her life, this had always been what she told grownups. No one ever had to worry about Shannon. It had been drummed into her to be self-reliant. She was determined to use that strength to forge a new path, alone, now that Frankie was gone. Last thing in the world she wanted was to depend on her parents or anyone else. She told herself over and over again she was fine. She could do this.

Frankie's favorite place to go on Sundays was Duckies, the frozen yogurt place where a lot of the Team guys hung out. She saw them, with their dark glasses and cargo pants, their canvas slip-ons or rubber sandals made from old tire treads.

She was a dark chocolate girl at heart. But that day she ordered Frankie's favorite, strawberry. He liked the fresh chunks of fruit they put into their cones.

She added a few white chocolate chips and sat at the little yellow-topped table in the corner, out of the wind, and where she could watch people walking down the Strand. She watched young couples, fingers entwined, older couples walking their little dogs, retired Navy, and new recruits. Everyone walked the Strand, looked into shop windows, and simply enjoyed being alive.

That sent a silent tear down her cheek. Maybe the strawberry was too sweet.

A couple of groups of older Team guys were walking back to their cars from a swim at the beach. Their crab-like walk pegged them. The sand going halfway to their knees told her they'd done a timed swim like Frankie used to do. Someone honked. Someone gave the finger to a pickup truck filled with rowdy young guys.

Being part of the things Frankie had liked didn't help. Her thoughts got sadder. She had to dump the rest of her yogurt and put her own sunglasses on so people wouldn't see how hard she'd been crying. She found her car and drove herself home.

Setting out her purchases, she hung two little frilly pink dresses in Courtney's closet. The first two things there. They were small, almost like they'd been made for a doll. But no question about it. They belonged to Courtney.


DAYS STRUNG TOGETHER, and soon another month had gone by. SEAL wives and girlfriends were at her house constantly. They held a shower for her, and both Frankie's mom and her own mother came. It was fortunate the two women got along so well, and Shannon knew they'd started phoning each other on a regular basis. One mother helping the other mother. Gloria was right, "We'll all get through this together somehow."

And then one day Shannon laughed again.

# CHAPTER 7

T J. HAD BEEN spending a lot of time at Gunny's gym. Timmons was practically living there as well. He'd sold his house, moved into an apartment nearby, and become a permanent fixture there.

The older man had dropped a bit of weight, lost most of his potbelly, and was developing definition in his arms. The frog statue, their Team mascot replaced some five times in the past, was braced to the wall. It stood on a glass shelf with a recessed light shining down on it. On that shelf were several pictures, including one of Frankie's smiling face, taken on his wedding day. T.J. looked at that picture every time he came into Gunny's. He recalled the promise he'd made, and the look of the beautiful girl on Frankie's left. He knew time was running out on his conscience, and he'd have to act soon or the mission would be labeled a failure due to abandonment.

Timmons had brought in several of his older friends, and soon a white-haired group was assembled there regularly. Detective Mayfield had retired from the San Diego P.D. and was now living with Armando's mother, and he and Clark Riverton, another San Diego policeman soon to retire, dropped by for the group. Sanouk called them the "Silver Senior Running Shoe Circle." But there wasn't anything senior about them, other than the fact that T.J. occasionally heard discussions of Viagra and special hair products.

Amornpan, Sanouk's Thai mother, took care of the older gentlemen's club like they were her boys and she was a Southeast Asian lounge singer. She was beautiful and ageless. She was a gracious lady. She made Timmons a better man simply because he walked in and greeted her every day. T.J. doubted they were lovers yet, but their paths were definitely heading in that direction, and the Team Guys talked about it all the time.

Good for him.

T.J. finished early and said his goodbyes. He always gave his final goodbye to Frankie with a kiss to his forefinger and then a point straight at the guy. Increasingly he also pointed one at Shannon. He was more aware that he needed to do the one thing Frankie had asked before he passed over. No matter how uncomfortable it was.

"I know, I know. You asked me to look in on her, watch out for her, and I haven't done that. Sorry, man. But, jeez, you know about the picture I look at every morning in my shaving drawer. You want me to get rid of it? If I give it back to her, she'll have a fit."

He wondered how Shannon was doing. He had a feeling she needed a little silliness in her life and wondered if he could help out with that.

He stopped by a toy store and inquired about playhouses. They happened to have a pink gingerbread house in the back that had been returned last Christmas since it was missing parts.

It was T.J.'s kind of gift. He bought it at a huge discount, threw it in the second seat of his truck, and, without calling Shannon first, headed over to her place.

He pulled out the partially opened carton, trying not to drop pieces. A small plastic bag of screws fell at his feet, and he cursed but picked them up without losing his grip on the wooden panels of the playhouse.

Shannon had already opened the front door when he got there. Her eyebrows were knitted into a frown. She inspected the pieces of wood under his arm and then looked up at him with questions she seemed unable to verbalize.

"Every princess deserves her own house. A playhouse," T.J. said as he lifted his shoulder to draw attention to the playhouse pieces.

"Is this a playhouse or a dollhouse?"

"I think it's a playhouse."

"You are aware she won't be able to play with dolls for probably at least two years."

"So, it will wait for her, then. Maybe in the meantime you can use it." He tried to smile, but the blush on her face and the fullness of her belly were too powerfully distracting. She was the most beautiful woman he had ever seen. She was the first pregnant woman he'd been within ten feet of.

Ribbons of jazz came from the house.

"I can just put this in the back yard, if today isn't a good day. I can come back another time to put it together, but I have time to get it done today, if you're willing."

"I hadn't even gotten to thinking about what she would play with once she's walking. You do know they have to be born first, start crawling, and then walk, in order to use an outside playhouse?" Her frown marks were easing, and a small, very tiny smile formed on her lips as she told him nonverbally she appreciated that he'd thought of the baby. He liked that he'd been able to think of something she hadn't yet.

*So far so good.*

She opened the door, gesturing him inside. He knew where the door to the back yard was, through the master bedroom at the back of the house. Once inside, he saw her unmade bed, the glass of water by the nightstand. A book was lying face down on the table.

"Did I wake you from a nap?" he asked as he walked past the bed.

"No. I was getting a snack and heard your truck pull up." She opened the sliding glass door and allowed him to walk in front of her into the yard.

She'd planted flowers along the edge of the lawn, ones which had not been there when he visited Frankie before their last deployment. The day of the funeral, he hadn't followed the others to her house for the reception, preferring to linger a little longer at the cemetery. He'd had private thoughts he wanted to share with his Team buddy.

The yard looked happier than he remembered. He was glad to see Shannon had maintained everything like before Frankie was gone. He'd seen a number of wives fall to pieces, not that he blamed them. But Shannon had moved forward and seemed steady.

He knew she must be hurting inside, but because of her dislike for him, hid it well. He decided perhaps he could change that a bit. Maybe he could bring her a bit of relief.

He laid out the pieces, putting the screws and washers on a corner of the box it came in. He crosschecked the parts to the manifest and discovered there were several bags of screws missing.

He began tracing his footsteps across the lawn.

"What are you looking for?"

"I think I may have dropped a few things. Any tiny bags of screws or wooden dowels?"

"I'll go look, but I didn't notice any." She disappeared from the screen door, returning a few minutes later carrying a glass of ice water.

"Nope. Not a thing." She slipped out through the slider and stepped down onto the concrete patio in her bare feet … with those hot pink toes he was having such a hard time ignoring.

"Here," she said holding out the glass.

"Thanks." He drank the whole thing, a bit of the cooling water sluicing down his neck and into the ribbing at the top of his T-shirt. He took a mouthful of ice and began crunching it as he handed the glass back to her.

Shannon watched him, expressionless, and said nothing.

He put together what he could, and figured he'd find the fasteners for the rest later. A couple of times he put the wrong side out. He cursed at the instructions, and decided they'd probably been translated from Chinese. At one point he discovered there was an important triangular-shaped piece missing, one supposed to hold up parts of the roof. Just gone. He had one side, but not the other. The clerk at the store said everything was there, even though the box was opened, but now he could see the young man had lied.

A couple of times, the angle of two panels he'd screwed together was compromised, and collapsed. If he'd been home, he'd have destroyed the whole thing, kicked it around, bent and broken it further, and tossed it in the garbage. But this was Shannon and Frankie's house, and this was for their baby, and dammit, he was going to get this done.

So much for playing hero. The pieces were so messed up he didn't know where to start. He sat down and concentrated on them, hoping a solution would present itself, like magic.

*Fuck it.*

When he was about to give up, he heard the sliding glass door pull open again, and this time out walked Frankie's dad, with his tool belt on and a red canvas hand tool caddy in his left hand.

"Shannon said I should come and do a rescue on this mission," Joe Benson said with a beaming smile T.J. found comforting, though he didn't want to admit defeat.

"Yup. I do believe we have a problem, Houston."

"Well I'm good at fixin' problems. Let's see what you got there," Benson said as he squatted down to peer at the roof and corners.

T.J. turned his back to the house and began showing Joe what he'd figured out, but he felt Shannon's eyes on him.

He kind of liked it.

# CHAPTER 8

S HANNON WATCHED HER husband's hard-bodied friend while he worked outside, struggling to wrestle pieces of pink and light green plywood, painted to look like the sides of a gingerbread house. He first read the instructions, and then quietly aligned the pieces, searching for fasteners, which, all too often, seemed to be missing. He looked for holes that weren't drilled.

By now Frankie would have given up, but in the hour that Shannon watched T.J. curse and nearly throw the pieces over the fence, she'd also seen him quell his anger, tell himself he could do it, and then sigh back into it. Until another problem arose.

Unable to bear the sight of his frustration any longer, she called her father-in-law. Joe was a regular guy and was never shy about helping out, especially if it required any carpentry or woodworking. And he was the most patient man she had ever met. Their personalities were total opposites, but standing side by side, though Frankie was nearly a foot taller, she could see they were father and son, no question.

"Be glad to help," he said, and then appeared at her front door within twenty minutes. Just in time, too, because Shannon could smell defeat brewing in the yard.

"He's getting awfully frustrated, Dad. He thinks there are screws missing, and maybe some wooden pegs." She scrunched up her nose.

"Always are, sweetheart. I got plenty," he said as he jiggled his tool kit. "Or they don't put the holes so they align, or give you the wrong sizes. I'm sure we can work it out."

Within two hours the little playhouse was constructed, complete with new trim around the eaves for extra sturdiness, which Joe had recommended. The two men worked well together, and on several occasions

T.J. burst out laughing at whatever Joe had said. She heard Frankie's name several times.

It occurred to her that it did Joe good to have another man Frankie's age to share the work on that playhouse, and if Frankie were here, Joe would have been doing this alone. But with T.J. he'd found a kindred spirit.

Or maybe it was the grief that brought them together. Whatever it was, it was working.

Shannon admired their handiwork. The two men were practically slapping each other on the back. Extra holes had to be made, and one piece was hand-cut to fit in where a piece had broken. "You guys want sandwiches?"

"I'm actually starved," T.J. said.

"I am too," said Joe.

"You want to come in or eat outside?" Shannon asked.

The men looked at each other and shrugged. "Whatever's easiest," T.J. answered. "Makes no difference to us."

She threw a wet towel at T.J., which caught him right across the kisser, eliciting a delicious pearly-white grin. She worked to restore her icy demeanor, but broke out in a brief laugh as she commanded, "Clean off the table and I'll bring the food."

Seated around the round glass-top table while they ate, the men continued to discuss their work. "You know, we work well together. No arguing or fighting. Kinda like working with the Team guys, like Frankie." T.J. caught himself, sighed and fell back into his chair. "I'm sorry, Joe. Couldn't seem to help myself."

Shannon had thought the same thing. She'd seen Frankie doing things with his buds on Team 3, but even that held a healthy dose of swearing, jousting and horsing around. The mission was always accomplished, no matter how much irreverence there was. She also knew that Frankie could be sensitive and very stubborn. T.J., for all his bad-boy qualities, had remained more focused on the task once Joe overcame the two key obstacles.

*Stop comparing. Not fair.*

Why was she doing it, anyway? The baby kicked as she brought the dishes into the kitchen. Joe was right behind her, carrying the rest of them. "You know, it's good to see you laughing again, Shannon," he said as he set things on the counter. He slung an arm around her shoulder and squeezed her to him.

"Thanks, Dad." She hugged him back. Then she placed one of his palms on her belly so he could feel the baby. "She wants to come out and play with you, Grandpa."

Joe was overcome. "Ahhh," he growled and wiped a tear from his eye. "She feels strong, Shannon. She does this a lot?"

"I have no comparison, but yes, I think she's very active now."

"That's the way Frankie was. His mama wasn't getting any sleep in the end." He pinched her nose. "Make sure you rest up, kid. You're going to need it."

T.J. had come from the restroom and was standing in the doorway to the kitchen, bracing himself with one muscled arm pressed against the top of the archway, hips slung at an angle. Though he was a good ten feet away from them, Shannon could see a tinge of envy there, and she picked up that perhaps he was holding himself back.

"You want to feel the baby?" she asked him.

He shook his head with a small shrug.

"Oh, come on, T.J. Get yourself over here." Joe stepped aside and Shannon walked slowly to meet T.J. halfway. Carefully he extended his palm, and she placed it against the lower right side of her belly. The warmth of his hand caused the baby to jump again, and they were rewarded with a kick and what felt like hiccups.

He stared at his hand, and she could see him soften and transform. When he looked up at her, she saw his need and his pain, which mirrored her own.

"Well, I'd best be going," Joe barked, collecting his things.

T.J. took a step back and jammed his hands into his front pockets. "Yeah, I've got things I need to do, too. I'd say we did well, Joe. And Shannon, thanks for lunch and all the ice water." His smile was gentle.

Joe and Shannon hugged, and then T.J. gave her a gentle embrace. Her belly rubbed against his lower abdomen, and she was surprised by a rush of intimacy. She felt T.J. hesitate to pull away. "You got anything else you need, give me a call, okay? I'm not as good as old Joe here with the hammer, but I can figure out most things."

She found herself saying, "Thanks," but felt the exchange was unfinished.

Joe was out the door with T.J. behind him when she decided to call, "T.J., there are a couple of things I think Frankie would want me to give you," she said to his back. She saw him stiffen, saw him share a glance with her father-in-law, and then hesitate, holding the door open.

"Bye, you two," Joe nodded and took off down the walkway with his toolkit.

T.J. closed the door behind him. Shannon suddenly felt awkward and shy about being alone with him. Something had shifted.

"We need to talk," she said, taking his hand and leading him to the living room and the brightly flowered overstuffed couch Frankie always said looked like it belonged in a hippie museum.

She sat an arm's length away from T.J., curling one leg underneath her. It was getting harder and harder to find comfortable positions as her belly grew. Placing her arm along the back of the couch, she rested her head there at an angle and looked up at T.J., who was focused on her eyes and nothing else.

"I've been missing Frankie a lot today," she said, looking away, unable to look at his face as she said it. Her shyness was coupled with a tiny shiver of danger, making her heart beat harder and sending the baby into another acrobatic routine.

"Yeah, me too," he whispered. He placed his hand over hers on the back of the padded couch, and rubbed her fingers. She saw no smile on his honest face. He knew what she was feeling. "Come here, Shannon," he barely whispered, waiting for her to make the next move.

She found herself leaning up against his chest, his arms wrapped around her, as his long fingers massaged the top of her spine and lazily dove into her hair, sending warm ripples from her scalp over the rest of her skin surface. Her arm had wrapped around his body, her other hand rubbing over his shoulder muscles. She was aware of his heat, the smell of him, which was all male, the sound of his breath as his chest rose and fell, the way her cheek felt pressed against the granite of his pecs. She allowed herself to wallow in the muskiness under his chin.

Then he tipped her face up to his, and he kissed her. Need sparked like a match in a dark room. How she'd missed the tender kiss and touch of a man! She'd told herself she needed to learn to live without it for now. But it flared up anyway.

She accepted his lips on hers, accepted his tongue that waited for an invitation before plunging into her mouth. It filled the vacant and hollow places of her loneliness. His moan flamed her passion, opening to him, and drawing him in deep. She was starving for him in every sense of the word. A tiny alarm bell off in the distance was ringing, but she put it out of her mind.

He kept one large, callused palm under her chin, rubbing her lips with his enormous thumb. His eyes were sharp with what she easily recognized as arousal, though he was masking it. He was also showing her a hint of something deeper.

He waited for her to speak, to give him an answer, put a label on what was happening between them. She'd been doing a lot of telling herself this and that, thinking about how she should feel, how she should be holding things in check, especially with the responsibility of carrying Frankie's child.

But she discovered her body ached for T.J. Her own needs were relegated to the place of someday, and became paramount. She missed intimacy with Frankie, the way it was so obvious he loved being with her. She missed the way he enjoyed her body, the way their lives had entangled and grown like two distinctly different vines covering the same trellis.

She laid her cheek against T.J.'s chest again and allowed the rhythm of his breathing to say what she wasn't ready to hear in words. Her own body responded, and their tandem breathing became background music for their hands, which rubbed and explored. His soothing touch on her back, her neck, down her arms. He laced his fingers between hers, kissing their joining, and she found it heightened her arousal.

She leaned back and studied his face again, tracing her fingers over his lips, begging him to speak what he probably wouldn't feel free to say. She knew it was loneliness that drew them together, the shared understanding that they both cherished the precious memory of Frankie as no other two people could.

His lips found hers again, found the spots under her ear and beneath her jaw as she lifted her face to the ceiling, closing her eyes and reveling in the way he explored her neck and the hollow between her shoulder and her upper chest. His thumb breached the crevice between her upper arm and her chest and then warmly squeezed her breast as he moaned into her ear.

Is this the talk she'd wanted to have? Was talking even appropriate? She'd have to slow things down and check her internal roadmap, even though she simply wanted to let go and plunge over the edge.

Other than his hand on her breast, he hadn't touched her in any sexual manner, the kiss being all the signal she needed to know he was willing to go further. But he seemed relieved to find she wanted to separate. Maybe he wanted the talk too. Maybe he regretted advancing on her. In any event, it needed to be addressed.

Her hands remained in his as he leaned against the couch, examining his thumbs brushing over the tops of her knuckles and down her fingers in a slow massage.

"T.J., it feels so strange to be sitting here doing this. We never got along before, when Frankie—"

"Was alive," he finished for her.

"Yes." Her eyes followed as he brought her knuckles to his lips and kissed them again, then spread out her palm and kissed it softly in a deeply personal and intimate kiss.

"I think what I'm saying is that I'm ready to try to move on."

She watched his eyes dart quickly to her face. Perhaps he hadn't gone there yet inside.

"I think I'll always miss him. But life does go on. He'd want that, Shannon. He said that to me at the end. He wanted—" T.J. stood abruptly. "I can't do this," he said as he tunneled his fingers through his hair and released a sigh of exasperation. "I'm sorry, Shannon."

Shannon got up carefully and stood close to him, wrapping her arms around his waist and pressing her face to his strong upper torso. "It's okay. I understand," she whispered to his shirt. She lifted the cotton fabric, exposing enough of his abdomen that she could place her bare palm there, and pressed. "Help me, T.J. Help me to heal."

He paused and took a deep breath. Could it be so hard for him to show her a little softness, a little kindness and affection for the memory of their shared past? Was it asking too much?

"The baby—" he began.

"Will be fine," she finished for him.

# CHAPTER 9

**T**J. COULDN'T BELIEVE he was walking down the hall of Frankie's little love nest, the floorboards creaking under their weight, the birds chirping outside in accompaniment to the sounds of an ordinary day. Except this wasn't ordinary. Her body was plumped with the evidence of Frankie's love for her and she was leading him to her bedroom—to do what? Make love to her? The pregnant wife of his best friend? A woman who was seven months along? Was this even possible? How would he feel if something happened to the baby?

He was going to need reassurance before he'd get naked with her, but no matter what, he knew it was going to happen. He really hoped he wouldn't feel like a dog afterwards though.

They walked past Courtney's pink bedroom, all set up with white furniture, waiting for the little one to imprint her personality upon it. What a miracle, he thought, how this happened. In two months another person would live here with Shannon. A little part of Frankie would grow out here in the real world.

The bedroom was rosier now, the afternoon glow deeper and more intense. She closed the door, and then walked around him to the bed. He watched her take off her top, revealing a heavy bra with her breasts huge and bulging behind the restraint of the white lace fabric. She undid the straps and let her breasts fall, deliciously exposed to him, moving with her breathing. The sight of a woman's breasts, so full and ripe with life had never turned him on more. His cock was fully erect, holding his pants out front in that famous tent.

He was mesmerized by her as she slid her elastic-topped pants over her belly and down around her ankles and stepped out of them. Her smooth skin stretched over the growing child made him want to drop to his knees. She was the most beautiful creature on earth, pregnant and ripe with new life, standing before him unashamed of her nakedness. She was showing herself to him in a most intimate act, one no woman had done for him before.

"Are you sure this is okay?" he asked.

"For now, yes. Not for a whole lot longer, though. But yes, having sex during pregnancy is normal and natural." She seemed to welcome the fact he had walked towards her.

She pulled off his T-shirt. He loved that she was undressing him, giving him time to get used to seeing her so big and so round everywhere. Her nipples were hard and enormous. Her belly button was protruding, almost like a little act of defiance. Her shiny hair smelled wonderful, and he felt her warm need as she rubbed her full breasts against his bare chest. She undid the button fly on his jeans and sat on the bed while she lowered his pants to the floor. His erection bounced to attention and hardened further when she wrapped her fingers around his shaft, squeezing and working up and down gently, then squeezing his balls.

She licked his tip and then pressed him through her lips folding her tongue around him. He'd have been content if she could remain there forever, if he could keep watching while she sucked and rolled her tongue over him. Her hands gently squeezed his butt cheeks and he allowed himself to be drawn deep into her mouth and down into her throat.

He'd never seen anything as luscious as her lips working on him, had never experienced anything that drove his own need so fiercely. Her shimmering hair in the afternoon sun and the smooth texture of her shoulders and thighs illuminated in the golden glow of the day moved him to tears. He thought perhaps this was what she had in mind all along. Part of him was relieved.

But that wasn't everything Shannon had in mind. She scooted back on the bed, knees slightly bent, her taut belly rising and falling as she inhaled and looked up to him with smoldering need.

"How do I—" he started.

She smiled and interrupted him. "T.J. Don't tell me you've never had sex before."

Now he felt stupid. "Not with a pregnant woman."

"Thank God I'm the first for you. I wouldn't want to be second or third."

She was toying with him. His cock was getting stiffer and almost pained him. The little challenge to his ego spurred him on.

*Holy cow. She wants me to fuck her.*

"You sure this is okay?"

"T.J., if you want to stop, I'd understand. I mean," she said as she rolled over on all fours and presented her sweet ass to him, "I wouldn't want you to do anything you don't want to do."

*Fuck it.* He could see her wet pussy peeking like ripe fruit from between her legs. She allowed her shoulders to fall to the mattress as she rolled her head to the side and looked over her shoulder at him with those eyes full of smoldering need.

He decided he could do this. "Help me," he said.

"First of all you have to assume the position behind me. Can you do that, T.J.?"

*Well, hell yes, he could.*

He knelt on the bed and allowed his thighs to touch the backs of hers, his cock rooting up the cleft in her smooth behind. His hands were on her ass, rubbing, squeezing and separating the cheeks.

"Touch me," she whispered.

His fingers found her soft lips. He rimmed her opening and played with her folds, but still felt hesitant to penetrate. She moved herself against him, asking for it, but he found himself almost afraid of her need.

He dropped a shoulder and angled himself under her, kissing her sweet folds and massaging her nub with his tongue. Her sweet and sour flavor, musky with need, was an elixir. Her body jumped as he ran his teeth over her clitoris and then sucked her to a peak.

"Oh God, I had no idea I needed this so much," she moaned.

He gently tipped her to her back, putting one knee between her legs and feeling her ride his thigh. Her face was a beautiful painting of softness and lust as she lost herself for him. His thumbs and fingers pinched her nipples, and she arched, moaning. Her sensitivity to his touch anywhere on her body was spurring him on like never before.

"Baby," he whispered as he nestled a kiss under her ear. His erection pressed under and around her belly. "I have something."

"Thank you, because I don't."

He reached for his pants at the foot of the bed, sheathed himself and returned.

"I don't want to hurt you."

"I'll tell you if it hurts, T.J. But right now, I don't want to talk anymore. I want you inside me. No more questions, T.J. No more," she said in her silken voice. She lifted her head off the pillow to plant a long kiss on him, sucking his tongue inside as she rubbed her sex against his thigh. "Please, T.J., I need you inside me."

He didn't want to press down on her abdomen, so was careful to brace himself, which was no problem. Her writhing form beneath him, the touch of her belly against his abdomen was actually a turn-on he hadn't expected. His cock ran the length of her and then found her opening, and he stopped.

He wanted to watch her eyes while he penetrated her. He wanted them to look at each other. This was not his usual way. But this time was different. He wanted the reality of what they were doing to be front and center. It needed to happen in the full light of the day, without the excuse of alcohol and without the intense foreplay and occasional light bondage he usually liked.

He wanted this woman because she was carrying his best friend's child, and because he'd promised to protect, defend and take care of her. He wanted to fulfill his promise, and maybe receive a little redemption in return. He hoped it would change him, perhaps exorcise his demons.

He leaned forward with his forearms at the side of her face, rubbed his thumbs across her lips and her eyelids and kissed them one by one while he crouched and angled himself to push gently inside her. As he did, little by little, he saw it in her eyes, all the pain for the past and the love for the future. All at once. Right there in her eyes. He gave himself to her in every way he could.

He'd never wanted to mate with a woman this way. Bring her pleasure, rock her world and be the man she could depend on. He wanted that. As he rooted, carefully at first, she accepted him deep. He felt no hesitation as he rhythmically drew in and out, changing the speed but pulling the edge off it. He poured intensity into the slow slapping of their bodies, the feel of the smooth surfaces of her skin, the little moans and whimpers of her soul. He wanted her to bring it all on, full force. He wanted to take all of her.

He didn't know what to expect, but gradually her body slipped into a long rolling orgasm that triggered his own. She rolled her shoulders up and to the side so she could look at their joining. He kissed her belly as she ran her fingers through his hair, massaging his temples. He kissed her nipples and she arched backward, her head falling back into the bed. His spurting inside her was prolonged, and he knew she could feel every drop.

Her eyes filled with tears that spilled over onto the vanilla-colored pillows underneath her.

"Everything okay, baby?"

"It couldn't be better," she whispered. "I thought I had no right to this. But he's here."

T.J. wasn't sure he was going to like what she would say next.

"I know he's here. I know this is what he'd want, T.J."

He remembered Frankie saying that very thing, but he also knew he would never be able to tell her that. His hand smoothed over her engorged abdomen again. He loved the feel of the taut skin under his fingertips and palm. He agreed with her, even though he'd believed he had no right to this.

But he also knew he'd belonged here all along.

# CHAPTER 10

R IGHT NOW HER body was sensitive everywhere. The changes in her hormone levels, the softening of her bones and toughening up of her nipples in preparation for birthing a baby and giving succor, mixed with the wonderful glow of a new love...not only growing inside her belly, but also in her heart, as she learned to accept the reality that she could expand that heart and open it to include T.J.

She could love Frankie and all that Frankie had meant to her, even including her occasional regrets, and she could love his child. But she found room in there for T.J. as well. Could T.J. be her forever man now? She was certain Frankie would approve. That was important to her.

They didn't speak of it while he helped her into the shower. As he smoothed the lemon shower gel over her body and kissed the back of her neck, he didn't speak of it. As she rubbed gel on his upper chest, down his shoulders, as she smoothed over his stiff cock, over his thighs, as she took him into her mouth, kneeling before him, while he palmed his way down her back to press fingers into her cleft and squeeze her buttocks, they didn't speak of it.

When he took her from behind, pressing her carefully against the tiled surface of a shower stall barely big enough for both of them, as she wanted him more after his release than before they'd started, they didn't speak of it.

Her connection to him was pliable yet solid. Not like rigid bands of steel. It was flexible. The golden threads connecting them grew with every contact of their bodies. The exploration was delicious, and still left her wanting more.

In the mirror she watched him drying her off with one of the white fluffy towels Frankie had bought. He wrapped it around her, put his face next to hers and stared back at her in the reflection. She loved seeing his face next to her own. She wore the blush on her cheeks from his stubble like a badge of honor, and was proud of how they were together, proud of how she felt and how her heart sang.

He was still stargazing at her.

"What?" she said as she turned to face him in the flesh.

"Marry me, Shannon."

"Oh, my gosh, T.J. Don't you think it's too soon?"

"Too soon for what? Look at what we've been doing all afternoon." He stopped her wandering gaze, raising her chin up so he could look at her straight on. "I'm serious as a heart attack, Shannon. Marry me. I won't rest until you do."

She loved his relentless attitude, the sure compassion of his voice, and his confidence in a future she was sure had been planned differently than it was presenting today. And she could see he wouldn't give up until she said yes. This was far from a game for him. He wasn't the same T.J. who had left on deployment two months ago. This was a man she could marry and live with her whole life.

"It would be my honor, T.J." As soon as she said it, fear crept in, but T.J. was overjoyed.

"Get dressed. We're going to go look at wedding rings."

"No. Not today."

"Yes, today. Today we tell everyone. Everyone. Your mom and dad, Joe and Gloria.

"You're so silly. Are you sure?"

"Aren't you sure, Shannon? Because if you're not, best to tell me now. Just get it out there, and I'll walk away." He didn't smile. She could see he wanted the reassurance, but didn't want to make it too obvious.

"T.J., we had time together with Frankie's dad. And now to call them and say we're getting married, well, I don't think it shows Frankie the respect he's owed."

T.J. got pensive. "Maybe you're right. Frankie would want us to wait, to be sure. String it out for a year or two. He'd want us to wait until after the baby was born, maybe have you date a few other frogs to make sure you were making the right choice, that sort of thing." His serious face showed not a hint of humor, but she knew him well enough to know he was just about to bust a gut.

She beamed up at him. "Have all those girls after you, have you dodging the frog hogs and high schoolers, sampling here and there," she said as she reached for his cock and squeezed it. Her hands were on his thigh as she dropped her towel, went up on her tippy toes, and pressed her big belly into him. "All those lithe young bodies moaning under your strength. The girls you could tie up and cuff."

T.J. stepped back out of her reach. "Whoa. Wait a minute. Somebody's been talking out of school."

"What do you think Frankie was doing after you described what you liked to do to your partners? I heard all about it." She stepped to him and took his cock in her palms again. "And I expect—after the baby's born, of course—for you to deliver. I've had a preview. I want the full fuckin' feature."

*Holy shit. Did I just say that?*

She realized then and there that things were back to normal in her life, if that was ever possible. She was starting to swear again.

Like a sailor.

# CHAPTER 11

T J. NOTICED A marked change in Shannon when her mother came to visit. The woman was built so solidly, the guys used to call her the Iron Maiden, whispering it so Frankie didn't hear, of course.

With one eyebrow raised, Mrs. Moore examined him like an ugly insect throwback in some nerd's bug collection.

"Nice to see you, T.J. You been helping Shannon do some things around the house?"

He worked not to blush. It was something like that. He was hopefully helping her get her life back, look forward to something. But he could see in Mrs. Moore he'd hit a brick wall. She might have noticed his duffel bag and some clothes strewn across the bed, a surefire indication he'd spent some nights there, but Mrs. Moore was purposely ignoring them.

She kept her eye on him even as he went to the head to take a leak. When he came out, she stopped whispering to her daughter.

"So, T.J. who are you dating these days? Anyone Shannon or Frankie would know?" Her eyes registered the cold blooded demeanor of a lizard.

He checked Shannon's line of sight and saw she wouldn't look at him.

"I have my heart set on the right girl, whenever she'll have me."

Mrs. Moore leaned back and roared. Her brittle laughter tinkled like pieces of shattered glass. "My understanding is that you'll probably have to forage somewhere outside of San Diego. I think you've bedded—"

"Mother, please."

T.J. was glad Shannon had come to his defense, but a sense of unease and dread began to grow. He felt a sense of danger the more time these two women spent together. And he didn't know why.

"I don't think that is very polite, Mother. T.J. has been a great friend, helping Joe build a playhouse for Courtney. You really ought to see it. Very impressive."

Mrs. Moore walked down the hallway to view the backyard from the master bedroom and shouted back, "You make a good carpenter, T.J. At least you could do that if the SEALs don't work out for you."

T.J. angled his head, looking for some sign from Shannon, but she shrugged and gave a puzzled expression in return. Mrs. Moore came back into the room.

"Well, I'm sure you have a lot better things to do than hang around a couple of old married women. I'm taking Shannon shopping. I'd invite you, but I think you'd be pretty miserable."

He placed his palms in his jeans pockets and nodded for a bit before answering. "You're quite right, Mrs. Moore. I'll just get my things."

"Why don't you wait for us?" Shannon posed. "Maybe we could have dinner after I drop Mom off at the hotel?"

"And do what? Clean the house? Straighten your closets?" T.J. felt the scab had been picked and he couldn't stop himself. He didn't like that Shannon was excluding him. Mrs. Moore reminded him of some of the foster moms and state officials he'd known. They'd talk civilly but their hearts were black as coal. Being around her made him nervous.

Shannon was frowning when he stuffed the duffel with clothes from the bed. Throwing his shaving kit inside and zipped it up. With the canvas strap slung over his shoulder, he leaned over and gave Shannon a wet kiss on her cheek, daring her to grab him and demonstrate what she'd been showing him for the past several days and nights.

But unfortunately that wasn't to be.

*Fuck it.* Definitely overdue for a bender.


HE WAS STILL cursing himself when he met Tyler at the Scupper later that evening. Tyler was trying to be helpful.

"So, she doesn't like you. Shannon didn't like you at first, either."

"Tyler, I'm not going to fuckin' have sex with Mrs. Moore to convince her I'm a nice guy. No, the bitch is made from body parts straight from hell."

"Come on, T.J. Lighten up." Tyler tried to punch him in the arm, but T.J. glared at him.

Tyler had the stones to wait until T.J. softened his eyes first. That was smart. Wait for the angry man to not debase himself and get things under control. Only jump in and call him out when it was getting into emergency mode. T.J. was glad he still had that control.

"I'm falling for her, Tyler."

"Tell me something I don't know."

"Probably isn't wise, but I am."

"So, can you distance yourself?"

"Not and keep my promise to Frankie. I said I'd be there."

"But not in his wife's bed."

"No he even said that too, in the end. Was the hardest thing I've ever heard. The guy knew he was dying and he made me promise—" T.J. didn't want to show tears, so he squinted and looked to the side at the string of muscled men sitting up to the bar watching a basketball game.

"Grief does a lot of things to a man. You should talk to Nick about that one. Kate says Devon has her hands full sometimes at the winery, Sophia's—you know."

"Yeah, I know. I really miss that sonofabitch. Frankie would know what to say to cheer me up. I never realized how much he did for me."

"I gotta ask you, man. What do you think Shannon wants?"

"Well, that's the thing. I thought I knew. But now I'm not so sure. Maybe she was just lonely."

"Hell, you both were lonely. Wouldn't be the first or last time a SEAL widow took up with another SEAL, you know. Maybe even someone she wouldn't have—"

That put T.J. over the edge. He'd been hit with the two by four called *She's only with you because she doesn't have Frankie*, and that smarted more than anything else he'd felt for months.


HE WASN'T IN good shape when Shannon called him. He was walking down the Strand, because he knew he shouldn't be driving. He was so drunk, he couldn't remember where his pickup was, anyway.

"I'll come get you," she whispered. In spite of his sour mood, his unit lurched, making him swear.

"What's the matter?"

"I'm fine," he argued.

"T.J., come on. This is me."

He watched the steady stream of lights from passing traffic and decided he'd not take a chance to cross the road and run to the beach. It was dark. He was drunk and cold. He wanted to go home and fall asleep in his own bed.

"I'm not much good company tonight."

"Don't do this, T.J."

He knew it wasn't wise, but he sat down on one of the concrete bus stop benches, leaned back and crossed his leg. "You think we did this all too fast, Shannon?"

He hated that she took a long time to answer.

"Can we talk about this in person?"

"You don't want to be around me tonight, Shannon."

"I don't want to leave you this way."

"What way?" He knew what she meant but he wouldn't let go. He knew it was so unwise to even talk to her right now. But he couldn't help himself. Just like Frankie and wanting to talk to the girls. He didn't, but he couldn't help himself.

"You're drunk."

"Well, la-dee-fuckin-da."

"You're an asshole."

"Yes, darlin' I am. I'm a fuckin' asshole."

"I'm coming to get you. Tell me where you are."


HE RELUCTANTLY TOLD her and then fell asleep on the bench. Next thing he knew, he was being shaken by a policeman he'd had a run-in with a time or two. Shannon arrived just in time to place her very pregnant body between the official and T.J. before he could be arrested.

"It's my fault, officer. I was late," Shannon started. "I got held up and didn't get here like I was supposed to."

T.J. groaned at the lie. The policeman helped her get T.J. into her car after some fancy explanations from Shannon.

He knew she was angry with him when she didn't say anything until they got nearly to her house. "So what brought all this on, T.J.?"

"Why didn't you tell your mom?"

"Tell my mom what?"

He couldn't believe he was hearing this. Did she forget already that she'd said she'd marry him? "You didn't tell her about us, Shannon." He saw pity in her eyes, exactly the thing he didn't want to see.

"T.J. We need to talk."

*Yeah, holy fucking right we need to talk.*

They arrived at the house, and Shannon parked the car in the garage. T.J. was struggling to get out on the passenger side when Shannon was suddenly there to help him up. He tried to push her arms away, but had to be careful, and in the end gave up and just let her guide him.

He loved the smell of her hair, the brush of her belly as she braced him, pressing her left breast into his chest, encouraging him with little words like he was a child. She led him to the living room, pulled his feet up onto the ottoman, covered him with an afghan and removed his shoes. He heard the buzz of a coffee grinder and soon the fresh smell of the black brew.

"You want something to eat, T.J.?"

He couldn't answer that question. His mind was completely blank.

"T.J.?" she asked, her hands on her waist.

"I don't fuckin' know."

She brought him a mug of steaming black coffee, but didn't trust him to hold it on his own. When he reached for it, she held it away from him. "Wait just a minute or two. I don't want you to burn yourself."

None of this was helping his mood. Finally she put the mug to his lips and watched as he slurped it and then pulled his head back when he'd had enough.

"So I gather you've changed your mind." T.J. didn't see any point in belaboring the point. He decided to confront her."

"I didn't say that."

"But you didn't tell your mom what we've been doing the last few days either. That indicates you've had second thoughts, Shannon. Or am I wrong?"

"You're right about one thing. Perhaps this was all too fast." She was studying her hands wringing in her lap. When she looked up at him, he wasn't sure what he saw in her eyes.

"What is it, Shannon? What's changed?"

She hesitated before starting. "Mom overheard one of the wives say you made a promise to Frankie to take care of me and Courtney."

"Yeah, I did. So?" He was getting a very uneasy feeling about her mother's communication.

"So, I have to ask you, T.J., would you even be here in the first place if you hadn't made that promise? Are you doing this for Frankie, or—" she turned and looked away from him.

"Shannon, honey, no." He tried to grab her but upturned the hot coffee and it burned his leg. "God dammit!" he shouted.

They both ran to the kitchen to get towels. The burn on his thigh didn't hurt nearly as bad as the ache in his chest. Before they returned to the couch, he pulled her to him. "Please, believe me. My promise has nothing to do with this. It got me here, but it's not what's keeping me here. Shannon, you have to believe me."

"Then why didn't you tell me? Did you think I wouldn't find out?"

T.J. was starting to lose his patience. He didn't like his honor questioned. "What the hell lies did your mother pour into you?"

Shannon reared up. "How dare you say that? These are my questions."

"Well, everything was fine until she came down here. What kind of infection did that woman lay on you?"

"She's my mother, T.J." Shannon shouted.

"Yeah? Well I had a mother too, for all the good it did me." He wished he could stop, but he couldn't. Something had become uncorked, something raw and ugly and vile.

He could see she was staring into that dark pit that was his past, and it scared her.

"I never had anyone who cared a shit about me until I joined the Navy, until I met Frankie. Family is just—I could never do what my father did to me, abandon my child. I want to be there for you both."

"I understand, but I think we should wait until after the baby's born to make all these permanent decisions."

He cursed to himself. He'd jumped the gun and gotten in the sheets with her first, and impulsively asked her to marry him, which was a huge mistake. If he could have just taken his time, been patient, perhaps she wouldn't be having this reaction.

And then there was that fuckin' big knot in his stomach that said perhaps he wasn't the right man for her after all. He'd made the promise to Frankie, but what if it wasn't what Shannon wanted?

"Look, Shannon, I'm sorry. I want only the best for you and for the baby. And yes, I gave my word. You have to understand I've never done this before. I fuckin' made a promise and I'm going to keep it. I'm just not doing it the right way, obviously. And maybe I never will. I'm not Frankie, and I fuckin' won't replace him."

"Nor could you, T.J."

Her steely tone stabbed him. Anger flared again in his belly. She was right. He never could be the kind of husband and father Frankie was. He was a completely different man. Different kind of man. Didn't matter how much he told himself, the fact remained he would never live up to Frankie's expectations of him. So why try?

"T.J., I care for you deeply. But I still want to cool things off a bit, catch my breath and figure out what I want. I don't want to rush into anything. I need some time."

"Of course." Tired and defeated, he spoke to his shoes. "I'll sleep on the couch."

Shannon agreed quickly and slept in the master bedroom. Alone.

THE NEXT MORNING, he felt the distance between them growing. He didn't want to be the one chasing her. The dull ache in his chest was unbearable and he told her he'd give her some space and return to his little apartment. She casually said she'd call him in a few days.

He forced himself not to call her and tried to focus on anything but how lonely he felt. First, he'd lost Frankie. He felt like he'd lost Shannon. Nothing he used to do to get himself out of his funk appealed to him, either. Worst of all was the feeling he'd let Frankie down.

T.J. WAS CLEANING his equipment at his apartment two days later when he got a call from Tyler.

"I think a little get together is way past due. You free Friday night, stud?" Tyler asked.

"Sure." He was pretty sure this would involve a blind date with someone they thought was perfect for him. And it never worked. "Who the fuck is she Tyler?"

"Kate's sister from Portland. She's a real nice lady. Got two kids. Very level headed, though, and pretty."

"Not really up for this, Tyler. Not really a good idea."

"So, you're gonna sit home and, what, watch TV?"

"That's pretty much what I've been doing, that and some PT."

"So Friday you're coming over for a barbeque. You're coming alone, right?"

"Probably. Haven't seen Shannon in about three days. And I haven't called her."

"Good."

Gretchen was in her early thirties, and an attractive, thoughtful lady, composed in spite of always being surrounded by her own little wolf pack of girls. Though it was far from anything he'd experienced, he found a new affinity for family, for connection. He knew Shannon would do what she needed to do. He couldn't change that.

But he still hoped she'd opt for staying in San Diego. Even if she wanted a separate life from his, he could still be a part of Courtney's life as he'd promised Frankie. He chuckled at the "old, gnarly guy" spying on the probably gorgeous Courtney at her soccer games or dance parties. The one who would take out anyone who as much as touched or looked at her wrong. The guy would be toast. In spite of himself, he cracked a smile.

Kate switched on the TV and all of them watched a news flash about threats coming from groups in the Middle East. They were threatening the lives of servicemen, saying they'd come get them at home.

Tyler and T.J. shook their heads. "Can't wait to hear what Kyle has to said about this. They've gotta be making plans," Tyler said.

"You check out all the new security on base? I'd say hell yeah they're making plans."

The newsflash was over in seconds, and Tyler shut the TV off. "Not like I have to listen to this thing play over and over again all night." He left to check on the barbeque.

"So how you holding up, T.J.?" Gretchen asked him after the girls ran past them to the backyard. Kate had given them ice cream.

"There are days which aren't so good. Most days, I'm okay. Trying not to do anything too stressful, just chilling. We'll get plenty of stress next deployment."

Gretchen nodded. "Does this stuff, like on the news, bother you at all?"

"I'm not going to lie, things are heating up everywhere. But it's our job. It's what we train for."

"Bad guys coming here?" she asked.

"I'm on a need to know basis." He smiled. "They'll tell us what to do when the time comes. Until then, we just live our lives and get ready for the next deployment."

His eyes landed on her pretty face, and he could see how a guy could fall for her. She had a quiet manner, but a wicked sense of humor he'd enjoyed earlier when she was trying to tell a story at dinner over her three daughters who interrupted her constantly. Surviving the public spectacle of her professional basketball player husband running off with a floozy, and surviving it with grace, added one more jewel to her crown. She was a solid woman.

"How you holding up?"

She stiffened. "Funny you should ask me that question. No one ever does."

He didn't get to hear her answer, because Tyler chose that moment to come barging back into the room.

"Okay, so guess what, pilgrims?" Tyler said. "Tomorrow night we're going line dancing."

"Nah, I don't dance," T.J. Said.

"Makes two of us," said Gretchen. "Besides, I'd have to get a sitter, and I don't know anyone down here."

"No problemo. I know a couple of Team guy daughters who would love to babysit. You aren't going to get out of this that easy."

She looked over at T.J. He hoped he didn't look too displeased, but he was mortified and hoped they'd drop the whole thing. He wasn't that lucky, and arrangements were made for him to meet Gretchen, Kate and Tyler at the Norwegian Hall the next night.

T.J. helped clear the table, bringing in the dishes to the very pregnant Kate, kissing her on the cheek. He wouldn't have done that, but the proximity to Shannon had driven off some of the fear he had about hanging around pregnant women. "Thanks, Kate. That was real nice."

"Well, it was Tyler's show. Loves to barbeque. As I recall, you love it too."

"Yes, ma'am."

"So how's Shannon taking things? I heard you were kind of sweet on her for a time."

T.J. was uncomfortable speaking about it with Kate. Women had a way of getting him to say things he didn't want to reveal.

"We're friends. I think she's trying to figure out what she wants."

"I can understand that." Kate dried her hands on a towel, threw it on the counter in front of her and asked him point blank, "And what do you want, T.J?"

It was a good question. He didn't have a clue. Then he thought of something. "I wanna get home from the next deployment with all 20 fingers and toes. And I wanna keep my promise to Frankie."

"You're a good man, T.J. Talbot."

He wished he could agree.


HE RAN INTO Joe at the store the next afternoon. "Hey Joe," he said with a warm, friendly smile. His compassion and respect for the older man had increased since their project with the playhouse.

But he was almost afraid to mention anything about he and Shannon drifting apart until Joe shared news he found very disturbing.

"Heard from Shannon's mom. Shannon's up visiting her in the Bay Area. I sure hope she doesn't relocate there, but I guess the Moores wouldn't mind. Said we should come up and visit any time."

*What? How could this be?*

He'd promised he'd look after Shannon, but now it was more than a promise. He wouldn't be the same without her in his life. He worried Shannon hadn't told him she was leaving town, taking it as further evidence she was planning on moving on, and perhaps without him. His heart sank to the bottom of the ocean.

"Joe, I'm sorry to hear that. We barely had time to get acquainted," he said to Frankie's dad.

Joe smiled. "You looked like you were getting along quite well, to my keen old eyes." T.J. couldn't look at him, so stared at his canvas slip-ons.

"Son—" Joe put one hand on T.J.'s shoulder, waiting until he returned his look. "I was going to tell you this a couple of days ago, but now ... well, I guess my timing kinda sucks."

Did T.J. want to know what Joe was about to say to him?

"It was hard losing Frankie. I won't lie. Probably harder on Gloria. Boy, was he the apple of her eye. She lived for that boy growing up. He never wanted for anything. Anything. I used to lie awake at nights, knowing she was dreaming about our son, planning his life, and worrying about all his needs. My job was to wait. Wait until she came back to me. And now she has."

Joe's eyes watered. T.J. nodded, reached over and gave Joe a bear hug. Why had the God of SEALs not given him a father like Joe? Why hadn't he gotten a father at all? And why did Joe and Gloria have to endure the loss of their boy? It should have been him. T.J. should have been the one to not come home. Frankie'd had so much to live for. Especially now.

After the men patted each other's backs, Joe wiped the tear away from one eye with a knuckle. He took a deep breath and continued. "I didn't know I would have to lose my son to get my wife back."

T.J. felt like a dumbass for being so wrapped up in himself he had missed the obvious pain the Bensons were still feeling. He became more aware than ever before how the cycle of life changed everything with each new addition or deletion. Little Courtney was changing Shannon's trajectory. Frankie's exit changed the trajectory of the Bensons' relationship.

*And me? What right do I have to expect anything from these people?* Frankie had been on loan to him courtesy of the U.S. Navy. Shannon on loan to him through Frankie. No one owed him an explanation. And no one cared, either.

There he was, thinking of himself again, while Mr. Benson stood before him, tears streaming down his face. Maybe he couldn't have Shannon and the child. But there were things he could do.

"Joe, I honestly hope she doesn't move. I'd miss her too. Let's hope she'll come home, to both of us."

The old man's lower lip quivered. He wasn't able to speak, so T.J. grabbed him again and allowed the man to sob in his arms. Several people passed by them in the cereal section of the grocery store, but T.J. didn't care what they thought. Giving Joe the loving arms he'd earned was way more important. They could think they were a gay couple, a couple of reconnected family members, or old friends. It made no difference to him. Letting Joe know he wasn't alone was the most important thing in his life.

The rest would simply have to take care of itself.

THAT AFTERNOON, T.J. left several messages for Shannon, all unreturned. He met Kate, Gretchen and Tyler at the dance hall. He told himself it was good to move, to feel the rhythm of the music, to concentrate on following the caller's directions. Gretchen was a good partner, and, while he didn't feel a sexual spark, he did feel something for her. He was ashamed to figure out he felt sorry for her. He could tell she liked him, and he wasn't going to be able to give her back anything at all.

The awkwardness intensified during the slow dances. It was so wrong for him to be here. He wanted to be anywhere but trying to play nice, when something was boiling inside him.

Gretchen licked her lips, perhaps expecting he'd kiss her. "Gretchen," he said as he squinted, moving away to a safe distance, "how long are you down here for?"

"I go back in three days." She was smiling, examining his eyes for signs she'd never see. He knew she didn't find it easy to trust men, and who could blame her? He wished she didn't trust him.

Images of that day at Shannon's, fixing the playhouse for the baby, the lovemaking, all of it came back to him. Along with a double dose of self-loathing. Why had he pushed things so fast? Why couldn't he have just kept his fucking hands off her?

"Hey, T.J. You didn't ask me to marry you, did you?"

Her statement stunned him out of the rut his mind had replayed over and over again. He frowned. "Last I checked, no."

"So why the long face? It's only dancing. I'm a good cheap date. I don't require much. I change partners gracefully, and I won't expect you to call the next day. But I get lonely, and I think right now you are, too."

She spoke the truth. He was lonely. Just like Shannon had been lonely and let him have his way with her.

His face was close to Gretchen's and he could have kissed her, saw her even prepare for it, but he began to pull back. Gretchen grabbed his ears and wouldn't let go until she laid a long, wet kiss on him.

But there was only one girl he wanted to kiss, and it wasn't sweet Gretchen. How he wished it was different.

# CHAPTER 12

A LTHOUGH HER MOTHER had extended the invitation, Shannon was going home to see her dad. She'd never been able to get enough of his love growing up. He'd worked long hours while she was being shuttled back and forth between piano lessons, ice skating, swimming and the Children's Theater, which was her real passion. Her well-run life was her mother's design, and there hardly was time to think about anything else.

Her dad was devoted to her mother. That same attentiveness was what originally attracted her to Frankie, who would be the same kind of husband her dad was. Now without her husband, it made the visit with her dad all that more important.

The neighborhood looked just as she remembered it, except the trees were bigger and the houses seemed smaller. She'd ridden her bike up and down the level streets, where the curbs were all rounded to make that part of town "kid friendly," or so her mother had touted to all her friends.

Her mother had been a social icon, PTA President and deeply involved in all of Shannon's school activities. Mr. Moore's devotion to her mother only widened the gap she felt growing up. Her mother's events and parties made the local society columns, and Shannon was known as "Mrs. Moore's daughter." She felt more like Mrs. Robinson's daughter from The Graduate, even though she didn't suspect her mother of infidelity. But, she thought, her mother could have played that role well.

When she went off to college and then met Frankie, his easy-going manner and devotion made her the center of his universe, and for the first time in her life she didn't have to share the stage with another Diva. Frankie was her ticket out. She'd never laughed so hard or loved being alive so much.

On this trip, she was hoping to extract some of her mother's iron will and bask in her father's love. She knew it would help her heal.

Not yet ready to face them, Shannon drove past her parents' house. One by one, her childhood landmarks came into view. The town was known for having one of the first children's libraries in California. It also had a children's theater around the corner from where Shannon had taken her swimming lessons. On an impulse, Shannon parked and got out.

She remembered the lifeguard instructor with shocking white-blonde hair and brown eyes, the one who always had a thick layer of white zinc oxide on his nose. He wore dark-rimmed sunglasses and had the physique of Michelangelo's David or Adonis. The worst memory was from when she was eight and would always belly flop if he tried to help her do a front dive into the pool. His habit of putting his hand on her tummy right before she launched her dive had flustered her and always landed her in disaster. Did he ever catch on?

She wandered over to the Children's Theater, finding the doors open. Several children and one adult were on stage, with a director sitting three rows up from the stage, barking instructions.

She turned left, sure that the room was still there, and it was. The wardrobe closet was her favorite childhood memory. It had been guarded by Peg, who had worked there for thirty years. Peg, was enormous, but somehow made it up and down the narrow rows of sequins, feathers and silks, remembering every jacket, every pair of pants, every cummerbund, petticoat or pair of wings, and what size child they would fit. Her loving hands and generous hugs turned plain children, petrified to get up on stage, into magical creatures. In their finery, they would parade back and forth, becoming kings and queens, knights and dragons, butterflies and birds and pumpkins, and a host of other things they'd never thought they could be. The imagination and silliness of childhood were allowed to run free in the theater.

Shannon imagined Courtney taking an acting class. She hoped she might get her first kiss from a boy covered in greasepaint, her little heart going pitter-pat, just like she had.

At the end of the first row of costumes Shannon got to her knees. Carefully, on all fours, she crawled under the red petticoats of the can-can dancers and lifted the glittery finery. She was looking for her inscription written in pencil on the wall.

*Shannon Loves Richard.*

She recognized her handwriting. Sitting under the mass of red petticoats, with her back leaning against the wall, the baby kicking in her belly, she touched the letters she had scrawled. With one hand on her abdomen and the other pressing against her letter to her future self, she felt the distance between where she had been and where she was now.

*This place could be good for Courtney.* She couldn't wait to tell Courtney all the stories and adventures of her youth, the piano lessons with the teacher who had performed at Carnegie Hall when she was young, but who lovingly placed her gnarled and crippled fingers over Shannon's small ones, asking her gently to stretch wide to reach all the notes her young hands struggled with.

"Grow into your piano hands, Shannon. You must stretch and grow into them." And gnarled and crippled or not, her fingers had felt smooth and soft, her handwriting perfectly formed as she jotted down the lessons with a soft pencil.

Back in those days, it had been pure pleasure to ride her bike with the breeze running through her hair. She'd watch the big houses with the beautiful yards go by one by one. Imagining the stories, the families inside, and wondering what they were doing, she rode almost invisibly down the heavily tree-lined streets of a community of people who cared about their children. Her stories were her future, riding her bike up and down the rounded curves from the sidewalk to the streets and back again, trying to envision a life like the one she was leading now.

But she'd also felt confined here as a child, with her parents' high expectations she could never completely live up to. Doing it her own way became more important the older she got.

Now, she appreciated the beauty of her childhood. She saw how it enveloped and protected her. She realized that this was the childhood she wanted for her daughter. The two of them together would find that safe, comfortable place.

She was alive and happy now, although a widow, with a child not yet born, living in a place that reminded her of a past she could not have any longer, wondering if it might be wise to move to a place where she could create a future all by herself.

She'd written down the address of a little house three doors down from the home she grew up in. Smallest house on the block, in need of the most repairs. But it would do. Shannon's past would shield her daughter's future.

She needed to do this. She needed to move away from San Diego. She was determined to be self-sufficient, but it made sense to have her parents close by, just in case. When she told herself that moving here would be no big deal, she knew there was a lie hidden in there, but quickly tamped down the feeling. She'd needed the space away from San Diego to make a clear-headed decision, away from the temptations of her body. Now that she'd decided, she was ready to face her parents.

And then she'd tell T.J. what she'd decided.


HER PARENTS WERE thrilled with the possibility she'd move up north, and wanted her to move in with them, which she declined.

"Oh, honey, it would be so nice to have little Courtney in this house," her mother had said.

Her dad's face was all the encouragement she needed.

"No, not here, but perhaps close by. There's a little house near the theater that's for sale."

They'd discussed it until late in the evening. She walked outside after her parents went to bed and looked up at the star-filled sky. The move wouldn't be like the last time, when she had just graduated from college, an eager young woman off for her first job, a great adventure in a town full of hunky Navy guys. *A safe place to be*, her friends had said. *Lots of sunshine and mild climate. Nights full of stars.*

It had been one of those starry nights when she'd met Frankie. He'd graduated BUD/S and was getting ready to deploy for the first time. She didn't even know what a SEAL was until she'd met him. He was forever with his sidekick, T.J., and her distrust and dislike of him was instantaneous.

Now she knew why. T.J. had wanted to insert himself between her and Frankie. He was protective. Never having anyone to protect him in a system that had failed him miserably, he wanted to take care of Frankie, even if Frankie didn't even know he needed taking care of. He'd fixed him up with girls T.J. liked, but who scared Frankie to death.

Shannon smiled at this. T.J.'d been so tender with her. She owed a lot to Frankie's best friend. Without her intimate afternoons with him, when she explored the depths of her heart and soul, she would never have been able to find the strength to contemplate moving back home. She hoped he would understand. And that one fine day he would have a woman and a home of his own.

His quiet confidence had instilled in her something special, like Frankie had. T.J. had shown her the way to go on, to deal with life on life's terms, that every day was a gift.

He would forever be special to her. And she'd make sure Courtney knew him as her daddy's best friend, but probably not as her mother's lover. Wrap up a few more details, and then she'd go home, sell the house, and get on with her life.

Telling T.J. he would be welcome to come visit, but not share her bed any longer, would be the hardest part. She hoped this gentle warrior would in time forgive her for parting them, even though she didn't have a clear-cut future.

For the first time in her life, she didn't have definite plans. Her plan was simply to live. To raise her daughter. To work hard to be the kind of mother Frankie would have wanted, give back to her parents the kind of love, through Courtney, she wasn't able to show them growing up.

The next day, she went shopping with her mother for things for the new house. They talked over lunch like they had when she had her first department store job when she was still in high school.

Shannon went with her mother to interview a new doctor, a woman doctor this time, who didn't ask where her husband was. She still wore her wedding ring, the simple gold band that was the only thing Frankie had been able to afford. She made diagrams and drew out the furniture she would bring up. She laid out Courtney's nursery. She thought about the vegetables she'd plant, and she interviewed her realtor's gardener. She found a new place to have her car serviced.

T.J.'s messages finally stopped, as if he'd had a premonition about her plans. Day after tomorrow she'd return to begin the packing and moving process. With her parents as co-signers on the loan, there wasn't an issue about her qualifying. The death benefit was more than ample for her down payment. She knew Frankie would approve.

Now if she could figure out a way to tell T.J. without breaking his heart. Would he be able to support her in this decision? Would he understand?

# CHAPTER 13

**T**.J.'S PHONE RANG early the next morning. It was Shannon.

"Understand you've gone up north."

"Yes, I came to visit my folks."

He wanted to say something but held his tongue. He wanted to tell her what a bad idea that was, ask her why she had to go way up there when everything she needed was right here in San Diego. But he didn't want to hear what she'd say.

"I'm actually considering staying here. I want you to think about that before we talk further."

So, there it was. Confirmed. His worst nightmare.

"Sounds like you've pretty much made up your mind."

"I think it would be good up here for Courtney and I."

"Where do I fit in that picture?"

"I'm not sure yet. Where do you want to be?"

"Well, I can't move up there. Sounds like you don't want to be here, with me. So that pretty much tells me everything." He thought he was prepared for this conversation, but now realized how inadequate he felt. He wished they were talking face to face, but realized perhaps that was Shannon's plan.

"I've had some time to think, and maybe staying down in San Diego isn't the best for me anymore."

"Why, Shannon? I already said I'd take care of you and the baby. Why are you running away?"

"I'm not, T.J."

"So you just don't want to be around me, right? It's me, then. Why don't you just fuckin' come out and say it?"

"Because that's not the truth."

"Why didn't we talk about this?"

"You don't owe me anything, T.J. I want to do this on my own. Away from the distraction of—"

He hated this. "So, now I'm a distraction?"

"You don't have to take care of me. I want to know I can do it on my own."

"I just have to ask you, Shannon. Is there someone else?"

"No. I wouldn't do that."

"I'm coming up to see you."

"No, don't. That's not a good idea."

"You saying you'll refuse to see me? That what you're saying?"

"Why do you have to be so in charge? Can't you see I just need to process things a little?"

"You know what you're doing to Joe and Gloria Benson?"

"T.J., that's between me and them."

"I'm fuckin' coming up there to talk to you, period."

"Fine." She sighed. "But I won't change my mind. You can't fix this, T.J."


T.J. GOT PERMISSION from Kyle to make a run up to the Bay Area and then took a transport to Moffet Field. He rented a car on the El Camino and rang Shannon.

"Where are you right now?" he asked.

"You're here? Now?"

"What did you think, I was kidding?"

She decided to give him the address of the little house she'd just made an offer on.

Within a half hour T.J.'s hulking frame blocked sunlight coming through the small rounded window in the heavy oak door. He pushed it open with a loud creek that echoed off the bare hardwood floors and stucco walls. The place was similar in style to the home she and Frankie had bought in San Diego, a Spanish style bungalow, but even smaller.

The sight of her as she walked around the corner from the kitchen took his breath away. She'd developed even rosier cheeks, and her belly looked like it had grown dramatically. He found himself gawking and then remembered himself.

As he got close to her he could see her apprehension. He wanted it to be anticipation of a joyful reunion, but that's not what she showed him. With her arms outstretched, palms facing him, she kept him from her, so he leaned over and kissed her on the cheek.

"Missed you," he whispered.

"Thank you, T.J." He could see she was choosing her words carefully. "I've been good. It's been good here." She turned, walking toward a sliding door that led to the backyard off the dining room. He could see the steam from the heat of her fingers as she placed her palm against the glass. "It's small. Only two bedrooms, but I can afford it, with Frankie's benefits."

He stood next to her. The overgrown yard was going to be a lot of work for her. There was a single swing hanging from the branch of a large shade tree. "You're gonna fuckin' do this?" he whispered.

"I think so."

"Doesn't have a playhouse," he mumbled.

That got her to turn towards him. God how he wished she'd take his hand, give him just some little bit of encouragement. It wasn't much, but she smiled. "Maybe you and Joe could bring the one you made up here. Do you think you guys could do that?"

He wanted to say no. He wanted to grab her and drag her butt back to San Diego, stay right next to her until she changed her mind. He told himself he'd let her drift too long. He never should have waited. He'd given her the space, and she'd gone and convinced herself she needed a separate life. And he knew Frankie wouldn't want that. It was eating a hole in his stomach like acid. He couldn't protect her from afar, and he wasn't ready to leave the Teams, even if she wanted him here, which she clearly did not.

"Shannon, I'll do what you want. I promised to take care of you, and if this is really what you want, well, I guess Frankie will have to forgive me."

"But you could still be part of our lives. I wouldn't ever exclude you from Courtney's life. My parents—"

"Fuckin' hate me, Shannon. Well, your mother does, anyway. How long before she'd convince you that I didn't belong anywhere near you and the baby?"

"I won't let that happen. I promise."

He decided he was ready to look at her. With her face upturned, her full lips so kissable, her nostrils flared slightly, warm breath washing over the delicate hairs on her upper lip, he wished he were the man she needed, she wanted. He wanted her in the worst way. He'd only had a taste of what it could be like. Frankie was right, had been right all along. Shannon was the real deal.

And he'd discovered it too late. He'd mucked it up. And now perhaps that chance would never come along again. He touched her cheek with the backs of his fingers, rubbing his thumb over her lips. "All right, honey. If this is what you want, who am I to ask you to change your mind?" He tried to smile, but couldn't.

She moved towards him and lay her head against his chest. As he rubbed the top of her spine, fingers sifting through her hair, he heard her whisper, "Thank you."

HE HELPED HER lock up the house. While she called the Realtor, he took her over to her parents. Forced to stay for dinner, he had no appetite and tried not to look at the beautiful woman sitting across the table, who might as well have been on the other side of the world. A week ago, he never would have dreamed he'd be sitting here, actually strategizing her move, offering to help her get all the people she'd need to make that move. His Team buds would help, of course. It would be painless for her, because he'd make sure it was that way. He'd make sure all she had to do was wait out the last weeks of her pregnancy.

Mrs. Moore was actually cordial to him. She hung back at the dinner table to talk with him in private.

"You've surprised me, T.J."

"Yeah, well I surprise myself sometimes," he said as he took the cup of coffee she offered. Shannon and her dad were looking through catalogs in the living room. He could feel her eyes on him.

"I can't imagine any of this is easy for you."

He told himself not to trust her. The sound of compassion in her voice came dangerously close to pity.

"Not up to me."

"Well, you're being a prince, T.J. I know we haven't always seen eye to eye. This is what's best for Shannon. You'll see. She needs to raise her child here, where her home is."

T.J. raised his eyebrows. "Used to be she thought of that house in San Diego as home."

"Things have changed," she said, and she was right.

"They certainly have." He'd be going home, alone.

But then, he was used to that.

TWO DAYS LATER, back in San Diego, T.J. agreed to meet Gretchen at a local ice cream shop. Kate and Tyler were babysitting the girls, who were hoping their Mom had found another guy. Always on the lookout for a new daddy, they weren't very subtle about it.

T.J. knew there was only one woman for him, though. And he also knew Gretchen understood that. Kate's sister was easy to be around, warm of spirit and gentle on the eyes. A man could do far worse, but he knew that wasn't what he was interested in. He was marking time until his life could start in earnest, giving Shannon all the room she needed, keeping a tiny flame of hope that she'd come back to him.

God, it had only been one day but already the waiting was hard. He'd hoped a little fun with Gretchen would distract him. She was easy to be around, and he found he liked making her happy.

On the way home, she asked him to stop. "Can we have a little talk?"

He pulled to a gravel shoulder on the road that wound through the foothills, angled the car toward the bay and turned it off.

"Shoot."

She adjusted herself to face him, bending the knee closest to him, but she stayed on her side of the front seat of his truck. "I meant what I said a couple of nights ago. I'm a good listener, a good friend. I'm not looking for anything long term."

"Gretchen—"

"Hear me out, T.J. What's wrong with a little recreational sex and some cuddling? You might find you like it. We might find a way to heal ourselves somehow."

"I don't think I can be fixed, Gretchen." He didn't want to look at her because he didn't feel worthy of even her friendship. He couldn't believe he was not interested in the "recreational sex" part. How much he had changed. Now the idea of using Gretchen to heal his loneliness or take the edge off his sexual desires made him sick.

He couldn't pretend with her. It wasn't right.

"T.J. look at me," she whispered.

He did. She was pretty, and she was totally willing. He could have kissed her, done far more, and she would have let him.

"Am I so bad to look at, such poor company?" Her smile was sweet, her eyes innocent and he couldn't go there.

She was on him in a flash, her fingers clutching the back of his neck, pulling him into her, her lips ravenous over his. She was going to move onto his lap, but he stopped her, holding her by the upper arms, stiffly.

"I can't, Gretchen. I just can't."

Her nervous laughter wounded him. "And here I thought you were the bad boy. Kate told me all about you, although she was careful to edit."

He smiled at hearing about his reputation.

"Yeah, well don't believe everything you hear. There are some things I'm not especially proud of."

"What about Shannon?" she asked.

"That chapter hasn't been written."

She watched him squirm. "You two dated a little, Tyler says."

"You could call it that."

Gretchen leaned forward, turned his face toward her. T.J. was wary, but he felt she wasn't interested in coming on to him. "Holy cow, you're *sweet* on her, aren't you?"

He tried to smile, but it was awkward. Involuntarily he looked away as his eyes filled with water.

"Oh. My. God. T.J. You've been hiding this. From everyone."

"No one to tell." He was glad Tyler hadn't broken his confidence.

"Does she know?"

There was *that* question. At least it was one he could answer. "Oh, yes, she surely does know."

"When does she come home?" Gretchen asked.

"Home? She hasn't told me. But I guess in the next couple of days. She's probably going to move away."

"Are you going to try to change her mind?"

He considered that statement. Was he going to try? Hadn't he tried already with zero results? "I don't think I can, Gretchen. Not sure that's possible."

"She's nuts. She'd be crazy not to want to come home to you. You've got to go for broke, T.J. You've got to make a stand. Don't let her get away."

"Gretchen, I love your optimism. But haven't you heard that saying, 'You can lead a horse to water...'"

"Is that how you got through BUD/S training? Is that how you do it when you go overseas?"

He had to admit she was right. That wasn't how he did it. They all had a plan. They had missions to accomplish. They didn't sit there and let insurgents and enemies come after them, they took the fight to them. They openly protected the people they were sent to watch over.

"You didn't ring that bell, T.J. Why are you going to ring it now?"

*Holy fuck, she was completely right.* He'd given up. He shook his head. What a dumb ass he'd been. Slinking around, feeling sorry for himself.

"Gretchen? I think I love you."

She giggled, and it made his heart sing.

"God I wish you could have said that earlier. I might have kept my big mouth shut."

He hugged her, kissing the side of her face. "I think you're the first woman I've told that to who hasn't had sex with me first."

"Then I take that as a compliment, T.J. And if Shannon is nuts enough not to fall into your arms, well, I'm not ashamed to say I wouldn't mind being a welcome distraction. I think I could do make-up sex pretty good, although I've never tried."

"I'll bet you could," he said.

He realized now what he had to do. He had to fight for Shannon. With everything in his being, he had to fight to keep her. Because it *was* a matter of life or death.

# CHAPTER 14

S HANNON FLEW BACK to San Diego, and the heaviness in her chest increasing the closer they got to landing. Joe met her at the airport, asking about her stay with her folks and how they were. She knew it was just small talk, because Joe had called several times while she was gone to inquire about her. She knew her mother had told them Shannon was considering a move back home.

Joe helped her with her bag, bringing it up the shallow steps to the front porch. One of the reasons she liked this house was the way the little concrete steps had been colored red. The concrete had been stained before it was poured, forever committed to that rosy hue. The heavy oak door had a small window in the center of it, covered by Spanish wrought iron detail. She'd loved this door and the way it protected her home inside.

She was surprised it still felt like her home. Or their home. Hers and Frankie's. And the home where T.J. had told her he loved her, the safe place where she'd learned that she could go on.

Joe quietly stayed behind her, allowing her entry, and without stepping inside himself, set her bag down on the wood floor and said his goodbyes, promising to look in on her tomorrow.

"You've gotten much bigger this week. Are you comfortable?" he asked.

"Not quite uncomfortable yet, still able to sleep, thank God. But soon. It will get dicey soon." She decided not to bring up her move.

She listened to the creaking of the floorboards, took in the way the house smelled. A large bouquet of red roses was on the dining table. Her fingers were trembling as she plucked the little card from its holder and read T.J.'s inscription.

*Missed you more than I thought possible.*

*I know we have to talk. But just know that I love you.*

She rubbed her forefinger over the words he'd carefully inscribed. This was going to be more difficult than she thought.

The doors to the master bedroom and the baby's room were closed. She smelled cleaning agents and realized someone had gone all-out to prepare for her return to this house, prepared it as though she was going to stay. The windows had been washed. Area rugs had been cleaned, and larger ones freshly vacuumed.

Opening the door to her bedroom, she looked outside at the play house T.J. and Joe had put together only two weeks ago. Someone had planted flowers all around the little house, as if she were staying. And she could just see a tiny table with a miniature tea set inside.

A small wading pool with pink mermaids on it and fresh, clean water filling it, with a child's seahorse life preserver bobbing up and down in the shallow water. Ready for Courtney...in about a year. There was a two-bucket swing set installed at the side of the yard. An old-fashioned bench swing with green canvas canopy sat under her maple tree, with a couple of new flowered pillows on top. Everywhere she looked, a bit of magic had been added, painted, or enhanced by colorful plantings.

She went back inside and felt like she was coming back to a lovely familiar dream. If a house could love the people who lived in it, this one did. Just as Frankie had. Just as T.J.—she had to stop thinking about him, or it would be more difficult to continue with what she'd decided to do.

Pulling her rolling suitcase down the hallway, she unpacked, put the clothes in the washing machine, and turned it on. She took a long shower, washing her hair, getting all the dirt and grime of airports and travel off of her skin.

After rubbing her hair with the fluffy white towels Frankie had bought, she combed it out and secured it with an antique clip, and then slipped on her favorite nightgown, noticing her belly almost didn't fit now. In her bare feet, she made herself a tall glass of ice water with mostly ice. The refrigerator was fully stocked with food. Fresh vegetables and fruit in baggies tucked neatly away. Two steaks marinated in a covered glass dish. Was she looking in on a fictional couple? Or was this part of her life?

She took her glass back down the hallway to Courtney's room. The mysterious welcoming committee had glued her daughter's name to the door in multicolored wooden letters. She brushed over the letters with her fingers, and then opened the door.

A bouquet of light pink roses, short-stemmed, sat on the baby's changing table and permeated the air with their sweet fragrance. Above the table, a framed poster was hung, inscribed with the words,

*May you touch dragonflies and stars,*
*Dance with Fairies and talk to the moon.*
*May you grow up with love and gracious hearts,*
*And people who care.*
*Welcome to the world, little one.*
*It's been waiting for you. We've been waiting for you.*

She walked over to the roses, and touched the letters on the poster. They were hard to read, because her eyes had filled and tears were streaming down her cheeks. She sniffled, overcome by the message T.J. had left for her daughter, the man she had decided to leave for...for what?

She wiped tears from her cheeks with the backs of her hands, then reached up to touch the words again, like she was touching his face, the man she had decided to leave behind, like her pencil scratch in the costume closet at the theater. Except this wasn't a memory. This was real time.

"I thought maybe you'd like it." T.J.'s voice filled the room, wrapping around her, with that warm, familiar cadence, snagging her heart, squeezing tight, and not letting go. "I have to admit, I got some help from Kate and Gretchen. They helped me pick it out."

She turned to find him leaning against the doorway. His long, muscular legs encased in blue jeans above bare feet, a light blue shirt opened to his tanned chest, revealing more muscles than he had a right to. His hips were cocked at an angle, his hands jammed into his front pockets. With his dark hair and blue eyes, the need written all over his face, he was a package she hadn't been prepared for.

"It's beautiful, T.J."

"I could say the same about you."

He didn't come over to her, but his eyes drank up the sight of her like it was the last time he'd see her.

He nodded to her flannel nightie, "I see you're not quite ready to entertain company. Perhaps I should come back another time, then?"

"Don't be silly. You're here."

"Yes, I am, Shannon. I'm here. But where are you?"

She examined her bare toes. She'd had them done in pink again. Her eyes began to tear up. Where was she? It was a good question.

"You can barely fit into that nightgown," he whispered.

"Watch it." She gave him a smirk and was rewarded with a tiny smile.

"But I love how you look, so full. You're the most beautiful woman I've ever seen, Shannon. I mean that."

She rested her hands on her stomach. "Never thought I'd need to be reassured."

"Oh, honey, I intend to remind you every day and all night long." His eyes pierced the veneer of her tough outer shell. She took in a deep breath and then walked over to him. "We should talk."

He reared back a step. "We will. But I've got something to say first, Shannon."

The distance between them felt achingly like the Grand Canyon.

"I love you, Shannon. I love that baby you're carrying. Whatever you're going to tell me next, I just want you to know that before we start." He looked down at his feet and then pleaded with his eyes. "And I've missed you. God, I've missed you."

It was natural to be drawn into his powerful arms, as she stepped in to feel him against her. He was careful. He simply held her tight, massaging the back of her neck at the top of her spine. She could hear his heart beating, strong and true. The sound of his breath surging in and out of his chest cavity washed over her like the soothing sounds of waves at the ocean.

There was something she had been protecting—what was it, anyway?—and now that protection was falling away. She felt herself open up to him again, and discovered the careful, familiar reassurance that all was well. In his arms, all was well.

That's when it hit her. She'd been shielding her heart. As she looked up at him, as his lips found hers, she knew she didn't have to steel herself against the pain of losing again, losing what she so desperately wanted.

He was respectful and chaste with his kiss, allowing her to lead. His hands came up to cup her face as he kissed her again, this time deep, but still tender. "Missed you, baby," he whispered to her lips.

She unwound from him. "Come. We need to talk, T.J." She took his left hand and led him to the living room, and then turned to offer him the couch, before she sat next to him. She became self-conscious of her wet hair, but she saw in his eyes that he loved her just the way she was. It was not conditional.

"Why, why did you do all this, T.J.?"

"That's an easy question to answer. Because I love you. Because I'm all in. I think the more important question is, what are your plans, and do they include me?"

She cocked her head to the side, lowering her gaze, not wanting to look up at him. He took it well. He straightened his back, sitting across from her, the leather couch groaning under his huge frame. He reacted like he'd been given an order, his chest filled, allowing the oxygen of his heavy breathing to calm him. It was what he did when he was nervous.

"I've been trying to sort it all out. Confused, here. I came home with one thing in mind, and now I don't know—"

"Well, Shannon, you're going to have to tell me to pack it up and quit, because not texting me or calling me back, or feeling confused, aren't going to cut it. You're gonna have to tell me to stop loving you, because I'm not going to unless you demand that of me."

"T.J., don't," she pleaded. But what did she really expect him to do? Of course he would react this way.

"Honey, I'm trying to understand. Did I come on too fast, too strong? Did I push you? Or is it that you don't like me, or is there someone else? Because I don't understand why you won't grab that big brass ring, that juice of life we have here, and go for it."

"That's what I'm trying to do. I thought maybe going home, back to where I was raised, would be good for me and for Courtney."

"Away from me, you mean? You want away from me? What have I done to make you want to run away? All I've done is love you, honey. Make me understand, please."

"I thought it would be good to go home, back to a place where I had happy childhood memories."

"So this isn't your home? This place. You and Frankie bought it right before you got married. I heard you say you never wanted to move. Ever."

"That was when Frankie was here with me."

T.J. nodded. "Well, that's true. I'm not Frankie, Shannon. No one will replace Frankie. You'll never find that, honey."

"I don't want to live in the past, T.J."

"Isn't that what going home is all about? *This* was your life. This was Frankie's life. These were the men and women he loved. His community." He looked up at the ceiling. "Oh, God, Shannon, I was hoping maybe I'd gotten it wrong somehow, but now I can see, you're just not that into me. As hard as it is, I know I have to accept that and move on."

He still wasn't leaving. He turned and asked her, "Is there anyone else?"

"No. For heaven's sake, no!"

"Then, can I ask you another question?"

"Fair enough."

"Are you going home or running away?"

He was right. She was running away.

"This place, this community scares me," she had to swallow because her voice wobbled. "Reminds me of what's changed. It's like I'll never be able to escape. I'll never be on my own."

T.J. chuckled at that.

"What's so funny?"

"You don't understand diddly about being alone. I've been alone my whole fuckin' life and never knew I'd missed anything until I found the SEAL family here. Do you know what it's like living in a community of people who would gladly die for you?"

He abruptly stood, walked around the couch and pointed down the hallway to Courtney's room.

"We do that. We make it so there are dragonflies and angels and fairies."

She quickly turned her back to him, weeping softly, but not wanting to show him her tears.

He came back, standing in front of her seated body, now uncomfortable because the baby was kicking up a storm as if wanting to be heard.

"You think it over, Shannon. Say the word, and I won't bother you again."

She was shocked at her own mixture of feelings. She'd been so set on her course, she hadn't prepared herself for the change of heart she was clearly having. Shannon hadn't considered this part, hadn't envisioned it.

He put his hand on the front door handle, and suddenly the importance of his leaving woke her up. Had she been cat-napping through life? The door he was offering her could give her the world. And she was giving it up...for what? So she could be independent? She could do it on her own, but was that reason enough to do it on her own?

She knew the answer to that. And she knew she'd fallen for this hero the moment she'd kissed him. And now she was being a complete fool.

His hulking frame filled the whole doorway as he prepared to step outside and out of her life forever.

"Wait, T.J.!" She stood and watched as the force of her shout out triggered a jolt in his neck and shoulders. His back was still turned to her. His hand gripped the door handle so tight she thought he might twist it off.

"Forgive me," she whispered.

When she saw his face, she saw his tears. Of course she'd never seen him cry before. They'd spent most of their time either jousting, angling for position, or sparking off each other. Even when she didn't trust his friendship with Frankie, the passion between them had been strong.

Was she grown up enough for this big, strong man with a heart the size of all San Diego? Was she ready for the next great adventure? Was she ready to keep the memory of Frankie beside her as she made her life with this man, who she now knew loved her so completely she'd never need to feel alone again?

And could she handle it if anything happened to T.J.? Would it be worth the incredible pain of possibly losing him in order to live with him in the here and now?

The answer was yes. He was waiting for that answer. He deserved that answer, she thought as she walked slowly up to him.

"Yes. T.J, I've been a fool. I need your forgiveness. I need your love. I need you."

He gathered her in his arms. "I'm right here, baby. Nothing to forgive. Never going to leave you. Never."

She knew he'd keep his promise until his dying day. And she would too.

# CHAPTER 15

T.J. WOKE UP with a start, and then remembered, unlike the last few mornings he'd awakened, all was well. Finally well.

Shannon's warm pregnant body was spooned in front of him. Her hair was all over the pillow, with his nose buried in that space he loved at the base of her skull, the place where her scent was strongest, fine baby hairs tickling his cheeks and sending shivers down his spine. He'd never felt as connected to anyone in his life. His hand smoothed over her giant belly, loving the feel of her ripeness and her motherhood. He couldn't wait to see the baby Frankie had placed there in her tummy, to love that little girl and let her know what a wonderful father she had. He promised to make sure she knew about Frankie. He could feel Frankie's love all around him now.

Shannon stirred. Then she pulled his hand up to her breast, turning her face to his lips, coaxing him to touch her cheeks. "Good morning, sweetheart," he whispered.

Her little moan told him she was sleepily aroused. He didn't want to be too urgent with her, so large with child, but his need was never-ending. He was rewarded when her hand dove down between them, and she gripped his shaft.

"I love how you're ready all the time, T.J."

"Anyone around you would be ready all the time, Shannon. Would be a fuckin' freak of nature not to be, honey." She squeezed him, and he sighed into her ear. "Sorry for the swearing, but sometimes…" She squeezed him again, and he couldn't think straight.

"You can swear all you like to me, T.J., as long as it's in bed. I love it when you tell me you like to fuck me. That's not swearing. It turns me on."

"Thank God. We're both blessed with the potty mouth gene."

"Should I take your cock in my mouth?"

"Um. Would you?"

"I'd love to."

Sure as shit, she slid down the bed, her nipples leaving a tingling sensation when they rubbed along his lower abdomen, and then pertly nestled against his thighs as she took him between her lips and sucked.

He laced his fingers through her mass of brown hair at his chest. He slid one hand down to her cheek and mouth and felt where her lips covered and pleasured him. Her belly nudged its way between his legs when he separated his knees. Warm pregnant Shannon was the most exciting sexual partner he'd ever known. This unexpected pleasure was something that filled all the gaping holes in his soul.

She was moaning, coaxing him harder, and working to make him spill, ravenous with that tongue of hers.

"Baby, love this, baby," he whispered. He pulled the hair from her face so he could see her. "Love watching you going down on me Shannon."

She smiled, pulled her mouth to his tip and sucked as her eyes gave him a sultry smile that ignited the bed sheets. He was so damned lucky. She loved like she lived, with a full heart and spirit. She had some magic he'd never felt before with any other woman, as if being around her would be just plain good for him. That her essence was good for him. Made him a stronger, better man. This gave him more than the erotic pleasure he craved, it gave him life itself.

She took his seed, drawing every drop from him and then asking for more. She was writhing on the bed as he spurted, taking him deep. Her fingers clutched his butt cheeks as she pulled him to her. When he was done, she kissed his thighs and smoothed her hands up his lower abdomen, kissing him all the way to his belly button. Then she snuggled under his chin as he pulled the covers over them both.

He reveled in the warmth between them, the way they just seemed so right for each other. They'd come together like two comets in the sky that should have exploded on impact, but instead fused together and became a brilliant supernova. The bright light of their love was strong, their desire fierce. He'd always known Shannon was like this, but that she could be like this with him, well that was the real miracle.

He rubbed his fingers against her shoulder while he thought about all the dumb things he and Frankie had done together, all the times he had made Shannon furious with him. Frankie always seemed to walk away unscathed, leaving him to battle with Shannon. Now he saw why. He and Shannon were so much alike they were the same side of the same coin. Her intensity was what he craved as sure as he loved that in himself.

He could tell by her breathing she wasn't going to fall asleep.

"What do you want to do today, sweetheart?" he asked.

"Um. This," she said, kissing and flicking a tongue over his nipple.

"You surprise me, sweetheart."

"Didn't anyone ever tell you that a woman has lusty thoughts when she's pregnant? She has certain needs?"

She looked up at him, and yes, he could see it in her eyes.

"Love those needs. You can show them all you like."

She smiled and snuggled her face under his chin. "We won't be able to do this too much longer. But we can for now. I want all I can get while I feel I can."

"I want to be careful too."

"You're careful, T.J. You're the most tender lover I've ever had." She looked up at him again, and he was nearly hard already.

He chuckled. No one had ever told him that.

"What's so funny?"

"I'm not normally known for my tenderness, honey, but with you, it's just the way I love to be."

"Because I'm carrying a baby, T.J. Our baby, little Courtney. We'll love her together. And then maybe later, you can show me some of your other side."

Her eyes called to him again, daring him to summon his strength. He couldn't wait until after the baby, when he could exhaust her and make her bones turn to rubber.

SHANNON WANTED HIM to move in right away. She dressed in one of Frankie's big shirts and her drawstring pants and announced she was going to help him move. That day.

"No hurry on all this, Shannon. I can get it. Not like there's a ton of stuff."

"All the better to do it now. And besides, I'm big, or haven't you noticed?" She pulled her shirt up, and damn, every time she showed him her bare tummy with the belly button that had started becoming an *outie* he grew hard. He silently cursed himself, but she had such an enormous effect on him, he could hardly be in the same room with her without getting hard.

T.J. promised he'd get things moved over in the afternoon.

"No. We. Do. It. Now."

"Shannon, honey, my place is—"

"I know. A bachelor pad. You probably never anticipated having to entertain me there."

"I never entertain there period." Even before Frankie had married Shannon, the two of them had little in the way of furniture, using cardboard boxes for tables where they cleaned their weapons while watching the TV set perched atop some fruit crates. They hadn't bothered to buy a couch, chairs, or even a dinette set. But they did have the biggest TV they could afford and a gas-fired barbeque. Frankie's room was bare, since T.J. hadn't had time to get another roommate.

When they got to the complex, T.J. tried one more time to ask her to stay in the truck while he went inside and got his things. The answer was the same.

First thing he noticed was the smell coming from the brown bag left by the front door since he hadn't invested in a garbage can. He'd left remnants of a sandwich and a sour half-quart of milk. He'd not turned on the AC because he had to pay the electric bill, which was not part of the lease. He never left it on, because he never knew when he'd be back home.

Shannon went over to the sliding glass door and opened it, looking for a non-existent screen. She quirked up an eyebrow.

"Football accident. Screen is downstairs in the carport, a little bent."

She walked to his efficiency kitchen. T.J. tried to place his body between her vision and the sink full of dishes.

"Shannon, stop checking me out."

She glanced down at his package. "I wasn't checking you out, but come to think of it, that might not be a very bad idea." She slid over to him and placed her palm warmly against him and smiled. "Nice, T.J. I can see all this turns you on too. Like playing house?"

"Seriously, Shannon, let's just get this stuff out of here and get out. You don't have to look over everything, do you?"

She stepped as close as she could to him, her belly being the obvious impediment. She squeezed and pressed her palm against the hardened ridge of his shaft. "What are you worried about, T.J.? We're all friends here, very good friends."

He was having a hard time liking it, but his groin loved the massage her strong little hand was giving him. Damn, he was filled with such confusing thoughts and feelings. A real mixture of dread and lust. He allowed himself to be led while she had her way with him. He was powerless to stop it.

"Show me your bedroom. Now," she demanded.

If she hadn't been so pregnant, he'd have refused and fucked her on the living room floor, but because she was rubbing that enormous belly against him, showing him her need, he took her hand and pulled her to the bedroom.

He had black sheets and a matching comforter cover. A used dresser from Goodwill stood in the corner. Other than the posters of naked women all over the walls, the room was empty. Some were just pictures of large asses and boobs. He also had a couple of pictures of women bound and trussed with black silk straps across their bulging chests.

She raised her eyebrows. "Seriously kinky, T.J. I had no idea."

"Really, Shannon? Really? You had no fuckin' idea?" He wasn't sure if he was mad or excited by her perusal of the things he liked to see just before he went to bed at night. "Like I said, I don't entertain here."

"No. You probably like the beach, or the back of a pickup, or a motel."

He nodded.

"I happen to like it. Turns me on, kinda." She took off her shirt and slipped off her pants. Naked except for the huge nursing bra trying desperately to hold her breasts inside, with her bulbous tummy swaying underneath her she crawled up on his bed. Her sweet ass waited for him, her sex wet with need.

"Not here," he whispered, fixated on the peach between her legs he so wanted to kiss.

"Here. Am I the first, T.J.?" she asked, peering around her thigh, making sure he couldn't miss her ass. "Am I?"

"Well, yes."

"Oh, that makes me so hot."

"But not here."

"Come to me baby. I need you," she said.

*Well, fuck it.* He wondered if it was because she was pregnant or if the posters really did turn her on. Didn't matter what she said, he would not be bringing any of these to their bedroom at the new house. He'd done too many unmentionable things to the sight of these posters, and there was no way he would introduce that to their world. He dropped his pants, as she backed up into him. He took hold of her hips and pulled her back onto his shaft, careful to slide in along her wet channel without forcing himself. She seemed to be getting tighter each time they'd made love. The cheeks of her rear jiggled as he gripped and released them, spreading them wider for his selfish penetration. She moaned like a cat in heat.

"Shhh. Shannon the walls are thin," he whispered.

She let out another moan.

The woman was out of control. He hoped to God the neighbors next door, two newbie SEALs, were out.

He thought perhaps he had pushed Shannon over when she lurched forward, grabbing his pillows and then squeezing them with her arms, pushing onto him deeper. She screamed into the pillows.

*Good idea, Shannon.*

"You like that, baby?"

"Yes. More, T.J."

"Glad to give you what you want, baby." He thrust inside her so deep he thought she'd split in two.

She jumped a bit at first, and he thought he'd hurt her or the baby. But then he felt her clamp down on him as her orgasm came with terrifying speed. She plunged her face into the pillow and wailed as he pumped her deep and slow.

He arched over her and finished, holding her breasts through the heavy cotton fabric of the bra that seemed more of a BDSM torture device. He made a mental note next time to get that thing off her first. He sure wouldn't be thinking of it later on.

# CHAPTER 16

S HANNON HELPED T.J. move his meager things into the house. She was surprised it all fit into half his trunk, and recalled how Frankie's things had been reduced to just a box as well. T.J. had more equipment than anything else. His kitchen things he'd agreed to give to whatever young SEAL would eventually take over his apartment. He had no furniture to speak of. She liked the fact that it was the man who was moving into her home with her and the baby, not the stuff he had. The man was who she wanted, not his stuff.

It moved her to see where he had spent his single days, where he and Frankie had stayed before Frankie moved in with her. The simplicity of his lifestyle and the private side of him that wasn't displayed to anyone else turned her on. He was embarrassed about his lack of decorating skill, and yet he had shown such tenderness with the flowers he'd planted around Courtney's playhouse and the beautiful words on the poster in her bedroom. She liked that he'd chosen to share intimate moments with her, intimate things about himself that no one else, and perhaps even none of his SEAL buddies, knew. All he showed the outside world was his equipment and the posters of naked women. She didn't even mind that he liked to look at them before he fell asleep. Even that was sexy to her. The man was a tight package, bound up in that hard body of his. He kept his personal life guarded, not public. No trappings to weigh him down. Everything he needed was inside *him*.

She'd cleared out Frankie's clothes two weeks into her mourning, knowing that it would help her heal. She'd held each one of his shirts up to her nose and inhaled his unique man scent, crying while she refolded the shirts and laid them in the box for donation. Though his clothes had been washed many times, she recalled how his scent remained, even after the man was gone.

What surprised her, as she laid T.J.'s shirts in the same drawer Frankie had used, was how comforting it was having him watch her do this little activity. She smoothed over the American flag-splashed boxers he wore, rolled up his socks in the same direction, and refolded his jeans to fit inside the shallow dresser. He let her position his clothes, ever careful to not intrude. She knew he was taking his lead from her. If she wanted it fast, he'd go fast. And fast or slow, he appeared to enjoy just watching her work out the details. She felt his respect for her private thoughts.

He took her hand, leading her to the kitchen, where he obviously felt most comfortable.

"T.J., I love watching you cook," she said.

"I'm not cooking, I'm making you a salad." His dazzling white smile sent a tickle to the top of her spine. His long fingers stroked the lettuce and caressed the tomatoes he was slicing. "You have to eat. You've exerted yourself this morning." He didn't look up at her, but maintained a Cheshire cat smile as he watched the sharp knife do its job.

"I still like watching you," she whispered.

"I know," he said, grinning down at the countertop, his cheeks slightly pink from a touch of shyness. "I kind of like it." He backed up a bit so she could see the tent in his pants.

"Wonder what we're going to do after the baby comes. We won't be able to be so selfish with our desires, will we?"

He nodded to the bowl he was preparing for her. "I'll definitely let you sleep a little more, Shannon. But honey, you can let me handle everything else but sleeping and feeding the baby. I want to cook for you." That's when she saw the deep blue of his soul. He passed the bowl across the countertop, handing her a fork.

"And here, I never pegged you for any of those domestic talents. Your kitchen couldn't have been sparser. Where did you learn to cook so well?" she asked.

"One of my foster mothers owned a restaurant. We learned how to do all sorts of things in there."

"Where's your lunch?" she asked.

"I'm going to fix something after you go down for a nap."

"What if I want you to nap with me?"

"I have a little research to do on the computer for work—which I can't tell you about, so don't ask, okay?"

She was hungrier than she'd thought. The crisp lettuce and fresh multicolored heirloom tomatoes looked like they'd come from a farmer's market.

"You get these at the Friday market?"

"Glad you noticed."

"I can't believe you know that about me too."

"You forget, Frankie used to talk about you all the time. We know more about you than I think even your parents do." He shrugged. "Guys talk to pass the time. You were his favorite topic of conversation. Shit, it was much better listening to him talk about you than his sorry life. I'm sure there wasn't a guy in the squad who minded his descriptions of all the things you liked, and the way they…" He hesitated, and then continued, "the things that turned you on, baby. Most of us had yet to find that. A woman who would love us like you loved Frankie. We could tell just by the way he described you."

Sadness crept over her like an old shawl. She took in a deep breath and found it helped when she let out all the air.

"This okay to talk about, honey? Don't want to upset you."

"No. I have to get used to it."

"Yeah. Helps me too, in a way. My promise to Frankie was to make sure his little girl knows him as her daddy. I intend to tell her lots of things about Frankie, the censored things, of course," he said with a warm smile.

She nodded and searched the remnants of her salad. "I'm moving forward, just not always easy."

"Roger that, Shannon. I'm right there with you."

She loved looking into his cool blue eyes, experiencing his passion and his pain. He was a package containing two powerful forces. *What does he see when he looks at me?*

"I'm grateful that I have you to walk me through this. Unfortunately, I suppose you have been through this before—I mean, losing a Team guy."

"Yes, but this time is different, sweetheart." He came over to where she sat atop the stool and smoothed a lock of hair back behind her ear. "You being here is helping me too. And in a strange kind of way, the promise I made to Frankie is helping too. Maybe he knew that, Shannon. Maybe that's why he made me promise him."

She gripped his forearm, feeling the corded veins covering powerful muscles. She let her palm glide over the dark hairs, then travel over his bicep and slip around his neck. "Thank you. Thank you for loving me, and loving our baby."

He massaged the top of her spine the way she loved. "My pleasure, sweetheart. My mission in life. Always will be. I'm never going to leave you, Shannon. I promise."

It caught her up short, tears spilling over her cheeks at the complex mixture of pain and the pleasure. She had a past she still mourned, but also a bright future. Remembering the past and anticipating the future was making her tired. Or perhaps it was the pregnancy.

Little Courtney kicked, a stunning reminder of her baby's demands to have a future more compelling than her past. Shannon smiled, and patted T.J.'s broad hand against her belly, disregarding the shadows that lurked. Courtney's coming was slowly stretching her, expanding her capacity to feel. Her love for her baby, and now the new love for this fine warrior were helping her heal the pain of Frankie's absence.

He pointed to her nearly finished salad, and she nodded, yes, she was done.

After he rinsed her bowl, he washed his hands and came around the counter to take her hand in his, leading her to the bedroom. "Cinderella has left the ball. She is going to go take a nap," he said to the spirits in the walls of the bungalow.

She followed behind him, loving that he towed her, drew her to the bed, like he was drawing her to the rest of her life. With T.J. she felt secure. Unafraid of whatever was coming next.

She slipped off her shoes and undid her drawstring pants so she could sleep loose inside her clothes. He'd pulled back the covers, and after she crawled in, he rested on top of the covers, holding her body through the comforter. He kissed the back of her neck, and tangled his fingers in hers. She found herself matching his breathing.

"What was it like for you growing up in all those foster homes?"

"Frankie never told you?"

"No. He said you never talked about it."

"He lied, Shannon. It was nothing like the life Courtney will have, I can assure you that. Made me a man at fourteen. You don't want to know all the details. Boring, really."

"I want to know. Tell me." She felt him tense behind her. "When you're ready to tell me. I want to know everything about you, T.J. I need to know."

"Well my parents, they say, weren't married and were young. I suppose I could feel grateful they placed me for adoption rather than, you know, the other choice."

"Did you go looking for them?"

"Nope. All I know is they lived somewhere in the South. And from then on, my foster caretakers—whatever they felt like telling me, told me stories. I don't think anybody really knew. I was told my mother was beautiful, a lady, but they were very poor. My dad was a war hero they said. Who really knows? What kind of hero abandons his child?"

"Maybe he didn't know. Happens."

"Like I said, the stories I was told are contradictory. As a kid I used to wonder what it would be like if they came, together, a couple, you know. It's every orphan's dream. I would lie there on my bed, look out at the stars and wonder if they were looking at the stars too, wondered if they ever thought about me. Ever."

Shannon was moved to tears again, but let them travel silently down her cheeks so T.J. wouldn't see them. Her life had been so different, but there was some toughness that had developed in her that matched T.J.

"I knew it was folly. Knew at the time it was just what I told myself to keep from crying at night, acting like a girl. It would take a while before I liked girls." The rumble of his chuckle rolled over her and nested in her heart.

"I can just see you lying on that bed looking up at the stars, T.J. I used to stare out at the lights and wonder whom I would fall in love with. Who would I marry? I didn't have your kind of childhood, but I still wanted a handsome prince to come whisk me away, take my vanilla life and ignite it. Take me away from the organized and ordinary and make it sparkle."

"I'm gonna work on that, babe. I'm gonna perfect that."

"You already have done a pretty good job, T.J."

She fell asleep dreaming of what it would be like when the baby was born, when she'd get to meet her little Courtney, hold her, and pass her into T.J.'s waiting arms.

SHE AWOKE TO the sounds of T.J. tapping on his computer keys. The nap had freshened her. She cinched her pants up, brushed her hair and put it up in a clip. Examining her face in the mirror, she saw her skin was pinker, and perhaps a little fuller, but she looked good. She looked rested, and for the first time in many weeks, content.

The T.J. effect was definitely good for her. She tiptoed to the hallway and watched him work on the computer, intent, focused. The man could do anything and it looked sexy.

Little Courtney kicked as if she agreed.

*Shhh, Courtney. You're way too young to have such thoughts.*

The baby kicked again.

# CHAPTER 17

T
J. TOOK SHANNON to a dance recital held by the wife of one of his Team buddies. Italian-American Sophia Beale was married to one of T.J.'s best friends, Mark. They'd met in Italy, where Sophia was living, before the two happened to find themselves on the same cruise ship. Their one night stand in Italy bloomed into a happily ever after while crossing the Atlantic, even surviving an attempted terrorist takeover.

The dance space was located adjacent Gunny's Gym, now owned and operated by the widow of the newly deceased Gunnery Sergeant. Amornpan had come all the way from Thailand to care for the aging Marine in his final days.

"Amornpan is Thai, a really beautiful woman," T.J. explained to Shannon. "Sanouk told us she never stopped loving old crusty Gunny, who used to describe her as an angel of the jungle."

"Who is Sanouk?" Shannon asked.

"He's the son Gunny didn't get to meet until his last year here. He got Amornpan pregnant when he was a young man in Thailand, but he never knew it."

Shannon nodded, frowning.

"Sort of a fact of life, really. Military guys do this all the time, litter the world with babies. I have friends that have four or five kids with like three different women, never marrying any of them."

Shannon's eyes were round with disapproval.

"Not me, Shannon. Never me."

"That you know of."

"Well, there is that." T.J. wondered why he'd even brought it up. Then he remembered. "Sophia has hired a bunch of instructors, from ballroom to belly dancing and everything in between. Sophia of course does all the Latin jazz, tango and most of the ballroom instruction. Amornpan teaches Eastern and some Middle Eastern dances and gives traditional Thai performances."

Shannon clutched his hand, weaving her fingers through his as they walked to the studio doors. Exotic reed, flute and drum music echoed out into the street.

"They're all going to perform today, along with some of their best students."

"You're going to get up there and shake your fanny if I call you to the floor, T.J."

He stopped so quickly, Shannon's huge belly rammed into his backside. "Sorry," he murmured.

"I've seen your moves. I'll bet you are a good dancer," she said to him, lips quirking into a smile.

This did please him. "As a matter of fact, I am rather good at it."

"I'm going to make you prove it."

He rolled his eyes and bent down to kiss her delicately, which got them both so distracted a skateboarder nearly hit them. The softness of her lips, sucking his, the placement of her hand at the buttons of his jeans were two of the little things he loved the most about how she loved him. She was never afraid to show affection for him. It filled a huge hole in his soul that someone so fine would find him so continually attractive. Made him want to think of dark corners and long nights with the crickets chirping in one of those no-name towns he grew up in.

He felt so lucky to be alive, and ached that it was his place to be with her now, not Frankie. That sadness never went away.

The music got loud when someone opened the doors.

"T.J. get your hands off that woman and get your butt in here," Timmons' gravely voice boomed just like T.J. remembered. "Glad to see you dressed proper, at least. Why, hello, Shannon."

Their old Chief, now retired, had taken an extra interest in the gym, and in Amornpan in particular. TJ opened the door wider to allow space for Shannon's large frame to get through.

"Timmons, you dressed up, too," she said to the older SEAL.

"I've been told I clean up real good. Sort of a special day for us here at the studio."

Shannon hesitated, like she was going to ask him about the "us" but T.J. gently pushed on her, and they brushed past his former liaison officer.

"Git yer butt over there by Mark and Nick," Timmons said, pointing.

T.J. had wanted to say something to Timmons about his new passion for working out, but was feeling so lighthearted, he didn't want to embarrass the man and ruin the mood for himself. He showed Shannon to a wooden folding chair next to Nick. Mark sat on the other side.

"Nick, how long are you down here for?"

"Just for the jump school course. Then back up to Sonoma County. We're in the middle of harvest. I shouldn't even be here."

"Glad to see you decided to stay in, my friend. We need guys like you," T.J. answered.

"Can you tell my intended?"

That caught Shannon's attention. "Good job, Nick," she said as she winked at him.

"Not like it's any secret. We've been living together for over six months now. This next workup will be our first real separation. We'd like to get married before that happens."

"What's your date?" Shannon asked.

"How about three weeks from today?"

T.J. whistled involuntarily. He leaned into Mark. "We have some serious planning to do, my web-foot friend."

Mark nodded with his arms crossed and shot T.J. with his imaginary forefinger shooter. When he turned back to Shannon it surprised him that she was frowning and staring into space, her face in profile. But T.J. could see the grimace and knew there were some unhappy memories. For his part, he'd never seen Shannon as lovely as she had been as a bride, and could now admit that was the day he fell in love with her. But he knew her memories of him were much different than that.

With an arm around her shoulder, he still managed to get his lips close to her ear. "Honey, I've changed."

The look she gave him, her doe eyes tearing up slightly but unwavering, told him he was going to have to work a lot harder at the convincing thing.

"I have," he insisted again and followed it up with a kiss to her cheek. He didn't notice the room had gotten silent, and someone had cut the house lights. A heavy-set woman in the row in front of them turned around and squinted.

"Shush," she said, reading him up and down.

T.J. rolled his neck and avoided Shannon's glare as the music began with a romantic ballad for a tango. Mark's Sophia, began a sultry number in her red form-fitting dress that left nothing to the imagination. Her dark hair was neatly gathered in a tight bun to the side of her face, adorned with a large bright red poppy matching the color of her full lips. The crowd was hushed. Mark sat with his eyebrows raised, and T.J. could see the beginnings of a crooked grin forming in spite of his tense jaw muscles. T.J. smiled too, and just as their eyes met, Shannon gave him another jab in the ribs.

Well, of course Shannon would be a little sensitive about her less than flat tummy. In her near-term condition, she couldn't move about the dance floor with such ease and grace. T.J. wrapped his long arm over her thin shoulder and squeezed her to him. "You're the most beautiful woman in here, babe," he whispered.

"Not that," she whispered, as the woman in front of them sighed and fidgeted. "Look." She pointed to a cluster of red-ruffled young girls with black low-heeled shoes similar to Sophia's. The oldest among them appeared not to be beyond six years, and two of them were barely out of diapers. When the music ended, Sophia took her bow to a standing ovation, and the cloud of red chiffon raced to take positions encircling her legs.

With arms raised above their heads, waiting for the music to begin, the young girls surveyed the crowd with wide dark eyes, glitter spray sparkling in their hair and over their young cherubic faces. As the Latin beat began, they twirled and strutted with remarkable skill, with only an occasional mishap. The audience spontaneously clapped in rhythm to the music, which seemed to foster enthusiasm among the young dancers eager to perform.

At last, the youngsters and their teacher were given a standing ovation. The group performed another routine and the girls were released to sit with their parents in the audience.

T.J. could see the excitement in Shannon's eyes, and he knew their little Courtney would someday take lessons here. "I can just imagine how cute she'll be," T.J. said, as he pulled several flowing curls back behind Shannon's ear. "She'll probably be the tallest, too!" Shannon nodded with a smile on her lips.

Sophia directed a series of partnered dances with the older children. There being a lack of boys in the class, most of the "couples" were two girls dancing together.

A modern jazz troupe with ragged clothing performed a difficult choreographed set of numbers, ending in a swing-fest the audience loved.

At last the music turned distinctly Eastern, and the house lights were turned down low. With the audience dark, a spotlight flashed on the golden vision of Amornpan, encrusted in a costume that looked like exotic chainmail. Atop her head was a headdress, over a foot tall. Her heavily painted features made her look like a china doll, T.J. thought. Just as with Sophia's performance, Amornpan moved with the grace and skill of a world-class dancer, her arms forming graceful angles, her head tilting horizontally as her fingers twisted backward, playing small bells and finger cymbals.

Nothing about the costume, the sounds or the dancing were familiar. T.J. found himself holding his breath in spite of the fact that this woman was old enough to be his mother. Her grace and beauty rivaled any twenty year old's. He found Timmons standing in the shadows in the back corner transfixed, arms crossed, and his face unreadable. T.J. knew the man's private thoughts were deep. He was happy for him.

After the performance, several of the SEALs and their wives and girlfriends went to a local microbrewery that also played sports on big screen TVs. Mark and Sophia were talkative, chattering and kissing, while feeding each other finger food. Timmons dropped by with Sanouk. Kyle and Christie were there, as were several others, including Fredo and Mia.

They all stopped and observed a news bulletin that interrupted the ball game announcing a terrorist beheading of another male American journalist, along with a female aid worker.

*The American journalist was captured over a year ago and several attempts to locate and free the man and two others, were unsuccessful. Another aid worker from the U.K was executed a month ago.*

The Team guys shook their heads, taking short looks at each other as they shared their private thoughts in mixed company. Team business was never discussed in front of the wives unless absolutely necessary. Since there was little chance they'd be deployed sooner than three months, all they could do was register their disgust, but T.J. knew everyone was thinking the same thing. The groups were getting bolder and bolder. It wouldn't take long before some of these actions would take place on

American soil. And that meant innocents would be targeted.

The announcer came on and showed a scratchy sign written in Arabic. Jones squinted and swore, being the most fluent in Pashto. T.J. could recognize some characters and saw the distinctive "U.S" letters on the sign.

*"The threat is considered credible. Members of the military and their families are being targeted. No one is safe, no matter where they live. No one.*

The announcer signed off, and the news station made a brief statement T.J. couldn't make out, and then the ball game went back on. Most everyone was looking into their water glasses and beers, but as if on cue they looked over to Kyle.

"Well, there's no fuckin' thing we can do about it right now, so let's toast to Sophia and Mark. Hooya!" Kyle boomed.

Glasses were raised and the chant was repeated, adding Mark and Sophia's names.

"Where's your mom, Sanouk?" T.J. asked the gangly kid, in the silence that followed.

"She's cooking something special. A dessert for …" Sanouk threw a thumb in Timmons' direction. T.J. had never seen the man blush before, but he was bright red.

"Oh, this is serious shit, man," Fredo began. "When the woman starts making desserts, you got yourself trapped, man. They break out all the stuff they do really well, and then later, it's all TV dinners and—"

"What the fuck you talking about?" Kyle blurted. "You've never been fuckin' married, Fredo."

Jones added his opinion to the mix. "As a matter of fact, I don't think any woman has been brave enough to cohabitate."

The crowd laughed at Fredo's expense.

"So you gonna just sit there and take that, or you gonna tell them?" Mia said to Fredo, who was the second man T.J. had seen blush tonight.

"I proposed to Mia last Saturday night, and she said yes." Fredo could hardly look at anyone, and ducked his head like a beer had been poured on him.

"I hope Armando's okay with this. Mister *don't mess with my sister*," Kyle added.

Christy stood, leaned into Fredo's back, and gave him a bear hug from behind with a kiss on the cheek. The cat-calls were long and loud.

"You done good, Fredo. Congrats you two," Christy said as she winked at Mia.

"Thanks."

T.J. felt Shannon stiffen at the early talk of Fredo's engagement, but he gave her a warm smile and a kiss, and she leaned into him with a sigh.

"So that's two weddings," Nick said as he drilled a look at T.J. and Shannon.

"We're doing it backwards, guys," T.J. said softly. "Having the baby first, and then if I do well enough in the delivery room, perhaps Shannon will marry me afterwards. But she needs to know I can handle myself in childbirth."

"Oh T.J., that's not what I said." Shannon had slapped his arm, but she was smiling in spite of herself.

"Wasn't what you said, honey. I read your mind." T.J. pointed to his temple and got another arm slap for his troubles.

"When's the funeral, Fredo?" Sanouk asked. Mia scowled.

Fredo cracked a smile that completely bisected his face and spread his already wide nose. "Going to Vegas this weekend. Who wants to give me away?"

# CHAPTER 18

S HANNON HAD FELT slightly sick to her stomach at the brewery, so T.J. took her home early. She noticed her fingers and ankles were swollen, and they hurt from the pressure.

"Gotta get you off those feet," T.J. said. "You going to be able to sleep, honey?"

"Not with this nausea."

"If you're not feeling better by later this evening, I'm calling the doctor."

"I agree." Shannon had to admit, she was a little concerned by how quickly her mood changed with her upset stomach.

She took a cool shower and donned a big shirt, readying herself for bed.

It was usually comfortable in San Diego, since the temperature never varied by more than a few degrees all year round, but today there was no breeze coming off the ocean. She got up and turned on the window air conditioner that looked nearly as old as she was, but nothing happened. T.J. was working on his computer in the living room with a headset so he could listen to his warrior music and not bother her. He had been obsessed with news accounts from North Africa, and although he never said so, Shannon suspected that was where they were headed on their next deployment.

Standing in the doorway, she watched him hunch over the blue light from his laptop. His enormous shoulders tapered down to an impossibly thin waist, which she noticed now more than ever, due to her condition. The baby had been lazy all day, but as she ran her hand over her eight-months-pregnant tummy, she whispered to Courtney. "Won't be long now, sweetheart. Can't wait to hold you in my arms." She rubbed back and forth and hummed a little tune she'd been sung as a child, and eventually Courtney started moving slowly, almost in rhythm to the music.

She knew she should try to get her rest, because she'd been advised these quiet nights wouldn't always be here. And then she'd be nursing a young baby with T.J. overseas. Knowing how she'd worried about Frankie, as it turned out for good reason, she wouldn't be getting any sleep even if the baby didn't keep her up all night. There were still so many unsettled things.

T.J. sensed her presence and came over to her, kneeled and spoke to Courtney. "You keeping your mama up all night, darlin? Gotta let her get her rest so she can be strong to handle you."

He stood up and she buried her head into his shoulder and wept.

"Hey, what's wrong?"

"I feel like it's the quiet before the storm, T.J. I feel like I need to be prepared, like something's going to happen that will rip me from this peace."

T.J.'s hands were all over her back, her neck. He knew just where to knead her upper spine so as to work out the kinks and make her feel rubbery. "Good that you recognize that. We have down time overseas, too, but we know better than to let our guard down." His breathing was heavy as he shook his head.

"What is it? What aren't you telling me, T.J.?"

"You saw that report on the news tonight, babe?"

Shannon nodded, but stayed wrapped in the safety of his arms.

"You gotta be vigilant, watch everything and everyone around you. Especially when I'm gone, but even now. Things are changing out there, and some of the arena we've been working in is coming home to the U.S. We'll get them, that's for certain. We're hoping to minimize the threat, but we can't be everywhere."

"You really believe that guy?"

"They went after the World Trade Center twice before they got it right. These zealots are different from us because they don't value human life, so their own death means nothing. What we don't understand is how someone who is raised here and given so much could turn and want to destroy us. Those are the ones we probably can't stop, until the entire movement is crushed or some cooler heads prevail. Contrary to what some media centers say, we didn't cause this. It's because of who we are that they come for us. And if they can't get us on the battlefield, they'll try to pick off some of our non-combatants, our families."

"I hate to even think about that."

"I know, sweetie. But you have to. Your instincts are good. Stay alert. Know where that loaded gun is at all times. Never be without it when I'm gone, understand?"

His warm hands cupped her cheeks as he savored her lips slowly. She felt his heat coming on, mingling with hers, and allowed it to deliciously subside. She was ready to not be pregnant and could hardly wait.

T.J. escorted her back to the bedroom. "Couldn't get the air to work. Can you?"

"I'll go get one tomorrow, but lemme look at it."

Shannon got into bed, covered herself with just one sheet and lay back to watch T.J. fiddle with the knobs and then finally pound the top of the machine with his fist. The unit slowly sputtered to life.

"You're so masterful!" She extended her arms to the sides to invite him into her bed.

"Not really, I just knew where to hit it. You heard about the guy who was hired to fix some big machine in a factory and insisted he be paid up front?"

"No. Who was he?"

"It's a story, babe. He gets paid ten thousand dollars, walks into the plant and hits a pipe with his wrench and the machine starts working. The factory owner cries foul."

T.J. pointed to the air conditioner.

"The fixit man said, *Hey, I did my job. It's fixed.* The factory manager said, *But all you had to do was bang on one pipe. That's not worth ten thousand dollars.* The man said, *One dollar for hitting the pipe and nine thousand nine hundred nine-nine dollars for knowing where to hit it.*

"I don't care. You're still amazing."

"I think it was frozen up, and a chunk of ice fell outside. That's all."

"But you knew where to hit it."

"Nope. I guessed."

# CHAPTER 19

T J. GOT A call from his liaison during breakfast. Shannon had finally fallen asleep and he preferred to leave her that way.

"What's up, Chief?"

"T.J., I got a collect call from Tennessee, and I didn't accept the charges at first. They never called back, but left a number. I could hear a man's voice on the other end, and he kept shouting out your name over the operator."

T.J. closed their bedroom door shut before answering. "Who was this guy?"

"He says he's your father, T.J."

He'd always known that someday something would surface about his family. He expected to be contacted by a sister or brother, or perhaps his mother, but not his dad. T.J. had always envisioned a beautiful woman who had given him birth, remembering one of his foster parents' words about how she'd been a beauty queen in Arkansas. So, perhaps his father was from Tennessee. That *could* be possible.

"Can I have that number, Chief?" he asked. Even as he blurted the words, he wasn't sure he really wanted to talk to the man. But reflex made him ask anyway.

"Well, son, I'm afraid I have some bad news on that front."

"I don't understand, Chief Collins."

"The call came from Riverbend Maximum Security Prison."

It was as if he'd run into the end of a telephone pole they'd trained with in his BUD/S class. A wave of nausea consumed him. Black blotchy spots formed before his eyes, and he fought back dizziness.

*Fuck me. My dad's a serial killer or child molester.* If it was a maximum security prison, he wasn't there for stealing a car or writing too many bad checks, not that that would have been okay with T.J., either.

He didn't remember much of what Collins had to say after that, but he did have his wits about him to at least write down the phone number. After he hung up, he saw that a similar number was showing on his phone without voicemail. Could these be from two different family members? Maybe his mother? He wasn't sure how he felt about that, judging from how well he'd scored with the last scenario.

He hit re-dial, and it was answered by a message.

*"You've reached the office of inmate special services Travis Banks of the Riverbend Correctional Facility in Nashville. I'm not available to take your call…"*

Before he knew it, a beep indicated he was to leave a message. *What the fuck do I say?* He hung up and cursed.

*What am I, in grammar school?*

T.J. stomped around the kitchen, opening cupboards, looking for something to eat. He grabbed an apple from a fruit bowl and took a bite out of it. The interior of the apple was soft and a little mushy and contained the remnants of a worm, probably less than half of what he had in his mouth. He opened the front door, spit out the fruit onto the shrubbery, and threw the apple like he was throwing a grenade, past the next street at least, over the tops of red tiled roofs, until it was out of sight. He knew he could throw it far enough to make it to the estuary. He thought he had enough on it to send the red fruit all the way to heaven, but after a few seconds he heard the unmistakable sound of a car alarm going off.

*Son of a bitch.*

Walking inside, he slammed the front door shut, rattling the walls, and then he remembered Shannon.

Her face was white as she ran to him, bolting from the bedroom like it was on fire. "What is it, T.J.? What's happened?"

"Nothing."

"Stop that. You tell me right now what's going on. I'm getting really freaked here. I haven't seen this side of you. Ever."

He tried to take her in his arms, but she slipped away, hugging herself, twisting from side to side.

"Tell me first," she whispered.

T.J. lumbered over to the couch and collapsed, his face in his hands, his elbows propped on his knees. He mumbled, hoping she wouldn't hear, "I found my dad."

"What? I can't hear you."

He really didn't want to tell her, but he would have to. This was going to ruin everything.

"T.J. I want to know what's gotten into you? I *need* to know what you're—"

T.J. stood tall, and for a moment he saw fear on Shannon's face. At the same instant, the nausea in his stomach increased. He held his forefinger up to her. "Be right back," he said as he ran for the bathroom and deposited his coffee, breakfast cereal and what must have been left of the worm in the toilet.

After washing up, he came back to the living room to face Shannon, who hadn't moved. It was painful to see tears welling up in her eyes. He gripped the rounded doorway trim, inhaling, and said,

"I think I found my dad."

At first Shannon had a broad smile on her face as her eyes widened, her forehead creased in happy anticipation of a reunion he knew wasn't going to happen. She angled her head, frowning, but her voice was hopeful. "That's great, T.J. You've always wanted to find them."

"No. I did not."

"Yes you did, sweetheart."

"I fucking did not! And I fucking wish they were dead, or at least my dad. No wonder they never reached out to me. He couldn't."

"Why not?"

"Because I think he's been in prison my whole life!"

"You don't know that, T.J. Did you talk to him?"

"Fuck, no."

Shannon stepped back. "You need to lower that tone. You're starting to scare me."

At this, his knees nearly gave way. He was mucking up everything. One royal fuckup after another. "You suppose he's known about me all along?"

"Beats me. You have a number to call him?"

"I've already—" Then he remembered he hadn't left a message for the guy from the prison. He pushed the red redial button and got voicemail. "Sir, my name is T.J. Talbot and you called me today. Someone also talked to my liaison. I'm in the Navy, sir. The person my Chief overheard said he was my father. I spent my whole life in foster care, so I have no clue if my name rings a bell at all. Fact is, I don't really know who I am."

He left his cell number.

He held up the piece of paper, "I'm going to call this one now."

The phone rang and rang and rang without anyone picking it up. He was going to have to wait for the prison official to call him back. If his father was in prison, he was guessing this was a payphone in a prison common area used by inmates.

Shannon was drinking a glass of water. Her complexion was still pale. T.J. looked at her fingers and noticed her rings were tight. She filled up another glass and sat in the living room to drink it.

"How're you feeling?"

"Not very good, T.J. I think I should go back to bed. Can you come?"

"I'm going to let you rest. I've got some Team stuff to do, to read over. Don't want to disturb you."

"You don't disturb me. I like it when you're there."

"Should I call the doc?"

"If I can't sleep, might as well call him. Come to bed when you can, okay? I like having you next to me. I'm a little stressed for some reason."

T.J. registered that now Shannon was feeling some stress, which might mean her blood pressure was rising. None of these signs were encouraging, but if Shannon wasn't in pain and could sleep, he figured that would give her the most benefit. He decided to stay up in case someone from Tennessee tried to call him back.

# CHAPTER 20

T.J. FINALLY CAME to bed close to midnight and Shannon was engulfed in a deep sleep. He said a little prayer of thanks for this. He snuggled next to her, spooning to her backside, like he often did.

As the sun was peeking through the curtains, T.J. woke up and found the bed soaked. The baby wasn't due for nearly another month, but the doctor had said it could happen any day and the baby would be fine. So he figured Shannon's water had broken. But when he looked over at her, her skin was pale and clammy. She woke up slowly, more slowly than usual.

Something was seriously wrong.

When he turned on the nightstand light and drew back the sheets he saw the brownish stain everywhere, not clear like he'd seen in his Corpsman training. And Shannon's lack of energy told him she was in real trouble.

He cursed himself for not checking on her earlier. *Damn, I should have paid attention.*

He dialed their doctor.

"Doc, she's pale and has cold sweats. The bed is wet, but the water is light brown, Doc." He was near hysterics.

"She needs to be admitted. Can you get her here fast, because if not, I'm sending an ambulance."

"Shit, Doc. She going to be okay? Is the baby okay?" He watched as Shannon nearly fainted, coming from the bathroom where he'd heard her vomit.

"Can't tell, son. But the longer we're on the phone the worse it's gonna get. You get her to the hospital STAT, understood?"

"Understood."

He hung up and ran to assist Shannon. He got out her favorite pair of drawstring pajama bottoms, and a big shirt. The SEAL wives had made a quilt for Courtney, and he wrapped it around her shoulders, which made her burst out crying. Her emotional reaction sent him into the stratosphere with worry.

"You need anything, honey?"

"I couldn't keep anything down, even if." She inhaled and then let her tears burst forth, grabbing him and pounding her fists to his chest. "This wasn't supposed to happen this way."

"No worries. Please, Shannon. I'm here. We're going to meet the doc at the hospital. He'll have everything ready."

She'd been complaining of her feet hurting, and her fingers swelling. Now he saw her ankles swollen, almost bulging over her feet. He knew if they were this way right now, after a night lying down, it was a horrible sign.

He raced to the hospital and got there within fifteen minutes. Shannon was in pain, and had been consumed with heavy contractions. He was supposed to encourage her, thank her for enduring the pain. But he wasn't sure the pain was normal, since something was seriously wrong with the delivery. And he knew Shannon was sick. He hoped little Courtney would be tough enough to survive.

Doc Peters met them already dressed in scrubs.

"I want to be there. I have medic training," T.J. whispered to him, trying to calm Shannon's frowns as another contraction hit her. They were coming more frequently.

"They'll get you prepped, but right now I gotta get her examined and then into surgery. We're set up for a STAT C-Section."

T.J. didn't want to let loose of Shannon's hand, but finally allowed the heavyset nurse to lead him through a side door after they entered the double swinging doors of the surgery unit.

Scrubbed and prepped, armed with a mask, the operation was well underway when T.J. and the operating nurse entered the cold, sterile room. The sight of Shannon's blood on the table was not something he was prepared for, though it was normal and he had seen blood hundreds of times and had it spill or spray all over him many times in battle. She had been put under a general anesthetic, a breathing mask over her mouth. Sounds of her heartbeat were strong, but irregular. He recognized a very faint secondary heartbeat and realized the baby was in serious distress.

A sensor rang out as T.J. stepped next to the doctor, just far enough away so as not to interfere. The belly incision was completed, and he could see the bluish webbing of skin that was the uterus. A quick slice revealed an unmoving baby with a sickening blue cast to the skin. T.J. caught his breath.

There was no crying as little Courtney was lifted from her mother's womb. She was carried to the lighted crib, the pediatrician rubbing her skin roughly with towels under the warm lights, and working to suction her nose and mouth quickly before starting CPR. A monitor was placed on the baby's chest but there was no heartbeat. T.J. was grateful Shannon wasn't awake to experience the pain of knowing the baby was stillborn.

More sensors were going off as they worked on Shannon's body as it went into convulsions. Orders were shouted over the din of beeping. He might have recognized what was being said, but he was in a state of shock.

*Come on, Shannon. You can't leave me now.* Being drawn between two horrible scenes, T.J. didn't know where he belonged, and he felt ripped apart.

He almost missed the little bit of good news as the pediatrician shouted, "And folks, we have a live birth." The baby still looked a light shade of pale blue, but had some pink to the chest and upper thighs, the face going from a light shade of purple to pink in the stretch of thirty seconds.

Doc Peters barked at him, "Go be with your baby. Nothing for you to do here, T.J." He immediately obeyed.

*My baby. No, this is Frankie's baby. And I'm not going to let anything fuckin' happen to her.*

The pediatrician's eyes showed a smile as T.J. touched little Courtney with his gloved hand. "Hey there, little Courtney. You're all right now. Mom's a little busy, honey, but you are just as sweet as can be. Love you, sweet thing." Hot tears coursed down his cheeks, blotting in his mask. He felt the reassurance of a tap to his back by one of the nurses as the doctor placed a breathing mask over the baby's mouth. Another nurse stuck a needle into her foot to extract blood, which drew a healthy reaction.

He was given a warm towel to continue to rub Courtney's feet, squeezing them, feeling the baby pull her toes back, raise her knees. At last he heard a raspy and tremulous cry through the mask. But it was one of the most wonderful sounds he'd ever heard.

"That's right, Courtney. You tell your mom you're here. Tell her you want her to get herself over here to hold you, Courtney, honey."

"She's a big girl," the doctor said. "Over eight pounds. That's good for her."

"Thank God, she's a girl."

"We're not out of the woods yet. She can't yet breathe on her own. But she's stabilizing. We'll know more in twenty four hours."

"Hear that, Courtney? Honey, you're gonna have to let them take care of you a little longer. You gotta breathe, sweetheart. We're all right here. You're beautiful, Courtney. My beautiful little girl."

Work on Shannon slowed as Doc Peters announced her vitals were improving.

"That a girl, Shannon. Hang in there. No more scares."

T.J. stopped rubbing Courtney's feet and looked over at Shannon's face, which had also pinked up. Trained to be even-keeled, to keep his emotions in check, he felt like he was going to explode. He didn't know if it was pain or delight. The mixture of fear and joy jumbled his insides. He wanted to rattle the walls and blow out the windows with a battle cry he knew would scare the entire ward. So he took a deep breath and swallowed. His hands were shaking and his guts were doing flip-flops.

One of the pretty nurses smiled up at him with her warm brown eyes, her long lashes glistening like she'd been crying too. "She's going to be fine. Everything will work out the way it's supposed to."

The comment didn't make him feel better.

She patted his shoulder again, like she had done before. "Relax," she whispered.

T.J. stepped back and almost lost his balance.

"He's done," Doc Peters said to one of the attendants, nodding in T.J.'s direction.

"No. I'm not leaving." He inhaled again and stepped to the table and took Shannon's hand, punctured with tubes held strapped in plastic tape. He rubbed her fingers and felt them warm to his touch. She was still way too cold, but her breathing was normal. "I'm here, Shannon. Courtney is in good hands now. I'm here, baby. Not leaving until you wake up."

The pediatrician wheeled baby Courtney from the operating room.

"She's beautiful, Shannon. Big strong girl, like you, sweetheart."

He felt her body stir. He looked up at the doctor, who had successfully stitched her belly up and was wiping her down with surgical wash. Peters nodded, so T.J. continued. "She's got Frankie's big jowls, fat cheeks. And her thighs, well, honey, those didn't come from you, sweetheart. Must have been on Frankie's side of the family because that one's going to be a high jumper. She's built like a rabbit."

A couple of the attendants giggled.

"I've seen lots of babies, Shannon, all wrinkled and misshapen. Little Courtney looks to be a beauty queen so far. Except for her—" He was going to say *coloring,* or something indicating she looked like a space alien, but thought better of it. "She's a blueblood all right. Not that she's blue or anything, just, just—" He wasn't having any luck recalling something appropriate, so he did something he was used to doing. "Fuck, honey, you sure gave me a scare. I'm here for the long haul, baby. Don't fuckin' leave me, Shannon. Don't ever leave me."

The pretty nurse's eyes sparkled. Dr. Peters grunted, but it was a grunt of approval. The gray-haired physician looked up at him and nodded. In muffled tones coming through the mask, he mumbled. "Go get yourself five or ten, T.J. She's not going to wake up for another hour or so. We'll come find you when she awakens so you can be there, okay? Go get yourself a quick nap.

"But I want to stay," he answered.

"If you don't leave, I'll make them get you, son. You've done all you can. Now leave us to do our jobs. You go do yours, which is buck up for the next round. I'll be out to see you in a bit."

With that, T.J. was led out of the operating room.

# CHAPTER 21

S HANNON FELT AS if she'd been run over by a girls' soccer team, cleats and all. Her head was pounding, her belly hurt, and when she moved her legs, it really hurt. She needed some pain medication, and right away. As she opened her eyes, for a second she wondered where she was, and then she remembered.

*Courtney!*

The white ceiling tiles moved back and forth as she started focusing on the sharp burning in her lower belly, intensifying until she heard a groan that sounded like it was from someone beside her, and then felt the last rumbles of it leaving her own chest. Instantly, there was someone peering over at her.

*T.J.*

She wanted to smile, but tears flooded her eyes at the intensity of the pain. She wanted to be happy to see him, but her body was in panic mode. If she didn't get something, she'd go mad with the sensations burning in her lower belly.

"You're okay, honey. I'm right here. Courtney's in the nursery," he whispered to her as he bent and kissed her forehead.

"Is she—" Shannon found she couldn't bring herself to say anything more.

"She's fine, sweetheart. She'll have to stay in the nursery for probably a few days, but she's fine."

"Oh God." A wave of nausea overcame her and she gagged, rolling her head back.

"Hold on a bit, Shannon. Honey, they're going to get you something. How do you feel?"

"I hurt."

"I know, sweetheart. It's coming."

An African-American nurse in white loomed over the bed. "Good morning, Shannon. How are you feeling?"

"I hurt. I'm sick."

"You sick to your stomach, too?"

"Yes."

"Okay, I'll get you something for the pain, and something for the nausea. You allergic to anything?"

"It should be in her chart," T.J. snipped back at her.

"I don't remember," Shannon interrupted.

"Why don't you let me do my job. I gotta ask, that's all, sir." She was stern with T.J., which bothered Shannon.

"Please hurry. It hurts."

"I know dear. I'm getting it right now. Just hang on for a minute."

T.J. talked to her, telling her how pretty Courtney was. She wanted to enjoy what he was saying, but she couldn't concentrate. Everything she saw, felt and heard coursed through the hot excruciating pain in her lower belly. She felt like someone had punched her there so many times she'd surely be black and blue. She had a faint recollection of some pulling and tugging coming from her insides, and wondered if she'd started to come to during the caesarean.

At last the nurse injected the clear liquid into the IV tube above her head and patted her forehead. "That should make you feel better, sweetie. Just take some deep breaths, and relax into it."

She tried to inhale, but wound up in a coughing fit. T.J. held her head up, supporting her upper spine so she was halfway to a sitting position. His powerful arms felt good as he held her steady.

"Let me do all the work, honey. Don't use those muscles just yet."

A warm glow emanated from her belly to her heart, and she remembered the new love she had for him, the fresh new glow of a bright future deliciously brightening everything inside her.

She reached for his face with her free hand. "Love you, T.J." She couldn't find him, and didn't have the strength to search the space in front of her for him. Before her arm hit the bed, his fingers found hers and he squeezed and supported her hand, then rubbed up the surface of her forearm to her elbow, which felt heavenly.

"Not going anywhere, Shannon. Right here. Love you so much, honey."

"So Courtney's okay, then? I was sure that—"

"Shhh. She's a sick little one, but she's going to be okay. It was close, Shannon. Real close. They think she's out of danger now."

"What happened?"

"Something went wrong. They aren't sure, but I hope to God I didn't—"

"Don't be silly, T.J. You didn't have anything to do with this."

"Sure hope not. But she's a strong girl, and she has to fight an infection in her lungs. It's something they all go through when this happens. With antibiotics, she'll be okay, that's what the doctor told me. He'll be in later on to talk to us."

"Thank God, you were there, T.J. I felt you there the whole time."

"I was, honey. They had to kick me out."

"When can I see her?"

"Dunno. Let's just focus on you getting better. That's what I'm here for."

"No, I have to let Courtney know I'm here. I have to talk to her so she knows I didn't leave her."

When she looked at the expression on T.J.'s face, the full impact of her statement forced tears to her eyes. Neither one of them could speak. He bent and tenderly kissed her parched lips. In a low growl, he whispered, "And I'll never leave either of you two. Never. Never, never going to leave you."

The shiny dark hair at his temple and around the back of his head welcomed her fingers as they sifted, as she pulled him toward her again to claim another kiss. "I know that now, T.J. I won't ever doubt you or your loyalty."

"Or my love," he whispered and nibbled on her lips again.

"Or my own. I need you so much, T.J." She had to stop because the tears were coming again. The jumble of emotions was making her heart flutter. As her pain subsided, some of her desire for this man's body came rolling back like a favorite blanket to warm her. She wanted him close, to climb into bed with her right there in the hospital room, and comfort her.

He chuckled, as he must have picked up on her feelings. "Can't wait to get you home, honey."

LATE IN THE morning, they were informed how sick Courtney really was. The fluid she had aspirated could cause a massive infection in her lungs. Blood work had come back with disturbing results, but they were reassured by the fact that the baby was responding to everything they were doing for her.

Shannon walked the halls with her IV, assisted by T.J., who chattered like a schoolgirl. He had more descriptions of Courtney than she'd ever heard before. It was as if he knew her whole personality. Knew what she would be like as an adult.

"She's got a cute face, and oh my God, her long fingers are so graceful."

He mentioned over and over again how perfect she looked, which told her he'd been concerned and perhaps she hadn't always looked that way. "How blue was she?

"Okay, Shannon. I'm not going to lie to you. She looked like a space alien." He was serious, and then broke into a warm smile filled with his bright white teeth. "Was beginning to wonder," he said as he bent down again and kissed her tenderly, "if you had done it with a guy from Pluto or something. But when I saw Frankie's big ears—"

"She has Frankie's ears? Oh. My. God. That's terrible." Then she realized his changing the subject from the baby's skin color had worked.

"On Courtney, honey, they look perfect," he whispered as he kissed her right ear. "Just like yours."

She was promised a visit with Courtney if she'd take a nap, but Shannon wasn't having any of it, insisting on seeing the baby. She'd agreed to follow the nurse's instructions about pumping her breasts since she couldn't feed Courtney yet, but there would be no real rest for Shannon until she could touch her baby. Even T.J. tried to talk her out of it, which made her wonder if there was something wrong with the baby he wasn't telling her. Something he didn't want her to see.

The neonatal nursery was filled with more equipment than a modern air traffic control tower. Several couples sat beside tiny babies hooked up to tubes and monitors that beeped. Courtney, at over eight pounds, looked like a giant. Although her color was good, she had difficulty breathing, her little chest moving up and down in raspy bursts of motion. It was clear the baby was fighting for her life.

Shannon took a chair at the side of the plastic tenting. A nurse helped her into Platex gloves and covered her hospital gown with another one, light turquoise in color. The instant she was allowed to rub her gloved fingers across Courtney's cheek and chest, she felt the connection between mother and daughter. As she had done while in the womb, the baby responded to the sound of Shannon's voice, even managing a squint that could almost be considered a smile. The forced little cry was sad and pathetic. Shannon spoke to her in a low voice.

"You're perfect, Courtney. You do have your daddy's ears, sorry to say, but you'll have beautiful brown hair that will cover anything you don't like about them. T.J. and I are right here."

T.J. squeezed her left hand, her fingers laced with his. He began massaging her neck and kissing the side of her face, which was just the encouragement she needed. He was such an instinctively tender and affectionate man, for all the warrior training he'd had. Knew just what to do to calm her down. She was so glad he was by her side, and couldn't imagine going through all this without him.

She closed her eyes and said a prayer. *Please, help Courtney to be strong so I can hold her, really hold her. I've lost Frankie. Don't take Courtney, too.*

T.J. must have seen the tear slipping down her cheek because he whispered, "It's going to be okay, honey. Everything's going to be okay." And that was the most wonderful thing he could have said.

"We're not going anywhere. We're here to keep you safe," she said to the baby. She looked up at T.J., kissed him and then turned back to Courtney.

"No one is ever going to leave you again. Ever."

# CHAPTER 22

T. J. KNEW AS long as he was in Shannon's room, she wouldn't sleep, but the bags under her eyes and hollow cheeks told him she really needed rest. He didn't want to leave, but it was better for her if he did. Best to not interfere with the nurses who were far better informed and equipped to handle their charge. T.J. had enough medical training to stop a man from bleeding to death in the arena, or do a quick stitch up or injection to stop an infection, but the fine tuning in the care Shannon required could only be done by a trained and loving nursing staff.

He was confident they were what she needed. He left the hospital on his way to the parking lot mulling over the situation with his father in prison. He'd always thought of himself as the guy who could solve anything, could "get 'er done," but this had completely blindsided him. He loved Shannon and Courtney, but the old friend Doubt and the evil twin Inadequacy had their hands all over him. It amazed him how quickly and almost comfortably he could go back to feeling like he was not good enough for anyone or anything.

He knew it was time to look up a Team Guy, but first he had to try to reach the numbers in Tennessee. He hit redial again, and got the same recording. This time, he didn't leave a message.

TYLER WAS HAPPY to hear the news.

"That's just awesome, man. Congrats!"

"Thanks, Tyler."

"Anyone else know? Or you want it kept private for now? You know Christy, Kate and Sophia will all want to go see her. Is this a good time or should they wait a bit until things settle down?"

"I'll give Kyle a call, but no, go ahead and give everyone the news." T.J. reserved his communication with Kyle for himself, in case he needed that one on one with his LPO.

"Roger that. Kate's going to be ecstatic. I guess you won't be joining us this weekend in Vegas to give Fredo the ol' send off?"

"Nope. Besides, I got something else I got to do."

"This sounds serious. You okay, T.J.?"

"Naw, I'm feeling full of shit, man, and I should be hopping for joy right now. Timing's a bitch, but I just found out I *do* have a dad, and apparently he's alive."

"Well, he's a grandpa then. Makes no difference the baby isn't your blood. That child and Shannon are a part of you now just as if they were."

"I got that. But there's no fucking way that man is going to be anywhere close to the baby or Shannon. No way."

"Come again?"

"Found out yesterday my dad's apparently in prison. In Tennessee."

"Fuck no. That sucks. What for?"

"Does it fuckin' matter, Tyler? Really?"

"Probably not. Sorry, man. Simply selfish curiosity on my part."

T.J. could hear music in the background, and Kate singing to it. The sounds of Tyler's ordinary life only accentuated how misplaced he felt. He was torn apart by his love for his lady and the baby, and struck by the harsh reality that the plan hadn't started out that way, that this still was Frankie's life he was stepping into. And T.J.'s background left scars that might not ever heal. He found no compassion for a father who was now reaching out to him on, of all days, the day he was working up to his new role as father and, hopefully soon, husband. No matter how bright his future could be, and he'd been grateful for this new chance on life, his past just wouldn't leave him alone. Wouldn't leave him alone to enjoy Shannon and Courtney for one whole fucking day.

"You still there, Talbot?" Tyler's voice was laced with concern, and to T.J. it sounded almost condescending.

"Yeah, I'm still here. I'm not a fuckin' schoolgirl."

"No sir. You're one of the baddest, meanest motherfuckers out there, the guy who saved my life, and the guy who's going to save Shannon and the baby's lives now. *That* guy. Don't forget *that* guy. To hell with everyone else. Even me. Pay no attention. You're *that* guy and always were, T.J."

"Got it. So I'll quit my pity party now."

"You want some company?"

"Nah. Hate to ruin your day."

"Fuckin' no way, man. Kate's on an organizational whim. I'm about to have the cleanest and most organized underwear drawer on the planet. Can you fucking believe that? They teach these things on TV. Screw the Home Decorating channel, or whatever the hell it's called. Kate watches it practically twenty-four seven."

That was funny, but T.J. almost couldn't laugh. His feet were encased in weighted boots like in astronaut training. He was fuckin' walking on the moon.

"So, you'd be fuckin' putting me out of my misery."

"Okay. I'll give Kyle a call, and then meet you at the Scupper? Mind if Kyle joins us, if it comes to that?"

"He'll be babysitting if Christy goes over to visit Shannon, but yeah, no worries."

T.J. hung up, and called his LPO.

"Hey Talbot, how's it hanging?" Kyle picked up on the first ring. T.J. could hear Brandon's incessant jabbering and knew that Kyle was probably being overrun by the preschooler.

"Just wanted you to know Frankie's baby was born today."

Careful hesitation preceded Kyle's comment. "You mean *your* baby."

"That's right, LT."

"What's wrong? Everything go okay?"

"Not really. She was born with some problems, and we almost lost her."

"Why the hell did you go through all this on your own, man?"

"Hey Kyle, cut me some slack. I'll bet you weren't thinking much when Brandon was born."

"That's a fact. So, how's everyone doing?"

"Baby is improving. She was born C-section, and she aspirated the—"

"Spare the deets, T.J. But everyone's doing good?"

"I think so. Shannon's a trooper. The baby is going to have to stay in the hospital, but the doc thinks she'll be okay, and then we'll do the tests, you know."

"I do."

"But that's only partly why I'm calling. I'm giving Shannon a chance to catch up. Then she can have more company."

"I'll make sure Christy tells everyone. She's gonna want to tell the whole team, you know."

"Fine by me. Especially those that knew Frankie, they would want to know."

"You tell Tyler?"

"Yeah, just called him. We're meeting up for a couple of brews."

"Good. So quit pussy-footing. What's up?"

"I just got a strange call from Collins. Apparently my dad is trying to reach me."

"Your dad? Didn't know he was in the picture."

"He isn't. And he won't be."

"Okay, you wanna explain that to me?" Kyle was working to hide concern, but T.J. felt it anyhow.

"I guess he's an inmate at Riverbend prison in Nashville."

"Wow."

"That's a maximum security prison, Kyle. I haven't spoken to him, but there's an inmate services guy I've left a message for. He tried to call me during the recital."

"Gotcha. Timing sucks."

"Doesn't it, though?"

"And you've told Shannon?"

"Of course. Kyle, this was one of the hardest things I've had to do, tell her this." T.J. reeled himself in, but just barely. He wanted to protect Shannon and the baby from the reality that was his past. How he wished it was a different story that was unfolding, rather than one with dark unknowns he wasn't sure he wanted to reveal.

"Not like you knew anything about this beforehand. This is just the hand you've been dealt, T.J. It isn't who you are. But I'm reading between the lines—"

A loud scream came from the background on Kyle's phone. It sounded like Brandon.

"Sorry, gotta go. Brandon's just pulled a table over on himself. He's into everything now. Just wait, T.J. You can't leave them alone for a *second*."

"Roger that, LT. Catch you later."


THE SCUPPER WAS cool and dark, which matched his mood and suited his needs. Tyler was dressed in cargo pants and a long-sleeved T-shirt with the SOC logos—skulls, tridents, and Latin phrases—covering up his tats. They'd been in the Scupper so many times with the Team, it wasn't as if any of the regulars wouldn't know who they were. Tyler could have worn a dress, and he wouldn't have fooled anyone.

He stood up and they embraced, his friend smacking him loudly on the back.

"You look like shit," Tyler said as he ordered his beer and searched the room. It was a habit they all had. Wasn't so much looking for people they knew as people they *didn't* know. That was the real problem. His scanning over with, Tyler glanced up. "Any more news?"

"Not a thing."

"Kyle coming?"

"You were right."

"Payback, I'd say."

"Double. Of course in my case, I doubt Courtney could ever do what I put my foster folks through. Like Rory, I burned down a woodshed."

"I know, because you could, right?" Tyler chuckled.

Images of being beaten bare-bottomed with a strap in that woodshed came flooding past, tugging on his gut and throwing his insides across the bar. He was so small then, and the evil foster dad he had at the time was huge with hands the size of basketballs. The guy could grip his upper arm with just one hand and swing that strap with the other so hard he had welts for a week afterward, and it hurt to go to the bathroom or even fart. He vowed he'd never be that small or helpless again.

"Something like that," he answered, and took a big sip of beer. He tried to remember when it was he received his first compliment or the assurance that he could trust someone, or that his little body wasn't going to be abused in some way.

All he could remember were the first days getting yelled at by his BUD/S instructors, by his Basic instructors at Great Lakes, and the odd feeling that he was home. He was *used* to it. He could *do* this. It was something he was made for. And that feeling grew every day he served, every day he packed and re-packed his parachute, every day he cleaned his equipment and stowed it away like fine pieces of china and crystal. This was, after all, his *real* legacy. Everything else was pure fantasy.

"So here we are. Wanna talk about it?"

"Nope. Wanna forget about it."

"So what are your plans?"

T.J. shrugged. He hadn't thought about what his plans were, since it was a moot point anyhow. No way would he leave Shannon and the baby alone, not with nuts running around the country spouting their mouths off about getting revenge against innocent military men and women's families. He wasn't going to allow anyone else but himself to protect them.

But even if he could, he wasn't so sure he'd want to talk to his dear old dad, if it even was his dad.

His phone rang.

"T.J. Talbot?" said the burly voice he recognized as Travis Banks from Nashville.

"That's me."

"I'm—"

"I know who you are, so let's just cut the bullshit, and you tell me why you're calling me."

Banks let the line go silent a little longer than necessary. T.J. felt a reproach was coming.

"You're father is dying, son. He wants to see you before he passes on."

T.J. looked at Tyler, who was chewing on his lower lip and not making eye contact. He wasn't going to tell the man about Shannon and the baby, because he didn't think his father deserved to hear it. "I'm afraid that will take some time to arrange. See, I'm in the military."

"We know that, son, but your father has maybe a week tops on this planet. He's tried to escape twice from our hospital ward bare-assed in his gown, everyone chasing after him. He's hell-bent on seeing you. Our hospital is in the Riverbend Maximum Security Prison here in Nashville, so his attempts were pure folly, as are the years those attempts added to his sentence. He'll die here, son, and probably this week."

"Understood. I'd say he's your problem, not mine. Sonofabitch didn't even think to try to contact me until he was getting ready to check out. What do you think that makes him?"

"Like you said, Mr. Talbot, a sonofabitch. But he's your father."

"Sperm donor."

"I stand corrected." Banks sighed into the phone. T.J. heard a wooden chair squeak and could just picture the place. It probably would be a tiny office with old government-issue desks and gray file cabinets with inventory stickers on them, a window that didn't open, with bars on it. The employees of a prison were behind bars as much as the inmates were. Probably would smell like all the Juvenile Halls he'd been in from Texas to California.

Banks tried another olive branch. "Look Talbot, there's no good reason to say good-bye to the man who gave you life, except just to do it. Just because he wasn't there for you isn't a good enough reason to not be a decent human being."

"You're wrong, Banks. I owe him nothing. And I am an honorable human being. Of that I'm certain."

"So I hear. Thank you for serving your country."

T.J.'s internal alarm went off, hoping that his dad didn't know, or this man didn't know he was in the Special Forces. Now of all times, this sort of thing should be kept quiet.

"I've got some personal things going on at home now, and it will take time to get approved for leave. Not sure I can do this so last minute. So don't get your hopes up." He wasn't inclined to lift one single finger to request any time off, but it sounded better to say it.

"Well, I'll let him know we talked. You do the best you can, son. I'm sure that will be good enough." Banks hung up.

It would have settled things much easier for T.J. if the guy had yelled at him, shamed him in some way. That kind of direct challenge was something he could handle, and he'd win at that game. But when Banks used the phrase, "Do the best you can do," it irked him worse than if he'd sat on a rusty nail. Not a mortal wound, but it would fester, hurt like hell and eventually need to be addressed. It wouldn't heal on its own.

He set his phone down and then finished off his beer. "My dad's dying. Got maybe a week to live."

Tyler knew better than to say anything. They searched the bar, looked up at who came out of the men's room, where their hands were, and if they carried a backpack. Looked for someone lingering in the doorway to the outside and listened to all the traffic noise. The news program on one of several big screen TVs was turned up, and it had stopped the ball game.

"...we're just getting word now that at least two family members of a retired Marine have been injured: his wife and one of the couple's four children. Mrs. Cole was able to shoot the attackers with a loaded gun from the couple's kitchen, but was injured in the altercation. One child was *spending the night over at a friend's. Mrs. Cole and her child were taken to Scripps Mercy Hospital in San Diego. It's believed the attacker had been looking for Cole, who was not home at the time."*

The banner on the screen said Homegrown American Terrorist in bright red letters. It continued to scroll across the picture of the Emergency Room of the hospital.

Shannon's hospital.

# CHAPTER 23

**"S**ONOFABITCH." T.J. SAID as he and Tyler stood at the same time. He didn't even ask if Tyler wanted to go. In a minute they were both in T.J.'s four-door pickup, headed down the freeway, stuck in traffic.

Tyler spoke with Kate briefly on the phone, and then hung up. "She's going over to Christy's to help out. Kyle's been called in."

"No shit. That was Magnus Cole's wife on the screen. You know, he's the guy who has been organizing all those Warrior Runs? We've sponsored them at Gunny's."

Magnus had been another foster care product, although he had fared better. T.J. had spent time with him. Magnus was working with a lot of at-risk youths in his retirement and was quite high profile and in the media all the time.

"Yes. I've seen him. I knew you were friends. Sorry, man."

"He's gonna go off like a powder keg," T.J. said, and spit out the window.

They rode the rest of the way in silence. T.J. kept the radio off so he could think. They got to the hospital just as several large TV motorhomes blocked the entrance to the Emergency Room.

"Christ, wonder how anyone who really needed help could get in there. Where the hell are the cops? There are people all over this place, like ants. No way this is secure."

"I'm packing, just so you know," Tyler whispered.

"Always."

They parked in the reserved doctors' lot and were slipping in a side entrance, when someone exited wearing bloody scrubs. They expected to be stopped and questioned, but the orderly ignored them. T.J. opted to bypass the elevator and take the stairs. At the door to the second floor, a bloody handprint was framed ominously on the ivory painted metal door. The door handle was also covered in blood. Tyler and T.J. instinctively drew their weapons.

"Maternity and nursery are on floor four," T.J. barked.

Tyler grabbed his arm, holding him back. "You know what you're doing here, T.J.? Remember, we're in the U.S. of A. And we got permits, but if there's been violence the cops aren't going to know if we are good guys or bad guys, and they'll shoot us down like dogs if we're not careful."

"Yeah, well can you inform those assholes that it's illegal to kill innocent women and children? Do you suppose that would help, Tyler?"

"Fuck sake, T.J. I'm not worried about anything but you. You don't need trouble. Protection, yes. But trouble? We gotta stay calm."

"Roger that. No worries. We trained for this, remember?" T.J. yanked his arm out of Tyler's grip and dashed up the last flight of stairs to the white door marked *Floor 4*.

Stepping out into the hallway, it surprised them there was no chaos. No screaming. No unattended posts. They walked along the hall to one side, keeping their side arms down and behind them. Tyler frequently checked for anyone coming up from the rear. T.J. felt the familiar touch from Tyler's hand on his shoulder, like they'd been trained. "So far, so good. I got no one," Tyler whispered.

The vinyl flooring rippled unevenly under the light of the overhead fluorescents. A stacked meal tray cart was conveniently parked between two rooms on the left. T.J. held onto it while they both took cover behind.

"She's down four rooms, on the left."

The nurse's station was packed with hospital staff and what appeared to be a doctor. The heavyset charge nurse rounded the corner holding a clipboard, and stopped in her tracks when she saw T.J. peering around the cart.

"Mr. Talbot, what in the hell are you doing?" Her voice carried such that everyone within twenty feet looked first at her, and then over to the two SEALs. A quick assessment told T.J. that nothing out of the ordinary was happening, so he stuffed his SigSauer under his shirt and secured it with the Velcro strap he'd fashioned at the rear of his belt. Tyler stowed his in the lower pocket of his cargo pants.

He stood up and stepped away from the cart. "You do know there's a whole lot of commotion downstairs, don't you?"

"We haven't been notified. It would come over the speakers. No one's called. What kind of commotion?"

"There are victims in an attack. I think they've brought them in downstairs. This was an attack on a military family."

One of the young volunteers put her palm to her lips. The doctor picked up the floor phone and started calling, and several people looked at their cells.

"There are bloody handprints to the door on Floor Two, in the stairway." T.J. exchanged glances with Tyler. "Holy shit, the guy we passed at the side entrance—he was covered in blood."

The charge nurse ran for the desk and began dialing the phone. "I'm calling security. You two are gonna wait right here."

The doctor interrupted her. "Already got through. They've had an altercation but everything's quiet."

"What about Shannon?" T.J. asked.

The nurse kept the phone to her ear. "She's fine. Probably wide awake by now. Are you satisfied?"

"Not until I see her."

"You carrying—yes—this is Four South, are we anticipating a lockdown or emergency? I see. When did that happen?"

T.J. walked briskly toward Shannon's room, but the charge nurse raised her voice, cupping the phone. "Hey. Hey. You wait right here. You can just sit and wait." She hung up the phone.

"No can do, Ma'am," T.J. said as he walked backwards, holding his hands out to the sides, palms up. T.J. and Tyler were in the room before she could stop them.

Shannon was sitting up, looking a much better shade of pink. Even without makeup, she was beautiful.

"I knew when I heard all the shouting that somehow, my T.J. was involved." Almost as an aside she said, "Hi there, Tyler." She re-directed her focus to T.J. "What are you up to?"

"I'm just checking on you. That's all."

"So what's with the altercation with the nurses?"

Tyler poked his head out into the hallway, then stared back at T.J. and shrugged. "Security must be pretty busy. Don't see a soul."

"Security?" Her frown leveled on T.J. "What have you done?"

"Nothing. Look, there's been a terrorist attack on the family of a Marine. It's all over the news."

Shannon picked up the clicker, and all three of them watched the announcer give a special report as again pictures of the hospital emergency room filled the background of the screen.

> "...by the Middle Eastern America group, with sympathetic ties to certain radical elements in Iraq and Pakistan. In recent weeks, the government and local law enforcement teams have been stepping up their security measures following the threat of attacks against our military men and women. In this particular case, we understand Mr. Cole was in Washington working on a bill that would help military veterans and their families. He's been an outspoken advocate for at-risk youths in our community and helped to foster and sponsor many charity events here."

A photo of Magnus Cole in his Marine uniform was shown next.

"Shit!" Tyler blurted out. "Who gave them permission to give out all that information?"

"T.J., he's in the news all the time. It's what he's been doing," said Shannon. "Even I feel like I know him, and I've never met him."

T.J. was seething. He was fisting and unfisting his hands, grinding his jaw. He desperately wanted to throw something.

A passage from his least favorite book in school, a book he was forced to read in three different high schools that year, *A Tale of Two Cities*, came to mind:

*It was the best of times. It was the worst of times.*

# CHAPTER 24

KYLE FINISHED HIS briefing with most of the other LPOs of SEAL Team 3, some of the Senior Chiefs who were stateside from Team 3, several Lieutenant Commanders and the top three Naval Intelligence officers at Coronado. Kyle had never met those guys, as they tended to keep a very low profile.

What struck him was that the task force was preparing for this day, yet nothing special had drifted down to the SEAL teams not on deployment. They were focusing on methods of ensuring that military families were being protected. It was also discussed that perhaps the perps were a pair of unknown lone wolves with an axe to grind, a local disgruntled recruit or two who had been forcibly DOR'd or had some beef with the military. This idea was roundly rejected. The method of the second assailant's death and the claim of responsibility made it pretty clear there was a Middle Eastern connection.

Then he learned the details of the attack. The first assailant was in the process of going after the youngest of the three children with a knife, when Mrs. Cole fired point blank with one of the couple's five loaded handguns. The other assailant was run off the property and blew himself up in the middle of rush hour traffic on a busy neighborhood expressway, injuring multiple drivers but without further loss of life except his own. It didn't take a rocket scientist to figure out that the terrorist was looking to make a splash on the evening news, and he got his wish, although Kyle hoped he was enjoying his time in hell without the virgins and would never know the bitter fruit he had spawned.

He called Christy, hearing the screams of little children, Brandon the loudest amongst them, and several women conversing quietly so Christy could talk to her husband, their husbands' boss. There wasn't any laughter as would normally occur at such a gathering.

Upon hearing the children in the background, he thought of the Cole children he'd met at a Christmas fundraiser last year.

"How are you doing, Kyle?" That was his Christy. Always watching out for him. Right in his face, asking the tough question. God, he loved her strength. She was going to be a great help to the other wives and girlfriends.

"It's bad. You saw the news?"

"Well, of course, until the kids and others began to arrive. Phone's been going nonstop. Kyle, they put T.J.'s picture on the TV, right next to Magnus's."

"You're kidding."

"No. Remember that run they did last year for the Warrior Foundation? Someone dug up a photo of the two of them together."

Kyle knew it wouldn't take long for the facial recognition software to find T.J.'s name and publish that, too. He wondered if the news media had any idea how they had put his guys in jeopardy. On days like today, he felt like the war was being lost.

And then he adjusted his attitude. It wasn't lost, because he was still alive, and he'd die protecting the ones he loved. It was the same deal whether at home or overseas. They never left anyone behind, and they wouldn't hesitate to save the lives of others, even at great personal cost. It was what he signed on for.

"I'm coming home. I gotta get hold of T.J. first. I think Shannon is at that hospital."

"Oh my God. Should I go over there?"

"Absolutely not. Stay home. Keep everyone there. See if you can have the gals get hold of their husbands. I'm going to call a meeting for Charlie Company. No one else, though. No one is to talk to family, except to answer direct calls to their phones. No details. Just reassure people they're okay. Don't do anything to attract attention, and if the fucking news media arrives on our doorstep, make sure you call me right away and don't, whatever you do, answer the door."

"What's going on? Why is this happening?"

"Because they can't win. So they'll cause as much pain as they can. They can't get us, so they'll target the families."

Kyle let Christy absorb everything he'd said.

"Any questions?"

"No. I love you."

"Love you too, babe. Gotta be extra vigilant. Better to plan than not be prepared, right?"

"Roger that."

Kyle snickered. "Cute. I like it better when you say that in bed."

"Well come home at a decent hour, and I'll give you a repeat performance."

"Now that's worth living for, trust me. Okay, Christy, gotta go."

"Love you. And Kyle?"

"Yes?"

"You're right, they won't win. Maybe this was what we needed as a country to wake up to the real world. You guys do too good a job making it so we don't have to think about it. Only fair that we have to share in some of the risk. I signed on for that when I married you. I'm still solid with that decision."

# CHAPTER 25

S HANNON'S CONCERN OVER Courtney's condition had lessened, but she began to worry about the darkness that seemed to descend around T.J. involving his feelings towards his father. It worried her that he had no use for his own family. She wondered if love alone was enough to heal his pain, and how much of this pain would become part of her life.

She also knew he wasn't going to be able to come to her, that it would be her job to cross that ocean, prove to herself that she could handle T.J.'s intensity. Frankie had been easy to love, like her dad. But T.J.'s black mood was completely foreign to her, and she felt inadequate and more than a little afraid.

The meds they'd given her were really beginning to kick in. She wanted to talk to T.J. when she wasn't so distracted with the pain she could hardly think. She wanted him to go home, and come back rested so he could be fully present to her and Courtney. He needed to be able to feel her love.

Tyler and T.J. had gone into the hallway to talk to security. She should have paid attention, but now she didn't want to meddle. She had to trust him. The emergency C-section had scared her. But the possibility of losing her man, again, scared her even more. She remembered the folly of thinking she wanted to raise her child on her own. What a stupid idiot she'd been. She was lucky T.J. was so insistent, that he'd made that promise to Frankie, that although Frankie wasn't perfect, he had the foresight to make T.J. make that promise. He knew perhaps better than anyone else did, that if T.J. promised, he would keep his word.

But that didn't mean T.J. would be able to make it smooth for her, despite what he might say. It was her job to toughen up, match him in every way. In grief and in joy. There would come a time when T.J. would need her as much as she needed him now, and she vowed to be there for him.

Just like the men on SEAL Team 3 he served with so honorably, the guys Frankie would rather spend time with than anyone else in the whole world, she'd never give up. She'd go to her grave trying to give T.J. what he so richly deserved. It wasn't about sex. It wasn't about being comfortable, staying out of trouble or any of the things she thought about that day when she married Frankie. It was all about being the best kind of woman she could be, rocking T.J.'s world and making sure he understood he was loved with every cell in her body. Was loved like he'd never been loved before, just like the words to her favorite song.

She would love the stuffing right out of him and heal all his sharp edges in the meantime.

Shannon wiped her cheeks just as T.J. and Tyler came into the room. "Everything go okay out there? I notice you didn't get carted away."

The joke fell flat. Tyler looked like he wanted to be anywhere but here.

"Tyler, can I have a word with my intended?" she asked. She liked that T.J. looked shocked. It wasn't joy, but she'd take it anyway.

Tyler wiggled his eyebrows. "You guys okay if I take a cab home? I'm kinda missing Kate right now."

"I'll drive you," T.J. said.

"No, he'll take a cab, because right now I need to talk to you, T.J. But we'll pay for it, right?" she said as she looked at T.J.'s puzzled expression.

"No worries, guys," Tyler said. "And congratulations! I think the ladies are arranging a visit tomorrow. Best to get some one-on-one time before the crowd arrives. Later, Talbots." He winked at the reference to a marriage that hadn't yet occurred.

"Sit here, hon." She patted the bed where she'd slid her legs to the side to give him room. The hospital springs squealed as he sat his frame down but avoided eye contact. "Tell me," she whispered, and then took his hand.

He allowed her to thread her fingers through his. She rubbed her thumb over his in a gentle massage. He watched in what appeared to be detached silence. The electric, erotic trance their touch usually created was missing. T.J. was in a deep freeze.

"Tell me," she said again, softly, this time touching his arm and gently rubbing up and down.

He stiffened, sat up straight, stuck his chest out and inhaled. Then he released her fingers and sat with his arms crossed, again not making any eye contact with her.

She was going to wait all night. It wasn't her place to speak up or ask him again. Twice was enough. She had to trust him. She watched the dark brown curls that were forming at his temples and behind his ears. His face in profile could have been the bust of an Native American Chief. She loved his broad nose and full lips, his leathered skin peppered with black stubble. She wanted to touch the dimple at the base of his chin, then kiss it softly as she'd done so many times. Shannon recalled what it felt like to lay her ear against his strong torso and marvel at his heart beating strong and true. He was a complicated package of strength and softness. He could be so fearless, like the day he'd hung those words on Courtney's bedroom wall, pulling his heart out and handing it over like an innocent trusting youth. Or, he could be shut down, like tonight.

The more he tried to be strong, the more she could see the soft, sensitive side of him. Why had she never seen these things before? Of course he would love her baby like his own. He was the kind of man who would love her more than he'd love his own life.

He'd been holding his breath, but this time he closed his eyes and let it all out. When he opened them again and looked down at her, some of the spark was back. Just a little, but enough for now.

"My dad is dying and wants me to come visit him."

"You talked to him?" She could feel his tension filling the room, and it scared her.

"No, I talked to the inmate liaison, or whatever he's called. The guy told me he has less than a week to live."

"Then you need to go see him."

T.J. stood, his hands in his jeans pocket. "I'm not doing that. I'm not letting that fucking man into my life. He didn't want me. Well, I sure as hell don't need him."

"Except that you would regret it your whole life, T.J."

"You have no idea what regret means, Shannon. Not like you ever had to worry about anything your whole life." He refused to have eye contact with her. She could see how hard he was working to hold in his anger.

The cruel statement had a ring of truth to it. She told herself he didn't really mean what he'd said. She was not going to let him see how much he'd hurt her with that comment. "I was scared today. We both were."

He said something under his breath she couldn't make out.

"I have regrets, T.J. I regret that I made Frankie wait two years to marry me. I regret that we didn't make love the night before he deployed. I regret I wasn't a more appreciative daughter growing up. I regret picking so many fights with you, when you were just trying to help Frankie grow up. I was jealous of how he loved you, T.J. You did for him what I would never be able to do."

T.J. was watching her hands folded neatly in her lap. She smoothed the pink blanket over her thighs until there wasn't a wrinkle or pucker anywhere.

It was her turn to take in a deep breath. "It would have been painful, but I regret not being there, to hold Frankie for his last breaths. That should have been me, not you. And he never should have made you promise what you had to promise him."

"No, Shannon, don't say that."

"Well, I didn't make it very easy for you, did I? I think you scared me to death, the way you looked at me. I was scared of the way you made me feel when I was around you. And I'm going to be scared when you go overseas, because now I don't know what I would do without you, T.J."

She didn't recall a time when they had honestly looked into each other's eyes the way they were right then. At the edges was the sexual tension, pulling them in that direction, but she wanted him to see that she could just as easily be his friend as his lover. For the first time, she just wanted to be there for him, without strings or expectations.

"You won't have to worry about that, honey," he said, as he held her right hand. "I may have to go places, but I'm not leaving you. Ever."

"Because you gave your word to a dying man. If you're reconsidering what you promised, just know that you don't have to—"

T.J. quickly knelt by the bed and put both her hands to his lips.

"Nonsense. Stop it," he said to her fingers.

"Would you have persisted if you hadn't promised?"

His eyes were watering when he answered, "That's an unfair question. That's not how it works."

"So you tell me how it works, T.J. How is all this going to work? How are you going to be a father to Courtney when you won't go see your own father, who's trying to reach out to you through time and space? I may not have a lot of things you have, but I do have love for my family. I know I could never live with myself if I let him die in a prison cell, knowing his son didn't want to see him before he went. You'd hate yourself too, I just know you would. I don't want that for you. I won't bring that hatred into our family."

He stood back up and turned his back to her. She could tell he was weeping. His shoulders slumped forward. She carefully got out of bed with the clattering of plastic tubing and the wheels of the IV squeaking, and he turned around just in time to pull her to his chest. His heavy breath was on her neck, his fingers digging into her back as he clutched her through the hospital gown.

She gently kissed the hair at his temple, whispering that she loved him while she allowed herself to melt into him, until the pain of her incision sharpened and she stiffened involuntarily and then stepped back slightly.

"Baby, did I hurt you? I didn't mean to—"

"Shhh. I'm fine. I got a little carried away is all. There will be time for that." She grabbed one hand and turned toward the door. "Right now I want to go see our baby, T.J. I want to watch as you touch her."

He brought his forehead to meet hers and nodded. "Okay. We'll do that."

With the assistance of the nurses, another chair was brought into the nursery, and T.J. was properly gloved and gowned. Shannon leaned into his side as he placed his hand through the plastic seam and gave Courtney a tickle to her cheek. The baby's complexion was a deep pink, but getting lighter almost before their eyes.

"Tomorrow I think maybe you can feed her," the head nurse said from the other side of the warming unit.

"Really?"

"Well, she needs your early milk as soon as you feel up to it. I'll help you pump a little so you'll be ready tomorrow."

"Oh, and I'd love a shower."

"Not for a couple of days. The doctor. has to inspect your incision tomorrow. Maybe day after. But I'll bring you some things to freshen up." She turned, and after giving T.J. a look that told him she didn't trust him to behave, left the room.

"I'm not letting that woman touch you. If there's going to be any washing up, I'm doing the washing."

Courtney was fussing, trying to push the mask off her face with flailing fingers and arms. T.J gave her his little finger and she grabbed it.

"Yeah. You're gonna play softball. You'll be a pitcher with that grip."

# CHAPTER 26

T J. HAD A hard time sleeping. The nurses made up a bed next to Shannon, and he'd fallen asleep off and on after watching her doze off, their fingers weaving together like they'd been doing it for fifty years. He'd tried several times to pull back his arm, which had fallen asleep from the elbow down, but each time, Shannon grabbed onto him harder, and he was unable to extricate himself without waking her. It made him smile and count his blessings.

Earlier, before he'd finished his private visit with Courtney, a young neonatal intern joined him. The young man patted him on the shoulder and took a careful look at the baby. He listened to chest sounds and nodded, raising his eyebrows.

"You've got a very strong little girl there."

"Tell me about it."

"Good thing she was so large. Hardly seems like she was, what, two weeks early?"

"Doc had told us just two days ago she could be born at any time. I'm guessing she figured she was ready."

"Under the circumstances, I'd say we got lucky." He repositioned his stethoscope around his neck. "I'm inclined to remove her mask and see how she does. Wanna do it?"

"You sure?"

"No, but I don't hear anything that disturbs me. I think she can breathe on her own."

"She's been fighting that thing ever since I got here tonight."

"Well, let's give it a go and see how she does."

Though T.J. had stitched salty combat vets up, the idea of pulling tape off little Courtney's fine light brown hair, ears and cheeks left him squeamish. "I think I'll let you do it, if you don't mind."

With the breathing mask removed, the baby eased into a deep sleep with regular up and down chest rhythms. He watched her for nearly a half hour, and then went in search of Shannon. There was a new crew at the nurses' station, so he informed them he was joining Shannon.

"We're gonna let her sleep tonight. She can have the baby tomorrow," he was told.

A young pretty volunteer brought him a set of turquoise scrubs to use as pajamas, blushing as she presented them. He didn't have the heart to tell her he never wore any, and thanked her with a wink.

Shannon was finishing up a sponge bath.

"You're gonna love this. Courtney is breathing on her own."

"You're kidding? That's awesome!"

"We just took the mask off, and the doc says she's breathing completely without difficulty. They've still got her monitors on and will check throughout the night, but that's a great sign, honey. Really remarkable, Shannon. I'm so proud of you both." He watched Shannon towel herself off.

"I can't wait to get a real shower," she said.

T.J. leaned over and kissed her. "And I can't wait to get you in the shower too."

He washed up in the private bath, but by the time he climbed into the hospital bed, Shannon was fast asleep. He extended her arm to his chest and held it there with both of his. Filtered light sliced into the room from the hallway. Outside, the sky was beginning to turn deep blue, and he willed himself to sleep. But as the early morning hours turned into real morning, the new sunlight was hard to sleep through.

He thought about the conversation with Travis Banks. He wondered what kind of man could do a job like that, and then figured it was some kind of calling, like the calling he had to become a SEAL. Not many people understood his motivation to jump in harm's way and not get any active recognition for it. The pay wasn't that hot, the life insurance was adequate, but then if that occurred, he'd not be around to enjoy it. It was a good way, though, to secure his family's future. Frankie's policy was going to pay down the mortgage on the house so they didn't have to pay PMI, and the rest would be saved. Courtney's education would be paid for, thanks to Uncle Sam. Shannon would get a new air conditioner for the back bedroom.

Voices in the hallway woke him several times. Each time, it got harder and harder to fall back asleep, so finally he got up, dressed and hung out at the nurses' station for some free coffee. He was informed the local donut shop would be making the rounds in an hour, mostly for the staff, but they told him a lot of the dads really enjoyed that service.

He was the only dad, of the several newly admitted couples, to spend the night, and he found that to be curious. How things had changed in his life. He wouldn't have thought he could enjoy sitting quietly by, watching Shannon or the baby sleep. It had all been about doing midnight HALO jumps, or training missions in the glaciers of Alaska.

T.J. decided to call Travis Banks.

"Maybe you can help me with some decisions, Mr. Banks."

"I thought you'd call back, son."

"No promises, yet. But I'd like for you to fill in the details, if you could. I don't know a thing about my dad." After he said it, he wondered if this was a good idea, but his curiosity was getting the better of him.

"I can't tell you anything without his permission. So much easier, son, if you'd just come out here, then ol' Bobbie Ray could decide for hisself what he wants to tell you."

"So his name is Bobbie Ray." Maybe it would be easier for Travis, but T.J. could see it would be more difficult for him.

"Yes, son. Bobbie Ray Stokes. He said he named you Bobbie Ray Junior, if you want to know."

"I could have gone a long time without knowing that." He felt the familiar lurch in his stomach from fear, followed by slight nausea.

"I understand." Travis' deep vocal tones ended on an even deeper, darker downturn.

"Is my mother alive?"

"I think that's what he wants to talk to you about. I think he wants to tell you where you can find her, if you're willing."

"I'm not sure I am."

"Well, it's your decision, of course. We're just here to help out."

"You enjoy your job?"

"Job? Oh, I see what you mean. No, son, this is not a paid position. I'm a volunteer. I have a little church about forty miles away. We do a lot of prison outreach. I'm only here three afternoons a week. The rest of my time, I'm tending to my other flock on the outside."

T.J. was pained with guilt he'd been so crusty to this man, who was obviously just trying to do something nice for the prison population. Guys like this were rare. He was glad that someone on the outside cared for these men, even if he couldn't go there himself.

"I'm sorry I got a little rough with you, Mr. Banks."

"You can call me Travis, and apology accepted. We all do the best we can do. You thought I was someone trying to insert hisself into your life without an invitation. A lot of people don't come 'round when a family member is in prison, and many don't have family to talk to. So we try to give them just a little lifeline. But they gotta do all the heavy lifting themselves. We're here to support that."

"I'll bet you've seen some drama."

"Oh, yes, I could tell you some stories. I work with many of the sick or hospice patients. They often want to clean up their lives as they prepare for their final destination. When you're livin' here, heaven looks like a lot better place."

"I can imagine."

"They might have messed up *this* life, but they can have a clean fresh *new* one, and that's what we focus on. Goin' home to rest."

T.J. couldn't speak, frozen by the man's story.

"Mr. Talbot, I *can* tell you this, your daddy has confessed his sins, of which he has many. I'm not goin' to lie to you. But give the man a chance to make his peace with you. He's told me it's the biggest regret of his life, and it has something to do with why he's here. That's all I'm going to say about *that*."

T.J. considered his choices. He was inclined to set up a visit, but mostly because he knew it would please Shannon. Wasn't going to be like welcoming dear old dad into his family circle. Courtney and Shannon would probably never know him. So what would it hurt? His dad would never live to meet anyone he cared about. So he reconsidered his decision, and found himself promising he'd work on it.

"And son, I'd hurry about that, if I were you. Hate to see you come all the way out here and not be able to talk to your dad. The sooner you can get here the better, if you want to connect at all."

He thought about Kyle's comments. "*This is just the hand you've been dealt. Not like you had any say in the matter.*" It was true, he was blaming his father for the abusive foster families he'd been so unfortunate to be placed with. He wanted to think his father would have chosen another trajectory for his son, but it wasn't within his power to do so. He'd have to be okay with that for now.


HIS PLANE TOUCHED down at Nashville International Airport two days later. He'd made sure Courtney was going to be completely healthy before he bought the tickets and called Banks, who agreed to pick him up at the airport and get him right over to the medical facility. The subliminal message was as clear as the orders barked at him from the instructors at BUD/S. His dad didn't have long to live.

Banks was younger than he'd imagined and much larger. He towered over T.J. by a good four inches and had a handshake that could crack walnuts. The African-American gentleman wore a black suit and quickly retrieved T.J.'s luggage from the carousel, then insisted he carry the bag to the car.

T.J. was concerned people would think Mr. Banks was in his employ, but it seemed to matter little to Banks, whose steady gait was damned hard to keep up with. He drove a dark-colored Chevy sedan that was old, but very well cared for.

"I'm afraid the air doesn't work too good. The heater does, not that we need that today."

T.J. was sweating before they hit the first right turn. "I left a reservation at the Rinwood Suites, and it's kind of on the way, I think. Mind if I check in?"

"Well sir, I'd be rude, wouldn't I, if I asked you to cancel your reservation? But I was planning on you staying with me at the parsonage so as not to be a financial hardship."

T.J. had to smile. Banks was a wily country preacher all right. He'd be a captive audience over dinner and breakfast, and that would give the minister two chances to save his soul. Well, that was okay. The man did save him some money on a rental car. The least he could do was listen to a couple of sermons. And who knew? Maybe some of it would take. Not like T.J. had much of a spiritual life.

"So you're a Navy guy, then. That right, Mr. Talbot?"

"Travis, if I'm not allowed to call you Mr. Banks, you sure as hell—sorry, you sure as heck can't call me Mr. Talbot. Can we get that straight, please?"

"Yessir, I get you plain. How long you been in the Navy?"

"Ten years."

"So you're gonna make a career out of it, then?"

"I haven't thought about that much. Playing it day by day. Had a rough tour last time over."

"I'm sorry about that."

"Wasn't your fault. Mine neither. War is messy."

"That it is, son."

"Travis, how old are you?"

"I'm almost thirty-six."

"So why you call me son? We're practically brothers as far as age. Not like I could be your son."

Banks was overcome by a deep belly laugh, letting go his straight demeanor and dropping his guard a bit. T.J. guessed he had some wild days behind him.

"Yeah, but we look alike. Gotta admit that."

They both laughed. T.J. liked Banks more and more as they drove to the outskirts of Nashville.

"How'd my dad find out about me?"

"I have no idea. He doesn't have access to anything on the internet, but he gets calls. Not many, but a few."

"My mother one of those calls?"

"Can't say, T.J. I really couldn't say. Remember, I'm only there three days a week." Banks hesitated and then he sighed. "I can tell you he only found out about where you lived recently, so I'm guessing it was a visitor or a phone call."

"So, who visits him?"

"Never seen a one. Not one."

"What's killing him, if I can ask that?"

"I don't suppose it would violate anything. Kidney failure. He's gone about as far as he can go. He's not a candidate for a transplant, unless you wanted to give him one of yours."

"You're not serious?"

"You mean would I expect you'd give your dad a kidney so he could die in a jail cell? No sir, I wouldn't bet on that one. Besides, he's way too sick now. If he knew about anyone he was a blood relative to, he'd have told the doctors at the hospital before now. But we hardly ever get those approved, even when we find a donor match."

"You're not considering one thing, though."

"What's that?" Banks had turned off the highway and was idling down a two-lane country road. The large prison facility was hard to miss, looking like a college campus.

"What if he wanted to die?"

"Well, I'll let you ask him yourself."

# CHAPTER 27

B ANKS SHOWED HIS prison ID at the external guard station. The heavy chain-link fence rolled shut behind them, temporarily sealing them in so the credentials could be verified before the second gate opened. After that, there was another perimeter fence around the prison hospital, this time with a guard shack, again denying them entry until their verification was run up the flagpole.

Travis parked in the staff parking lot, as opposed to the completely vacant visitor lot much closer to the front entrance.

"They're gonna check your person, so if you have anything you normally carry that could be construed to be as a weapon, you'd best leave it in my trunk."

T.J. removed his SigSauer and placed it in his canvas duffel before Banks slammed the lid closed.

"You got your wallet, right?"

T.J. nodded.

"They'll keep that with your I.D. until you turn in your visitor badge. Never leave any money in it, I always recommend."

"I got credit cards mainly. A few bucks."

"I think you're good. Staff here is all paid, no honor farm workers, so I think you're safe, but I don't mind opening the trunk if you feel uncomfortable."

"I wasn't until you started talking about all this."

"Fair enough. Forewarned is forearmed." Banks flashed him a bright white smile, and T.J. noticed for the first time he had one gold tooth in the front, one of his canines.

"That's an impressive crown you got there."

"Well, there's a story behind that, too. Stories. Everywhere we got stories, all *kinda* stories here." Banks waved his hands through the air like he was arranging a large flower display.

The two men mounted the four shallow concrete steps, and then T.J. remembered he needed to check in with his LPO. Most of the Team was in Las Vegas for Fredo and Mia's wedding.

"You get there okay? You okay?" Kyle asked.

"I'm fine. I'm at the hospital now. Looks like I'll be able to see him in a few. Give my best to Fredo and Mia."

"Will do. How're the little one and Shannon doing?"

"About as good as can be expected. I mean Shannon's doing great. Courtney is going in the right direction, they say. Shannon's mom and dad came down to be with her."

"Awesome. So I gotta tell you they posted a picture of Magnus on the local television station. Haven't seen it on the national stations, thank God. But it was that picture of the two of you at the Warrior's run, remember?"

"They posted my picture on TV?" T.J. felt powerless being so far away from Shannon and the baby. The thought that his face might bring them danger scared him.

"Yes, I'm afraid they did. I think it's only a matter of time before someone recognizes you, or uses that recognition software and they dig out your name. I need you to keep a low profile and be properly warned. Hoping these are a couple of nuts working on their own, but if not, you keep your eyes peeled for any signs someone recognizes you who shouldn't, okay?"

"Will do."

"Okay, be careful, and thanks for checking in."

"No problem. I'm going to stay over at this reverend's house. He works with the inmates." T.J. looked over at Travis, who tilted his head to him in acknowledgement. "I'll be coming back tomorrow. You staying over in Vegas after the wedding?"

"No. This isn't a good time for a couple of days R&R for me."

"Gotcha. Well, again, give my best—"

"T.J. you sound real good. Glad you're doing this. But don't linger there, okay?"

"No, I'm definitely coming home tomorrow."

After the call was over, T.J. thanked Travis for waiting. They continued their journey through a set of automatic doors that opened to a reception area. Unlike the hospital in San Diego, this one was completely devoid of female nurses or staff. He chuckled to himself that he was right about the smell too. Straight institutional eau de pee/vomit/bleach, just like juvenile hall, or at least the ones he'd "visited" in Texas and Nevada.

His guide brought them down a wide corridor with rubber bumpers as wainscoting, stopping at the first door on the right with a sign on it that read, *Chaplain.* Travis unlocked the solid core door with the brass handle, and inside T.J. actually felt like he was experiencing déjà vu. The room was filled with gray file cabinets along one short wall, a well-worn and stained leather couch on the other. The file cabinets had large red inventory stickers, just as he'd envisioned.

"You keep files on your flock?"

Travis chuckled. "No. Those would be death records. I guess they thought no one would want to break into the chaplain's office, and the chaplain, with a direct line to the man upstairs, wouldn't mind housing the last written evidence that these souls ever existed." He walked over to one cabinet with a large dent in the bottom file drawer as if it had been kicked in on purpose. His hand placed on top, he gently tapped with his palm to some imaginary rhythm. "These are my flock, in a way. The ones that flew the coop." His gold tooth gleamed in the morning sunlight filtering through the missing mini blinds like a spotlight.

He could have been the Grim Reaper himself.

Banks placed a call and informed someone on the other line they were headed down to see one Bobbie Ray Stokes. As he followed the large chaplain down the hallway and into the elevator, T.J. thought that he should have some kind of reaction to the sound of his real name, and found he did not. He was relieved to discover he didn't fit into Bobbie Ray's world, even though a tiny part of Stokes was imbedded in T.J.'s DNA.

Travis didn't say a word as the old elevator machinery groaned and slowly went from the first floor to the second. They could have walked the stairs faster.

As the doors opened, Travis examined the hallway, first right, then left, and then moved out of the way so T.J. could exit the tiny elevator car, much the same as T.J.'d blocked women and children behind him when he was on a rescue mission or was trying to get the injured to safety in a war zone. Well, he guessed sometimes this was a war zone. Despite his hardened heart, he found a little uptick in his right upper lip, the beginnings of a smile, at the vision of his father running down the hallway, or the stairs, or ducking into the elevator with his butt hanging out in all its glory.

The first bone-chilling scream came just as T.J. had turned the corner with Travis, on their way through a set of double swinging doors some-one had the poor taste to paint in a blue sky and clouds motif. Only thing worse than that would be if someone had painted black wrought iron gates and labeled the outside *Hell*. Now that would have been funny. And it would have complemented the scream that came from a scrawny man in the first room to the right just past the doors. An attendant was attempting to calm him down, perhaps medicate him.

Travis was probably immune to it now, having been through these doors more times than T.J. wanted to think about. He kept walking, so T.J. followed quickly, shortening the gap Banks' long legs created when he wasn't paying attention. He had to admit, he was relieved the screamer wasn't his dad. He kept telling himself it would be all right, no matter what he saw, no matter how surprised or caught off guard he might be.

But that was before he entered the room. Travis stepped aside, and T.J. was face to face with his past. The graying man had sunken cheeks, his skin quite orange, and he had a feeding tube down his nose. They'd restrained him to the bed with 3" nylon straps like the TRX units they worked out on when they were deployed. One strap was pulled tight across his chest and under both arms, fastened to the bed frame under-neath with special welded hooks probably designed for that purpose. What bothered T.J. most was that both the man's ankles were cuffed to the metal foot rail. The bottoms of his feet were blackened. Red welts had formed where he'd apparently tried to move. They were doing a good job keeping him in one place, in the same position. Probably the position he'd die in.

But that left his arms free, with one hooked up to an IV. With his unencumbered side, T.J. watched a bony finger rise from the bed and point at him.

Gray-white stubble covered the man's face, more than a few days', maybe even a week's growth. His liver-colored lips were spotted with dark stains that looked like droplets of blood, and there was a dark brown blood stain the size of a silver dollar on his gown, over his heart. The bony finger continued to rise as his lips pulled back into something that would have looked like a smile if he weighed more than eighty pounds.

The man was tall, which made him look like death itself.

"That's him," he said with difficulty. "That's my boy. You takin' me home today, son?" The man's raspy voice was what T.J. had expected, but it still was uncomfortable to hear.

T.J. looked at Travis, who was focused on the dying man. "Bobbie Ray, he's come to visit with you. We've talked about this. You can go home anytime you're ready. You speak your peace now. I'll leave you two alone for a spell." Travis backed up and motioned for T.J. to sit by the bed in a metal chair that had chipped beige paint.

His father was able to follow along as T.J. sat, adjusting his focus a little slow and late, but winding up having full eye contact when T.J. sat. There were tears in the man's eyes. T.J. worked hard not to give him the satisfaction of seeing his own, but couldn't stop them from welling up and spilling over his lower lids. And fuck if his lower lip didn't start quivering too. He held his mouth shut, feeling the rush of emotion, the years of pain, the years of wonder and how he'd told himself every day of his life how he hated this man.

But he could not call upon that hate to control his tears. So, he just gave up and let them stream down his face.

# CHAPTER 28

T HE WEDDING PARTY clustered around the closed door of the wedding chapel in the Bellagio, which was decorated with flowers and had all the luxurious details of a much larger setting. Through the windows they could see another wedding in progress, the flowers and padded chairs drenched in the colorful hues of ambient light were worthy of any beautiful cathedral in Europe. The fact that it was small and intimate actually added to the festive mood. It wasn't like any Las Vegas venue Kyle had ever been to before. And he'd been to a lot of them. It was the favored destination for his Team guys, who often got married and divorced quickly.

*That's just the way they are.* He took Christy's hand and felt the searing heat that struck him every time he touched her. Married now five years, with two children, and if she'd let him, he'd have two more and love them all just like their first, Brandon. She worked like a son of a gun, and if it weren't for her income, they'd have a whole different lifestyle. And Christy would seriously have to alter her shopping habits.

Fredo and Mia arrived. Mia was stunning in a very low-cut bright white gown that she was practically poured into. With her bronzed skin and long black hair done up and cascading down over her shoulders, she was one of the most beautiful brides he'd ever seen. Several of the Team guys removed their dark glasses and bowed to her, clearing their throats. He'd never seen Mia blush before, but she was clearly moved by the experience.

And Fredo was in a tux. First time he'd ever seen his explosives expert dress up in anything but an ill-fitting borrowed suit. They wore their dress uniforms for funerals. His shimmery brocade vest in white was a perfect complement to his dark slacks and white shirt, but the white tie looked like it was going to garrote him. Or maybe it was just that Fredo looked nervous as hell. His man frowned and nodded to the door of the chapel, as if Kyle was in charge.

"They not letting anyone in?" he asked, his furry eyebrows tenting. Kyle chuckled to himself remembering the numerous discussions Christy had with him, along with a couple of the other wives, trying to convince Fredo to tweeze or at least thin out his unibrow. As with many things about Fredo, once he set his mind on something, there was no stopping him. Just like the way he pursued Mia, Armando's bad girl sister and troublemaker, who rejected him for nearly three years. Fredo kept after her until she finally came to her senses.

And that was why he was one of the best go-to guys around. Why he was so deadly with his explosive charges and gadgets in the arena. He was irreverent and careful, a rare combination.

"There's another wedding finishing up," Christy whispered to them. "Mia, you are just—" Christy could hardly continue. "You are a complete knockout, sweetheart."

Mia beamed. "I'm doing this all the way."

Fredo bent, whispered something to her lips and kissed her. Kyle was happy his man got the girl of his dreams, although he'd always thought he deserved someone with less baggage. But Fredo was a rock-solid warrior hell-bent on saving people, and he was going to be the best husband Mia could have ever chosen. And that's the role Fredo wanted to play.

Felicia Guzman, Mia and Armando's mother, held little Ricardo. The charcoal braid woven atop her head was laced with fresh flowers enhancing her handsome, dark features and her bright brown eyes. She and Sergeant Mayfield had gotten married this last spring, and Mayfield doted on his new adopted grandson like he was raising him as his own.

"Mrs. Guzman," Kyle nodded to Mia's mother. He shook Mayfield's hand. "Heard you're retiring, really retiring now?"

"Yup. Sent in the paperwork." He started to say something else when the doors to the chapel opened, and the crowd separated for the other bride and groom to exit the church. They were young and without family or friends. Surprise registered on the bride's face as she made her way through the crowd of SEALs, wives, girlfriends and other family.

An attractive older woman wearing a pink suit ushered them inside to their seats. She took Mia's hand and led her around to a doorway off the tiny vestibule, where they disappeared. Organ music flowed from a decent sound system.

He looked over his Team Guys. Cooper was there with Libby, holding hands with their son, Will, who was smartly dressed in a little short pants black suit and red bow tie. Jones was with a new girl, as he usually was. Nick and Devon were there, Armando and Gina, Kate and Tyler and Sophia and Mark. Rory and several of the other single SEALs on Team 3 were clustered in one powerful girl-chasing unit and would be engaged in that kind of activity as soon as the wedding was over. He'd already overheard plans to rent a limo and do the town and anyone who came their way who was willing.

But the new crop of SEALs was coming along, and Kyle was proud of the respect they showed their senior man by showing up. These new young additions to SEAL Team 3 hardly drank and stayed away from the ladies, unlike their older mentors. Some of the immoral or lewd behavior allowed among the teams in the past was coming under more scrutiny. They were even asked not to get full sleeve tats any longer, something that had been a time-honored tradition. These new guys had a dedication to country and perfecting their trade unlike what he'd seen before. Kyle knew the recent blowups in the Middle East were driving a whole new breed of fighting men into the arms of the Special Forces.

Several of these new men shook his hand and bowed gently to Christy with the brief, "Ma'am."

They'd left Brandon and little Maggie with a hired hotel sitter, and Kyle was happy for the alone time with Christy, even though he was surrounded by people. They were his people. It was about as safe as it could be. And he knew most all of them were packing, so heaven help the sorry asshole who might want to challenge them. There wasn't any need for the firepower, but he felt naked without it and knew everyone else felt the same way.

The music changed and winks and nods continued amongst the attendees. Fredo stood up front by the black-robed minister, and Kyle wished he'd insisted he stand up for him. He actually felt sorry for the man. Coop was in the front row whispering some encouragement, and then probably following it with some kind of verbal joust, as was Coop and Fredo's pattern. The first swear word he heard of the day came from Fredo's mouth, which caused the minister to take a step back and cough.

Mia made her way down the aisle to the Wedding March, standing next to Fredo. The short service was over in less than ten minutes. The rings were exchanged, and then Fredo kissed his glowing bride while the crowd whooped and shouted, "Hooya S.O. Chavez!"

Around the corner from the chapel was an Italian restaurant, Izzy's, where they'd agreed to meet for lunch. Izzy was the father of a Team guy on the East Coast, and it was nearly sacrilegious not to give him a visit when in town.

His heavy New Jersey accent fit right into the ambience that was Las Vegas, and Kyle had often wondered if he had "connections" somewhere. And he was known for sometimes paying for a wedding party out of his own pocket, if there was the need. They were all family, every one of them. Family takes care of family.

Coop raised his glass for a toast. Fredo looked uncomfortable, but Mia kissed him on the cheek which seemed to lighten his mood.

"So when I showed up for Indoc there was this guy they told me about. This little short asshole who thought he could be a SEAL. Everyone was laughing at him." Coop nodded to the bride and groom, winking at Mia. "We had to settle things, of course. I mean, boys will be boys, and everyone was nervous as hell about trying out for the Teams, knowing there was an eighty to ninety percent chance they'd wash out."

The nodding and verbal affirmations were lavishly strewn about the room.

"We had a couple of professional footballers trying out, and they definitely thought they had more of a shot than this little Mexican prick sitting over here."

Fredo gave him the finger, and the crowd loved it.

"So to settle things, someone suggested they wrestle." Coop stopped to properly apprise Fredo before he continued. "And that stopped just about all talk of whether or not Fredo could make it. Fredo, I don't think you lost one of those, did you?"

"Still haven't."

"And he cheats."

"Fuck you. I don't cheat," Fredo barked.

Those that knew Fredo well knew that he did put his hands inappropriately on the other guy's junk during wrestling matches. This usually caught them off guard, and Fredo would get the quick take-down. Kyle knew it was part of what made him such a good, innovative SEAL. Fredo had a plan and a strategy for everything.

"Here's to the guy who counts the number of dryer sheets I use when I used to do laundry at his house, and he calls *me* cheap."

The crowd loved it.

"The guy who thinks there is something unholy about tofu and green salads—"

"*Not* unholy, just not natural," Fredo quipped back.

"Who thinks that anything green, except green chili salsa is also unhealthy," Coop continued. Fredo shrugged, guilty as charged.

"To my best friend, and absolutely someone I would stand right next to and take the bullet for, to someone Mia will never have to worry about because he'll go through hell itself to come back to you every time, and heaven help the guy who tries to mess with you, darlin', I give you Mr. and Mrs. Alphonso Manuel Esquidido Chavez." Coop raised his glass. The room shouted, "Hooya Mr. and Mrs. Chavez!"

Gina Guzman, Mia's new sister-in-law, stood up next to toast for the bride.

"Mia, you were one wild child there, and I was thinkin' man, I don't know if I can keep up with her." Gina was referring to the fact that she had worked an undercover detail and had befriended Mia originally as a means to help take down a local San Diego gang she was hanging with.

"Then I met your brother." She bent down and gave Armando a kiss. She continued, fanning her face. "Who knows what would have happened if I'd not met him, huh? But I thank my lucky stars every day that I did, and that you and I became friends. You watched my back. You also gave me some fits, too."

The crowd laughed.

"But it is so nice to see you so happy, and with the best guy you could have picked. This guy is as solid as they come."

Armando stood up, and said, "Excuse me—"

Coop pulled him down to allow Gina to continue.

Kyle's phone went off, and he saw from the display it was from T.J. He whispered to Christy, "Gotta take this."

He exited the restaurant as Gina was finishing and heard the shouts of acknowledgement from the revelers.

# CHAPTER 29

**"A**RE YOU IN any pain?" T.J. knew he should address this dying man as "Dad" but that was not something he could do. Not that he didn't feel anything. He felt a lot. He felt too much. He just couldn't make anything out of it. And that wasn't what he was used to.

The old man searched his face, back and forth, squinting in a smile of recognition.

"You grew up strong, son. I can tell. It was better that way. Better for you."

T.J. had to break away at that remark. *In your dreams, you old prick.* There wasn't any point to make him suffer even more than he already was, so he kept his mouth shut.

"They treating you good here?"

His father's laugh lines preceded the grimy grin he got back. T.J. noticed he was missing quite a few teeth. He tried to visualize him young and healthy, and just couldn't.

"I can't complain." His graying blue eyes were still bright, though his body seemed to be rotting away from them. "So I guess you want to know about your family then, T.J., or did your sister get hold of you?"

*Well isn't that something choice. A sister. I have a sister.* He was still feeling somewhat numb, but this news began a slow thaw.

"No one from 'the family' as you say, has ever contacted me, or if they tried, they gave up."

"Don't you want to know about your sister?"

"I'm here out of respect that you wanted to see me, and you haven't long for this world. I'm here so you can tell me whatever you want to tell me."

"Okay. First things first. I killed a man. I laid in wait for him, and I killed him. I shouldn't have, but I couldn't help myself." The old man didn't take his eyes off T.J. "I loved your mother. Loved her too much."

"Well, you're here. Where is my sister?"

"She lives about a hundred miles that way." He pointed west. "And your mother is buried nearby."

Bobbie Ray looked vacant, his eyes staring off at a distance, and at first, T.J. thought he'd passed away. He stood up to lean over and check, slightly alarmed, when his father lurched forward involuntarily, like he was coming back from the dead, which totally freaked T.J. out. He also smelled of death. He'd learned to recognize that smell over the past few years.

"You taking me home today? You got a nice car?"

"No, you're staying here. I'm going back home. This is your home now."

His father shook his head. "Did you drive or fly?"

T.J. was getting more impatient by the minute. He knew there wasn't anything he could do for his father, except listen to his stream of consciousness wanderings. He actually prayed that he'd go peacefully, and soon. And if he was in a dulled state, perhaps that would be better for everyone.

But T.J. did have questions. He just wasn't sure it was appropriate to ask them. Or, maybe he just wasn't sure he'd like the answers. His mother apparently was dead. But he had a sister, and that changed things for T.J.

"I met a real nice girl," his father started. "She looks a lot like you. Has your eyes. Beautiful girl. I'm going to ask her to marry me."

"That's nice." T.J. thought he might find out details by just listening and not asking. Perhaps there would be some pearls in the old man's words that would give him some of the clues he was seeking.

"I messed up. She loved him. She loved the man I kilt."

"My sister? What's *her* name?"

"Lois. Lois Foster. Old Mr. Foster died many years ago. Never did like me and when I got sent here, well, there wasn't any way for me to get in touch with her. I fucked up, son."

"So, my mother's name was Lois?"

"You know Lois? Did they introduce you to her? Don't you think she's pretty?"

T.J. wanted to get up, run away and never come back.

"I thought about this day for many years. What would I say to you if

I ever found you."

"Have you talked to my sister?"

"Twice."

"What's her name?"

"She has a boyfriend. I met him once too."

"What's her last name?"

His father looked back at him like he was the crazy one in the bed. "*Who?*"

*We're losing time.*

"My *sister*. What's my sister's name?"

"You have a sister?" his dad asked. "Congratulations. Wonder why they never told me!"

He had that far away look again.

"Hey, son, you taking me home? I'm ready anytime you are."

He could see his father's body shutting down by the minute. His speech was starting to slur. T.J. reached out and touched the old man for the first time in his life, placing a gentle palm on his frail shoulder which felt like all bone and very little flesh. "Dad. You *are* home. Remember what Travis said? You can close your eyes and go there anytime you want."

His father seemed to get half of what he said. "They're really good here, you know. Take such good care of us. Really topnotch place. I'd come back here anytime."

*Great. Dad thinks he's in a vacation resort or something.* It was funny, if it wasn't so sad. His father didn't register in the slightest that he'd been physically touched by his own son for the first time ever. "Tell me her name, Dad," he asked softly. "Tell me my sister's last name."

But his dad had checked out of the resort and was on his new adventure.

"GLAD YOU GOT to see him," Travis said as they traveled down the highway toward the town of Dover. The reverend managed to do a little digging and had found the address of one Connie Fallon through an ancestry.com account, checked the phone book and found she had a listed phone number as well as her address. Dover was only about twenty miles from Travis's church and parsonage, so he agreed to accompany T.J. on the trip. They'd tried to call ahead, without luck.

Next, T.J. called the hospital, reaching the nurse's station to check on Shannon.

"I don't want to talk to her if she's sleeping."

The nurse checked and confirmed she was asleep.

"Wonderful. How's she doing?"

The nurse was shuffling through some paperwork, probably checking the permission slips Shannon signed on admittance. "Everything's going in the right direction, sir. I'd let her sleep."

"How's little Courtney doing?"

"I understand there is an update, but not until the patient has been informed."

"Good news or bad news?"

"You're going to have to get that from your wife."

*My wife.* He liked the sound of that. He wanted to celebrate, but there were too many unknowns and he wouldn't let his heart go there. He told himself it would be easier when he had an update on Courtney. That was, if it was good news. Something in his gut told him it was.

"Would you ask her to give me a call when she awakens?" He gave his cell phone. "Tell her I will be coming home tomorrow, okay?"

"I'll do that. She's had a lot of visitors. She really needs to rest right now, so I'll give it to her when she awakens."

T.J. wondered who would be pestering her so much, when most of their platoon on Team 3 were in Las Vegas.

"Can we cut out the visitors?" he asked.

"Sure, but the police have been in several times. And a newspaper reporter. We got rid of *him*."

"Police?"

"We didn't know you knew the Marine whose wife was injured."

"Okay, I'm going to get someone to come stay with her. Her parents been by much?"

"Oh yes. Both sets, yours and hers."

T.J. didn't correct her. Frankie's parents had every right to see their new grandchild. He was going to make sure that always was allowed.

Next he called Shannon's parents and got her mother on the phone. T.J. and Mrs. Moore had a difficult relationship going back to Shannon and Frankie's wedding. He guessed his taking off for Tennessee was just another example to Mrs. Moore of a lack of good judgment. She was frosty, more so than usual.

"You kids are in the middle of all this media circus, and Shannon needs to get her rest while you're streaking all over the countryside searching after lost relatives."

"My father died this morning."

"Okay. You sound *devastated*," she said mockingly.

He was wondering if he'd ever have a normal relationship with her. Probably not. "I'll be home tomorrow. Turns out I have a sister I didn't know about, so I'll be stopping by to see her if I can, and then I'll come home."

"How nice for you."

"Look, the reason for the call, although I *always* enjoy our calls, Mrs. Moore, is that there have been some police and other people bothering Shannon. And there has been a reporter snooping around. I need her left alone as much as possible."

"Well, well, we finally agree."

T.J. was so glad Shannon hadn't gone through with her plans to raise little Courtney on her own in the Bay Area where her parents lived. Her whole life would have been changed by the proximity to this woman. But she was Shannon's mother, and he wasn't going to interfere, especially when he needed her keen eyes doing a stealth mission to order people around, which was exactly what she was well suited for. She could have run a whole platoon.

"We want to cooperate with the police. But in light of what happened to Magnus' wife, and that hospital area not being that secure—"

"Yes, we were told you actually saw one of the terrorists."

"*One* of the terrorists?"

"Apparently small cell, they've taken responsibility."

"All the more reason. I need you to stand guard over Shannon and be extremely picky about who she talks to. Be rude if you have to.

"I can do that."

T.J. knew she definitely could.

# CHAPTER 30

COURTNEY WAS RESTING comfortably in Shannon's arms when Shannon's mother and father arrived. The baby had been transferred to a regular nursery crib, which was sitting nearby.

"Oh, hi, guys," Shannon called out to them. She hadn't expected them until this evening.

Her mom gave her a hug and kiss, and sat for a minute on the edge of the bed, brushing her fingers over her granddaughter's pink fuzzy head. "She's really beautiful, Shannon. Ears are a little big."

This tickled her. Long past caring about this little feature of her anatomy, Shannon was happy the baby was going to be allowed to go home with her today. When she told her mother, they were thrilled.

One of the nurses came in after Shannon buzzed her.

"Yes?"

"Say, I'm wondering how soon before we are allowed to leave?"

"Leave?"

"Well, the doctor said he was going to release me. My parents are here to help me. We're ready now if everything is okay."

"Let me check. Is she nursing or just sleeping?"

"Mostly sleeping."

"You want her to nurse, honey. She'll get comfortable and all warm and snuggly, but she needs to eat so you keep your milk in. You'll have problems when you get home if not."

"I think she's getting plenty. But this is my first."

"All right." The nurse came over to the bed and addressed Mrs. Moore, "Excuse me, honey." When Shannon's mother stood next to Mr. Moore, the nurse leaned in. "I'm gonna take the baby, get her weighed, take a final blood test and get her cleaned up for you. Then I'll bring her back. She'll be good and fussy when I get done poking around with her."

"That woman is rude," said Mrs. Moore.

Nothing could dampen her mood, except she hadn't heard from T.J. She'd gotten the message he'd landed safely while she was resting. But his call was overdue, and she needed to hear his voice, curious how the meeting with his dad went.

"I wish T.J. would call," she said to her mother.

"He didn't call you? That's why we came right over. He's coming home tomorrow, he said."

She wondered why he'd not called her directly, but instead called her mother. "Hope everything went well."

Mrs. Moore glanced at her husband, and then added, "Honey, I'm afraid his father passed away this morning."

"All the more reason—"

"He should be home with you and the baby," Mr. Moore asserted. "You are unprotected here. and I don't like that. With that reporter yesterday and all the questions the police are asking. T.J. felt it too, asked your mother and me to come over and stand guard. We're not leaving until they release you, Shannon."

An attractive male intern in scrubs, a stethoscope draped across his neck, popped his head inside. "Can I have a word for a second?"

"They can stay here," she answered.

"Sorry, confidentiality rules. I'm really sorry." He smiled at her parents who looked at Shannon for direction and when she shrugged, they exited to the hall.

As the door to her room closed, he came over to Shannon's bedside and sat down, which alarmed her.

"So, where's your husband?"

"You guys know he's—" All of a sudden it began to dawn on her there was something wrong about this man. He had a faint accent, which normally wouldn't bother her, but the nametag on the scrubs identified him as being with housekeeping. Why would he need a stethoscope?

He was drawing something from his pocket. She saw the flash of a syringe containing a light yellow liquid. Adjusting her weight, she pushed back away from him just before he lunged forward attempting to inject something into her neck. She wanted to scream but his hand covered her mouth. With a quick kick to his hip, he was thrown off balance and fell to the floor, scattering her IV and several other items, including a plastic water pitcher on a nearby stainless steel tray, all over the ground.

But the kick had had also thrown off her balance, and she found herself reaching for anything to avoid falling from the hospital bed onto the other side. She clutched the air, knocking over a vase filled with flowers, sending it shattering to the floor as she fell hard. She tried to scream but found the air had been knocked out of her. Pain seared her abdominal area.

At last she found her voice and screamed.

The next instant, he was around the end of the bed and, reaching over her, attempted to grab her hair. Her hands swept the floor. She felt the wetness of the broken vase as well as the sting of a piece of broken glass that had gotten stuck in the palm of her hand.

In the meantime, something was happening outside the door. She could hear her mother shouting for help. Sounds of a struggle, with something heavy being thrown against the door. Was there someone else outside? She remembered the warning T.J. had given her mother.

*Hopefully Courtney is safe. Please, let her be safe. She has to be safe.*

She heard a definite gunshot sound and screaming. Her assailant yanked her hair, pulling her head up like a rag doll with a jerk. Now he wasn't holding a syringe any longer. He held a heavy knife like T.J.'s KA-BAR, the one she had looked at several times. She knew where his intended trajectory was. Her legs flopped and scraped on the wet, slippery floor as she tried to throw his balance off from the lethal crouch position, a tight tripod. His center of gravity was too low, she realized.

*This is not acceptable. This is not going to happen. Never. Not at any time.* She was not going to die, wind up another statistic on the evening news.

He was twisting her head to get a lethal angle at her neck. She knew what he was after. She remembered something T.J. had explained to her.

*Sometimes when you're in a struggle, best to stop fighting. Go in the same direction as the attacker, because if you resist, you cause them to use deadly force to restrain you.*

Instead of pulling back, trying to avoid his body and the knife that was gripped in his right hand, she leaned forward into him. He lost his balance for just a second, enough time for her to bring up her palm, drawing her arm over and outside his left. The glass wedged there hurt like a son of a gun, but as her fingers gripped it tightly, cutting her further, she drew strength from the pain. She hoped it was big enough to do what she needed it to do. Using her own fist as the hilt of the glass blade, she swung upward and rammed it into the assailant's neck, remembering to throw whatever weight she could muster from her own body following behind, and then pulled down.

She felt the satisfying crunch of cartilage and muscle tissue being sliced open, followed by a warm spray of his blood, covering her face and chest. He tried to adjust, dropping his knife in order to hold onto his neck, but his knees slipped in the pool of blood. Shannon seized another opportunity, drew one knee up to her chest and then pushed with everything she had, her bare foot landing square in the middle of his chest, sending his body backward.

He was skidding across the bloody floor when the heavy door swung open and knocked him solidly in his head.

Seeing her parents in the hallway, worried but apparently unharmed, the bevy of staffers behind them and the two uniformed guards hauling up the unconscious assailant by his armpits, she allowed herself to collapse and breathe. Other than the pain in her palm, and something intense burning in her lower belly, she felt pretty good, considering.

She looked at her bloody hands, the sloppiness of the mortal combat she'd just engaged in, her heart pounding so hard it nearly exploded her chest, and she discovered something.

It felt damn good to be alive.

# CHAPTER 31

**"Y**OU LIKE LIVING out here, don't you?" T.J. asked Travis.

"Yessir, I used to. It does me good to be in this beautiful part of the world. And the cost of living is a lot less than other places. I won't lie, part of the charm, part of the charm."

Travis' gold tooth was glinting in the sunlight. "So you gonna tell me about that tooth?"

This gave the big man a belly laugh. "You're gonna think me quite insane. Maybe a bit more eccentric than you like."

"But you forget. I'm in the military, and let me tell you, I see stuff all the time on deployment that is pretty fuckin'—sorry, man, just force of habit."

"It's all right. You're an all right dude, Mr. T.J. Talbot. I think you're one of God's warriors. And God's warriors get to take special liberties with their language." He smiled broadly and then swung his eyes back to the road.

He sucked in air as if he could create a vacuum in the old Chevy, then blew it out so hard T.J. thought the windshield might cave.

"Okay, here goes," Travis started.

T.J. could already tell he was going to dig the hell out of whatever the man was going to say.

"I met this lady when I was twenty-five, over a decade ago now. We didn't obey any of God's commandments, in fact, I think this woman was hell bent on breaking jus' about all of them."

Travis stopped and threw out a throaty laugh, his belly rubbing against the steering wheel of his car. If it involved a woman, now T.J. was even more sure he was going to like the story.

"I've known a few of those," he admitted to the preacher. "They don't interest me any longer either, but man. I haven't thought about those days for a while now, but that's all I used to think about."

"You was just finding your way, son."

"That's a fact. Not there though. It was never there."

"No, it never is. And that kind of relates to this story. See, she and I, we got married. The woman was one of those who would get something into her mind, and then she'd never let up, you know what I'm sayin'? She was one wild child. I thought at first it was cute. I mean, at twenty-five, she was the most exciting thing to ever come my way, and I wanted excitement."

T.J. remembered the hundreds of girls he'd slept with over the years. Luckily, most of his liaisons he couldn't remember. He couldn't even remember their faces. Maybe that was a good thing.

"Well, Mr. Talbot, that woman wanted excitement too. And when I was no longer her drug of choice, she moved on. And when I say she moved on, I mean she took it upon herself to sleep with anything that would walk, know what I'm sayin'?"

"I do." T.J. felt sorry for the man.

"It cost me every penny I had, which wasn't much, just to complete the divorce."

"You married now?"

"Nope. Not looking yet, either. I'm still wearing off the effects of my last one. Some days, T.J., the sight of a woman scares me all the way down to my toes."

"I understand."

"When it was all said and done, I was left with two gold wedding bands. And that's where they is," he said as he tapped his gold tooth with his forefinger. "Right there so every time when I looks in the mirror I gets to remember I'm a survivor, and I'm never goin' down that rabbit hole again. I gets to smile and look back in the mirror at the face of a free man."

T.J. was smiling and he knew Travis was interested in hearing what he thought. He kept looking over at him as they turned off the highway and onto a small single lane country road. In the distance a small town took shape.

"You know, Travis. I think that some time soon you'll meet the right woman, and she'll want you to get that tooth fixed. I think the sight of her will light that golden path to heaven itself for you."

"You think so?"

"I know so. Yup. I know so." T.J. was feeling more comfortable with the preacher the more time they spent together. "I sure found the right gal." He told Travis about the baby, about Frankie.

"You're a good man, Mr. Talbot."

"You know, I almost didn't want to come here at all. It took a while to shed off all that dead skin. I was worried it would suck me right back into that angry place I grew up in. God, how I hated that man. And today, I just realized I didn't hate him at all. I hated myself. I was exorcising demons." He watched Travis' face in profile. "You've done that too. So now you can give that to someone else, or rather, let someone else give that to you. You help everyone else. You tend your flock. Time to let someone tend to you, my man."

"You could be right. I'd like to think you are."

"And speaking of which, I need to give my intended a call." T.J. dialed Shannon's number and got her message. He dialed his mother-in-law and got the same. He double checked to see if he'd missed anything and found he hadn't.

They drove into the little town with one stoplight.

"Kind of peaceful here. This a nice place to live?" T.J. asked.

Travis bobbed his head. "Yes and no. We got something strange goings on here. I notice it because I see the change in the prison population, which comes more from this area than any other. Lot of poor folks here. But a lot of angry folks coming in from other places. Big cities. I'm just one preacher at Riverbend. They's groups here that send their guys in every day."

T.J.'s attention was sparked. He had to ask, because they'd all been talking about it on the Teams. "Religious types?"

"Doing the conversions, yessir, but I don't take my flock out and do no target practice. They have a big communal camp right here in this little town. News media says there are known camps operating, dozens of them, and we got one right here. Can you explain to me why no one is asking questions? And I see men I grew up with changing, becoming hard. Mostly I see strangers in this area where I used to know everyone's name. So, if you ask me, T.J. I say no. Not any longer."

"I've seen the bloody effects of fanatical groups overseas. A lot of people are getting killed. A lot of innocent people, and that's just wrong."

"Sort of feels like it's all coming to this country, don't it?"

T.J. knew for a fact it was.

CONNIE DROVE UP just as Travis and T.J. were getting back in their car. They'd been standing on the porch, knocking on the painted old screen door of a bungalow that could have been in any small town in America. The birds were chirping, and there wasn't any traffic noise or car horns blaring. A single airplane overhead made its way across the sky, leaving a white tail behind it.

She was holding a bag of groceries in one arm, shielding her eyes with her other palm. "Can I help you?"

T.J. figured she was about his age. He could definitely see a family resemblance to his own face.

"Holy Mother of God. Is that you?"

"I think so," T.J. started. "You're Connie?"

"Yes. Yes. I'm your sister. Your twin sister." She set her package on the hood of her car and ran up to him, but stopped just in front. They both took a tentative step toward each other and embraced safely. She had lighter brown hair than his, but the same light blue eyes.

This was another surprise in a day of surprises. His father hadn't mentioned anything about him being a twin, so T.J. was skeptical. "We came from the hospital, and I'm sorry to say, Dad has passed on."

He expected a different reaction than the one he got.

"Well, that's done, then." She returned to the car, closed the door and picked up her packages. "Come on in, and we'll toast to dear old Dad."

As T.J. passed Travis, the preacher's eyes got wide.

Over the next hour, Connie told him she'd been raised in Colorado and had been adopted into a good family. T.J. let her know his was quite a different path, but spared her the gory details.

"When my mother died last Spring I figured that would free me up to go looking for my birth parents. I got here just in time to see Mom before her passing, and I took care of her a bit in the end. She told me her father forced the adoption, and it was one of the biggest regrets of her life. I'm glad I got to tell her I had a good upbringing. Now I'm glad she never found out about yours."

T.J. remembered what Kyle told him, about living with the hand he was dealt. He realized that that was the life he was supposed to lead, just like he was supposed to be Courtney's father.

"She lived in this very house her whole adult life. Never married again. Never had any other children. And she never went to visit him, even though she was a couple of hours away all that time."

"Wonder why?" T.J. pondered.

"I don't think we'll ever know. They weren't married, you know." She brought out pictures to show him what his mother looked like, and she gave him a smiling photo of her that was his favorite. "Here, so you can show your little girl, someday."

"Funny how that happens. Now I have something physical to show of the past I never had. Thank you."

Connie then pressed a small envelope into his palm. "Keep this too. Open this after you've gone."

T.J.'s cell phone rang. It was Shannon.

# CHAPTER 32

"**O**H GOD, T.J. It's so good to hear your voice," Shannon said. She'd told herself she would be strong, but upon hearing him, she lost all her composure. He began firing questions at her, and she lost the ability to speak all of a sudden. "You have to come home. Please come home now."

"Is everything okay with you and the baby?"

"Yes. But almost no." She told him about the afternoon's events, explained that her parents took her home, and that Kyle had insisted a couple of Team Guys stay with her until T.J. could get home. "I know you said tomorrow. I need you here as fast as you can get here."

Shannon was relieved T.J. headed straight for the Nashville airport where they determined he could catch a flight back to San Diego that would get him home near midnight.

Just over an hour later, he texted:

*Made the plane. Taking off soon. Coming home to you. Get ready. Love you more than I thought possible.*

His text thrilled her. She ached for him, missed him now more than before. With giddy relief that he was finally going to be home tonight, she texted back:

*Ready? All I can think about, sweetheart. Safe travels. I might never let you out of the bedroom. Ever. Love you too.*

She got the little ping that told her she had a return message:

*Hmmmm. That sounds yummy. I don't belong anywhere else. See you in a few. Kiss Courtney for me. All my love.*

The Moore's settled in the third bedroom, while the two new SEAL Team 3 members were given pillows and blankets to sleep on the couch. Shannon had wanted to go to the airport to meet T.J., but knew it was not wise. Ollie, one of the young SEALs, would go while the other one would stay behind and keep watch.

She dashed into the shower, wrapping her stitched hand in a plastic bag, the plastic covering her abdominal stitches. Anticipation was boiling in her stomach as she carefully changed the sheets, placed fresh candles all around the bedroom. She tried to eat the food her parents had prepared, tried to make small talk with the young SEALs while they all waited, but in the end, she was so distracted by anticipation of T.J.'s homecoming, she couldn't focus on anything but what it would feel like to be wrapped in his strong arms. He was coming back home to her, and that made her feel giddy as a school girl. Seven hours was waaaaay too long to have to wait.

Courtney was demanding a feeding, and this eased her nerves. She lit a candle in the bedroom and leaned into the soft pillows of their bed, nursing her, telling her about her daddy.

"He's tall and handsome, and he loves you so much. He'll shower you with kisses and you'll love falling asleep in his arms."

She placed her little finger close to Courtney's waving hand and fingers. The baby grabbed it like the lifeline it was, and they rocked together on the bed by candlelight.

"Little strong Courtney," she said, and kissed her.

A few minutes later, she put the baby to sleep in the portable sleeper by her bed, covered herself up in the quilt the SEAL Ladies had made for her, and let herself fall asleep.


WHEN SHANNON'S CELL phone pinged with another text, she awoke to a darkened bedroom. The screen on her cell glowed on the night stand.

*Just landed. Found Ollie. We're headed home, sweetheart.*

She returned his text with hearts and flower images.

The baby began to fuss, so she changed her, nursed her again and then put her back down. Just as she stepped into the hallway she heard Ollie's truck, and knew he was home. Her heart was racing as she saw the front door open, and there he was. Her parents flocked to him immediately while his brothers stood nearby. Ollie leaned forward and peered down the hallway at Shannon and gave her a wink.

He hadn't taken his eyes off her since walking through the doorway.

Dropping his bag, he ran to Shannon, pulled her inside the bedroom and slammed the door behind them. She could hear a generous serving of chuckling coming from the other side.

Alone in the darkened room with the candles lit, T.J.'s honest face danced in the glow of candlelight. He wrapped his arms around her waist and hoisted her up off the ground as she felt the urgency of his deep kiss. She could feel his chest expand as he inhaled her, gave her that gravely groan from deep inside.

"God how I missed you," he whispered through his kisses. "Shannon, I'm so sorry for all that's happened, and for not being here."

She placed her fingers over his mouth. "Shhh. No talking now."

"But seriously," he insisted. "Is everything okay? Are you both okay?"

She showed him her bandaged palm. "Just five stitches and maybe some surgery later on, but I was lucky."

He unwrapped the gauze outer wrapping and then peeled back the adhesive tape to examine the work. She watched as he calculated its adequacy and saw the slight nod, giving approval. He pressed the wrapping back down, securing the bandage and then carefully wrapped it back in the gauze, kissing her palm gently, kissing every layer of the wrapping. "Does it hurt?"

"Just a little."

"And here?" he placed his palm on her belly.

"Better now that you're here."

He smiled. "You need anything for the pain?"

"No, sweetheart. All I need is right here."

The baby stirred, so T.J. let Shannon slide down his frontside, drawing her over to the crib. "She's beautiful. God, I'm a lucky man."

"We're the lucky ones," she said. The tenderness she saw in his face for Courtney filled her heart to capacity. "We were so lucky they'd taken her away before the—"

"No," he said, stopping her with his kisses. "You were right. No more talking. Besides, we'll wake her." He took her hand, examined the room full of candles and brought her over to the bed. "Our time now."

"Yes," she said as she felt his hands slide up her front, squeezing her breasts. She helped him remove her clothes, and then took her time removing his shirt, kissing his warm flat stomach muscles, up the center of his chest to under his chin. She undid his belt and button fly carefully, one by one, slid her hands into his pants and then around to his butt cheeks and pulled the denim fabric down until his jeans fell. When he stepped out of them, they were completely naked together, his erection pressing into her belly.

Her hands massaged the full length of him, massaged his balls as they kissed. Their heat ignited, and he pulled her down into the bed. He kissed a trail under her ear, and whispered, "God, Shannon, I don't know what I would have done if anything—"

"I know, love."

"You were so brave. So very lucky," he said to her mouth. He kissed her neck, down to her breasts and then back up again. She held his head between her hands, and he leaned into her bandaged palm, kissing her again on the wound. "So strong. Do you know how incredible you are, Shannon?"

She rolled back into the pillow, placing her arms back above her head. "Show me."

His answer was swift, and with another guttural moan he was rooting for her opening. "Sorry, but I have to—"

"It's what I want too. I need you inside me, T.J."

"I don't want to hurt you, honey. You sure this is okay?"

"I need you."

He thrust deep, being careful not to press against her lower abdomen, but matching her urgency. The delicious feel of him made her arch back, raise her knees and press her pelvis into his. His long strokes were tentative and careful. Then he began a deliberate rhythm that was long and smooth, enough to absorb every motion, but fast enough to heighten her arousal with each thrust. He kissed her eyes, whispered *I love you's* to her mouth over and over again.

He arched up, slid his knees under her thighs, bracing her back with his powerful arms and moved her down on his shaft, carefully grinding her down and then releasing her to writhe against him. He was so deep she was melting as her internal muscles milked him, as she felt him tense and then thrust several more times deep into her tender soft tissues that burned for him. On one final thrust he allowed himself to release into her, holding her pressed against him as she felt him lurch and begin to spill.

"Oh, God, T.J. I need this."

"Yes, baby." The sound of his voice triggered a slow rolling orgasm as her body exploded. She pressed her chest against his, grabbed the hair at his nape and let her pelvis ride down onto him, her legs balancing them as he pushed up and deeper inside her.

He held her firm, slowly pressing harder, then releasing, working her insides with deep, short movements as her spasms subsided and her bones turned to rubber. A forlorn moan sounded somewhere, and then she realized it came from her, so completely spent, and yet craving more.

At last they collapsed back into the bed, a tangle of arms and legs, kisses and caresses.

*This is the life I've always wanted. This is the way it's supposed to be.*

Turning to the man in her arms, her rock, his eyes searching her face, she realized that whatever came with the intensity of loving this man, whatever it was, she was in for it one hundred percent, and always would be. This was the life she was destined for.

THE NEXT MORNING Kyle came over, and the family held a strategy meeting.

"We have only a few choices," Kyle said. "The Navy is working hard with local media outlets, who have promised no more inappropriate posting of pictures of family or Team members. This has been a tradition going back many, many years, but oddly enough, we have to keep repeating it."

"Can't believe they didn't know that, Kyle," added T.J.

"Well, we have to be ever vigilant. You know that."

Everyone nodded. Shannon sat on the couch between T.J. and her mom, and she was holding hands with both of them.

"It's a double-edged sword. We can have you guys move, which in essence disrupts your life, changes your plans, maybe permanently, or we stay and fight." He lowered his eyes. "And we're not supposed to be fighting here on our soil. But everyone understands we need to be prepared and, if attacked, we defend."

Shannon felt T.J. tense up. "What does your Navy liaison suggest? Should we move?"

"We don't know what they know about you, Shannon. We know they are probably studying T.J., because the news put up his picture. It may be that T.J. being here poses more of a danger to all of you, which totally sucks, because he's the one that could defend you better than anyone else."

"But if we move together—" Shannon began.

Kyle shook his head. "Still no guarantees, Shannon. Should we house our families in a compound somewhere to keep them safe? Are we going to do that just to make sure they are? That's not what we're about. That's not how we live. We live free."

"Just that we have to root out the bad guys," Ollie added.

"How do we do that?" Shannon asked.

"Two schools of thought there. What we're not going to do is go on a search and destroy mission. We don't do that here. Ever. We hide in plain sight, or you move to a location that they don't know about. We don't know how long that would work. Will you have to be looking over your shoulder for months, years to come? No guarantees even if you do move, you will be safe."

Shannon could see the dilemma. She knew her answer, if T.J. would allow it.

"I can't take that chance," T.J. said. Shannon closed her eyes. She'd known he'd say that. "I'm the one who is exposing this family to more danger. You're right, Kyle."

Shannon knew she had to be careful with this next part. "But they came after me in the hospital. They found me somehow." The room remained quiet.

"It has to be your decision. I don't know how they got your information, Shannon. Maybe it was one of the hospital staff, someone who knew you were in labor, and knew what T.J. did for a living. Just hard to say. We don't talk about what we do. We were never supposed to. But especially now, we don't talk about it."

Everyone agreed with this.

T.J. squeezed her hand. "Honey, I am causing further danger by staying here. I say we move, or—"

Shannon stood up and addressed the seated circle. "I won't *be* safe, T.J. if you leave. We stay together. If we move, we move together. Or we stay here, and we keep our eyes and ears open. But I'm not running away."

Kyle smiled. "That's exactly what Christy would say. You gals are tough, I'll grant you that."

"Look at what she did yesterday. They'll be asking her further questions. Won't that trigger curiosity with the neighbors here?" Mrs. Moore asked.

"We can arrange for all interviews to be done at the jurisdictions. None here. I think that could be carried out," Kyle added.

"What about Frankie's parents? What if they stayed there?" Shannon's dad asked.

"That would be putting them in danger. I couldn't ask them to do that," Shannon answered.

"Come here, Shannon," T.J. said and stretched out his arms.

The group chuckled in response as Shannon sat on his lap, legs across his thighs. The protective shield of his arms warmed her and calmed her nerves.

"I say we ask them, honey."

Shannon couldn't believe he was actually proposing this.

"I think they'd want to help, in fact, I know they'd love to help. And they'd love spending time with Courtney."

Kyle nodded. Shannon could see he thought it was a good idea too. "I don't think they'd be on anyone's radar," he said.

"If they know I live here, or know anything about you, Shannon, they'll come here. But they may not know about Frankie's parents," T.J. followed up his statement with a kiss. He ducked his head to make direct eye contact, "Or, do you not want me to be there with you? You could stay there alone, if you want."

"Don't be silly." Shannon was beginning to warm to the idea.

"Shannon and the baby could come stay with us in Palo Alto," Mrs. Moore cut in cheerfully. She got an immediate reaction.

Kyle, T.J. and Shannon all answered with a resounding, "No."

# CHAPTER 33

T J. KNEW THE Bensons would be happy with the arrangement, and he really didn't mind the fact that he'd be spending time with Joe Benson, one of the best dads ever. First day they stayed with the couple, Joe reached out to T.J.

"I was real sorry to hear about your father," he said, his warm eyes not following the smile on his lips. T.J. could see the death of his son still pained him, and probably always would.

"Thanks. That helps, Joe. We both lost someone. I lost a brother, and you a son. Although I also lost my dad, I didn't have what you guys had."

"Everyone does the best they can, son."

"I've heard that a lot lately. Too much, I'll admit." T.J. had thought he'd purged it all out of him, but some of the familiar loathing for his horrible childhood came roaring back.

"Well," Benson said as he removed his hand from the top of T.J.'s shoulder, "We just take it a day at a time. We celebrate when we can, and we cry when we must."

Nothing was ever discussed further. Shannon and T.J. moved several items in two trips from the old house, enlisting the help of a couple of the Team guys. The rush of every day life, with a newborn and with grandparents to dote on the child, started to make everything seem normal.

But that was a problem for T.J. He did not feel normal, and it was getting worse. He was filled with pain, and needed more and more time alone. He retreated to the back bedroom often and lay down while Courtney slept beside the bed. The sounds of the baby's breathing were healing, reminding him of new life and future miracles. But it was short-lived. He couldn't put his finger on it. This was not something he was used to, a family routine. Loving relatives who were gentle and civil to one another. The more he was around it, the more he began to feel out of place.

Today was an especially bad day. He'd tried to work it out down at Gunny's, overstaying the meter and getting a huge parking ticket. Fredo and Mia were back from their honeymoon in St. Thomas, and all of a sudden everyone on the Teams wanted to know when he and Shannon were getting married. The police interview today was especially hard, because they brought up his juvenile record.

*Like I'm one of them? Do they really think that?*

The FBI agent in charge of the questioning separated him and Tyler and kept harping on the fact that their stories didn't entirely match and kept grilling them for several hours. Even Tyler was upset by it, but took it a lot better than T.J. did.

"You getting along with your wife?" the heavyset agent asked him. The guy had a grease spot on his tie T.J wanted to cut off with scissors.

"Of course. Never better." He knew the man knew they weren't married and had said it on purpose to pick a fight.

"You're living with her in her dead husband's parents home. Why are you not living in your own place? You're not married, right, and have no plans to?"

"We have plans to."

"Yet nobody here seems to be able to give me a date. Have you set a date, Mr. Talbot?"

"What do these questions about my personal life have to do with this investigation?"

"You have a problem talking about your personal life?"

"Fuck no. Except it's personal."

"You've always been known as kind of a loose cannon, Mr. Talbot."

This one really got to him. He fisted his hand under the table and purposely didn't grind his teeth. "Who told you I was a loose cannon?"

"Your LPO, Lansdown. Said you had been kind of a party animal, and now you were more domesticated. Surprised him, he said."

"Then I'm sure he meant it as a compliment." T.J. didn't think Kyle would have said this, or at least didn't mean the implication.

"You like being domesticated? That idea appeal to you, or are you itching to get out there and do something wild and crazy?"

"We all do that. It's what we do. But no, I don't have any plans to go chase girls or go off on a stupid drunken bender. I don't do that anymore.

Kyle's right."

The agent leaned back in his chair and took his time answering. "I'm wondering if all this bliss, without the ring and the date, has got you feeling like your balls are in a vice. Know what I mean?"

T.J. hated the man now. He looked back at him like he wished he could've looked at his father years ago growing up, not the kind of look he had to give him as he was dying in the hospital bed. He didn't care what the man thought of him now. He knew it was a danger sign, and he was powerless to stop it. He decided no response was the safest course of action. He was used to some professional jealousy, but this was over the top.

But the agent couldn't stop either. Something was growing between them, and it stunk up the little interview room.

"You ever get angry with your girlfriend? Strike her?"

That was enough. T.J. reached across the table and grabbed Agent Asshole by the greasy tie and yanked his face close. "You fuckin' prick. Get off my back. I don't ever raise my voice or my hand to Shannon. I'm not the one you're looking for. I was clear across the country paying my respects to my dying father, you asshole."

T.J. released the agent before the door burst open and two other agents poured in. They were sent outside immediately. Agent Asshole straightened his tie and smirked. "I don't like you, Talbot. We can do this hard or soft. But something tells me you like it hard, so I'm not going to play that game with you. We got us some homegrown terrorists with special knowledge of your particular family's whereabouts. We've got stories of bloody handprints in places where you were, conflicting witness descriptions, and an assault on your girlfriend while you are in Tennessee visiting a man you hated your whole life. It just doesn't all add up.

HE WORKED AT adjusting his mood before he got home. It did feel restricting, trying to play nice when he was angry at so many things. He was angry Shannon had gotten injured. Angry that she was naturally so understanding and compassionate towards his family, when he found it difficult to even think about them. Shannon was consumed by the baby, and although he expected this, he didn't expect that it would pick a scab with him. He felt invisible.

In the old days, before Shannon, a good old night of doing all kinds of things he'd regret the next morning was the call to order. But it was out of the question, and up until now, that had not appealed to him.

He told the Bensons he was going to take a short nap before dinner, retreating to the back bedroom where Courtney was sleeping. Looking down on the baby, he asked himself again why circumstances had taken Frankie, who was loved, cherished and honored by this family and by Shannon, and left him behind in the man's place. A reject. A raging war still brewing inside him. Full of flaws. He was unfamiliar with not being in control, worried about being good enough, deserving enough to be able to protect Shannon and his new daughter. Did Shannon deserve better? Was it right for him to reap the rewards someone else had sowed? Was this stealing?

He moved to the high-backed reading chair and let the mood wash over him. *We celebrate when we can, and we cry when we must.* It was just like the arena. The waiting was the worst.

Shannon entered the room with a basket of laundry.

"Whoa, T.J." She set the basket at her feet and knelt in front of him. "Where did you go?"

"Sorry, Shannon. I'm not doing this very well, am I?"

"Doing what?"

"I feel Frankie—" He had to stop because he didn't want to show her the depth of his darkness.

Shannon slipped onto his lap. Her easy demeanor usually lessened the burden, but tonight it annoyed him. He didn't want her pity.

"I feel Frankie all over this house too. His pictures from his Little League teams are still on their dresser. Our wedding pictures are in the hallway, did you notice?"

T.J. nodded. One of the first things he noticed was that. He remembered how he felt that day. He was focusing on trying to get laid, and still knew that Frankie was one of the luckiest men alive. And now she was *here* with *him*.

"I think your mom was right. I never should have gone to Nashville. I should have been here. Maybe we could have caught all those guys, and we wouldn't have to move or impose on the Bensons."

Shannon held his face between her palms. "Hey. T.J. This isn't you. Where is all this coming from? No one is saying those things except you. We don't know why things happen. You were honoring the request of a dying man, your father."

"Who was a prick and an asshole."

"But the important thing is that you did the honorable thing. I can't believe I'm hearing this." She stood, hands on her hips. "Is this the way you're going to be? Because if so—"

"Don't say it, Shannon."

"What? You mean I can't tell you the truth? After what we've all been through in these past two months? We have to start couching our communications around each other? We're not strong enough to face the facts?"

"That's unkind, and you know it." He was seething. He felt his anger was becoming directed at her. He felt as hopeless as the child he was in the woodshed. He couldn't solve the problem. He had to wait to do anything, and waiting was totally the pits. He hoped Shannon had the control to stop, because he wasn't sure he did.

"I'm not buying this, T.J. I'm not going to spend my whole life walking around on eggshells, pretending things are one way, when reality says it's another."

"Whose reality? Yours? Mine? The Bensons? Those assholes? My dear old dad?"

"You're confused."

"I'm *not* confused. I fuckin' know who I am and don't need you fuckin' telling me otherwise." His voice boomed and bounced off the walls, waking Courtney.

"Well, I hope you're satisfied." She turned her back to him and picked up the baby. On her way out of the room she delivered the kill shot. "You're not the only one who's lost someone, T.J. Man up."

He grabbed his car keys and stormed out of the Benson's house without saying a word. He got in his pickup, wanting to make a public display, to squeal down the road, but at the last minute remembered who he was and what he was really fighting.

And then he knew what he had to do.

# CHAPTER 34

THE BENSONS WERE understanding after hearing the argument, but clearly didn't know what to do. Shannon and T.J. hadn't really settled in. This loving couple had been delighted to spend so much time around the baby, and now T.J. was going to mess this all up.

She'd been telling herself she had to be strong, and all this nightmare would be over soon, but now she had serious doubts. Perhaps the attack in the hospital was the easy part. Maybe she and T.J. were not going to work out, and she'd go back to considering raising a child alone, back full circle from where she'd started a couple of months ago right after Frankie's death.

Mrs. Benson brought her a hot cup of herbal tea, which was a lifesaver. As soon as she took a sip, she felt her milk let down and Courtney nearly choked on the stream that came towards her.

"Thank you," she said to the kind woman.

"Used to work for me every time with Frankie. As a baby, he'd get so hungry and frustrated. The more he fussed, the tenser I became. Then of course the milk didn't come. It's always touch and go with your first, they say. You start worrying about everything."

"You're right. The little argument with T.J. didn't help either."

"It happens. You know, Joe even asked me after Frankie was about a month old if I still loved him. Can you imagine? Here I was trying to be the best mom, thinking I was doing all the right things, and I'd forgotten to let him know how special he was to me."

Shannon thought that was very good advice.

"He's probably trying to work out his grief at losing his father. It comes on in strange ways. We've certainly learned a bit about that. When you least expect it, something will—" She abruptly stopped and gave her a warm smile. "I'm sure everything will work out just fine."

Shannon wished she could feel as assured.

Courtney went down again, and the three of them ate dinner together without talking about T.J. Shannon was mulling their earlier words and grew more and more concerned she'd done irreparable damage to their relationship. She wanted to call him, but thought he'd feel chased. She decided she needed to trust him to come home soon.

Ollie and Rory stopped by the house looking for T.J.

"He left about an hour ago," she told them.

"That's when he tried calling us. You know where he went?"

"No. Sorry. He needed to do something. I'm not exactly sure what it was."

After the boys left, Shannon decided she would turn in early. She took a long hot shower and settled in to bed, reading herself to sleep.

Two hours later, T.J. awakened her, kneeling at her bedside. "Wake up, Shannon," he whispered.

She could smell alcohol on his breath as he tenderly kissed her.

"Come on honey, we have to talk." He picked her up out of the bed and sat with her across his lap in the reading chair. She found the shelter of that spot just below his chin where her head fit so well, the warmth radiating from his body along with the sound of his heart and the ebb and flow of his breathing.

She spoke to the top of his shirt, her forefinger tracing over his lower lip. "Where did you go?"

"I went over to the house. I got out Frankie's 30-year old whiskey we brought back from one of our cross-country trips and opened it. We were saving it for some special occasion."

"What's the special occasion?"

"Well, maybe I got ahead of myself." His fingers worked over the tension he felt in her shoulders, her upper spine. Hear me out, Shannon. And then you tell me."

She lay back against his chest as he began again. His raspy voice was something she could listen to forever.

"I was thinking about what was wrong with me. I have you. I have beautiful Courtney. My past is, well, behind me now. I have a sister. All the right parts are so right, and the wrong parts are gone. Except for this homegrown threat, which is real and considerable, everything about my life, our lives, is going well."

She snuggled closer to him and sighed. "Yes, T.J. we have it all."

"What happened in the hospital made me realize that anything can happen at anytime. We can't control it all. Ever. We try, we pay attention, but it's an illusion to think we can. We have to live with it."

She wasn't sure where he was going with this.

"And I've been fighting it, Shannon. I've been holding my breath and resisting this."

"Resisting what?"

"Taking life on life's terms." He squeezed her tightly. "I was waiting until the baby was born. Then waiting until we were settled here. And honey, I don't want to wait any longer. What if we all die tomorrow? I mean, Frankie taught us that."

She sat up and searched his face. She could see his full lips in the light of the moon and the reflection of light in his eyes. But she felt the warm arms that held her, the words that soothed her soul.

He fumbled through his pockets until she heard paper rustle. He brought out a small brown envelope not any larger than a couple of inches long. He slipped his fingers inside, and she saw him draw out a plain gold band and hold it to the moonlight. "This belonged to my mother, and is all I have, all I can give you from my family, from my past. But if you'll marry me, Shannon, it and everything else I am, everything else I own, is yours. Forever, honey."

She didn't have to think about it. She placed her finger into the ring opening, allowing him to slide it on. Then, clasping his hand, she said, "It would be my honor."


HE TOOK HIS time with her. The careful, gentle nourishment he gave her in bed was more than sex. She let him start slow, matching his actions with her own. Her touch mirrored his. As he kissed and caressed her delicate places, sending her on a mind-bending journey of passion, her fingers traveled over the scars and wounds of this warrior, tracing the tats she could not feel but knew were there. She kissed the invisible scars in his heart, loved the little abused boy and the brave man who never gave up hope even in the face of tragedy. She could give him everything he needed. Frankie's parents could be his parents. She and Courtney would be his family in every sense of the word, a better family, a family that would mirror the joy he brought to them.

She pushed on his shoulders and guided him to lie on his back. Mounting him, she lowered herself on to him slowly. Her hands braced against his upper torso, she ground her pelvis down slowly, watching his face in the moonlight, and feeling the delicious sensations of their joining. She rocked and angled her body back and forth on him, squeezing her muscles, enjoying every inch of him deep inside her. She watched his eyes sparkle and non-verbally let him know how much she loved and cherished him.

Their lovemaking was a sacrament. She felt her heart would forever be the sanctuary of his soul.

His lips on fire muffled her cries. He waited for her explosion, before he plundered her deep, lodging himself until he began to spill, holding her so close she could barely breathe. He loved her with everything he had, and she knew that she would willingly take all the intensity, even the pain sometimes, and claim it for her own.

She asked him for more lovemaking during the night, not able to get enough of him. She held up her hand with the ring shining in the midnight light and he kissed it, as he kissed the palm of her other hand where she'd been cut.

"You are my warrior princess. Nobody should mess with you," he whispered.

"Except you. I want you to mess with me. Promise it will be like this every night?"

He chuckled. "I'm not Superman."

"Yes, you are. We'll train together."

"I like that kind of training."

EARLY IN THE morning, before the sun rose, Courtney needed another feeding. T.J. changed her very wet diaper and brought her into bed with them. He watched as the little mouth latched onto Shannon's breast, while his fingers laced through her hair. He rubbed her temples.

"So beautiful. I am the luckiest man in the world," he said.

"To me, you are the *only* man in the world."

# CHAPTER 35

T J. GOT UP at sunrise, slipped on some pajama bottoms and tiptoed quietly into the kitchen to brew some coffee. Movement outside got his attention, and he saw two men dart into the yard of the neighbors across the street. They were holding semi-automatics.

He grabbed the landline and dialed Kyle.

"I got two men outside the Benson house, I think with AKs."

"Shit. I'll see who I can get on the way. Be there in ten. Hang on."

"Roger that one, big time."

He woke the Bensons from the master bedroom, who quickly made it into Shannon's room. T.J. threw her a pair of his pajamas while she grabbed his shirt from last night from the floor.

"I only saw two, but there could be more. You guys stay in here and wait." He pulled a SigSauer from his duty bag, pulled the hammer back and handed it to Joe Benson. "If you have to. You got twenty-one chances."

"Right," he answered.

"This door is no cover, so move the chair in front of you, or use the mattress if you have to. Do not let anyone in here unless they knock four times, got it?"

"Got it." Benson said.

"That means shoot them through the door if it starts to open without it."

"Got it." But T.J. could see Joe's hands shake and hoped the man wouldn't shoot himself first.

He grabbed his H&K and kissed Shannon. "Try to keep her quiet. She's gonna freak if she hears gunfire."

He closed the bedroom door and wondered why they hadn't come in the middle of the night, when the element of surprise would have helped them.

Hiding just inside the second bedroom, which would be out of the line of fire if they came from either front or back, he texted Kyle:

*Family, closed door. Your ETA?*
*Here. Got 3 more.*
*!!*

Just then, he heard glass breaking and knew they were already in the house.

*Glass broken in kitchen.*

At the sound of movement in the kitchen, he knew they'd come in through the garage. Checking the windows in the bedroom, he did not see movement. He heard the staccato of a Middle Eastern tongue and decided the two were together in the kitchen.

*Conf 2 Cajuns.*
*We're coming from the rear. Armani front.*

He stored his phone, adjusted his grip on the H&K short barrel he'd brought with him, and readied himself. A dark shadow crossed the end of the hallway, just as he saw Armando on the outside run forward. If he was planning on a front door breach, T.J. would not have the shot he wanted or he'd hit his own guy. He'd have to wait for instructions.

One gunman dressed in a black headdress but wearing sneakers and blue jeans came down the hallway, causing one of the floorboards in the old house to groan, and he stopped. T.J. saw the shadow form outside his door and couldn't risk a peek. The door moved slightly so he blasted through it chest-height and heard the drop of a body and retreating footsteps.

Courtney screamed, revealing the family location.

Hearing glass crunch in the kitchen he guessed the gunman was headed back to the garage area but he couldn't risk a shot. Nothing was moving on the other side of the door. Just then, the front door shattered in an explosive charge. Mere seconds later he heard the staccato of gunfire and a few seconds later heard the word, *"Clear!"*

He was never so happy in his life to hear that word. Opening the door, he checked the body in front of him and confirmed he was shot through the heart.

"Not so fast, you dog," a voice said from the master bedroom behind T.J. "You will drop your weapon."

T.J. tried to turn.

"Now! You will drop your weapon now!" And then the gunman addressed whoever was in the kitchen. "I have your man. You will surrender, or I put a bullet in his brain."

T.J. was still crouching, and he knew the gunman's sole interest was to carry out the mission and probably not to take prisoners. He didn't buy the stall. As the seconds ticked by, and he heard the man back down the hallway toward the closed door of his family's hiding place, T.J. inhaled and yelled as loud as he could, "High."

Armando's kill shot hit him in the middle of his nose, and his head exploded. T.J. scrambled to the back room to make sure there weren't any others.

"Clear," he shouted.

Armando's smiling face appeared in the hallway.

"Way to lie low, Talbot."

"Roger that. Knew you could make that shot."

"With my eyes closed."

T.J. stood up, knocked four times on the door and then stepped in.

Joe Benson had been holding the gun out in front of him and was so rigid with fear that when T.J. entered he kept the gun aimed at him.

"Whoa, there, Joe. I'm one of the good guys, remember?"

Joe sighed, dropped his arms and his shoulders, and nearly collapsed. T.J. took the Sig away from him, and uncocked the hammer so he wouldn't shoot himself in the leg.


POLICE AND RESCUE squads descended all over the house. Kyle and the others retreated and disappeared. Armando had to stay, as did T.J. Their liaison, Collins, as well as other Navy personnel showed up to run interference and guarantee neither of the two SEALs were exposed to the public. It was decided the attack would be classified a robbery stopped at gunpoint by a sharp-thinking retired carpenter who happened to be pretty good with a gun.

Lined with tears, Shannon looked exhausted. Of course, Courtney was nursing and didn't seem to be affected by the sea of activity around her. Mrs. Benson attempted to bring coffee and water to the investigators and crew who had shown up. She tried to engage the services of her husband, but Joe appeared to be in shock still. T.J. sat him down.

"Joe, you did real good, there."

"Man, I'm sure glad I didn't have to shoot that thing. I'm not sure I would have."

"Trust me, you would have. The way you looked at me and pointed it right at my chest, you would have. Just took you awhile to register who I was, but you were ready."

"I could never do what you do, T.J."

"You would if you had to, and you would have tonight. But you didn't have to, and that's what we're all about." He draped his arm around the man he would forevermore consider his father. "Frankie was right there with you. He's jumping up and down in heaven, Joe. Believe me, he is."

That brought a smile to Benson's face.

The local police were able to control the two news vans that showed up at the scene and worked to keep a wide perimeter of neighbors.

Collins brought T.J. two yellow ponchos so they could exit as part of the rescue squad. They concluded their questioning, Collins observing everything. "I'm afraid I can't have you leave with the family. It just would draw too many questions. They'll be here awhile and I'm going to sit in on Benson's interview, make sure the story goes the way it should."

"Only guy I'm worried about is that prick from the FBI who interviewed me yesterday."

"May not be able to keep you away from him, but I'll try. Now you and Armando go crash at his place and get some rest. I'll get the family over there as soon as I can, okay?"

T.J. put on his yellow rubber slicker and looked for Shannon, who was changing Courtney.

"You did great, sweetheart," he said as he wrapped his arm around her waist. Shannon collapsed into his chest. With one hand on Courtney and the other arm squeezing the love of his life, he propped her up until her sobs ended.

"I'm so grateful, T.J. I'm—"

"You guys were troopers. You got nerves of steel, Shannon. I'm gonna need that in the months and years to come, honey. You're my rock.

"Dad was—"

"Awesome," he interrupted. "He was freakin' awesome."

She chuckled. "He was kind of, wasn't he? I thought he was going to shoot you." That brought a smile to her face.

"I think you would have jumped him, rather than let that happen," he joked. "You're tough, babe. Really tough. You guys kept your wits about you. That's what it takes."

"And training."

"There is that."

"Do you think this will end it?" She picked up Courtney and held her against her shoulder, patting her back.

T.J. didn't want to answer, but he had to be honest with her. "No. Unfortunately, no. But I think this group is done, for now. I think we can expect more. I'm going to have to wait to see. Might be they relocate me to an East Coast team, but the Navy's got their work cut out for them. Getting this close to our families is going to be something they're going to have to look at.

She smoothed his cheek with her right hand. "Thank you, T.J. for coming into our lives. You kept your promise to Frankie. You protected me and Courtney. I love you."

Armani and Collins interrupted their long kiss at the doorway.

"Gotta go, Talbot," Collins' voice was curt and efficient.

T.J. kissed Shannon one more time quickly and then addressed her, "I'm going to slip out with Armani, and we'll meet up later at his house. Collins here is the man you want if you have any questions. He'll be here when they formally interview Joe and Gloria. He'll make sure you get to where you're supposed to be without the news media or nosey neighbors getting in the way.

"Right."

"Okay, then."

It was hard to leave them behind, but for their best interests and for the circumstances, it was their only option. As he made his way toward a waiting unmarked van, next to the Puerto Rican sharpshooter, he discovered something else about himself.

The anger and anguish he'd been feeling before he'd gone over to the house, before he'd given the ring to Shannon, before the gunfight, was completely gone. He knew it was something he'd be dealing with his whole life, but one huge problem had been solved.

Shannon said it earlier.

*You kept your promise to Frankie.*

# CHAPTER 36

T J. WAS DRESSED in a tux and felt like a stuffed penguin. Kyle, Armando, Tyler and Fredo were beside him as they watched the last of the attendees filter into the little chapel. Green leafy vines covered the side of the building, with a large terrace at the back where the reception was going to be held. Sounds of birds echoed throughout the mostly stucco surface of the Spanish-style complex.

It wasn't the grand, lavish wedding Shannon had the first time, but it was what she wanted, and T.J. was grateful for that.

Cindy, Shannon's former maid of honor, flounced by wearing a bright blue dress, on the arm of another SEAL T.J. recognized from one of the other Teams. She twiddled her fingers at him with a sultry smirk.

*And I'm not even slightly interested.* But he winked for her benefit, and gave her a warm smile anyway. Fredo, Kyle, Armando and Tyler followed the two women until they disappeared into the church. It was just what they always did. No one said a word.

Mrs. Moore was to be escorted to the front row, and that was T.J.'s responsibility. Though it would normally be his best man's duty, T.J. had insisted it be his job. She appeared before him, looking wound up tight but gorgeous. He noticed she smiled at him a lot more, which gladdened his heart. Maybe the truce they'd called during the wedding planning would work after all.

"Why, Mrs. Moore, you look absolutely divine," he said as he bowed in her direction.

"Glad to see you haven't taken off for Alaska," she said and winked at him. T.J. could clearly see where Shannon got her fiery spirit.

"Never. I messed up Shannon's first wedding. I won't mess up the second. I promise."

She dazzled him with her smile, her eyes filling with tears, just the way Shannon's did when she was overwhelmed by emotion. "I know I can count on that promise."

The groomsmen each punched T.J. in the arm and went ahead to stand at their places in the front of the chapel. Organ music wafted through the hallways and mixed with the sounds of the birds. He would always remember this as a perfect day. He was going to be stepping into a role he had never had before, to complete a mission he was made for.

He took Mrs. Moore's arm and accompanied her toward the entrance to the chapel. Mr. Moore appeared out of nowhere and stood behind him. T.J. turned, and they shook hands.

"Son," he said, "I'm very proud you're marrying my daughter. Nothing could please me more."

As he escorted Shannon's mom down the aisle, he looked at his side of the church. They'd talked about someone else standing in for his parents, but T.J. told everyone to leave those seats vacant. Joe and Gloria Benson defied his edict and stood tall in the front row anyway, next to his sister Connie. He brought Mrs. Moore to her seat and stopped to give her a warm kiss on the cheek. "You're beautiful, just like your daughter," he whispered.

Mrs. Moore straightened for a second, her eyes darting up to his face, unsure about the compliment, but then he could see her insides melt. Something else was on the tip of her tongue, but she tempered it. "Thank you," she breathed back to him softly.

T.J. took his place next to Tyler, held his hands together and winked at his sister.

The audience began rustling as the music changed and everyone turned to see the vision of Shannon, standing in the same wedding dress she'd worn before. He was surprised and wondered about the protocol of this. He remembered that day, how Frankie had fallen and her bodice had been pulled down. He blushed and cleared his throat as he relived that memory.

Whatever possessed her to wear the same dress?

Looking at Mrs. Moore, he caught her wink at him. This had been her suggestion, he realized.

But as he watched her lightly drift down the burgundy carpet towards him, a proud Mr. Moore on her arm, he saw that yes, this was the perfect choice. He was stepping into the role that had been created for him. He was on a path that had been blazed for him, part of the tradition he'd always shunned, veered away from. As a SEAL, he was following the brotherhood of those who had fought before him, some of whom had perished. He wasn't independent of them, he was *part* of them. The living and the ones who had passed on.

As it should be.

Shannon stood before him as Mr. Moore gave him her hand. He kissed her palm, the one with the now-healed scar in the center. Her eyes were glistening, her breathing ragged. "I am the luckiest man in the world."

She slipped her fingers into his hair and shook her head. "I wish you could kiss me right now."

"Very well." He pulled up her veil, and, completely without regard to protocol, pulled her to him and kissed her, as she exploded in his arms. They listened to the crowd titter, but he didn't care. He could see she didn't care either. He kept his hands around the small of her back and no lower, but damn, he wanted to.

Just as he had the day of Frankie's wedding, though it was so inconvenient, he was getting a hard on. *It's the dress.* Something about all the flouncy, crinkling material flowing everywhere. It brought out the familiar wild side of him.

The minister cleared his throat, and again a ripple of laughter waved through the audience.

"I guess I should get you properly wed before I get you out of this dress," he whispered. She remained in his arms, waiting for him to take the lead. She'd have stood there half a day if he wanted, and he loved that about her.

"You can take your time, I understand you're a special operator, and I'm going to let you special me all you want."

"Let's get you mine, legally. I don't want you slipping away on me."

"Never going to happen, T.J."

The crowd was laughing now heartily. Several Hooyas enthusiastically gave him encouragement. He turned to the audience and gave them a thumbs up, and several returned his gesture.

"I'm ready now," he said to the minister, whose face showed a mixture of concern and amusement.

"Good. Okay, ladies and gentlemen …"

But T.J. had kept his arms around Shannon as she leaned in all her perfumed glory against him, her breasts pressing against his biceps. He matched her breathing, as they stared into each others eyes at several places during the reading of the canon. The minister had to interrupt their gazing for the presentation of the rings.

For the second time in his life, he slipped his mother's ring on Shannon's finger, looking over at his sister. Connie immediately lowered her chin and could not look back at him. Shannon was now his for all eternity with the pronouncement. Her veil was already tucked back from her head. He lifted his hands to cup her face and spoke, "If you can find it in your heart to love me a tenth of the amount I love you, you'll make me a happy man, eternally."

Their kiss was brief. Shannon wanted to say something, "T.J. you are the man I was always destined to be with. My heart is filled to bursting. I'll be here for you forever."

T.J. picked her up and whispered, "Honey, I hope you don't mind, but I've got the biggest hard-on I've ever had, and I need some cover."

She threw her head back and laughed. "Perfect. Don't ever change, T.J."

"Not to worry, baby."

He carried her down the aisle, as he winked and she waved to faces in the audience. He continued carrying her down the brown tiled floor to the minister's office, which was locked. Still with Shannon in his arms, he found a Sunday school room open and slipped inside.

His hands were all over her, first pulling down the bodice to expose her breasts. He knelt and suckled them, at the same time reached under her white skirts and found she was not wearing underwear.

"How did you know?"

"I was hoping. And I liked the feel of walking down the aisle without them on."

"You're a wicked bride."

"I am that. So wickedly in love with you."

He sat her on a countertop, brushing the contents aside.

"Hurry," she whispered as he began unzipping his pants.

All he could do was fumble. He'd never had so much trouble with his zipper in his life. Then it got stuck in the fabric of the front closure.

"Fuck!" he said.

"Please, yes."

"No, I mean, the zipper is stuck."

"Let me." She squeezed his package, massaging lower, pushing his hands away. Her fingers deftly found the zipper, untangled the fabric from the teeth as she pulled the device down slowly and her hands found his shaft. "Ah, there we are, T.J." She slipped his trousers over his thighs.

She guided him to her entrance, and he at last felt her moist folds around him as he squeezed her buttocks, pulling her onto him.

SHANNON WAS NOT going to leave his side. She didn't want to dance with anyone else, but in the end she caved and socialized. She watched him from behind as he talked to his Teammates. She watched how delicately he treated her mother. He even danced with his sister.

She was happy that at last they would be able to move forward together.

Joe Benson asked her for a dance. "I think I am just as happy today."

Shannon's eyes filled with tears. "He would be happy for me, for all of us, Dad."

Benson looked down and lost his timing for a second, stepping on her gown, and apologized. "I think he would. Gloria and I have no regrets, Shannon. None."

At last she was able to dance with her handsome groom. T.J. swung her around the room with the practiced composure of a professional dancer, and it surprised her.

"You've been practicing," she said.

"Sophia's dance lessons. Secret stealth mission."

"Ah, I see. And what else have you been practicing?"

"You'll just have to wait, Mrs. Talbot. That has taken a lifetime of planning. I may have to do a lot of practice, but I plan on becoming absolute master and commander."

"Counting on it. And I'll be your second in command."

Thank you for reading SEAL's Promise. If you'd like to continue with the Bad Boys of SEAL Team 3 series, won't you pick up SEAL My Home? It's Book 2 in this popular series. Or, you can pick up the Big Bad Boy Bundle, which has all three of the Bad Boys books in it. And if you're an audio book lover, you can get the audio book of this bundle, as well as all my other bundles and series books on Audible. It's 22 hours of listening fun!

Now, stay tuned for Lucas, inspired by visiting my son as a newby SEAL, living with three older SEALs, a couple of them married with children. Juggling multiple child support payments and divorces, these older guys were sometimes a good example to a younger newbie tadpole of what *not* to do. But, all of them find their happily ever after, one by one.

Enjoy Band of Bachelors: Lucas!

# LUCAS

**Band of Bachelors**
**Book 1**

SHARON HAMILTON

# CHAPTER 1

L UCAS WOKE UP with the sun slicing daggers of light into his eyes.
*Fuck me.*

He rolled over to shield his face from the bright morning and fell off the couch, right onto his tailbone.

*Goddamit.* The sharp pain added to the bruise he'd already created from previous sleepless nights. His ass had made divots between the second and third cushions of the sectional, which was as equally uncomfortable to sit on. The couch's grey scratchy fabric was Scotchguarded, making his back and balls itch. His buddies on SEAL Team 3 had picked up this wonderful piece of *loungery* for two hundred bucks four months back. The San Diego Goodwill had been so happy to get rid of it, they gave the team the matching loveseat without charging a penny extra.

From the floor, Lucas stared eye-level at the hunk of junk he'd battled with all night long and knew it would still go up like a torch regardless of the Scotchguard. As he pulled his body up, the matching loveseat veering off to the right gaped at him, its bent footrests looking like huge gumless jaws. The thing was laughing at him.

It was nothing like his king-size bed with the Egyptian cotton sheets at home—the home he'd been kicked out of a month prior. He hadn't expected to have to sleep on his buddies' couch this long. When he'd first been shown the door, he hadn't been too worried, convinced Connie would soon change her mind and invite him back.

He'd envisioned that 'welcome home' party every day and night, in spite of the fact that his last vision of her was of her screaming at the top of her lungs, those delicious blue veins at the sides of her neck protruding like they were fat, blue birthday candles. His sobbing three-year-old daughter stood next to her mother, burying her face in Connie's thigh as the toddler screamed in her arms. It broke Lucas' heart to see his wife clutch the baby, his horror-filled expression showing fear and confusion.

That was one shitty day, but he knew in his heart of hearts that at any time, she'd soften and he'd be back home, in their bed, sliding against her smooth thighs and kissing the place between her legs, making her scream his name. Oh, he was the candy man, all right. His dick got hard just thinking about it. She'd never had a man go down on her before they got together. She'd been a good Catholic girl, and the nuns had filled her head with stories of how the germs from his hot tongue would poison her womb.

*As if they knew.*

His arousal meant only one thing: he'd have to finish it in the shower or he wouldn't be able to get his jeans on without pain.

Someone swung open one of the four bedroom doors with enough force they nearly ripped it off its hinges. "What the fuck just happened?" asked Jake, his mop of black hair sticking straight up like an unclipped Mohawk. "We just have an earthquake, Lucas?"

Lucas grimaced. "No, that would be my ass hitting the ground."

"Would you quit that? You'll wake up the whole fuckin' household."

Lucas stood in his shorts, bare-chested and barefoot. He inclined his head to the side, arms outstretched, palms up as if listening for the complaints—which didn't materialize—from the other three rooms. "And your point is?" Lucas asked, after a few seconds of silence.

"Geez, Lucas, would you put your fire hose away? I've seen it, re-member?" Jake pointed to Lucas' groin.

Standing at full attention, Lucas' *unit* had found freedom from the hole in his American flag shorts and was ready to par-tay. He quickly tucked it back in, but it popped out again. That time, he turned his back to Jake, properly stowed his cannon, then whipped around to find that Jake had disappeared back into his room.

Only two of the bedrooms had their own private bath with a shower, since the guest bath only contained a toilet with a cracked seat and a sink. Lucas didn't want to wake anyone else up, so he headed for the half bath, looking forward to perhaps working on his aim while studying the raunchy posters pinned up all around the little room. They didn't have to worry about entertaining females in the men's club of an apartment, since most of the SEALs who lived there had sworn off any women, except professionals who would definitely not be looking at the posters.

He washed his hands twice, feeling more relaxed, then padded into the kitchen to make some coffee. He covered the coffee grinder with a towel to muffle the sound and inhaled the only luxury the boys allowed themselves: fresh ground coffee.

He paused his musing to glare at the coffee pot, performing its death gurgle. He surveyed his temporary 'home sweet home'. The garbage can was overflowing—even the recycle side—with beer bottles, pizza boxes, and half-gallon plastic orange juice containers. A wet bath sheet and t-shirt hung over an old, paint-splattered folding chair, one of four, surrounding a square card table with coffee rings stained into it. Their big-screen TV sat on top of two pallets they'd hauled from the dumpster. The light beige rug was mostly *dark* beige from oil, food, and coffee stains, and one plate-sized red stain from someone's Hawaiian Punch spilled a week back. They'd been trying to clean up each little accident, until the punch mishap. After that, they understood that when they deployed, they'd not get their deposit back on the apartment. Ryan said they might even owe the landlord something.

*Look at me...already considering myself part of this sorry band of bachelors.*

Lucas chastised himself for even considering this to be the case. He'd be out of there so fast it would take them a couple of days to miss him.

*Sorry-assed sailors.* Unlike his Connie, the bachelor frogs had only themselves to blame for their poor choices. Jake had children littered all over the world, just like their old pal, Gunny, who used to own the gym they all trained at. He wasn't exactly sure how many he'd fathered, but knew it would take two hands to count.

The coffee pot began to shut down, as he took stock of his friends.

Cory Brown was a preacher's son, way too trusting, and had started dating girls from his father's church after high school, until several parents complained he was deflowering the future generation of Sunday school teachers. And then he knocked one up, and that was it. Reverend Brown made sure the right thing happened. That marriage didn't last more than a month after the baby was born, and then Cory was being sued for child support that would take over half his pay, including his SEAL bonus.

Ryan and Alex got married in a double ceremony in Las Vegas, and had similar stories of woe.

No, none of them had spent much time finding a fine, quality girl like Connie. Yes, she was a bit hotheaded, but Lucas kind of liked it when she got steamed up, as long as it was something he could wiggle his way out of. The unfortunate bachelor party in Vegas was the last straw, though. And the stripper he'd had his photograph taken with turned out to be a transvestite, not that it made any difference to Connie. Lucas had been hoping it would.

But all that would be over soon.

He turned off the coffee maker, poured himself a cup, added a shot glass full of real Half and Half and walked out onto the deck overlooking the valley below and Coronado Island in the distance. He considered getting the boys up because a Specialist from Virginia was coming to do some training with them, even though it was Saturday. The military didn't observe weekends if the upcoming mission was urgent. This one apparently was.

Below him in the parking lot, a sweet brunette in an impossibly tight, short skirt stepped out of a cherry-red VW convertible. She looked up at him, shielding her eyes with one hand and slinging her large bag over her shoulder with the other. Lucas straightened himself up and sucked in his gut, smiling as her gaze found him and gave him an appreciative perusal.

He told himself it wasn't really a bad thing. One thing to look, another to, well, partake. He didn't want to blow his chances of sliding back into Connie's expensive silk sheets, or being buried deep inside her sweet little jellyroll. But looking was okay. He'd just not chat her up. So he waved.

Her grin was fine. She looked like the kind of girl who had all manner of dirty little thoughts. She licked her lips, straightened her upper torso and smoothed over her tummy and hips with those palms of hers. One wrist had a charm bracelet that tinkled in the distance. Without an invitation, she headed straight for the entrance to the upper floors, right below him.

*Holy hotness. Did she think I invited her up?*

Inside, he found Ryan, Alex and Cory up and showered, making a barefoot line in the kitchen like old men at a rescue mission.

"I say strawberry waffles before we head over to the base," said Cory as he poured his coffee.

"Ask them to leave the whipped cream can this time," said Ryan.

Jake exited from his bedroom, followed by a cloud of steam, matching the shirtless wonders in the kitchen.

Cory nearly spit out his mug of Joe. "Dayum, Shipley. Good thing we're not shooting this morning. I'm going to be shaking for a week," barked Cory.

"Use more cream," was Lucas' answer. "Hey, guys, you know anything about this Thom guy? He's some kind of security expert?"

"Something to do with a little pod of terrorists they encountered over in Mosul." Alex sat down on the floor, back straight against the wall, his feet out in front of him. Ryan soon joined him.

"Kyle said they've got information the group plans to do something here in California. A retaliation," added Jake.

"Helluva thing to do on a Saturday, haul us in there," said Cory.

"What the fuck difference does it make?" Jake wrinkled his nose and forehead. "Not like I've got a date."

Lucas snorted. "Oh, so you call those hookups 'dates' now? You really go on dates, Jake? Man, I must be rubbing off on you."

"You should talk." Alex and Ryan were punching each other in the arm, which escalated into a coffee fight. Alex continued, caramel-colored liquid dripping off his chin. "Don't see you dating anytime soon, shit-face."

Lucas hated the fact that his last name had taken the ugly moniker ever since the unfortunate bachelor party he didn't remember.

"Geez. I hang around you guys too much and I might stop believing in true love."

Lucas was pelted with coffee, one of the SEALs throwing the ceramic mug itself, which hit him at bicep level.

"Okay, okay. I get it. It's just that I'm not ready to give up on my marriage like you guys. I may not have as many kids as you do, Jake, and I may only have known her a little bit longer than you two knew your wives, Groves and Kowicki, but I *definitely* know how to fuckin' use a condom, Cory—*especially* if I'm gonna screw a girl in the back of my father's sanctuary."

"Hallelujah, praise the Lord," someone shouted.

"A fuckin' religious experience, I call it," Jake said as he high-fived Cory.

"See, that's where you guys go wrong. You don't treat women with respect."

No one said a word. Then the unofficial spokesman for the group, Jake, inserted his opinion. "So, if you feel like you don't fit in, why don't you fuckin' leave?"

The silence that followed made Lucas nervous. He could sense more than a couple of his buddies felt he'd crossed the line. There were some hurt feelings they often didn't verbalize, but he sure could feel it. He knew he had to be careful.

"You don't know a damned thing until you've really walked around in another man's shoes. Or, in Cory's case, his high heels." Lucas delivered it straight and for just one second he thought he'd made thing worse.

But then the catcalls began, which was a signal things were returning to normal. Lucas relaxed enough to apologize and make it sound like he meant it. And he did. The doorbell buzzed.

"You know," said Jake, who walked over to Lucas and fist-bumped him, "you're probably right. You're the one who's gonna make it in this relationship game. For us assholes, well, I think we're pretty much fucked."

All of them laughed.

The doorbell buzzed again twice this time, and Cory jogged over and opened it. Lucas couldn't hear anything but a sweet voice asking if she could talk to Lucas. He didn't know how, but he just knew it belonged to the lady in the red VW. *She knows my name?* He was flattered, until he remembered his situation, and Connie.

"Sure, come right in, ma'am," Cory offered, showing her the way with his arm.

Her bright red lips were the same color as the VW. She had the whole ladybug thing going on—with her black skirt, the black and white polka-dot blouse that was a bit sheer, showing him she wore bright white, lacy underthings—his personal favorite. She kept her knees together as she carefully stepped over their dirty carpet, her spiked heels making her balance a little difficult. She extended her hand with the charm bracelet softly clinking, and he extended his.

"Holy crap, Shipley, you've been holding out on us," someone said. The team separated and gave Lucas and the girl space like a drop of oil in water.

"So, you're Lucas Shipley," she said sweetly, and then gave him a devilish smile that made his shorts erupt.

He nodded nervously as she shifted her bag, which had fallen off her shoulder.

"Excuse me," she said as she extracted her hand and unzipped her purse. Bringing out a large white envelope, she didn't give him time to stop admiring her shapely form.

"You've been served."

# CHAPTER 2

MARCY GELLAND LOOKED over at the woman who was ending her marriage of five years. Connie Shipley was initialing and signing where the little orange arrows indicated. It wasn't easy, Marcy knew, to just wash your hands of a marriage, especially a marriage with property and children. She saw how resolute Connie was, how firmly she pressed, signing her name with a big script flourish like she was autographing a bestseller in front of a crowd of people. The baby was trying to grab her pen, then her hair, the top of her dress, her earrings, but still Connie persisted, gently peeling back his chubby hands. Her young daughter was coloring with felt-tipped pens on the dark blue carpet at her feet.

She knew there would come a time during the process when Connie would wonder if she was doing the right thing. That was always the risk in taking on real estate listings where the couple was divorcing. One moment they hated each other, then the next they were doing the hot and dirty on the kitchen floor. She'd worked with couples who started out being adversaries, requiring her to take a neutral stance. But if one of them wanted to keep the marriage together, it was a fifty-fifty chance that party would prevail, and then suddenly representing them became impossible. Harder still were the cases when the house had already sold, and the buyers were looking forward to moving in.

But as she watched Connie with the paperwork and discussed the numbers with her, Marcy had the impression the woman was completely sure of her decision.

"So, when can I get Lucas' signature?" Marcy asked the attractive blonde Navy wife as she bounced her baby on her knee.

"Sorry. That's your job, Marcy. I'm hoping he'll cooperate, but I'm not sure."

"So you are the one forcing this, then?"

The baby was fussing. Connie drew a bottle from the large satchel under the table and unceremoniously stuffed the nipple in the baby's mouth. "Excuse me. What did you ask?" She frowned, bouncing the youngster.

"It was *your* decision to sell everything off, then? Did you try to work it out, go to counseling?"

Connie gave her a look she knew quite well. Her half-lidded eyes told her she was tired of trying to explain it, even to herself. "Not sure whose great idea it was to post the pictures of the SEAL bachelor party online, but it was irrefutable evidence."

"Ah." Marcy studied her. She decided to let it go without asking for further clarification. "But he won't be surprised, I guess."

Mrs. Shipley laughed, tossing back her head. The baby's arm had traveled down Connie's shirt, between her breasts, while his other hand fisted his blond curls at the temples. That's when Marcy saw an anchor tat on Connie's right breast, and underneath the anchor was the name *Lucas*, written in fancy script. She wondered what Connie would do to cover up or alter that message.

"I'm pretty sure he expected to be invited back. But I don't think it was me he wanted. Just my bed." Connie followed the comment by raising her right eyebrow and giving Marcy a sultry look.

Marcy sensed it was not a good idea to pry any further, but she did need some help getting the listing contract signed.

Connie put the empty bottle back in the diaper bag and put the baby over her shoulder. Marcy thought she handled the little one with callused indifference, as she lifted him up and down against her shoulder and chest until they heard a gargantuan burp followed by sounds of spillage.

"Dammit," Connie said as she stood up, handed the baby to Marcy, and then retrieved a cotton cloth from the bag, wiping her neck and shoulder, her front, and her back. Then she wiped down the chair and dabbed the carpet.

Marcy had never held a baby before, so she continued to grip him under his armpits as the blue-eyed cherub stared back, then promptly spit-up clotted milk, which dripped down his chin and soaked into his cotton t-shirt.

Connie came to her side, taking away the baby before the smelly liquid fell on Marcy. "Did he get you wet? Oh, Marcy, I'm so sorry," she said, holding out her cloth.

"He's got a bunch of stuff—," but before Marcy could complete her sentence, Connie had eliminated the evidence.

"Look, next is going to be a huge explosion," Connie said as she patted the baby's underside, "and you don't want to be around for that one. So I've got about two minutes." She fished out a card and handed it to Marcy. "Here's his cell phone, but the email no longer works. He's getting something else set up, since he no longer lives at the house."

"Gotcha. So I should call him?"

"Yes. Now, let me just tell you a couple of quick things and then—" Connie sniffed in the baby's diaper area—"so far so good. I feel like I should warn you: do not believe a word the man says. He's a sweet talker, and he might even come onto you, you know, try to seduce you so you'll go easy on him?"

"Oh, not to worry, Connie. Besides, I have a boyfriend," Marcy lied.

"Well, that doesn't matter one whit to him. I could tell you stories. I got tired of being all alone and scared to death while he was overseas. And then when he came home, he either wanted to screw day and night or he wouldn't want to do anything. He'd just watch TV. The kids would be screaming, and he'd be near comatose. I needed a big fuckin' break. I'd been stuck with them for months sometimes and here he couldn't help out, lift a finger."

Marcy was filled with compassion for the woman who felt abandoned, tied down with kids she was responsible for raising nearly on her own. Whatever glue had held this marriage together was gone.

"Then there was the staying out late, drinking with the guys—Marcy, he was hanging out more with them than with me. If he didn't have some bar thing to go to, some fuckin' *Macho Brotherhood* thing to do, he was in bed." She wiped a tear from her cheek. "Those guys are always getting married, divorced, their ladies leaving them. It's all just one excuse to Par-Tay. And he's got these loser friends who have messed up their marriages, too. They're a bad influence on him."

Marcy had gotten the picture minutes ago, but Connie seemed hell-bent on smashing her points in with a dull knife. "What about counseling?" she asked.

"Counseling? Those guys don't do that. Deathly afraid someone will label them as unstable and they'll lose their precious Trident. He didn't like to talk about feelings, especially *my* feelings. He was like, 'So, join a gym, or why not take up a hobby, like quilting or gardening.'" Connie rolled her eyes. "I mean, really? I'm trying to raise two kids all by myself, and he was streaking out there clear across the world from me, and doing who knows what that he couldn't talk about. Marcy, it was all just too much."

Like it was an exclamation mark to Connie's speech, they both heard the explosion in the baby's diaper. Those big blue eyes looked to Marcy as if she had an answer for him.

Marcy wrinkled her nose at the smell. "What do you need?"

"I need to get my life back. I need a nanny."


AFTER CONNIE LEFT, Marcy gave the SEAL a call. She heard loud music in the background, some whistles and "Oh yeah, yeah, baby." Marcy knew Lucas Shipley was at some sort of strip club.

"Hallo?" The husky, inebriated voice boomed in her ear.

"Is this Lucas Shipley?" she asked timidly.

"Who the fuck wants to know? You drive a red Volkswagen?"

"Pardon?"

"It's a simple question," he slurred. "Do you fuckin' drive a red Volkswagen? Inquiring minds want to know, darlin'. You might as well jump on in with the good news. Everyone else has."

"No."

A loud cheer went up as she heard a female voice in the background. The bump and grind music was so loud, the phone was beginning to cut out.

"Hello, baby. You have a fine ass." His sexy whisper was barely audible.

"Excuse me?" Marcy's back straightened as she felt the jolt travel down her spine.

"Ah, fuck, honey. I'm hanging up the phone right now." He whispered to Marcy, "'Excuse me, it's been nice, but I gotta go." She heard him shout out to the stripper, "No! Baby, don't go!"

The line went dead.

Marcy nearly threw her phone against the wall. It was all the evidence she needed to be totally convinced Connie Shipley was indeed doing the right thing for herself and her young family. She could completely understand why she wanted to separate from this scumbag of a husband.

Marcy was going to help her make him pay.

# CHAPTER 3

T HE MORNING BEGAN just like it always did. Lucas fell off the couch.
Behind Jake's closed door, Lucas heard, "Fuck!" Climbing back onto
the scratchy couch, he tried to bury his head under his pillow as Jake let
loose a string of invectives. That started another SEAL yelling at him, and
then Cory swung open his door and came running out so fast, Lucas
thought he was going to get thrown over the balcony.

"Would you fuckin' quit this shit, Lucas? We gotta tie you to the so-
fa?"

"Maybe I should get a rollaway?"

Alex appeared right behind Cory with his eyes narrowing. "I think
you need to get yourself another crash pad, Lucas. It's clear this is a more
permanent arrangement—and you're becoming a pain in the ass. Around
here, sleeping in on Sunday mornings is sacred. *Sacred!* You need to find
yourself another king-sized bed somewhere, and fast."

Lucas thought about the night before. They'd dropped Thom off at
his hotel, but the SEAL from Virginia Beach couldn't walk, so they'd had
to carry him into the room. It had fallen to Lucas to fish the room key out
of the man's pants, and that wasn't pleasant at all.

He vaguely remembered Thom's wife calling. *Wait a minute.*

"Did Connie call?" he asked, sure someone's wife called. Or girlfriend. His mind was totally fuzzy.

He was about to ask the little crowd gathered again when the sound
of the coffee grinder jolted him harder than if he'd been hit in the eye
socket with a dull spear. Holding his ears with his palms did nothing to
stop the pain.

Lucas collapsed again and waited for silence.

"Check your phone, asshole," Jake barked. "Now, in addition to having you over here at no rent, out of the goodness of our hearts, you want us to be your answering service, as well?"

"Okay, fair enough," Lucas said as he checked his cell. "I don't recognize this number." He hesitated and decided to hit redial later. "So, on that other point, I'm willing to share in the rent. I can pay in advance, up front. Question is where do I sleep?"

The unanimous answer was, "Not in my room."

Jake stepped up to deliver the final ultimatum. "I think you're shit out of luck, sailor. You need to find some place permanent."

"I really think she's gonna change her mind. Something tells me she's just bluffing." Lucas thought about all those deployments he came home and all he wanted to do was stay in bed and screw. Connie wanted relief from the kids. Why didn't he see that? But Lucas was so damned happy to be alive, to be home, to be in his bed again with the woman who made him feel terrific, when she was into it, he thought she'd be just as into him. Wasn't that what she missed all the time he was away? He couldn't figure her out. He was, after doing it for Connie, for all the people in this wonderful country. Why couldn't she get that?

"Seriously? You really think she'd go to all the trouble and expense of filing for divorce—that had to cost her at least a grand—*and* have it served, and you're still thinking she's gonna take you back?" Alex was shaking his head, his mouth puckered like he'd just taken a spoonful of motor oil.

"What fuckin' planet are you on, man?" Ryan asked.

Connie had accused him of being insensitive. But he *was* being sensitive. He was going out with his buds, not leaving them alone. Some of them had gotten home to find their wives with other men, even pregnant by other men. Other fuckin *regular Navy* guys and that was just tight. Nothing good about that. They were all responsible for each other. He wouldn't expect they'd abandon him, so why shouldn't he support them? It wasn't about the drinking or the strippers, it was about the community, and the healing that occurred when they all hung out together. Everyone returning home whole meant fixing stuff on the way back, as well as the adjustment to being home.

He could see now this would never be good enough for Connie. She had to be the center of attention, even ahead of the kids, and that bothered him. She just didn't get it. And she never would. She was like a clock that had been over sprung and would never again purr like that kitten he liked in bed, the lady who drove him wild with fantasies all during his time overseas.

"Redial, my man. Then I'm going back to bed," Jake added.

Lucas punched the red arrow on his phone, and the call was connected.

*'This is Marcy Gelland from the Coronado Bay Realty. I'm either on the other line or assisting clients. If you would leave your name and number and the reason for your call, I'll get back to you as soon as I'm free. Thanks, and make it a great day!"*

Lucas hung up. "Realtor," he said sheepishly. The day was suddenly turning dark.

Jake started to laugh. "You son of a gun, Lucas. Don't you have a clue what's happening to you? Your wife is trying to sell the house right out from under you."

"I'll just give my tenants notice and move into it. Mom left it to me when she passed. I can't afford both houses anyway," Lucas answered. "She's stupid to sell it. Don't know how she'll afford to get another place since she's not working."

Ryan leaned in, handing Lucas a fresh mug of coffee with the usual dosage of cream. "She doesn't have to work, my man. *You* do."

MARCY SOUNDED A bit frosty on the phone, Lucas thought. She insisted on a meeting, requesting he come down to her real estate office.

"Couldn't we meet at the house? Haven't seen the kids for a week, and you'll need Connie's signature anyway."

"Already got it, and I don't think she wants to see you."

It pissed him off that she would have such an opinion about the details of his marriage, since she'd only been hired to sell the property.

"Lucas, I can't find the information I need on the home at Linda Lane, and the property in Sonoma County. Do you have mortgages on those?"

Lucas fisted his right hand and nearly cracked the cell with his left. "Wait a minute. My mother left that house on Linda Lane to me. That's *my* house."

"Did you ever get the transfer done after your mother's death?"

"You're not hearing me. I'm not selling that house. I'm keeping it. I need some place to live."

"I'll require the rent rolls and how much the taxes are. Is there a mortgage? Connie thought it was given to you free and clear."

"You know, I'm talking and you're not hearing me. That was *my* house left to me by *my* mother."

"Except you were married at the time."

"So?"

"So, half of it belongs to Connie. You know California's a community property state. I'm no attorney, Lucas, but I think maybe you should get one and right away. Connie intends to sell this property, and the house up in Sonoma County, too."

"That fuckin hunting cabin has been in my family for a hundred years." His voice cracked like a teenager. "No way is that going to Connie."

"Look, go get an attorney. In fact, I insist you do so."

The cold bitch didn't sound like she had an ounce of compassion.

"I could give you three names as recommendations. But in the meantime, you can't stop Connie from putting the house, the house you two lived in together, on the market. She can't *sell* it without your permission, but she can encumber her half. And if she goes to court, the judge will order it."

He felt her voice soften just a touch, but she was still all business and still too pushy.

"Maybe if she gets the house sold, and she gets some money, she'll ease up on the other properties. Maybe not. But you need to get an attorney right away, and you need to meet with me to get this paperwork signed."

"I need time to digest all this. I just got served with papers yesterday."

"Oh." He heard the hesitation in Marcy's voice. "So, this was a surprise, then?"

"Yeah, it was pretty much a surprise."

"Can we compromise?"

He could hear some sweetness, but he didn't trust his ears yet.

"I won't have you give me any signatures on the Linda property and the cabin in Cloverdale, but can we at least do the paperwork on the house so I can get it on the market Monday morning?"

He'd agreed because he didn't know what else to do. He'd trained for everything under the sun, every eventuality, but he'd not been prepared for the attack coming from the one person in the world he always thought would be there for him.

Connie was taking the house they'd picked out together as newly-weds, with money for the down payment that came from his SEAL signing bonus. She could try to take what his mother had left him, as well as the cabin up in the woods, but she could *not* take his dignity. That, no woman would ever have, *especially* not Connie.

# CHAPTER 4

**M**ARCY DIDN'T EXPECT the tall SEAL to arrive so soon. She'd been involved in checking the new listings and had begun to upload some of the Shipley house information to the multiple listing service. She was waiting for his signature before she hit send.

The pink stucco home was on one of San Diego's nicer streets. The picture she'd taken that morning didn't do it justice. It had a rounded doorway like many of the bungalows in the area, with a red-tiled roof and iron grates over the tiny windows on the whole front side of the building, including the front door. Built just after the Depression, every house in town of that vintage was nearly identical, except for some interior remodeling and reversal of floor plan. The living room was always on the right or left and the kitchen was opposite, on the other side of the dining area. The homes had been built for younger families, but younger families could barely afford them anymore without help from outside.

She was admiring the pleasant picture on the screen when she heard his deep voice behind her.

"You're Marcy Gelland?"

When she turned, his dark hair and deep blue eyes threw her off-balance for a bit. He was stuffed into jeans that were baggy at the calves and knees, but well filled out in the butt and groin area. And he'd caught her checking him out.

His eyes smiled while his lips didn't move except for a tiny muscle on his left, which was a good thing. The resulting dimple at the left side of his mouth was giving her palpitations.

*Well, of course he's handsome, Marcy. What did you expect?*

He smelled of fresh soap, wore a white button-down shirt with rolled-up long sleeves, showing his corded muscles and multiple forearm tats, including a string of frog prints going from his wrist to the crook in his arm. She was glad she'd decided to wear her dark blue suit, her power suit. She needed the strength and resolve it gave her.

Standing, she extended her hand and felt him give her a full-contact handshake ending with a little squeeze. He returned her palm in an altered state. Her heart was pounding so hard she was sure her little dangle earrings were shaking.

Picking up her file, she asked him to follow her to the conference room. She could easily imagine him gazing at the movement of her hips under her skirt, so she attempted to walk completely without swagger, so as not to encourage him further. His mannerism wasn't at all what she expected when he pulled out a chair for her. She was forced to say thank you, and then felt his fingertips glide across the top of her shoulders as he returned to his side of the table, sat with his fingers folded on the tabletop in front of him.

Marcy recalled what Connie had told her. He could be a charmer, and no doubt he was on his best behavior right that moment. If he expected any special favors, he was sorely mistaken. She inhaled, elongated her neck, settled her jaw and applied her professional mask as she met his stare.

He was stoic, seemingly unaffected by her in the slightest, leaning back against the padding in the office chair, breathing shallowly, but drilling her with his gaze. She could tell he was checking her out elsewhere, with his peripheral vision, but was skilled enough to hide it.

In spite of herself, she was dying to know if she'd measured up.

*Get hold of yourself. He's a predator, after all. Good at sizing up people, assessing his odds and calculating weaknesses.* "So, Mr. Shipley—"

"Lucas. You can call me Lucas if you're going to rob me. No need to be all formal about it."

"I'm not robbing you—"

He put one paw on her hand, the one clutching the legal-sized manila folder with the listing information in it. The action made her jump and immediately pull away.

"Marcy, may I call you Marcy?" He didn't wait for an answer. "Let's cut the crap. I've given it some thought for, oh," he pulled out his cell phone and checked the time, "about thirty minutes. She can have the house. She can keep it, sell it, give it away to a homeless shelter for all I care about it. That's no longer a place I want to have anything to do with," he said, pointing to the folder.

"Mr. Shipley—"

"I said call me Lucas," he interrupted.

"Mr. Shipley, this hasn't been negotiated and until you get yourself an attorney, you shouldn't be offering anything like that to me. I'm supposed to be an impartial neutral party to this transaction, represent-ing both of you—"

"Sure you are." His arms were crossed and his left eye squinted, pull-ing up the left side of his lip.

"Well, you're certainly not making it very easy for me."

"What freakin' rule says I'm supposed to make it easy for *you?* You think this is freakin' easy for *me?*"

"No. But I'm here to get your signature on the listing contract for the house. *Only* the house. I'm going to tell your wife—"

"Soon-to-be ex-wife."

Marcy nodded and stared back at his oversized fingers. She saw cut marks on the inside of his bent and misshapen forefinger and a scar running up from the knuckle of his middle digit to above his wrist. The scar was nearly covered by a patch of dark body hair. He was missing the last joint on his fourth and little fingers. The vision distracted her until she saw him dip his head down, looking up and across to her side of the table, expecting an answer.

"You were saying something about my ex-wife?"

She took a deep inhale. "Mr. Shipley, I was offering a peace pipe, of sorts. We can do this contract, and I can get the house on MLS tonight or first thing in the morning. I'll tell her you wouldn't agree to the other two houses. Perhaps, with your cooperation here, this afternoon, I can convince her not to pursue the other two homes."

He leaned back in the chair, hiding his hands underneath the table. His chest fully rose as he gulped in air, and then his shoulders dropped as he exhaled. The scent of his body laced with what smelled like menthol shaving soap hit her in the face like a blast furnace and, in spite of herself, made her panties wet.

"And just why would you do that?"

She didn't really have an answer, because it had just come to her as a strategy and she had no idea from where. "Just…I don't know." She shrugged, seeking words to describe what she couldn't. Her insides were a jumbled mess. "I guess I feel like we should take this in little bites. The whole enchilada is probably hard to swallow at this point in time, Mr. Shipley."

*Oh, no. There it is again, looking at me that way. The edge of his upper lip curled in amusement.* If they were familiar, if they were a – *What in the devil are you doing, Marcy?* By the arch of his dark brow, she could tell he was tempted to say something dirty about the size of her mouth and the whole enchilada, and she worked very hard to put it out of her mind.

She closed her eyes so as not to watch him, putting her forehead into her palm, trying to seize back control of the conversation. It was no use, when she opened her eyes, and regarded the hunky SEAL sitting in front of her, with that sexy way he objected to everything she was trying to do, even the favor she was trying to bestow on him, the butterflies in her stomach instantly multiplied. Connie was right. He was a charmer of the professional class. A sheer force of nature. Her heart was beating like she'd just run a marathon.

Normally, the calmest person during a negotiation, but today, right then, she was losing it, big time. She'd never before met someone who affected her so. Was she excited for the challenge, or was it something else?

*God help me.*

# CHAPTER 5

THOM GRANDE WAS waiting in the warehouse where the rest of Kyle's squad assembled. The SEAL from DEVGRU in Virginia studied each man carefully, as Lucas knew he'd been trained to do. Lucas had deployed with the Varsity Group, as Team 6 was known, two summers before, although not during the deployment that took out BinLaden. It was a special operation of four weeks, which gave him a nice signing bonus—enough for the down payment on the house Connie now wanted to sell.

When Thom's blue eyes met Lucas', he winked, acknowledging the antics of the night before at the strip club. Lucas wished he could remember more of it. He hoped he hadn't blown his chances to do a rotation with them, or perhaps join Team 6 in the future. Since he didn't have anyone around to hold him back, doing the most dangerous tours overseas was suddenly looking like the cure he needed. Way better than waiting for legal papers and the inside of courtrooms. He'd be crying, the kids would be crying, and sure as shit, Connie would drill him with a look that would send him straight to Hell.

Thom walked over to him, and they shook hands.

"How's your head, Shitface?"

Lucas turned to Jake, who snickered.

"I'm fine," Lucas mumbled. To Ryan and Jake, he whispered, "You fuckin' told him?"

"It slipped," Ryan whispered back. "But it was kind of obvious."

Jeffrey and Danny entered the room, and Kyle called the meeting. "Okay, gents, yesterday was the briefing on that terrorist Jihadi John and what Thom and his boys have been dancing with. We have some late-breaking intel we were waiting for before we gave you the whole story."

They waited. Thom stepped forward and stood next to Kyle.

"So, I've got some bad news, gents," Kyle said.

Lucas could taste the juicy deployment he knew was coming up. Wouldn't that make his soon-to-be ex shit her pants? Turf the little hottie realtor, although he wouldn't mind hanging out with her again. He'd enjoyed the sparring the previous afternoon. He hadn't been able to sleep much that night, thinking about all the things he could do with her, all the positions…

"You think something's funny, son?" Kyle said.

Lucas saw bodies turn in his direction. His shit-eating grin and pleasant fantasy went right out the window as he realized they were waiting for him to respond.

"Yeah, asshole, I'm talking to you." Kyle had his hands on his hips and a mean scowl on his face.

"Sorry, sir. Was thinking about something else for a second."

Kyle's jaw clenched. "You see what I'm talking about? You guys do that over there and you'll get your brains splashed over all your buddies. Focus, goddammit. We're not in high school." Kyle sighed and continued with the monologue, but gave Lucas a nasty glare. Thom was standing half a body width behind Kyle, with his palm to his lips, having a hard time keeping a straight face, so the SEAL looked down.

Alex rubbed his dick against Lucas' left butt cheek, messing with Lucas' concentration, so he whipped around and tried to pop him.

"You wanna just sit this one out, Shipley?" Kyle barked.

Lucas knew if he told on Alex, he'd lose the respect of the team. He had to take it on by himself. "Chief Lansdowne, I got the runs. Got them last night. I was going to make a dash for the head, but I suddenly got control."

He knew they were all busting a gut inside. Thom broke out in a full smile that Kyle couldn't see.

"You want to go to the little girl's room, then, Shipley? Or are we good now? Can we go on with our meeting?"

"Yes, Chief Petty Officer Lansdowne. I'm good."

Kyle took one step back, folding his hands at his waist behind his back. "This here is SO Thom Grande, and he's going to tell us what we just learned today."

"Thanks, Chief Petty Officer Lansdowne," Thom Grande said in a soft voice.

His smirk was subtle. Lucas could see his affable nature made him a natural-born leader. He couldn't remember everything that was said the night before, but he remembered SO Grande had confided he'd had his share of difficulty with an ex-wife himself.

"We spent about four months last year on deployment, jumping in and out of Mosul, trying to rescue sensitive information and looking for one mean motherfucker, Jihadi John. I'm glad to say drone strikes have nearly wiped out the network he created and grew. But we don't really know anything further since that region is off limits to us now, as you know, or at least officially."

Thom paced in front of the thirty-man squad, walking a nearly straight line right down the middle of one crack between two poured slabs of concrete flooring, like the precision footwork was enjoyable to him.

"The nature of the enemy—of any enemy, for that matter—is to adapt to their environment and to stop doing what's not working and expand what is. This cell is no different. The drone strikes and night raids we used to do a couple of years ago were eating into the propaganda value of their campaign. They went quiet after we captured the cluster of leaders at the top, and those bastards are now housed in Kurdish prisons, guarded by men who would rather kill them than guard them."

Lucas waited for the first shoe to drop. He was salivating, the mantra *deployment* ringing in his ears.

"And when they went quiet, we thought perhaps they'd had a change of heart, or that the younger generation didn't have the stomach for war. We considered it a good sign."

Thom stood within two feet of the front line of SEALs from Alpha squad. "I was sent here because we received some intel we think is credible, and it involves Teams 3 and 5. Today, it was confirmed, and that confirmation was what I was waiting for before I could level with you all, completely." He locked gazes with everyone in the front row. Then he paced back the way he came, gaining eye contact with every man in the second.

Kyle watched them all, as well. Thom completed his analysis of what was to be their future. Lucas couldn't wait to hear the words, *We'll be deploying within the week.*

"We have reason to believe there was a death squad sent specifically to go after members of Teams 3 and 5, as retaliation."

He let it sink in a bit. No one said a word.

"Somehow, they got it that Team 3 and Team 5 were the ones who rounded up their leaders. They intend to bring some of you boys back home with them as hostages. To return the favor, so to speak. To show that it can be done—"

Lucas was hearing things he never thought possible, things so far from his imagination he had a hard time understanding the actual words. It was as if Grande was speaking Pashtu.

"—that terrorists could come here on U.S. soil, could kidnap a bunch of Navy SEALs and bring them back to Iraq. Their own twisted version of a snatch and grab."

The squad erupted in a string of expletives, each mumbling their favorite words of disgust.

Jake was the first to speak coherently. "You have to be shittin' me. That's the dumbest idea I've ever heard."

Thom smiled, even though his gaze remained hard. "I agree. It sounds farfetched." He looked right at Lucas as he continued, "But *if* they could, and that's a pretty big *if,* the propaganda factor would be huge. Even if they halfway carried some part of it off, their mission would make headlines all over the world."

Kyle took one long step, coming to sharp attention as he joined Grande. "Unlike our side, those bastards don't care about the loss of life. They're looking for sensational things they can do to swell the ranks with new recruits. Trust me, gents, something like this would be huge for them, even if they fail. And make no doubt about it—they *will* fail."

Lucas still had one last hope for deployment. "So, what is it we do, exactly? Like when do we leave and get these assholes before they try to come over here and attempt their suicide mission?"

"You boys aren't going anywhere overseas; not yet, anyways. You're not due to deploy for another five months, at least. You get to stay here while the other teams are out. Team 5 will deploy in thirty days, as planned. But you guys—you? You get to hang around Coronado and become bait."

Lucas was getting sick to his stomach.

Alex rolled his shoulder and growled, "SO Grande? Could you answer a question that's bugging me?"

"Sure. Go ahead. I'm here for your questions. All of them," answered the Varsity SEAL.

"Why don't we just meet them in combat over there, like Lucas here just said?"

It was Kyle's turn. Sucking in air, his back erect, he answered, "Because, Kowicki, they're already here."

# CHAPTER 6

**M**ARCY WAS UPLOADING the rest of her listing, sending out the reverse match emails to agents who were looking for property in this price range and location, when her cell phone rang. It was Connie.

"Hi, there. Just uploading your listing right now, Connie."

"Thank God. Do you have to inspect the other two houses, Marcy? I found keys for both of them."

"Well, Connie, I was going to talk to you about that." Marcy was trying to dart between the divorcing couple, noticing how anxious Connie was to untie their bond of marriage. "Why don't we just take it one step at a time? I think Lucas has shown some cooperation. Maybe we can get a great offer on your house right off the bat, and that would take some of the financial pressure off you both for a bit until you get settled. We can always handle those other two listings later. We could perhaps offer to be reasonable if he cooperates, which would be much better for you."

"And why would I do that?" Connie's cold tone sent Marcy a chill.

"Well, I think it's in your best interest to have his full cooperation on the sale of the house, Connie, don't you?"

"I don't care about getting cooperation. I want to make him pay."

"But Connie, don't you want to walk away with the most amount of money?"

"You mean, would I rather walk away with a ton of money or the satisfaction of screwing him six ways to Sunday? If you have to ask that question, Marcy, you don't know me very well."

The baby started crying in the background, and Connie went to retrieve him. Marcy really didn't know Connie as well as she was going to, but she did know this wasn't headed anywhere good.

Connie picked up the phone again and continued, "If you're coming out here today to put the lockbox on, I can give you both keys. I have no idea if either of them are occupied—"

"He told me the house on Linda Lane had a tenant in it."

"See? I told you he'd cooperate. That's more than he's told me. He hides that rent money, spends it on God knows what. Gambling. Girls. Drugs—"

"Drugs?" Marcy's hackles raised a bit. The suggestion seemed to be completely out of character, even for Lucas. He was, after all, an elite Navy man.

"Sure, why not? I mean, he does everything else. The man's a fuckin' human tornado. He and those boys of his are wreaking havoc wherever they drop their pants—"

"Look, Connie, I don't want to—"

"Maaaaar Seee. Did that asshole try to charm his way into your pants? He can, you know. I told you he can."

The dance Marcy had started became very tedious and she began to wonder if she had the skill to stay out of the frying pan, or avoid getting hit by it as it went flying past her head. "Look, Connie, can we just keep it simple? I don't think he wants any trouble, he just—"

"That sweet-talkin' dickwad."

Marcy was walking on quicksand. These two were going to be a real piece of work. Suddenly, she wasn't so confident she'd be able to keep them in their own corners and avoid killing each other. "You have to give the tenant notice for those kinds of things. I don't even have any way to contact them."

"Then I'll go. I'll just fuckin' walk right up to the house, knock on the door, put little Jack on my boob, and ask to fuckin' walk around the house that I half-own. I can take pictures, right?"

"Connie, you're not hearing me."

"I'll tell them if they want to stay, they'd better cooperate with open houses, tours coming through, people walking through at all times of the day and night."

"All things you'll put up with on your house, is that correct?"

"*Hell, no.*"

Jack started to fuss. Again.

"Look, you've talked with him about it. He didn't react."

"He most certainly *did* react. He strongly objected. Only way I could get him to sign the contract for your house was by telling him we'd do it one step at a time. Same as I'm telling you now, Connie. Seriously, this is in your best interest."

"Why don't you just fill out the paperwork, and I'll sign those two new contracts today. He can sign when he realizes I'm serious. Oh. And how much equity is in both?"

Marcy was beginning to see why they were divorcing. Connie was every bit the piece of work he was. "He didn't tell me about the mortgages or taxes, but I did ask him."

"That jerkoff."

"I don't think he would have signed the listing agreement on your house if I held him up for all three listings, Connie." How many times did she have to repeat that fact before it sunk in?

She could hear Connie telling something to their daughter. "I have to go, Marcy. What time will you be here?"

"I can get there within an hour. After I finish a couple of things, I'll be right over."

Connie hung up without saying another word.


ON THE WAY over to Connie's, Marcy couldn't understand how two people could make babies together and still act like children themselves. And how he could go through the grueling training to become a Navy SEAL, have all the stamina—mental stamina—to do that job and not be able to reel in his emotions. That was her first thought.

Her second thought was about how completely *unboring* the guy was. She imagined he would be a piece of work in the bedroom if he loved like he argued. He had skin in the game. Life mattered to him. *Things* mattered to him. Was it because he had to control his breathing, his fear, and his thoughts of impending death so many times in the battlefield he just let it all hang out in real life?

*Yeah, that's probably it.* Being a trained warrior, he was out of his element stateside, having to do things like be soft and gentle and worry about someone else's feelings. He'd married someone else who also had a hair-trigger and needed the intense relationship a guy like him could bring. That not only wasn't in his training, but he'd probably been trained to funnel everything emotional away from the job as a stress-coping mechanism.

And so the wife and family received the brunt of his inability to connect. The family got what was left over after his deployments, not his best side, either.

Still, she wondered what they'd been like when they first married. She imagined they'd exploded like rockets lighting up the sky. Those two were probably incapable of doing anything halfway.

She allowed herself a smile. Maybe she was going about it wrong. Maybe she should just sit back and enjoy the show. At least they weren't turning on her.

Not yet.

She rang the doorbell, and Connie's disembodied voice told her to come in. She laid her paperwork down on the dining room table, including the folder with his signature on the contracts and disclosure statements, and then sat and waited. She needed Connie's John Hancock on the disclosures.

Connie wafted into the room wearing the tightest pair of jeans Marcy had seen, along with a push-up, low-cut cotton top that revealed her ample cleavage.

"He filled out the Transfer Disclosure, Connie. I gotta have you review what he put down, initial and sign these."

The SEAL wife sneered at the stack of papers. "Wow. He musta been there for hours and hours. The guy can't read, you know. He covers it up well, but the Neanderthal doesn't read anything. He likes graphic novels and—"

"Connie, he reads just fine. It didn't take long. I helped him with some of it, but he filled it all out."

Connie crossed her arms over her chest, sending her boobs north. "Sure you did." Connie's look was a challenge.

"What does that mean?"

She huffed and leaned over Marcy's shoulder, grabbing a pen. "Just sayin'. Okay, where do I sign?"

Marcy indicated where she was to initial and then sign beneath his signature. "Fuckin' jerk signed in my spot."

"Makes no difference—"

"So, you don't think it makes a difference who's on top?" She wiggled her eyebrows.

Marcy looked away and felt heat creep across her cheeks.

Connie laughed. "I'll bet this is the last divorcing SEAL you'll ever represent, huh?"

"No. It isn't the first, and it most certainly won't be my last, either."

"Well, if you can keep the cows in the barn and keep his pants on, you might get paid. One of my best friends is a realtor, and she wouldn't touch this with a ten-foot pole."

"I'll bet," Marcy said under her breath, slipping the contracts into the folder. So much for feeling lucky about winning the listing from the agents she'd had to battle it out with. Unless that was a lie, too. Sensing Connie's unfriendly stare on the top of her head, she pulled out the blue lockbox and held it up. "This goes on a water pipe or, if there is none, the front door, but it scratches the wood. It has to be on something that won't go anywhere."

"Put it on his fuckin' flagpole. And I'm not talking about his dick."

The woman's cursing was beginning to wear on every last one of her nerves. She'd never have guessed wives cursed like sailors, too. Marcy fought for composure. "So, that's where, exactly?"

"Oh, that's right. His huge honker of an American flag isn't on it. Some days, when the breeze picks up, I'd have to battle that damned thing so I could get out the front door. He likes 'em big, like everything, except his women. He likes them with huge tits in fancy white lace, likes skinny waists and loves to talk dirty in bed."

Marcy felt heat begin to crawl up her neck, but managed to will away the blush. She wondered how the Lucas she'd met could have hooked up with this woman, and though it wasn't really her business, for her own sake, she needed to know. A slight worry for the health of the children began to grow as well.

Connie gave her a little wink and a half-smile.

"Gonna miss that part of things a bit. But I'm working hard to find me a replacement—quick."

# CHAPTER 7

A FTER THE MEETING, Thom Grande came up to Lucas, the rest of the team barely within earshot. "Understand you're having trouble with the missus."

"That's fuckin' putting it mildly."

"So that explains your behavior last night. Not that I minded tagging along."

"You forget yourself, Grande. I think you forgot the part about us helping you walk and plopping your sorry ass on the bed at your motel. Or don't you remember that?"

Thom nodded and grinned at his cowboy boots. They looked expensive to Lucas, but then Lucas, being a California kid, didn't know anything about boots.

The SEAL peered up at Lucas and gave him that knowing look. "Been there, done that."

"What, the going to strip clubs or the domestic wars?"

"Guilty on both counts. But that kind of action at clubs and bars and shit, Lucas, there's nothing there except a fake good time. It's all fake, man. Save your marriage if you can."

Lucas started to chuckle. "Well, it isn't up to me, Grande. The woman has her own ideas of where the boundary lines are, and I fuckin' crossed into enemy territory when I wasn't looking."

"And she won't forgive you?"

"Nothing to forgive. She thinks I did the thing with a transvestite who takes a really good picture. Not that the big guy wasn't attractive, just not my thing. I've never been unfaithful to Connie, but I can't convince her otherwise."

"So, you keep pushing the envelope, hoping some woman will just grab your balls and make you forget your wife? That's your plan? That what you're saying? You know how dangerous that is?"

"Look, man, this is all good here, but you're not my fuckin' psychiatrist. No offense intended. I got Kyle and the guys here watching out for me. I'm good. I'm just going through a rough patch. I got kids I won't be able to see, a wife who wants to have nothing to do with me for nothing I've done, and now she's taking me to the cleaners. I fucking re-upped for four years to get the down payment for this fuckin' house she's taking away from me. And now the bitch wants my granddad's hunting cabin and the house my mother left me."

Grande stepped back. "No worries. I feel you. Didn't mean to butt in, Shipley." He held his palms out to the sides as if demonstrating he didn't hold a weapon. "Just if there's any advice I can give you, the best advice I didn't get until it was too late, is to get a good divorce attorney."

"Fuck it. She can have it all."

"And she'll keep taking it until you fight her, my man," Alex said as he slapped Lucas on the back.

"Listen to him, Shitface. This guy has the scars to prove it," added Jake.

"Come on, assholes," Kyle called out. "Get the hell out of the building. I gotta lock up."

THEY MET FOR beers at the Scupper. The usual parade of high school students and college party girls was in and around the bar, sliding up and down seats like they were working a pole at a club, the skirts shorter and tighter than Lucas remembered. They were looking younger and prettier the more beers he drank.

One of Kyle's old-timers, Calvin Cooper, sat down across the table. "You're gonna have to face your demons, Lucas, or you'll be no good to us. Being sober is no joke, my man."

Cooper's gentle rolling voice was soothing, but a warning nonetheless. His plain talk and even sharper stare made Lucas sit up. Coop's huge six-foot-four frame loomed over the table like he was the king at court.

"I can handle it."

"Oh, sure you can. Until you can't, and then you'll be balling one of those sixteen-year-olds with a fake I.D., and bam, you're off the teams. You gotta ask yourself what's really more important, being married or being a SEAL. 'Cause right now, you can't do both. It's eating you alive, man. You're hooked up with a woman who can't handle the heat. She's gone over the edge. She's bent. And you're in some la-la land, thinking you can turn her back into the little kitten she was when you married her."

"How many times you been married, Coop?" Lucas liked the big SEAL medic.

"Mentally? Lots of times. But nah, I tried out a lot for all those teams, but in the end, there was only one lady for me. Just once, man."

"So, how can you talk?"

"You forget I've been doing this over eleven years. I've seen it all. If Kyle doesn't toss you, I will. I'll give you a mental so fast you won't be able to find your dick. Just imagine how the Navy will put you to use with that in your folder."

As one of the team medics, Coop could easily end his career. He wouldn't want to, of course, but if it meant saving the life of the others on the team, weeding out someone who wasn't paying attention, it would be something he'd have to do for everyone's safety. And though Lucas would be off the teams, his obligation to the Navy would continue. He'd get stuck cleaning toilets on a ship or perhaps being a BUD/S instructor and dishing out his brand of hate on all the young, new recruits.

"One more piece of advice, and then I'm going to get these gentlemen to escort you home. Get yourself a fuckin' lawyer. Stop feeling sorry for yourself. Quit reacting and start making a plan. Either walk away or fight. Those are your only two choices."

The giant stood, threw down a twenty, even though he'd been drinking mineral water, and in a couple of long strides was out the doorway.

Minutes later, Lucas left as well. The night air was crisp and the stars were out. The warm, salty breeze was something Lucas loved more than just about anything.

Just about.

They had five days until they started training for hostage rescue and house-to-house searches. They'd all have to requalify on the range, and anything less than expert was not acceptable. Lucas decided he'd go visit the cabin, get in touch with his childhood and see what the ghosts of Northern California had to say to him.

Besides, it beat waiting for Connie to serve him with more papers. And the ghosts were a helluva lot kinder than Connie's mouth.

But his dick still got hard when he thought about what wonders she could do with that mouth.

# CHAPTER 8

**M**ARCY HAD A friend from college who lived in Sonoma County and sold real estate. And she happened to be married to an ex-SEAL. They had a small winery operation a lot of the San Diego crowd had invested in. She decided to call her.

"Hey, Devon. I've got a property I need to check out in Cloverdale. Was thinking maybe I'd drive up and see you and Nick for a day or two. What do you say?"

"That would be great. You want my help with the listing in any way?"

"I don't have the listing yet. Divorcing couple. He's a SEAL, and they don't exactly see eye to eye on everything yet."

Devon giggled. "They never do, unless *you* screw up, then they get reunited."

"In this case, I'd actually walk away. They have two beautiful kids. A shame, really."

"Not everyone can make it. Lots of divorces in the community. What day are you coming?"

"How about tomorrow?"

"Sure. My place is open. We just finished the guest cottage, and I don't have anyone renting it until the weekend. The place is yours."

"Thanks."

"Does Nick know him?"

"The SEAL? Name's Shipley, Lucas Shipley."

"I'll ask him. Safe journeys. Why don't you fly up? We got direct flights now, just like in the big city. I'll pick you up at the airport. Would save you a whole day each way, unless you want the drive to ease your mind."

"You know, I think I'll do that. But let me pick up a car at the airport.

I'm going to need my own wheels."

"Yup, unless you want to drive one of our tractors."

MARCY DROVE FROM the Charles Schulz airport down the freeway into Santa Rosa, and then took the two-lane country road to Bennett Valley. A small shingle sign at the end of a crushed granite driveway marked the property as Sophie's Vineyard. The rows of lush green vines under a bright blue cloudless sky welcomed her. The rich black soil of Sonoma County provided stark contrast to the colors of the fresh crushed straw covering it. Something emotional was building inside, and she wasn't quite sure what was happening. She felt like there was a new adventure looming—something unexpected was about to happen. It would alter her path forever.

Devon and Nick's modern home was built on the site of Nick's sister's nursery grounds, a nursery that had failed as an enterprise, but succeeded in bringing together Nick and Devon, a couple who were living out their dreams in the wine country. Though Nick had retired from the teams without a pension, he was more than content running the day-to-day operations of the small winery. Devon made enough money for them to live on while the grapes were developing. It was a storybook romance from beginning to end.

Devon wrapped her arms around Marcy and gave her a squeeze. "So great to see you, Marcy. Wow. Things in San Diego must agree with you."

"Thanks." Marcy blushed. "I've been lucky, I guess."

Nick appeared at the doorway. He was as handsome as Marcy remembered—tall with wide shoulders, blond hair and green eyes. Wearing jeans with suspenders and a khaki long-sleeved shirt rolled up at the sleeves, he was wiping his hands on a rag.

"Hey there, Marcy," he said as he gave her a quick hug and kiss on the cheek.

"You're looking all farm boy-like, Nick. No body armor, guns, or tats covering half your body?"

"Oh, I got the tats," Nick said, showing her the line of frog prints extending from his wrist to inside his elbow joint, just like Lucas had.

"All the guys on Kyle's squad have them. Sort of a rite of passage. You're working for one of us?" Nick squinted and asked, tossing the rag onto the seat of a riding mower.

"Lucas Shipley. You know him?"

"Yeah, Devon asked me. Can't say that I do, but there were a bunch of guys at the end, coming on board. How long's he been with the teams?"

"All I know is he re-upped a couple of years ago. His bonus was what gave them the down payment on the house I'm selling." She allowed her voice to trail off. This was part of her job she wasn't proud of.

"Ohhh, ouch. Well then, I probably knew him. Some of the guys do extra training, though. Languages, medic long course, details at Quantico, burn center in Texas. He could have been doing one of those."

"And you took a lot of time off, Nick, when Sophie—"

Marcy had been told the story of how Nick's sister had been poisoned with arsenic in her well water by a neighbor who was now serving time for her murder.

Devon frowned and then drew herself out of her private thought. "Well, I'm not being very hospitable leaving you out here. Nick, you want to get Marcy's bags?"

Marcy opened the truck as Nick picked up two overnight suitcases and slung her briefcase over his shoulder.

"I still get to do all the heavy lifting around here," he said as he widened his eyes and pretended to be overloaded.

Devon slipped an arm around Marcy's waist. "So, tell me about yourself. What's new? And I need to hear about all the hunks in San Diego you're dating."

As Marcy stepped into the doorway, she was stunned. Far from looking like a house, the place more aptly resembled a church. The living room was two stories tall, with a large glass garage door facing out to the hillside garden beyond. The carefully crafted rock walls and meandering garden paths she could see from the large window were stunning. Inside, the living and dining room contained eclectic things from all over the world, including a couple of flower boats from India and a carved sandalwood cabinet that looked like it came from a palace. She smelled fresh coffee and heard light jazz playing in the beautiful room.

"This is amazing. I guess I had a hard time visualizing it when I was up here for the wedding." She turned around a couple of revolutions. "It doesn't look like the same place."

"That was before we got all the furniture in the house. Was a great place for a wedding, though," Devon said.

Nick came back from the hallway and took his wife's hand. "I've set your things on the bed in there. You have a fireplace, but I'd keep it off. We're getting some heat these days. The pilot light keeps the room toasty, sometimes too warm."

"Thank you so much," Marcy said.

"You want something to drink? We were going to have an early supper."

"Wine. You have any wine?"

Nick walked over to a huge floor-to-ceiling wine refrigerator cabinet with double doors, housing more than a hundred bottles of wine. He turned to Marcy and said, "We got white. We got red. You get to pick."

"You have any that came from here? I'd love a red wine."

"Excellent choice." Nick presented the cool bottle to Marcy, where she read the label, *Sophie's Choice.*

# CHAPTER 9

T HE TRIP UP the coast was always enjoyable. Except for a couple of areas of commuter congestion, the ride was uneventful and stress-free. Lucas used the time to listen to several audio books he'd not made time for in San Diego. The beautiful ride went by quickly, even with the three stops for gas. Like most men on SEAL Team 3, he owned a Hummer, something Connie had been bugging him to get rid of because of the expense. Today, he was glad he'd prevailed in this one thing.

Watching the landscape change from ocean to rocky shoreline in the Monterey area, back to farmland north to Silicon Valley, and then back out to the coast at Marin, all the way nearly to Bodega Bay, it was hard to envision the beautiful scenery as a war zone. But if Thom was right, that's exactly what it was. Stopping for oysters at Marshall's Cove, he drank a beer and watched the sun as it began dropping to the water's horizon. A local motorcycle club was loud and apparently staying nearby. Listening to their language, he pegged them for cops, not bandits.

It touched him as he watched the band of brothers play together, how the cops from the East Bay were trying so hard to have a normal life, just like he and his SEAL buddies did in Coronado. These men had seen the carnage left by society and chose to serve honorably, just like the SEALs. And just like the SEALs, in their off time, they didn't want to look anything like cops. They wore their red bandanas and black leathers. Beefy arms sported tats. And every one of them had all manner of ear piercings. Some of the bikers were alone, some with wives or girlfriends. The ladies were in all sizes, shapes, and ages.

*Good for them.*

The public had no idea what evils lay out there, even in the brown and green hills of the wine country of California. Evil was everywhere.

Lucas knew it was his job to keep evil at bay. And now he'd be doing that at home, as well.

He knew from the talk and the reaction from the other guys that this was a hard thing to wrap their minds around. Danger at home. Sure, the cops were used to it, but SEALs? Having to watch their six at home, in the land of freedom? Where everything was apple pie, and it was easier to tell the good guys from the bad guys?

Forget politics. Leave it to a bunch of politicians to make treaties and agreements they knew no one would keep, and leave it all to the fighting men and women to enforce the unenforceable. Wasn't their fault they were losing the war, and now was it really coming over here? No one could win that kind of war. Even the zealots wouldn't win.

It was just like the cops, trying to deal with the complexities and political decisions of local laws. Up to them to enforce the unenforceable, too.

He finished his oysters as he mentally said goodbye to the guys acting like badasses down at the designated fire pits on the beach. He drove east, and then in an hour arrived in Cloverdale.

He'd forgotten how the sound of the crickets made him feel safe. As long as they were doing their two-toned chirp thing, it meant no strange animal or person was on their way. Just like frogs at the local frog pond he'd played at as a child. When the din stopped suddenly, that was when you paid attention to your surroundings. His grandfather had taught him that.

Lucas fished for the old brass key, slipped it into the lock and instantly he was taken back twenty years, even though it had only been less than ten since he'd been here. That was the summer Granddad had passed away, and his dad soon after that, as if the two were brothers, instead of a very close father and son.

He'd always envied his dad's relationship with his grandfather, probably forged because he'd been raised without a mother and there wasn't anyone to dilute their relationship.

Their whispers in every corner still haunted him as he examined the crude, knotty pine cupboards the three of them had made one summer. He opened the cabinet next to the sink and, sure as shit, there were the holes in the cabinet door where he'd had to re-drill for the screws attaching the hinges three times. His dad wanted him to do it, until he learned how to do it right. The puttied holes were testament to a lesson learned, and no one ever talked about it after it was accomplished. As he grew into a teen and came up to hunt with the two most important men in his life, he liked to look at that door just to remind himself of where he'd come from. It was like proof of his existence.

The cabin had only one bedroom. The old brass bed sported the quilt his mother had made, and when he checked out the spongy mattress that always squeaked when his father happened to take his mother up sometimes, a small cloud of dust rose. Lucas quickly removed the quilt and took it outside, shaking it furiously. He left the colorful patchwork quilt over the porch handrail to air out.

Lucas reset the refrigerator switch and plugged it in, hearing the familiar purring of the old turquoise Philco appliance, stowing the milk, eggs and beer he'd brought, along with some meat for a barbeque he was looking forward to the following night. He found rags and cleaning supplies and did a thorough scrub down of the whole cabin, working until well after midnight. It was a labor of love, homage to a time long past and perhaps never coming again. Just like the refrigerator, he felt his reset switch had been tripped. He was ready for the change.

The cold shower he took before bed was exhilarating after the twelve-hour drive. He found a flannel nightshirt of his father's in the bureau drawer, stowed his Sig Sauer under his pillow, brought the quilt from the porch inside and, draping it over the bed, crashed.

AT FIRST LIGHT, the birds began chirping, and Lucas found it impossible to sleep any further. He checked his gun, made his bed and unpacked the few things he'd brought with him. The tall highboy dresser with its cracked mirror stood faithfully to serve him, like a butler, showing a reflection of himself in the darkened glass. He took another cold shower, this time not feeling so cold, considered shaving and decided against it. He put on his jeans, a new t-shirt, and then a sweater of his father's he'd found hanging in the closet.

He was going to make some coffee when he heard a car drive up. Quickly stowing his gun in the back waistband of his pants, covered by the sweater, he looked through the window to the driveway outside. Next to his burgundy Hummer, a white sedan was parking. Out stepped Marcy Gelland.

He opened the front door and leaned into the frame, arms crossed, until she looked up and saw him.

"Oh. It's you!"

"Yes, Miss Gelland. I do own this cabin—at least for a little while longer, anyway."

Her oversized satchel was slung over her shoulder. She had on a pair of forest green recycled ankle gardening boots, and a big white, silk shirt with a pocket stitched over one breast, covering long, tan slacks that were going to be way too warm in a couple of hours. She'd done her hair up in a clip, and she wore no makeup. He liked her better that way.

"You following me now?" he asked, not moving from the spot, daring her to try to gain entry into his private domain. "I told you I wasn't going to sell this place."

She turned around, glancing at the tree line before her eyes at last landed on the thatched roof of the cabin. Then she tilted her head and spoke to him. "Beautiful here. I don't blame you a bit."

"So, you've seen it. Now, you can go, Miss Gelland—or is it Mrs. Gelland?"

Her lips parted slightly, one side turned up, amused. "Marcy. You can call me Marcy. Unlike you, I've never been married."

"Touché." The sting in her comment hurt like a pinprick, but it sucked him back into his impending court battle with Connie. He dropped his arms at the sides, suddenly not knowing what to do with them. "Well, that's it. Show's over. I have nothing else left to offer, unless you like strong coffee and scrambled eggs."

"I love strong coffee and scrambled eggs. I'm afraid I can't make either one successfully."

He didn't know why he said it, but before he could take it back, found himself whispering, "Well, perhaps you're better at other things."

"I should hope so," she said timidly. "I guess, according to you, I rob people for a living."

"Ah, an honest woman who admits her vices. How refreshing. Do you ask for forgiveness before or after you fleece them?"

At first, she didn't smile, just stared back at him. She wasn't afraid, which was such a turn-on. "I solve problems. Most of my day is spent solving other people's mistakes and problems. And I'm damn good at it." She narrowed her eyes, as if taunting him to say something nasty.

Lucas was struck with the inability to fight with her. Whatever was going on, he couldn't dislike her, and he wanted to, perhaps needed to.

Marcy still didn't move an inch. There she was in the middle of the fuckin' forest, way far away from anyone who could hear her scream. He was trying to stand up to her, trying to hate her and everything she stood for. He wanted to blame her for what his life was going to become. She was a willing accomplice to his wife's selfish attitude.

She remained standing, as if waiting for instructions. Defiant, almost petulant, daring him to cave in and show his ungentlemanly side. She hugged her file folder and oversized purse, looking way more desirable than she probably knew. But when she broke a smile and stepped closer to his perch, she finally dropped the hand with the folder, catching it at the side of her hip, and giving him the view of her chest he'd wanted to see. Although he wasn't going to let her catch him at it, his peripheral vision took in the whole lovely sight of her.

She glanced up, recognizing something, and gave him a playful, narrowed look. "I think we got off to a bad start. I'm not here to cause you any pain, or to rob you. Mr.—"

"Lucas. If I'm calling you Marcy, you're calling me Lucas."

"Yessir," she said as she straightened her spine, her pert little lips doing that pouty thing.

What a blessing she was. What a fresh piece of something he'd never had and wanted desperately.

"Like I was saying, *Lucas*..."

Her large brown eyes smiled up at him, and his heart melted. He hadn't realized he was so starved for mature female attention, the kind that wasn't tipped or bought and paid for.

"I think you misunderstand my intentions. I'm not here to sell your cabin. As a matter of fact, I'm not sure I can, or that Connie has the right to order either of them sold. That will have to be worked out in a settlement agreement between the two of you."

He could see that the longer he watched her speak and focused on her lips, the more talkative she became. Words were nervously stringing together, and all he could think of was her light pink tongue darting out behind her white teeth, and the way she licked her lips and nervously bit her bottom one.

"You haven't taken my suggestion and gotten an attorney yet, have you?" she finished and took in a deep breath.

"That was only a little over a day ago, Marcy." He was thinking to himself that his perspective was changing by the minute. "But I'm all ears. Perhaps you can recommend someone for me."

The double meaning seemed to make her blink very slowly, considering what he'd said. She quickly looked downward toward her ridiculous boots.

"Where'd you get those?" he asked with a chuckle.

"Costco."

"No socks. Can't go into the woods without socks. You'll get ticks on your ankles, or worse, traveling up your pant legs."

Marcy cocked her head and frowned then gave him that full gaze that did him in. She forged her response. "You going to continue to defend the perimeter, or am I invited in for those scrambled eggs and strong coffee? Or have I said something to cause you to change your mind?"

There was an exchange between them without words. It fell to him to speak up first, perhaps acknowledge what was going on inside him, hopefully inside her, too. He knew when a woman liked what she saw, and she was definitely transmitting it. "On the contrary. But enter at your own risk."

He let his words linger there until she dropped her gaze again. Stepping aside, he turned and opened the door for her to walk into his life.

Once inside, she slowly took stock of the place, carefully examining the pictures on the walls, the cabinets, the hooked rug in front of the fireplace, the kitchen area, and the sparse furniture of the living room with one table lamp he'd made as a Boy Scout.

"It's lovely. I can see why it has special meaning to you. Lots of memories here. I can feel them, I think."

He'd been holding his breath. "Thank you." He stepped closer to her, and slowly brought his palm to her cheek and cupped it. Letting his fingers brush against her flawless skin, and then dropped his hand. He wanted to be careful, not push his boundaries, but the granite in his pants was making him very uncomfortable.

She turned once again, and he wanted to lace his fingers through her hair, take that damned clip out and muss it all up real good, before he gave her the kiss she so deserved. Hell, *he* deserved that kiss. It had been a long, insane dry spell.

She set her folder down on the table, placing her bag on top of it. "Can I help you with something?"

*Oh, yeah, darlin'. You can help me heal that big wound in my soul. Get me feeling right about myself again, about the world.* "Let's see. Can you crack eggs?" he asked as he brought out a carton from the refrigerator and set them next to a green bowl from the cupboard. "I even have the right implements." He drew out a wire whisk from one of the drawers.

Her fingers wrapped around the base of the whisk, and for a moment, their fingers touched. It would have been so easy to curl her into his chest, kiss the top of her head, and feel her blood pumping in her neck as he nibbled there. She smelled divine, and he was fairly sure her temperature had risen, since there were tiny beads of sweat on her upper lip.

He moved away from her to light the propane stove and pull out an iron skillet. As she cracked several eggs, he brushed behind her to get the butter. He felt her jump at his proximity, and it gladdened him. He would take the whole day cracking eggs and eating breakfast if she'd let him. Suddenly, he wasn't in a hurry to go anywhere or do anything.

He poured water from a gallon jug into a saucepan on the stove, and after boiling it and cooking the eggs, filled the coned coffee filter to the top and watched as it drained into a ceramic pitcher.

He added cheese and some spices to the eggs, made toast in the frying pan, poured their coffee, and put the cream on the table.

"Breakfast is served, Madame," he said with a bow, placing the two plates on the table across from each other.

"So how often did you come here growing up?" she asked.

"Some of the best times of my life. My grandfather and father used to bring me up every summer. Sometimes my mom, but only occasionally. Learned to hunt and fish. They told stories about being a man that scared this little boy to death."

Lucas worried he'd revealed something perhaps he shouldn't.

The silence was awkward and in need of filling. Marcy beat him to it. "Wow. These eggs are terrific—I think the best I've had."

"Not my best skill," he said, smiling into his coffee mug.

She answered him with a smile. "You want an update on the house?"

"I don't care about that right now, really."

"Okay."

"No offense."

"None taken," she said breathlessly. "Lucas, this property was yours before your marriage, from what I can see. Unless you encumbered it in some way." Her eyes were soft.

"The bank asked me to use it as additional collateral on the loan, because Connie had a couple late payments on her student loan."

"But you didn't borrow against it, right? Pull any money out of it?"

"No. Just used it as a kind of guarantee for the house loan."

"So, if *that's* paid off through escrow, then *this* house would be, what, free and clear?"

"Yes, ma'am."

"I'm no attorney, but I understand that if it was yours before you got married, it remains your sole and separate property. I don't think you can be forced to sell it."

"That's good news," he said, letting out a breath. "So, I have a question for you, Marcy, since we're talking about business sorts of things." He was about to risk a little more, feeling suddenly comfortable and intrigued.

"Shoot," she said as she finished her eggs and took a gulp of coffee.

"Why are you here?" Her eyes widened at first, and then she returned his honest gaze.

"Well, you'll probably have to submit a valuation for this place during your divorce proceedings, when they start. And, I don't know." She shrugged, brushing some crumbs from her lap. "I guess I was looking for something. Not sure what."

Those eyes again searched his face.

"Did you find what you were looking for?" he asked as he covered her hand with one of his.

She hesitated a bit, giving a jolt as their fingers wove together, and then he drew her hand to his face and kissed her palm.

She swallowed hard. "Yes. I think I did."

"Is this wise, Marcy? You're going to have to stop me, you know, because I can't."

She closed her eyes again, as if searching the back reaches of her mind. "I don't want you to stop," she said, her eyes still closed.

# CHAPTER 10

**M**ARCY QUIVERED WITH anticipation as he took her by the hand and, without looking back, brought her to the little bedroom. In front of the patchwork quilt, he reached around her waist and drew her to him, holding her as her hands traveled up his arms. She arched back and they parted. He bent and kissed her. When his kiss went deep, she was lost.

This wasn't the smart thing to do. Somewhere, she knew this, but she'd been starved for this meal. She knew deep inside, she'd always regret it if she didn't just take a chance and let herself glide into something unwise and dangerous—with him.

*I'm going to have to cancel the listing and give it to someone else in the office*, she thought while he kissed her neck. He removed her hair clip, tossing it to the corner, his fingers lacing through her hair.

Other equally ridiculous thoughts flew past her when his fingers probed down her front as he slowly unbuttoned her shirt. She'd worn a lace bra. White. Exactly what Connie had said. The look on Lucas' face told her it wasn't a lie. *Lucas likes his women big-chested,* which Marcy was, *and in white lace,* which she also was.

"Lucas, wait a minute."

"No." He continued exploring her top, trying to get his tongue into the cup of white lace to taste her nipple, kissing her in other impossible places.

"If we do this—"

"Honey, we're doing this."

"Then I can't represent you."

"Ask me if I care," he whispered in her ear. "I need this. I think you do, too."

He was right, of course. But her job, her morals, every alarm and bell were sounding off the wall.

"I—I don't think this is a good idea."

"Same answer. Ask me if I care."

"I feel like I'm taking advantage of my position."

He continued kissing her neck and between her breasts. In spite of herself, she felt his hard ridge, and instead of backing away, she pressed into him.

"I intend to take full advantage of you taking advantage of me," he answered in a whisper.

"It isn't wise."

"No, it isn't."

"It isn't smart." She sighed as her lips told him something else.

"Not smart at all," he murmured before he completely covered her mouth.

When their lips parted, she was leaning in to him, holding on to him like he was her lifeline.

"But is it right, Marcy? Ask your soul. Is this something you should have, something you *deserve*?" He ducked his head a bit to gaze into her eyes. She could see he was giving her the choice.

"Is it, Marcy? Is it right for you, because it's sure right for me." His thumb brushed against her lips.

"Would you stop if I asked you?"

"Yes, after I kissed every inch of your body. After I made you come so many times, you didn't remember your name, baby. Yes, I'd stop. If you begged me."

*Dayum. Dayum.*

"I don't do this. I'm not that kind of girl."

"I know what kind of girl you are. The kind of girl you're showing me is just fine. I like your kind of girl very much," he said as he continued kissing her, his long fingers reaching into the top of her panties after his other hand unzipped her skirt, and it dropped to the floor. The heavy bulge in his jeans against her nearly nude sex was such a turn-on she sparked a fever.

She crossed her arms behind his neck, pulling his head down to hers. "I'm lost, Lucas. Help me."

His long groan had her bud pulsing. She could feel the moisture preparing her channel for him. He lowered his crooked forefinger, and she sucked in air as he inserted it in her opening. "Does that help, baby?"

"Oh, yes, Lucas. But I need more."

"Of course you do. Show me. Show me what you want."

Suddenly, she was timid, but she smoothed over his button fly.

He groaned. "You want that, baby? I want to fuck you so bad right now. Take it out for me, sweetheart. Let me feel your fingers around me."

She undid the top three buttons on his fly. He was commando, no underwear. "You like it quick," she heard herself say.

"No, sweetheart. I like to be ready, is all. Not quick. I like it slow. I like you to ache when I ram my cock inside you."

She had never been more ready in her life. His jeans fell to the floor. She took the enormous girth of him, squeezing him, pressing him between their abdomens. She whimpered when she saw a little of his pre-cum leaking. Her ears were buzzing. He was peeling away all the layers of her ladyhood, all the good girl parts of her, leaving the wild child unfettered and free and aching to perform on a stage for him.

She opened his shirt, popping the buttons.

The rest of the clothes went quickly. As she stood before him completely naked, he dropped to his knees and kissed her leg from her knee all the way up. When he reached her sex, she jumped and her lower lip quivered. She gripped the tops of his shoulders at the intimate act.

"Tell me what you're thinking," he whispered against her mound.

"I'm scared, Lucas."

He leaned back on his haunches, grinned with lips wet with her own moisture, and then dropped his gaze to between her legs again. "You've never done this before?" He reached out and touched her. "Has a man ever played with this?"

She couldn't speak; all she could do was nod. She'd had a man touch her there, once. And she'd asked him to move his hand away.

His gaze narrowed. "But you're not a virgin, right?"

"No, just not—"

"Ah! Now I understand. Just not this. You haven't done this," he whispered as he moved forward, looking up at her while he lapped at the slit between her legs. "Baby, you taste sweet. You like that?"

"Yes."

"You want more?"

"Oh, my God, yes."

"That's my girl. Ride my hand while I taste your juices. Just a little." He held her hip and tilted her pelvis back and forth, dipping his head to bury his tongue inside her as he rocked her back and forth.

God, it was getting hot in the room. The backs of his fingers rubbed against her thighs, gently smoothing and parting them. "That little bud is working hard, Marcy. You feel the pressure there?"

"Yes," she whispered.

"I'm gonna take some of the pressure off, so it doesn't ache so much. You okay with that, honey?"

"Um, oh, yes." She couldn't think.

He sucked the lips of her sex and slid his fingers up and down. "You tell me if you want me to stop, and I'll stop." He slipped both thumbs inside her opening, breaching her core, giving him full access.

"Don't—"

His head jerked up.

"God, *don't stop*, Lucas. Please. Don't. Stop."

"I have no intention of stopping. We got all day and no where else to go."

His tongue found her opening again.

She felt an orgasm coming on quickly. She pinched her own breasts, and then looked down on his head buried between her legs, where he feasted.

"Come for me, baby. Let me taste it, sweetheart," he whispered below her.

The friction of his tongue against her clit made her shudder as she felt herself lose control. His deep guttural moan told her he tasted the gold he was seeking. "God, Marcy, more, give me more," he said just before he dove in again.

As the spasms overtook her, she was filled with crazy need to have him inside her channel while she pulsed against him. "I need this so much, Lucas. God, I can't tell you how much I need this."

He withdrew his hands. "I know, baby." He fished for something in his pants, she heard the tearing of a foil packet and then he stood. Her hands went down to his shaft. She rubbed the ridged surface of the condom, and her eyes grew wide.

"Something else new, am I right? Oh, baby, what I'm going to do to you," he said as he picked her up quickly and dropped her back on the bed. "I'd normally like to get you screaming before I come inside, but I think you're there already and I can't wait any longer."

He mounted her, spreading her thighs. He yanked two pillows from the head of the bed, stuffed them under her pelvis and let a finger rub up and down her wet slit so achingly slow; she arched back and spread her legs further apart.

With his gaze locking with hers, he put his forefinger in his mouth. "Ah, baby, choices, choices." The tip of the condom had filled slightly and the plastic looked like it was going to burst.

"Lucas, please. Don't tease me any longer. Please."

"Please what, sweetheart?"

"I need you. Inside me."

He let the tip rub up and down, and then he pushed enough to have just the head inside her and held.

"Please, Lucas," she said, raking her nails over his chest.

"Ask me. Beg me, baby."

"Please, I need you to…"

"To what? What do you need me to do? Tell me, sweetheart."

"I need you inside me."

"Yes, baby, but ask me nice and sweet. Tell me what you want."

His gaze became devilishly dark as he stroked himself, ready for entry. "I need the command, baby."

She inhaled as his large hand squeezed her breast so hard it nearly hurt.

"That, that thing you were thinking. That thought. I want to hear that thought," he said as he smiled, squeezed, and slid his knees under her thighs, readying himself.

"Fuck me, Lucas."

"Yes, my dear. That's exactly what I'm going to do. With pleasure." He grinned again. "Pull me inside, baby."

She leaned forward, gripping his buttocks, and pulled him with her muscles deep inside her, holding him there, milking his length and feeling the hardness of his tip against her cervix. The dull ache had her squeezing her eyes shut. She rolled back and arched her abdomen. His hands held her hips, then pulled her knees up over his shoulders, and he ground down into her, rotating and drilling, holding firm and then deepening his pressure. "Is this what you need, baby?" he asked.

She couldn't speak. He thrust and held her tight, holding his breath as she did the same, then released her and soon thrust deep inside again. Her spine began to tingle as the little precursor to her orgasm began. She desperately needed him to fill every part of her insides. The calm between his powerful hip thrusts left her vacant and needy.

"Deeper," she whispered.

He hitched her knees up again, burying his shaft without holding back. "God, Marcy. I can't get enough."

The soft hairs at the back of her neck began to stiffen. She felt her internal muscles clamp down on him hard. Her breasts felt hot, her nipples engorged. Her body was at the edge of an explosion of passion unlike she'd felt before. Her eyes flew open and through her hair, she saw the smile cross his lips as he felt her pulse against him, as he watched her pleasure, kissing her eyes, her neck, the warm space between her breasts.

Then a sudden frown wrinkled his forehead and his lips formed a perfect O. "God, I can't help it," he said with difficulty as he exhaled, pumped and held, until he collapsed on top of her. As her breathing slowed and perspiration traveled from his chest to hers, she allowed her fingers to sift through his hair, pushing it off his forehead. He kissed her nipples gently, then tucked his head into the space beneath her chin and pressed his cheek to her.


IN THE LAST few moments before she fell into a deep sleep, Lucas still buried deep inside her, she played with the damp curls at the back of his neck. Her fingers stroked up and down his spine and she squeezed his butt cheeks. His enormous torso pressed her breasts until their bodies breathed in tandem. Holding him, she'd never felt happier, and she knew, if she ever had to let this man go, she'd miss him the rest of her life.

# CHAPTER 11

THEY NEEDED A cold shower after the third time they made love. Lucas insisted on washing her all over, slipping fingers into every crevice, because it was like seeing her all over again. Her body was like silk. The bubbles over her breasts made them slippery. She was built perfectly for him, and he loved the feeling of her slick body brushing up against his torso.

He tried to envision the faces of other lovers and exciting conquests from his past, but he couldn't see a single one. He couldn't even picture Connie's face anymore. The connection was so strong between him and Marcy he didn't care if they never left the cabin.

Where was it all going? And did it matter, really? He knew Connie would blow a gasket, and he hoped she wouldn't retaliate against this lovely creature he'd found, this woman he barely knew. He wasn't going to fuck it up. Not this time. The bonfire they could build together would be enough to last their lifetimes.

*What the fuck am I saying*? he asked himself as he watched the water sluice down her perfect back, ending at that perfect ass. She was using his palms as her washcloth, letting him touch every inch of her.

He knew they needed to talk, but he wasn't in any hurry. This was what he knew: The sight of her nude body shuddering in front of him, and her little shouts and wiggles as the cold made her jump, had him smiling and fucking melted his heart.

Oh, he was snagged all right. He was so fuckin' hooked and hog-tied. There was no way out. No way he'd let anyone get between them.

But then he remembered he was a team guy. He was a warrior, and there was a job to do in just a couple of days. They'd have to talk between their fucking. She liked to talk during sex, just like he did. He could pump her little pussy until her lips were so swollen she'd walk funny.

And even then, it wouldn't be enough.

"Are you hungry, Marcy?" he dared to whisper. He hated to end their little romp in the shower, but he honestly wasn't sure if they hadn't already drained the well. "We're gonna burn up the pump if we keep this up," he said as he kissed her under her ear.

She turned, and her smile tempted him further. Half-lidded eyes did him in. "I'm starved. What did you have in mind, sailor?"

THEY ATE THAI food on Cloverdale Boulevard. He began to get his bearings, watching people through the dirty glass window. He liked the little town. Things hadn't become all yuppified. There were cowboys, jazz musicians, pot smokers, and little hotties trying to get modeling jobs in San Francisco, so they could escape from their little town. He couldn't blame them. People lived here because they didn't aspire to do many big things. And that meant things were safe—if there ever was a really safe town in the U.S. anymore.

He pushed his leftover food aside and took her hand. "I gotta explain a couple of things to you."

She set down her fork, took a sip of water, and gave him a sober look.

"You know what I do, right?"

"I do."

"So, I don't think I'm breaching protocol when I tell you the world is a much more dangerous place than everyone thinks."

She shrugged. "I know that."

"No, sweetheart," he said as he leaned in, putting his elbows on the table. "You don't know the half of it. Involving you in my life, and I'm assuming we'll be involved—"

"Involved?" She raised her eyebrows.

"Well, pardon me, but I just assumed that—"

She giggled, and it was such a wonderful sound. "You and I are in a boatload of trouble, Lucas. We just jumped out of an airplane without a parachute."

A smile tugged at his lips. "That's a pretty good way to put it, honey." He could see she was hesitant to say something.

"I'd say we're more like blended. Like all those bodily fluids we exchanged all morning."

"I like all those bodily fluids. I want to make more," he whispered.

Marcy blushed.

"What is it? You re-thinking all this?"

"Not sure I can. It's just that I can't believe I'm here, with you. Connie was all wrong about you. I'll bet you never cheated on her either."

"Never. Not after we got married."

"For the life of me, I don't understand why she thought you did, how she could just could walk away."

He stiffened. He didn't want to talk about Connie. "Long sad, story, Marcy. We sure had fun, but we had no staying power. She had one station, Marcy. It was to be all Connie's way. Always Connie's way. She could never understand why I wanted to do this. Looking back on it, I don't think she really supported my decision to become a SEAL. Not really."

"So much for easing into things to find out what's going on, Lucas."

"You and me? I told you it wasn't smart."

"You did. And I didn't listen. I've been a bad girl." Her eyes sparkled as she dipped her chin in an obvious flirtation.

Oh, that was such a dangerous thing to do to him. If she only knew.

"I haven't even gotten started, Marcy, with all the things I want to do with you."

She blushed and looked down at her lap. "Are we going to think about all this before we spend another few hours getting lost in each other's arms?"

"That's exactly what we're doing right now, honey."

She watched their entwined fingers, his thumb caressing the back of her hand. "No, *you* were starting to warn me about something," she said.

He adjusted his hips, rolled his shoulders and tried to get comfortable. "We're deploying in a few months, but in the meantime, we're doing some training out of state."

"What kind of training?"

"See, that's the problem—I can't tell you."

"Are there girls there?"

"Honey, there are girls everywhere. Anywhere there are SEALs, there are girls. But if you don't stop letting those nasty thoughts run naked around that cute little pink brain of yours, I'm gonna spank your sweet ass until it's welted and red."

Her eyes widened. "Another thing I haven't tried before."

It was no use. Only thing left to do was work up a good appetite for that nice steak barbeque he'd planned. The big difference was that this time, he was going to do it all naked.

# CHAPTER 12

M ARCY CALLED DEVON and Nick and told them she was going to stay in Cloverdale and wasn't coming home until tomorrow.

The following day, she and Lucas shopped for provisions in town, and then about noon, went to Nick and Devon's home, where Lucas seemed impressed with the small winery.

Devon was giving them scrutiny after Marcy introduced Lucas to both of them. Marcy could tell she'd figured out who Lucas was, and what they'd been doing.

"I'd heard about this place from some of the old guys," Lucas said. Nick's head jerked up.

"Old?"

"Well, the guys who have been in longer than ten years. You got out at ten, right? About the time I joined Team 3."

"That's right."

"You okay with leaving the teams, Nick? I mean, did it give you trouble?"

"You heard I got injured? It was an easy choice after that. And Devon does really well. I think it would be harder if we lived down in San Diego, seeing all the guys every day. Here, we just blend in, man. It's a good life."

Lucas' phone chirped. "Hallo," he said as he watched Devon and Marcy whispering in the kitchen. He recognized the number as Kyle's.

"We've stepped up the training, Lucas. I gotta ask you to come back."

"When?"

"Yesterday." Kyle's tone told him not to argue. It was a command.

"What's up?" This wasn't anything good. Something big had happened.

"Not over the phone."

"Okay, well, I'll get going tonight. Be home in about twelve hours."

"No can do. Bought you a ticket; it's waiting for you at Sonoma County Airport."

"Today, as in this afternoon?"

"Yessir. That direct flight leaves at three. You better be on it."

"I got my truck, Kyle."

"So get someone else to drive it home, Lucas. This is something we can't wait about."

It wasn't optimum, but Marcy agreed to drive Lucas' truck back to San Diego. "You can stay a couple of days up here with Nick and Devon, if you want. Makes no difference to me when I get the truck back. I won't be anywhere I'll need it."

He knew Marcy wanted to ask him where he was going. He liked that she didn't even try. He worked to calm his breathing. He didn't want her to get as nervous as he was. "I can't even go back up to Cloverdale to clear out the place, and there's one thing I don't like leaving there."

"No worries, Lucas. I can bring your things back."

"Cabin's pretty out in the middle of nowhere, Marcy. I don't want you going up without someone to help." Nick was watching nearby.

"Promise."

"You unplug the refrigerator and take home all the food. Make sure the water's shut off. I got a couple of things in the closet, in particular, a heavy black zipper bag full of crap. Don't forget that one, Marcy." Lucas saw the black bag registered with Nick, who added his nod.

"We'll go up there tomorrow. Soonest I can do it."

"Thanks, Nick."

"So, other than making sure everything is locked up tight, nothing else needs to be done." He handed her the truck keys and watched her frown with downcast eyes. "Marcy, honey, no worries. You guys get up to Cloverdale tomorrow. You show them the way, okay?"

Marcy agreed.

"Some of that stuff's heavy. Especially that bag." He glanced over at Nick, and they shared a look. "You don't know the area and there's some crazy shit going on."

Nick gave him another brief nod.

Marcy reached for his arm. "I'll be fine, Lucas. You just come home safe," she whispered.

He put his arms around her and felt her shaking as he held her close.

"I will, baby. You just keep the truck until I get back into town." He paused. "And I can't tell you when, either, but I'll call when I can."

Marcy took him to the airport in Lucas' truck so she could practice working the stick shift. He showed her all the little gadgets, like the keyless entry and the locked storage compartment she was never to open, which sat underneath the front seat. "You put the heavy black bag here in the back seat and you cover it up with the blanket there. Don't forget it, promise?"

"What's—?"

"Don't ask, Marcy. Just have Nick help you with it."

When they arrived at Schulz International, Sonoma County's only airport, Lucas checked his duty bag separately, having the talk with the security agent. He had to take some of his things with him, since he really didn't want to leave all of his firearms back with Marcy for the road trip home.

As they waited for his plane to San Diego, she brought it up first. "I'm going to have to tell Connie, Lucas. I just wanted you to know."

"Your funeral." The line was getting shorter, and then he was at the x-ray machine. "Tell her we don't get along."

"And what if she sees me driving your truck when I return it. What's she going to say then?"

"The likelihood of that is nil, Marcy. You know that. I doubt she'd ever come over to the place. She never has. You want to avoid Connie at all costs."

"I have to cancel the listing, Lucas, have to give her a reason."

"Don't mess with her, Marcy. If she does find out, don't be surprised if she doesn't try to go after your license or something like that."

"Just such a risk. I'll park the truck at your place, maybe get someone to help me with your stuff. And mysteriously slip away. Geez, Lucas I'm so nervous about all of this. I hate all this sneaking around."

"You go by Gunny's Gym and ask for Sinouk, the owner's son. He can help you with the stuff." Lucas saw she'd been pouting. "Hey, not to worry." He elicited a smile from her as he coaxed another kiss from her lips. God, he hated to leave her now.

"Sir, I'm afraid visiting hours are over," the guard barked. "You're gonna miss your plane."

He gripped the back of Marcy's hair. "We'll talk, Marcy. Not to worry. We'll figure something out."

"But I'm going to give up the listing anyway, Lucas. I just can't in good conscience—"

"*Sir!*"

"Just one fuckin' minute, okay?" Lucas shouted over the small crowd. A mother shushed him and covered her daughter's ears. "She's gonna have a pretty hard time getting my signature now, Marcy." He was rewarded with a smile, and a kiss.

His parting thought as he turned and headed for the plane: *I like the way you do business, Marcy Gelland!* He hoped he had one more time to say goodbye before they deployed in earnest. Finally, he tore himself away and tried to focus on the mission at hand.

SHE WATCHED HIM walk out onto the windy tarmac, following a trail of travelers, including one older man in a wheelchair. He quickly turned around and ran past the security guard, who chased him back inside the terminal.

On the other side of the glass security doors, he pounded with his fists and shouted, "Marry me, Marcy Gelland!"

"Yes. Yes, I'll marry you, Lucas Shipley," she shouted back, her heart bursting, crazy, totally crazy for the guy and completely not caring about any of the reality of what she'd just plunged herself into. One thimbleful of rational thought made its way out at last.

"But first, you gotta get divorced."

# CHAPTER 13

MARCY DECIDED TO go straight up to the house in Cloverdale after dropping Lucas off at the airport. She didn't want to bother Devon and Nick, who would be waiting for her to stay over tonight. Driving all the way back down to Santa Rosa, picking them up, and then going north to the cabin and then back home was just too many trips on the 101 Freeway, and inconsiderate of her friend's time. And she wanted to do the lockup in the daylight hours.

She'd promised Lucas she wouldn't go up there alone, and now she was going to violate that promise. *Always easier to ask for forgiveness than permission.* It had served her well for most of her life. Now was certainly no exception.

Traffic was coming the opposite direction as she headed north. When she pulled into the little town of Cloverdale, she stopped at a coffee shop and picked up a cappuccino and a sandwich, then took the winding road off into the woods north of town.

She took one wrong turn, then doubled back and found the correct trail to the cabin. Using the large brass key, she let herself in. As she stood, feeling the warmth and the wash of memories of what they'd been doing for the past twenty-four hours there, she blushed. It was so peaceful and quiet. On the front stoop all she could hear were the sounds of the tall trees rustling in the wind and an occasional bird. Somewhere off in the blue, cloudless sky a small plane sputtered on its way. A faint smell of campfire and woods was soothing to her nerves. It made her sleepy being so peacefully alone.

Back inside, she washed the dishes and put them away, unplugged the refrigerator and shut off the water main to the house. She made the bed, folded and straightened the towels in the bath, put Lucas' clothes in another nylon shoulder bag she found in the closet, and added her own clothes. She picked up the heavy black bag Lucas had mentioned and gingerly carried it to the truck, depositing it on the rear floor like she had been instructed, covering it with the old blanket. Returning to the house, she took one more look around, loaded the other bags up, and then went back, pulling out all the supplies from the refrigerator and put them in brown paper bags, and locked the door behind her.

Before taking off, she walked around the outside of the cabin to make sure all the windows were secured.

The roadway going out looked different than she'd remembered and again, she took a wrong turn. The drive ended in another cabin nearby, with several metal outbuildings and a stable behind it. A slim man in jeans and a light blue shirt was working with a hoe in the front yard where he was growing a small vegetable garden. A battered red pickup truck and a rusted white passenger van were parked at the side of the structure. The man looked up. He wore wire-rimmed glasses and sported a full beard.

Marcy knew there were communes and pot growers out in the woods between here and Mendocino County. The young man looked like he could have been a settler from a Jewish kibbutz with his full beard and well-tanned skin. He leaned on his hoe and squinted in the late afternoon light at her, frowning, his wire-rimmed glasses glinting in the sunlight.

She rolled down her window, leaning out. "Sorry. I'm a bit lost. Looking for the way out to the highway."

She noticed the front door of the cabin opened and she could see a face, perhaps two in the crack created. The man looked up to the door and shouted something and the door immediately shut.

He walked toward her, pointed with a thin finger, and in accent he said, "Left. Then right. All the way right."

"Okay, so I go out this driveway, turn left, and then take the first right?"

"First right, all the way right," he repeated in his thick accent. "Freeway." He nodded.

"Thank you very much."

The man bowed slightly, smiling as if blushing, averting his eyes down and away from her. Marcy put the truck in reverse, grinding the gears, which had the stranger abruptly raise his head in alarm. She hit the gas and too quickly let out the clutch and the truck stalled. She put the truck in neutral, restarted it, and took off down the road in a cloud of dust. In the rearview mirror she saw two other young men leave the front door, both standing side by side, intent on watching her truck barrel along the dusty drive. Just before she turned left, she noticed a small wooden sign she'd missed on the way in. It was the sign of the cross, with sunlight grooved in and painted in faded yellow. Underneath the insignia were the words, "Sonshine Haven."

Marcy made a mental note to ask Lucas and perhaps Nick and Devon about this obviously Christian camp so close to Lucas' cabin. In a way, it was reassuring to have a neighbor so close nearby, in case anything were to happen with the cabin.

By the time she hit Highway 101, the sun had fallen low. She got a text message that Lucas had arrived safely in San Diego and would call when he could, later tonight or tomorrow morning. She texted back hearts and kisses to him, which he returned.

Next, Marcy telephoned Devon, gave her the news and told her she was on her way back to their house.

Nick was particularly quiet over dinner, causing Devon to ask him what was wrong.

The handsome green-eyed former SEAL gave Marcy a serious look, cocking his head to the side. "Marcy, I don't know you very well but I'm bothered about one thing. And you're gonna have to forgive me on this. I'm a very careful man."

"Okay, shoot," Marcy said.

"Nick?" Devon slipped her arm under Nick's and squeezed herself next to him. "What's up?"

Nick smiled at his wife, but it quickly evaporated.

"Lucas told you not to go up there alone, and the very first thing you did when he was on that plane was go right up there."

Marcy felt her cheeks flush. Nick's direct approach to her disobedience made her feel ashamed, naked in front of them. It was time to beg for forgiveness.

"I didn't want to bother you guys—"

"But Lucas asked you *not* to do that. He made quite a point about it, and probably had good reason for that, Marcy. It has to do with your safety."

"Nick, come on," Devon pestered him.

Nick stiffened, removed Devon's arms from his, separating himself from her, and sat up straight. "It's not funny, you two. If Lucas mentioned it, then it was important. You have to trust him when he tells you things like that, Marcy. You don't know what's at stake."

"I know, but nothing happened. I just got all the things out, did what he asked, and I buttoned up the house so you guys don't have to be bothered with it."

"Except he's going to want me to go up there and make sure it's okay. So you didn't save me a trip after all."

"Nick? What the heck is going on?" Devon asked. Her frown cut deep into the bridge of her nose.

"These are strange times. Lucas even said it. I've been told about all sorts of stuff you guys don't want to know about. It's for your protection you not know. But you have to follow directions. Nothing optional about it."

Marcy knew he was right, but she didn't care for Nick's method of delivery. She felt prickly. Devon had obviously picked it up.

"Nick, get over it, will you? No harm no foul. That's one of your favorite expressions. So just chill. The main thing is that she got it done. Lucas' stuff is safely back down here."

"Not the point, Devon."

"I'm done with this, Nick. You need to go to bed. Now." Devon was getting angry. "Marcy and I will clean up here."

Devon pointed to the stairs.

Nick gave her a hug and quick kiss. Then he addressed Marcy. "Sorry, kid. I'm going to be a stickler about this. Tomorrow we go back up there and double check everything, not that you didn't do everything correctly, but he wanted me to go so I could confirm that it was all done. We're like that. Thorough. Checking, double-checking. Sometimes our life depends on it. No reflection on you."

"I understand." Marcy thought she did a pretty good job of hiding her hurt feelings.

Nick turned and ran upstairs. Marcy followed Devon to the kitchen, and then remembered the food she'd left in the truck. "Holy crap. I've probably got a back seat full of sour milk and melted cheese."

"I'll help you."

The two of them carried the two boxes inside the kitchen. Marcy was going to get the other bags later. They stowed the perishables, cleaned up the dinner and placed dishes in the dishwasher, turning it on. Devon made a couple of glasses of ice water and handed one to Marcy. "Come on, let's sit in the living room for a bit."

"I'm for that," said Marcy settling into the comfortable couch.

"Let's catch up on some juicy gossip," Devon started. "I want to know all about Lucas' wife, or soon-to-be ex-wife. What's she like?"

"She's a piece of work, Dev. Gorgeous, but a basket case. She's bitter, and I don't think he did anything to deserve that. She's jealous of his connection with the Brotherhood."

"From what I've heard, some of the guys play around a lot. Father children all over the place. Many of them lack good judgement. Don't get yourself caught, Marcy. Be careful."

"I might be stupid, but I believe Lucas. I really do," admitted Marcy.

"Some women aren't made for this lifestyle. I might not have been very good at it, actually."

"I don't know much about the community. Maybe you can help me there. All I know is Lucas is on her list. She seems to genuinely hate him. I feel sorry for those kids. Just too bad what she's doing."

"They're pretty intense. But I remember I asked one of the wives about them before Nick and I got married one time when I visited—have you been to any of their get-togethers?"

"No. This happened so fast. I mean, we're only at day three here."

"Right. I forget, Marcy. They rarely let in outsiders, so having you here, involved with him like this, well, it brings you into the inner circle. They have a funny way about them, a code. You're either in, or you're out. You're in, Marcy, and Connie is out. But none of the guys will date her. If she's out, she's out."

"It just seems over the top."

Devon laughed. "In the beginning, I thought so, too. I mean, Nick seemed just like a total asshole at first. So full of himself. But boy, when we got involved, man did sparks fly."

Marcy felt her cheeks pink up again.

"You have to love the way they live, their intensity. Sometimes they're right on, and sometimes they have shit for brains." Devon continued. "They get all this training, all this fantastic equipment. They pretty much feel invincible. Hard for them when they come home. The wives are taking care of everything, running the house, paying the bills, and then he comes home and suddenly he's the king. All she wants to do is get some help. Especially with the kids."

"Makes sense. Connie more or less told me the same thing." Marcy was hesitant to ask Devon so she started softly. "You guys going to try anytime soon, Devon?"

"Have been. It will happen when it happens. At least I don't have to try to space the births around deployments, like some of the other wives do."

"Impossible." Marcy shook her head. How *did* women handle all that, not knowing if their men would come home? But she realized it was what women and families of soldiers have to deal with all the time. Always been that way for those who chose to love warriors, not a stock broker, insurance man, or another realtor.

"So what's her main beef with Lucas?"

"I think the tipping point was a bachelor party, and some of the pictures taken were a little revealing." Marcy giggled. "They had some dancers and such."

"Strippers," interrupted Devon. "Seems to be a custom for these guys. I don't even ask what Nick's party was like."

"Well this one was worse, from what I understand."

Devon frowned.

"Someone posted them on Facebook, and when Connie saw them, she flipped out."

"You can be sure I didn't check Nick's FB page for a month afterward."

"Smart. But, honestly, I think Connie didn't want anything coming between her and Lucas. I think she began to resent the Navy, resent his closeness to the other team guys, perhaps asking him to choose between her and the brotherhood."

"Ouch! Not smart."

"Just my guess, Dev. So when Lucas didn't agree or side with her, I think she decided she was done. I hate to think it's about the money she'll make with the sale of the house, but you know, Devon, I couldn't even rule *that* out. She's one of the meanest people I've ever met."

"And you have to deal with her?"

"I think I'm handing the listing over to someone else."

"Probably wise. I mean, I can only imagine what would happen if she found out—"

"Gives me chills, Dev. Not looking forward to that."

"And you have to drive his truck all the way back to San Diego, too?"

Marcy shrugged.

"How is the market down there?"

"Going gangbusters. That's why I have to get back. Been one of the busiest times I've had. How about you?"

"You know what they say. How do you make a small fortune in the wine business? Start with a large fortune and you'll soon have a small fortune."

They shared a laugh.

"Everything I saved and did has gone into the winery. We start crush soon, fingers crossed for nice temperate weather for harvest. Hoping we get a good yield and the grapes are better than last year. We're at year five now. Another two to go and we'll know."

"Are you still selling real estate as much as before?"

"As much as I can. But Nick needs my help here, too. I represent some big investors who are buying right now, so that part's been good for me. We have investors too, some of the SEAL families are part owners, so that takes the burden off, but adds the pressure to turn a profit."

Marcy looked around the house, hearing the crickets through the screens overlooking the patio. The large harvest moon was just rising over the vineyards in the distance. It was a special evening. Felt like the calm before the storm, for some reason, and she was grateful her college friend could give her the time to just sit and chat.

"You own a little piece of Heaven, Devon."

"That we do. Sophie, Nick's sister, always said so, and she was right. I wouldn't trade my lifestyle for anywhere else in the world. I'd like to raise my family here one day. I'd love this to be a Northern California Wine Retreat for SEALs and their families."

"Wouldn't that be something?"

# CHAPTER 14

L UCAS WAS MET at the airport by Jake and Alex. The warm night air
smelled of the salty inlet, something he'd forgotten he missed.

"So what's up with your truck, man?" Jake asked as Lucas climbed
into the second seat of the Hummer.

"It's getting driven back in the next day or two. Kyle wanted me back
here ASAP. You tell me, what the fuck's going on?"

"All shit is hitting the fan. We got a lot of chatter about some groups
all over the U.S. They're making us do some specialized training with the
guys from Little Creek. Team 6 uncovered some stuff in Turkey. And
someone tried to take out a military surgeon on vacation in Oregon with
his family. They were just camping."

Lucas felt guilty he'd been so head over heels loving Marcy, he hadn't
been watching the news. Other than X-rated movies, international news
was as popular as sports at the bachelor pad.

"Everyone okay?"

"Cut up, especially his wife, but the kids were okay. Lucky thing he
was carrying a gun, though he'll get written up for it." Jake drove them in
the opposite direction of the apartment.

"You're shitting me," Lucas said.

"Federal lands. Not allowed to carry," Alex said over the back of the
seat. "They might not have survived without it, though."

"That's messed up," said Lucas. No one said a word. Lucas noticed
they seemed to be headed toward Coronado. "Hey, we going over to the
Team Building?"

"Yup," said Jake.

The injustice of the attack and the fact that the man might get in
trouble for defending his family had him fuming. "Just can't believe

they'd actually put a letter in his file." Lucas continued to shake his head as he watched the lights of the Coronado base come into view.

"Kyle thinks they'll go light on him, but they have to make note of it." Jake's shoulders rounded as he continued, "A very strange world out there, Lucas."

"That it is. You guys do any training yesterday or day before?" Lucas asked.

"Nope. We start the briefing tonight. Couple of guys coming in tomorrow," answered Jake.

They passed the guard shack, parked the Hummer, and walked toward the entrance to their building. Kyle was locked in serious conversation with a small group of team guys, including T.J., Cooper, Tyler, Rory, and Luke. All of them looked up and behind Lucas as the team erupted in a warm welcome for a dark-skinned man wearing western wear, including cowboy boots.

Kyle put his arm around Jake, as he pulled a group of newbies over to introduce them. "This here is the baddest motherfucker on the whole planet."

The dark-skinned man nodded and looked down at his boots. Though he wasn't one of the newbies, Lucas had never met the man before, even on his DEVGRU deployment.

In a heavily accented voice, the newcomer answered, "Only when I have you guys at my back, or dropping in like flies all around me. Then I can be very, very brave. By myself, not so much."

T.J. and Luke came over and gave the man a bear hug. "Come here you lying sonofabitch," T.J. said to his ear. He made a grand gesture of kissing him on the side of the face. "How the fuck are you?"

"I'm good. My wife's pregnant again. Hoping to create one of those, how you say, 'anchor babies'?"

"Why am I not surprised?" Rory Kennedy said.

When T.J. let go of him, Kyle stepped up and repeated the hug. He turned and presented the man to Lucas, Jake, Alex, and several newbies at the end. "This here is Jackie Daniels, our interpreter. We don't know his real name—"

A couple of the older SEALs started laughing. Lucas hadn't seen so many white teeth since the last time they'd had a bachelor party and half of them were completely shitfaced. Fredo and Armani entered the warehouse building, along with several others Lucas thought looked like transplants from other teams.

Cooper added his hug to the lineup. "Yeah, if he told us, he'd have to kill us, so we call him Jackie. And T.J.'s right, he's the baddest mother-fucker in the whole Navy."

"No. Your government will not make me a Navy man. I am working on my citizenship, but soon, they will give it to me, and then I can be a taxi driver like all of my other countrymen."

Jake stepped forward and shook Jackie's hand. "Honor to meet you. Heard a lot about you, Mr. Daniels."

"Jackie," the interpreter corrected. "Mr. Daniels sounds like some guy who is the principal at my daughter's school."

Jackie gripped Lucas's hand, tilting his head and giving him a wide smile, but his eyes didn't blink or waver, and Lucas felt like he'd just had his mind read. Jackie took a respectful step back and seemed to sense the new introductions had some uneasy around him. Lucas also knew it didn't bother the terp, Jackie, one bit.

They'd been told the stories about how he'd risked his life on several missions with their team, as well as several others he'd worked with in the past. Their highest level capture was on a mission that nearly cost six SEALs and a CIA agent their lives. Unlike several of the other interpret-ers, Jackie was not opposed to be carrying a weapon and protected them on this mission when they freed several SEAL hostages taken captive. This was before Lucas joined the team.

Like a skilled warrior, Jackie didn't force himself on any of them, nor make them show loyalty without it being earned. Lucas knew he was a big-time asset to whatever mission they would be tasked with.

Kyle came to attention, regarding several men in and out of uniform who walked through the Team 3 Building doors. Lucas and everyone else faced them, and several addressed the new audience in hushed tones.

Collins, their SEAL liaison, walked over to a small group of tables and chairs, followed by one Lt. Commander and a non-uniformed, who Lucas judged to be CIA. Kyle took his place next to them, making a fourth. Lucas knew something big was going on as another couple of unidentified, but well-built, gentlemen took to some rear seats in the pit. This was a nighttime briefing, conducted without the whole Charlie Team being present, which meant they were in a hurry. He was glad he'd texted Marcy when he landed, since he doubted he'd be able to be in much communication very soon.

"Gentlemen, take your seats," Kyle said to the group, who had already started doing so before the order was given. Lucas sat next to Jake and Ryan. Looking around, he nodded to Alex, Cory, and several others.

No one standing was smiling. T.J. and Luke sandwiched Jackie, the terp. Danny and Jeffrey sat together in the back row, both wearing sunglasses, though the building was low lit. Rory sat just in front of them.

"This here is Lt. Commander Ian Forsythe, Office of Naval Intelligence. He's going to brief you on a situation we have going on now. Lt. Commander?" Kyle backed up and the highly decorated veteran cleared his throat and took the center stage. Though the SEALs were not required to salute, each man in his own way sat up straighter, uncrossed their arms, and showed they were paying attention, unlike their normal demeanor.

"You've been briefed before about terrorist group formations in this country. I know you had a representative of DEVGRU, SO Thom Grand, speaking with you recently about death teams who we now know have landed here. We have it on good authority some have been spotted in several areas in the southwest, south, and now with this recent incident in Oregon, we believe some are in the Pacific Northwest. We're still scrambling a bit to gather all that intelligence without tipping our hand."

Lucas' stomach lurched as he realized he hadn't eaten anything since boarding the plane, except for some peanuts and a coke. Or, maybe it was the news. He would have anticipated getting geared up and ready to roll if he was with Team 6 again, or even Team 3 in Iraq. But he wasn't sure what the plan of action was for the situation at hand. This was a threat on U.S. soil, after all.

Forsythe continued. "We know members of the military, especially SEALs, are being targeted. Our families are in danger. Our friends too, perhaps. Time to take measures, hopefully preventative measures to ensure our community stays safe."

Forsythe turned to Collins, who stepped up next to him. "Gentlemen, we're going to institute some rules that will not be broken, do I make myself clear?"

Affirmations trickled from the group, a combination of nods and whispers and grunts.

"While we are doing some specialized training, and this will all be explained to you in detail, we're going to organize a com schedule, so no one on this team is out of the loop. And this is going to extend to your wives. And I gotta also mention there will not be the usual recreational use of females, or something that involves you getting shitfaced and making a scene, or getting caught in some place by yourself with people you don't know. We aren't sure how they'll come after us, but we're staying vigilant and, of course, prepared. Being prepared keeps us alive, right, gents?"

Again a wave of affirmations filled the room.

Kyle added his comments. "Newbies especially, listen up. We're doing something that's never been done before. We're going to create an old-fashioned phone list. You are to be in phone contact with five other men on our team every day, morning and evening. And you are to pass along anything you see that is out of the ordinary. Each five-man group will have a senior man who will be responsible for relaying information. But, make no mistake, you can't get hold of someone? You call me, you call Coop here, Fredo, Armani, or Collins."

Forsythe added, "Your training is going to coincidentally take place next to two well-known and documented terrorist training camps. Active camps. Camps we believe have recently imported some talent, and that talent has been kept hidden, which means they know we're surveilling them, and they're still doing it."

A hushed silence fell over the group. Someone let out a loud and long, "Fuuuuck."

"Gentlemen, those of you who've been over in the arena know that not many of these guys fear death. They don't fear getting caught, because that makes the news. Making the news is what they're after. They won't win in the end, but they want to make the US of A feel like a self-imposed prison camp." Forsythe exhaled and paced back and forth.

So that was the gig, Lucas thought. They were supposed to look like they were just living their lives as usual, but they were going to go dangerously close to the bee and not get stung, or be ready for the swarm. They were going to tempt the group to try and snag one of them. But he wasn't sure, so he thought he'd asked.

"Sir, SO Shipley here. May I ask a question?" Lucas stood.

"Go ahead, son," Forsythe answered.

"I'm just not clear, and you probably have much more to tell us, but from what our brothers at DEVGRU, SEAL Team 6, told us, weren't they interested in perhaps doing a reverse snatch and grab?" Lucas could see a couple of newbies had no clue what he was saying.

"That's right. We think they're looking to take a target back with them, possibly a SEAL, and more specifically, one from Team 3 or 5."

More muttering and private discussions continued until Lucas continued. "Okay, then. Why are we going to train near them, if our goal is to avoid being captured or killed?"

Kyle inserted himself before Forsythe could answer. "You mean did we just confirm the CIA and Naval Intelligence is using us as bait? That your question, SO Shipley?"

Lucas nodded his head. "Yes, Chief." He heard a couple of the older SEALs swear, crossing their arms and legs. It was something apparently, several of them were thinking about, but none were excited by the idea.

"Who else would you suggest, SO Shipley?" began Forsythe. "Your wives and children, innocent civilians?" Forsythe drilled his stare into Lucas, his breathing very slow and deep, like he was bracing for a punch and was completely calm and ready for whatever anyone would dish out. All sound was sucked out of the room and nobody moved. "I'm asking you a serious question. I'm as serious as a heart attack, Shipley."

T.J. Talbot snarled out, "Oh yeah. 'Come on over here said the spider to the fly.'" The big SEAL examined the fingernails on his right hand as Jackie and Luke started chuckling. Lucas sat.

Coop was more sober. "I'm going to ask you what I always need to know, sir."

"All ears here," answered Forsythe.

"The women and children. What the fuck are we supposed to do with them?"

After a brief moment of silence, while everyone looked at Kyle, Jones added his comments. "You dumb-fuck." Jones waved his long arms around his head. "You white boys are real slow in the bedroom. You're supposed to keep them barefoot and happy. Nekked I think, too. Yo mamas never teach you nothin?"

Everyone started adding their two cents. But Coop and Kyle were staring at each other like they shared something no one else knew about. Kyle hushed the raucous spouting off. Lucas knew it was nervous repartee, helping to mask how uneasy everyone felt about this whole situation. "Wait a minute guys," Kyle continued. "Coop has a point. So listen up." He turned to Collins and then glanced over at Forsythe.

"I'll take that," said Forsythe. "We're instituting something for them, too. Similar. We're going to embed some extra protection. We're also coordinating with the local sheriff and police, on a very limited basis, not with the rank and file, so while you're gone on training, or, if we don't have a more favorable outcome, we may delay deployment. Just not sure yet what that's going to look like."

"In the meantime, we're traveling out of state," said Kyle.

Fredo shouted out, "Snow gear or swim trunks?"

Some of their jungle training was in Baja, some in Florida, or desert training in Las Vegas. Alaska was always good for cold-weather exercises.

"Neither," barked Forsythe. He took two steps to the side, assuming the wide stance some of the officers were known for, arms crossed behind his back. He inhaled sharply, gave them a half smile and shouted, "Gentlemen, we're headed to Tennessee."

# CHAPTER 15

**M**ARCY AND NICK drove up to Cloverdale in Lucas' truck mid-morning.

"Sorry about the inconvenience, Nick. I thought I was saving you some time."

"No need to apologize, but you gotta pay attention, Marcy. It comes with the territory."

She knew he was right. "You know we hardly know each other, Nick. There is so much about Lucas I'm just learning."

"Afraid I can't help you there. But even if I could, we don't do that."

Marcy knew it was an uphill battle. It was a long-shot that the two of them would wind up together, and now she began to feel guilty she'd said yes to marrying him. In fact, as she thought about all the decisions she'd made, especially the one about "screwing the husband of the divorcing clients," which was a huge no-no on every scale possible, she was ashamed. She might have even jeopardized her job at Coronado Bay.

Nick tuned in on a country satellite station, taking some of the tension out of the air. She crossed and uncrossed her arms and legs and began chewing down a nail. The countryside was green with rows of vineyards, but the brown earth and commercial buildings detracted from the beauty of the several wineries they passed on their way. Traffic bothered her. The bugs on the truck's windshield bothered her. She didn't like one of the songs, and she wished she was back in San Diego, near the ocean, near the blue water and the breeze that was ever present.

Her cell rang. Nick turned down the radio station so she could answer it. "This is Marcy."

"Where the devil are you, Marcy?" Her broker's voice sounded shrill.

"Sorry, Joe. I'm up here in Sonoma County, looking at my client's real estate. She asked me to do it."

"Are you sure about that?"

"Yes." Marcy's stomach flip-flopped, and she squeezed the phone against her ear.

"I've had some complaints from other agents; they can't get hold of you."

"I've gotten no calls, Joe. I'll be back in a day or two."

"Good idea, Marcy. Say, you give that SEAL's wife your cell?"

"I did. Why?"

"Not sure, but she's been talking to Gail here in the office, you know, the new agent married to the football player?"

"Oh yes."

"I guess they're friends. I'd watch my back on that one."

"Joe, there's a little situation there I need to go over with you." Marcy looked sideways at Nick who was pretending he couldn't hear. "I'm going to give up their listing. Coming up here, well, it's changed my perspective a bit." Then she felt Nick's eyes on her as she tried to speak to the passenger window softly, seeking some privacy. "I just can't represent them. I don't feel like I can get along with Connie."

"Then talk with Gail, or someone else about referring it, Marcy. But do it quick."

"Will do. As soon as I get back."

"I'd do it by phone. I'd talk to your client today." Joe hung up.

Was she ready to confront Connie, and do it by phone, not in person like she'd planned? She'd thought she would have the long drive home to San Diego to rehearse and think about how to tell Connie, so it wouldn't blow up in her face. Not being present in person was more dangerous.

"So the wifey doesn't know you and Lucas are an item? That what I'm hearing?" Nick asked.

"Afraid so."

Nick was mercifully quiet. Marcy knew what he was thinking. This also wasn't a very good way to gain points with her college friend and her husband either. Marcy sighed. She was messing up on all fronts.

"I really screwed things up, Nick," she said at last.

"Roger that, Marcy. You got yourself one hell of a problem. And it's going to be a problem for Lucas, too, even if he didn't think about all this beforehand."

No, they certainly hadn't thought about anything. All that mattered at the time, and for the two days afterward, was the chemistry between them, how she felt being around Lucas.

The sounds of the truck filled the deadly silence between them.

Nick continued. "We do so many things well overseas, because we're trained to do it over and over again. All this stuff? Divorce, selling houses, dating? I can't say our community does it very well. We're used to jumping in without thinking. Can't do that at home. And that's a hard lesson to learn. Took me awhile to settle down to being a civilian."

She appreciated his candor and realized she was getting more of a glimpse of the community, way more than she probably deserved.

"But you eventually did, Nick? You eventually made the switch over?"

He nodded, staring right as they pulled off into the woods north of town. "I got injured and that helped the choice. But I couldn't do it back down there in San Diego. It would've driven me nuts. But yes, eventually." He smiled back at her, his honest green eyes giving her a steady hand-up. "Not saying I don't miss it sometimes, though." He splayed his right hand as it rested on top of the steering wheel. "Just being perfectly honest."

Marcy gave him instructions, and in a few minutes they pulled down the now-familiar dirt driveway.

"I can see why he wanted you to come here in the daytime. And you *do* know there are pot growers all over here, right?"

"He told me."

"Used to be a big problem when people would stumble onto someone's field and get shot. Now I think these people grow inside temperature-controlled buildings, the big operations, that is. And they don't do the pot forests like the old days."

"Speaking from first-hand knowledge?" Marcy said as she opened her door and hopped out.

"Not me. My folks, believe it or not."

"You know I got lost coming here yesterday. There are little roads and trails all over the place up here. When I came the first time, I used my GPS. But not everything up here is on that map."

Nick walked to the front stoop. "Nice up here. Very remote, though. You don't ever want to be at this place alone."

Marcy nodded and inserted the key into the front door. Fear coursed through her when she discovered it was unlocked. She was sure she had locked it when she left.

She instantly knew someone had been inside the home even before she saw the mess left behind. The cupboards had been ransacked. Cushions in the living room had been torn open, white pieces of cotton stuffing fell like snow over the floor. A long wooden cabinet door was broken off the hinges, splinters covering the braided rug in front of it. A metal lock was discarded. Nick ran to the bare cabinet first.

"Was this empty?"

"I have no idea."

He peered through checkerboard kitchen window curtains, while Marcy noticed someone had thrown darts, hitting the wall instead of the game board. Nick searched the rest of the cabin, including the closets and the bathroom.

"I'm going to go look around outside. You check for anything that might be missing, if you can tell."

Contents had been removed from the bathroom cabinet and strewn over the floor. Several vitamin and aspirin bottles had been opened and their tablets were absorbing water, turning to paste. Someone had used the toilet, not been very careful about their aim and not flushed it.

Marcy checked the bedroom closet. Every box or bag was opened, and open-ended. Books were removed from the desk in the corner. The cushions on the overstuffed reading chair were sliced open and stuffing was removed just like in the living room.

She wondered what the motive of the break-in had been. The urine left in the toilet made her think druggie kids might be the culprits.

Nick entered the bedroom just as she'd discovered the bedroom window latch had been pried off the wooden sash, which still remained open. "I think this is how they got in," she told him.

Nick fingered the cut marks in the window frame. "I'm not liking this. I've got to get hold of Lucas. You sure you never saw this gun cabinet loaded with weapons?"

"No. I think the weapons are still in the second seat of the truck."

"What the fuck?" Nick's eyes squinted. He cocked his head. "What are you saying, Marcy?"

"The large black bag he was most concerned about is in the back seat of his truck. He wanted me to make sure you helped me. I forgot all about it when I got home last night. It's still there."

Nick ran outside, ripping open the second seat door, removing the blanket and placed the bag over the other items on the bench. As he unzipped it, Marcy could see over his shoulder a huge weapon nearly four feet long. There were several smaller bags, which Nick quickly checked through, and she noticed several contained large sharply-tipped brass rounds in neat rows. Another weapon, much shorter and stubby, looking like a small machine gun, was wrapped in a dirty blue towel. He undid pockets on the front of the bag, pulling out a couple thick knives with serrated edges. Marcy was looking at the bag belonging to a killing machine. Something deep in her stomach churned and her mouth became parched.

The sun was making her dizzy and she stepped back.

Nick made sure the black nylon was well hidden under the old blanket, and turned to address her.

"You're not used to all this, so I have to forgive you for some of your stupid mistakes, but Marcy, no more. You've made a whole boatload of bad decisions, starting with leaving unattended a very dangerous weapon and enough rounds of ammo to kill a hundred people. In the wrong hands, these things are deadly. Could cost you and everyone you love their lives. So, I'm going to give it to you straight. Don't make this fuckin' mistake again. I'm not letting you drive to San Diego alone to return them to Lucas. And I know sure as shit he's going to need them very soon."

"Sorry."

"No. Just doing what he'd do if he was here. Marcy," He stepped forward so quickly she jumped, flinching when he grabbed her shoulders. "You don't do shit like this again. You watch everything. You never leave a weapon lying around where it can be stolen, or found by police, understood?"

"Yes." She couldn't help it, but her lower lip was quivering. If she wasn't so afraid, she'd be breaking down into a sob, seeking the comfort of Nick's arms.

"Okay, gotta call Lucas. You feel okay about starting to clean up in there?"

"Yes. Again, Nick, I'm—"

Nick had dialed Lucas and interrupted her. "Hey, asshole. You wanna tell me what you were doing with an M27 and a fuckin' MP5 in the back seat while your girlfriend and my wife go shopping for bagels and coffee and shit?"

Marcy was glad she couldn't hear Lucas' response.

# CHAPTER 16

**M**OUSTAFA WAS GLAD he'd seen the woman who was fated to come into his web yesterday. He'd dreamt about her all night long as he pleasured himself lying on the mattress out under the stars. When he'd heard an owl hooting in the distance, he grew cautious, washed his hands in the hose bib by the garden and retired inside for the rest of the evening.

His two recruits read their books by candlelight. Moustafa was trying to use as little energy as he could, and liked the idea that the boys were learning their sacred studies just as the Prophet had centuries ago, by candlelight.

*God is great.*

He knew where she had come from, and he'd scouted the little cabin earlier in the month. So he had reason to go back now. As the dawn was breaking he and the others hiked a path through the heavy woods. He chuckled that the recruits would be scratching their skin off the next day, as the forest was full of poison oak. Moustafa knew the best thing was to take a cold shower afterwards, use his Tech-Nu and then blot his skin dry. He wouldn't get the pox of western man that way. But the boys needed to experience the uncomfortable results while they meditated and did their prayers.

*God is great.*

He'd seen the gun cabinet on the previous scouting and was most anxious to open it and steal what he thought would surely be some weaponry inside. But that was not to be. The flimsy pine cabinet only held cobwebs and spiders. Even the refrigerator was empty.

He relished shredding the couch pillows, tossing all the dishes and glassware like they were made of paper. His recruits took his lead and destroyed the bathroom. Nothing was found that was of use. The books were unreadable, the magazines worse, although his recruits stole the ones with the naked women in them, thinking Moustafa wouldn't catch them hiding the folded lust books in their clothes. They were like schoolboys upset with being harshly punished, angry that there wasn't anything to eat in the refrigerator, which was still partially cold, justified to help themselves to the infidel's debauched way of life.

He was going to turn on the water and let it run, perhaps burn up the pump and drain the well, but he wanted to watch her shower again, like he'd watched the night before when the big man was there fucking her on his knees with his lips, fucking her from behind and letting her fuck him between her breasts. He would enjoy taking her apart bit by bit, if the opportunity presented itself. It could be a teaching moment for his recruits, who would soon have to do the same. He'd show them an infidel was not like a real woman, one of their believers. They were too used to their mothers and sisters, but they'd learn, in time. Showing them how to properly kill an infidel would toughen them up.

He heard the high-pitched whine of the infidel's truck from a mile away only an hour after they'd started searching the cabin. They'd had just enough time to run back toward the mother house. Moustafa jumped in the shower and put on clean pajama pants and a loose fitting Humboldt State t-shirt, watching as one by one, both of his new recruits began to scratch their skin. He didn't feel a thing.

*God is great.*

By now, she would have found the cabin altered. Moustafa would wait until nightfall and then creep back and perhaps spy on her sleeping there. Perhaps look for items in the vehicle she wouldn't think to lock up.

He got out his yellow lined tablet, working on his plan for new recruits arriving this fall, all arranged through a refugee humanitarian program administered by the church group they bought the camp from.

*God is great.*

America was indeed the land of opportunity. They had no idea what they were willingly giving away. It was a sign from the Prophet they could walk right in and claim what was theirs. The Kingdom of Heaven would reign supreme for all the true believers. And those who did not submit, would be eliminated. There was only one path to Heaven and all roads led there, whether or not the hapless Americans knew it or not.

He smiled as he looked out the window at the bright sunshine. In the dialect of his adopted home, Northern California, he said to himself, 'God is Awesome!'

# CHAPTER 17

LUCAS HADN'T BEEN able to reach Marcy, but the call with Nick got him worried. They'd all been asked to stay off their cells, unless it was an emergency, so he'd had to end the call quickly without asking how she was doing.

"Can't talk, Nick. I'll be dark for a few. Bring that shit home." He hated to hang up like that, do that to a former teammate, even though they hadn't served together. But he knew Nick would figure it out.

Their transport was waiting on the tarmac near lunchtime, the big beast gobbling all sixteen of them, with another group coming the following week from two other teams that were redeployed from the Pacific and East Africa. They landed in Park Field as part of the Naval Mid-South command base. The temporary training hangar and cyclone workout area looked like old prison grounds. A small track bordering a roughly patched lawn with goalposts at the end seemed out of place in the dusty heat of the afternoon.

Tyler Gray was the first to say something after they walked their gear toward the yard. "Holy mother fuck. We got ourselves a soccer field."

Fredo nodded his head. T.J. and Cooper looked toward the sky at the heat of the sun and shook their heads. Lucas stood next to them all, feeling suddenly joyful. "We can have ourselves a scrimmage, gents."

"Gets mighty hot this time of year," said Rory.

Lucas turned back to survey the rest of the base. Old planes and bunk buildings, long since unused, littered the area. It did not look like a high-level SEAL facility, but Lucas reminded himself it didn't take lots of shiny new equipment and paint to make a good target. Even a fresh patch of green lawn wouldn't do it. They weren't there to impress anyone. They were flesh and blood bait on a stick.

The team was greeted by a petite woman in blue camo. She wore a whistle around her neck and a stopwatch. She singled out Kyle somehow and shook his hand. "Donna Grant. I'm one of your trainers here."

Several of the team regarded the diminutive woman, but respectfully not a word was spoken. "Chief Petty Officer Kyle Lansdowne. Where you want us, ma'am?"

She dropped her hand and did an about face, motioning him to follow toward one of the run-down barracks. Several vans were parked nearby and a Skilsaw was being operated inside one of the rooms.

"We don't have much, but what we have is yours, Chief. Had to install internet and some extra plugs, replace part of the bathroom fixtures, some broken windows, and got rid of the crusty urinals. These buildings haven't been used for over twenty years." She turned to the group, smiling tightly. "Downsizing and all that shit," she said, wiggling her eyebrows.

Kyle angled his head and frowned, but his eyes grew to twice their size. "Good to know." He winked at Coop and Fredo.

Lucas regarded the grins and white teeth surrounding him and knew the little lady had just made one hell of an impression on the whole group. Someone mumbled, "I think I might like this training after all."

Donna walked like a basketball player, but without the tall lanky build. The hallway floor was covered with speckled puce gray vinyl tiles the Navy used boatloads of all over the world. The building was cool and dark. When she flipped on the buzzing overhead lights, some of them blinking and barely glowing behind yellowed plastic covers, it wasn't much of an improvement.

"Okay, you campers can choose your rooms. Trust me, take the ones on the ground floor. Upstairs can be for the poor frogs who have to come next week."

The rooms were not large, but bedrooms opened to a central quad area, so four men could share the common area. Single mattresses in each room were brand new, still in plastic, one set of white sheets and a pillowcase folded neatly and perfectly centered. The rec room at the end of the building was completely sparse. No TVs, tables, or couches were anywhere in sight. A stainless steel all-in-one sink, stove, and dishwasher was bordered by light green Formica countertops with stainless steel, real authentic retro trim. Plywood cabinets overhead had no doors on them.

"Looks like a Costco run is in order, gents," whispered Kyle.

"Do they even have a fuckin' Costco in Tennessee?" asked Fredo.

"Oh yes. We have three," added Donna. "We got more bars, more churches, and the biggest Costco in the whole state not more than a few miles away."

Donna announced the evening dinner would be served at twenty-hundred and pointed to the hall where it would be served. "And tonight, we have something special for you. Providing you behave yourselves, you'll get to train with the Navy Soccer team. They're joining us for dinner tonight, gentlemen."

Lucas and Tyler grinned at each other. Both of them had played with the boys before and were looking to a rematch.

"When do they arrive?" asked Tyler.

Donna checked her watch. "They're on their way now. Just finished up a game against Tennessee State, and they won, so the ladies are going to want to celebrate."

"Ladies?" Lucas asked.

"Yes. Didn't I tell you? They're the Navy *Women's* Soccer Team."

The announcement had room choices happening quickly and the showers were suddenly full, which limited the water pressure to a trickle.


KYLE CONDUCTED A briefing before dinner. "We're about ten miles from the camp run by the MOA group here. Occasionally we'll see members on the freeway, or in town at various places, primarily grocery outlets and secondhand stores. You are not to engage them. I'm good with you looking casual, sharp and military, but no insignias of any branch, please. I'm okay if they think you're a paramilitary defense contractor group here for some specialized training, or, better yet, Army Corps of Engineers working on one of the dams or waterways nearby. But don't volunteer one fuckin' thing. Don't talk to them, or to the locals who have befriended them. You can't trust a one, not one."

Kyle continued with some of the ground rules. "Any of you want to grow beards, be my guest. You know how that registers and identifies us overseas. But again, and I can't stress this enough, you stay off social media as far as posting pictures and letting people at home know you're okay or where you are exactly. Only cell phones, and only if it's extremely important. We have internet just to get and send information about our finds, and not for your pleasure, okay?"

The team grumbled.

Kyle handed out a list of names. "This is your phone tree, like your mom had when you were playing soccer. You check in with your men on this list every morning and every night. You know where they are, when they'll be back, when they get up, and when they go to bed."

"Do we have to find out when they take a shit?" T.J. asked. The group started adding other bits of helpful advice.

"I'm thinking no," said Kyle, who grinned neatly and then turned to all business.

Lucas had chosen a room with Jake, Alex, and Ryan. They'd already made a list of furniture for their crib, as well as the electronic equipment, including a big screen TV and a couple of blenders.

"We gonna be allowed to watch streaming video?" Jake asked.

"Working on it, Jake. Security is our main concern, so stuff like that has to be checked out, and the ONI office hasn't finished their work. We'll work something out."

Kyle distributed pictures of the camp bordered with tall metal fencing covered with razor wire in the remote forested region up the road, which also encompassed a rocky crag nearly two hundred feet tall. Kyle told them the group had twenty-four-seven guards posted in pairs atop this vantage point.

He also told them all aerial surveillance was current. The group had purchased a small dozer-tractor and they appeared to be enlarging a large swale or earthen dam, harnessing one of the tributaries into a man-made lake that had begun to fill. "We don't know what's going on here, but if you'll notice they have some small watercraft so we're guessing some kind of amphibious training exercise area." He showed them a picture of a target range and one long metal hangar with no doors or windows in it. The structure looked brand new.

"We are trying to find out what that building is. I'm sending a couple of you over to the contractor's office to find out. Whatever it is, you can bet it's no good. We don't have authority to trespass, so keep your distance, but understand these guys are for real, and they've spent a lot of money getting set up."

The jovial nature of the possible meetup with the soccer players was dashed as the team studied the glossy pictures being passed around. Kyle held up a picture of a graying rotund gentleman in a long Afghani robe and gray pakol cap. His wide face and near mid-chest level beard streaked with light brown made him look grandfatherly and harmless. Lucas had seen many of these tribal members before on previous deployments and it was difficult to tell the good guys from the bad guys.

"You see this guy, you let me or Lt. Commander Forsythe know right away. This is Sheik Hammid Rushti. He hasn't been picked up by birds in a month or more, so he's either escaped without detection or he's still inside. And if he is, we'd guess he'd be here." Kyle pointed to the long, ominous building.

Kyle went over the training schedule as Donna Grant entered the building and announced dinner.

Most the SEALs wore white V-necked t-shirts, and jeans or cargo pants, and canvas slip-ons. There was more aftershave and clean-shaven cheeks than Lucas had remembered at a high school dance. He knew, after tonight, everyone who would be growing beards.

He'd gotten two text messages marked urgent from both Nick and Marcy to call, so he tried to reach Marcy first.

"Lucas, someone's broken into the cabin."

"What? You get my black bag?" He tried to hide the edge to his voice.

"Yes, not to worry. That bag and all your things came back with me. Everything you asked me to get, I did."

"So, what do you mean? Broken in and busted the place up?"

"Yes."

"Nick was there with you?"

"Yes, he went with me to, well, to double-check everything I'd done. I came right up after I dropped you at the airport." Marcy was hesitant to finish. "And I cleaned out your place, like you asked, but I did it alone. So he took me up there this morning—"

He swore and hoped she didn't hear it. "Marcy, I told you not to do that."

"I know, Lucas. I've already gotten the lecture."

"So what did they take?"

"Nothing. Just threw things around the house, broke the dishes, and messed up the couches and bathroom. Nothing that couldn't be fixed."

"How'd they get in? You *did* lock it, right?"

"Of course. Looks like they pried open the bedroom window and came through that way. Didn't break a window, just trashed the contents, the furniture, and…and your gun case. *Was* that a gun case?"

Lucas concentrated and didn't remember checking the case, which had been locked. He'd lost the key years ago.

"It was, but I don't think there was anything in there. Haven't opened it since high school, but my dad and grandpa never left weapons up there. We always brought everything."

"Well, that's good. That's the one thing Nick asked me about."

"I'll bet. So they busted it open?"

"Shattered it."

"Is Nick there?"

"He's outside checking the perimeter. We're preparing to leave here in a few. He's gonna be responsible for that heavy black bag getting to your apartment. That *is* where you want it, right?"

"I'm thinking my locker at the team building. No one's at the apartment."

"Where are you?"

"Can't say."

"You can reach Nick on his cell. We'll be driving all night, so call us anytime you can."

"Thanks, Marcy. Glad you weren't hurt." His mind was racing to think who could have damaged the cabin. It had been there so long without an incident, it was so unusual, but then, lots of unusual things were happening.

"I'm fine. Don't worry about me. And Nick will drive with me all the way to San Diego."

Lucas saw the others gathering for dinner. "I have to go. Tell Nick I'll call later, if I can."

"Will do. Miss you, Lucas."

"Me too, Marcy. You have that talk with Connie yet?"

"Was going to wait until I got there, but don't think I can now. She's already making a little stir at the office."

"Do *not* tell her about us, Marcy. Big mistake. Trust me on that."

"No argument here, Lucas. You take care of yourself. Is it customary to say keep your head down? Like 'break a leg' for an actor?"

Lucas found himself smiling and it felt good. "Would be better if you told me you were in the shower rubbing that gel all over your body."

"Well then, sailor. I'd say it's still appropriate to say, 'keep your head down.'"

"Roger that, baby. Soon. Be safe. Be smart."

"Love you, Lucas."

He hadn't heard those words for at least two years. Marcy's confession of love to him was just in time, too. Not that he needed something to live for. "Love you too, kid. Talk soon."

He hung up, the hard-on in his pants very inconvenient, but easily covered up by a food tray. He hoped.

While they waited for their food, the soccer team bus drew up and one by one the ladies exited, each carrying a large blue and gold leather bag. The players unceremoniously slipped the leather straps off their shoulders and dropped them just inside the doorway. Several disappeared into the restroom while others washed their faces and hands in the cool drinking water dispenser and sauntered over to the food line in their matching blue and yellow flip-flops with the large block letter *N* on the outer edge.

Tyler was the first to speak to them. "Congrats on the win."

One player towered over all the others, being nearly Coop's height, which would make her nearly six and a half feet tall. She cut in front of the line without looking at any of the SEALs, without asking permission. Their captain was still wearing her red armband.

"Thanks," the captain said. "And we beat the *guys* in a twenty minute friendly game too." She flashed a perfect white smile back at Tyler, then winked up at Jake.

Their shorts and tanned legs were scoring big-time points with the team, both married and single guys. All of Lucas' bachelor buddies were pulling out chairs, tucking napkins into their shirts, and asking politely for salt and pepper instead of standing to reach in front of each other. They brought glasses and pitchers of iced tea for the ladies, not paying attention to a couple of SEALs who had their hand out for a cup. The swearing was clipped as well.

Kyle, Cooper, Fredo, and Armani sat together at one end of the table with several other of the married guys. Though married, Tyler sat next to their captain and the two started talking soccer immediately.

Lucas overheard Tyler whisper, "Who's the Amazon?" to his neighbor.

"By the way, it's Lacey," she said shaking Tyler's hand.

Tyler began, "This is Jack, Lucas, Alex, Connor, Danny, Jeffrey, and the rest of the guys are married."

"And what are you, Tyler?" said Danny Begay. "Lacey, don't trust him. We're both married."

Lacey began her team introductions, and then added, "Husbands and boyfriends are not suitable topics of conversation on the road."

Jake and Alex shared a smile.

"But I'd recommend staying away from our keeper, Chloe. She's the short one in her family and her dad plays for the Suns."

Chloe lifted a fork and nodded acknowledgement, but otherwise sat expressionless and focused on her food.

One of the pretty blonde-haired brown-eyed players asked the table a general question. "So why are you guys way out here? And how come we've been sent to babysit you? Aren't you guys SEALs?"

The question left the table completely quiet.

# CHAPTER 18

MARCY AND NICK started to drive Lucas' truck back to San Diego in the afternoon. He called in at dusk, and Nick reassured him he was going to keep Marcy in plain sight.

"Honestly, Lucas, the gun cabinet would have been of interest to anyone. Because it had a lock on it, it was attractive to kids. That's who I think they were. Normal thieves don't do destruction. They just look for valuables. This was a concerted effort to damage and destroy."

She watched the dusk send an orange glow to the western horizon. They'd gotten so busy cleaning everything up and disposing of the broken things, she'd completely forgotten to call Connie. They had another six hours to drive, so she decided to put it off until she could do the *in person* conversation.

Nick chuckled. "Nothing like that. But they did pee all over the toilet." Nick gave Marcy a wink. "Your lady made that place shine when we were done. I screwed the window frame shut because I didn't have a new latch. You'll have to fix that when you return."

He finally asked Lucas the question Marcy was wondering. "You in country or out?"

She heard the, "Yes," in response from Lucas.

"Meaning you are or are not out of country?"

She heard the tinny, "Yes" from the other end of the phone.

"You asshole."

Lucas said something else while Marcy waited to get her chance to talk to him.

"Hey, punk, you have any beefs with your neighbors?" Nick rolled his eyes and gave her another wide smile.

She heard the scratchy swearing and objection on the other end.

"I know, I know. You guys were angels growing up. I can only imagine you terrorizing the little church goin' sweethearts when your dad and grandpa weren't paying attention. No, asshole, I'm talking about the fuckin' neighbors who live in that commune next door." Nick held the squawking phone out to Marcy. "You tell him."

"Nice to hear your voice twice in one day, Lucas," said Marcy. "Everything okay?"

Lucas laughed. "The beach is awesome, babe. Those umbrella drinks are strong. Good music. Missing you real bad."

"That's the only part of this conversation I believe, Lucas."

"Nick said we have new neighbors? What's this about a commune?"

"Well, looks to me like they've been there for awhile. Doing a bunch of things. Buildings out back. Nick said it was an old Christian camp. Sonshine Haven. You hear of it?"

"Nobody has used that place for years, Marcy. I didn't think they even had a road cleared anymore."

"Trust me, it's been worked on. Bunkhouse-like cabin in front and a covered riding arena in the back. Some new metal stables, and hay barns. The guy tending the vegetable garden looked like he could be a pot grower."

Lucas didn't say a word. "You stay away from there, Marcy. I'll check it out when I get home, but for now, no one goes up there."

"Don't you think someone should check on your place for you? How long will you be gone?"

"Not your concern, and to be honest, none of us knows that. But you stay away. Understood?"

"Yessir."

"Seriously, Marcy. Especially with the break-in, you don't go up there anymore."

Marcy agreed with him completely.

They said their goodbyes and Marcy handed the phone back to Nick with a "Thanks."

Checking her cell phone, she noticed she'd missed a call from Connie Shipley. "Oh shoot. I had the ringer turned off. I have to call my client."

"I'm going to pull over for a quick bite. You want a burger or something? There's a great Mexican restaurant a couple of miles west."

"I'm game. Let's go Mexican. I'll finish my call with Connie and then meet you inside."

Connie's phone went to voicemail right away. "Hey, Connie. This is Marcy Gelland with Coronado Bay Realty. I'm—"

Just as she watched Nick walk inside the restaurant, she saw Connie had returned her call. She hung up the message and answered her.

"Sorry to call you so late, Connie. I'm on my way back to San Diego. Thought maybe we—"

"Well, holy shit, Marcy. How good of you to wake the baby up."

"Sorry. I can call in the morning—"

"No. You don't get off that easy."

"Pardon?"

"I've got a screaming baby, but I got a boob that will do just fine."

"Okay." Marcy tried a nervous laugh on for size. Connie was more than prickly.

"All good now. Little shit won't sleep the night, but then that's nothing new." Connie took a deep breath and let it out before she continued. "So, I've been doing a little research. Very interesting what you can find out if you ask the right questions."

"Not sure what you mean, Connie. What questions?"

"When were you going to tell me you were fucking my husband?"

# CHAPTER 19

PT STARTED AT o-six-hundred with a timed five-mile run around the track. The girls joined them. On the other side of the cafeteria was a small gym with rusty equipment Lucas could smell just as soon as he walked through the old double doors. One window had been duct taped down the middle, cheaply repairing a crack that threatened to destroy the whole frame. Fredo was making a list of things to get at Costco. He'd put down a water dispenser, some white towels to wipe the equipment down with, cleaning supplies and some free weights.

The smell of fresh coffee reminded Lucas of home, causing a twinge of homesickness. He missed her.

The training went by fast as they focused on pull-ups and sit-ups before they began doing stretching exercises. Several of the team guys remarked they missed the ocean. Coop and Fredo had created a ritual of diving in after an especially long and arduous workout.

Kyle asked T.J., Armando, Lucas, and Jake to join him for a hike up toward the ridge overlooking the camp's compound. It was classified a training exercise.

The five of them made less noise than one of the local deer as they jogged through sparse woods and a meadow with a small stream coursing through the middle. Close to the compound, the terrain was dotted with large granite boulders and became steep. Midway up the bluff, Kyle motioned with hand signals pointing to a sentry. The team fanned out around the back side of the outcropping so his line of sight would miss them. The thin, dark-skinned man was wearing shabby ill-fitting clothes and shoes that laced up, but appeared several sizes too large for him.

T.J. nearly ran into another sentry sitting on a large boulder, an AK-47 resting across his thighs. T.J. signaled and everyone froze in place.

The team waited nearly an hour, settling against rocky crags and high meadow brush, easily camouflaged, to make sure no one else appeared in the area. Since these men were not breaking the law, the SEALs were only tasked with observing, making note of what they found and not to engage. Unless fired upon, they would not be allowed to use their weaponry, either.

They heard a vehicle approach from several hundred yards behind them. Country music was rising into the blue overcast sky. The heat was stifling hot, and Lucas studied the gray clouds with more than a passing interest. A quick shower, even a downpour would be welcome in the nearly one-hundred-degree noonday heat.

The vehicle came into view. Both sentries watched the red Jeep advance into the woods, following the off-road trail. They were speaking to each other from about ten yards apart, their dialect sounding Pashtu, but Lucas couldn't be sure. Kyle held up a small recording device with a plastic cone boost, trying to capture what was being said.

Two young girls in tank tops and cutoffs were in the front seat of the open-air Jeep, wearing baseball caps and sunglasses. One was singing to the words of the song on the radio.

Lucas was concerned at first they were wandering into a den of bad guys, but when one of the sentries waved to the driver of the Jeep, and the other one didn't ready his weapon, he knew it was a planned or announced visit. The girls did not look Middle Eastern, but extremely westernized and young.

Lucas quietly cleaned the lenses on his binoculars, wiped down the scope he'd mounted to his H&K, inserted his fifteen round magazine, and then clicked off the safety, which was all they could do, since they weren't on a snatch and grab or kill on sight mission. Armani was laying flat and had already sighted the camp below, while Kyle was focused on the sentries. That left Jake to be their eyes behind them his Glock at the ready.

Below them, the Jeep stopped, motor running, as the two girls inside began a conversation with the perimeter guards. The ladies turned down their radio and spoke with one of two guards, who leaned over the door of the Jeep as the other scanned the roadway and the hill above. Without knowing it, the guard looked directly at the Team's position, and Lucas heard Armani hold his breath as his finger rested against the trigger mechanism after selecting his firing safety setting. As the guard looked away and the girls were waved through, Lucas noted Armando quietly release his breath, closed his eyes, and then retreated back.

Kyle took pictures of the compound, the approach, and close-ups of the guard gate and the sentries and where they were placed. There were several large trucks with closed beds parked at the side of the long building. A satellite dish and radio tower was installed atop one of the pine trees nearby. Kyle took pictures of that too.

Their LPO motioned for them to make their way back down the hill, and once at the bottom and out of sight, sprinted the way back to the creek, where they splashed water on their faces and down their shirts. Then they continued with the jog until they got back to their camp mid-afternoon. Lucas headed for the shower, for a cold one, soon followed by Kyle and the others.

Alex and Ryan hung around the doorway, waiting for him to finish in privacy.

"So what'd you find out?" Alex asked.

Kyle put his head under the water, rinsing off before he answered. "They're used to having female visitors."

"How'd you get that?" Alex asked, scrunching his eyebrows and forehead.

"They didn't make the local girls cover up. Especially their heads."

"Then there were the cut-offs," Lucas added.

Alex was still not convinced. So Kyle hammered it in. "That would *never* happen to an un-westernized Iraqi." He dried off and threw the skimpy towel around his waist. "Still can't decide what's in that building, but they're moving something in and out of there with those trucks. They're smart not to have people out in the daytime for the birds to spy overhead. We need to get our IR gear and visit them after dark. Begay has natural night vision so he's coming. You in, Alex?"

"Sure, anything, Chief. After all, I don't got a date."

"He's working to fix that as soon as is humanly possible. But the job comes first," added Ryan.

"Tyler's got his eye on Captain Blondie, that married sonofabitch," said Armando.

"I think she's sweet on Jake, from what I can see," said Alex.

Lucas knew Tyler would not go outside his marriage, that the chance to converse with someone about soccer was the real draw. "I agree. Never thought the bachelors would hook up on this training. God is looking out for you guys."

"*You* guys?" asked Kyle. The skimpy white towel barely tucked around Kyle's trim waist and narrow hips. "Aren't you in that league, Lucas? Connie's got you by the balls, I hear."

Lucas nodded in agreement. "Actually, I'm a little attached to my realtor. Got serious quick."

"Holy fuck. You're dumber than I thought, Lucas," said Kyle. "That the realtor Connie hired?"

Lucas didn't see any point to keeping it a secret. "Well, yes."

"You ain't even fuckin' divorced yet."

"That's been pointed out to me, Chief," Lucas answered.

"Unbelievable," Kyle said as he pushed his way past the crowd.

Back at their room, Jake sat down on Lucas' bed. "I need to talk to you a minute."

Lucas was putting on his jeans and a black Team 3 t-shirt.

"He said no logos."

"Shit, you're right. Just second nature." Lucas removed the shirt, tossing it in the built-in cabinet, and unwrapped a new white t-shirt. He slipped it over his head. "Thanks, man." He could see Jake was conflicted about something. "You okay?"

Jake looked at his hands, forearms resting on his thighs. "I've been dating that friend of Connie's, remember?"

Lucas had forgotten all about it, mostly because, since his divorce, Jake never stayed serious with one woman for more than about a month. He figured that ship had sunk long ago.

"So this is serious then, that what you're about to tell me?"

Jake grinned. "You know me. Fucked it up good this time. How did I know she had a sister that didn't look anything like her? Still a babe and all, but man, I had no idea sisters could look so opposite and yet act so competitive. Real catfight. And then they turned it all on me."

"Some people like that action, Jake."

"Shut the fuck up motherfucker. I'm not talking about *that*."

"Come on, Jake, you know sisters are bad news."

"Like I said, I didn't know!"

"Sounds like you dodged a bullet, my man." Lucas slipped on his shoes. He combed his hair and put on aftershave. "Weren't you the one all spouting off to me about staying single? Distrusting women? Didn't we have that conversation? So she, or they, whichever it is, broke up with you. Big deal."

"Well, yeah, that part's okay. I mean, I'm used to it. But boy, these ladies these days talk. They even talked to my ex. Connie gave me an earful."

"Well, you didn't exactly behave, Jake. I mean, mine was just a picture. You went and did the dirty."

"Not with a transvestite hooker."

"*Dancer.* I don't go with hookers."

"That you know of."

"Jake, just where the hell is this conversation going? You know full well I don't date or sleep around at all. And I never did that while married."

"You're married now, asshole."

"Yup, but she served papers on me."

"You're still legally married, you dumb-fuck."

"That's a minor detail. Thing is, Connie got some bad information, and believed I was—"

"That's what I have to talk to you about."

"Okay, I'm listening." Lucas could see Jake didn't want to tell him something and it was eating a hole in his gut.

"So the four of them are having lunch together, and—"

"Jake, you are one unlucky motherfucker. The four of them? Your ex, the sisters you've been banging and who else? Someone *else* you were banging?"

"No. Not exactly."

"Jake what part of '*banging*' don't you understand? That's like being just a little pregnant. We've had that talk, too."

Jake's expression became more painful.

"Holy fuck, you got the sisters pregnant, both of them?"

"Nah, man. Like I said, the four of them were having lunch, and apparently they told Connie—"

"Wait a minute, *my* Connie?"

"She isn't *your* Connie anymore, Lucas."

Alex and Ryan appeared at the doorway, as if on cue. Lucas glanced over at them and then put his hands on his hips. "Fuckit," he said as he grabbed Jake by the shirt. "You fucked Connie, too?"

Alex and Ryan sprang to action and separated them.

"No way, Lucas. I wouldn't do that. Honest." Jake's eyebrows tented upward, eyes squinting like he'd just smelled something terrible. He rubbed his forearm where Alex had grabbed him roughly. "I must have mentioned it to the one gal on our way out here. They wanted to arrange a double-double when we got back. Remember those, Lucas? Like we did before you married Connie?"

Lucas could never forget those nights. "Before you were married, too, asshole."

"That's right. So, I told them you were seeing this realtor Connie had hired. They told Connie you were banging the realtor."

Even though he'd confirmed one of his best friends hadn't slept with his wife, Lucas still wanted to punch Jake as the deliverer of the bad news. Very bad news.

"Why did you have to tell me this?"

"Because it's the truth, man. Thought you ought to know, since you said you were sweet on her. Knowing Connie and her temper, I'd put protection on your lady, Lucas."

"Except I'm stuck in fuckin' Tennessee. How the hell am I supposed to do that?"

"Well, call her, when you get the chance. At least give her a warning."

Kyle stood behind Ryan and Alex. "We good here?" he asked.

Lucas nodded his head while the others just watched.

"We're meeting in five. Rec Room." Kyle said as he left.

Lucas knew it was the end of their private conversation. He was good at burying all his feelings over any deployment. One by one, the team collected in the rec area, as instructed.

Kyle was poring over his computer. "Okay, I've uploaded the photos and sent the audio clip back to Coronado. Hoping we can get some confirmation on what to do next."

Rory asked the next question. "You make them out to be Afghani? You think they were speaking Pashtu?"

"Yes," T.J. said. His language training was the best in the team. "See if you can amplify it, Kyle and I'll take a listen."

"Roger that, T.J."

The door burst open at the end of the bunkhouse and in walked Fredo, carrying boxes. "Hola, amigos! We got our Costco shit here,"

Accompanying him were Coop, Jeffrey, and Danny. Coop and Fredo unloaded boxes to the kitchen counters while Danny and Jeffrey sat down to assemble two tables and chairs and a TV stand which had all come in boxes. Soon several other members of the team took up positions in a circle.

"Okay, we got nice, fluffy towels," said Fredo. We got two cases of beer, some waters, and sodas and shit. Kyle, got your fuckin' turkey jerky."

"Thanks man," said Kyle.

"I bought condoms, toothpaste, deodorant, and aftershave for those dating, Red Bull, Gatorade, Monkey Butt powder, moist towelettes and some medicated ones for the old guys, hand sanitizer, detergent and dish soap," Fredo continued. "Coop got his dryer sheets and mineral waters too, so he's happy."

"Razors?" Lucas asked. "Forgot to mention it."

Fredo came over and put an arm on his shoulder. "Got you covered, my man, since you're beard is ugly as shit."

Lucas punched him in the arm.

"And for the record, no tofu or fresh vegetables. I figure frozen shit will work, lots of tortilla chips and salsa. Those of you into the healthier lifestyle can go to the fuckin' market tomorrow."

"Awesome!" Jake said as he opened up a box of chocolate bars.

Within ten minutes, all the furniture was assembled without anyone being in charge. The directions were passed around as needed. It was obvious the TV stand needed something on top, which would be one of the missions for tomorrow.

Two blenders and a coffee maker were set on the countertop. Coop filled new ice cube trays and placed them in the freezer. Fredo doled out a towel for each man.

"Okay, I'm going to say this one time, because about six of you have asked me," started Kyle. "Yes, we're having the ladies over tonight for a meet and greet. And here are some of the ground rules."

Lucas and Jake looked at each other and rolled their eyes. The disagreement of earlier seemed to have dissipated.

"First, the bedroom doors are to remain open while they're here. If you're going to be unsociable and go to bed early, you go to bed with your door open and the light on in your quad room. Got it?"

The grumbling continued until Donna Grant showed up to announce dinner.

"Hold on, Boy Scouts," Kyle shouted. "Got two more things to say. I need a volunteer to organize a scrimmage tomorrow afternoon."

Lucas and Tyler's hands shot up.

"Okay, we got two. Perfect." Kyle looked over at Fredo. "You need a donation of how much, Fredo?"

"Hundred bucks, gents," Fredo said.

"That has to happen before the weekend. We have a signup list over on the refrigerator for anything you want that you can share. No promises, of course. Fredo here keeps all the money and there are no refunds."

Lucas noticed a lined piece of yellow paper had been pasted to the refrigerator door with duct tape.

"I'm going to choose several to go up later tonight for a look-see at the camp with some IRs. We aren't telling the girls anything about this, get my drift?" Kyle surveyed his men in front of him. "We might get a visit from DC and Forsythe in a few days, depending on what we find up there at the camp. He's to bring some equipment I've requested. Again, no word of this to the ladies."

Alex asked if the phone tree was in effect tonight.

"What do you think?"

That seemed to settle it.

"I'm sending Coop and Lucas to town tomorrow to talk to the barn contractor. On the way back, they're to pick up a big screen and Blu-ray. We'll wait for them before we start the scrimmage, okay?"

Lucas nodded to Coop, who returned his acknowledgement. They both understood neither would have the night shift tonight. It also meant Lucas might be able to call Nick and Marcy, and perhaps use the internet at a coffee shop.

"Anything else you need to know about?" Kyle searched the room. "Everyone good on the home front?"

Jake and Ryan punched Lucas in the arm.

"Not you, Lucas, you're fucked," said Armando.

Several of the men started to chuckle. He had to defend himself. "At least I'm not the only one. How many times has she taken you to court, Jake?"

"Every time I knocked her up."

Amid the laughter, Kyle signed them off. "Okay, then. We'll have a briefing after PT in the morning. Be safe tonight and get to bed at a decent hour. The midnight hike will be with Armani, Fredo, Danny and Alex."

Kyle let them head for dinner. On their way to the door, he announced behind them, "Last one up cleans up the kitchen."

Lucas knew that meant there'd be a race for early bedtimes, which was probably what his LPO intended.

# CHAPTER 20

**N**ICK AND MARCY arrived in the early dawn, stopped for breakfast, and then drove to Lucas' apartment, the place he told them was temporary and shared with the other bachelors.

"This is going to be new for me too, Marcy. Never met Lucas before you came into the picture."

"Do you know Connie?"

"Only by reputation. You've got your hands full."

"Tricky part is getting someone *else* to keep the listing. I can't in good conscience represent them. I mean, I *could*, but the appearance would be otherwise."

"I totally get it. Devon has had similar issues."

Marcy checked out Nick's expression. "Not really," she said with a teasing smile, followed by a wink.

"Oh, yes. She gets divorcing couples all the time. About half her business."

Marcy had to laugh at how naïve Nick was, something she also saw in Lucas. Here he was this big tough guy and was completely blind to some personal things. "I think I went a little beyond where Devon has gone. I know her and she'd never do what I did."

Nick blushed and would not look back at her. "Gotcha. Sorry. It didn't even cross my mind."

He set the black clothes bag on the floor near the front door. "Don't know which is his room," he added as he began searching the bedrooms for something that would indicate it belonged to Lucas. "You recognize anything?" he asked as he walked out of one bedroom into the next.

"Afraid not," she sighed. "And I don't know the other guys either."

Marcy unzipped the duffel and pulled out clothes she'd added back at the cabin. Some of her underwear accidentally dangled from one hand in front of Nick.

"You need a bag," he said, and pretended he'd not seen the unmentionables. Returning with a recycled plastic shopping bag from the kitchen, he continued not making eye contact.

Marcy loaded up and dropped the bag by the door. Then she walked slowly through the apartment. The living room couch and matching loveseat looked more than well-used and wasn't anything she'd sit down on. There were nude posters in every room. Several hard-oiled women in handcuffs, blindfolds, and various states of mostly undress lined the walls of the guest bath.

A set of folding chairs sat around a small stained table in the kitchen. The rugs were brightly stained. The slider to the balcony overlooking the valley below was covered with handprints and a torn screen hanging on a bent frame.

Two of the bedrooms had cultures growing from half-eaten food or glasses. The kitchen sink was filled with four bowls with old cold cereal stuck to the sides.

"If I had a couple of hours, I could fix this place up," she said.

Nick smirked.

Marcy continued. "And I'm thinking they'd hate it. Am I right?"

"With those guys? From what I understand, anything approaching domestic bliss would be totally off limits."

"Okay, so what's next?"

"I was thinking I'd get the equipment bag over to the Team building, but I'm detached, so I'll have to get someone else to do it. Can you drop me off? I'll stay there tonight and try to take a plane up to Santa Rosa in the morning."

"Sure thing. Thought the whole team was with Lucas."

"They have someone who injured his leg in a jump and didn't go."


MARCY SLIPPED BEHIND the wheel of Lucas' truck and watched as the sandy-haired ex-SEAL hoisted the heavy weapons bag over his shoulder and resumed a path to his friend's front door. He met another well-built young man with an ankle to hip cast on his leg. Marcy shook her head.

*Am I ready for all this?* She'd barely knew Lucas, and already she was running guns, cleaning up ransacked cabins, and riding in his truck with another SEAL she barely knew. And somehow, she was *okay* with it?

*How my life has changed.* With a heavy dose of apprehension, Marcy noted how fast her world had tilted on its axis. She waved goodbye to Nick and his friend like they were people she'd known her whole life. The day was already getting long and she needed a shower and an early to bed.

But first, she had to face the wife of the man she was screwing.

THE CORONADO BAY Realty office was on a corner in the neighborhood of expensive designer boutiques, high-end burger bars, vegetarian restaurants, art galleries and espresso coffeehouses. Marcy had always enjoyed working at the attractive, highly-visible, upscale office, unlike some of her other realtor friends. Many of the agents there didn't need the income and worked there just to hobnob with local celebrities and wealthy businessmen. It was also known far and wide as a great place to pick up a wealthy second or third husband for singles or soon-to-be singles, either male or female. She was one of the few who did not have all the cosmetic surgery to make themselves into sufficient eye candy.

Their lobby was decorated by a designer regularly featured in Architectural Digest. Imitating an abandoned villa in Tuscany, broken pots spilled water fountains and colorful beds of flowers decorated outside the entrance doors. The lobby featured a large, textured steel waterfall, giving a serene and peaceful effect, like a high-end spa. Bird calls and a Tuscan orange room scent piped into the air ducts drifted around the reception and waiting area.

Today, none of those things did anything to cheer her mood.

Gail Burnett, married to the famous wide receiver, Barry Burnett, was the first to greet her. She had been chatting with the young receptionist, her long, tanned form outfitted in a white designer suit. Her blonde hair cascaded over her shoulders and back like spun gold. As she turned to face Marcy, her eyelids closed slightly. She licked her lips and tilted her chin up. Her green eyes sparkled with mischief. On another day and under different circumstances, she would have been someone Marcy could enjoy spending time with. But as a competitor, she was a feral cat used to successfully taking down lions.

Gail was all the wrong kinds of dangerous.

"There you are, sweetie."

It always annoyed Marcy when someone only a few years older could take on the aura of a critical parent.

"Hi, Gail." It was always wise to give the realtor what she wanted. "You look terrific today."

"And you look like you've just come from a demolition derby." Gail winked at her, making it overly obvious she didn't really mean the comment.

Except she did.

"Just got back from up north."

"Yes, heard about your interesting road trip." Gail checked her nails and then fluffed her hair.

Marcy wondered why her broker would have disclosed this little factoid. She put it out of her mind. "How's everything around here? Keeping busy?"

Gail smiled. Marcy held her breath.

"Can't complain. Barry's in Detroit, so I'm actually getting some work done."

Marcy figured Detroit wasn't the shopping destination Chicago or New York or even Atlanta would be. "Well, good. I've got some catching up to do myself," Marcy answered. "Let me get settled, and then could you and I have a little chat in the conference room?"

The receptionist, seated behind the curved bamboo counter, tore her eyes off her computer screen and shot a worried glance at Gail's profile.

"Sure thing, Marcy. Kind of wanted to talk to you as well." The fetching smile she used on her best clients looked dangerous.

"Give me about five. I'll meet you there."

"You bet." Gail turned and continued her conversation with the receptionist. Her skirt could not have been any tighter, revealing she wasn't embarrassed to show she wore thong underwear.

Several minutes later, Marcy and Gail stepped into the warm bisque-themed meeting space. A mural of vineyards and tiled roof spires perched atop rolling hills was painted along the long wall. Marcy sat at the head of the table, laying down her listing information and several other forms she'd dug out.

Gail had a thin file folder she held in long tapered fingers accented with pearlescent polish. Her open-toed sandals made small scratching sounds as she took up her place on Marcy's right, and sat.

Marcy looked at the painting before her and took in a deep breath as if she was vacationing in the little Tuscan village, not staring at a plastered wall. Her nervousness was uncharacteristic, but then, there were so many things she hadn't fully thought out. Normally, she liked to calculate every move in this chess game of real estate sales. Now she was trying to execute a retreat with her job and her pride still intact.

It was not what she was used to doing.

"Gail, I've taken this listing for a house on Apricot Way, and—"

"Connie and Lucas' house. I know it well," Gail interrupted.

"Good. Well, I've decided I'm going to refer their listing, and wanted to know if you'd be interested in taking over for me." She didn't spell out that normally there would be a referral fee shared between the agents, and just decided to let the implication stand, without bringing attention to it.

Gail hesitated a couple of seconds, tapping her fingernails on top of her file folder, as if she was considering a move she wasn't sure of. Her surgically plumped lips pulled back, without a wrinkle, into a thin line. Her eyes were able to give more expression. "Your timing is pretty good, Marcy." She opened the folder. "Because I got this letter from Connie earlier this morning."

She handed the sheet of paper across the table. Marcy read:

'To: Marcy Gelland

*I hereby request that you withdraw my listing at 442 Apricot Way, San Diego, California, immediately. I no longer wish to be represented by you.*

The letter was signed by Connie Shipley and dated this morning.

Marcy sat back and waited for the other shoe to drop.

"You know we're always trained to give the client whatever they want, Marcy. I didn't solicit this, not in any way." Gail watched her words sink in. "Marcy, she wants *me* to represent them. Connie feels there's a conflict of interest." Gail's eyes got hard and cold. No smile lines appeared on her flawless face.

Marcy was going to sidestep the elephant in the room, hoping she wouldn't have to bring it out into the open. Instead, she decided, again, to give Gail what she wanted.

"Well, Gail, I agree and have no objection to this. Like I said, I wanted to—"

"And I'm *not* paying a referral fee, Marcy. Don't you think it's a little beyond that anyway?"

"Fine."

"Really?" Gail made a point to raise her eyebrows and bat her big green eyes with the eyelash extensions.

Marcy didn't want to press a fight. If all this could just go away, she'd be fine with the lack of income. She didn't have Barry Burnett's income as backup, but she was the top office producer and could absorb the cut in pay. What was more valuable than the commission earned was her standing in the office, especially with her broker, Joe.

She pulled out a Change Order form and began to fill it out for Gail, when they heard noise coming from the lobby. Marcy had just signed her name to the form when Connie Shipley appeared at the conference room door, her left hand splayed as she slapped the glass, her wedding ring making the metallic tapping sound. She was holding the baby in her right.

Marcy didn't realize Gail had locked the door, so when Connie began yanking on the burnished copper handles, the rattling sound shook most the nearby walls. Connie's face was shriveled in anger. "You let me in there, right now. Where the fuck is Lucas?"

Gail stood to unlock the door, but before she could get there, Connie continued with her tirade.

"Release me from your fuckin' listing contract or I'll tell the whole world you're fuckin' my husband!"

Even through the thick glass, Connie's voice was loud and menacing, but not nearly as loud as Marcy knew it was to the whole office. It would be impossible for anyone present to miss Connie's accusations.

*So much for a clean exit.*

# CHAPTER 21

AFTER DINNER, THE music began. Jake was the center of attention, often dancing with three or four soccer players. He kept encouraging Lucas to join in, but Lucas was preoccupied with the reveal Jake had given him about Connie, and he worried about Marcy and how she was doing.

He slipped into the bathroom and tried to text her, but couldn't get a signal. In the old days, he'd have been mixing the margaritas and making sure everyone had a generous helping of alcohol, but this time they'd only bought a limited amount and that was mostly beer. He started a list he'd be going over tomorrow when he and Coop paid the visit to the contractor and the shopping trip planned for afterward.

A coed poker game was in full swing. Lucas was normally right in the middle of the action, but his somber attitude prevailed.

Donna Grant wasn't participating in the alcohol, the dancing or the cards. She took a seat next to him and toasted his beer with her mineral water.

"You got a girl at home, Lucas?" she asked. The lady was probably five years his senior, but he'd seen lots of relationships with older military women and the young SEALs. It gave them a problem sometimes with the other branches of service they had to work with closely.

"Complicated, but yes," he answered her. If she wore a little makeup, she'd be pretty. He noticed she had a barbed wire tat around her left wrist. Her hair was cut short, but was shiny brown. With her large brown eyes, she had a classic look and would be stunning if she wanted to be. That had him curious.

"What exactly does that mean?" she asked, without looking at him.

"Means my wife's divorcing me, and I recently found a girlfriend."

"Can't live with them and can't live without them, that right?" she answered.

Lucas rolled his shoulder and cracked his neck. The loud noise had her wincing and even caught the attention of a couple of the card players. "That sounded painful. You better get that checked out."

"I'm fine. You?"

"I like the travel, and I prefer working with men on the job."

Lucas pegged her for being perhaps sweet on women. He nodded, not bothered one way or the other.

She smiled to her shoes. "I like men all right, Lucas. I'm just more of the best friend kind of person. Don't much care for chasing after the steamy romance, if you know what I mean."

No, he didn't know what she meant.

"Sometimes, Donna, it just comes to you. Sometimes you don't have to chase after it at all."

"That happen to you?"

"Sometimes," he answered.

"So that's what happened to your marriage, then?"

"No. That's not what I meant. I'm not like that, although my wife—" He stopped himself until the alarms in his head stopped screaming. "All that was before I got married. My wife is the one who found and chose me."

Donna peeled her gaze from the poker table and looked at him honestly. "And here I would have thought you knew."

"Knew what?"

"The woman always chooses, my friend. That's why you guys have to wait. When you're single, that means no woman has chosen you yet."

He wasn't sure he liked the tone of her implication. She was complicated. Secretive. That was a dangerous combination.

"I still say you be patient. It will happen for you. You just wait and you'll see."

"Great advice, but I'm afraid it doesn't really apply to me."

"But you *are* looking?"

She rocked her head from side to side. "Everybody looks, Lucas. I apologize, but it's a long story. It's not that I'm into ladies, I just have issues with men."

"Except you like to work with them?"

"I know, sounds nuts, doesn't it?" She smiled and he did think she was pretty. "You trying to pick a fight?"

"No, ma'am. I don't fight with women."

She giggled and said something under her breath that sounded like a swear word. "Long story, my frog prince, and I don't know you well enough."

He decided to add a little levity into the conversation, since he was getting a bit uneasy with her secrets, not that he had any right to them of course, but he was used to being direct and forthright, answering and asking questions. He thought he'd just push a little to see if he could crack that tough exterior. "I don't have to worry about you taking a knife to my throat late some night, right? You're not one of those?"

She showed him her white teeth again in a grin. "Only if we're forced to sleep in the same bed and you snore, which I can already tell you do, so give it up, sailor, and leave me alone." She stood and walked away, still looking like an athlete slowly departing a basketball court or a track somewhere. He realized she was probably way stronger than he'd given her credit for.

And lethal.


EVERYONE TURNED IN before nine o'clock, with the exception of the group going with Kyle to the top of the hill.

"I'm good if you need me, Chief," said Lucas.

"Sure you're just trying to get out of cleaning up? But if you want to tag along, be my guest. You got your FLIRs?" he asked, meaning the SEAL-issued forward-looking infrared goggles.

"Roger that."

"Okay, you still up to the shopping trip tomorrow with Coop?"

"Fuckin' A, Chief."

Kyle and Danny led the team back through the woods. With their thermal gear, they saw eyes of forest animals such as fox, raccoon and deer light up and move quietly out of their path. The sky was cloudy, which was good for visibility. The moon was over half full and very bright.

Lucas was amazed how much easier it was to see the outline of the lone sentry with the equipment they brought. They would be back up as time permitted on other nights, just to verify the single guard was not an anomaly.

Kyle directed Danny and Armando to position themselves higher than the sentry to give the rest of the team cover in case they were discovered. The rest of the team took the best clear vantage point nearly twenty yards below the sentry so they could get a closer wide-angled look.

Scanning the campground, Lucas watched the end on the long metal building slowly move to the side, its large, metal, gear-type wheels squealing as the metal door rolled out of the way. Inside, he saw what looked like a warehouse with tables and storage shelves. But down the center of the building was a lush garden of plants, reminding Lucas of pictures he'd seen of the Panhandle in Golden Gate Park. He counted approximately twenty men, all carrying small automatic weapons similar to their short barrel H&Ks slung over their shoulders.

Lucas heard the whir and click of the scope camera as Kyle documented everything, including the sentry. Lucas adjusted his magnification, got out his vest pocket spiral and jotted down the license plates of every van or truck he could identify. Kyle gave him a thumbs-up, adjusted his scope, and took more photos.

Boxes were being loaded onto dollies and placed inside rear doors of two trucks they'd seen earlier that day. Just before the door shut, Lucas caught a glimpse of a sandaled pair of feet peering out of a long kaftan, or robe.

He tapped Alex on the shoulder, pointing straight ahead and saw the faint nod of acknowledgement in return. Alex laid a hand gently on Kyle's shoulder, passing the information along. Lucas could see he'd already started taking pictures of the figure in the doorway.

He wasn't surprised when the gentleman didn't go fully outside, but remained in the doorway. Lucas could see he had a long beard, which the goggles showed in near-perfect detail. With the man's wire-rimmed glasses, the girth of his upper torso, his height, and the tribal cap he wore, Lucas knew he was looking at pure evil.

*Fucking Sheik Hammid Rushti!*

There was no doubt in his mind this was the gentleman whose picture they'd been shown yesterday. He was amazed at the quality of equipment they'd been issued and the detail it provided.

*God bless the U.S. taxpayer and the United States Navy Spec Ops Command.*

Surveying the rest of the area, he found someone sitting in a small sedan, under cover of a large willow tree. Once again he gave the signal to Alex, while Fredo watched from Lucas' left side. Kyle took photos of the car.

The howl of a dog of some kind startled Lucas and nearly had him lose his footing. Pitching forward, he braced himself, which knocked a small round rock loose. It slid down the hillside, picking up steam along the way, making too much noise on its journey. The sentry turned in their direction, angling his gun to waist height. Lucas, Alex, Fredo, and Kyle stayed perfectly still, holding their breath.

Lucas wondered where the animal noise had come from since the sound reverberated all over the small canyon. Without turning his head, he glanced to the left and saw two scrawny dogs playing in the dusty campground yard below. The man in the sedan got out, whistled to the dogs who jumped to him and whined as he chained them to a metal clothesline dog run. The movement distracted the sentry, who sat with his rifle across his thighs, studying the compound below.

Kyle and the rest of them stayed calm and within seconds their infra-red picked up the shape of Danny backing away from the guard not more than a few feet behind the man. Their only Native American SEAL, Danny made a habit of sneaking up on everyone on the team and playing pranks. Lucas was pretty darned glad he was part of the mission today. If need be, that guard wouldn't have heard a thing before Danny's blade did its job. It was reassuring to know someone so skilled was there to protect them all.

They waited until they could no longer see Danny's outline before Kyle ordered them to get ready to return to camp. His Chief whispered something to Danny, who got out his slingshot, picked up a pea-shaped pebble, aimed without use of the IR goggles at one of the dogs. The animal yelped and started to howl, backing up in circles and trying to get loose of the chain. In the safety of the noise the commotion caused, the team retreated and was halfway down the back side of the hill before it got quiet again.

Lucas realized he'd been holding his breath nearly the whole way down.

# CHAPTER 22

THE DAY ENDED mercifully and at last Marcy got her long bubble bath She retired early, which was also something she needed. She propped up pillows and took out her favorite romance book. She loved the lavender hand and body crème she'd used; it would calmly put her to sleep. Just before cracking open the book, she checked her phone. Still no text or call from Lucas.

She fell into the love story, feeling sad she was missing Lucas. That new scratchy feeling in the pit of her stomach, indicating a new love and desire to grow and explore that love brought delicious anticipation. It was something she'd only felt a few times in her life. This was not just the lusty parts of their steamy and rather sudden crash into each other. It felt like something long sleeping had been awakened. The passion and intensity of this SEAL took her breath away. She knew a relationship with him would be a wild ride, and not all of it would be fun.

But, boy, would it be exciting.

She snuggled in bed, relaxed but unable to sleep. She could still feel his callused hands move up and down her thighs, the way his stiff fingers moved the hair around the back of her ears, or unclipped her hair to let it fall. He didn't make love to her, he *consumed* her like a man who'd been starving. His neediness was something that filled a void. She also realized very few people would ever see that neediness, or how strong his desire was to love and be loved fully. Every other man she'd ever been with was a pale copy of the color and life and energy Lucas brought her. It was something the SEAL training would never drum into him. It was who he was and what he brought to the SEAL team. It wasn't anything a man could learn.

As her eyes closed, the screaming and yelling of this afternoon faded into a sensual dream. Connie's ugly face, the screaming baby and scared to death toddler weren't so scary as she felt Lucas's body behind her, warming her back, his hands around her waist, holding and protecting her, while his lips and tongue tasted the sensitive skin at the back of her neck.

It was what life was all about: the ugly and the beautiful. One woman's horror was another woman's lifeblood. She was sure she was the woman for him, just as she'd felt the first time she'd kissed him and her eyes opened for the very first time to what could be her new future.


THE MORNING LIGHT brought fresh appreciation for the warm glow she felt inside. She lay back in the soft pillows, hearing the diffused spray of a sprinkler outside her bedroom window. The day would be a tough one. But for right now, she was savoring one of the first mornings of her new life. Someday, she'd look back on it and remember how she felt, and perhaps she'd tell someone, perhaps a son or daughter, what it felt like to fall in love.

She held that thought, letting her heart beat faster, feeling the blood pumping all the way to her fingertips. She never wanted this feeling to end.

And then her phone rang. It was her broker, Joe Reed.

"Marcy, we need to talk. Can I buy you lunch or a cup of coffee when you can spare some time?"

"Sure, Joe. I was planning on coming in to the office in an hour or so. Have some paperwork to handle."

"Well, you know what? I'd like to talk to you some place private. There's a lot of stuff going on right now, and I just needed a private place to clear the air a bit. That okay with you?"

"Absolutely. The Coffee Bean near the office?"

"Maybe some place else. We'll run into agents on their way in. I just need to talk, Marcy."

Her stomach fell to the floor. His normal friendly tone was distinctly missing, though she could tell he was working hard to mask it. "Okay. Where and when?"

"That new place off the strand? They have ice cream, candy, and coffee? How about that one? Haven't been in there yet and my kids are dying to go there."

"Sounds good. In an hour?"

"Perfect."

Marcy decided to finish shattering the rest of her bucolic morning by asking a question she didn't want to ask. But it would prepare her for the meeting, and that was the best she could do right now. "Is there a problem?"

"Marcy, I like you, but yes, there's a big problem, I'm afraid."

MARCY FOUND A parking place for the truck in a lot behind one of the storefronts that was under remodel. She'd planned on dropping it off at Lucas' place and then taking a taxi back to pick up her own car. Rounding the corner, she walked down the half block to the little specialty shop. She didn't see Joe anywhere until she heard the tinkle of the front door bell and saw him standing right beside her.

Joe had been a good mentor, although they hadn't been close. He'd helped her get started in the business and ran a very tight office for a local celebrity chef, who owned Coronado Bay Realty. One of the things Joe did exceedingly well, and the reason he was such a good manager to work for, is that he had a no-drama policy at work, and so his stable of agents weren't going and coming like so many of the offices in San Diego. Everyone was happy, and Joe didn't hire people without something to bring to the company. Several retired Navy veterans with heavy combat experience, pilots, and sports figures worked at the office.

"Always be the calming voice in the negotiation," he'd taught her. Marcy knew some of the drama now occurring between her and Connie was not anything he'd be happy with. She hoped Gail had backed her up, somehow shifting some of the blame off her shoulders.

"You go get us a table. What can I get you?" he asked with a smile that looked difficult to produce.

"Latte. Medium."

Marcy found a corner and sat against the wall, leaving the comfortable plastic padded bench to Joe. He'd put on a little weight in his middle, but he was still an attractive man with a dusting of gray hair. The office had been very busy with the uptick in sales all summer long, and she thought perhaps he'd not made the time to go to the gym.

He came back bearing two identical coffee drinks, set one down in front of her and slid into the padded seat. After his first sip, he opened his eyes and peered right into hers, slight worry lines developing between his eyebrows that all of a sudden disappeared as he began to talk.

"Thanks for coming, Marcy. I've been talking with Gail Burnett."

"Yes, I met with her yesterday afternoon, and my client on Apricot came by the office. I transferred the paperwork to Gail."

"Okay. She told me as much." He let his fingers scratch at the brown cardboard heat sleeve on the side of the cup. "Your former client, Connie Shipley, has been very vocal, even after yesterday. She barged into the office this morning and broke up a meeting with the staff. I couldn't get her out fast enough."

"Where was Gail?"

"Not in yet. But Connie came in to see me. Insisted on it."

Marcy waited for him to gather his thoughts. She knew this was difficult for Joe. Whatever he was going to say next, she wasn't going to like.

"She's made some rather severe accusations." His sad eyes were apologetic. He slowly inhaled, his chest getting full and his shoulders rising. He leaned over the table and bent down, coaching his words, lowering the timbre to a whisper. "She said that you had sex with her husband, *while* you had the listing." His eyes did not smile. He tilted his head in the other direction, but didn't take his gaze from her. "We don't do that here at Coronado Bay, Marcy. And I know you know that."

She had wanted to return his gaze, but inside she felt ashamed. "I'm sorry, Joe. It was a mistake," she said to the tabletop.

He sighed with the confirmation she'd given him, shook his head, and looked up to the ceiling as if he'd find an answer there. "God, I was hoping you'd say she got it wrong." He looked out the window onto the traffic passing by on the Strand.

"I'm not going to lie, Joe. It was just plain and simple a mistake. I'm sorry."

"Damned *right* it was a mistake," he said, his temper beginning to flare. She'd never seen that in him before. "She's talking about suing the company."

Her steely resolve, the fantasyland that everything would turn out somehow crashed all around her like a porcelain doll. Her eyes got hot, and soon tears welled up and started running down her cheeks. Joe handed her a napkin which she used to dab her eyes with.

"What in the devil were you thinking?"

"I wasn't. That's the problem."

Joe sat back and watched her work to repair her composure. With his back erect, he examined the coffee shop, making note of the clerks behind the bar and the new customers who'd entered. His eyes also lighted on the empty seat on his left. "Well, here's the thing, your problem has now become my problem. My problem will be Guy's problem and I don't want to lose my job."

He didn't have to tell her anything more. She was going to try one more time to save the situation. "Is there something I can do to fix this?"

"Not really. I'm in damage control here. I have to tell Guy, and your little lady has a big mouth on her."

"She's mean and vindictive."

"She has some choice words for you too, Marcy. Words she's screamed all over the office. We had clients in the conference room, sitting at agent's desks who heard all this. It was the last thing I wanted to hear at the top of her lungs. We handle a lot of divorcing couples, as you know. That's all we need is to have some divorcing wife hear our agents sleep with their husbands. Get my drift?"

"Yes. I fully understand. I take full responsibility, Joe."

"And you of all people. From a nice family. I mean I have gold-diggers in this office. I try to weed them out before they get hired, but you know this can be a problem. I never expected this from you. You are usually so levelheaded. What the devil got into you?"

If she was crass, she would tell him exactly what had gotten into her, or whom. Now she understood why Lucas wanted her to lie, but that wasn't going to be the way. She knew that was wrong. Why didn't she stop herself from making the other mistake that would, in all likelihood, cost her her job?

"Joe, tell me what I can do, and I'll do it. Anything. You want me to talk to Guy?"

"God no!"

"What can I do to fix this situation for you? Forget about me. What can I do to make it up to you, to the company and its reputation?"

He bit his lower lip, then he smiled. "I'm going to have to ask you to leave."

Marcy expected it, but it still didn't take away the shock of hearing the words delivered to her. Her parents would be so disappointed in her. Every meeting she would go to from now on would be painful. She could feel the whispers behind her back, the gossip. All the embellishments to her character as salacious details were spread throughout the professional community. And it would be more vicious because of the company's long-standing reputation for being more professional and a cut above the rest of the offices in town.

"I understand. I wish there was some way I could get a second chance. Believe me when I say it will never happen again."

"Well, you're right about one thing. It *will* never happen again at my company." He stood, extending his hand to her. "I'm sorry, Marcy. Very, very sorry. You get your things taken care of, I want you releasing all your listings and we'll close the escrows you have, send you a check. But after today, I'm going to ask for your key and ask you to vacate your desk."

She shook his hand and tried to be firm about it. "Okay, I'll get right on it today. Do—does anyone know yet?"

"The secretaries, that's all."

That meant Gail and the rest of the gossip crew knew every detail, and what they didn't know, they were making up. She wanted to go home and just throw herself in her bed, but it wouldn't get any easier than this morning, before the office got busy, to remove all her things. Someone walking out with a Banker's Box full of stuff always indicated one thing: they were permanently leaving. And in her case, everyone would know she was fired.

Marcy watched Joe walk out into the sunlight, the glass door shutting behind him, ringing the tinkle bell. Her stomach was in knots. She picked up her half-sipped Latte and tossed it in the garbage.

Walking toward the burgundy Hummer, her cell phone rang.

It was Lucas.

# CHAPTER 23

"**W**HAT'S WRONG?" LUCAS asked.

"I was asked to leave."

"Leave? From where?"

"Basically, the company fired me, Lucas."

Lucas knew this had something to do with Connie. Hell, it had something to do with him, too. Guilt was not an easy emotion to feel, and he found it stuck like black tar in the pit of his stomach. "What are you going to do?" He held off saying he was sorry, as that cow had already gotten out of the barn.

"You mean right now?"

He felt Marcy's defenses rising. Perhaps his making the phone call was a bad idea. But being in town, he had to try.

"What are you going to do about your job?"

"I don't have a job, Lucas. I'm not sure what I can do. First, I'm going to deliver your truck back to your apartment. Then go by and pick up my stuff at the office. Then look for a job, I guess.

"So this have to do with us?"

"Of course it does. Connie found out, you know."

"Yes, that was partly why I was calling. I just discovered that out too. Jake had dated one of her friends. I think that's how it got to Connie."

"God, Lucas, you guys sound like a bunch of gossipy women."

It frustrated him, too. So many uncertainties about relationships, and women were so darned complicated. He didn't have that with any of the guys he served with. But then, it was life and death and a little screwing around in between. They got serious about really serious things. Everything else was like quicksand, something to avoid at all costs, and usually meant someone other than himself would be crying. He'd be left with that uneasy feeling in the pit of his stomach that he'd been a disappointment, but was powerless to sort it out and make things right. He didn't like not being in control.

So now he'd gotten her fired. That was on him, not her. And that just wasn't fair. She'd been a casualty of his desires. Oh yes, the desires were real, but she paid a heavy price for it. And could he be trusted, really?

Now, so far away from her, maybe that was the safest for her. Not for him. God, he wanted to see her, but it was better for *her.*

Her frustration speared him through the long, tired sigh he heard over the phone. He'd wanted just to touch base, yet he couldn't tell her anything about what he was doing. Nothing like, "Oh, we're just having a normal day, checking out terrorists, searching for bad guys at midnight, fraternizing with the Navy Women's Soccer team. We're buying big screen TVs and checking out contractors and little hottie Nashville chicks who want to hang out with these assholes we're watching. We're locked and loaded and nearly cut a guy's head off last night, but other than that, we're fine."

He really didn't know what to say. And he knew he should say something, and quick, too.

"That's too bad, Marcy." He winced, doubling over, socking his thighs with his fists. Coop looked up from his computer and grimaced at him. The tall SEAL held his palms out to the sides as if telling him, *'What the fuck are you doing?'*

"Too bad? Did I hear you right, Lucas?" He deserved every bit of her frostiness.

"I mean, what do you want me to do?" He tried to be soft. He was listening for every little detail over the phone, any sigh, anything at all telling him she was okay with it. But he had a really bad feeling about their chemistry right now.

The silence sliced down on the back of his neck. *Shit. Here it comes.*

"You know, I might be some minor inconvenience to you, Lucas, and I do appreciate the call, but right now, I've got to sort out the rest of my life, since I don't have a job and I won't be able to afford to live in my place for more than a couple of months and no one in San Diego will hire me anyway."

"You're being a little dramatic, aren't you?" He bit his tongue at what an asshole he was being, but if there was nothing he could do, why pretend? She needed to calm down and solutions would come to her. In any high-stress situation, making a decision while upset could get you killed in the battlefield. And this was beginning to feel like a war. The love wars, like the boys had been telling him. But he also knew he was sounding like a royal jerk to suggest it. He didn't know what to say to her. He cared about her so much and wanted to spend the rest of his life with her, but he freakin' didn't know what to say right now.

He could feel what her face probably looked like. He knew she'd be bright red now. Her chest would be blotchy and she'd be shaking like a leaf.

The last line she delivered, he knew he fully deserved.

"You know, Lucas? I didn't understand how Connie felt until today. Now I do. You are every bit the asshole she said you were—"

"Marcy, wait—"

"Wait? Wait for you to come back here to California so you can charm the pants off me again? You know, Connie warned me about you. I didn't believe her. Now I'm thinking—no, I'm *knowing* she's right."

"Marcy, calm down. You don't have to get upset—"

Coop was looking at him like he had black warts all over his face.

"No, of course not. Who needs a fuckin' job, Lucas?" She sucked in air. "I could go stand on a street corner here and pick up SEALs who want to screw, maybe make a few bucks to tide me over—"

"No, Marcy. That's just nuts."

"You know what's nuts? Believing your horseshit. You remind me of the guy my sister dated. He'd put a big fuckin' engagement ring on someone's finger so he could get all the sex he wanted. When he broke it off, she gave the ring back. It was the best deal in the world for him."

"I didn't get you a ring. I have no ring."

"Which means it was an even worse idea to agree to marry you."

"Marcy—"

"Please, Lucas. I don't want to hear another word. Let me cling to that tiny ounce of self-respect I have left. I thought you really cared."

"I did."

He realized he put closure to their entire relationship with that one. Coop covered his face with his hand and was shaking his head.

"Oh yeah? Well listen here, sailor. I never did."

The line went dead.

"Fuck," he said and almost tossed the phone.

"You are a seriously stupid asshole, Lucas. I don't think I've ever heard anyone at your level. Ever. So all the stories are true. You and that stripper?"

"Dancer."

"The trani dancer?"

He was going to argue the point, but looking at Coop, he knew he should just shut up and get drunk.

LUCAS WAS STILL festering, consumed in his head as they drove over to the building contractor's office.

"Would you stop with the fuckin' sighing, Lucas? You're acting like a teenager." Cooper downshifted the van and pulled around the corner, sending Lucas into the passenger door. "Get your fuckin' seatbelt on, man."

Lucas complied.

"And get your mind off that phone call. We have to concentrate here."

"I know," he said softly. He told himself he wouldn't have taken it so personally if he'd been overseas. Over there, you knew you had to concentrate. Here, on home soil, it was something he was having a hard time getting used to. Terrorists here. Possibility of danger. Here. In Tennessee, of all fuckin' places. It just didn't fit.

Coop drove them to the office of the contractor who built the barn at the complex.

Inside the front door, a large fuzzy-haired dog slept by the metal reception desk. He rose up, blinking his dark eyes underneath soft bangs, regarded them casually and then laid his head back down over his outstretched paws.

They were greeted by a young, ponytailed blonde girl who appeared to be high school age.

"Can I help you?" She wore tight blue jeans, ones she looked poured into, and a pink flannel shirt in a plaid design, and pink cowboy boots. Her drawl was soft and sexy and Lucas again cursed his lack of judgment.

Coop cleared his throat and took out a piece of yellow-lined paper with a building design drawn on it. "We're looking to get some quotes on a building for my friend's ranch. He drew this from a magazine."

She took the paper, regarding Lucas briefly, and then studied the drawing.

"Let me get my dad. Just a minute." With the drawing in hand, she exited through the glass door to the shop area in the rear. Lucas couldn't help but follow her perfectly formed ass through the doorway. He told himself it reminded him of Marcy, but he cursed himself for the lie.

A country station was playing in the background. Pictures of stalls, hay barns, and paddocks adorned the walls. The owner apparently supported several kids' baseball and soccer teams. Framed letters from satisfied customers also cluttered the walls in small black frames. Although clean, the office was sparse. Two imitation leather chairs in an olive green color sat in the corner, bordering a corner table with a large amber lamp that looked like it had come from someone's living room thirty years ago. A space heater in the opposite corner next to the dog kicked in, but the dog didn't move.

"Where did you get the picture?" Lucas asked.

"Traced it from one of those farming magazines."

"Looks like the one—"

"Shhh. Sort of. That was the idea."

Lucas took three steps to the side and bent down to pet the dog, who promptly rolled over and exposed his full underside, including an empty ball sac.

"Sorry there, boy," Lucas said to him. "You're a friendly thing aren't you?"

A red-faced gentleman with a belly bump walked through from the back with the paper in his hand. He extended his hand. "Hunter Boles. I'm the owner."

His thick accent was difficult for Lucas to understand. Coop returned the shake. "Calvin Cooper here, and this here is Lucas."

Boles pursed his lips, a frown developing on his forehead. "Hey, Jake, get over here," he ordered the dog. The animal scrambled to obey. His legs were long and thin, with a slim waist and large chest. Lucas thought he might be part Greyhound. "Some guard dog, right?"

Cooper gave him a half smile. "I got a dog, Bay. About the same size, and he's real friendly when I'm around. Not so much when I'm not. I'm sure your dog is the same way."

Lucas saw Jake hang his head as the door was opened and he walked slowly to the back. "Yeah, well, he's supposed to earn his keep. My wife doesn't like him at home because he sheds on everything, so this here's his home and he's workin."

Boles put the paper on the desk, smoothing it over.

"This is just a rough drawing of what he saw."

"This your friend here?" Boles said, pointing to Lucas.

"No. My friend lives west of here."

"Um hum." Boles studied the drawing again, tilting his head to the side and scratching the back of his neck, then stood to address Coop. "So what's he doing with the building, then?" Boles squinted up to Coop's considerable six-foot-four frame.

"Hell if I know. Gentleman farmer. Grows pot? He hasn't told me. And I don't ask."

"Gotcha. Yeah, we got a few of those around here."

"He's got money."

"I would expect he'd pay cash." Boles said as he narrowed his eyes.

"Sure. He's just looking for a good deal."

"So how did you get my name?"

Coop shrugged. "No clue."

The owner pulled his pants up onto his waist, which was wider than his hips. "So don't 'spose you know what size he wants, either."

"Big."

Boles grinned and Lucas could see a wad of tobacco stuck to his upper teeth, staining them a dark brown and making him look like he was missing them.

"No windows, I guess."

"That's what he drew. I thought he just forgot to put them in here. I mean, why would anyone want a building like that without windows?"

"Well, it kinda depends on what you're doin' inside, Mr. Cooper. If you don't want anyone to know, whole lot safer not to have windows."

"You build anything like this he can take a look at?"

"Sure. Baptist Free Will Church over near Paris, but that one has windows. This here is really a warehouse. No animals?"

"Again, Mr. Boles, I have no idea."

"Well, I need to know that. Ventilation? Air conditioning? He want it on a slab?

"I'm guessing so, yes."

"Well, keeps the varmints out, too. Until it rusts." He held the paper up. "Can I make a copy of this?"

"Help yourself," Coop said.

Boles handed him back the drawing. "I'm a little uncomfortable talking price without the owner, you know, the guy who's paying for it, being present. Don't like to talk to representatives, no offense."

"No offense taken, sir."

"You shopping this around?" he asked Coop.

"You're the first person we came to."

"Why don't you let me have a first crack at it? I'll see if I can find you an overrun or slightly damaged building, if that's not important to him?"

"Sounds good to me. If I don't have to drive halfway across the state, I'm happy with that."

"You fellas aren't from around here, are you? You sound like a Midwestern boy."

"That's right. Nebraska."

"I knew it."

"And I'm from California," added Lucas. Boles completely ignored him.

"Well, Mr. Cooper, I'm going to need the size, though, so you'll have to get him to give me a call with that. I'll have to see the site, study the road access for the trucks carrying the steel."

"Of course."

"How soon does he want this?"

"He said as soon as possible."

Boles studied both of them slowly, focusing on their shoulders, forearms, taking special note of their tats. Cooper had turned his forearm toward his side, as did Lucas, to hide the identical frog print tats that nearly everyone on Kyle's team had from inside their elbow to their wrists. Lucas made a note to himself to wear something long sleeved the next time.

"You boys military?" Boles had taken on a somber tone, trying to sound more casual than he was thinking.

"Ex," said Coop.

That seemed to satisfy Boles. He handed Coop a couple of business cards. "That's got my cell phone on it. Use that number. I pick it up all the time, day or night, but never when I'm on top of a building doing an erection, okay?"

"Thanks, sir. I'll have my friend call you."

They both turned to go, Lucas opening the outside door first. From behind them, he heard Boles shout out, "What's your friend's name?"

Coop slowly turned. "Kyle. Kyle Lansdowne."

Boles shook his head. "Never heard of him."

# CHAPTER 24

**M**ARCY DROVE LUCAS' Hummer to the complex the bachelors lived in. Of course, she felt completely different now than when she and Nick had returned Lucas' items. She had been in some fog then, clinging to some oversexed belief this was true love and Lucas was The One.

*Thank God for reality*, she thought. Though painful, she made a mental note that a fresh start was what she needed. And maybe San Diego would remind her too much of the failed experiment that was her SEAL, Lucas. It would be a good thing if she never had to talk to another SEAL for the rest of her life. Except Nick, of course. But then, he wouldn't really count, since he was out and Devon was her friend.

Thinking about Devon's career in Sonoma County gave Marcy an idea as she turned off the truck. She fiddled with the keys and saw what looked like a front door key on the fob. Perhaps that was to the apartment. She decided to try it, and perhaps call the Taxi from inside Lucas' place.

She examined the area, including the parking lot that was near drained of cars. *That's right. Everyone's at work.*

She told herself it would get easier. Shrinking from the reality of her firing wouldn't help. She'd face it head-on. Get used to the idea that, unlike the rest of the world, she was on a precarious footing, but she would definitely find a way out. And whatever was out there, was going to be a good thing. *Not* a bad thing. When had she not landed on her feet?

Marcy knocked on the front door, and when no one answered, used her key. "Hello? Anyone home?" she said out of practice. The place smelled just like before. It was still a man cave. If she still harbored any warm loving feelings for Lucas, she'd stay and clean the place up, but she figured they wouldn't notice any tidying up, and it would send the wrong message. The men had nothing living in the place that needed tending, like plants or fish tanks. Everything could be left to rot or dry up as she was sure they were used to doing.

She examined the sagging ugly brown couch, and got the impression perhaps this was Lucas' bed. *Serves him right.* The SEAL was freeloading on his buds too.

She walked toward the dirty sliding glass door entrance to the balcony overlooking the parking lot. The barbeque was still covered in plastic, but the wheels and undercarriage were getting rusty from the salty air. The view was nice, seeing the bay and a large cruise ship pulling out, getting ready for a grand voyage.

*Maybe I should sail away. Take a vacation.*

She thought of Nick and Devon's place, the winery, the beautiful scenery she'd seen on her way up to the house in Cloverdale. She did have a California Real Estate license, so relocating up there might work. Might. Maybe Devon could grease the way a bit. Hanging around Nick would be safe too, since he wasn't really close to Lucas and probably wouldn't have much to do with him. And somehow, she trusted him.

Marcy discovered there was no apartment phone, but she did find a phone book and called a taxi with her cell, instructing him to meet her next to the Hummer. She peeked one more time at the four bedrooms, and again at the disgusting hallway bathroom with the raunchy posters and, as if she was saying goodbye one final time to Lucas, did a complete 360, not finding anything she wanted to memorialize. She was done. Time to go. Next fish to fry was moving all her stuff out of the office. She dropped the keys under the sand-filled ashtray pot standing guard by the front door.

Halfway down the hallway, she ran straight into Connie Shipley, who was carrying a Banker's Box. She had the baby in a front backpack and the little girl was tugging at her impossibly tight jeans.

"You just keep turning up like a bad penny, Marcy," the SEAL's wife said.

"Just dropping something off." It was a partial truth, though she really had no reason to be inside the apartment.

"Well then, you can open the door so I can give Lucas this shit."

"He's not here."

"Do I care? Did I ask that?" Connie balanced the box on the metal railing. The toddler was yanking on her leg, begging for something.

"Well, I'm just leaving." Marcy tried to walk past Connie, but her former client stepped into her path.

"Hey. You got a key? Then I don't have to leave these outside the door."

Marcy cursed inside at the thought Connie would leave a man's stuff outside for anyone to steal. She knew Lucas wouldn't be back right away, and she guessed Connie did as well. "Yes. I have a key. You don't?"

"Of course not. So you can let me in, and then leave it with me."

Marcy wasn't sure what to do with that one. She whirled around, walked past Connie, stooped down and found the key and unlocked the door. She stood next to the frame while Connie and her box and two children entered. The way the woman wandered around, Marcy ascertained she'd never been inside the place before.

"Where's his bedroom, Marcy?" Connie asked, pursing her lips and raising her eyebrows. She was still holding the box, while the little girl began running from room to room. "Lindsay, stop it," Connie yelled.

"I have no idea. I was never here when Lucas was."

"So how come you have a key?"

"Because I drove Lucas' truck home from Sonoma County with Nick, his friend."

"Oh, so now we're working on another SEAL? Is that right? He *is* another SEAL?"

Marcy wanted to get herself as far away from this woman as she could. She was having unclean thoughts about saying or doing something unladylike. "Connie, Lucas was called away so fast, he had to fly back. That left the truck behind, and I was conveniently available to drive it back."

"With your new boyfriend."

"I don't *have* a boyfriend. And what difference does it make to you, anyway? Let's just get this over with, and then we don't have to speak to each other again, okay?"

"Fine." She dropped the box beside the entrance to one of the bedrooms. Marcy could hear something clatter inside, perhaps break. "Lindsay, we're going."

The little one grabbed onto her mother's hand and continued looking back at Marcy with wide eyes, her little feet running to keep up with her mother.

Marcy locked the door, tucking the keys back into her pocket this time, and followed behind them. At the parking lot, she stood by Lucas' Hummer to wait for the taxi she'd called. She would ask Nick for the name of someone in the area she could safely leave Lucas' keys with.

Connie hadn't forgotten her earlier request. Holding out her hand, she gave a triumphant smile. "The keys."

"I'm sorry, those weren't Lucas' instructions."

"You have no right to my husband's truck keys or the keys to his apartment!"

Marcy's fury didn't interfere with her judgment and she bit her tongue, swallowed, and reeled in everything she had to stay calm. "I'm afraid you'll have to take it up with him. I'm merely following orders. But in case it matters, I'm not coming over here or taking his truck anywhere."

The unkind scowl Connie gave her did nothing to her already churning insides. Marcy was confused, hurt, angry, and tired of everything, ready to put it all behind her as quickly as possible.

"You know, Marcy, my divorce attorney has suggested I sue your broker."

"Really? That surprises me," Marcy lied. She thought perhaps the woman wanted to gloat about something. "I'd love to stand here and chitchat," she said as the yellow taxi pulled up and she waved to the driver, "but I have to go over to the office to pick up my things. As you may or may not know, they fired me because of the stink you caused. So I get to move on with my life. I guess I should thank you. But I do have work to do."

She didn't look back at Connie as the taxi did a U-turn and came back the way it had entered the parking lot.

IN FIFTEEN MINUTES, Marcy was at her own apartment, located within walking distance to the Coronado Bay Realty office. Once inside the door, her defenses dropped and she ran to her favorite overstuffed reading chair. Her tears had begun before she hit the cushions. The familiar hollow angst in her chest, the hole through her heart, was something that began to spread all over her body, causing her to shake. The tears desperately tried to wash away the hurt and memory of something lost, perhaps something that never was. Her neck ached.

She leaned her head on the padded back of the chair, staring up at the watery ceiling. Big gulps of air helped, and she began to calm with each deep breath she drew in. At last, the warm familiar aura of the place she'd enjoyed living in finished the soothing job of bringing her back to herself—the self that she'd relied on, the person who had been successful, enjoyed life, and made good decisions. Not the reckless self so easily influenced by that wrecking ball of a man. He was like an Alaskan ice breaker ship, crashing through all her defenses, making a waterway for himself where there wasn't one before.

She'd been so dumb. She'd been no match for his intensity. And yet, being perfectly honest, that intensity was what she had been attracted to in the first place. She was like a moth to the flame, and, unlike her usual self, powerless to stop it.

Marcy decided to call Devon in the privacy of her own space. She made herself a glass of ice water, brought it back to the chair, and dialed.

"Hola, Marcy. How are things?"

"Nick get back okay?"

"Fine. He had a good time driving down with you."

Marcy's stomach lurched. She'd not had breakfast, just the coffee. "He's a really nice guy. You're a lucky woman."

"Hey, hands off."

It was a light-hearted comment, but it cut to the bone. She covered the phone in case Devon would be able to hear the heavy breathing that came along with more tears. She tried to speak, but the words were more like a whisper.

"Marcy? Are you okay? What's wrong?"

"They fired me." There. She'd said it.

"Oh my God. When did this happen?"

"Just today, just now really. It's a mess, Devon."

"Yeah. I can imagine. Your broker is taking a hard line. You gave up the listing, of course?"

"Absolutely. But Connie—that's the wife—she's a real pistol. Lots of drama with that lady, and, well, she caused a scene in our office, with all the high-end clientele, celebrities, and such. My manager worries about—"

*Oh hell, who am I kidding? I made a mistake!*

"It's all my fault. Never should have happened." She tried to laugh, but it didn't come out right. "Devon, I was such an idiot."

"Love is blind."

"And stupid. There isn't anything there. I gave up my career—a good career too—for a couple of days of self-indulgence. That's the long and short of it. I'm ashamed."

"Oh stop it. I think you guys are great together."

"Except that's not happening either."

"What?"

"Lucas called right after I met with my manager. I know I was upset, but he sounded like such an asshole. I ended it, Devon."

"Oh no! I'm sorry to hear that."

"Well, Dev, this has been a couple of just terrible days. I'm working to get my head on straight. And I was wondering—"

"*Of course.* You get your butt up here. You can stay as long as you like."

"Under the circumstances, I've had to turn over all my listings to the office, so there isn't any reason for me to stay down here. I really appreciate it if I could bunk up there until I sort out what I'm going to do. But I'm not one to impose."

"Nonsense. You can help me with the crush and all the holiday party planning, Marcy. Get your mind off everything. Just get the soonest flight out you can."

"I think I'm going to drive, bring a few of my things, if that's okay. *Not* moving in, of course, but I will need a car. I plan to look for work up there. Maybe, you know, a winery hiring?"

"You can use ours—the old beater or the Kubota, of course!"

They both laughed.

"I'll get your room ready and you just let me know when you leave. We'd love to have you."

"Thanks, Devon. Really appreciate this."

"You'd do the same for me."

"I would."

Marcy was about to sign off, when Devon added, "Hey, and sorry about the comment about hands off on Nick. I didn't realize—"

"I'm so over that, Devon. How would you have known? Eventually, I'd like to find someone just like Nick. When I'm ready. Right now, I just gotta land on my feet, figure out what I want to do."

"I got it. And where, right? You need to figure out where you're going to live? You're not giving up real estate, are you?"

"Well, perhaps we could talk about that too, but let's just wait and see where this takes me. I do appreciate all your help."

"I'm going to talk to my broker, or do you not want me to do that?"

"Hold off for now. I'll see you in a couple of days."

"No problem. But get up here so I can keep an eye on you, okay? I'm going to worry myself sick until I see your smiling face."

Marcy was so filled with gratitude, she nearly started crying again. It wouldn't totally fill the hole in her heart, but it lessened the size and gave her the doorway to another future, so she could turn her back on the poor decisions of her recent past. In time, she knew she'd scratch her head and wonder what had come over her. It would look like just a little blip on her timeline. She'd be able to notice it without feeling like she'd lost something.

After all, she *was* gaining a future, somehow. It just wouldn't be with Lucas.

# CHAPTER 25

L UCAS DIDN'T LIKE the contractor. "You trust this guy?"

"Well, we're not going to fuckin' build a building on the Navy site. Not sure how much trust we need."

Coop's steps were longer than Lucas' He began to speed up to stay slightly ahead of the tall medic.

"But with the proper encouragement, I think we can get his cooperation."

Lucas stopped in his tracks. Looking up to Coop, he asked the question: "How we going to do that?"

"Up to Kyle. He has ways, believe me, and he knows more about this whole thing than he lets on."

Lucas nodded. He knew Coop was out of sorts about something. He could ask the giant about it, but decided he'd wait for Coop to seek him out. He didn't have to wait long.

"Look, Lucas. I'm going to say this once to you, and then I'm going to shut up about it because I really shouldn't be having this talk with you."

*Oh fuck, here it comes.*

"Ladies. This is about ladies."

"I don't need it, man." Lucas wondered why everyone felt they had the right to tell him where he'd fucked up. "I'm not a perfect man, Coop. I make mistakes just like the other guy. I don't need to hear all about it, is all." His shoulder ached and he rotated it while cracking his neck.

"Holy shit, Lucas. You gotta get that looked at."

"Shut up and go ahead, tell me what I can't stop you from saying. Just for the record, and for the second time, I. Don't. Need. It."

"Oh, you're gonna need it, or you won't make it on the team. I've seen guys…" He was quiet as a couple of young girls passed by them, giving them a long hungry stare. Coop turned around to make sure they were out of earshot, and Lucas heard their giggles. "Girls are funny," the tall SEAL whispered.

"I don't get that same reaction, Coop."

"You know what it is? They know I'm nice to them. I've never mistreated a lady. Worst thing I ever did was turn them down, and that's hard. But sometimes, it's the most compassionate thing to do."

Lucas tried to let Coop think he was considering his words, but he didn't believe a word of it.

"A man wants to do things, you know, sweet talk himself into a little nice situation. A little pleasure party, you know. It makes us feel good. Makes us feel like a man when the ladies fall for us. Flirting is one thing, being a gentleman is another thing. *Not* being a gentleman or not realizing the consequences of your actions is very dangerous."

Lucas was hoping Coop would shut up soon or he was going to lose it.

"THEN YOU'LL BE like your friends at the bachelor pad. Hating women. Leaving them crying all over the place. Kids in every port, you know what I'm sayin'?"

"Coop, that's not me. I used a condom."

"Fuck's sake, Lucas. I think you're the dumbest frog I've ever met. You seriously think that ends your responsibility? How the hell'd they let you on the teams with that attitude?"

"No one asked me about condoms, man."

"I can't believe what I'm hearing," Coop said. "Unbelievable."

Lucas was starting to get pissed off. "Coop, could we just stop talking about all this shit and go buy the fuckin' TV and maybe some groceries, including some beer—a lot of beer—and then you can leave me to have my own pity party?"

"Sure. I expect you'll be rooming with those guys for the next ten years. Better start looking for a five bedroom place, or you'll start sleeping with each other."

"Asshole."

"I've been called that before. I expect you'll be called that a whole lot now. Good luck with that, by the way." Coop stopped in his tracks. "One more thing—"

"You said that already. This makes the second thing."

Coop ignored his words and punched him in the chest with his fore-finger. "You stay the hell away from my wife, Libby, or any of her friends. And if she's real nice to you and tries to fix you up with one of her lady friends, you just say no. You stay away from all of them, you hear?"

"Sure, Coop." He had to look up to the tall Nebraska former farm boy, but he wasn't intimidated. "I can do that. Your lady and her friends are probably way out of my league, anyway."

"You just have to learn the facts of life, Lucas. Don't listen to Jake and Ryan and those losers."

"They're not losers. And Connie and I had a great time in the begin-ning."

Coop started laughing. "I'll bet you did. Not doubting that."

Lucas still didn't like the advice giving, but Coop was senior to him on the team and he knew it was smart to show him the respect he was owed, even if he didn't agree or like the advice.

"You'll figure it out, kid."

He didn't take offense at Coop's comments, even though they weren't even ten years apart. But Coop had paid his dues, and Lucas had one third the deployments the tall medic had.

That counted for a lot. He figured he could put up with some of Co-op's shit and then go his own way. No need to start another confrontation, or a fire.

THEY BROUGHT THE large screen TV into the temporary team building to much celebration. With quiet concentration, the Blu-ray and cable was connected, and soon the 55" screen was streaming action-adventure films. Another poker game was started, but Lucas grabbed a couple of beers and retreated to his bedroom. He thought about his conversation with Marcy, especially her words that Connie had been right. Were they both right? Perhaps he had no business being with a woman.

When he'd moved in with Jake and Alex and the rest of the boys, he thought it would be a temporary gig, that Connie would tire of her single life, she'd start to miss him, and voila, they'd be back together again.

He'd been wrong on that one.

Then he found himself attracted to Marcy. That was not only wrong from her standpoint, it made things worse with Connie. And it ruined

Marcy's employment situation. He never intended for this to happen. He didn't wish any ill to come to either of them. Was he really that dangerous?

He finished his first beer, set the bottle down on the concrete floor, where it tipped over. Jake was at his doorway in an instant.

"You're being rather unsociable, my friend."

"Bad news. That stuff with Connie is a real mess. Wish Connie hadn't been told."

"Hey, I wish a lot of things. I wish my ex hadn't gotten the hots for the pharmacist. I wish I hadn't been on such a long deployment. I wish I hadn't dated the sisters—"

"That one," Lucas said as he pointed to Jake while still holding the bottle, "that's the one that fucked us both up, and got Marcy fired."

"Fired?"

"Yes. Fired."

"Wow, that sucks."

"Jake, the company she worked for is real high-brow and everything. Not everyone understands these things. I mean, we do, but it didn't go over very well with her boss."

"Geez. I'd never make it there," said Jake.

"No kidding."

"Half the population screws around, and here it was just one night of sin and all."

"It was a couple. But that's not the point, Jake. She was working for both Connie and I, and how do you suppose Connie took it?"

"Yeah. I knew that." Jake sat down with his beer. "So what's your plan?"

"What do you mean?"

"Well, what did you tell her?"

"Oh that." Lucas sat up, rubbed the back of his neck and took another long sip of the second beer, finishing it as well. "We're done."

"Done?"

"Yup. I screwed this one up royally. Really great lady. I wasn't thinkin'. She's better off without me." Lucas looked at the bottle and set this one down carefully beside the first one.

"If it makes you feel any better, I've been told that a time or two."

Lucas nodded his head and he imagined Jake had been told that many times over. "We aren't the type who are good for women, Jake. I didn't believe it at first, but you know, in the brief time since I've been bunking with you guys, you've got me convinced."

"Well, glad we could help on that score at least," Jake said as he stood up. "Come on, it's going to be time for dinner soon, and then maybe we can wreck some hearts on the Navy soccer team. You game for that?"

"Not sure about the girls, but the food? Yeah. I could take some right about now. And then I'm going to have a few more beers and see where it leads me."

"That's a good plan, Lucas."

Lucas watched him leave the room while he stayed behind, sitting on the bed, with the light of the day waning, waiting for dinner, considering having one more beer before.

It was a shame Marcy had to pay the price for his stupid mistake. But hell, at the time, it sure didn't feel like a mistake at all. It felt like one of the best couple of days of his life. Everything was possible. He was finally into a woman who was just as into him. How in the world could that be a bad thing?

# CHAPTER 26

M ARCY WAS GOING to attend to her office things, but after the call with Devon, she started making a plan, writing a list of things she would pack and take up to Sonoma County. To heck with the prying eyes of the office. Besides, if she went in there right now, she would be the talk of the place. Marcy decided to wait until late in the day when she knew the office would be completely deserted.

She picked through her clothes, thinking there could be a few boxes she would give away. She straightened up her apartment, changed her sheets and towels. Something about this little ritual made her feel more like a whole woman. She lit two new candles and played a streaming Spa Radio channel. She made herself a light lunch, brewed some fresh, strong coffee, sat at her tiny dining table overlooking the flowering crepe myrtle tree that went up three stories, its showy deep rose pink flowers blooming happily just for her. It had been a nice place to stay, but she realized she would move on without regret. Some place equally as nice in Sonoma County awaited her. And in the meantime, Devon and Nick's home was a safe place to land for a few days.

She called her hairdresser and found out she'd had a cancellation, so Marcy took the time to have some highlights and a trim. Next were her nails and a pedicure at her favorite Asian spa with the waterfall. She even managed to return Lucas' keys to the friend who had taken the heavy duffel. She no longer trusted leaving them at Lucas' apartment, where Connie had watched her retrieve them.

Strengthened by doing all the things she liked, she decided to go face the office, just as the sun was hanging low and threatening to melt into the ocean. Tomorrow morning she'd get up early and go to the gym in the complex, finish her packing, and then perhaps leave for up North early the next day.

All the good self care she'd done buoyed her mood, so that when she pulled into the parking lot at the Coronado Bay Realty company's lot, squeezing her Nissan between large Mercedes, Teslas and Bentleys, the three cars of choice for the Realtors in her office, she felt strong and ready to take on anyone or anything.

Until she rounded the corner to her semi-private office. Someone had already started moving her things and had brought in several boxes of their own. Marcy's plaques and awards, even the oil painting a client had done for her as a thank you, some of the celebrity photos she'd had signed, were all stuffed roughly into a couple of cardboard boxes without being careful about the quality of the packing job. It was an obvious slight. The painting had a small hole in the bottom right corner of the canvas where a sharp cornered black-framed award had poked its way into it.

*Son of a bitch.* She worked on keeping her emotions in check, the painful memory of Lucas' advice to do so washing a prickling wave over her skin surface, making her hot, frustrated and needing to take it out on something. She kicked the brown box belonging to a stranger, heard something inside tinkle like it had broken and frowned.

"Hey, Marcy. That's my stuff," Gail said to her back.

*Of course it would be Gail.*

Whipping around, Marcy stared back at the woman who was dressed in skinny jeans and an expensive designer t-shirt, showing her ample surgically enhanced cleavage, dressed for a designer work day. "Who gave you authorization to take my stuff down? You put a hole in my painting."

Gail sneered, reared her head backwards like Marcy's comment had an odor. "Geez, Marcy. That thing? I'm sorry. I thought a little kid did it. I was careful with your awards." She crossed her chest, arms revealing long white fingernails. "As for who gave me authorization? Joe did. He said he'd *fired* you." Her eyelids lowered and Gail didn't seem to have any trouble using that "F" word. She examined Marcy's face through the bottom half of her eyes, head thrown back again. "Sorry about how all this has happened."

"I'll bet," Marcy mumbled. Her composure had flown right out of the room. "I need a little privacy to go through my things, if you don't mind." She took two steps toward Gail, pulled the door away from the wall and swung it in front of the agent's body. Gail had to step back to avoid getting it slammed in her face. Marcy made sure she gave it an extra push for the satisfying sound effect as it rattled the other doors and windows in the building.

She pushed Gail's boxes to the corner and out of the way first. Then she loaded up the items on her desktop so she could use it as a staging area for other things she needed to quickly go through. Gail stood outside the glass window overlooking the bullpen of other agent's desks, talking on her cell phone, while giving a disapproving look back to Marcy. The agent's lack of consideration for anyone else's feelings actually helped with the process. Marcy was looking forward not to have to deal with Gail and the other whispering hens who could say whatever they wanted, once Marcy was safely away, living a great life in Sonoma County.

Surprised it only took barely a half hour to complete the sorting, Marcy brought a large box of papers and folders to the shred bin in the reception area, unlocked the box, and dumped her things inside. The rest of her things fit into three remaining boxes. She'd been short one, so removed the contents of Gail's things from one box and placed them on the near-empty desktop.

A picture of Gail and Connie caught her eye. It was taken in Hawaii, in happier times. The two ladies were tanned, drinking umbrella drinks at sunset. Behind them were two tanned men: Lucas Shipley and Barry Burnett. The visceral reaction she had seeing Lucas' face was a surprise to her. His wide smile and white teeth contrasted the twinkle in his eye. She could see all the way through to his bad boy soul. It made her heart beat faster.

*Damn.*

Carefully, Marcy grabbed the framed picture and turned it over on the desk top. She loaded up her items and took each box out to her car. Before she removed the last box, she righted the foursome picture, turning it to face the side wall, surrounding it with other things from Gail's collection, turned around and left without searching back.

"All yours," she said with a quick smile. Gail stood in the lobby area alone, without expression.

"Good luck to you, Marcy. Where are you going to work?"

"Not sure yet."

"Well, I can call your cell, then?"

"Excuse me?" Marcy set the heavy box down on a reception chair.

"If I have questions about your other listings."

So Joe had given them all to Gail, which felt like a stab in the back. Suddenly her trusted feeling towards her broker was gone.

*Better. You are so outta here, Marcy. Who cares what any of them do now. Not. Your. Concern.*

"I'm probably not going to be available, Gail. It's up to you."

"Oh."

Marcy was planning on calling all her former clients, to say a proper good bye. Perhaps lay the seed they could still use someone else from the office if they were unhappy with her replacement. Something like that. Do it classy and quick. Let them know it wasn't her choice.

"Where are you going, then?"

"Gail, I have no idea." One of the receptionists was leaning to the side to watch her communication with Gail. Marcy walked up to her and presented her office key. "Give this to Joe, okay?"

"Sure will."

Marcy walked out the lobby doors, past the scored faux columns and broken pottery vases bursting forth with color, down the crushed granite walkway to the parking lot beyond and set the box down in the trunk. Marcy and her Murano drove off. She had no impulse to want to see what the office looked like. There was nothing there any longer she wanted to remember.

THE TRIP UP to Sonoma County the next day began after Marcy did one last hard workout in her complex gym. The morning commute was thinning. She texted Devon before leaving and then promised she'd let her know when she was near San Francisco. She double-checked messages and confirmed Lucas had not called, which was as she expected.

Near dusk, she was close to San Francisco, stopping by an Italian place she knew about, had some soup and good San Francisco French Bread, a cappuccino, and then texted Devon she was an hour and a half away. Devon texted her back a smilie face and a heart, *'Can't wait.'*

Near eight o'clock she turned down the winding Bennett Valley Road, into the crushed granite driveway of Sophie's Choice Vineyard. The stress of driving the distance and the awkward meeting at her office lifted as she pulled up to the beautiful modern home, golden lights from the many windows illuminating the silent green vineyards tucked in neat rows.

Devon ran outside, grabbed her Murano's door handle and swung it wide. "Welcome home!" She nearly pulled Marcy from the little SUV and then gave her a big hug. "So glad you made it safe and sound."

Devon was quickly trying to struggle with Marcy's bags when Nick appeared. "Hold it there. You get your butt inside the house, little one. I got this."

Marcy started to take one of the bags and Nick swatted her hand away.

"I *said* I got this." Then he broke a smile. "Welcome." His familiar blue-green eyes were warm and friendly. With his straight jaw, slightly unshaven stubble, his blond hair wildly growing like cropped golden hills of California, he exuded confidence, health and a good dose of sex appeal. She had trusted him since the first time she'd met him, but now, she realized she'd missed their easy conversation and banter on the trip down to San Diego.

As the tingling began forming in her belly it dawned on her that the person she was really missing was Lucas. The loss of that sexy friendship she had with him hurt like a wound that would never heal.

She and Devon laced their elbows together as Marcy slung her red computer case over her shoulder and walked arm in arm with her best friend. Her eyes filled with water with the welcoming she'd received in just under a minute. It was something that helped take away the bitter sting of her firing and painful scrutiny in San Diego.

They were playing soft music that echoed up throughout the house. A melodic soft African singer's voice filled the large rooms with warm sound.

"You have dinner? Want anything?" Devon asked.

"I'm fine. I stopped in San Francisco and had some soup and French bread."

"Vesuvio's?"

"What do you think?"

"How about some hot chocolate?"

"Sounds perfect."

Devon pointed through the sliding glass door off the kitchen, "You go on outside to the guest house and get yourself situated. I'll brew you some hot chocolate with a little chili, okay? Come on in after you get settled."

Marcy set her computer case down and crossed the kitchen in three long strides to hug Devon. "Thanks so much, Dev. You guys are a lifesaver."

Devon's body was warm, returning her hug with a squeeze. "I'm just so excited to have you here. We've got some wonderful news I'll tell you all about it after you come back. Now scoot." She said as she spanked Marcy on the rear.

The cottage brought back the memory of when she first came up to Sonoma County, the day she met Lucas. It was the cottage she'd hoped to spend a few nights with him in, before he was called away. A single lemon-scented candle glowed on the glass coffee table in front of the burgundy loveseat at the foot of the bed. Bright oil paintings adorned the walls as well as collages of work done to the winery. She examined one picture with a bunch of boys working shirtless, spraying each other and dancing. She saw Lucas among them.

"Where do you want these?" Nick asked, standing in the doorway behind her.

"Just put them on the bed. I'll unpack later tonight and tuck them away." She smiled up at him as he lay the suitcases down on the bed, waved and started to leave.

At the doorway, he turned to ask her a question, "So Marcy, you hear from Lucas?"

"No. Not sure I will ever again."

"Ever is a long time." He was right, of course, but Nick's wicked red eyes bored into her like she was target practice.

"I know, Nick. I appreciate all you guys are trying to do for me. This was very generous of you."

He departed.

The property had been Sophie's struggling nursery and Marcy could still feel her presence, her spirit somewhere. Sophie had been Devon's mentor and friend, but she was also the older sister of Nick. Marcy knew the story of how she'd died at the old home, had been poisoned with arsenic in the water tank. Shortly before her death she had to endure the fire that nearly burned everything to the ground. She looked at a picture of Nick and a very frail and thin Sophie, which must have been taken just before her death.

Marcy washed her face, put on a stretchy top and bottoms she could sleep in, hung up a few things and placed underwear and other items in the dresser drawers she'd been provided. She removed her shoes and slid into some felt slippers, making her way back outside along the pathway nearly overgrown with honeysuckle, to the rear kitchen door. Devon had just poured them each a steaming mug of hot chocolate.

"Here you go. Let's sit here for a bit," Devon pointed to one of the overstuffed chairs in the living room. A fountain outside bubbled and spattered loudly, working its magic on Marcy's soul and she relaxed further. Nick sat on the wide arm of Devon's chair, making her look like a child easily lost in the big cushions. Devon's feet couldn't touch the ground when she was seated all the way to the back.

"So, can I ask you what happened with you and Lucas?"

"Nick, stop it. None of our business," Devon interrupted him. It elicited a shrug from Nick.

"Sorry."

"If it makes you feel any better, when Lucas gets home, I'm sure we'll talk. But only if he initiates it. Not holding my breath," said Marcy. "In all fairness, it was just one conversation, a long-distance conversation." She examined her fingernails. "Nothing I can do about any of it until he's back. I could tell his focus had changed. He was a bit stressed."

"I'll bet," Nick whispered looking far away.

"What's happening, Nick?" asked Marcy.

"Crazy sh—stuff." He shook his head. "We are living in strange times."

"Well these are certainly strange times. I meet Lucas, and less than a week later, I'm without a job, relocating to Northern California. I'll be lucky if I still have my real estate license left when all the dust settles."

"Lucas is a one-man wrecking crew."

"We all are," Nick corrected her. "Remember, Devon? We get this tunnel vision, especially when we're on deployments. I've seen guys lose it when they get into arguments with their girlfriends or wives. Here they are, hiding in some boxcar of a home, hot, tired and maybe a little scared. Waiting for all the action to start and wham, a call to or from home, puts them on their ladies' shit list. Not a damned thing we can do about it, either."

"So, maybe it's best that everything is over before too much is made of it." Marcy's words trailed off and she slowly felt herself getting sleepy. "I gotta turn in."

"Me too. We'll talk in the morning. I have a noon appointment in the office, so why don't you plan on going in with me and I'll introduce you to my manager. That sound good?"

"Thanks, Devon."

On the way back to the cottage, Marcy saw a shooting star, and made a wish, just as she'd always done as a child.

*"If there's a way, and a reason for it, bring him back. If you can. And only if he wants."*

# CHAPTER 27

THE SOCCER GAME after lunch between the Navy players and the SEALs was a complete wipeout—for the SEALs. The girl's goalkeeper wasn't afraid of a muscled hero coming at her. What she couldn't stop with her body, she would push back with her spikes. She drew blood on three forwards, tackled another and did a from behind slide tackle as her only defense of the box when she'd been caught off guard by a quick pass. With no refs to call a maybe questionable foul, she got away with it. What was apparent was that, for all their strength and stamina, because the SEALs had not worked together as a team on the field, the girls would be able to kick their butt each time they played. And the games wouldn't be close either. They called it quits after an hour, and although there was a dispute about the actual score, what wasn't in question was that the girls scored at least ten times, and the SEALs had only made one.

It was something that would eventually even out, but it would take several more games than they had.

A party was arranged to go up to spy on the training camp in the daylight. This time, Lucas stayed back at base. Jeffrey had brought a prototype of his new Battlefield Zombies video game Lucas and Jake lost themselves in.

"Holy shit, Jeffrey, do you suppose you could have any more blood in it? Alex asked the handsome former Bachelorette contestant.

The game had blood spurting in every direction when one of the good guys died, and greenish black ooze that worked like acid on the good guy's skin for the zombies. Lucas laughed when a new zombie appeared dressed as a cheerleader, complete with a couple of heads she used as pompons she held by long stringy hair. He wasn't so sure he'd have much of an appetite for dinner. It didn't affect his ability to drink red bull and beer in alternate doses.

"Red sells really well in China," Jeffrey answered.

"That's death to Chinese."

"Prosperity and long life, good luck too," he answered. "That's what they asked for. Lots of red."

"Who the fuck is supposed to win?" Jake asked. "Looks to me the zombies have an edge."

"Can't make it too easy. I think they expect for a novice there'll be lots of red. They asked for that. Then we get the kids to watch the online tutorial I'm working on now. You tell me what parts you like, would like to see more of."

Lucas switched with Rory and T.J. while Lucas, Jake and Ryan went outside, sitting on foldup lawn chairs he and Cooper brought back.

"So you guys think we can find a five bedroom in the complex?" Lucas asked.

Ryan sniffed the air, "You smell that, Jake? I can smell it a mile away. This here is a kiss-up."

"Nice and sweet," He smiled back at Lucas. "You stay the hell away from me in the shower. Recent breakups can do a lot to a guy, and you got two inside of one week, my friend."

"Shut up. You should talk."

"Seriously, Lucas," Began Ryan, "You're lucky man. I'd say you dodged a big ol' bullet. These married guys, they can talk all they want, but we all know what some of those ladies can turn into. And as you've noticed, you don't get any warning or chance to plan."

"Ryan's right. You're much better off playing the field."

They all turned their heads when Rory screamed, "Fuckin' A" so loud it nearly rattled the windows. The video game was getting lots of attention. The noise made it difficult to talk, so the three bachelors retired to Lucas and Jake's bedroom.

"In time, it goes away, and then you wonder what the big deal was," said Jake, pulling from a bag of chips.

"What goes away?" Lucas wondered.

"You know, dreaming about your ex, and trying to get back together. That goes away in time."

"What about your kids, Jake?" Lucas had identified what the real pain was.

"I get to see them. They're actually happier to see me when they don't see me every day. Our times are special now. And they can't say no."

Lucas had to laugh again. "You should see mine. Connie's scared the shit out of them. They cry whenever –well I've only seen them once since the—the—"

"You just got served man. You haven't had enough time for them to adjust. Now for another piece of advice?" Jake started. "Get back in good with that Realtor, and make Connie jealous. She'll start trying to get you back, Lucas. Women like a little competition."

"You don't know Connie."

"No. Sadly, no," Ryan said.

Lucas threw his beer at him and the arc of amber liquid sprayed across Jake's chest. It started a pileon—Jake was on Lucas immediately and then Ryan jumped the pile, causing them all to hit the floor.

Rory and Jeffrey appeared and quickly separated the brawl by pulling Jake and Ryan up to standing position, then shoving them out into the common area between the two bedrooms.

Lucas tore himself off the bed, straightened the mattress that had been dislodged from its base. He wanted to watch some news, feeling a little isolated from the rest of the world, but the game players were monopolizing the big screen. Depending on how long they were there, another TV might be in order to satisfy all camps.

Kyle and the rest of the men who had gone with him up to the hills made their entrance. Kyle headed for the bedroom he shared with Coop, who was burdened with some equipment in a pack that looked heavy. In his other hand, he held a camera with long lens attached. Lucas walked over to his LPO, leaning into the doorway. Kyle sat at a makeshift desk, and was writing some notes, copying some measurements from a crumpled piece of paper they'd prepared in the field.

"What's up, Chief?" Lucas asked, but he looked at Cooper.

"No sign of Rushti. Kind of a quiet day," Coop said. Kyle's back was to the two of them, until he turned around to face them.

"I gotta call CentCom, gentlemen. I'm gonna need a little privacy."

"Sure thing." Coop set the equipment on a table against the wall, which also housed three black duty bags Lucas knew to be filled with ammo and IEDs. Lucas entered the hallway with Cooper right behind him, closing the door.

"We saw him though, right? I mean they know that back in San Diego?"

"And D.C."

"You know what the plan is?"

Cooper grinned.

"There is a plan, right?"

"Oh yeah, there's a plan."

"Spill."

They heard the hallway door open. Lacey and several members of the soccer team sauntered in, freshly washed, looking lovely, and smelling even lovelier. Lucas momentarily forgot his question to Cooper, until the giant stepped on his big toe.

"The plan is that we focus on what the plan is, young froglet. Keep your eyes and ears open."

Several of the girls shuffled slowly past them, their running shoes barely making a sound. Cooper nodded. Lucas mumbled, "Ladies."

"We weren't sure we'd be welcome after today's game," started Lacey. She gave Lucas a wink.

Jake and Ryan had joined the group. "Apology accepted. But you owe us," Jake said. The two accompanied the girls to the living room/kitchen. Rory demonstrated the new video toy.

Coop cleared his throat. "So the plan is that we don't do anything to provoke them. Can't do a damned thing until we get the okay. Now, if they pick a fight, well then, all bets are off."

"You don't think they'd be stupid enough to—"

"Stupid's got nothing to do with it, Lucas. They're worked up with the heavenly fever, I call it. That knife cuts both ways."

"That it does," Kyle said behind Coop. "We stop talking about this right now. We have company."

"Roger that," Coop said. "Lucas, you hang with Kyle and I and stay away from those friends of yours or you'll go crazy. There's a reason they're single and we're married."

Lucas thought about the comment from Jake about being better off, and he agreed with his buddy one hundred percent. That's when he decided Cooper wasn't nearly as smart as he thought he was when it came to women. Eventually, he'd find out.

# CHAPTER 28

EVON AND MARCY rode together to Devon's office for a scheduled appointment with her Broker/Manager.

"I know about Coronado Bay. Good company. We've shared referrals over the years, although we don't get many coming up here from San Diego," Ted told the two women.

"Just want to be totally honest and above-board," Marcy began. "I made a terrible mistake, and this lapse in judgment isn't something I'm very known for. I've never been close to this. Ever. I think this couple just rattled me. I've worked with very high-end and powerful people, Admirals, CEOs and heads of hospitals who are used to hiring and firing doctors, and never had a problem."

Ted smiled. "Well, Devon's husband is the exception, of course, but most these guys are pretty wound up tight. I can see where that would bring some extra tension into an already stressful situation."

"Thank you, sir."

"So is there any fall-out about all this? Are you being sued? The company being sued? Anything like that and I need to know? Anything that comes up, I have t be kept in the loop."

"Of course. No. Nothing like that. I've turned over all my listings to another agent in the office, as instructed. I have nothing that should pull me back there. I need—" Marcy's left eye twitched as she stared down at the carpeting. "I want," she corrected, "to make a fresh start of it. I know Devon. I hope to make friends and get involved in the community and perhaps forget I was ever in San Diego. Besides, it's lovely up here."

"It is. Don't let the people fool you. Lots of money here. We are what they call the blue jeans tofu crowd."

All three of them chuckled.

"Down south, they try to show their opulence. Opposite up here. We don't like that sort of thing. We hate scandal, drama, too much rushing around, being cutthroat or unfair. Most agents here don't care how much they do, as long as they do it right. And I couldn't agree more. Lucky, really, to live here."

"I can see that. Well, if you'll give me a chance, I'd like to join your team."

"I think you'd fit in well, Marcy. Welcome aboard." He leaned over the desk and gave her a firm handshake. "I'll have the Independent Contractor agreement drafted for you in the morning, and of course we'll have to request your license."

Marcy held out her business card for him to get the broker address and her license number. "That's my cell."

"You want a desk here? Or, are you working out of Devon's house, like she does?"

Marcy smiled at her friend. "I'm going to impose as little as possible on Devon and Nick, although I'll be staying there until I can find my own place. So yes, assign me a desk and I'll try to start as soon as it's arranged. That way I'll be around your staff and people who can show me what to do until I learn.

They got up to leave, shaking the Broker's hand, and he tilted his head to the side. "You still seeing the SEAL?"

"Well, he's on deployment, but no, I don't think so. Part of the reason I need a fresh start."

"I understand completely. It's a shame, Marcy. Sorry for all this mess. But I figure you'll want to get busy to bring in some income. That works for me."

The two women had lunch downtown at an open-air pizza restaurant, watching people, sitting in the late autumn sun.

"I'm going to go looking for a place to stay, Devon. I intend not to be a burden to you guys."

"Don't be ridiculous. You've been through a lot—"

"Everything of my own making."

"Yes, that's true, but what kind of a friend would I be to dump you out on your own? You take as long as you want. Why don't you start making some calls for me? We could share the listings, if you get the appointments for me. We can work as a team."

"I don't want to impose."

"Now you're just being silly. I've got phone lists at home. You could even get started today, if you wanted."

Devon stopped for a newspaper, handing the classified section over to Marcy to search for properties.

At home, Marcy called on several rental cabins. Not being familiar with the area, she ran the addresses by Devon, who immediately eliminated those that she wouldn't find to her liking. Marcy was left alone when Nick returned and took Devon shopping.

Her rental car had GPS, so when she found a cabin up in the woods near Lucas' cabin, she decided to head up to Cloverdale area and check it out. Along the freeway she passed rows of vineyards, splaying out in order, leaves beginning to turn yellow and red at their tips. Assorted white tents were set up in the rows as a sun shield for field workers picking the grapes for harvest. Underneath the green and golden leaves, the ground was a rich charcoal color. Bins of grapes stacked up between rows. Several large estate wineries were perched like crystals atop rolling golden hillsides.

Cloverdale came up soon after. The two lane road through the center of town was nearly devoid of traffic. A dog made his way across the highway, barely glancing in Marcy's direction, sensing she'd slow down and let him cross without him having to make a run for it.

Before she made it off the highway, she stopped for a coffee. Espresso machines squealed their protest. The heavily tatted barista was playing light jazz in the background. Marcy examined artwork hung along the bright orange walls of the little coffee house. A lending library stood in the corner with a full two rows of books, several of the romance. It was a place she could sit and think about things, on another day when she wasn't on a mission. Some day, when she could ponder the complexities of life. She got in her car and headed left when she passed the outskirts of the town, as her GPS had instructed.

The drive through the redwoods was lush and green. Unlike the scrubby oak and madrone wilderness where Lucas' family home was located, this area was cooler, closer to the ocean by a few miles, the damp green carpet of foliage making a perfect place for a nap in the forest. The tall trees were thicker and let in little light. The road soon turned to a red-brown color. Her GPS instructed to go further, when all of a sudden, something hit her rear bumper from behind. She dared not look into the rear view mirror since she was having so much difficulty maneuvering her car, but one quick glance and she saw a dirty white van with tinted windshield. In the limited light from the forest, she couldn't tell who was driving. The van continued to push her car as she fishtailed in front of it. Unable to keep up with the switching back and forth. Eventually she was forced off the road, down a small embankment and into the path of a redwood tree.

In a flash of color, she saw the impact. Her windshield cracked and burst forth into a rain of crystals while her head was forced into the steering wheel, and then ripped backward from the impact of the crash. The airbags deployed before her head could hit the steering wheel a second time.

The last thing she heard was a door opening with a squeak. It wasn't from her vehicle. She smelled gasoline and wondered if she'd be able to move if the auto should catch fire. Black spots appeared in front of her eyes. She felt something warm trickle from the side of her mouth as her forehead pressed into the sticky wet plastic of the white airbag. Blackness shrouded her in a deafening silence.

# CHAPTER 29

L UCAS TRIED HIS hand at Jeffrey's game after dinner. He noted Donna was sitting just a little too close to him, and her thigh stretched the length of his. While he didn't think she meant anything by it, he also felt it was more than a sexual advance. Her close proximity, her scent, the way she laughed and so expertly worked the controls of the game when it was her turn, and competitively tried to beat him at every round, intrigued him. But he also felt something dark was looming just under her surface. She wasn't a woman to talk much, and she'd been blabbing all evening, and drinking more beer than he'd seen her do the previous two days.

Something had shifted. She trusted him. He wondered if that was very wise.

Kyle went outside to greet someone who drove up in what sounded like a large diesel truck. Lucas tried to angle a way to see through the building windows, but couldn't make out who it was.

"The barn builder," Coop said.

Lucas excused himself and followed Cooper outside. When Boles laid eyes on them, he didn't smile or extend his hand like he had in the shop.

"You guys got a lot of fuckin' nerve getting me to come out here after dinner. Urgent, you said. What the fuck's so urgent about this place? This is government land. I don't want any of that goddamned paperwork filled out in quadruplicate cluttering up my system. I deal with small time rural farmers." His face was bright red. One eye had a popped blood vessel, which was new. Lucas saw he could have a temper. "I don't have to wait months and months for my cash. I get it before or the day of installation."

"We had to do it this way, sir," Coop started in. He peered over at

Kyle, asking for help. They'd not discussed him coming over today. Kyle must have gotten the urgent call from Forsythe and made the invite himself.

His LPO sat down on a picnic table, leaned into his thighs and spoke slowly to the man, who was scanning the scene in front of him. Boles scratched the back of his neck and breathed hard like he had a medical issue.

"We're looking for information about our neighbor over the hill there." Kyle pointed to the ridge of dark green trees casually. By the way he studied the builder, Lucas could see he didn't trust him either.

"Not sure what you mean by that, son."

"You know, the people who have the little group thing over the hill. You've been there I'm sure. You helped them build it, am I right?"

"Of course. But if you think I'm going to go gossip about them—you guys have no right coming in here under false pretenses. I keep to myself. I don't ask questions and I certainly fuckin' don't answer any asshole's questions unless I got a good reason to do so."

Kyle stood up and was toe-to-toe with the man. The contractor's belly pushed into Kyle's abdomen but neither man backed up. "I got a good reason. Trust me I got a good reason," Kyle said between his teeth.

Boles managed to take a step back. "You guys military? You look military. What, we gonna have a fuckin' war on our hands here in the great state of Tennessee?

"Not if we can help it sir, and that's where you come in." Kyle's voice was practiced and gentle. Calming. It did little good.

"Like I said, I don't want any trouble."

"And we're not looking for trouble either," answered Kyle.

Boles scanned the three of their faces. He nearly jumped out of his pants when the back door to the building opened and out poured several SEALs. Lacey came behind them, kicking a soccer ball. Two of her teammates had removed their jerseys, exposing their sports bras underneath, and stuck the t-shirts inside the backs of their pants. The SEALs were bare chested, having tucked their shirts in similar fashion. Within seconds a lively pickup game of grab ass ensued, both sides trying to capture jerseys while others members attempting to bury the soccer ball into the post nets on either side. One goal was well defended, the other had no keeper.

Fredo had been on the sidelines and at last jumped in. With his speed and superior ball handling skills, he was dodging other players and easily scored a goal. He was on his way to scoring a second, when Chloe tackled him and left him limping for a bench.

"Who the hell are all these?" Boles finally asked.

"U.S. Navy Women's Soccer Team," Kyle answered.

"Navy, huh? So you guys are Navy?" Boles squinted into the remaining sunlight. The lights on the field came on as the dusk sensors kicked in.

"Um hum," Kyle answered him and didn't break his line of sight.

"Fuckin special forces. That's what you are." The builder spit on the ground.

Lucas cracked his neck again and all three turned quickly, alarm written all over their faces.

Kyle refocused on Boles. "So all we want is information." He brought a picture from his vest. "This man. Did you see this man?"

"Never saw him before."

Lucas didn't believe him. The telltale widening of the eyes before his uber-quick response told him the contractor had seen him, maybe even talked with him.

"Try again," Coop said as he picked up the contractor by his western style denim shirt. Lucas heard a loud rip in the fabric. His feet nearly dragged in the dirt although he probably outweighed Coop by forty pounds. Coop let loose of him, brushing the fabric flat against the man's chest. "I apologize for ruining your pretty shirt. I'll see to it Uncle Sam brings you another one."

"Get your fuckin' hands off me. You think I'm stupid?" Boles adjusted his clothes, stepping back for a safe distance.

Kyle looked at Cooper and then to Lucas and shrugged. All of them shook their heads. "No sir," Lucas said. "None of us thinks you're stupid. That's why you're gonna cooperate with us."

"This isn't fuckin' Afghanistan or Iraq. You can't just come in here and manhandle me!" His voice was attracting attention from the field. Fredo limped over to add assistance. Two of the girls stopped and put their hands on their hips. Even Chloe stopped, holding the ball at her hip with one palm.

"So, I'm gonna ask you one more time. Have you seen this man?" Kyle held the picture of the Shiek up to the builder's nose.

"He was there. Didn't talk to him, though."

"How many are they?"

"How the fuck do I know? They have some young ones that stay in the other buildings. Saw them through the windows. Never saw them outside. I only went inside their bunkhouse one time when I got paid. We made a point not to stare, if you know what I mean."

"Sure." Kyle sighed. "So guess. Humor me."

"Thirty? No telling how many inside those other buildings."

"So what's the scene like? You were there, what, three days?"

"Four."

"Okay, so what did you see that you remember? Anything unusual?"

"What, besides the fact that they pray several times a day? They wear long white robes in the fuckin' ninety degree afternoon? They got sandals instead of cowboy boots? You wear sandals here when you're a full grown man and you're, well, we don't do that here."

"I got you. So they're different. What else. What about this guy?" Kyle tapped on the picture.

"His look. The way he looked at me."

"How was that?"

"He looked like he fuckin' hated me." He pulled his jeans up, bringing his belt buckle up into the middle of his "pregnant" belly. "After the first day, I had the creeps. I asked for all my money. I gave it to my wife in case I didn't make it out of that place alive. The Mexicans in my crew didn't seem to have a problem with them. They're used to not understanding the conversations I have with clients."

"So what gave *you* the creeps?"

He looked up at the trees as if the camp's spies were looking down on all of them, and bit his lip, following along the horizon. He watched the soccer players for a few silent seconds without showing any expression, his lips pursing in fleshy puckers, and then smoothing back into a grimace. At last he took a deep breath and made a line in the dusty dirt with the side of his cowboy boot. When he looked up at Kyle, the man's eyes didn't stray a quarter of an inch from side to side. Lucas could see there was a little courage, a little fight left in the man. But not much. And though he was trying to mask it, Lucas could tell he was more than a little intimidated.

"One night we were working late. I saw this guy walk between the buildings. The sun had gone down. They'd finished their prayers. We were picking up our tools but the moon was bright so we could see. I wanted to get out of there so fast it made me sick to my stomach. We knew we'd be done in one more day, and that was one day too long."

"Okay. So what happened?"

"He walked into one of the houses. Before that, I never once saw or heard a woman. But that night, I heard a woman crying, like things were being done to her, you know? Those animals were doing things to her."

Lucas could see Kyle wanted to punch the guy, but his mission was more important than his own satisfaction. Instead of chastising him, Kyle showed mercy. Not many men, especially men who weren't trained to see the kinds of things they saw over in the arena, would know how to deal with this. It wasn't something people in the U.S. were used to seeing. Unfortunately, it was something all three of the SEALs standing before this man knew without a doubt occurred in the world of evil men. Lucas knew it hit all three of them the same. Someone innocent was being violated. Someone needed rescuing.

Kyle spoke softly, making the man lean towards him to hear. "Now you know why we must be here."

# CHAPTER 30

MARCY'S HEAD HURT with a dull ache, which is what woke her up. She was confused, but gradually the fog lifted and she remembered what had happened before she'd passed out. She also remembered hearing voices in a strange dialect, and hands holding her body, carrying her somewhere. But the splitting pain forced her to keep her eyes closed, keeping the room from spinning, knowing even limited light would hurt worse. And then things would go black again. This happened several times before she woke in earnest.

Now, nausea plagued her. She needed to roll over and vomit, but when she tried, discovered she couldn't move. As she struggled with her own mind, trying to will her legs to slide off the bed, and found she wasn't on a bed at all, but a hospital gurney. She smelled the sweat from her body and knew she'd been there more than a day. She had to go to the bathroom.

The tiny room was cold, like a closet off a main living area, without heat. Someone had covered her with a blanket that smelled like it hadn't been washed in months. And then she discovered she was nude underneath the blanket. So where were her clothes? Did she require surgery? Was she in a hospital or clinic of some kind?

Light crept under the doorway, where she heard muffled talking, again in a foreign tongue.

She checked herself over, closing her eyes and concentrating on what hurt and what didn't, discovering her head was still the most painful. She willed her bladder to hold and to her surprise, it worked. Wiggling her eyebrows up and down, she felt the welt on the right side of her forehead. The rusty taste in her mouth and clots of blood on her lip made her heart beat faster. It was one thing to be involved in an accident. But to be drugged and kept in a storage closet, without any medical care, meant only one thing: the accident had been anything but an accident, and the same people who caused it now held her.

They hadn't gagged her, so Marcy deduced they weren't concerned about her screaming for help. She guessed they were somewhere out in the boonies, since she could hear neither traffic, airplanes or other sounds of civilization, except for the faint middle eastern music and the sing song of the unfamiliar dialogue in the background.

The room smelled of bleach, or some sort of pungent cleaning fluid she didn't recognize.

Because one ankle strap immobilized her left foot, toes pointing down, Marcy developed a calf cramp in her left leg that began to drive her wild. She focused on the cramp, pushing into it, while her other leg developed another cramp. She willed herself into accepting it and stopped fighting, which gradually sent the dual cramps into remission.

She steadied her breathing, promising herself that, as more and more memory began to dawn on her, that she would not panic. What had Lucas said?

*'Aren't you being overly dramatic?'*

"Fuck," she muttered softly. She hated to admit it, but being overly excited *would* interfere with her problem solving, and she most definitely had a problem. A life or death problem. She harbored no illusions as to their intentions.

Marcy struggled against her foot binding and a small metal tray fell from the gurney, crashing onto a concrete floor. The door to the lighted room opened, flooding her with bright white light. She squeezed her eyes shut.

Someone closed the door partially, giving her eyes time to adjust. Standing before her was a young man in white robes. His full beard framed the smooth, young face of the man she recognized near Lucas' cabin from three days ago. He saw in her eyes the recognition she bore.

His teeth were white and perfectly straight. His smile tilted upward to the left as he scratched his chin. But the eyes of this man carried a coldness she'd not seen before.

He removed a large ugly knife, brandishing it from palm to palm, showing off the highly polished glint of the blade. His eyes studied her as he peeled back the top of the blanket and lowered the tip of the knife to her abdomen. He jerked it upward, tickling her skin without penetrating.

Still dangerously clutching the handle in one hand, the man pulled back the blanket to below her belly button. His sharp inhale told her he was turned on by the violence he anticipated. She braced for a stabbing, a deep cut, or perhaps a beheading.

One more time the blade was lowered and this time she felt the cold metal on the flesh of her upper abdomen, causing her to shiver. With a flick of the wrist her captor scraped her left nipple. He stared down at her chest, licking his lips.

He was muttering a prayer. Marcy accepted the fact that there was nothing she could do, except perhaps throw her weight to the side and topple them both. But being strapped to the gurney would put her at a disadvantage.

And then it hit her. They wouldn't kill her until they abused her. The way this man looked at her flesh, she became convinced his pleasure would be extracted from her pain. If she showed fear, or struggled, it would enhance the experience for him.

She vowed to hold out for as long as she could.

The robed man shouted several Arabic names and instantly the room was filled with several young boys barely old enough to shave.

He waved the tip of the blade at her while he spoke to them. None of them would look her in the eyes, but remained focused on her breasts. The robed one squeezed her left breast first, muttering something in a sneer, citing a verse the rest of the room repeated. He fondled her right breast, but this time, tweaked her nipple, twisting it until it caused pain.

She arched up as much as she could, but did not scream. That action drew a reaction from the young boys. One by one, they each took a nipple, twisted it until Marcy finally cried out. She watched in horror as the boys were encouraged by her terror.

Her stomach finally could hold out no longer as the nausea swept up from her abdomen, quickly sending bile and contents of her lunch up and out her mouth, spraying the group with her vomit. Pandemonium spread over the little gathering, as the room emptied, no doubt sending the boys to the showers to wash up.

She got what she'd been hoping for and didn't have time to brace herself against. The robed man's hand came crashing down against her left cheekbone and again the room went black.

# CHAPTER 31

E ARLY NEXT MORNING, Donna Grant went for her usual five mile run.
The faint scent of burning leaves was in the air. Heat from yesterday's sun had soaked into the soil and the asphalt she ran on at the side of
the country lane, but the air was crisp and cool, perfect for her run.

As the road veered off to the left, she heard a vehicle approach from
behind so she moved further onto the shoulder to make sure to give the
driver clearance. But the motor slowed and began following close behind
her. She tapped her watch, sending her personal signal through the Apple
device. The watch would clock her location and send that information as
well.

The motor continued to run but when she turned to look behind,
three dark-skinned men in green camo caught up to her, despite the fact
she'd put on the speedburner sprint most men had difficulty keeping up
with. They grabbed her arms, one of them put his hand over her mouth
where she was able to bite down and take a sizeable chunk from the
man's palm. She could feel freedom within reach when suddenly a moist
rag was placed over her nose and mouth and she succumbed to spotted
dizziness fading to black.

"FORSYTHE IS COMING today. We're gonna show him the camp. He's
bringing sat photos, and another special honored guest," Kyle reported to
the group before breakfast. "We do our PT here. No one leaves the
compound until Forsythe okays it, understood?"

"Who's Forsythe bringin'?" asked T.J.

"T.J. because I'm not totally positive he's coming, I'm going to wait.
But you'll find out when all the rest of us do."

Tyler raised his arm and was called on. "How about a rematch with the ladies? We're looking at O for three."

"Not a fuckin' chance. Besides, I think they're leaving soon, maybe even today. I don't want Forsythe to get the impression this is a Club Tennessee all inclusive fucking resort, catch my drift?"

Lucas noted how disappointed Tyler was. "I'll kick the ball around with you after breakfast, if you want. We can do that without the girls, right? You still remember how to play with men, don't you?"

The team laughed at Tyler's expense. Tyler took off his sweaty shirt and threw it at Lucas.

Breakfast was somber. The girls obviously noted none of the SEALs sat with them, as was the custom. Everyone on Team 3 had one eye on the entrance to the mess hall's doors, looking for Forsythe.

Lacey cornered Tyler when he went back for seconds. "You guys sore losers?" she asked loud enough for the entire room to hear.

"Nah. We got—" he looked at Kyle for reassurance he could mention Forsythe and got the nod, "We got brass coming in today. We're supposed to show our bad-ass side, not the fraternizing side. Nothing against you ladies."

"What a load," Chloe said under her breath as she walked past the men on her way to hand in her tray. Lucas thought it was funny as hell.

"See, that's what's wrong with women," Jake started. "They win a little bit, and then they take over. Mess with your head. Talk about sore losers. They hate to waste an opportunity to pound us into the ground."

"Fuck sake," said Alex. "It's their job to win. That's what they train for. We train for something else. They get in your head, Jake, because you let them get inside your head. Your fault, man."

Cooper leaned forward to be able to deliver his message to both Jake and Alex. "Boys, I'm having a hard time imagining you ever being married. I mean ever. This isn't about winning. You don't treat a woman like that. You continue with that shit and you'll be jerking off to the TV when you're seventy. Broke and lonely."

"Fuck, already broke," Jake said after standing. Tyler nodded to Lucas and the two of them cleared their spots, then headed over to the bunkhouse to retrieve the soccer ball.

A black SUV with darkened windows pulled up and three men stepped out. The security team consisted of the driver and two details. Ian Forsythe extricated himself from the rear passenger side, while Jackie

Daniels got out on the other side behind the driver. Kyle was quick to appear and give the man a shake, and give Jackie a bear hug.

Jackie was roundly welcomed. Lucas knew then, that if the mission was successful, they'd be interrogating the Sheik or his underlings, and that would require someone with native language skills. Jackie was the only man any of them trusted for this job. And he had saved their lives on several other missions. Not only was he deadly with his interpreting, he was deadly with any weapon they gave him, and never hesitated to use it. He was as close to an Afghani SEAL there was.

Several minutes later, the team was briefed. Forsythe showed photos of satellite surveillance on the camp.

"You'll see these trucks are in constant use. We've tracked them as far as we can. Gonna have to paint them somehow, or install tracking devices. We're bringing in some drones, but understand only Coop operates them. I don't want any incidents, or alerting the camp to our presence."

Coop nodded. "Can I take pictures?"

"Being fitted now as we speak, Coop. Daytime only, I'm afraid, though."

"We'll do the best we can."

"Chatter is up, indicating we got something coming very soon. The Oregon incident was apparently orchestrated by a group in Northern California, but you know as well as I do, there are over thirty training camps operating in the U.S. today. Our leadership hasn't been comfortable spying on them, although God knows they should be. I mean what the fuck do they want with training camps, learning how to shoot while crawling on their bellies, breech boats and blow shit up."

"Wonder if that guy who got away– remember that guy, Rory?"

"Sure do. The sidekick of the dude Megan went all Bobbitt on," said Fredo.

Jackie piped up. "I do not understand why your government does nothing. They know. It's like they want to allow these people to do evil things to the good citizens of the United States. This should never have been allowed."

"And it's getting worse," Forsythe said.

"Not like it's a church or Boy Scout camp," added Jackie. He continued to shake his head.

There was a general mumble of approval from the group.

"You know what they say. Evil exists when good men do nothing." He paused. "When Kyle reported your builder guy heard a woman crying out, that escalated this mission into a primary target. We can't engage unless they engage first. Be very clear about that. We in no way want to bring in local news crews or garner criticism about SEALs doing work inside the U.S. borders, so we're still considered a training mission. Doesn't hurt to take pictures, and if need be, stage a rescue if we can get the approval."

Armando stood. "Sir, wouldn't it be a good idea to inform the locals? Isn't this something the Sheriff's Department or Marshall's Service should know about?"

"We're studying the situation. Not sure it will work that smoothly. We got three jurisdictions and they don't always cooperate. But yes, we will if we can. If we have time. That would be ideal. But gentlemen, we're here to learn about this verified threat of militias kidnapping and taking hostages—SEALs, *not* civilians. So we're taking the broad interpretation it's our mission. But again, I have to underscore we keep it tight. We say nothing to anyone. No one. Understood?"

The Team was in agreement.

"We will have to verify there's a hostage situation. We can't just send guys in there, even locals, unless we can verify this. So far, we have nothing on what we've taken by air. Hope the drones work better, Coop."

"If she's able to be seen, we'll find her."

"I'm working on VIR equipment for your two drones, too," said Forsythe.

"Two? Hot damn!"

Lucas knew Cooper was their gadget guy and could rig up anything to look harmful or not harmful, depending on the requirement. In his single days he lived in a motorhome by the beach, outfitted with more devices than some small police departments had. His home on wheels, before his marriage to Libby, was affectionately called the Babemobile and had been used on some surveillance and rescues in the past, before Lucas' time on the Team.

Jackie Daniels spoke up. "You get something to record their conversations, and that will be more incriminating. They have to speak to someone by cell. They probably have computers, which would be good to try to capture."

"I got some little devices with a pretty good range. Problem is, we need to be line of sight to work them. That means someone has to stay buried up on top of the mountain."

"Then we'll plan that. You look today for what you'd need and plan where we put them. We'll do the rest," answered Kyle.

"Okay, then. Kyle, give me the grand tour," said Forsythe.

Lucas accompanied Forsythe and Kyle, Cooper, Armando, Jackie and Fredo to the top of the ridge. They were surprised to find two guards posted on the hill today, and, unlike before, one was upper ridge, one was lower ridge. With his high-powered scope, Armando was able to determine there were two other sentries across the small valley overlooking the camp. This meant they had beefed up security, for some reason. Nothing could be discussed until they were away from earshot.

Lucas heard the buzz of a high-flying drone before anyone else did, and he pointed it out to Coop.

"Shit," he said softly. He pointed to his chest, shook his head, "Not ours," he whispered.

Armando finished taking pictures. Lucas noted the vans were lined up as they always were, with the exception of one backed up to the end of a building. The doors were not visible.

Forsythe was comparing their photos with what he was seeing live and made a couple notations to Kyle. Lucas kept scanning the skies for evidence of the drone's return. Movement down in the valley piqued his attention and he found a drone operator using a small laptop computer was guiding it home. He handed his scope, taken from his H&K, to Coop. After several seconds of study, and watching the drone land near the lake's shore, Coop nodded and handed him back the scope.

"All good," he whispered.

Lucas gave him the thumb's up.

They began to leave the site when they heard a car approach the guard gate to the camp. The occupants were two ponytailed blonde ladies, both wearing short shorts and tank tops. Lucas examined the ladies as they were ushered through the gate. What he saw made the hair stand up all over his body.

"Holy fuck!" he whispered.

Kyle faced him and angled his head.

He whispered, "Builder's daughter" to Kyle's ear. Armando had them in his site as well.

"Wonder if papa knows," said Armani.

"I'm guessing not." Kyle added, "If he felt the creeps when he was there, I'd have a hard time thinking he'd let his daughter go there."

"He must have told her, right?" Lucas asked.

Armando shook his head. "I say no. She's doing her little wild child thing, but that's a dangerous game. Very dangerous."

The ladies parked outside one of the buildings and were shown the way to the building doorway. The girls looked at each other, shrugged and walked inside.

The SEALs waited a half hour without further incident. It appeared no foul play was at hand, or whatever the girls were doing was consensual, so Kyle and Forsythe checked with Jackie for any clues, and then called their surveillance off and the group headed back to camp.

After they arrived at the meadow at the base of the ridge, Lucas asked Coop what he was dying to know. "What the hell are they doing with that drone?"

"Same thing we are. We gotta hope to God they don't know we're here," Coop answered him. "Hard to tell, but I didn't see any equipment saddled on her, so I think she's not taking pictures, but you never know. They get hold of one of those micro cameras and we may be on their evening news."

Forsythe turned to them. "We're going to have to consider not going up anymore in the daytime. At least at night, we aren't as discernable."

"But our signature will stand out more," said Kyle.

"Only reason you'll be there is if we can't get the air support, if we go in. We need eyes on the ground," said Forsythe. "I'm going to get on the horn and find out if there are any updates. But I think our next mission will be to verify there is a hostage there."

Lucas didn't like the fact that, due to it being on U.S. soil, they'd have to be extra careful before they were granted permission to go forward. Going in and still having to get permission to go forward didn't seem tactically sound. But he wasn't the one calling the shots.

# CHAPTER 32

MOUSTAFA INTENDED MARCY would be the training whore for his young men, something to use as reward for jobs well done. He cleaned her body and even put first aid salve on some of her scrapes and the bump on her forehead. He enjoyed washing her, preparing her. The training would be long and delicious.

He found that forbidden fruit was the best kind of motivator. They studied it was wrong to have sex with an infidel, but an infidel being used to train boys into becoming men, was allowed. The fact that she would never give her consent made the whole scenario complete. Consensual sex with an infidel was punishable by death. Rape with a subhuman infidel was not only allowed, it was doing the Prophet's work and moving them all toward the Kingdom of Heaven. Moustafa knew he'd be rewarded.

In the meantime, he'd be quiet about his designs on the woman. He would let them touch her, pinch and lick her, perhaps draw a little blood, but the first entry into her body would be performed by him. He'd like to do it in private, but it was important to show the men how it was done. In the old days, they would have themselves to practice on, but now they had a live woman, a woman they could defile and not be punished.

*God is good.*

He'd given her another dose of heroin, when she started to come to as he was washing her. She quickly succumbed to a deep sleep and he could do anything he wanted to her. Such a thought was thrilling.

The heroin was part of the supply they were leaching out into the local high schools in Northern California, which accomplished two things: they raised funds for their cause, and they got the local population hooked on the substance. As far as he knew, they were off the radar.

The government was not only letting them operate these training camps, which emboldened his leaders back in Iran, but had expressly put out public communications to law enforcement they were to be protected. How the Prophet managed to arrange this, Moustafa could never figure. But it was a fact, they had nearly full immunity from prosecution, or persecution. Being isolated in the woods made them virtually invisible. Only thing missing was a fence. Every other compound had installed one. His would be coming soon.

*God is good.*

Marcy was in such a state that the restraints were not necessary. Besides, he liked having her drape over his body, her limp form still lusciously curvy in all the right places. He loved the smell of her perspiration, and the scent of old cologne behind her ears, on her wrists and between her breasts.

Today, while the boys were delivering their drugs to Cloverdale High School, he locked himself in the room with her, removing all their clothes and let her sleep on top of him. He fingered her clit, stuck a thumb into her anus and she moaned like it was pleasurable. But he knew better.

It had been a stroke of luck when they'd found her at the coffee shop. He'd hungrily watched her athletic body order her coffee, watched her out of the corner of his eye as she added cream and stirred the liquid mixture. Her backward tilt of the head exposed the silky white flesh of her neck. The more he watched her, the more he felt he owned her. His fantasies came in wild colors as he imagined things he could do to her, things like that warrior had done. He knew what her skin looked like at midnight, in the shower, even when she was relieving herself. He'd watched her shave her legs, shave other parts of her more intimately. Just for him.

They'd followed her at a distance, but when she drove off the main road leading to the coast, and onto the dusty dirt roads of the redwood forest, he decided on his bold plan. He would take her and the taking would happen nearly five miles from where they were living. It would surely take a week or more to find her car, locate her body, if at all. That was more than enough time for the events he knew were coming.

Capturing her was thrilling. He allowed someone else to drive while he made sure her body was sufficiently intact. Her arms were strong, thighs unharmed. Her forehead was bruised, but her abdomen was flat and unmarked. Her butt cheeks smooth and squeezable. He took just a few liberties, when the students were not looking over at him.

Soon it would be time to use her the way the Prophet intended.

His erection was deliciously hard. She was unconscious. He grasped her hand and squeezed her fingers around his shaft, jerking off into her belly button. He longed for the day he could take her several times and spend an entire day doing it.

When he heard the boys' van drive up, he quickly clothed himself, gave her another dose of heroin, placed her still naked body under the fleece blanket he'd taken off his own bed, and left her alone in the dark.

"Have you found anything?" he asked his young apprentices.

"Nothing."

"Then have you developed our next target?"

They nodded. "She's under age, Moustafa. Does it still count?"

"It counts double."

His young students beamed with delight and anticipation, handing him all the money they'd raised.

"Tomorrow, then. We will continue our training with the infidel whore. Later in the week, you all will become men together. Then you will have the chance to choose your own vessel. After that, we will kill them all. Together."

*God is indeed good.*

# CHAPTER 33

REVEREND TRAVIS BANKS ministered to his flock at Riverbend Maximum Security Prison, ten miles away from their base camp. Banks had met T.J. Talbot at the request of T.J.'s dying father, who was an inmate at Riverbend before he passed.

Because the SEAL team was asked not to leave camp, T.J. asked for and was granted permission to have him come visit at the camp the next morning. A year ago, Banks had informed T.J. about some of the activity that had been going on in the greater Nashville area, and the trending toward radicalization in the local prison population. T.J. thought perhaps Banks could be of some use.

The giant of a man with the gold front tooth made even T.J. look small, something that never happened.

"You never did stop by and I been waitin', T.J. We gots some catching up to do," Banks said, showing off his tooth in the wide smile pasted to his face.

"No excuses. But with little Courtney, it's been tough. We're expecting again."

"Halleluiah. God blesses those who do the good work."

"If that was the case, you'd have a dozen kids."

Travis stopped a bit, tilted his head and dropped his smile, as if offended.

"Oh shit, Travis, I'm so sor—"

"Jes messin' with ya."

Lucas could see T.J. was relieved. "Honored to meet you, Reverend Banks. T.J. has talked about you non-stop since we found out you were coming out here," Lucas said as he shook the pastor's massive hand.

Forsythe was going over some photos and stopped to greet T.J.'s friend. "We're most grateful for any help you can give us."

"That's partly why I'm here."

Kyle showed Banks the photo of the Sheik. "This is the guy we're looking for, reverend."

Banks studied the photo. "Hmm. Reminds me of a real bad dude came through here last year, just before Christmas, but it wasn't this guy. Big, grown bad-ass men at the prison were bowing on their knees to him. He swept through here, had a couple huge services at the Mosque and there were crowds clear across the street, blocking traffic. Police had to shut down the whole area and it was on the news. I don't remember his name, but he was someone big, very big in their circle."

"Like an advanced guard," Forsythe commented.

"Kyle," Jackie slipped between them. "You guys find some news footage. Let me listen to what he's saying and I'll tell you exactly what he was all about. This guy I don't know, but he must be a powerful Imam from Iraq, maybe Syria," offered Jackie Daniels.

Forsythe indicated he'd get someone working on it.

"So you wanna catch us up as far as what's been happening in the community?" T.J. asked.

"Word has it there's going to be a coordinated effort at a strike, or something of that nature. But the thing that bothers me is that this prison isn't the only place. I got a friend out west works in the central valley of California, and he's run across the same thing. This Imam I was telling you about went to all those places, too." Banks looked around him at all the SEALs. "So what're you doing here in Tennessee? Not exactly a place I'd expect to see this kind of crowd."

"Training mission," Kyle said. His voice was flat, but Lucas knew it belied apprehension. Kyle wore the mantle of leadership well, but anyone who spent any time around him knew he carried more than they saw publically.

Reverend Banks was hesitant to offer more help but finally agreed to check the visitor logs, which was a violation of his volunteer agreement.

"Now can me and T.J. here just sit and shoot the bull a bit? Or is this all serious, being that it's a *training mission*." He winked at T.J.

After getting permission, the two men headed to the corner. "Your sister looks good, T.J." Lucas heard the pastor say as they left earshot.

"How did we not know this, Forsythe. You guys uncover this?"

"I'm sure the Bureau has knowledge of it. Politics, Kyle. Stay as far away as possible from politics. No winners there, except the most ambitious, the ones who will do anything."

"That kinda fits us. We'd do anything to save this country," said Co-op.

"Ambitious here, to make sure everyone stays safe. A lot of our guys are dying out there and it's still coming this way," said Lucas.

"Well, that's geography catching up to us. We can be thankful for that big old Atlantic. Pacific too, for that matter," answered Forsythe. "With limited resources and the public retreating from their taste for war, as opposed to 9-11, we have to decide what to put to good use. Can't do it all. People need to understand that."

"Until something big hits us," whispered Kyle staring off into space.

"And maybe that's coming," said Forsythe. "Either that or we'll be ready. That's why you boys are here, mainly to watch and learn. We weren't putting you into the middle of a fight, but right next to the bad guys."

Lucas couldn't help but think about the timing of all this. Someone knew a confrontation was brewing. With over thirty camps in the U.S. it wasn't going to be possible to stop them all. Maybe, just maybe, they could stop one here in Tennessee.

He thought about Marcy and was glad she was some distance from harm's way, living in San Diego, where there were more military and retired military per square mile than just about anywhere. Even if he couldn't, some soldier down there would make sure she was safe. Of that he was sure.

# CHAPTER 34

D ONNA GRANT HEARD the voice of another woman, which was odd because she lived alone. But within mere seconds, she heard not one voice, but several. And they were all women's voices. One was sobbing uncontrollably.

She wondered if one of the soccer players had managed to call a meeting with several of the others while she was sleeping. It felt like she'd slept a whole week, and then remembered she'd been drugged. Then Donna recalled the strange truck, the rag across her mouth and nose, and the odd noises while she fell backward into someone's arms.

She'd been running. That was the part she was sure about. And they'd come up behind her and—and they'd kidnapped her! She remembered sending off the text SOS just before they came up behind her with the rag.

The sobbing continued. Several women's voices tried to soothe the pain, but if anything, the crying continued at an even higher decibel. Donna was now wrestling with two conflicting feelings. She felt perhaps they were all in danger, but before she could do anything, she needed to know whether or not she was intact or gravely injured. It was her training: to assess the damage to her own person first before attending to someone else's.

Her left shoulder was sore. Her head felt groggy, but other than that, she was good to go, provided they stopped giving her the heroin. She assumed that was what it was from her previous experience in Iran.

That had been nearly four years ago when their convoy had been picked off by a warlord and his small band of militia. While most of her unit was killed, they'd taken her captive. The days and nights blurred into one long nightmare that lasted nearly a whole month before she'd been rescued by SEAL Team 5.

But now it was happening all over again. She was a captive this time in the U.S., not some foreign hellhole. And there were other women here as well.

She arched her back and found she had no pain. She brushed the hair from her forehead, opened her eyes and began to feel her life had been spared so she could exact revenge. That required clear-headedness, planning. Taking in a deep breath, she pushed the screaming voices of insanity rattling around in her brain all the way to the back of her skull, where it could sit in a corner until she was ready to call it out. It was time to focus on what lay in front.

The zip ties they'd fastened to her wrists were easily removed by wiggling the ends back and forth until they crumbled in her fingers. She did the same with her ankle restraints.

"Who's here?" she called out.

The sobbing stopped immediately.

"I'm Jenna, and I'm here with Shelley. There's another young girl here, very young, but she doesn't speak English."

"Anyone know how long I've been here?" Donna asked.

"They brought you in this morning."

"Okay, I'm Donna. Coming over. Don't be afraid," she said.

She felt her way on the concrete floor stained with water and what smelled like blood, until her eyes adjusted and she could see the outline of three women in seated position.

"Anyone hurt?" she asked.

"She is," one of the girls said. We just got thrown in here. But from the feel of her face, she's been cut and beaten."

Donna reached out to the girl and immediately the poor thing jolted and pulled away, working against her restraints.

"They even have a collar around her neck," one of the girls said.

Donna used soothing words like she would do to a frightened young child, holding out her hand until she felt the familiar leather collar she knew all too well. The pictures of her abuse flooded her brain until she closed her eyes and willed them to be gone.

"There should be a buckle at the back, or perhaps a lace up device. Do you have use of your hands?" she asked them.

"Yes." She heard the clanging of metal as the collar was removed. The young woman spoke in a Pashtu dialect. Donna remembered the word *whore,* and *animal,* shouted to her multiple times, and she heard those words again uttered by a frail young girl.

She spoke a few words to the girl, and got some single word answers she could barely understand. Donna put her palm on the girl's shoulder and told her that there were people near who could help them all. It was the truth, however, getting word to those people, her SEAL friends, would be a whole other problem.

Her wrist hurt and that's when she discovered they'd not taken her watch, probably not realizing it had internet and wifi capacity. Donna pushed the light button on the right of the small screen and noted she had a decent signal. She tapped in an SOS to her procurement officer's cell phone in Norfolk. She didn't have time to look for a return signal, but started to focus on the other women.

Donna removed the zip ties from the others while one of the American girls held the light for her. Her fingers were stiff and swollen from the drugs, but eventually the plastic ties fell away.

The young girl looked to be no more than a preteen, which sickened her. Her clothes were in rags. Her pretty face was marred with large purple and blue bruises that had been dished out over multiple incidents. The girl's right wrist also appeared to be broken, the swelling forming a lopsided red lump that was hot to the touch. If she had time, Donna would make a sling to immobilize it, but for now she had to address the issue of where they were and what their options were.

"Why are you here?" she asked the American girls.

"Well, we know these guys. We've been coming here for weeks."

"Where is here?"

"Their retreat, you know, this is where they bring in the people from the cities and give them some country experience."

Donna couldn't believe what she was hearing.

"So this is the camp on Pine Flat Road?"

"Yes."

They heard voices outside the door. Donna scooted over to the other wall, lay on her side and pretended to be sleeping.

The door opened and a slice of yellow light fell on the room. Donna heard the young Middle Eastern girl whimpering as two men yelled at her and threatened to hit her about the face. Donna could tell they wanted to know how she'd managed to get out of her restraints. The girl didn't have to act to be scared, and didn't give them an answer. They grabbed her by the elbows, lifted her up, and despite her protests, carried her out of the room.

Donna heard the distinctive beep of her watch, thankfully just after the door was closed behind the enemy. She disabled the sound and then looked at the words on her tiny screen.

*Message received. ST3 en route.*

She doubted no text message would ever make her so happy again as those few little words.

"Okay, we got help coming I think."

"That the special forces guys?"

Donna's hackles stood up. "Who said anything about special forces guys?"

"My dad. He built this complex, well most of it."

"Okay. So he knows you've been coming over here?"

"No. He'd be pissed. We just like to hang out, you know. They have some awesome weed. They've been really nice to us."

"You call this *nice?*"

"Up until today," the other American girl said.

"Yeah," the other one whispered, her voice fading.

"So that should tell you, what?" Donna answered. "How long have you been here?"

"Since yesterday afternoon," one of the girls said.

They were silent. Finally one of the girls spoke up. "We came over to warn them. We thought they were friends."

"Friends?"

"People don't understand them. Once they get to know them—"

"No. I don't want to hear any more of this folly," said Donna. She looked for a window and found none. The only way out of the room was the door they'd come in through.

The air was punctuated by the sounds of their young co-captive screaming. "Still think they are friends?" Donna willed her nerves to calm, but terror was looming at the edges of her mind. She knew what a full on panic attack felt like, and she was close. She needed to be able to think.

The room was some sort of storage closet. With her wristband light, she was able to see cleaning supplies and an old mop, a broken wooden chair. All of a sudden she remembered what the girl had said. "Warn them about what?"

"We wanted them to know about the Special Forces guys who came in to town asking questions. I think they put us here just to ask us some questions. They're not going to harm us, you don't think?"

"They've been holding you against your will."

"Maybe they were provoked. They almost seemed happy about what we told them."

"I'll bet. Part of that devious plan they have. You've put yourself right in the middle of extreme danger. These are bad men. This is a terrorist training camp, not a Boy Scout camp for R&R. I can't believe how stupid you were." Donna took the broom, laying it against the wall on the floor. Her fingers squeezed the wooden handle, as if there was some support there. She sat back and tried to breathe. There wasn't anything in this closet she could defend herself with, except for this broom. After a few seconds she sent another text.

*4 of us here. One young girl badly beaten.*

Donna's eyes began to water. Her face began to flush, her fingers swollen and stiff. Her mouth was parched. Her heartbeat nearly threw her against the wall. She wondered how long before she'd completely lose it. She had to get out. Being confined for any length of time would kill her, not to mention what the group's intentions were, and she had a pretty good guess at those, too.

Memories began to sift into her head. Those long thirty days came flooding back again and she knew it was useless to try to push them aside now. Donna began to shake. She closed her eyes and banged her head against the concrete walls of their prison, like she had done before. After awhile, she knew it would no longer hurt. The back of her head would hurt later, if she survived.

But today she couldn't knock those visions out of her head. The trauma she'd suffered, the acts of debasement she'd had to undergo were so horrible, she'd become grateful for the heavy doses of heroin they'd given her that day and the days after.

Donna watched the outline of the two girls who had been unwilling accomplices. More memories poured in, her shakes became more pronounced. All of a sudden, she was transported back there as if it was happening all over again, right here, right now. She inhaled and braced herself for what she knew was going to happen next.

She remembered on that worst day, when she'd been forced to have sex with multiple men in an endless stream of hell, she wished they'd just given her an overdose. She'd tried to fight the effects of the drug, to make them give her more. She'd sought death with everything inside her. The more she fought, the more they beat her. She fought the cattle prods, the foreign objects forced into her mouth, her vagina and her ass, defying them, seeking to draw their anger to perhaps finish her off.

That day, she crossed the threshold between life and death. It wouldn't matter what they did to her. She felt like she was dead already. There wasn't anything further they could take. She was sure they'd already taken away her womb, cut and disfigured her such that her life as a normal woman would forever be lost to her. But while they'd altered her physical appearance and capabilities of her body, they didn't change the woman she was on the inside.

At the end of that day, she'd come up with a slogan that sustained her, "Dead people feel no pain."

She'd lived through that. She could wait the time it might take for the SEALs to stage a rescue. She hoped the tipoff didn't mean the SEALs would be running right into an ambush.

Donna left one more message for her boss.

*They know you're coming.*

# CHAPTER 35

JACKIE THREW HIS headset down on the table. "This is definitely the Sheik."

Lucas ran to find Kyle, who was on the phone. He gave his LPO a thumb's up.

"Okay, Jackie says it's him," Kyle said into the phone.

Jackie came up behind speaking over Lucas' shoulder. "The girl they are holding is from Michigan," he said in his heavily accented dialect. "I cannot make out the name, but she's been given in exchange for favors. She herself was a ransom."

Kyle relayed the information into the phone.

Lucas couldn't believe what he was hearing.

"Chief Kyle, she's only thirteen years old," Jackie added.

"Fuck me," Lucas said. "Sorry."

"No I completely agree," said the terp.

Could this mean they were getting permission to actually perform a rescue mission in the states? As far as he understood, this was the first of its kind performed by a SEAL Team on U.S. soil.

"How's Donna holding up, do you know?" Kyle was looking right at him while talking on the phone with someone from SOC.

Lucas felt like the air had been knocked out of him. Could Donna be in danger?

He ran to the poker game. "Anyone seen Donna?"

"Last I saw, she was going for a run," said Rory. "But geez, that was hours ago."

"Kyle's talking to command, and asked how she was doing."

Cooper shot up to his feet and ran to where Kyle was just finishing his call. They shared a private conversation, then Cooper departed to his room. Lucas guessed it was to retrieve his medical kit. That meant something big was happening.

Lucas began letting the other members know something was up. The faces of their team went from relaxed to stoic attention. The games were left right where they'd been played. Cards left overturned at each man's seat. The activity level began to intensify.

"Jake, we're gonna go do something. Get your shit together," he said to his roommate who was outside reading a book.

"Gotcha."

Lucas changed his clothes and put on his full camo gear even though it would be hotter than hell. He heard Kyle shout orders and they all came running to the common area.

"Okay, I've just been given the go-ahead for a mission to rescue confirmed hostages, one of whom may need serious medical attention over at the training camp."

The audience of SEALs were silent, except for some muttered cursing.

Lucas interrupted Kyle. "Excuse me, sir, but is Donna among the hostages, or do we know?"

"That's a confirmed yes. And we don't believe she's injured at this point, but we really don't know. There appear to be four."

The room erupted in every man's personal choice of profanity, so Kyle had to draw them to order.

"Listen up! We have permission to engage only if fired upon first. This is a rescue, not a search and destroy mission, and I want every man to fully understand that." Then he added, "Get your shit together and let's be on the road in thirty."

"We're driving?"

"We're borrowing Donna's two vans. I'm hoping she won't be too pissed."

Everyone grinned.

As the orders sunk in, the group got vocal, as had been their routine on deployments. Conducting a mission was what Lucas lived for. All the cares and concerns for his personal life, including Marcy and his kids, were secondary to the mission. It pained him that there was no one to call, no one to leave a message for. Before he allowed it to rot a hole in his heart, he sucked it up, took on a deep breath and started packing gear.

Kyle pulled the barn builder's card out of his pocket. "Lucas, go call him and find out where his daughter is. See if she's missing, okay?"

"Roger that."

"Hold it there, son. Get your gear together first. Then you call him. We think we already have the answer."

"Got it. So the girls we saw yesterday are still there, then?"

"That's what I want you to find out. There are at least four hostages right now. We just don't know who anyone is, except Donna. You get on the horn when you're done getting you shit."

"I'm on it."

Lucas moved down the hall, walking just outside the barracks doors and dialed the number. He got a recording.

*This is Hunter Boles. I'm not available to*—the phone message was interrupted by Boles' gruff voice.

"Mr. Boles, this is Special Operator Lucas Shipley. We have a situation here and wondered if you could give us some information."

"I'll do what I can." Boles sounded pissed he'd been interrupted from something and was helping out begrudgingly. "I'm a little short staffed here today, so you'll have to forgive me. Let's keep this short."

Lucas could hear another phone ringing in the background.

"That's partly what I'm calling about, sir. Do you know the whereabouts of your daughter, sir?"

The silence on the other end of the line screamed volumes.

"I have no fuckin' idea where she is. She's not at work, that's for sure. You know anything I should know?"

"When was the last time you saw her?"

"Yesterday afternoon. Just after lunch. But she's not here today. She and her girlfriend took off to run some errands yesterday, and I just figured she stayed with her friend Jenna last night. She does that all the time."

"Have you tried to call her?"

"Well, of course I have. Her phone doesn't pick up. Is she in some kind of trouble, Lucas—was it Lucas?"

"Yes, sir. We think we may have located her."

"Where?"

"Not at liberty to tell yet, but as far as we know, she's not injured and she went of her own will."

"What the hell's that supposed to mean? You mean like she wasn't kidnapped or something? That what you're sayin'?"

"In essence, yes. We'll let you know as soon as we have anything further."

"So if I was going to go look for my daughter, give me a guess where I should start."

"Does she often stay out of communication this long, sir?"

"No."

Lucas knew he couldn't reveal anything to the girl's father. "Her phone's probably dead. When we can, we'll have her contact you. Keep the phone by your side, okay?"

"Will do."

Lucas was going to hang up when he heard Boles ask him another question he didn't want to answer.

"Should I be wearing a gun?"

Lucas decided to give the man something to do. "I'd say stay armed until we find her. Now, if you'll excuse me—"

"Wait, wait, where is my daughter? You gotta tell me!"

"I promise to let you know just as soon as we confirm a few things."

When Lucas returned to Kyle, he shook his head.

"She didn't come home. He hasn't seen her since yesterday after lunch."

"That's what I was afraid of. Hey, thanks, Lucas. You packed?"

"Yup."

"Okay, see you out front in a couple."

"Chief? Can I ask a question?"

"Shoot."

"So are other places, like San Diego—are they experiencing this type of behavior too? I mean, how safe is it near one of these camps?"

"Right now I think your girl, the girl you broke up with, is safe, Shipley. We don't have any intel this is going on in any coordinated effort. We just know they're up to something. But as far as I know, no one else has experienced a hostage situation."

"Except there is that girl Jackie says was from Michigan."

"And that's a different story. Unfortunately, that was cultural blackmail. Any way you slice it, we gotta rescue those ladies quickly. We can't wait for a terrorism task force to get assembled."

"Thanks."

But Lucas decided he would have to swallow his pride, and as soon as they were back from whatever mission this was, he was going to find Marcy, apologize for being a complete dickwad.

# CHAPTER 36

IT WASN'T THE nakedness that bothered Marcy, it was the fact that she'd been injected with so much heroin she could hardly think.

The "boys" in the compound were getting bolder, showing their disgust of her, which of course she did in return. She felt like a piece of meat in their eyes. She was a plaything for amusement, similar to what a person would do if they were going to torture an animal. But she knew the longer she held out, the better chance she had of survival. She had no illusions the wait would be in any way pleasant.

Thinking about these men, she understood a little more where Lucas went on deployments, mentally. There was evil in the world. She'd seen her share of wicked people, but pure evil—until now—she'd never been exposed to it. If the world knew what she knew, what Lucas and his brothers knew, they'd spend less time being politically correct trying to run a gentlemen's war and more time seeking results. She knew that she was the least of those being tortured, held captive just for believing what they believed, for being an American, for having a lifestyle worthy of the envy of the whole rest of the world.

Lucas was part of that line of defense of the Homeland. And he was paying the price for it. He did and always would come to the aid of his brothers in arms, even though it would look like he was abandoning his wife and children. He had to have that singleness of focus. She understood that now more than anything.

How ironic, she thought, that now, after they'd broken up at her call, not his, that she should figure that out. She was grateful for what he had to do. She understood now what he needed in life: a woman to help him heal, bring him back, not make him jump through a bunch of hoops of her own selfish choosing. She also understood how Connie felt, but she was sure the woman had her own set of issues that warped her worldview and made it impossible for her to be the support he needed. Being totally honest with herself, Marcy wasn't sure she had it in her either. But she knew she'd feel like a complete heel if she didn't at least try. She owed the man an apology.

She closed her eyes and pretended to be asleep when she heard footsteps at the door.

The familiar voice of her oldest captor spoke in broken English. "You are awake I think. Time to prepare you for your new life as the vessel of our pleasure."

"I'm not the vessel of your pleasure, or anyone's pleasure. I'm a woman whose freedom has been taken from her, but who still has her dignity left. Nothing will ever make me a vessel."

He smiled and patted her arm. "We'll see about that." He pulled back the blanket and peered down at her naked body. "I can help you with a shower, if you like. Would you prefer to wash up before we get started?"

Marcy calculated what she'd have to give up for the chance to have her wounds cleaned and decided the most important part of her current survival plan was her health. She attempted to sit up and found she had been bound about the waist, to the rolling hospital cart. Her arms felt heavy and though unrestrained, were useless to her. She suspected her legs would be the same as she couldn't feel her toes.

"Yes, the effects are wearing off, so I had to restrain you. That means I will have to help you to the shower."

She wished she had more choices, but needed to see what was outside the room, and she needed to get as clean as possible.

"Yes."

"Yes, what?" he asked.

"Yes, I'd like a shower."

"Very well. The boys will be pleased when they get back, that you have prepared yourself for them." He pulled back the brown blanket that stunk of him, unbuckled the large leather strap around her waist, and slipped an arm beneath her, lifting her to sitting position. She tried to lean away from him, but there was nothing to hold her up. He adjusted her balance so she didn't do a backward roll off the gurney, bringing her forward and against his chest and abdomen.

His hand softly thread through her hair while she drooled a bloody mixture down his shirt, unable to stop him. His wild scent as pungent, without cologne, smelling more of rancid oils mixed with days of sweat. Her stomach churned and she heaved, but without anything in her aching stomach, she produced nothing.

"Yes, a little nourishment, too. Would you like that?"

She didn't trust his feigned sweetness. She tried to imagine what he'd look like eviscerated, or hanging from a tree, or torn limb from limb. The violent thoughts came easily, her fear fueling her imagination. Or perhaps it was the effects of the drug he'd given her.

"Water. I need some water," she managed to mumble.

"You can drink in the shower."

He was a small man, and had difficulty getting her out to the living quarters off the storeroom, down the hallway to the bathroom. Her toes dragged on the concrete surface and she knew they were bloody with patches of skin scraped off. Again she tried to raise her elbows, and was more successful than before, but at last her strength gave way and she allowed them to flop down over his arms wrapped around her waist. As he moved her into the shower, her head bobbed back, and although she tried, she was unable to hold it upright.

He sat her on the tiled handicap bench seat, leaning her back against the cool tile wall of the shower. She looked at her bloody feet as he disrobed, slipped off his sandals and then stepped close to her.

"I have watched you shave yourself."

She tried not to react. The water began to flow ice cold, and she shuddered. "Sorry we have no hot water here, but I think you'll enjoy this anyway."

He hoisted her up, into the spray and she stiffened, found the cold sent blood pumping to her legs and for a minute, she had enough traction to fight him off. But it was short-lived. Her knees collapsed and he was once again propping her up, facing into the spray. She opened her mouth and drank the cool water. It smelled of sulfur and rust. The drain and shower floor was light orange.

Marcy felt tingling in her extremities and allowed her heart a moment's triumph. It did feel good to get the sweat and remaining vomit from last night off her. It felt invigorating to have a drink of water. When he positioned her back onto the wooden bench seat in the corner she looked at his face for the first time that morning.

Though the young man smiled, his eyes were hard and did not smile. The covetous stares seemed to inflame something inside him that did not appear human. She could see how mad he truly was. He was living in a bonfire of hell, and it was of his own choosing.

She slumped forward involuntarily, and he pushed her back again as her head lolled forward.

Her eyes were focused on the tiled floor, fixated on something that was blurry at first. As her eyes came into focus, she saw a bottle with a large plastic pump spout in the corner. He bent and squeezed some of the clear gel into his palm, rubbed his hands together making a lather and began to rub his palms over her now-slippery flesh at the shoulders and then on to her breasts. She couldn't react as he squeezed her flesh, as he pinched her nipples. Her eyes continued to focus on the shower gel in the corner.

Slowly he lathered her arms, her belly, her thighs and legs, kneeling like a servant in front of her. Though she didn't show it, her spine became rigid. She could push her feet against the floor of the shower, felt the cool water and for the first time, she was able to squeeze her fingers into a fist.

Staring at the bottle still, she pushed herself forward over his shoulder, draping her body over him, and then allowed herself to topple, sliding down to the floor. He was frantically trying to right her, but with her slippery skin not giving traction, was unable to lift her up to set her back down on the bench. Her right hand reached for the shower gel and she watched as she tried to hold it one-handed, which would have been impossible even without the drugs, and the bottle tipped, scooting out of reach. She released the support from her legs and she collapsed to the floor under the stream, her back curved against the wall, her feet pushing against the wall perpendicular to it.

Her captor began to say things she didn't understand. But he was unhappy and getting more agitated by the minute.

Bending over her, he managed to get his arms around her lower back and tried to pull her up, but Marcy resisted, feigning lack of control. She rotated to her upper torso, to her back, looking up to him. His feet were slipping on the slick shower surface. He was focused on his arms, and when he squeezed his eyes shut to pull her limp body up, Marcy put both palms around the shower gel bottle and with all her might, forced the spout into his neck just below his chin. Even after the spout entered his skin, she pushed, feeling the delicious crunch of cartilage that was his windpipe.

Her captor screamed. The spray from his blood covered the walls and poured over her, coating her with the deep red of his precious fluids, momentarily blinding her. She pushed with her legs and managed to head butt the man out of the shower, where he fell onto the bathroom floor, still struggling to get the spout from his neck. His legs frantically bicycle-kicked as he tried to find something else to push against. He was trying to get air. His gurgling screams got less intense. His almond-shaped eyes stared back at her in panic, and she realized the same time he did that she had just successfully inflicted a mortal wound.

His struggle was over. A light bloody spittle leaked from the right side of his mouth. With brown eyes fixated on her, she saw the moment when life left his body. She continued to lay on her belly, gasping for air, the water sluicing over her backside and upper thighs, sending her ribbons of calm and bursts of hope. She didn't know how she was going to function against the men who would be coming back, but she knew she couldn't wait around to find out. Somehow, she had to get out of the cabin and to some place safe. Some place that had tools and sharp objects she could use to defend herself.

Carefully she sat up. Her legs were coming back to near full strength, the activity in the shower and adrenalin pumping through her veins apparently aiding this process. Marcy grasped the wooden slats on the bench and because it was bolted to the side, supported herself as she stood for the first time. She placed her palms on the tile, pushing until she was balanced and was standing on her own without aid.

Each movement was slow motion for her. She allowed the water to wash off all the blood, rinsed her mouth, taking more drinks of the precious liquid, and emerged, trying to avoid the growing pool of blood forming from the gash in her captor's neck.

Using the doorway as a brace, she stepped out and into the hallway she knew led to the living quarters.

Her own clothes were left on the floor in the storage closet where they'd been discarded next to her purse. Though they were dirty, she welcomed something familiar, something that smelled like freedom, grateful for shoes she would need to run through the forest to find help. Pawing through her purse, she found her cell phone and anxiously checked for service.

Her stomach leapt as she realized the battery was dead. She placed the phone back in her purse, slung it over her shoulder, picking up a couple of bananas and a half-full bottle of water and exited the dwelling.

Outside, she heard Middle Eastern music pumped loud, echoing throughout the long building on her right. She was grateful for this. Whomever was inside, then, could not have heard the screams of her captor. She bent her knees, crouching, and slipped into the edge of the forest. Once protected by the cover of greenery, she began to run. She knew right where she was going to go.

# CHAPTER 37

L UCAS HELPED COOP bring the drone cases. Kyle had Fredo continue to monitor with SOC, so he could lead the team. They all had their specialties. Armando was their best shooter. Coop was their medic with the most deployments with SEAL Team 3, but if he was working the drone, T.J. would take over in that department, with nearly the same experience.

Lucas was also trained at the Army course at Ft. Bragg, certified by the SEAL instructors there. He was also their second sniper. Fredo was their communications and explosives expert and had lovingly said to Lucas one time when they were relaxing, "If they don't want to talk, I send a little fire their way. And guess what? They talk!"

As a unit, everyone was trained for one specialty, but cross trained to be able to work in more than three others, if need be. Lucas breathed slowly and deep to calm his nerves. He was put up on the ridge out of sight, but nearly fifty yards from Armando. Fredo was next to Armando working the comm. Coop was over on Lucas' side, getting his drone out, clicking the wings into place. With a flick of the switch they heard the soft whir of the drone's belly. The small tablet screen lit up as the drone was readied for it's mission.

Coop searched his spot, searched the sky and then leaned over to Lucas. "Eyes for their birds, Lucas. I got interference, I need to know."

"Roger that, Coop," said Lucas.

Cooper stood, leaned back, clutching the drone in his right hand, then propelled it forward and let it go. At first the white bird swooped down, then was corrected to stay high until Coop got her tracked. With a thumbs up to Fredo, Kyle was told, "Eyes in the air, Kyle. Good to go."

Jake and Tyler had disabled the sentries when they first took up their positions. The sentries were bound, gagged and tied and wouldn't wake up for several hours. They now joined the plateau where Lucas and Coop were perched.

With his high-powered scope, Lucas followed the two teams below, who separated, coming from different directions. Two SEALs were left near the entrance to disable the guard shack after their breech was discovered. Everyone else was going to go through the holes they were cutting in the fencing material. One breech was behind the long warehouse, the other was in the area of the camp's vehicle storage, well masked behind a fleet of white vans.

Their Invisios clicked to life. "On three, two, one, go!" Kyle's voice commanded.

The front gate exploded, the doors bursting wide open. Small explosive devices and smoke bombs were tossed into the long warehouse, starting a fire as chemicals began igniting, ending in plumes of flame nearly fifty feet high. Several earth-shaking explosions took out the side of the metal building, sending burning debris and pieces of twisted metal all over the area. The thick black smoke nearly made it impossible to see.

The team near where the hostages were was taking on fire. Armando picked off three combatants within seconds, sending others, who had ventured out into retreat. Lucas followed as several of them hid behind a storage tank of some kind. Lucas' one well-placed round caused the tank to explode in a hail of fire. Tires on several of the vehicles began to burn.

He studied the area where they knew the girls had gone yesterday and saw the front door to the structure open slowly. One gunman had the girl with a forearm across her throat, a pistol aimed at her temple. The sheik, whose robes were bloodied, walked behind one of the local girls. Lucas recognized her as the daughter of the contractor.

Armando was shifting position, adjusting his range, checking the wind and then, as the young girl stumbled in front of the gunman, took his shot. The blonde girl and the Sheik behind her were covered in the spray from the man's exploded head. The Sheik was armed with a small automatic and as he pointed it in the direction of the screaming young girl, Lucas took the shot Armando wouldn't be able to make and the tall man dropped to his knees first before one of the SEALs did the double tap to his head.

Having lost the two leaders, the rest of the group dropped their weapons.

Fredo was giving out information. The SEALs pushed the captives to the ground on their faces.

Lucas had only seen two hostages, but both appeared to be out of danger, for now. He spoke to Kyle in his headset. "Where are the other two?"

"We got 'em. Donna's okay."

Lucas breathed a sigh of relief. Something about Donna told him it was important she didn't have to stay overnight in the camp.

THEY UNLOADED THE girls over at the dorms where the soccer team was staying. Coop worked on the girl from Michigan while Donna sat by her side, holding her hand, speaking to her in broken Pashtu. Donna herself had a pretty good-sized bump on her forehead, but was completely focused on the girl.

She nodded up to Lucas and smiled her thanks.

The blonde girls were brought food and drinks by the soccer girls, allowed to shower and were given changes of clean clothes. Jenna called her dad, who was on his way over. Sheriff and fire crews were on their way to relieve the SEALs who had stayed behind with the prisoners.

"I think she's gonna be good to go here," Coop said. "See if you can get me an ambulance, Lucas."

"Sure thing. What about Donna?"

"I'm staying with her. I'm fine. But let's get her to the hospital," Donna answered.

Lucas ran the hundred yards to their buildings and sent an EMT crew over to the ladies dorm.

DECOMPRESSION WAS A bitch, Lucas thought. Easier to stay pumped up, but when you went through a firefight, and usually they were short and sweet, like this one, it took awhile for the adrenalin to subside. Everyone retreated to their own brand of recovery while their bodies adjusted. The mission was a success, but wasn't really cause to celebrate. This was, after all, an operation on U.S. soil. They had gotten all the way over here, had set up a camp—hell, had set up multiple camps—and nearly pulled off a tragic loss of American life. It was all handled small, which was their way of saying it caused as little disruption as possible.

When his cell chirped, Lucas jumped, having forgotten he even owned one. It was Nick. That's when he realized there were two other calls from Nick as well.

"Hey, what's up, Nick?"

"Man, you're not going to want to hear this, but we just got a call from Marcy. Devon and I were sick with worry when she didn't come home last night."

"What do you mean? Marcy's in San Diego."

"No, she's not. She's up in Sonoma County. She left yesterday to go look for a place to stay—"

*Fuck me. I've messed up again.*

"—escaped, she thinks she killed one of them. We've called the cops."

"Where, Nick?"

"Cloverdale, man. She's at your cabin."

"What the fuck?"

"There's one of those groups up there. She escaped, but she's all alone in the cabin waiting for the cops. Just wanted you to know."

Lucas searched his memory

Immediately Lucas' heart began to race. He had to find Kyle. Somehow he was going to have to get to her, even though he was clear across the country. He knew he was probably too late, but nothing in the world would be able to keep him away. He just hoped the Navy would understand.

# CHAPTER 38

MARCY WATCHED AS the bars went back down to zero on her phone. She knew Nick would send the police. She knew she'd feel more relaxed when her cell had enough power to be in permanent communication.

She looked through the windows, searching for evidence the camp members were coming after her, and wondered if they even knew about this place. She'd broken the bedroom window, the same one that had been used for the thieves—and then it hit her. They *did* know about the house, because they were here!

The remaining captors were all young, and she doubted they would have done the damage to the place without their leader, so perhaps she was safe. Maybe they had outside help. Maybe they'd be blinded by revenge. Every bird, every sound coming from the forest put her at edge.

Lucas told her earlier that there were no guns stored in the cabin. So that meant she was going to have to improvise. Other than knives in the kitchen, she couldn't find anything else that would work as a weapon. She did have a broom handle that looked solid. She picked up pieces of glass stuffing two of them into her pockets where she could safely hide them until needed.

Nick told her he'd be right there, but Cloverdale was nearly an hour from their home in Bennett Valley. She just had to get through the next hour, or however long it took for the police to arrive. She hoped they'd not get lost.

Her eyes wandered over the cabin where she'd spent a beautiful two days. She could smell him. When she closed her eyes, she saw what he looked like when he talked to her, the angle of his head, the way he smiled, what the touch of his kiss on her lips felt like. So many little things came racing through the fog of fear.

She prayed she'd have the chance to tell him all this.

It startled her when her cell phone rang.

*Lucas!*

"Is that really you?" Her heart was pounding, and surely he would be able to hear her ragged breathing.

"Absolutely, baby. Are you hurt?"

"I'm okay."

"But did they hurt you?"

"No. Big goose egg on my forehead."

"God, Marcy, I've been a total and complete fool."

"Where are you, Lucas? I'm all alone here and—"

"Nick called me. We just finished up an operation and I'm coming to California right now as we speak. Waiting for the transport. Won't get there for a few hours. Nick says the police are on their way."

"Good."

"You have battery on the cell phone?"

"It was dead, charging it now."

"Okay, nothing to do but hang tight. Let's hope they decide to bale instead of coming to the house."

"What do I do if—" Marcy saw three of the young boys come out into the clearing at the kitchen side of the house. "They're here!"

She heard Lucas swear on the other end. "Get a knife. Hide in the bedroom closet. There's a hatch there in the floor of the closet. See if you can get yourself in there before they come. Leave the phone on, but try to hide it."

"Right. Bye." She placed the device on top of the refrigerator where only part of the cord showed at the attachment to the plug in the splashboard.

Marcy wanted to say more, much more, but she knew they'd find the broken window and she didn't have much time to get herself hidden.

The closet floor was covered with empty bags and a suitcase. She brushed them aside and found the ring of the hatch, pulled it toward her and saw the dirt beneath the cabin floorboards. Carefully, she pulled the closet door closed, and tried to distribute the bags so they would fall over the hatch opening, perhaps giving her more time. She was small enough to slip down through the square hole and then touched the ground, stopping to listen.

Chatter from the young men trickled down to her from on top as she heard them climb through the window and begin searching the house.

She wondered why Lucas had asked her to leave her phone on, but she guessed he wanted to listen to whatever was going on, since he couldn't be there.

Fingering the glass chard in her left hand and the serrated knife in her right, she sat on the cool dirt and waited without making a sound. Her stomach growled so much for a second she wondered if they'd be able to hear it. She wished she had the water she'd left on the counter, or the bananas she'd brought from her escape. No doubt the boys would find them and realize she was near.

Orders were being given between the men. They removed themselves from the place the way they'd entered, and soon all was quiet.

Except for the crackling she could hear. Then she could smell it.

They'd set fire to the house.

# CHAPTER 39

LUCAS HEARD THE unmistakable sounds of fire raging through the cabin. Already at thirty thousand feet, there wasn't a thing he could do, except text to Nick and Devon and let them know. He'd lost connection to Marcy' cell. He hoped she'd be able to get out before the smoke got to her, as this was more of a threat than the fire itself.

*Lost contact with Marcy. House on fire.*

*Holy shit. I'll call the PD. They should be there by now. You in the air?*

*Yes. Taking direct to SF. Renting a car.*

*Hold it, let us pick you up.*

*If you can, sure would appreciate it.*

*Okay BRB.*

Lucas was crammed into the oversold airplane, but because he was active military went to the head of the standby list. He texted Kyle to let him know he was on board. Kyle let him know the soccer team was leaving and Donna still wouldn't leave Alfari's side.

*Good. I think she needs it,* Lucas texted him back.

*Thinking the same.*

He decided not to add any further worry onto his LPO's shoulders, so didn't tell him about the fire.

He relaxed the seat back and pulled his baseball cap down over his eyes, and attempted some sleep. No telling what he would be doing later. He'd be no good to anyone if he was exhausted.

An hour into his rest the phone pinged with a message from Nick.

*Fire out. No sign of Marcy or the others. Will update if any news.*

Lucas managed to sleep the whole rest of the flight. The stewardess tapped him on the shoulder and asked him to reset the seat to its upright position. He barely had enough time before the wheels hit the pavement, in a landing far from smooth, the big plane swerving and rocking as if driven by a fighter pilot landing on a carrier. He checked his phone as they taxied to the gate and there were no further texts. His stomach turned over. When he mentally counted the hours since he'd last eaten, he discovered it had been nearly twelve.

He followed the line off the plane, his legs and neck stiff from sitting in one position for so long, but all the same, he was grateful for the shut-eye. Now he needed to find Marcy. He was hoping Nick had something he could go on.

Nick was waiting by baggage claim, but since all Lucas had was his carry-on, they made it out to the curb just in time for Devon to slip by and pick them up. The two men sat in the back seat of Nick and Devon's Land Cruiser.

"Not going to lie to you, Lucas. The cops in Cloverdale and the Sheriff's Department have an ongoing battle over the hearts and minds of the town, with the public pretty much split. So anything that is slightly controversial, you can bet there's a fair amount of finger pointing."

"Okay. I'm sort of used to that, on a much grander scale," Lucas answered back. "Shit, we never know who to trust, so we don't trust anyone."

"That would probably work well in this case, too."

Devon made a quick swerve to avoid a small car with blackened windows from hitting them. They had merged onto the freeway and took the overpass headed to 280 North.

"You okay, honey?" Nick asked as he leaned forward and put his hand on her shoulder.

"I'm fine. That asshole just doesn't know how to drive is all."

Lucas knew she was hauling ass to get them up to Sonoma County as soon as possible, while they had some chance to do some searching in the woods. But he wanted to get there without an incident, and he could tell Devon wasn't used to driving fast.

"So you were saying there's a pissing match going on. Is anybody focused on finding Marcy?"

"Oh yes, nothing like a murder to get the community all worked up. You know Cloverdale is a small town. That's part of the problem. Everyone knows everyone else's business."

"Right now, I'm thinking that's a good thing," said Lucas.

"See, I made the mistake of calling the Cloverdale P.D. But your cabin is in the County, Sheriff's jurisdiction."

"So who did you tell about the trap door?"

"I told the Cloverdale P.D."

"Okay. So who's taking lead here on the search?"

"That's what gets kind of interesting. We got some worried about stumbling onto a pot farm and getting shot."

"Shit. We got terrorists with a training camp and they're worried about pot?"

"Nope. They're not worried about the pot. They're worried about the gangs who guard the pot."

Lucas checked the passing lights as they swung their way onto the five-lane 280 Freeway. There was practically no traffic. He tried to think about where she would go. Could she have gotten herself safely out of the house and was hiding in the forest? Or, did they capture her as she was forced out, take her some place else? Marcy had told him about the neighbor and the young boys. Lucas didn't think they even knew how to drive.

"Someone's helping them. We just have to find out who that is," said Lucas. "The one in Tennessee? They had a whole house filled with paper money. Floor to ceiling. They've been making so much money selling drugs, they have plenty to buy political favors. They did it in Nashville. Those guys run the prison there. They could do far worse in a little town of less than ten thousand people, no problem."

During the two-hour drive, Lucas and Nick discussed all the scenarios they could think of. If Marcy was on her own, it would only be a matter of time before she'd find a way to contact one of them. Eventually, she would. If she could stay hidden.

But if she was being held by yet another group, or worse, being transported to one of the larger training camps up in Oregon, they were screwed. That would involve a plan taking up hundreds of man hours and probably the FBI, just like when they had a large scale drug bust. The jurisdictions fell all over themselves for the percentage rights to the drug spoilage, but they had to play nice with the Bureau.

Lucas wasn't prepared for the site of his little piece of Heaven, looking more like a burned out building in Bagdad or Mosul. Smoke still filtered up to the darkening sky. Perimeter lights had been set up, juiced to one large engine unit from downtown Cloverdale. Blue and red lights flashed, the vehicles fanning out like at a drive-in movie. Lucas walked like a zombie through all the noise of the radios, the generator and sound of the water pumps occasionally kicking in as a four man crew continued looking for hot spots.

The fire investigator introduced himself. He was one of the only men who wore a yellow jacket, but did not wear a hat.

"How did it start?" Lucas asked.

"They found something as an accelerant. I think you had lighter fluid or cleaning supplies under the sink, like most people? We think they poured it, ignited it and left."

"Can I?" Lucas asked, pointing the charred spines of the once-beautiful cabin.

"Sure, just walk the perimeter. There are still hot spots inside, so don't step there."

"No problem." Lucas and Nick began walking around the edge of the debris field.

"We cut the power of course. Your propane tank exploded," the inspector said as he followed behind them pointing out the highlights of the destruction, like he was giving them a tour of an art gallery. "Any idea why someone would want to torch this place?"

"No clue," Lucas answered him. "But it was broken into and vandalized not more than a week ago. Kind of a teenage thrill thing, we thought at the time. This goes along those same lines."

"What did they take?"

"As far as we can tell, nothing."

"I'm told you never met these people?" the inspector asked Lucas.

"That's right."

"The woman who is missing, Marcy Gelland, saw them," offered Nick. I did see the break in, helped with the cleanup, and Lucas is right, it did look more like some kids having fun at his family's expense."

"And what makes you think it was kids, like the kids from next door?"

"Because they shredded some girlie magazines, right, Nick?" Lucas turned to Nick, who confirmed it.

"They peed on them, too."

"So all they did was destroy? They didn't take anything?"

"Not a damned thing." Lucas made his way over to here the bedroom closet would have been, swiped the charred detritus to the side with his shoe. The hatch cover was burned all the way through. Partially burned pieces of furniture and flooring had dropped down into the five foot space. Lucas remembered his grandfather telling him it was the safest place to hide if anything dangerous happened to them. He remembered playing in it when he was a child. It earned him a fair share of scoldings.

Lucas jumped into the space and searched the walls with his penlight flashlight. Someone had written "Boathouse." He looked up to the inspector. "There a lake with a boathouse around here?"

"Over toward the camp there's a man-made lake and I think a small shed protecting a pile of stacked canoes," answered the inspector.

"Wonder how the hell she knew about that," said Lucas. "Where is this lake?"

The inspector gave him a hand up. "If she came over from the compound next door, she would have run right past it."

"Wonder how the hell she got out while the house was burning," muttered Nick.

"I have no idea. But I hope to God she did. Let's go."

AT THE FIRE scene, Marcy had managed to scramble out through the flames, the smoke giving her cover. She hid in the scrub behind the cabin, undetected. A green van picked up the boys, who had obviously been waiting for it. The van barreled off down the road before any of the emergency vehicles arrived. The driver's door was marked with some sort of official insignia she couldn't read.

She wondered if other men were still at the complex and would soon be looking for her. She needed to make it to the boathouse so, if need be, she could wait it out until she was safe. Until someone she trusted showed up.

Seeing the coast clear, she ran as fast as she could until she got to the old red structure, pried open the locked wooden door and let herself in. She stayed in there while emergency crews were working in the distance. She wasn't going to go out there in her sooty clothes and be arrested for being an arsonist. The only people she would reveal herself to were Lucas, Nick or Devon.

None of the fire crew or investigators even came close to looking at the boathouse, so she began to feel safe. She worked to stop from falling asleep in the warm space but was having difficulty. She was tired, dirty, and her lungs were filled with soot. She desperately needed a drink of water.

Marcy scrambled out the back of the structure, stooped down, lay against the dock landing on her belly, and splashed water on her face, taking long sips of water to quench her thirst. She quietly returned to the relative safety of the wooden structure.

Finally, the number of flashing lights diminished, and several vehicles left the scene. In spite of her efforts not to, she leaned against the doors of the little structure, and fell into a deep sleep.

Hours later, she was jarred awake when she heard a noise. Through the slim crack between the doors, she saw four figures jogging straight toward her. She braced herself, waiting until they stepped into the moonlight and out of the shadow of the forest, her hand firmly gripping the knife handle. If it came to it, she'd go out fighting. She was ready for the final showdown.

# CHAPTER 40

LUCAS CONSIDERED THE message might be a trap, but his heart couldn't afford to wait any longer. If something had happened to Marcy, if she was injured or being held, or worse, the sooner he could find her the better. Devon held back to the shadows, just in case, while the three men approached the door.

As he got to within twenty feet of the outside of the building the red doors burst open and Marcy came running out, jumping into his arms.

"God, you're safe, Marcy. Thank God," he whispered as he held her shaking body. He felt her break down, as sobbing overtook her.

"Shhhh, shhh. You're safe. We got you. Nothing's going to happen to you anymore." He was rocking her from side to side. Nick put his arms around both of them. Within seconds Devon was there as well.

"Are you okay? Are you hurt in any way?" Lucas asked as he set her down. He brushed the hair from her face, blackened from the fire. He noticed a patch of her hair had been singed, but other than that, she looked pretty damned good.

"I'm fine," she beamed back up to him, tears making white lines down her cheeks. "I was hoping you'd see my message." She glanced over at the inspector.

"This is—"Lucas turned to the investigator with an apology.

"Russ Butler, ma'am. I work for the Cloverdale fire district."

Marcy nodded and allowed Devon to grab her, but her eyes came back to Lucas.

"So glad you're okay. What an ordeal. You held up like a champ, Marcy," said Devon.

The long looks Marcy was giving him as she spoke with Devon and Nick speared his heart.

"Come here," he finally said as he opened his arms. She nearly collapsed into him. She was mumbling words he couldn't make out. "It's all over, Marcy. Nothing is going to happen to you. I'm here now."

IT TOOK NEARLY an hour to finish with the Sheriff's Department. Lucas was still combing through the rubble for anything left untouched by the fire and was coming up completely empty. The house was gone, completely gone, but it had done its job and protected her from harm, just like his grandfather had instructed those many years ago. Little did he know that some day those safety instructions would save the life of the woman he loved.

He had a new appreciation for how fragile life was. He also knew that he wouldn't be able to put anything in front of his feelings for Marcy, and for her safety again. They needed to have a talk. He hoped she felt the same.

On the trip back to Bennett Valley, she leaned into him as they sat in the darkness behind Devon and Nick up front. His arm was draped around her shoulder as she snuggled into him. It had never felt so good to have someone need his protection.

His fingers traced up and down her upper arm. Marcy brought her right palm to his face as she lifted herself to look him in the eyes. "Thank you, Lucas. Thank you for everything."

"No, sweetheart. You are the hero of the day." He bent down to brush his lips against hers. "Not sure what I would have done if anything had happened to you, baby."

"You were there. You told me what to do. You gave me the courage I needed, Lucas. I would not have been able to survive without your help. I—"

He covered her mouth with his and allowed her wild scent to completely overtake him. Her lips needed him. He was trying to be gentle at first, but her need slammed up against his chest and he was soon consumed in the flames of her desire again. Her breathing became deep, their tongues mingling. He heard her faint moan which caused him to hitch his own breath.

"Sweetheart, love you, sweetheart," he whispered between kisses.

She grabbed his hand and kissed the center of his palm, then looked up at him with her twinkling brown eyes and placed his hand against her breast, and squeezed.

He chuckled. "Honey, if you don't think I'm getting the message, you're not as smart as I thought."

He knew Nick and Devon were aware of their fooling around in the back seat when he saw Devon take Nick's hand and they shared a smile.

Marcy slipped his hand under her bra and he felt the pillows of her flesh, warm and fragrant, waiting for him to enjoy. His pants were getting tight. He squirmed in the seat as she ran her fingers over the bulge in his jeans and she squeezed his package.

"We need that shower in a hurry, sweetheart," he whispered.

"I need you, Lucas. Your ass is mine until I tell you it's okay to go back to work."

"Yes, ma'am. The Navy doesn't own my body. You do."

"Glad to hear it, sailor. I have plans for you."

"I can't wait."


THEY ARRIVED AT the winery. Nick handed Lucas his backpack and winked. "Guest house is all ready for you guys. I think Devon and I are going to sleep in tomorrow," he said as Devon wrapped her arms around her husband. "Depending on when we all surface, we'll have food should you be in need of some nourishment."

"Thanks, man," Lucas said. "Thanks for everything." He gave Nick a quick hug, hugged Devon, giving her a peck on the cheek, and took Marcy's hand, squeezed it, and led her around the back to the guest house.

He could see shadows inside the main house as lights were turned off, including the bright patio light that threatened their privacy. With the crickets chirping in the background, a light cool breeze running off the rustling grapevines all around them, he placed his hand to Marcy's neck, letting his fingers lace through her hair, tilted her head back and looked down on her glowing face. Her eyes smiled back at him. "Seeing your dirty face is one of the most beautiful things I've ever seen, Marcy."

She drew her arms up around his neck. "Lucas, I need you to undress me."

"Of course," he said, thrilled. "Wouldn't want to—whoa," he said as she quickly unbuckled his belt and shoved her hands into his pants.

"I bet I get you naked before you even get started," she whispered through half-lidded eyes.

"Not a chance." But he got snagged getting her pants off. The feel of the lace of her panties against her smooth rear end put him in a trance he wanted to savor.

He kicked off his shoes and his pants fell to his ankles. He stepped out of them, kneeling in front of her as she pulled his shirt off his back from his waist up over his head.

"See, you're slow," she teased, removing her own shirt and bra, her breasts in full view.

He reached up and squeezed, watching her arch her back with the pleasure of his touch. He dropped his hands to his thighs, his erection pointing to the stars above.

"I'm going to go real slow Marcy. I'm taking my time. I'm gonna make you beg me to stop."

"Another promise you won't be able to keep. There's no way I'll ever stop. You'll have to peel me off your body a week from now."

He stood, taking her hand and leading her into the little cottage.

The room was lightly scented with a fresh vanilla aroma. She followed him to the tiled shower. After turning on the warm water, he soaped her arms and neck as she pressed her backside against the wall, watching his face as he smoothed gel all over her body. His fingers kneaded down her spine, starting just under her hairline, and one by one, working his way down to the crack in her butt. With both hands, he pressed her forward against his groin, squeezing her cheeks, lifting her as she pushed against his hardness. She raised one thigh over his hip and rubbed the lips of her sex over his cock.

She gave him a long lingering smile. "My turn."

She placed her palms on his shoulders, moving him to sit on the tiled bench seat. His fingers found her opening, but he massaged all around it as she arched back, took some gel and rubbed her palms over his chest, his neck, his shoulders, and then lower stroking his cock and squeezing his balls. She stepped aside and let the water sluice off him, and then she placed her knees on each side of the bench and lifted her lithe body up over him. In one long fluid movement, her breasts leaving a hot trail down his chest, she angled her pelvis and came down on his shaft.

She began a slow rhythm up and down, raising and lowering her body on him, writhing like his private dancer. He buried his head in her chest, bit her nipples, helped her move up and down on him by palming her butt cheeks, and supporting her body's weight. She ground down against him, kissed his temple, hugged his face to her chest, massaging his temples with her probing fingers. Into his ear she whispered, "I want you to come in my mouth."

"Yes, baby," was all he could say.

She began to lift off him, and he grabbed her hips and ground her down on him again. "Please, Lucas. I want you in my mouth," she whispered again.

This time he allowed her to slide off him as she kneeled before him on the shower floor. The water was starting to get cold, so she arched her upper torso and turned the valve off. As the steamy water dripped around them, the drain gurgling, she placed her lips at the tip of his head, running her tongue over him, sucking him gently.

He moved his pelvis forward as she fully took him in her mouth. One hand found his balls and squeezed as she swallowed all of him deep. Back and forth, her movements were long, careful, and needy. He never wanted it to end. He felt himself get harder the more she worked on him. She registered her pleasure with little whimpers, coaxing him up and down. Several strokes later, he was bursting inside her mouth as she sucked against his pulsations.

He was near completion. Her fingers formed a ring at the base of his cock and one last time she squeezed the full length of him, then sucked his tip. Rolling back on her haunches her sultry smile teased him further.

"Let's rinse off and try something else," he said to her. His fingers had already found her opening before she could stand.

He turned her around and pressed himself, still hard, into the soft valley between her butt cheeks. She turned on the water as he continued to rub against her soft flesh, stimulating him further.

He pulled her to him, spreading her cheeks, finding her opening and helping himself inside her. Marcy moaned, pressing the wall with her palms as he entered her, thrusting up deep. His thumb pressed against her clit from the front, and she jumped, spreading her knees and pushing him deeper still. He stroked in and out of her tight opening, making her little organ stiff, feeling her give way, start to let herself go.

The cold water was delicious. He bit her shoulder, the side of her neck as she melted into him, giving him full access to all of her. He felt her juices begin to flow as he pressed her clit again, holding firm while he impaled her deeper still. She stopped breathing, held her breath and then exhaled as her body began the rolling orgasm he knew had been waiting for him right at the edge.

She covered his hands with one of her own, the other against the wall, giving her traction as she helped his fingers press against her while she came.

THE FLUFFY WHITE bath sheet wrapped around both of them, hot and sticking to her thighs as they lay together in bed. Marcy was going to try to keep her promise, but more importantly, she wanted to keep up with this brave warrior. She needed to show him she had all the stamina he had, and perhaps a little more, if possible.

When she found his cock, he angled his pelvis, pressing against her, a smile affixed to his lips. The morning sunlight made the sheets whiter, and the scruffy beard on his chin and cheeks gleam golden in the new morning light.

He opened his eyes as she massaged him to a full erection. "Will it be like this every morning, Marcy?"

She nodded her head. "I promise."

He touched her cheek with his fingertips. "You happy?"

"Never happier."

Lucas inhaled, rolled on top of her, spreading her thighs with his knees. "Every morning, then," he whispered and bit her ear lobe. He kissed her ear, sending an erotic zing down her spine.

"Every morning. Night too. I'm in for it, the whole way," she heard herself say.

She was looking for some hesitation on his part, some indication she'd gone round the bend faster than he had. Was he uncomfortable with the intensity between them that had started nearly from the moment they met?

He was bending down, watching her.

"What? Something wrong, Lucas?"

"Not at all." He pressed his cock against her opening, waiting for her to make the next move.

Marcy watched his eyes change as she grabbed his cheeks and pulled him deep inside her. It began to build an intense session that left them both wrung out and gasping for air.

## LUCAS

"I HAVE SOMETHING for you," he said when she woke up. He was sitting across the bedroom in an overstuffed chair, still deliciously naked.

"Well I thought you already brought something. And then something else, and then another one, and so on. So get over here and give it to me," she laughed back at him.

He jumped back into bed, his long warm body lying against hers. He held her hand up, kissed each finger, inserting them one by one into his mouth. When her fourth finger came out, it was wearing a ring. It was a beautiful dark ruby in an antique setting.

"Belonged to my mom. I want you to have it."

"It's beautiful, Lucas. Thank you." She kissed him, then examined the ring again.

"I asked you once, and you said yes. Marry me, Marcy. Say yes again."

"On one condition."

"Shoot."

"Ask me every day. Ask me to marry you over and over again. I promise, the answer will always be yes."

"Done deal."

"But Lucas, we still have the same problem."

"Problem? What problem?"

"You gotta get divorced first, my love."

So did the Bachelors grab your heart? Thanks for reading Lucas and Marcy's story. If you want the whole Bachelor Series, you can read the Big Band of Bachelors Bundle, which has all of the bachelors falling, one by one: Alex and Jake.

Next up is Tucker and Brandy's story. You'll love this couple. Brandy is a plus-sized girl with a healthy libido, but who is frustrated with a series of one-night stands, always the bridesmaid and never the bride. Tucker is a typical 5XL type guy, has been off the Teams for nearly ten years, still handsome and even at 40 can outrun and outperform most the younger guys. He's missed the Teams, and coming to a wedding on New Year's Eve, he gets to have a taste of the Brotherhood he's missed all these years.

But he also falls in love with Brandy, lovingly stuffed into a bustier, with the curves and size he loves, marching down the aisle, as Dorie's maid of honor. What starts as another one-night stand turns into a forever love for the most improbable of couples! See why Brandy and Tucker's story has captured my readers so....

# NEW YEARS
# SEAL DREAM

## Bone Frog Brotherhood
## Book 1

SHARON HAMILTON

# CHAPTER 1

"**N**O THANKS NEEDED, Tucker. I didn't ask you to be part of the wedding party because I didn't think you'd fit into a 5X tux on top with your XL waist. You're an action figure, Tuck. Besides, you drool."

Tucker growled as he turned his back on the groom, Brawley Hanks. The dressing room full of handsome penguins grunted and politely guffawed, since they were all dressed up and on good behavior.

"And there's no room for even a Barbie on his arm. Damn those church aisles," barked Riley Branson.

Another former Teammate, T.J. Talbot, grabbed Tucker's arm and drew him out of the Room of Doom, as the single SEALs called it. "Pay no attention to them. They're assholes. Also, who wants to walk down the aisle with a Barbie Doll?" He winked at Tucker.

He felt at ease immediately. Tucker's huge hands and fingers knotted themselves to oblivion, having no place to hide and looking like a bushel of antlers he was carrying. "Thanks, T.J. I hate these things," he said, pulling on his lapel. "But I've been out of commission so long, thought it would be nice to see some of the guys."

"And now you've seen that nothing has changed." T.J. was nearly as tall as Tucker, perhaps an inch shorter. He bumped foreheads. "But the girls will be younger because of Dorie, and that's probably a good thing," T.J. whispered.

"You having regrets, you old married fart?" Tucker murmured back.

Brawley's dad appeared in the church hallway before T.J. could answer and slapped both the former Teammates on the back simultaneously. "Glorious day, isn't it?"

Tucker knew old man Hanks was relieved his son had finally settled down and picked somebody. Brawley had more breakups than a pre-teen homeroom class.

"Yessir. Just took the right woman." T.J.'s face was shriveled up, like his last comment had soured his tongue. Tucker knew he was lying through his teeth. Privately, he thought, it took more alcohol than could fill a battleship to convince Brawley it was time to man-up.

"Dorie's a real nice gal," Tucker offered up. "You're gonna be a lucky father-in-law. She should fit in well with the rest of the family," he added, trying to keep a straight face. He knew it would be painful for T.J.

Both gentlemen looked back at him, T.J. not showing an ounce of expression. Mrs. Hanks was raised in the local Mennonite community. She was as plain as a saltine cracker, without any makeup or hair curling or adornments. Her two daughters were younger, even paler copies of her. Whereas Dorie looked like she could handle a Las Vegas pole and entertain a whole room of men. Those were going to be some interesting family dinners during the holidays, Tucker figured.

When he had the courage to look back into Mr. Hanks' eyes, he realized old man Hanks married her probably because little Brawley was on his way, and for no other reason. He felt the man's pain.

"You believe in miracles, son?" Hanks said, his eyes folded into thin slits.

"Yes, sir, I do. I surely do. That and redemption, too."

T.J. cleared his throat. "Well, congrats, sir. Must be a load off to have Brawley settled. I think those two will be happy together."

The far away look Mr. Hanks gave them back was difficult to read. Tucker had been feeling a little lonesome and sorry for himself until he encountered Hanks Sr. today. Now he was damned pleased he'd never hooked up with anyone.

*Sure, they're pretty, but they're dangerous. Unpredictable. Who needs them? Certainly not me!*

At last, Hanks pushed through the two younger men, heading for greener pastures, having exhausted any thought process he was following. He turned his head back to them and whispered, "Happiness' got nothing to do with it. All a state of mind, gentlemen." His fingers pointed to his temple, oddly positioned to look like a gun. "All a state of mind." He sauntered off, straightening his jacket and making room for his crotch as he walked, swinging his feet at the ankles to shake off wrinkles.

"Close your mouth, Tucker. You're gawking," T.J. reminded him.

"That's a complicated man right there," murmured Tucker. "I can see how he gutted out twenty years on the Teams. Thank God Brawley made it. Would hate to be a son of his and not make a Team."

"You know the family better, but I'm guessing being on the Teams was summer camp compared to growing up in the Hanks household."

Tucker knew T.J. was right. They'd grown up together in Oregon, and the two boys got acquainted by competing for spots in high school sports teams. They joined their BUD/S class together, but Tucker disengaged after ten years. Brawley re-upped for a short tour and was going to leave as well. Then he met Dorie, so he extended and used the bonus to buy a house. Dorie had a lot to do with that decision.

The rest of the wedding party began to spill out onto the walkway leading to the sanctuary. Blossoming orange trees gave off a gentle and pleasant aroma. Tucker punched Brawley hard in the bicep, nearly knocking him over before he gave the groom and his groomsmen a fat-fingered wave. He was going to find a seat toward the front, but not too close, give himself enough room to spread out in case he fell asleep during the wedding. His goal was to keep his big mouth shut and his eyes glazed over so he could just swim a little with his former Teammates without getting into trouble. That meant he'd keep his hands to himself and wouldn't ask anyone to dance. He'd also pretend not to look for cleavage or evidence of a proud bony mound or ample ass beneath layers of swirling chiffon and taffeta.

*Piece of cake,* he thought as he entered the sanctuary. Organ music played, accompanied by a violin and flute combination.

*Hospital music.*

The two Hanks sisters were dressed in identical maroon dresses with white lace collars, revealing their beanpole stature. Both girls had their long brown hair parted in the middle, tied in a bun at the back of their neck. No curls, ribbons, or sparkles to adorn them. Each had a deep pink lily wrist corsage on their right hands, folded identically next to each other.

The moms were ushered in next. Mrs. Hanks wore a darker shade of maroon, but her brownish grey hair was pulled back similar to her daughters'. Mr. Hanks looked around the room, catching eyes of friends and landing briefly on Tucker's face. He sat down hard, making the pew squeak.

Dorie's mom was lead in by Riley Branson. The lady was the same kind of bombshell for the older crowd, and Brawley had told Tucker stories of her younger years growing up in San Diego. Though she was close to sixty, her hair was as blonde as her daughter's gorgeous locks. She wore a tailored light pink suit with a flared waist jacket covered in glistening crystals that flashed all over the interior of the narthex and the aisle going down. The skirt below her tiny waist didn't leave much to the imagination. She wasn't as tall as her daughter, so the high heels were giving her some trouble on the cushy rug.

Dorie's mother sat next to her already seated boyfriend, an obvious sign that he might not be a permanent fixture in the family, but he gave her a peck on the cheek anyway.

The organ music crescendo rose, and a majestic non-wedding style march was on, signaling that the audience should rise for the bride and her father. Everyone came to their feet, Tucker one of the last to stand. He turned to the narthex and saw beautiful Dorie all decked out in bright white. Ahead of her were several bridesmaids, all Barbies, except for one, who was a big girl with about the largest chest Tucker had ever seen. He found himself praying for a clothing malfunction as she paraded down the aisle with Riley. Her tight bustier looked like it was going to explode any second, which might even knock Riley off his feet. He found himself chuckling under his breath at the image in his head until someone in the row ahead of him turned around with a frown.

But Tucker's daydream was shattered by the presence of Dorie, looking every bit the virginal angel. She was probably the prettiest bride he'd ever seen. Her veil was loaded with little crystals, like her mother's suit. By candlelight at the evening service, it created the effect of a thousand little faeries dancing down the aisle all around her. Mr. Carlson looked tanned and about as proud as a father could be, since his daughter was marrying a war hero.

Brawley was gaping and looked pale as the creamy skin on his bride's beautiful face. His best man whispered something to him, which caused a quick glance to his crotch, followed by an annoyed sigh as he realized his best man was messing with him. He presented his elbow to Dorie as her father kissed her good-bye. Dorie grabbed Brawley's hand instead.

Tucker prepped himself so that he wouldn't fall asleep, but found he needed very little help. The girls were ten point fives, even the heavy one. He told himself to stop it several times, but he was used to ranking women in front of him. Dorie would be number one, of course. Then there was that red-head, but the dark-haired heavy one kept catching his eye. He matched them all up to her, and, to his surprise, his dick preferred her.

The Hanks sisters began a duet that was about as bloodless as the middle-aged female lab tech at the VA who actually sported a five o'clock shadow. It was about as pleasant, too. The slightly off-key rendition of a country song he couldn't remember had people in the audience coughing to clear the pain in their ears. Tucker was going to burst out laughing if he wasn't careful. He opened a package of gum, made too much noise, and found people frowning at him.

*Who cares?* He chomped his gum silently and appeared not to notice.

With that out of the way, he tried to concentrate on the words of the reverend's message to the audience, and that's when he fell asleep. He startled from a very pleasant dream to find several in the crowd reminding him they still didn't approve. An older bony fist leaned over his shoulder to hand him a tissue because he had drooled on himself.

*Can I help it? Sermons put me to sleep.*

Then he noticed the dark-haired plus sized girl staring right at him with daggers. Okay, so he messed that one up. But he wasn't there to take home a date anyhow, so he shrugged, stopped looking at the girls, and started staring back at the people in the audience who had caught the snoring or grunting or drooling—maybe all three.

*I need some spiked punch.*

He knew that someone was going to do it. Mrs. Hanks had forbidden alcohol, but she was about to learn a lesson. It was no SEAL wedding if there wasn't a heavy dose of alcohol.

*Come on. Come on. Let's get the party going.*

The rings were exchanged. The kiss was pornographic, as a good SEAL should behave, and included a gentle squeeze of the bride's ass, which made her giggle when they both got tangled up in her veil. Tucker noticed the big girl didn't like that, either.

Mercifully, the wedding was over. Brawley and his young nymph floated down the aisle, followed by the bevy of lovelies, Tucker was suddenly jealous that T.J. had accompanied the brunette. The shit-eating grin he gave Tucker in exchange meant he knew full well what he was doing as his elbow leaned a little deeper into the lady's chest, which extended her left boob and created about eight inches of mouth-watering cleavage.

*I got assholes for friends.*

But since T.J. was happily married to the lovely Shannon, Tucker didn't have to worry about anything.

Except to keep from drooling, get drunk with dignity, and pretend this was a good idea.

Because it wasn't. He knew he'd made one of the biggest mistakes of his life.

# CHAPTER 2

B RANDY WAS GLAD the party was beginning. Her plan was to get considerably sauced, dousing and putting out the fires of a disastrous year. She'd been let go earlier in the year for speaking a little too plainly to a customer of the advertising firm. A competing agency hired her the next week—until she found out they were moving their operation to Silicon Valley from San Diego. Her father still owned and operated the local organic grocery store, and so Brandy came back to work for him until something else came on the horizon.

When Dorie asked her to be part of the wedding party, her decision to stay in Southern California was set in stone.

Thinking it would be helpful to meet her diet goals for the wedding she took up a part-time job as a weight loss counselor. The free meal plans and extra income were at first a double bonus. She had some early success, but then her diet stalled and crashed. The food started tasting like cardboard, and she was secretly supplementing with things from her dad's store. Her lack of progress and her MIA at weigh-ins caused another termination.

But that was last year. This was New Years Eve, and she was going to have a great year. She'd land that dream job after all, get down to a size eight or ten—one she'd never achieved before—and who knows what else could happen? Perhaps Prince Charming would notice her new svelte physique. She'd start lifting weights and perhaps learn to run so she could enter a 5k with Dorie.

She watched the bride and groom glide over the dance floor. The weather was spectacular and clear, surprisingly warm. By candlelight, they swayed and swooned, and there wasn't a woman in the crowd who didn't want to trade places with Dorie and her handsome new husband.

The hush that fell over the group made her begin to cry. The glittery twinkle lights and silky drapes at the sides of the tent blew in the gentle breeze coming right off the bay.

She approached the group of her fellow bridesmaids and noticed their chatter stopped the instant she was upon them. Several brittle smiles greeted her.

"Having a good time, Brandy?" asked one of them.

"Isn't it the most gorgeous wedding you've ever seen?" she answered, aware she was gushing like a schoolgirl.

"I'm looking at all the eye candy," one of the other girls remarked, nodding to the group of nearly twenty young men, all fit and handsome, dressed in black tuxes and suits.

"Your Randy is deployed, Sheila. You can look, but better not touch."

"I hear that the guys on SEAL Team 5 don't have much to do with these boys. They're all Team 3."

Brandy was disgusted with her attitude, but the rest of the crowd tittered, and closed ranks. Soon she was left alone as they wafted off to grab some punch. On the way, two girls were asked to join the dance floor, as other couples from the partygoers began to pour into the revelry. In a matter of minutes, the bride and groom were hidden by other dancers. When the tune turned lively, the dance floor got even more crowded.

Earlier, she'd watched one of the SEALs on Brawley's team add some rum to the punch, along with something else, so she was fairly sure it would be strong. But just in case, she had a flask of brandy, her namesake and always a good companion in case the evening turned lonely.

She checked her watch as she headed to the punch and saw it was forty-five to midnight, the beginning of the New Year. Soon all those bad dreams of this year would be wiped away forever.

As she reached for a glass, another hand crossed hers. In the collision, several drinks fell to the floor, and several more fell over on themselves on the pretty lace tablecloth, making a light pink stain. The hand she'd collided with could easily palm a basketball or clean off a windshield with one swipe. Enormous beefy fingers, dripping in the sweet mixture, shook, sending droplets of punch all over her face and upper chest. The surprising spritzer caught her off guard.

A deep voice made an apology to the plain woman behind the punchbowl who looked like she'd faint from fear. Then the voice came her way.

"So sorry. I didn't mean to make a mess."

It was the beast from the sanctuary, the one who reminded her of Shrek. And now he even sounded like Shrek. She stared up at massive shoulders and a puffed out chest so large he could have trouble getting through a doorway without going sideways. He wasn't young, like the other men, with a healthy dose of salt and pepper in his hair and a solid white full beard. It was a lot to take in, but she finally found his eyes, and that settled her nerves just a bit.

"Are you okay?" he whispered. His warm eyes twinkled and were kind.

"Y-Y-Yes." Then she felt the coolness of the punch covering her. "Napkin."

It was quickly delivered to her flailing hand.

"Another one. I need another one," she said since the small napkin began to fall apart as she dabbed her face.

He handed her a fistful nearly an inch thick.

"Oh! That's too many," she mumbled, but took the wad anyway.

"You got a lot on your-your-your chest there. I hope it doesn't stain." He pulled her aside to make way for one of the caterers to mop up the floor.

The slip made her angry. He gave her a fistful of napkins because of the *size* of her chest. She turned her back to him and continued to dab off the droplets dripping down between her breasts. Out of the corner of her eye she saw one of the other bridesmaids whisper to her neighbor.

She abruptly turned again so she could address the monster, but the area was vacant. She caught sight of his back and head as he ducked under the tent cover and walked out into the night.

The young catering staff member brought her a filled cup of punch. "Here you go. Don't be concerned about this. That guy looks like an accident waiting to happen. Not your fault."

"Thanks." It was all she could think of to say.

The punch was indeed strong, and Brandy discovered upon finishing it that, although she was relaxed, her breathing was still just as difficult. She tried not to think about the help she'd needed getting the big undergarment on before the bustier could go on. It took two of the bridesmaids to work alternating to get the large zipper to close. At one point, she thought her breasts would reach her chin, but she was able to position herself until she was somewhat comfortable. The bustier was easier, since it closed with a row of large hooks and eyes.

She wobbled her way to the women's restroom and reapplied lipstick, really laying it on heavy. She loved the bright red shade of her new purchase. Adding a little blush, removing two dried droplets of punch, and rinsing her dress with a little water, she felt put together and ready to take on the world. It was only twenty minutes to midnight. All this would go into the folder of old news in just a little while.

Brawley was standing at the edge of the dance floor, watching his friends taking turns dancing with his bride.

"She's lovely, Brawley. I'm surprised you share her," she said and smiled.

The handsome SEAL had always been nice to her. Her crush on him was hard to hide. He leaned over and whispered in her ear, "Well then, let's make her jealous. You game?"

When he leaned back to check her expression, she gave him the biggest smile she could muster.

"Game on, mister."

They danced a modified swing to a lively Motown classic. She knew Brawley had benefitted from the instructions he had taken with Dorie. Brandy had taken lessons with her father after her mother passed. The two of them moved around the floor like a choreographed routine, causing a clapping circle to be formed around them. Brawley's bow tie was undone, as were the top two buttons on his shirt. Brandy wished she could remove or disconnect something, too, but in the end, she stopped just long enough to take off her shoes and throw them into the corner. Brawley swung her around with his powerful arms. She felt lighter than air.

*This is a good way to usher in the new year.*

Finally the music ended and the crowd cheered them. Brawley gave her a big bear hug that nearly toppled them both. She regained her balance, and, breathing heavy, she accepted his polite kiss to her cheek— a cheek she would hate to wash off.

Dorie was smiling as she re-attached herself to her beau, using his handkerchief to wipe the sweat from his forehead. All Brandy could do was watch them.

The room seemed to rumble behind her, but it was only the sound of the beast's voice.

"Tell you what. I'll go kidnap Dorie, and then you can have him."

Even the hair at the back of her neck stood straight out. Her shoulders felt the tiny beads of moist breath against her flesh. It set up a vibration that traveled briefly down her spine. It was a curious reaction, especially for someone so beast-like.

Upon turning, she faced his warm brown eyes again. They were still twinkling little laugh lines evident at the sides. Somewhere the bevy of bridesmaids and their friends were laughing, and she didn't care.

"That would never work. Brawley would be too heartbroken. He'd probably throw himself off the Coronado Bridge." Her tongue nearly stuck to the roof of her mouth. "I need something to drink."

"I think we should try this punch thing again, don't you?" His voice was gentle, almost melodic, but very, very deep. She felt the words vibrate in her chest.

"Yes, let's try to do it better this time. I think they're out of napkins," she answered.

Was that a growl she heard? She wasn't sure. But it was a wicked growl that could fend off anything.

They walked together side by side.

"I'm Tucker," he said flatly.

"And I'm Brandy."

At the table, he chose the larger clear plastic cups, handing her one and taking the other for himself.

"To a new year. No accidents," he said.

She met his cup with a dull click. "No accidents. To a perfect year."

The cool drink was refreshing, and she finished the whole glass faster than he did. His face was full of surprise.

"All that dancing," she said between deep breaths, "I needed that. Probably should have had water—"

All of a sudden, she felt light-headed. The air constriction had finally caught up with the alcohol floating around her stomach and brain. As she began to see black spots in front of her eyes, she felt his arm underneath her back, holding her, keeping her from falling. Just before she blacked out, she heard the words,

"I've got you. No worries."

# CHAPTER 3

T UCKER CARRIED HER to a row of chairs setting just outside the tent. He hurried to get her out before they attracted much attention. Instinctively, he knew she'd be embarrassed if she caused another incident.

She was beginning to moan as he did a light jog towards the chairs. He laid her down, then removed his coat and placed it over her, pulling it up all the way to under her chin.

"Brandy, stay right here and stay warm. I'm going to get some water and a clean washcloth for your forehead. But stay here, okay?"

He saw her nod. Her face was pale, and she'd attempted to open her eyes, but closed them again with another moan. He suspected she'd be sick next.

He ran to the curtains where the catering equipment and staff were housed and got a clean dishcloth and a bottle of sparkling water. When he returned to Brandy, she had already rolled over on her side and was starting to vomit.

"It's okay. You eat anything today?"

She shook her head and then retched nothing but a pink liquid. All she had on her stomach was alcohol.

"You need to eat something. That will soak up some of the alcohol."

She ignored him and retched again. He held her hair back from her face before wiping her forehead, cheeks, and then finally cleaned her lips. He helped her roll back.

"Not too far back. Stay on your side. It might help."

She sighed and snuggled under his jacket. "I hope I didn't get your tux."

"Nope. All's safe. You were actually quite dainty about it. You should see it when I get sick. Not a pretty sight."

"I can only imagine," she mumbled. Then her hand searched and grabbed his as she opened her eyes. "Sorry. Sorry. I'm so sorry. I didn't mean that."

"Yes, you did." He held her hand, and then his thumb began to rub over her knuckles. He stopped himself. "You didn't eat anything before you drank. It happens to the best of us. I'm going to get you something."

"No. I'm on a diet."

"Hogwash," he said as he got up and headed for the food tables. Glancing back, he saw that her gaze followed him. He loosened his tie and unbuttoned his collar. Brawley was on him with concern written all over his face.

"Is she okay?"

"She's gonna be fine. Liquor on an empty stomach. She just needed some fresh air, and I'm getting her something to eat." He searched the small finger sandwiches and bypassed the frittata and vegetables.

"You let me know, promise?" Brawley answered. "We're cutting the cake at midnight. Just a couple of minutes now."

"I'm on medic duty, but I can only imagine what that kiss is gonna look like. You gonna mess up her face with it?"

"Nah. I wanna get laid tonight, Tucker. It's my wedding night."

"Smart move. Don't worry about Brandy."

"She's in good hands." Brawley winked and left to join the crowd gathered around the cake.

Tucker piled the dish with the sandwiches and returned to Brandy. She was attempting to sit up. He knelt in front of her. "I've got some bread here, which should be good for your stomach. Some kind of mystery meat in the middle, so go easy."

She had pulled his jacket around her shoulders. She smiled. Her beautiful chest and cleavage was hard not to stare at, so he focused on the plate offered to her. She popped the little sandwich into her mouth and closed her eyes.

"Hits the spot."

"Good." He took one. "They're not bad. You should have another."

Brandy did as she was instructed.

"Feeling any better?"

She nodded. Her hair was hanging down over her shoulders as she put her elbows and forearms on her thighs. The gap in her bustier was enormous.

"I wish I could take this damned thing off and go topless."

"A dangerous thought," he said, slightly embarrassed she'd caught him looking.

She smiled. "So tell me something, Tucker. Did someone put you up to this? Be nice to the fat girl?"

The thought had never occurred to him. He was surprised.

"No. No one put me up to anything. Why, you think there's something unattractive about you? Are you an axe murderer or serial killer or something I should be afraid of?"

She shrugged and gave a small laugh. "You know the expression. Age old tale. '*Always a bridesmaid, never a bride.*' That sort of thing."

"Whoa!" Tucker handed her the plate and stood up. "Who said anything about being a bride. If you're thinking—"

"Happy New Year," came the shout from the tent.

He looked down at her. She'd set the sandwiches to the side, took a deep breath, and said, "Shut up and kiss me, you idiot."

With the room erupting in horn and popper noises, Tucker came back to his knees, reached for her face, and melted his lips into hers. It wasn't the wedding cake kiss Brawley would have, and tasted like a ham sandwich, but it definitely got the sparks going deep inside him. Almost painfully, his libido lumbered into full action mode. He felt like a battleship heading out to sea on its final mission. His heart pounded, almost hurting from inattention and need. The subtle scent from her perfume and the way her hair felt on his cheek nearly made him dizzy.

He pulled back and looked into her eyes.

"You okay?" he asked.

"I'd be better if you kissed me again. I needed that."

Her fingers sifted through his hair. Their deep kiss left them both breathless. As his cheek set against hers, he whispered, "What was that?"

"You okay?" she asked, twisting the conversation and letting her eyes flirt. Her forefinger traced over his lips as she focused on them. He squeezed her shoulders but kept his hands in place. He desperately wanted to explore what was being so cruelly smashed underneath all that fabric.

He'd promised himself he wouldn't be looking tonight and would keep his hands to himself. But his promise was going down in flames. He just wasn't sure what he should do. He knew what he desired, but he didn't want to take advantage of her, since he was fairly sure she was still pretty drunk.

"I don't do this," he finally said.

"I don't, either."

"I mean—what I meant was, you're drunk, and I don't think it's right to—"

"If you've changed your mind, just say so. Don't blame it on honor or some other BS, Tucker. I'm a big girl. I can smell a turn down when it's coming. I'm used to it."

His heart was breaking for whatever her experiences had been in the past. It was clear there was some damage there. But it just didn't add up. He could not see any reason she should feel that way.

She'd started to stand, began to remove his jacket.

"Wait, Brandy. You got it all wrong."

"It's okay. Don't patronize me."

"Damnit. I'm not patronizing you. Would you get that goddamned chip off your fuckin' shoulder, Brandy? What I'm telling you is I'm attracted to you. And I don't want to take advantage. I'm not that kind of guy."

He stood with her, putting the jacket back around her shoulders.

"Cake?" A silver tray with slices of wedding cake was presented to them by one of the wait staff.

Brandy eyed the tray, and Tucker could tell she wanted a piece. He took two plates. She was weaving slightly, so he guided her to sit back down. Then he got on his knees again, setting one plate aside. He cut a piece without frosting and held it in front of her. "Probably not the best thing for you to eat, but it might not be that bad."

She watched him while she opened her mouth. He placed the cake on her tongue.

"Perfect. Delicious. More. With frosting," she said.

"Brandy, you sure?" He could see some of the earlier dreaminess return to her eyes.

"What if I put some frosting here," she said as she touched the top of her cleavage with her forefinger. "Or what if it got smeared lower. Would you lick it off?"

Tucker's knees were shaking as his groin refused to behave. He inhaled her scent and the way her eyes were half-lidded while she dipped her finger in the frosting and slowly slid it down between her breasts. She leaned back on the chair, spread her knees, and dared him with her eyes.

His mouth watered as his tongue tasted her flesh beneath the sweet fluffy frosting. He sucked, pulling the top of her right breast into his mouth just short of creating a mark. But he wanted to. He wanted to see her naked, her nipples dripping with frosting, her sex wet with her desire for him. He needed to lose himself in those breasts as he took her deep.

Her fingertips touched his temples. She kissed his forehead, holding his head to her chest. Then one hand slid down the outside of his shirt to his waistband.

"Can I take you home with me?" she breathed into his ear.

"Darlin', I'll go with you anywhere. You just name it."

"I should go get my shoes."

"I'll get them. But I don't think you'll need them."

"Why?"

"Because, sweetheart, I'm going to carry you."

"Really? Why?"

"Because it's just what's done on New Years. You stay right here, and I'll go get them. You think about having that perfect year. You think about what a perfect night would be like, and then let's go do it. Okay?"

He could feel her eyes on his back as he made his return to the party. One of the bridesmaids tried to drag him to the dance floor. She got his shirttails untucked from his waistband before he got away. In the corner were Brandy's heels. He dipped to pick them up and sauntered right through the center of the dance floor, carrying his trophy in his right hand.

He saw the looks. He saw the surprise. He saw Mr. Hanks nod and smile some secret appreciation. Dorie winked at him. Brawley gave him a thumbs up.

He was back. Tucker was back in the real world. The night had turned from the biggest mistake of his life to something else quite extraordinary.

It was going to be the best night of his life. And this was only the start of a new year.

# CHAPTER 4

B RANDY SAT BACK in Tucker's bright red truck that set so high she doubted she'd be able to mount it without help. But Tucker had placed her delicately on the seat, strapping her in securely, and then pressing a warm-up kiss to her willing lips. In his own way, he was gentle, but it took effort to not break or hurt things, she noted. The engine revved, and then the truck lurched, headed to Brandy's cottage. She decided not to tell him her father lived in the house in front.

The inside of the cab smelled like him. He fiddled and adjusted the heater, asking if she was comfortable. It was only a ten-minute ride, but in that short time, she noted how he and the huge truck were one giant machine, like a Transformer. The dash and black leather seats were immaculately polished. The floor mats washed like a brand new vehicle. She noted a little decal on the driver's side of the windshield, shaped like an anchor.

When they arrived at her cottage, she was grateful all the lights were out at her father's house. Tucker insisted on carrying her to the front door and then let her slide down the front of him. There were bulging body parts she rubbed against, which would be impossible to miss.

She fumbled for her keys and then led him inside.

Tucker made her small living room feel even smaller. The cottage was a converted outbuilding. Therefore, the ceilings were a few inches lower than normal. He ducked and followed her to the single bedroom. Along the way, she asked, "You want anything to drink?"

His eyes were fixated on her. The slow shake of his head was sexy and deliberate. "No ma'am."

"I'm going to need some help getting out of this."

"Just show me what to do."

"There are these hooks at the back," she said as she turned to show him. "You have to undo them one at a time."

Tucker fumbled with the fabric and the closures. She could tell he was getting frustrated. "Holy cow, Brandy. How in the devil would you get yourself out of this thing by yourself?"

"I can pull it over my head, but it would be easier if—"

At last several of the hooks were released, and she was grateful for the extra breathing space.

"You got it."

The bustier fell to the ground. Brandy unzipped her skirt and laid it over a chair. The ugly diaphragm-squeezing undergarment was the only thing between them. She removed her stockings and panties, and once again presented her back to him.

"This is going to be hard. You have to unzip me here."

Tucker was on it, his huge fingers slipping beneath the off-white fabric, while his other hand grabbed the zipper and had it undone in just a couple of seconds.

"Piece of cake."

The rush of air to her lungs was so sudden she nearly fainted again. He braced her before she could fall over. He pulled her to his chest while his hands took hold of her ass and squeezed until it hurt.

She began to unbutton his shirt, then lifted the cotton tee shirt up, and kissed him, placing her palms over his pecs. She reached below, fingers creeping into his pants when he quickly undid his belt and stepped out of them.

She was going to step to press herself against him, but he abruptly picked her up and brought her over to the bed, where he gently placed her down.

"You have some protection?" he whispered as he kissed her neck. One callused hand squeezed her left breast and then slid down lower.

She started to sit up to grab the condoms from the bedside table, but he pressed her back, rising to his knees and staring down at her.

His hands massaged both boobs now. "You're incredible. I think I've died and gone to Heaven," he said as he nuzzled her cleavage, sucking and pinching her nipples. His scratchy beard tickled as his kissing moved lower until he was at her core. His thumbs pressed her open, rubbing her nub as she shuddered with anticipation.

She watched him pleasure her, his giant shoulders rising and falling as he dipped lower. He kept one hand massaging her breast. He was nearly delicate the way he explored with his fingers and tongue. It filled her with electricity as she heard him moan between her legs. She pulled his hair, massaged his temples, and then writhed to the feel of his fingers inside her, calling her to ride his hand and lose herself for him. She came up to her knees, reaching for his cock while she pressed herself into his giant palm.

She gripped him, moving up and down, squeezing his balls and covering his tip with precum. After some minutes of play, she raised herself up and reached for the drawer, bringing out the condom, then tearing it open with her teeth. As she looked up to him in the moonlight, their mouths closed on each other, tongues exploring, becoming more and more intense. Her fingers slid the thin condom down his shaft and massaged him while they finished their slow, sensuous kiss.

Tucker leaned back and brought her up on top of him. With her knees hugging his hips, he gripped her body, snagging her sex on his cock and then pressing her down so he was deep inside her.

He was urgent to move against her, raising and lowering her on him, drawing the rhythm faster and faster until he quickly picked her up, threw her back against the mattress, and mounted her. Plunging deep, he buried his head in her chest.

They moved together like old dance partners, reveling in the miracle that was their bodies. Beneath him, she felt delicate. She melted under his kiss, rising again into multiple orgasms as he plundered and then softened his penetration.

He was an innovative lover, consumed with desire for her, yet very attentive to her needs, begging her to come and then thanking her as she shattered beneath him over and over again. She knew that as the minutes turned into the early pre-dawn hours of the morning, she had never before felt so loved, so coveted and consumed. As the first rays of early dawn shone through the window, he held her close as he came hard and deep inside her, then folded her into his arms, and fell asleep.

She worried her beating heart would wake him as she luxuriated in the heat between them. Every cell in her body screamed for him. Her ear was pressed against his chest, and she listened as air filled his lungs and then expelled. Her skin was bathed in the sweet sweat between their bodies, the way her legs wrapped around his enormous thighs, and how his arms squeezed her so tight it rivaled the bustier just before she fell asleep.

But in the shelter of his arms, there was room to breathe, and finally to dream about a perfect evening, and the beginning of a perfect year.

# CHAPTER 5

A SLIVER OF bright sunlight traveled slowly across Tucker's face like a laser. At first, he startled, since his own apartment was heavily draped in blackout shades. Even on workdays, he was able to sleep in until at least eight. This seemed just minutes from when he'd last closed his eyes.

And then he felt her moist flesh melting all over him. He carefully opened one eye to peer at the lovely brunette resting on his chest. Her lips were still puckered and red, her cheek bulging against her nose. *And she drooled!*

He tilted his head back to avoid giving a belly laugh that would surely wake her. He didn't want to be robbed of these delicious moments. How could he have met a girl who drooled in her sleep?

He scanned the walls of her bedroom. She had tacked several tissue paper sketches of what looked like produce labels and several other ones of large flowers done in chalk or pencil. There was a sketch of a light pink sandy beach cradling white surf coming from a bright turquoise ocean. He noticed a poster made from a picture of Brandy dressed in a large purple grape costume. She was holding a bottle of wine and standing next to Dorie, in an identical costume. Their legs were bright purple from the knees down as they stood in a large stainless steel vat, stomping grapes.

She had a calendar with pictures of beaches from around the world and a photo of her as a young girl sitting beside an older gentleman driving a tractor at a pumpkin farm. Her burgundy bustier and bridesmaid skirt were draped over an easy chair, mixed with his black pants, white shirt, and red white and blue cotton boxers. He was a little embarrassed at the rah rah in his underwear, but he couldn't help it. It was the way he was.

Her bookshelf burst with paperbacks, spilling over onto the floor in several stacks. It appeared every one of them had a picture of a naked man on the cover. The bedside table still gaped with the open drawer containing a box of condoms. He noticed she owned a bright pink vibrator, and that nearly ruined his composure.

But it was all good. All normal. These were the trappings of a woman he'd been trained to protect. Her precious way of life was valuable, something worth saving. This was evidence that what he'd done as an elite warrior was all worth it. He hoped to God she never had to endure some of the things he'd seen out there on the other side of the planet, where children inhaled a steady diet of uncertainty, misery, and smoke from the ashes of their crumbling civilization that knew nothing but war. His job was to make sure that war stayed there and didn't come home.

Brandy was moving against him, stroking him like she'd done so delicately last night. Her pubic bone pressed into his thigh. He raised his knee to help intensify the feeling.

At last, she placed her chin on his sternum and fed from his eyes. What did she see? He hoped she wasn't disappointed. He wasn't. He remembered every kiss, every stroke, every shudder, and every time he pinned her to the bed with her arms outstretched, as if he could will himself to climb inside her and shelter in place.

She was twirling his frosty chest hairs, biting her lip, and waiting to say something, or waiting for him to speak first. But he didn't feel under any pressure to talk so he just watched this dark angel with the red lips he was ravenous for. He wanted to see her enormous breasts bounce in the morning sun as she writhed above him. He wanted to see her face as he filled her, made her come.

She opened her mouth to say something when the door to her living room opened and a man's voice called out, "Brinny?"

Brandy scrambled to sit up, taking the sheet with her, which left Tucker completely exposed. If the man in the next room came to the doorway, he'd also notice the enormous hard-on Tucker had developed.

She smirked, whispering, "My father."

He sprung to action and quickly slipped on his patriotic boxers, but remained seated on the bed.

"Just a minute dad. I've got someone here," she shouted to the next room. Twisting the sheet around her, she stepped to the doorway. Tucker got a nice view of her shapely rear, her long mahogany hair falling everywhere about her shoulders and upper back. He'd kissed every vertebra last night, kneaded the cheeks of her ass until she squealed. She could take everything he could give out, and then some. He hated having to be careful in his sex play. Brandy played at the same intensity.

"Oh, fine. Look, I'm headed off to the store. You coming in today?"

"Maybe later this afternoon. Would that work?"

"Sure. Sorry I didn't let you know yesterday, but I'm going to be one short today. If you can, that would really help me out."

"No problem, Dad. How about one or two o'clock?"

"Great. Hey, how was the wedding?"

She adjusted her sheet again, briefly shooting him a gaze as Tucker lay back on the pillow, his hands clasped behind his head. "Dorie was gorgeous. You should have come. They had a great band, lots of people you knew were there."

"A friend of Brawley's?" her dad whispered, but Tucker could hear it clearly.

Brandy nodded. "Dad, I've gotta go."

"No problem. See you later on this afternoon."

The door closed behind him.

Tucker watched her face recovering from the blush that also sent pink blotches to her upper chest. "That was awkward," she mumbled, fiddling with her fingers and refusing to look back at him.

He was charmed with the blush, but even more interested in getting the sheet off her. "Come here," he whispered.

Her face pinked up again, and he chuckled.

"After all the things we did last night, you expect me to believe you're really shy?"

She began twirling her hair around her forefinger, still avoiding eye contact.

"Come here, Brandy. Just for a little bit. Then I'd like to take you out to breakfast. I'm thinking pancakes."

Her large brown eyes snapped to attention. She crawled on all fours toward him. By the time she reached him, the sheet had been left behind. Her breasts overflowed in his hands as her young body undulated over his groin, pressing against the ridge of his hardness. Her fingers deftly slid his boxers down over his thighs while she guided him to her core. He held the sides of her hips, raised her up, and then plunged her back down on him.

Then he remembered. They'd forgotten the condom. Again. With his fingers digging into her flesh, he stopped her movements completely, knowing he had to ask the question and leave it up to her.

"Is it okay?"

"It's perfect," she blew back at his face, and then she kissed him.

THE SAMOAN PANCAKE House was always a Team favorite on weekends. But today was a holiday so the place was packed. He nodded to several former Teammates, a couple of whom were at the wedding last night.

She chose a corner at the back of the restaurant, and ordered.

"So you used to serve with Brawley, right?"

"About ten years ago. We grew up together in Oregon."

"You're from Oregon?"

He noticed she had a dimple to the right of her mouth, which was cuter than all heck.

"What?"

"You have a very sexy dimple right there." He touched the spot and loved her blush, as she held his hand.

"I love it up there. My parents had plans to retire near McMinville, but my mom passed before they could sell everything and go do it. Now Dad's stuck with the store."

"That's close to where Brawley and I grew up."

"That's what I thought. So your family was farmers, then?"

"Still are. My sister and her husband and kids live with them and they all work in the family business."

"Sounds nice. What do they grow?"

Tucker was hesitant to explain the details of his parent's venture, so he deflected the question by giving a half-answer. "They do hydroponics, greenhouse stuff. They used to grow wheat, but over the years, they've sold off parcels so now they only have a few acres left. It's all they can handle."

"You miss Oregon?" Brandy asked as their breakfast was served.

Tucker poured syrup all over his pancakes and even his eggs and the extra biscuit he ordered. "I worked up a regular appetite, Miss Brandy." He winked at her, amused by the way her jaw dropped as she watched him take his first bite. Then she blushed again.

"I don't miss Oregon at all. I like it here. More sun, less rain. More to do outside, and I don't have to prepare for monsoons to do them, either. San Diego suits me just fine."

"Yup," she agreed.

"You grew up here, then?" He knew she had, but wanted to keep the conversation going.

"Right here. I'm not sure if I stay because of Dad or he stays because of me. I work for him, help him out a bit, since I'm between jobs at the moment."

"I thought you worked with Dorie at the ad agency."

"*Used* to. I guess I pissed off a customer. I don't think the advertising business is for me."

"Brawley said your dad's store is quite upscale? Can he make it with Amazon and all those other players fighting for the retail dollar?"

"I think he makes just enough to live on. Dad's not someone who could ever work for anyone else. He owns the market outright, and the half-acre lot behind. He has some fantasy of doing a little truck farming, perhaps grow his own organic produce."

"Farming, even on a half-acre, is a lot of work."

"I think that's the point, Tucker. When he gets tired of it, then he'll sell. This gives him something to do. Keeps him from missing my mother. She was everything to him." Then she added, "I don't think our family does well with retirement. It's kind of a dirty word."

Tucker nodded and completely agreed. "Smart man. Men have to do things. They can't just sit around and watch the world go by. They have to get into action, or at least the men I hang with do."

"So now that you're off the Teams, what do you do?"

"I run some trainings for guys, mostly high school age, who are interested in joining the SEALs. I try to get them in good physical shape to help them pass BUD/S. I'm kind of the guy who tells them the truth, dispels the garbage the recruiters fill them with. I make sure they know what they're signing up for."

"They're lucky to have you."

"It's only part-time, but it gives me a chance to give a little back to the community. I also do some personal training and I work at the glider port, instructing for the skydiving school."

"Skydiving? Wow."

"You should try it sometime. You'd have a ball."

He was surprised to see she appeared resistant.

"No, thanks. I'll stick to the ground, thank you. If God had wanted me to fly through the air, he would have given me wings."

"Or an expert tandem buddy. It will change your life, Brandy."

"Or end it."

"No. These guys are safe. They train all the SEALs down here. Some of the most experienced skydivers and stuntmen in the country. It's all completely safe." He drew her hand to his mouth and kissed it. "All about trust, Brandy. And finding out about your limits."

They finished breakfast, and Tucker reluctantly took her back to her car. She turned towards him before she got out of the truck.

"I had a great time, Tucker. I had a goal to have one perfect evening, and it was all that and more. Sorry I got sick on you."

He leaned over and cradled her jaw with his palm before kissing her. "I did, too. I don't want to tell you my goal because you dashed it all to hell. This is the part where I ask you if I can see you again. I'm hoping the answer is yes."

She held his hand between both of hers. When she looked up, he thought at first she might say no.

"I was just looking for one perfect night. I guess I could handle two."

# CHAPTER 6

B RANDY CHANGED HER clothes and put on her comfortable cross trainers since she'd be standing the entire afternoon. She drove down the strand past the SEAL Qualification course and thought about what it had been like for Tucker and Brawley going through the training together. Many times, she'd watched the boat crews of new recruits working their way over the rocks or running down the beach carrying telephone poles over their heads. She mused that Tucker could actually make a telephone pole look small.

She turned off the highway and into the tree-lined streets of an older suburban neighborhood then headed away from the bay where things were a little more spread out. Small ranchettes dotted the landscape. She came upon the boutique strip mall containing a cluster of specialty stores with her father's organic grocery and deli at one end. She could see his silver pickup truck parked at the side, as well as Kip's beat-up VW. The five time college freshman had worked for her dad ever since he'd mastered the art of riding a bike. He was practically family. There were only a couple of other cars in the lot, indicating they were having a very slow day.

She loved the smell of the produce and the bright colors of the vegetables and fruit every time she arrived. It was like the smell of flowers at a florist. Her dad was famous for carrying unusual fruits from all over the world, but he specialized in California and Florida citrus and always did a huge business every Christmas sending fruit baskets to customer's relatives all over the globe.

She ducked under the portable canvas awnings shading the lovely displays, piled up in pine boxes. Two shoppers wandered down aisles inside the building itself. One was headed in the direction of the checkout, having spotted Brandy arrive.

"I'll be right back," she told the woman. "Just got to grab my apron and punch in."

Inside the store's tiny office was her father's desk, covered in catalogs, papers, and envelopes—most of them unopened. It was obvious he needed help with his bookkeeping and office organization. She intended to have a discussion with him about that very thing, and soon.

Brandy placed her purse inside the top file cabinet drawer, noticing it had been pushed aside and was slightly crooked. With a couple of shoves she righted it to stand snug against the desk, where it belonged. Her dad's chair was pulled out, and his glasses were folded on top of the closed laptop that was so old the Apple store refused to work on it any longer.

Slipping the kelly-green apron over her head, she deposited her cell phone in the large center pocket, tied the straps behind her waist, and began to look for her father.

"Dad?"

There was no answer so she figured he might be in the large cooler room at the rear.

That's where she found him. He was sprawled on the floor, his face turned to one side. A trickle of blood had seeped into the floorboards coming from under his upper body somewhere. His face was pale, lips slightly purple. She was immediately worried he might be dead.

"Oh my God. Dad! What's happened?"

She fell to her knees and tried to revive him, but his body remained limp. Then she checked for a pulse and was relieved to have found one. And he appeared to be breathing, but when she tried to arouse him again, he didn't respond. His face was cold and clammy.

With her own pulse racing, she dialed 911 and gave instructions to the paramedics who promised they'd be there within minutes.

She called out for Kip, but again received no answer.

"Hang in there, dad."

But her father didn't register any response, which sent a spear of panic down her spine. She wasn't sure if she should roll him over on his back and decided it would be safer to just leave him on his side. Beneath his head she felt the sticky dark red blood. Finding a clean hand towel, she applied slight pressure, hoping to stop the bleeding. In mere seconds, the towel was bright red and soaked. Her hands were dripping in her father's blood. She carefully rested his head against the soaked cotton and staggered out front to see if she could find Kip. It was hard to concentrate, but she managed to calm her nerves.

The customer was waiting not-so-patiently by the checkout, but when she spied Brandy's bloody hands, she began to scream. Brandy jumped as if she'd been slapped.

"Hold on. My father has taken a spill, and the paramedics are on their way. Give me a minute to get myself gathered. Have you seen Kip?"

The woman closed her mouth and merely shook her head briskly. "Who's Kip?"

"He's the other clerk here."

"I didn't see anyone."

Brandy looked at the woman's basket, then at the counter and discovered the cash register drawer had been pried open and was completely empty. A check was crumpled at her feet. It began to dawn on her that perhaps this had been a robbery attempt gone badly.

"Ma'am, it looks like we've been robbed, too. You sure you didn't see anyone?"

"No. No one was here. These folks," she said, pointing to a couple behind her, "arrived after me. Is your dad okay?"

"No. I'm worried. He's unconscious, but help is on the way."

Just then, she heard the familiar sound of Kip parking the company van. He entered the store, tossing and catching his keys. Upon seeing Brandy, he gave her a big grin. "Hey there."

"Kip, Dad's fallen. He's in the back. I've called the paramedics and they're on their way. This woman wants to check out, but I need to stand guard with Dad until the paramedics come. Can you get the backup working? If not, can we just close down the store?"

"Sure thing." Kip was already on his knees, extracting another register from under the counter, connecting the telephone feeds, and adjusting the paper. "I've got this. You go be with your dad."

She jogged to the back of the storeroom. Her father still hadn't moved.

She was relieved to hear the sirens getting closer until she saw just flashing red lights. Someone must have directed them to the rear because two paramedics ran through the back door and bent over to attend to her father. Their fingers deftly poked and repositioned his head and neck, checking out his neck, arms, and legs.

"Did you see him fall?" the handsome dark-uniformed rescue worker asked her as he scanned her bloody hands. He turned his attention back to her father, focusing on the bleeding from his head.

"No. I got here like ten or fifteen minutes ago. I expected to find him in the store, so I went looking for him and found him here. Just like this. I put the towel under his head. But there was so much…blood." Her voice wavered.

The other paramedic was up on her feet, barking instructions into the com strapped to her shoulder.

"Are you a relative or co-worker?" the male paramedic asked.

"I'm his daughter."

"What's his name?"

"Steven Cook."

"He have any illnesses or things I need to know? Medications?"

"Geez." Brandy wracked her brain, trying to remember if he'd told her anything about his health, and came up blank. "I don't think he takes anything. As far as illnesses, not that he's told me."

"How old is he?"

"Sixty-two."

"No pacemakers, history of stroke or heart attack?"

"No. Not that I know of. I really don't know. He's been healthy."

"So you didn't see how this happened?"

"No."

"Anybody angry with him for some reason?"

"No, why?"

"Sorry to have to tell you, but this was no accidental fall. It appears he was hit at the back of the head, you see here?"

He showed her a dark mass of clotted blood, hair, and tissue at the back of his head, slightly underneath him.

"And then it appears he fell, because this other wound looks like it happened when his head hit the floor. So we got two head injuries to deal with."

"I see." Brandy tried to sound as calm as the paramedic was. But in spite of her efforts, her teeth began to chatter.

"You going to be okay?" he asked.

"I don't like blood," she whispered. Black dots began obscuring her vision, and she could tell she was close to passing out.

The paramedic's quick thinking had him grabbing her upper arms with his bloody gloved hands and positioning her on a nearby chair. "Put your head between your knees if you need to. I'll get you some water in a minute. Better?"

She was starting to get confused and could feel her breathing becoming labored. So much was happening.

"Breathe. Take deep breaths," he commanded.

Her father still wasn't moving. His dark lips were getting darker by the minute. She abruptly threw off his hands. "Dad. He looks terrible! He's worse!"

"We got it. Just don't want you to die on me, okay?"

The woman paramedic returned with a gurney, which she lowered and positioned next to her father. She cut his long-sleeved shirt with scissors and then started an IV before helping her partner lift him onto the bed. They raised the legs on the cart, clicked it into position, and ran toward the back of the van. The woman stayed behind while the male worker came back to check on Brandy.

"Where can I get you some water? This *is* a store, right?" he asked.

"There's a case on the other side of this wall. Take a couple for yourselves, too."

He was back in seconds, snapping open the plastic cap and holding the bottle up to her mouth.

Brandy guzzled the cool liquid, trying to keep up, but wound up spilling much of it down her front. She didn't care.

"That help some?"

"I'll be fine."

"You have someone you can call?"

"Kip's here. I want to go be with my dad at the hospital."

"No, not in your condition. But we're taking him to Scripps. You can meet us there. No way I want you driving by yourself."

"Gene?" his partner inserted herself in the exit. "We gotta go now."

"Okay, we're outta here. The police will be arriving soon, so you'll have to give them a statement. Then get someone to bring you down. Right now, we gotta focus on Mr. Cook. So, you take care."

"Thank you so much." She started to stand, but he pushed her shoulders down.

"Don't be stubborn. Be smart."

She didn't like the comment, but she didn't have the energy to fight him back with some quick witty thing. If he only knew.

*Stubborn is my middle name.*

THE POLICE INTERVIEWED them both, promising to be brief so she could get to the hospital to see her father.

Kip answered another question. "He asked me to do the home deliveries because he knew you were coming in." He spoke directly to her.

"How long were you gone?" the officer persisted.

"Hour? Maybe an hour and a half. Normally, I'd go later, but I asked to get off early." He turned to Brandy again. "I got a date."

That's when she realized so did she. She'd promised to meet Tucker at the Rusty Scupper after work. He was working at the skydiving school all afternoon.

"You know of anyone who would want to hurt Mr. Cook?" the officer asked.

Brandy shook her head from side to side. "He doesn't have any fights or enemies of any kind. Everyone loves him."

"Well," Kip interrupted, "there is this one thing. He had a guy he let go last week. Several customers complained about him. Too friendly with the younger girls. I'm talking thirteen, fourteen-year-olds."

"When did this happen?" the officer asked.

"Thursday, I think. Jorge Mendoza. I never liked him. Steve got him from some church group recommendation. He'd been staying at a halfway house. I told your dad he was stealing beer and drinking on his breaks, but he didn't care until he started getting the complaints. Tats, even on his face. He stared at people. Cold eyes. Not a good dude at all. I was glad Steve let him go."

"I didn't know about any of that." Brandy admitted it was just like her dad to give someone a chance.

Several customers came asking questions, after hearing the sirens and seeing the police activity. Brandy told them they were closing for the day, and that her father was in the hospital. The police reminded her afterwards not to give out many details.

"Your father keep records here? Any way we could get this guy's address?"

"Um, yes. He keeps his records in the office, but I'll have to dig a bit. He's not the most organized owner out there. Some of it, he keeps in the safe," Brandy answered. One of the officers followed her, and she was able to get the employee folder from the second file drawer. She lifted a heavy canvas seed sack to access her father's safe and found it gaping open. "Holy crap."

Kip was at the doorway in a flash. "Ah shit. I was afraid of that." He put his hand over his mouth. "Sorry, Brandy."

"Did everyone who worked here know about the safe?" one officer asked.

"I wouldn't think so, but then, Dad was pretty trusting." shrugged Brandy.

Kip added, "We were really busy over the weekend with New Years coming up. Everyone was shopping for last minute things. I think he closed early last night. I'm sure he didn't make it to the bank. It's a shame, but I'm guessing he had a lot of cash in that vault."

"Which points to Mendoza again," said one of the officers.

Brandy took another long gulp of her water, finishing it off. Her eyes filled with tears. Her day had gone from spectacular to tragic. She needed to go be at her father's side. And what if he didn't survive? What would she do? She just couldn't bear to think about it.

The officers agreed to let her go if they could question her further at the hospital. Kip was in charge of closing the store. Brandy agreed to keep the place closed until the police had finished their work, and Kip agreed to open it for them in the morning.

Alone and headed back down the freeway, she left a message for Tucker, and then she burst out in tears, flushing out all the pain and pent up worry all the way to the hospital. By the time she arrived, her eyes felt like her lids were made of cardboard.

This was not the way she'd expected this day to go. As she entered the Emergency Room doors, she began to find some of her courage. She hoped it would be enough for whatever news they'd give her. She said a little prayer before she approached the admitting desk and strained to keep her lower lip from wobbling, Taking a deep breath, she told the admitting clerk, "I'm here to see Steven Cook. Can you tell me what room he's in?"

# CHAPTER 7

TUCKER HAD REMOVED his flight overalls, stowed his equipment, and repacked his chute and the tandem chute, double checking each fold twice. He felt the vibration from his cell and noticed he'd gotten a message from Brandy.

"It's me, Brandy. I'm on my way to the hospital. Scripps ER. Dad's been hurt, and they rushed him by ambulance. I'm meeting the police there. I have no idea how long I'll be, but I don't want to leave him until I know he's going to be okay. So I'm afraid I'll have to take a rain check on that burger and beer. Call me when you get a chance."

He dialed her back, sorry that he'd missed her call earlier. It had been nearly an hour. She picked up on the first ring.

"Brandy, what happened? Is he okay?"

"I don't know yet, Tucker. He was unconscious when they took him away. I'm waiting to find out if they'll let me see him. He's alive, and that's a good thing, but I don't know anything else. I wasn't able to talk to him. I don't know if he's still unconscious."

"But how did he get hurt? Why are the police involved?"

"It was a robbery at the store. They got the cash in the till, the contents of his safe, everything. The police are following up on a lead Kip gave them."

"Kip?"

"I'm sorry. He's dad's helper."

"So how did he get hurt?"

"Apparently, he was hit at the back of the head, and then fell. I found him on the floor near the cooler. He didn't look good at all, Tucker. Lots of blood. I'm worried."

"Of course you are. Listen, can I meet you there? I'm about a half-hour away."

"I'd like that," she murmured.

Tucker could tell she was trying to stay collected but was having difficulty holding herself together. Her breathing was forced and ragged.

"He's at Scripps you say?"

"Yes. I can call you if they take him somewhere else. But their ER and critical care is one of the best in the country."

"You got that right. Okay, I'll be there as fast as I can. You need me to bring anything?"

"Honestly, I'm not focusing on me at all. I think I'm still in shock. Just come. That would help."

Tucker stopped by his apartment, wanting to take a shower, but knew he didn't have time. He changed his clothes, picked up a pillow and blanket, threw a couple of waters in a bag, and headed up the freeway.

The sunset was a rosy pink, which sent a glow throughout the waiting room at the ER. His arms overflowing with the blanket and queen pillow, he scanned the seats and didn't see Brandy, so asked the desk clerk. He peered over the top of his bundle, since the woman was taller than he was.

"Are you family?" she asked, examining his armful.

"Yes," he lied.

"Well, hon, the daughter is waiting outside the treatment room. They're getting ready to take him up to ICU."

"How's he doing? Can I come in and wait with her?"

"Sorry, can't give you his status, but let me ask her if she'd like some company. I'm betting she would," she said, scanning the pillow again, squinting her eyes and smiling. "Can I have your name, please?"

"Tucker Hudson."

"I'll be right back." The heavyset nurse winked at him and then moved with the speed of a linebacker, disappearing around the corner. It wasn't every day Tucker spoke eyeball to eyeball with a woman who towered above him. In a few seconds, the side door opened, and the clerk called out, "Mr. Hudson, this way, please."

Brandy was in the hallway, speaking to a uniformed female officer. She abandoned the conversation temporarily and ran to his arms. An instant before she collided with him, he dropped his load and pulled her to him.

"You holding up?" he whispered to the top of her head.

"Better now." She snuggled to press herself hard against his chest, wrapping her arms around him beneath his jacket.

"How's you dad?"

Brandy pulled away, biting her lower lip. "Haven't talked to the doctor yet, really. Dad's had a brain scan and some bloodwork and some other tests. They told me his vitals were strong, but I don't know anything else. Hoping someone will talk to me before they take him upstairs."

The female officer appeared behind Brandy. "If you give me just a couple more minutes, we can get my questions answered, and I'll get out of your hair. That sound okay with you?"

"I'm sorry." Brandy walked back to the row of chairs they'd been sitting at, remained standing, her arms still about Tucker's waist. Good as her word, the police officer finished her questions and then was gone within a handful of minutes. Brandy leaned against him as they sat down together. A male nurse had picked up the blanket and pillow and placed them nearby, neatly folded.

"So how did this robbery occur? They hold him up at gunpoint? In the middle of the day?" Tucker asked.

"We still don't know that. Don't even know how many of them there were."

"Your dad have cameras in the store?"

"Only for looks. They don't record."

"All this is appearing like it was someone who knows your dad. Knows his way around the store. Knows the routines."

"I think that's what the police are going on. But, honestly, I don't care about the money. I just want to be sure he's okay, without any major—"

"Ms. Cook?"

Dr. Harrelson shook her hand and motioned for her to remain seated. He extended his hand to Tucker. "I'm Dr. Harrelson. You the husband? Boyfriend?"

Tucker found himself stumbling for his words, a bit put on the spot. "Family friend," he answered grasping the doctor's paw.

"Now *that's* a handshake!" Dr. Harrelson barked, feigning injured fingers.

Tucker thought he'd been rather careful and wasn't in the mood for jokes. "Sorry, sir."

"Okay, well we have good news and bad news, Ms. Cook. We're not seeing much brain damage on the scan, and the wave patterns are normal. He's got a little swelling, especially in the back here." The doctor demonstrated on his own head, palming an area behind his right ear at the base of his skull. "There's probably some pressure, which also could be from blood pooling, but we will monitor that, and it doesn't seem to be increasing, thank God."

"That's good. So what's the bad news?" she asked.

"He's lost a considerable amount of blood, and he definitely has a minor skull fracture, probably a concussion as well. The next twelve to twenty-four hours will be the most telling, but we should know more once we see how he weathers this."

"Is he awake yet?"

"No, and right now, I'm not anxious for him to be. I think we need to watch him, let his body heal and stabilize itself. There's a chance we'll have to go in there to relieve the pressure, but the bleeding has been stopped. We're thinking the bones in his skull will heal on their own."

"That's good news." Tucker was feeling encouraged and hoped Brandy felt the same.

"I was able to contact his primary care physician. Your dad's in remarkable shape for sixty-two. His doctor gave me his medical history. That's going to help us out a lot."

"So what's the plan?" Brandy asked.

To their side, they all watched as her father was wheeled out of the treatment room and down the hallway by two male attendants.

"His color is much better," she remarked.

"Yeah. We were a little worried when he first came in, but he's responding quickly. We hope that continues," Dr. Harrelson added. They followed Mr. Cook's gurney as it entered the elevator.

Tucker noted the strong jawline and the shape of her father's nose, indicating a strong family resemblance. His face looked relaxed. A large white bandage was wrapped around his skull down to the level of his eyebrows and ears. Tufts of graying hair stuck out the top where it had been left open, some of it still caked in dark red blood.

"So we're taking him upstairs, now," the doctor started. "He'll be in ICU, on the fourth floor, tonight. Once we get him situated, if you want to briefly come in and say goodnight, that would be fine, but no more than five minutes. He probably won't hear you, and he definitely won't respond. Just preparing you for this."

"Thanks, doctor."

"I have rooms upstairs, if you need a place to crash, but honestly, it would probably be best if you just went home and got some rest. Nothing like sleeping in your own bed."

Brandy searched Tucker's face. "What do you think?"

"I think he's right." He knew his apartment was not more than five minutes away, but he was hesitant to suggest he take her there. He hadn't entertained a woman at his place in several months and was in the habit of trying to avoid it at all costs. He was trying to recall how bad the place was, since it would be Brandy's first impression of how he lived. Though a tiny niggling voice whispered caution, he found himself overruling it.

"I don't live too far. But if you want to stay here, I'm willing to sleep in a chair by your side. I've learned to sleep just about anywhere."

"You a Team Guy?" Dr. Harrelson asked.

"Former."

"That explains the handshake. So, you two talk about it and then let me know. Give us about ten minutes to get him all situated, okay?"

Brandy nodded as the doctor left.

"I think he's doing really great, Brandy." Tucker had never seen the man before, but in light of what he'd been through, he thought Mr. Cook was looking good. "If he's stabilized, no reason for you to get worn out trying to sleep here. Hospitals make me nervous. Just too much going on."

Tucker had an aversion to hospitals. Even when he'd broken his legs twice in combat, he demanded he be able to walk out on his own, whether in cast or crutches or both. The first time it was nearly impossible to navigate. He got good at asking people to get out of the way by swinging his crutch high above his head like a hammer throw. He even resumed his skydiving, until his LPO found out and put a stop to it.

"You sure it's no trouble?" she asked. "Do you have a roommate?"

"No roommate. It's sparsely decorated and probably not to your taste, but I guarantee the bed's great."

She smiled, slowly swinging her head from side to side. "Why am I not surprised?"

"There. That's what I've been looking for." He angled her chin up and kissed her lightly. "I wanted to see that pretty smile. Ready to go?"

"I want to see him first."

An ICU nurse accompanied Brandy to the expansive room housing several beds, most of them filled. Tucker waited against the wall, sneaking a peek through the wide open doorway. He was able to see Brandy sit in the chair provided, reach over, and take her father's hand. She spoke to him, but too softly for him to make out. A few minutes later, with a gentle pat on her shoulder, she was ushered out.

"How's he look?" he asked her.

"He actually looks comfortable, but the nurse told me they'd be on high alert all night in case something happened. It's amazing he didn't break his arm or one of his legs, the way he must have fallen."

"Someone definitely looking out for him," Tucker answered back. "Let's go."

He drove in complete silence the short ten blocks before he arrived at the gates to his complex. He was grateful he didn't have to ruminate any longer than five minutes over his choice to bring her to his place. He'd have been a nervous wreck. Putting it all out of his mind, he helped her climb down from his truck, tucked the blanket and pillow under one arm, and took her hand with the other.

The first thing that hit him when he opened his front door was that he'd never before noticed that his room smelled of man sweat. Her room smelled of lavender and other floral fragrances. Before he turned on any lights, he stumbled in the dark, picked up the clothes he'd worn skydiving today under the jumpsuit, and tossed them behind the closet doors. Before he could choose the right lighting, Brandy turned on the bright kitchen lights, exposing the sink full of dishes. It was over three day's worth, even though he ate mostly frozen dinners on a regular basis.

*Why hadn't he thought about this?*

He hung his head sheepishly, hoping it didn't leave too much of a negative impression. "Between housekeepers," he mumbled, rolling his neck and left shoulder.

"You already warned me, so no worries. You also mentioned you don't have a decorator." She smiled, seemingly to enjoy his squirming. "I wasn't expecting an extreme makeover," she said, batting her eyes at him.

Tucker was definitely not feeling the least bit romantic. He was scared out of his gourd. He was on uncharted territory and regretted not paying attention to that little voice that usually gave him pretty good advice.

She wandered around his living room, examining the walls and bare corners. He had one couch, and it conformed perfectly to the contours of his large frame, even if it was ugly as sin. The table in front was a wooden shipping crate. She leaned over it and studied his choice of reading material. Several nudie magazines with specialty titles like *I Love Titties* and *Booty Call* were stacked five or six issues deep. All he could do was close his eyes and wait for her reaction. It was too late to whisk them away out of sight.

She picked up one cover and showed him the enormous boobs on the unfortunate girl. "Do mine look anywhere like these?" she asked, her face showing no expression.

"Holy cow, Brandy. No. *Fuck* no! Yours are…well, they're just right. A nice, full," he began to hold out his palms, fingers splayed and pointing up, "handful, just overflowing."

She had her hands on her waist. It was one of those attitude things women frequently gave him. He knew he was in some trouble, but wasn't sure how much. With his lack of sleep last night, his radar was not working, and his blood was inconveniently pooling elsewhere. He hoped she didn't notice. He wished she'd say something.

"But completely inadequate, compared to these." She held the magazine up, covering her chest.

"God, Brandy, those are unnatural. I mean if I wanted to play with a couple of deflated basketballs, I'd go take a drive to Sports City."

She flipped the magazine over to examine it again. "They do sort of look like basketballs."

Since she wasn't smiling, he carefully waited for the whole scene to pass. He tried to reassure her he liked her just the way she was built.

"And you have lovely curves, sweetheart. She's like a human tuck and roll. I like nice, curvy hips. I mean look at me. I want a woman I don't have to worry about breaking her pelvis when I make love. I hate skinny women."

He wasn't sure it was enough, so he waited, squinting as if bracing for a blow. She tossed the magazine back onto the table, and picked up one of the big butt issues. "Big Book of Booty. Nice."

Her darting glance at him was painful, but his dick was having great fun at his expense. Luckily, Brandy didn't look there. Instead, she smiled and asked him, "Does my ass look like this?"

Tucker was stumped. Brandy's ass did indeed look like the cover model's. She was round in all the right places. He decided he'd have to live or die, but he'd be honest with her.

"Yes, your butt looks sort of like that, only better. Smooth as silk. I love the way it looks and feels, sweetheart." He was hoping she didn't catch on that this was his favorite magazine.

"So why'd you buy this other one if you don't like basketballs with nipples? Or are you lying to me?"

"Look, Brandy, we're going places we don't have to go. But the truth is, there are some nice pictures on the inside. They aren't all like this. This is shock value, to make men buy the magazine. That's all. This is like a cartoon, a comic book, something men do to pass the time, like playing a video game or something. It's all fantasy."

He carefully maneuvered himself behind her, removing the magazine from her hands and turning her around.

"I don't need those things anymore. I got the real thing right here. You were created perfect for me. I mean that, Brandy." He massaged the top of her spine. With the other hand, he slipped it around her waist and slowly pulled her to him. "Perfect, in every way," he whispered. He let his hands massage her ass, squeezing and pressing her against his hardness.

"Why can't I be your fantasy, Tucker?"

"You are. You totally are. Men look. That's what we do. You do it, I'm sure. I mean, I saw all those romance novels overflowing your bookshelf. Some of those guys were *naked*. I'm sure it's done to sell those books to women, right?"

He suddenly felt like a louse. Here her father was in ICU, and he was having this discussion about boobs and booty. His lust was driving the conversation, clouding his better judgment. It wasn't fair to her. It wasn't even fair to himself. He wasn't acting like a real man. He was acting like a wolf—and everything he didn't respect. He was disgusted with himself.

He stepped away.

"I'm sorry, Brandy. This isn't right. I brought you here so you could get a good night's sleep, to help you rest." He chanced stepping back to her until he could feel the heat of her body again. "Let's just keep things simple and do that, okay? Let's forget about all this crap. I'm beat, and I'll bet you are, too. Can we call a truce and just sleep? I'll even keep my clothes on if you like."

He could feel her soften as she bridged the gap between them, all those lovely curves fitting so nicely, making him come alive. She placed her palms on his chest.

"It was my fault, Tucker. But I think you have a good idea there. Why don't we just go to bed?"

"You're on. No objections here," he lied. He tried to keep his grin from looking too lecherous. He took her hand and gently pulled her to the bedroom. He pretended he didn't notice the posters of well-oiled ladies on motorcycles, stark naked, or how she was staring at them with interest. She approached the poster with the row of ten perfect asses. He heard her inhale and hoped she wasn't going to object. If she did, he was going to rip all of them off the wall and toss everything from his balcony to the pool level below.

But what she did next surprised him. She removed her clothes, giving him one of those looks that made him nervous. It was the thing that scared him most about women. He had no way of knowing what was really going on inside her mind. While she stood in her bra and panties, she undid the center clasp and allowed the magnificence of her breasts to shine in the moonlight, beckoning to him. He was holding his breath, mesmerized.

"I like your idea. Let's just sleep." She pulled back the sheets and slid her naked body under them, invading his man bed, defiling his private sanctuary that would forever after smell like her and bring back memories of what it was like to have her there lying next to him.

He hurried to discard his pants and shirt and then his red, white and blue boxers, turning to sit on the edge so she wouldn't see the enormous hard-on he had for her. She snuggled close, wrapping her arms around his upper torso and squeezing her lovely upper chest against him. She moved her head just enough so her lips touched his ear when she said, "And then maybe tomorrow morning you can fuck my brains out."

Tucker knew he was hopelessly flawed. But he also knew he was utterly hooked on this woman. And he'd only known her for less than twenty-four hours. This had never happened to him before. If he wasn't careful, he'd be taking her to dress fittings and window shopping jewelry shops.

It would be the end of his life as he knew it.

And he'd love every minute of it.

# CHAPTER 8

A S THE DAYS and weeks flew by, Brandy's father recovered with only a slight amount of memory loss. He still had headaches that drove him to bed from time to time. He was able to identify his attacker as Jorge, his former employee. Although both the Sheriff and the San Diego PD searched, when they couldn't find him and he stopped reporting for meetings he was required to attend, it was assumed he had fled to Mexico. With his prior record, when he was apprehended, he'd be going away for a long time, since the assault caused injury that necessitated a hospital stay, and drew blood.

Brandy and Tucker spent time with Dorie and Brawley when they returned from their honeymoon in Hawaii. She also worked longer hours at the grocery, and assisted her father in hiring two more experienced clerks. She hired a professional organizer to work with her dad to get the office looking more like an office than a storage unit.

But Brandy knew she'd have to get another good job like she had with the ad agency. The rents in San Diego weren't cheap, and with Tucker staying over at her cottage so much of the time, she wanted to get someplace more private and not under her father's watchful eye. But she was in no hurry. She allowed her relationship with Tucker to take it's own path. The longer she was around him, the less of a difference their fifteen-year age spread made.

But today was going to be an important test of their relationship. Tucker had worked on her non-stop until she finally relented. She was going to allow him to take her tandem skydiving. Although she'd visited the glider port and watched him jump and land safely a dozen times, it did nothing to remove her fear.

"You just have to ignore it. Just like you did when you learned to ride your first bike," he'd told her.

"But I wasn't going to fall thirteen thousand feet if I had a mishap on the bike." She couldn't imagine she would enjoy falling through the sky, even with Tucker securely strapped to her back.

"Trust me, it doesn't feel like you're falling. It feels like there's a blast of wind coming straight from the earth, holding you up so you can fly. It really does feel that way, Brandy. You'll see."

The old converted bomber with the door removed loaded everyone and their buddies up after some ground instruction. Brandy and Tucker were to be in the middle of the jump, since it was her first one. Several SEALs and former Teammates of Tucker's jumped solo, doing cartwheels and in-air formations. At last it was their turn. She stood at the edge of the door, barely able to see cars moving below. Houses looked no bigger than her pinkie fingernail. The air that blew back through the jump door was freezing cold.

She wasn't sure when she was supposed to jump, and worried she'd catch her foot or shoelace on the flange at the opening.

"When do we—" she began to shout, until she felt Tucker's weight behind her and effortlessly they were out of the plane and freefalling. As her heart rate began to return to normal, she realized he was right. It didn't feel like she was falling at all. It felt like the earth was slowly moving to reach out and touch her, but very, very slowly. He tapped her arms, signaling her to make a human "W" as she extended them out to the sides and spread her feet.

He kissed the top of her head and shouted, "Close your mouth. I'm getting slimed."

Her wonderment and awe had caused her to forget that little part of the training. "Sorry," she shouted back at the top of her lungs.

Tucker handed her the cord to the chute and together they pulled it, which yanked her straight up several hundred feet, or so it seemed. As the glider extended, Tucker steered them around in circles, even driving them through wispy clouds, soaring up and then doing high-banked turns in mid air. As she came closer and closer to the earth, the air began to warm.

He pointed out the border. "That's Mexico right over there." He also pointed out several other landmarks. The San Diego Bay appeared like it was a shallow bowl of silver pebbles as it glistened in the morning sun. She took his hand and kissed his palm.

"Thank you," she said to him in the quiet. It felt like the ride went on for an hour, that they would be suspended all day, but finally the ground began to loom large. She threw her legs out in front of her as they landed on Tucker's, collapsed and rolled together in the long grass, entangled in the chute.

Looking up to the sky, it appeared twice as big as before, and twice as blue. A gentle breeze rearranged her hair when her cap fell to the side. Tucker's face and beard was pressed to her cheek. "I knew you could do it," he whispered. But even that whisper had the deep raspy tones that made her whole body vibrate.

"Amazing," was all she could think to say in return, as she continued searching the blue spans above her. "It wasn't anything at all what I imagined."

"It's like a lot of things. Scarier to think about than to do. We do thousands of these jumps on the Teams. Twice as high. At midnight when you only have your night vision specs on. You see oceans of glittering lights and hope that they're harmless animals, not the eyeballs of the enemy."

"I could never do that," she answered. "But I can see you doing it. Must have been fun."

Tucker hesitated before he said anything at all, and then she couldn't make out the words. She left him to his private thoughts. She knew he missed the life, and would ask him sometime how he replaced the adrenaline he used to have coursing through his veins. She wondered if being a farmer, or a father or husband would ever be really enough.

"Come on, we gotta get up before we get overrun with the newbies." He pulled her up by the straps, unhooked her from him and from the chute and began gathering the colorful fabric, shaking out the blades of grass and small rocks. She noted how happy he looked, with the sun shining behind him, greying hair blowing in the breeze.

She touched his cheek, making him stop, his hand wrapped around her wrist.

"I mean it. Thank you, Tucker." She stood on tiptoes and kissed him until he swept her up and carried her off the field, the lightweight nylon chute tucked under his arm.

Afterwards, they went for a seafood lunch down by the marina. She scanned the million dollar vessels and the people out walking their dogs or jogging on this sunny Sunday. Every day was sunny here.

"See, you wouldn't have this in Oregon," she chided him.

"That's very true. This suits me."

"Me too."

Over their soup he asked her, "Where do you want to go for Valentine's Day?"

That sent a zinger up the back of her legs. She recovered quickly, but couldn't make a decision. "Anywhere. You just name it."

"How about we go up north? Several of the guys and some of the wives are doing a road trip to Sonoma. Can you get a couple of extra days off? It takes a day up and a day down. Gotta stay and do some wine tasting. And I understand you're proficient at grape stomping."

"In February? You know anyone who has grapes this time of year?" She wrinkled up her nose and then winked at him.

"I love that picture with you and Dorie."

"Ah, the good old days, when I thought I had a job." She allowed her voice to wander off.

"You want me to move in? I could help with the rent."

Brandy's pulse quickened as her stomach turned. "I was thinking I'd move someplace else." She drank her water and didn't look at him for a couple long seconds, not sure she understood how he'd take it. "And no, your apartment is completely out of the question."

"Why would you ever want to move? Your place is perfect."

"And it's right behind my father's house."

"So? You don't think he understands what we do all night long, Brandy? Come on. He knows his little girl is all grown up, with grown up appetites. Besides, I think he'd be relieved you had someone to watch over you when he wasn't there to protect you himself. Give him a break. Let him relax. I'll do the heavy lifting for awhile."

The "for awhile" stuck in her chest. But, she had it coming. The conversation had come to the edge of their limit on what was safe to discuss. They never talked about long-term futures. It was way too soon.

"I think dad likes having me around, but it's hard to make ends meet with what he pays me. It's like my life's on hold each week I stay there."

Tucker was quiet, and then he spoke down to the tabletop. "Why not look at it like you don't have to decide right now. If you stay there you'll probably make him happy. He gets to see more of you than most fathers get. You're not pressured to go knock yourself out trying to swim upstream with all the other people clamoring for a fat paycheck."

She knew there was more he wanted to say, but was finding the choice of words difficult. She reached out and took one of his hands. "And I'm hoping you wouldn't mind, right?"

His brown eyes saw everything about her. He saw her insides, how her heart was beating, saw all her uncertainty. Saw how grateful she was that they'd met.

"That would be an understatement." His thumb caressed her knuckles and she thought she saw traces of a blush. "Can I ask you a question?" he asked.

"Shoot." She inhaled deeply and braced for something momentous.

"If we did decide to move in together, could I keep just one of my posters?"

# CHAPTER 9

TUCKER HAD SCHEDULED a fishing trip to Baja for early March, but that wasn't going to change his plans to take the road trip to Sonoma County. As they were preparing, he received an enormous rent increase, so Brandy presented him with a key to her cottage.

"You sure?" He was thrilled, but surprised.

"Nope. But I think it's time and I did ask Dad. You were right, he said he was relieved."

"Just human nature."

"So have you decided which poster will come with you?" He loved the way she teased him.

"I'm leaving them *all* behind. Why have an imitation when I've got the real thing?"

He'd been doing extra workouts with several new boys graduating in June, looking to enlist after the summer. His back and knees were bothering him somewhat, so he decided he'd take his time moving his stuff, do it gradually so he didn't send himself over the edge. For the first time in his life, he was feeling his age. He could still bulk up, and work all the machines at Gunny's even better than when he was on the Teams, but his agility and speed was lacking. He was stiff in the mornings and sometimes woke up with leg cramps.

But when Team 3 got orders to do a temporary deployment back to Baja, everything changed. The Team Guys were to work on the sex trafficking ring they had slowed, but now had flared up again. The fishing trip was still on, but Tucker was going as the real civilian, and it would be no picnic for the active duty SEALs. He'd gotten special permission after initially having his participation rejected. He was excited to be of service, even if it was logistics support, to the men he'd previously served with.

Brandy wasn't pleased.

"I think the Navy is using you as bait, Tucker. I mean, you have to pay for your part of the trip, but you don't really get to do whatever you want to. You have to hang with them. They should at least pay for your way down and back and the cost of the rental when you're there."

"I'm actually happy about spending more time with them than I would if it was a real vacation. We usually can only get two or three days, like our Sonoma trip."

But she didn't understand Tucker would have paid anything he could afford just to be embedded deeper within the community. He knew it was a hard thing to explain, so he didn't try.

He was nearly settled with the move, just ahead of their road trip. He had so little furniture, only the closet revealed the secret of his residency. Brandy got rid of her bed. He got rid of the old couch. Everything else he left behind for a young recruit who was beginning his first workup in BUD/S—someone who also appreciated his stash of magazines and posters.

He offered to rototill the back lot for Mr. Cook as a thank you for letting him share the cottage with Brandy. He even offered to pay a little more in rent, but Cook wouldn't have any of that.

Tucker fixed the clutch wires on the "mangler", as he called the tiller, switched out the gasoline after installing a new gas tank and filter. The machine purred like a kitten. Afterwards, the sandy light brown soil looked like chocolate sugar. He imagined Cook would have a field day while they were gone, planting all his early spring seeds.

At last, they took off for Northern California, driving in one long caravan of ten vehicles. Their destination was Frog Haven Vineyards, where several of the SEALs had invested some of their re-up bonuses. Brawley told him it was run by the infamous *Pirate*, who had also been a member of Kyle's squad. Tucker had never met the man.

But he'd also been on earlier road trips when he was active and knew all about Nick Dunn's winery in Santa Rosa, which was on the way. His sister had left the property to Nick. He and Devon converted the nearly bankrupt nursery site into a world-class wedding center, lavender farm and winery. Tucker had been part of several work parties in past years, but had never seen the final result, and knew Brandy would love it.

After only two stops along the way and nearly ten hours later, they arrived in Sonoma County, not stopping until they got all the way up to Healdsburg and the famous Dry Creek Valley. Traveling the winding country two-lane freeway through the valley floor, they found it covered in blooming bright yellow mustard flowers between rows of blackened and gnarled old grapevines. Vineyard workers were cutting back last year's growth to make way for trellising new ones. The air was lightly scented by the smoldering piles of clippings and farm debris all along the way.

"I can't believe I've missed this area," Brandy remarked. "Never thought I'd find anything prettier than Coronado, but this comes pretty close."

"People come here from all over the world just to drive around, eat incredible food and taste great wines. Barrel tasting is really big in the early fall."

"Sounds like Heaven," she answered back.

"These guys have it good. Zak's nickname is the pirate. He got injured on his first deployment, shot in the eye and is real lucky to be alive."

"I'd say. But except for the eye, he was okay?"

"Yes ma'am."

"Were you close?"

"He came on board after I'd gone, so I never got to meet him. But after the injury, he wanted to come back. He worked like a dog and qualified Expert with his other eye, and went through most of the BUD/S training again. You don't find many guys who could do that."

"So he went back?"

"Well, Kyle wanted him back, I was told, but in the end, the Navy thought better of it and asked him to scratch. He met a local Realtor and they found this property and bought it, along with a whole bunch of Team Guys and their relatives. Now they're making beer, along with the wine. I hear it's real tasty."

"Zak sounds like one tough dude."

The caravan slowed down, the first car turning up a crushed granite drive, quickly disappearing from view. As Tucker began his approach up the driveway, he drove past a handful of mailboxes, and pointed out the winery sign.

"Frog Haven. That's it. Got the Bone Frog logo and everything, not that the average tourist would know. You won't see a Trident anywhere."

They drove past more vineyard workers doing pruning and cleanup. A herd of small goats was grazing between several rows, hedged in by portable fencing.

"Am I seeing this correctly? Goats?" asked Brandy.

"They keep the grass down, leaving behind nutrients. A lot of the wineries in the valley are doing the same. Pretty smart. Rent-A-Goat." Tucker could see she was amused.

"No way. Really?" she asked.

"I don't lie. This herd is special. They make artisan cheeses the owner sells for big bucks. Your dad might even carry some in his store."

Once they approached the top of the swale, the jockeying for parking space began, with a couple of the big trucks nearly colliding. One by one everyone poured out, stretching and adjusting themselves after the long ride. In front of them was a quaint farmhouse with a large covered porch surrounding three quarters of the sides. It had been restored to perfect condition. An attractive woman in a smock apron, with two children hugging her legs stood at the entrance. Leaning against one of the porch posts next to her was a handsome man dressed in black, sporting an eye patch over one side. It had to be Zak. Tucker was looking forward to meeting him, finally.

Brandy shuffled over to Brawley and Dorie, striking up a conversation. Kyle's wife, Christy, ran to the porch and gave Zak's lady a big hug. A couple of the other wives did the same. Zak and Amy's two kids scattered into the vineyard to go play with a group of workers kids.

Tucker took Brandy's hand and they joined the small crowd that had gathered in front of the house, just as if Zak was going to make a speech to all of them.

Instead of Zak giving the speech, it was his wife.

"Welcome to Frog Haven. I'm Amy and this is my husband, Zak. I guess the kids are around here somewhere, so be careful pulling in or backing out of the driveway, *please!*"

The group chuckled.

"We're so excited to have you with us for a couple or three nights. We can sort all that out later. I don't think Zak has been able to sleep for a week, he's been so looking forward to your visit."

"Thanks you two," directed Kyle, taking charge. "Let's give them a big round of applause for making this one of the more frugal vacations we've been able to take."

The group clapped and several whistled or cheered.

Amy thanked them with a big smile. "Now, we have two unoccupied bedrooms here in the main house, but the bunkhouse sleeps twenty-four. No queen or king beds, so you'll have to put your singles together and negotiate the crack down the middle."

"Notice she said two beds together? No threesomes!" yelled Kyle.

After the laughter died down, Amy continued. "I'll let you sort all that out on your own. We eat in an hour, family style out back on the other side. I've got some heaters but there's no way I can feed you all in my little dining room, so wear your sweatshirts and jackets. If it's too cold for you, tomorrow we can arrange for supper to be served in the bunkhouse."

"Dinner attire?" T.J. Talbot asked her.

"Something you wouldn't mind getting stained with tomato sauce. We're going Italian all the way."

A cheer broke out, and as the crowd dispersed, Zak called them all back.

"Almost forgot. Short showers or only the first five of you will get one. My personal favorite is sharing, two-by-two. We have a nice hot tub you can take your time and soak in after dinner, if you like." Zak checked his cell phone. "On my mark....Go!"

The group took on the atmosphere of a church camp. The men were in sync because they were used to working together that way without anyone having to bark instructions. Tucker noticed several of the newer wives and girlfriends were completely confused, and Christy was a big help with some timely advice, discretely placed here and there.

Tucker and Brandy selected a dark corner in the bunkhouse. Wire cables worked like stringers, attached with hooks to the walls in both directions so old sheets could slide into place, giving each couple some privacy like in a hospital room. Tucker moved their two mattresses together and then re-made the bedspread to stretch over both sides. He'd been told to bring some comforters, so he retrieved them from the truck, and added them as well.

At the opposite wall, there was an old Franklin pot-bellied stove and a generous pile of wood stacked halfway to the ceiling. Several rocking chairs made a semicircle around the stove for evening chats. Against one wall was a tiny kitchen with a sink, a refrigerator, a picnic table that could seat eight and a microwave toaster oven.

But the highlight of the entire bunkhouse was the bathroom, containing a two-stall unisex toilet and one shower. Tucker was looking forward to the hot tub after dinner to work out the kinks in his neck and shoulder. He doubted he could even fit in the shower, let alone share it with Brandy.

They washed up quickly and then joined the whole group outside on

Zak and Amy's patio. Zak placed both their kids at the head of the table on a loveseat with pillows so they could see everyone. They were bundled for the ski slopes, wearing matching bunny hats.

At this time of year, the vines were bare, so the trellis they sat under left gaping holes where Tucker could see the stars. Some of the magic rubbed off when it turned very cold, with a slight breeze. He excused himself and grabbed their comforter from the bunkhouse and wrapped the two of them together while they devoured their steaming hot lasagna, green salad and a little too much red wine. With the slight buzz relaxing him, soon even the nippy night air stopped bothering him. He'd forgotten how different Northern California was from San Diego, where no matter what time of year, the temperature never fluctuated more than ten degrees.

Brandy was laughing at Christy's story of how she met Kyle, when she attempted to hold the wrong house open and found him naked and asleep—stretched out on the master bed.

Although the ladies were last to bond as a unit, as the wine continued to flow and the stories got louder and more daring, Tucker could tell they were already well on their way to coming together on their own team of sorts. It was important that the sisterhood of the wives and girlfriends stay strong and tight, since they would help hold each other up in case the unthinkable were to happen. Dr. Death stalked them all: men, women and children. And with the world exploding more and more every day, he was making house calls at home, in the good old US of A.

*You son of a bitch.*

Tucker had only had to hold one of his buddies as the young man's life passed from him. He never wanted to repeat the experience.

By candlelight, he studied the faces of those men he'd served with, and served under. He felt so lucky to have had that opportunity to be a grown up Boy Scout, doing crazy dangerous things, all the while making the world a safer place. He'd been able to push himself to his limits, the adrenaline nearly exploding from the veins in his neck, but as a force for good. Never evil. It was hard to explain to someone who hadn't experienced it for himself. It was probably the heavy wine, but right now he couldn't explain why he'd ever left. There just wasn't another job on the planet as good as being a Team Guy.

Amy put on some music and the ladies rushed to their feet to dance. It was fascinating to watch how women could just be so demonstrative, so ready to just throw their heads back, laugh and toss their cares over their shoulders.

Brawley scooted over next to him, and shared part of the blanket.

"You guys are getting along most excellently, my man. Brandy's a good influence on you."

"Nah. I still got the dirty thoughts, same as ever."

The two men chuckled. Brawley's eyes were sparkling in the candlelight as he watched his new bride dance with Brandy. Christy and several of the others became the girl group backup singers, line dancing in unison to the funky rhythm from an oldies satellite channel.

"We've missed you, Tuck."

"Missed you too," Tucker returned without looking at Brawley. "So you're staying in for another turn?"

"For now. Honestly, I don't know what I'd do if I didn't have this community or these things to do with my friends."

"I hear you." Tucker was trying not to dwell on it. He wanted Brawley to change the subject, but it was awkward sitting next to him, wrapped in the same blanket. He was sensitive about that sort of thing. As a youth, he'd probably spent more time with Brawley than he did his own parents.

"You'll have to hang around more when we get back to San Diego," Brawley said just before he finished his wine. Zak placed another opened bottle in front of the two men.

Tucker read the label out loud. "*Frog Haven Winery. A little piece of Heaven.* That's about how I'd describe it up here." He was hoping the change in focus would get the discussion off the Teams.

"First time I've seen it all built out. When they first bought it, I thought they were nuts." Brawley scanned the patio, smiling at the girls. "Now look at it. Piece of Heaven, indeed."

"Thought you invested like Kyle and Coop and everyone else," remarked Tucker.

"Nope. I bought a house with my re-enlistment bonus instead. Maybe the next time."

"So you're going career, like your dad?"

"I'm thinking PA school, or maybe med school, if I can get some tutoring."

"Geez, Brawley. You won't have any time if you do that. And you'll owe them another ten years at least."

"Well, it's a pipe dream." Brawley casually glanced at the ladies again. "They're getting smashed."

Tucker found this funny. "I think living here and doing this would be a whole lot easier. And no schooling or the cost of it."

"We'll see. First, I have to get in."

"By then, you'll have chipmunks running all over the place," Tucker reminded him. "Bills, gymnastics lessons and soccer practice. You ever spend any time with Kyle and his brood, or Coop? We can hardly get them to come out with us to the Scupper."

Tucker was convinced Brawley had forgotten his earlier remark, until his friend cruelly drove the point home again.

"Hell, Tuck. What's stopping you? I mean Kyle says you're paying for a vacation chaperoning the Team all over Baja next month. Some vacation. Why don't you just re-up? Come back to us."

"Because I'm thirty nine, Brawley."

"So am I, nearly."

"But I've been doing other things. I'm just not sure I could get through BUD/S again."

"They'd have to give you a pass on that," Brawley barked.

"Nope. I already checked."

The two of them sat in the few seconds of quiet while the ladies searched for another station. In San Diego, there would be crickets on a night like this, even in February. Tucker had heard an owl earlier, but no crickets.

Brawley turned, speaking to the side of his face. "Well, you just confirmed what I've been thinking for the better part of five years now. Don't deny it, Tucker. You want back in."

He wasn't going to make a big objection to Brawley's remarks because that would make him look guilty as charged. But his friend had nailed him fair and square. That little confidential talk with Collins about whether or not the Navy would consider a re-entry for him was kept under wraps. But he had to go open his big mouth tonight and tell Brawley he'd checked. He wondered if he'd done it on purpose.

*Wouldn't that be something if I could do it?*

Brawley stood up and positioned the entire blanket around Tucker's shoulders and gave him a gentle pat on the back. "I think I'm going to go out there and rescue Dorie before someone gets hurt."

Tucker nodded. "Think I'll do the same," and stood to join him.

Brawley grinned like he'd been told a dirty joke.

"What's so funny?" he asked the newlywed.

"I think everyone's gonna get laid tonight."

# CHAPTER 10

"WE SHOULD HAVE taken a week off, Tucker. I had no idea there was so much I wanted to see." Brandy was folding her clothes when Tucker made his way into their sheeted cubicle. He'd been stacking wood and making sure the fire was fully stoked so they didn't have to wake up in the morning to a cold building.

"Next time. I promise." He pulled her to him, fingering the red lace bra she'd bought for the trip. "Where on earth did you get this dangerous device?"

"You like it?"

"Turn around. Let me think about that for a couple of minutes."

She loved taking direction from him. She peered over her shoulder. "Like this?"

"Keep going."

Brandy slowly kept moving until she was facing him again. "Should I take my bra and panties off now?"

"I can't make up my mind."

His smile was bringing on a wave of hot, wet lust she could smell.

"Is it my imagination, or are these lovely lace things even more sexy looking when they're so—so—ample?" He darted a worried look her way. "Did I just make a huge mistake?" he said as he winced. He bit his lower lip and, in spite of his enormous size and white beard, looked like a little boy about to be punished.

"I used to let things like that bother me." She slowly slid her panties down her thighs. "But—"

"Don't touch that!" he whispered.

Brandy had her hand on the front clasp of her bra, ready to peel it away and stand before him naked. Instead, she splayed her fingers over the satin and eyelet lace, squeezed her flesh and took two little steps until their bodies touched.

"How is it that I'm always the one who's naked first?" she asked, her lips just barely touching his. She could hear his heart pounding in tandem to hers and took a gentle moan from him as they kissed.

"I guess it's because I always like to watch, and I forget myself," he whispered.

"I think it's healthy to forget yourself now and then, don't you?" They kissed again, but deeper. "You want me to leave it on or take it off?"

"I think you should leave it on for now. I'll get to it in about an hour. I have other things I want you to do first. Is that okay with you, Brandy?"

She watched him remove his jeans and underwear, his erection bouncing with anticipation. She held him between her palms like she was praying.

"It's perfect."


IT WAS PAST midnight when she awoke, grateful Tucker held her tight because the room was freezing. Someone in one of the other spaces was snoring up a storm and would have rattled the windows if there were any.

Her heart was still racing from their urgent lovemaking. He'd played her body like an instrument, hard, and incredibly deep, expressed both in body language as well as their frantic whispers. It had been so intense, at one point she broke down in tears and Tucker thought he'd hurt her somehow.

But in a way he had. She was forever altered as if she was a willing participant in her own destruction.

It was hard not to notice a man as tall and strong as he was. But now that she knew him better, had kissed every inch of his body and answered his need with her own, she understood that everything he did he was the master of, except sometimes finding words. But he loved with abandon, never holding back, pushing her to the edge, and then just a little further, until she'd collapse in his arms. The coiled, cloud-of-butterflies-feeling in her belly were physical manifestations of what she knew to be true in her heart. She was falling in love, as she never had before. She also knew this came with risks, since there would be no getting over that kind of intense love. In fact, it was delicious and painful at the same time, even with the absence of a breakup on the horizon.

She tried not to think about where it all was going. She'd been included in the community of brothers, felt herself blend in with the ladies who were lucky enough to also be loved by one of these warriors who turned their worlds upside down. Brandy just took the waves of emotion and passion as they engulfed her and tried not to focus on what it all meant. She knew that was a rabbit hole.

It hardly seemed possible they'd known each other for such a short period of time. He'd been the missing piece she didn't even know she'd been missing. If she ever had to be without him, life would never be the same.

She thought about Amy and Zak, who was nearly killed on his first deployment. Shannon had lost her first husband, T.J.'s best friend. She'd also heard stories about the women who couldn't handle the lifestyle, the intensity of their play and their hearts. Still, it was a family, a community of brothers and the women they loved.

But one thing bothered her. Tucker had been talking with Kyle and Brawley, and she knew he missed being a SEAL. What would she do if he decided she wasn't the right one? What if he tried to re-join his team and failed? How could she ever make up for that incredible loss he would feel.

Or, what if she never could keep him happy enough to stay? Could she meet him halfway, match his energy, and carefully tend to him if he ever fell apart? She wasn't sure she was cut out for it, any of it.

*Try to sleep. You have to rest. You'll drive yourself crazy with all these thoughts.*

"Everything okay, Brandy?" His words startled her.

"I'm sorry, did I wake you?"

He sifted his fingers through her hair. "Yes."

"I can't sleep."

"That happens to me sometimes too when I drink too much. It's like I'm over-drunk."

She lay on her back and enjoyed the feel of his large callused hand caressing her breast. The plank beams on the ceiling were barely visible in the reflection of moonlight. Brandy waited, trying to notice some sign her eyelids were heavy and her mind was quieting, but that sign never came. She inhaled and tried to sigh very carefully so he wouldn't detect her worry. But even that was unsuccessful.

"Talk to me, Brandy."

"I don't want to do it here."

"Hot tub?"

They threw on some clothes and took their towels, discovering that they were able to be alone under the stars. The warm water helped Brandy put her thoughts into words.

She wrapped her legs around his waist and floated with her arms about his neck. The white in his hair and beard made him appear to glow in the dark.

"Is it that bad?" he teased.

"What?"

"Whatever it is you don't want to tell me."

"No, Tucker." She paused and thought carefully before she spoke. "Let me ask you a question. Does the speed of all this scare you just a little?"

"You mean does it fall somewhere between skydiving at midnight and getting my ass shot off by a sniper? That what you mean by scared?"

Now she felt ridiculous. "I got the impression you weren't the kind of guy who just jumped into relationships."

"Oh. Okay. So now we're talking *relationships*. Is that what this is?"

She would have been worried but saw the goofy grin on his face. "Watch it. Don't you make fun of me. I don't like that, as you know."

"Well, you're right about me. I don't do this. I've never done this."

She didn't want to look at him in the eyes, thinking he might begin to get uncomfortable. The last thing she wanted to do was put him on the spot. But she wanted to know where she stood. And maybe that was the right way to put it.

"Tucker."

"Yes ma'am."

"Would you be able to give me some indication of where all this is leading? Like, do I fit into your life anywhere other than in your bed?"

He tilted his head and stared back at her without smiling, and her heart fell to the bottom of the hot tub.

"First, if you'd have asked me that about ten years ago, I'd be gone by now. Maybe even five years ago. But, believe it or not, I've mellowed. When I went to the wedding on New Years Eve, *my* goal, and remember I told you I didn't want to tell you what it was?"

"I remember."

"My goal was to keep my hands to myself and to not rank or otherwise check out the ladies at the reception."

"Okay. And how did that work out for you?"

"I didn't even come close to achieving my goal. I sat there in the church, and I watched as you walked down the aisle, and into my life."

Brandy was stunned. It wasn't what she'd expected at all.

"I've been watching you when you were sleeping, talking to other people and didn't know I was looking. I watch you from across the room and out of the sides of my eyes when we go places. And I've come to the conclusion that I don't ever want to spend a day when you are not a part of my life."

She scrambled to her feet, separated herself from him and stood with her back pressed against the other side of the hot tub. Her heart felt like it was going to jump right out of her chest and go running down between the vines.

Tucker just waited. And then that grin overtook his face. "Oh my God. You're scared." He approached quietly, relentlessly, and without hesitation gently took her head in his hands and kissed her. "It's just like skydiving, sweetheart," he said between kisses. "You put your arms out to the sides, and fly. And I'll be strapped right there behind you. I will never let you fall. And I'll never stop loving you."

How did you like the beginning of Brandy and Tucker's journey? You can read along on their journey through courtship, marriage, and starting a family in the other books, starting with book 2 of the Bone Frog Brotherhood Series, SEALed At The Altar, or, go all out with the Bone Frog Brotherhood boxed set, which contains all 5 books. These are also available on Audible.

This series of books was the first time I wrote about the same couple, Brandy and Tucker, instead of what I usually do, write a different couple for each book in the series. I loved doing this, and readers have called this series their favorite for that reason!

I just want to say thank you for reading about my SEALs and their ups and downs, how they are a force for good, but are sometimes flawed or struggle to accept the challenges of being a husband, a partner or a father in today's world. In their struggle, comes the story.

A hero isn't a hero because he's perfect. He's a hero because he usually does the right thing. Writing about these fictionalized, wonderful men with large hearts, egos and bodies, has been a lifelong dream of mine, and one that I hope to be able to do forever.

Thank you so much, and please, if you enjoyed this book, leave me a review.

Fair sailing!

# ABOUT THE AUTHOR

 NYT and USA Today best-selling author Sharon Hamilton's award-winning Navy SEAL Brotherhood series have been a fan favorite from the day the first one was released. They've earned her the coveted Amazon author ranking of #1 in Romantic Suspense, Military Romance and Contemporary Romance categories, as well as in Gothic Romance for her Vampires of Tuscany and Guardian Angels. Her characters follow a sometimes rocky road to redemption through passion and true love.

Now that he's out of the Navy, Sharon can share with her readers that her son spent a decade as a Navy SEAL, and he's the inspiration for her books.

Her Golden Vampires of Tuscany are not like any vamps you've read about before, since they don't go to ground and can walk around in the full light of the sun.

Her Guardian Angels struggle with the human charges they are sent to save, often escaping their vanilla world of Heaven for the brief human one. You won't find any of these beings in any Sunday school class.

She lives in Sonoma County, California with her husband and her Doberman, Tucker. A lifelong organic gardener, when she's not writing, she's getting *verra verra* dirty in the mud, or wandering Farmers Markets looking for new Heirloom varieties of vegetables and flowers. She and her husband plan to cure their wanderlust (or make it worse) by traveling in their Diesel Class A Pusher, Romance Rider. Starting with this book, all her writing will be done on the road.

She loves hearing from her fans:
Sharonhamilton2001@gmail.com

Her website is:
sharonhamiltonauthor.com

Find out more about Sharon, her upcoming releases, appearances and news when you sign up for Sharon's newsletter.

Facebook:
facebook.com/SharonHamiltonAuthor

Twitter:
twitter.com/sharonlhamilton

Pinterest:
pinterest.com/AuthorSharonH

Amazon:
amazon.com/Sharon-Hamilton/e/B004FQQMAC

BookBub:
bookbub.com/authors/sharon-hamilton

Youtube:
youtube.com/channel/UCDInkxXFpXp_4Vnq08ZxMBQ

Soundcloud:
soundcloud.com/sharon-hamilton-1

Sharon Hamilton's Rockin' Romance Readers:
facebook.com/groups/sealteamromance

Sharon Hamilton's Goodreads Group:
goodreads.com/group/show/199125-sharon-hamilton-readers-group

Visit Sharon's Online Store:
sharon-hamilton-author.myshopify.com

Join Sharon's Review Teams:

eBook Reviews:
sharonhamiltonassistant@gmail.com

Audio Reviews:
sharonhamiltonassistant@gmail.com

**Life** *is one fool thing after another.*
**Love** *is two fool things after each other.*

# REVIEWS

## PRAISE FOR THE
## GOLDEN VAMPIRES OF TUSCANY SERIES

"Well to say the least I was thoroughly surprise. I have read many Vampire books, from Ann Rice to Kym Grosso and few other Authors, so yes I do like Vampires, not the super scary ones from the old days, but the new ones are far more interesting far more human than one can remember. I found Honeymoon Bite a totally engrossing book, I was not able to put it down, page after page I found delight, love, understanding, well that is until the bad bad Vamp started being really bad. But seeing someone love another person so much that they would do anything to protect them, well that had me going, then well there was more and for a while I thought it was the end of a beautiful love story that spanned not only time but, spanned Italy and California. Won't divulge how it ended, but I did shed a few tears after screaming but Sharon Hamilton did not let me down, she took me on amazing trip that I loved, look forward to reading another Vampire book of hers."

"An excellent paranormal romance that was exciting, romantic, entertaining and very satisfying to read. It had me anticipating what would happen next many times over, so much so I could not put it down and even finished it up in a day. The vampires in this book were different from your average vampire, but I enjoy different variations and changes to the same old stuff. It made for a more unpredictable read and more adventurous to explore! Vampire lovers, any paranormal readers and even those who love the romance genre will enjoy Honeymoon Bite."

"This is the first non-Seal book of this author's I have read and I loved it. There is a cast-like hierarchy in this vampire community with humans at the very bottom and Golden vampires at the top. Lionel is a dark vampire who are servants of the Goldens. Phoebe is a Golden who has not decided if she will remain human or accept the turning to become a vampire. Either way she and Lionel can never be together since it is forbidden.

I enjoyed this story and I am looking forward to the next installment."

"A hauntingly romantic read. Old love lost and new love found. Family, heart, intrigue and vampires. Grabbed my attention and couldn't put down. Would definitely recommend."

## PRAISE FOR THE
## SEAL BROTHERHOOD SERIES

"Fans of Navy SEAL romance, I found a new author to feed your addiction. Finely written and loaded delicious with moments, Sharon Hamilton's storytelling satisfies like a thick bar of chocolate." —Marliss Melton, bestselling author of the *Team Twelve* Navy SEALs series

"Sharon Hamilton does an EXCELLENT job of fitting all the characters into a brotherhood of SEALS that may not be real but sure makes you feel that you have entered the circle and security of their world. The stories intertwine with each book before...and each book after and THAT is what makes Sharon Hamilton's SEAL Brotherhood Series so very interesting. You won't want to put down ANY of her books and they will keep you reading into the night when you should be sleeping. Start with this book...and you will not want to stop until you've read the whole series and then...you will be waiting for Sharon to write the next one." (5 Star Review)

"Kyle and Christy explode all over the pages in this first book, *[Accidental SEAL],* in a whole new series of SEALs. If the twist and turns don't get your heart jumping, then maybe the suspense will. This is a must read for those that are looking for love and adventure with a little sloppy love thrown in for good measure." (5 Star Review)

## PRAISE FOR THE
## BAD BOYS OF SEAL TEAM 3 SERIES

"I love reading this series! Once you start these books, you can hardly put them down. The mix of romance and suspense keeps you turning the pages one right after another! Can't wait until the next book!" (5 Star Review)

"I love all of Sharon's Seal books, but *[SEAL's Code]* may just be her best to date. Danny and Luci's journey is filled with a wonderful insight into the Native American life. It is a love story that will fill you with warmth and contentment. You will enjoy Danny's journey to become a SEAL and his reasons for it. Good job Sharon!" (5 Star Review)

## PRAISE FOR THE
## BAND OF BACHELORS SERIES

"*[Lucas]* was the first book in the Band of Bachelors series and it was a phenomenal start. I loved how we got to see the other SEALs we all love and we got a look at Lucas and Marcy. They had an instant attraction, and their love was very intense. This book had it all, suspense, steamy romance, humor, everything you want in a riveting, outstanding read. I can't wait to read the next book in this series." (5 Star Review)

## PRAISE FOR THE
## TRUE BLUE SEALS SERIES

"Keep the tissues box nearby as you read *True Blue SEALs: Zak* by Sharon Hamilton. I imagine more than I wish to that the circumstances surrounding Zak and Amy are all too real for returning military personnel and their families. Ms. Hamilton has put us right in the middle of struggles and successes that these two high school sweethearts endure. I have read several of Sharon Hamilton's military romances but will say this is the most emotionally intense of the ones that I have read. This is a well-written, realistic story with authentic characters that will have you rooting for them and proud of those who serve to keep us safe. This is an author who writes amazing stories that you love and cry with the characters. Fans of Jessica Scott and Marliss Melton will want to add Sharon Hamilton to their list of realistic military romance writers." (5 Star Review)